Y0-BZY-602

"Alive with character, action, and passion, a complex feat requiring exceptional virtuosity. For all its surface lucidity, even simplicity, we are always made aware of subsurface meanings.

"The two chief protagonists, Chief Clumly and The Sunlight Man, represent forces above and beyond themselves. Clumly is middle-class, traditional, Law and Order, the status quo. The Sunlight Man, a bearded illusionist, speaks of the world not as it is but as it could and should be. Whenever Gardner poses the two in confrontation, the novel rises to heights of eloquence and relevance rarely encountered in current fiction."

*John Barkham Reviews*

Also by John Gardner
*Published by Ballantine Books*

GRENDEL

NICKEL MOUNTAIN

THE WRECKAGE OF AGATHON

THE KING'S INDIAN

FREDDY'S BOOK

OCTOBER LIGHT

# THE
# SUNLIGHT
# DIALOGUES

## John Gardner

*Illustrations by*

John Napper

BALLANTINE BOOKS—NEW YORK

Library of Congress Catalog Card Number: 72-2226

ISBN: 0-345-30492-6

This edition published by arrangement with
Alfred A. Knopf, Inc.

Manufactured in the United States of America

First Ballantine Books Edition: December 1973
Fifth Printing: May 1982

Cover art by Paul Bacon

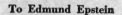

To Edmund Epstein

# Contents

List of Characters   xi

Prologue   1

I

The Watchdog   5

II

When the Exorcist Shall Go to the House
of the Patient . . .   63

III

Lion Emerging from Cage   135

IV

Mama   195

V

Hunting Wild Asses   227

VI

Esther   301

VII

The Dialogue on Wood and Stone   331

VIII

The Kleppmann File   363

vii

IX
"Like a robber, I shall proceed according
to my will."  393
X
Poetry and Life  419
XI
The Dialogue of Houses  441
XII
A Mother's Love  473
XIII
*Nah ist—und schwer zu fassen der Gott*  497
XIV
The Wilderness  535
XV
The Dialogue of the Dead  559
XVI
Love and Duty  593
XVII
Benson *versus* Boyle  601
XVIII
The Dragon's Dwelling-Place and the
Court for Owls  623
XIX
Workmen in a Quarry  637
XX
Winged Figure Carrying Sacrificial Animal  675
XXI
The Dialogue of Towers  691
XXII
Luke  703
XXIII
*E silentio*  711
XXIV
Law and Order  739

# Illustrations

*Facing page*

vi   FRONTPIECE: "The male nurse who looked
     after him stood in the doorway cleaning
     the fingernails of his right hand with the
     thumbnail of his left."

48   "From the darkest corner of the room came
     a harsher whisper. 'He's not the one.' "

104  "There was something there—even Nick
     saw it . . ."

204  "She stood in a white dress waiting at the
     underpass . . ."

276  "The Sunlight Man lifted his arm to hide
     his ugliness . . ."

325  " 'My kid,' Miller said. He sounded
     proud . . ."

345  "He was well dressed, almost elegant, the
     beard neatly trimmed, the grayish blond
     hair curling around his ears like the locks
     of an angel of ambiguous allegiance."

422    "He stood a moment between the two
       cars . . . savoring the queer sensation of
       being neither Boyle nor Benson."

442    "His prisoners in the cellar were asleep up-
       right, sagging in the ropes that tied them."

552    "He never saw her face and afterward he
       sometimes was not quite sure that she was
       real."

585    "That was good, right? You were mystified.
       Admit it!' "

634    "Kleppmann smiled, still hiding behind his
       curtain . . ."

734    "Figlow had shot him through the heart."

List
of
Characters

## PRINCIPAL CHARACTERS

*(All characters in this novel except for May Brumstead, Mr. Perkowski, Pete Mollman, and Dr. T. M. Steele, are purely fictitious.)*

**Fred Clumly** (b. 1902), Chief of Police, Batavia, N.Y., 1957–1966
**Esther Clumly,** his wife
**The Sunlight Man,** a lunatic magician
**The Hodge Family:**

Hon. Arthur Hodge Sr
m.
Sarah Ruth Judd

| William (Sr) | Arthur (Jr) | Ruth | Benj. (Sr) | Taggert |
|---|---|---|---|---|
| m. | m. | m. | m. | m. |
| Mildred | Florence | Geof. | Vanessa | Kathleen |
| Jewel | Hyde | Uphill | Woodchurch | Paxton |

| Will (Jr) Luke | (seven daughters) | | Benj. (Jr) (two sons) |
|---|---|---|---|
| Mary Lou | | | |

*Arthur Hodge Sr*, U.S. Congressman, builder of Stony Hill Farm
*Will Hodge Sr*, his eldest son, a Batavia attorney
*Millie Jewel Hodge*, Will Sr's wife (divorced, 1964)
*Clarence Jewel*, her father
*Gil*, her favorite brother, a suicide at eighteen
*Will Hodge Jr*, son of Will Sr and Millie, a successful Buffalo attorney
*Louise*, his wife, mother of their children Madeline and Danny
*Mary Lou Hodge Carter*, daughter of Will Sr and Millie, wife of *George Carter*
*Luke*, Will Sr's youngest son, a farmer
*Arthur Hodge Jr*, the Congressman's second son, an electrician, a man of system; father of seven daughters
*Ruth Hodge Uphill*, the Congressman's daughter, married to the brother of the Fire Chief in Batavia
*Ben Hodge Sr*, the Congressman's fourth child, a farmer and man of religion
*Vanessa*, his wife
*Ben Jr*, his son; died in the Korean War
*Nick* and *Vernon Slater*, young Indians paroled into the custody of Ben Hodge Sr (The elder, Nick, was later transferred to Luke Hodge)
*David*, Ben Sr's Negro hired boy, also a parolee

## SECONDARY CHARACTERS

### THE POLICE:

*Dominic (Miller")* Sangirgonio, Clumly's right-hand man
*Jackie*, his wife
*Tommy ("Einstein")*, his son
*Stan Kozlowski*, Prowlcar 19; son of a farmer
*Mickey Salvador*, eighteen, a guard in the city jail
*His mother*
*His grandmother*, a seer
*John ("Shorty") Figlow*, sergeant at the desk; a nervous man, unhappily married
*Ed Tank*
*Wilbur Haynes*
*Larry Lewis* } patrolmen
*Clarence Pieman*

*Borsian,* a State Trooper
*Baltimore,* Negro janitor in Batavia City Jail

### CITY OFFICIALS:

*Walt Mullen,* Mayor
*Judge Sam White,* brother to Congressman Edward ("Ted") White
*Phil Uphill,* Fire Chief
*Jerome Wittaker,* Mayor Mullen's assistant
*Mr. Peeper*
*Mr. Moss* } members of the Batavia City Council

### OTHERS:

*R. V. Kleppmann,* a confidence man and survivor
*Mrs. Kleppmann,* his wife
*Walter Boyle,* a thief
*Walter Benson,* a good citizen living in a suburb of Buffalo, N.Y.
*Marguerite,* his wife
*Oliver Nuper,* the Bensons' boarder
*Gretchen Niehaus,* one of Nuper's mistresses
*Albert Hubbard,* owner of a nursery inherited by his sons
*The Woodworth Sisters: Agnes* (deceased), *Editha* (aged 108, a poetess), and *Octave* (aged 97), daughters of Rev. Burgess Woodworth, original pastor of the Batavia First Baptist Church
*Clive Paxton,* owner of a trucking firm; father of Kathleen Paxton
*Elizabeth,* his wife
*Professor Combs,* her elderly lover
*Freeman,* a rootless wanderer

## MINOR CHARACTERS (A SELECTION)

*Merton Bliss,* the last of the New York State liars
*Robert Boas,* a drunkard
*May Brumstead,* beloved matron of the Batavia Children's Home
*Ed Burlington,* a news reporter, former Sunday School student of Mrs. Clumly
*Helene Burns,* a teacher; good friend of Taggert Hodge

*Dr. Burns*, a psychiatrist
*Bill Churchill*, a professional mourner
*Edna*, a madam
*Bob Faner*, next-door neighbor of Will Hodge Sr
*Mr. Hardesty*, neighbor of Luke Hodge
*Pete Mollman*, a publisher and printer in Millstadt, Ill.
*Harold ("Buz") Marchant*, a Chicago physician, friend of Will Jr
*Mrs. Palazzo*, Will Hodge Sr's landlady
*Mr. Perkowski*, a Batavia grocer
*Jeff Peters*, friend of Millie Hodge
*Chief Poole*, Batavia Police Chief when Clumly was young
*Raymond*, hired man to Will Sr when he ran Stony Hill
*Solomon Ravitz*, Buffalo TV personality
*Dr. Rideout*, Genesee County Coroner
*Rosemary*, a madam
*The Runian Sisters*, former occupants of Luke Hodge's farmhouse; murdered by their nephew and hidden in the manure pile
*T. M. Steele*, well-known Batavia physician and surgeon
*Walt Sprague*, last of the true Upstate New York Republicans
*Bob Swift*, a foolish newsman
*Rev. Warshower*, Will Hodge Sr's minister
*Rev. Willby*, Esther Clumly's minister

The earth in its devotion carries all things, good and evil, without exception.

—THE I CHING

# Prologue

Riding horses in a back pasture, gone wild. Woods. Inside, on a hill, a house as black as dinosaur bones. Grass grows up through the driveway's broken asphalt, but there is a car. This is the house of the oldest Judge in the world. The Judge has company.

"Take any ordinary man, give him a weapon—say, $x$ caliber —" (he chuckled wickedly) "—put him in the middle of a wilderness with enough ammunition to fire three times in four directions—these are Holy numbers—and behold! you've created order." He blew out smoke like dust.

"As to that," Fred Clumly said, "I wouldn't know." He had turned his badge in long ago, and even before that he had found the opinions of his friend the Judge, if the Judge was his friend, obscure. It was now no longer necessary to figure out what the Judge was saying. Clumly was retired. In Batavia, opinion was divided, in fact, over whether he'd gone away somewhere or died.

The Judge leaned forward, parting the yellow tobacco smoke with the side of his hand, so that Clumly could make out somewhat more clearly the great gray concrete head and the glint of the eyes. "The world is a vast array of emblems," he said, "exactly as the old hermetic philosophers maintained. I state it for a fact." His large fist closed.

Clumly nodded thoughtfully for a long time, his shrivelled

1

head bobbing like a dried pod on his frail stick of a body. "As to that—" he said.

The Judge sighed and, like an old, slow lizard, withdrew to the gloomy secretness of his smoke. They were both silent for a long time. The room grew darker, as the time of day required. The Judge said, "What ever happened to that boy of yours—the religious one—what's-his-name's son, your top man?"

"We lost track of him," Clumly said. "Went away, I heard. A town like this—"

"Tragic," said the Judge, nodding.

The former Police Chief scowled, considering. "As to that—"

"They all go away somewhere, sooner or later," the Judge said. "I've been watching it eighty-some years. Do you know where they go?"

Clumly shuddered. They'd been through this many times.

"Entropy!" the Judge squealed. Then he laughed, as soundless as a snake.

"Maybe," Clumly said.

The Judge asked kindly, "Your wife?"

"Dead," Clumly said.

The Judge nodded once more, remembering. "There's some meaning in that." He took a long, slow drag on his pipe, casting about like an old woman in an attic for the meaning.

"I doubt it," Clumly said.

"I don't suppose you ever hear of that magician," the Judge said then, "—the one you had in jail that time."

"Dead too," he said.

"Pity." He rubbed his hands together clumsily.

You could not see either one of them clearly in the yellow smoke from the Judge's pipe and Old Man Clumly's cigar. The bars on the window of the Judge's room were as vague as lampposts bathed in fog, and the whiskey in his glass was gray. The male nurse who looked after him stood in the doorway cleaning the fingernails of his right hand with the thumbnail of his left. He was not listening. In the dusk outside, four miles away, a traffic light changed, and a police car started up, clean and precise as a young child's tooth. The policeman, driving, waved to a man he knew on the sidewalk, and the man waved back with a smile. It was like a salute. The tyrannic scent of May was in the air; it was the time when young hearts blossom and burgeon, and boys try to think of heroic deeds. But it was winter in the Judge's room, for <u>nothing in this world is universal any more</u>; there is neither wisdom nor stability, and faithfulness is dead. Or, at any rate, such was the Judge's solemn opinion. But Clumly would say, "Well, so—" and would say no more.

"It was good of you to visit," the Judge said.

"No trouble," Clumly said. "A man—"

"Well, nevertheless," the Judge said. He raised the glass of gray whiskey. "Good whiskey," he whispered with deep satisfaction, without tasting it.

"Mmm," Clumly said.

The room grew darker. The Judge half-closed his eyes and thought about it. "Well, nevertheless," the Judge said, "we've had some times, we've done some tricks." He chuckled. "We've seen some curious things."

Clumly nodded, mechanical as an old German clockmaker's doll. His mind was a blank.

Later, after Fred Clumly was gone, the Judge said to his bored attendant, "I made that man. I created him, you might say. I created them all. The Mayor, the Fire Chief, all of them. I ran this town. I made them, and then when the time came I dropped a word in the right place and I broke them." He smiled and his gold teeth gleamed. The attendant looked at him indifferently, as if from infinitely far away, and the Judge sipped his whiskey again, uneasy. His spotted hand shook. One time in a nightmare he'd dreamed his attendant had shot him in the back. "I like you," the Judge said suddenly. "You're like a son to me!"

"As to that," the attendant said, "I'm what I am."

The Judge was not certain afterward that this was what he really said, and probably it was not.

# I

## The Watchdog

> *His watchmen are blind: they are all ignorant,*
> *they are all dumb dogs, they cannot bark. . . .*
>                                                        —Isaiah 56:10

### 1

In late August, 1966, the city jail in Batavia, New York, held four regular prisoners, that is, four prisoners who were being kept on something more than an overnight basis. Three had been bound over for trial; the fourth was being held, by order of the court, until the County could administer a psychiatric examination. The identity of this fourth prisoner was not yet known. He seemed to be about forty. He'd been arrested on August 23rd for painting the word *love* in large, white, official-looking letters across two lanes of Oak Street, just short of the New York State Thruway. As the police were in the act of arresting him he had managed to burn all the papers in his billfold (dancing up and down, shaking like a leaf), and he refused to say now a halfway sensible word about himself, ex-

5

cept that he was "an anarchist, a student." His face was slightly disfigured by what looked like a phosphor burn—the kind
men get in wars. Whether he was actually a student (he was
an anarchist, all right) there was no way of telling. He seemed
too old for that, and there was no college in Batavia; but the
town was not large and they knew he was not from there.
There were of course plenty of colleges elsewhere in Western
New York, and there was always the possibility that he'd come
from someplace far away. The Chief of Police—it was then
Fred Clumly—would sit in his office in front of the cellblock
and talk about it with whoever happened to be there—one of his
men or Judge Sam White or May Bunce from Probation. "I
think he's from California," Clumly would say. But he
wouldn't say why. "It's the way he talks," he would explain,
squinting, sitting with his bare white elbows planted on the
desk like trees. Clumly's whole body was creased and white
and completely hairless. He'd had a disease when he was in
the Navy, years ago. Aside from the whiteness and the hairlessness, his only remarkable features were his large nose,
which was like a mole's, and his teeth, which were strikingly
white and without a flaw. The whiteness, the hairlessness, the
oversized nose all gave him the look of a philosopher pale
from too much reading, or a man who has slept three nights in
the belly of a whale.

It was of course not true that the prisoner's way of talking
was noticeably Californian. But Clumly hated California, or
anyway felt alarmed by it. He would sit with his *Look* magazine, at home in his livingroom, squinting irascibly, fascinated,
at the blurry color photograph of a waitress with breasts completely bare, smiling, standing in what looked like a kind of
cardboard window, holding out a coffeepot to Clumly. Clumly's wife was a blind woman with bright glass eyes and small,
pinched features and a body as white as his own. Her small
shoulders sagged and her neck was long, so that her head
seemed to sway above her like a hairy sunflower. He minded
the way she filled her teacup, one finger over the rim to watch
the level, and he minded the way she talked to herself perpetually, going about the house with her lips moving as though she
were some kind of old-fashioned priestess forever at her prayers, or insane. Also, she whined. But Clumly was not bitter.
"Nobody's life is perfect," he sometimes said to himself, which
was true.

"Also," he said to Mickey Salvador, the new man, "what makes me think California is that beard."

"Like the riots," Salvador said.

"That's it," Clumly said. "You ever see a beard like that around Batavia?"

"Only Old Man Hoyt," Salvador said.

"Correct."

"And Walazynski."

"Correct," Clumly said. It was all coming clearer in his mind.

"And that Russian guy." Salvador tugged at his collar and stretched his neck, thinking. "Brotski. The one that sells *Watchtower*." He laughed. "With the leather pants."

Clumly scowled, and Salvador stopped laughing.

"I was out to L.A. once myself," Salvador said. "I wish to hell I'd got up to San Francisco."

A little daintily, Clumly picked up the half-smoked cigar from his ashtray, pressed the end firm, and lit it.

Salvador said, "My brother Jimmy had a beard once. It came in red. Jesus to God."

But Clumly was shaking his head, gloomy. "San Francisco," he said. "What's this country coming to?"

"I guess they all got beards in Vietnam there. But I guess that's different. My old lady's got a moustache. Shit, my old lady got hair all over her, just like a monkey." Salvador looked thoughtful.

"California," Clumly said solemnly. "That's what he'll be." But on his hands, where the flesh had not been damaged, the prisoner had no tan, and that was strange. He had large white hands like those in pictures of King David in the Bible. The tip of the cigar was sharp and acid on Clumly's lip and he thought again of quitting, but he knew he wouldn't. It passed through his mind that there was a beach somewhere in California where there was a car, a 1935 model, he couldn't remember what make it was, and inside the car a couple of lovers made out of old wire in the back seat, and some ladies' underpants. It was supposed to be an art work. Clumly had used it in a speech to the Rotary once. A sign of the times. "That's it," he said. "That's where he's from all right."

"Monkeys," Salvador said. "Shoo!"

That night Chief Clumly stood for a long time at the door of the cellblock looking at the scarred and bearded prisoner.

Then he went out to his car and sat there awhile, brooding, half-listening to the radio, and then he drove home, shaking his head, thinking. He was sixty-four, and he'd lived in Batavia his whole life, except for the three years he'd spent in the Navy, and half of that he'd spent staring at a hospital wall down in Texas.

"It's a funny business," he said aloud, above the noise of the police radio. He searched for words, squinting into the half-dark of the treelined street. (He was driving down North Lyon now, past tall, narrow, two-story houses with porches that went the full width of each house, old latticework at each end of the porches, and here and there a bike leaned up against the steps. Even with their lights on, the houses looked abandoned, like habitations depopulated by plague. You had a feeling there would be dragons in the cellars, and upstairs, owls. The curtains in the livingroom windows were drawn, and there was no one out, not a car on the street except his own. No light showed but the incorporeal glow of television sets. On some of the lawns there were bushy evergreens, and yet he could remember when all this was new, the lawns plain and bare, the trees along the sidewalks all small and straight and as self-conscious-looking as the new, white houses, now gray or dark green or fading yellow. He could remember when the evergreens were six feet tall, full of colored lights at Christmas, and the snow on the lawns reflected the light, pale blue and yellow and pink. He'd driven a Wonder Bakery truck in those days—Good Bread for Six Reasons—and before that he'd been the Watkins man—panaceas and potions—for the Indian Reservation.) But no words came, only the light of a cat's eyes beside the curb. At LaCrosse, he slowed almost to a stop and turned. The houses were older, even taller here, like old-time castles. They stood in the cool, cavernous gaps between oak trees a century old. He went up the gravel driveway to where his garage sat half-hidden under burnt-out lilacs and surrounded by high weeds. In the glow of the headlights, the weeds looked chalky white and vaguely reminded him of something. It was as if he expected something terrible to come out from their scratchy, bone-dry-looking obscurity—a leopard, say, or a lion, or the mastiff bitch that belonged to the Caldwells next door. But nothing came, and only the deepest, most barbaric and philosophical part of Chief Clumly's mind had for a moment slipped into expectancy. He put the car away, locked the garage, and walked around to the front of the house for the paper. It took him awhile to find it. The trees blocked the light from the streetlamp, and as usual there were no lights on in the house. He'd told her and told her about that. He found the paper by the side of the porch steps, almost under them, where you'd swear the little devil could never have put it except on purpose. Then, very slowly, weary all at once, he went in, unfolding the paper as he went. "Funny business," he said again thoughtfully, as he locked the front door behind him. He could hear her in the kitchen. The house smelled of stew with cabbage in it.

"Is that you, Fred?" she whined.

He held his nose lightly with his left hand and thought, as he'd occasionally thought before, how weird it would be if it were not him but some stranger, some lunatic escaped from the hospital up in Buffalo. The man would stand smiling, not answering, his glistening eyes bugging out like a toad's, surprised at the sound of a voice in the unlighted house, and after a moment he would appear in the near-darkness at the dining-room door, her high, chinless head alert and listening, white as death.

"Fred?" she called again, "is that you, Fred?"

"Just me," Clumly said, calm. He snapped on the lights.

He sat picking at his food, across from her, saying nothing while he ate, as usual. If there were hairs in the stew, he did not notice. Years ago—so long ago he could hardly remember it—he'd said something to her once about a hair in some food, and it had set off a terrible scene. She'd cried and cried, and she'd locked herself in the bathroom and said she was going to kill herself. "I'll cut my throat with a razorblade," she said. "Where are the razorblades?" And he'd stood bent over outside the bathroom door calling to her through the keyhole, begging her not to; he'd even sobbed, but purposely, hoping to persuade her, not really from grief. She had complained that he didn't love her, she was a burden to the world; and even as he reasoned and pleaded with her Clumly had realized, calmly, sensibly, that all she said was, well, sad but true. But in the same rush of clear-headed detachment he had recognized, like Jacob of old when he found he'd got Leah, whose arms were like sticks and whose mouth was as flat as a salamander's, that he'd have to be a monster to tell her the truth. What would the poor woman do, no beauty any more, without a skill or a talent in the world? He'd made a mistake in marrying her, one he might never have made if he'd been a few years older when they met, but his mistake, nevertheless. A mistake he was stuck with. He'd been twenty when they met, and she'd been eighteen. He was in the Navy, just getting his eyes opened. He'd gone to his first house of prostitution when they'd put in at the Virgin Islands, and they all sat in one small room with a radio playing foreign music, three other sailors and himself and the four brown, queerly familyless women (it seemed to him) in their slippery dresses and no underwear, their black hair as slick as silk—all of them drinking sludgy black stuff which smelled like Luden's Cough Syrup, but which they said was rum. He felt caught in an ominous spell. They looked like gypsies with crowns of plastic flowers in their hair. The room smelled rotten, the drink was poison, and touching the woman he had happened to end up with thrilled and repelled him— she was thirty if she was a day. Vockshy, Vasty, her name was. Something. Before long, whether from the poisonous drink or from Presbyterian shame, Clumly was vomiting in the street more violently than he would have thought possible for a human. He had to stand watch bent double the next day, and ever since that night his liver had been bad and whenever he was tired he'd walk slightly bent at the waist. Nevertheless, this is living! he'd thought. "Work like the devil, play like the devil," they said on the ship. Bam. When he went back to the whorehouse, Vockshy or Vasty was "occupied," he had to take a different girl. This queerly upset him. And then, home on leave, he'd found the pale and musing blind girl standing there soft as a flag beside an oak tree with burning green leaves—or, rather, the nearly blind girl: at that time she had sight enough to be put in charge of younger children from the Blind School, to lead them around laughing like circus people in time of pestilence, help them with their schoolwork, or, like the eldest orphaned child, punish them when they were bad. They were playing in the shaded hollow below her, and she, standing by the oak tree, was watching and listening and smelling the wind, she said. Her talk was like poetry in those days. She'd grown out of that later, as one does. Her voice was as soft as a southern breeze on the Mediterranean, so soft Clumly had to lean toward her to hear—blushing, twisting the sailor's hat in his hands. And so for two weeks they met every day, as if by accident, to walk and talk among the large trees or make pictures in the dirt with sticks or stones, or to listen to the Metropolitan Opera on Saturday afternoon (the thought of her breasts beneath the brassiere and high-collared blouse made him pale), and when he had to leave again she promised she would write. Eventually they'd gotten married. She seemed saintlike to him, and noble as a queen. He felt such an ache of tenderness for her, such reverence, almost, for what he called then her quiet courage, he could hardly sleep nights. He wrote to her constantly, slavishly, after the first two weeks, before he'd even thought about marrying her, and the letters that came to him from her (on pink or blue scalloped paper, awkwardly typed because she couldn't see well enough to read over what she'd written or even make sure what she said made sense) he read over and over and kept at the head of his bunk where he could smell them as he went to sleep. The others had teased him some, but not for long. People could say what they liked about them, sailors were the gentlest people in the world. Even now it could make his eyes mist, thinking about sailors. It was the sea that did it, old and bottomless with mystery, as people say, capable at times of unbelievable rage, and capable, too, of a peace that baffled you. As he'd tried to explain to Mayor Mullen once, to a man locked up in a steel ship, the sea was, well, really something. It *changed* you. Especially at night. Then the sickness had come, turning Fred Clumly to a grublike, virtually hairless monster, and he'd stopped writing, hoping to spare her. But his parents had sought her out and spoken to her, of course. She'd written to his buddy. Dog, they called him. He looked like a fancy dog with a too-erect head and large pink eyes. (Clumly could no longer remember the boy's real name. Walter Brown?) Dog had told her how it was with Clumly—how he felt about her and how he felt about, poor devil, himself. And so Clumly's love had bravely borrowed the money for a bus trip to Texas. "You look as beautiful as ever to me," she said in her soft voice, and they both wept. Her voice was unmysterious, faintly alarming. Dog came to the hospital and wept too. She read to him from a book in braille about Sir Lancelot, some story of adventure and romance so touching and foreign to them both that it made them blush and stop the reading for a while from embarrassment and fear. They were married, soon afterward, there in the hospital. That was all far in the past now, nearly forgotten; and even that night when she'd locked herself in the bathroom he could remember the beginning of it all no more clearly than one remembers a dream days later. She'd been plain to start with, except for her chestnut-colored hair. As she grew older she grew pinched and sickly-looking as a witch, and her hair became streaked with wiry gray. She began to tipple wine a little when he wasn't at home. Standing at the bathroom door that night, calling to her through it, he saw the years stretched out before him like a cheap hall rug in a strange and unfriendly hotel, and he thought—with such violence that it made him shaky—how it had felt to be totally free, standing looking down at the prow of a ship dimly lighted at night, with the ocean stretching away on all sides ambiguous as an oracle and glinting with unearthly silver, as calm and steady in its rhythm as the blood in your veins. Though he'd firmly put it behind him, he had not in all his years forgotten that vision, that temptation. One's struggle with the devil never ends. But he'd made her come out of the bathroom at last, groaning and stretching out her arms to him, and if there were hairs in the food tonight, or last night, or sometime last year, Clumly did not know it. If her slip showed or she smelled of wine, he did not notice it. Chief of Police Fred Clumly had renounced the world.

She said, "You look tired, Fred." Clumly's wife went out of her way to find phrases like "you *look*" or "I *see* that . . ." They all did that, blind people. He had a theory it was something they taught them at the Blind School, the same as they taught them to walk slightly faster than normal people, with their heads drawn back so they wouldn't hit first with their chins.

"Aye-uh," he said. "Tired. Gets harder every year." For all his annoyance, he spoke kindly, as was right. He glanced at her. She was shaking her head, the eyes turning with the face, and he looked down again.

After a moment she said—too loudly, as always, as though her voice had to be loud to get past the darkness she inhabited —"Vanessa Hodge called."

"Mmm," he said. He pushed the last of the gray stew against his bread and put it in his mouth, then wiped his hands on his napkin.

"It's about those Indian boys you've got locked up. Hodges

are their guardians, you know. Or they used to be. Poor Hodges."

He pushed the plate away and drew the coffeecup closer.

"It's been terrible for the Hodges. Poor Vanessa's not up to snuff since that little stroke or whatever it was, and she's not getting any younger. Even when things are running smoothly, she doesn't get around like she used to. She said they'd come in at all hours of the night, and sometimes their drunken friends with them. She said one night last winter Ben found that oldest boy lying on his bed just as naked as the day he was born, not a cover on him. She said when Ben touched him he thought he was dead. As cold as clay. She said Ben said he never knew before that when they say 'stone drunk' that's exactly what they mean."

Clumly sucked in the lukewarm Sanka and said nothing. He minded the way she went on and on and the blankness of her face, as though it were not a woman talking but the face of a horse on the merry-go-round, but though he minded, even now after all these years, he did not think about it. He was thinking of the bearded one from California. Could be he really was a little crazy. You heard sometimes about people going crazy from a bad burn. He prattled and babbled from morning to night, bothering the guards, bothering the other prisoners, and when he saw you watching him he made faces, or said a prayer for you, or he jerked up his hands like an animal about to claw you. But it didn't really seem like lunacy to Clumly. It seemed like an act, no less an act than those magic tricks he did, and the fact that the man went on with it day after day made Clumly uneasy. What went on inside their minds, people like that? Oh, they'd find out he was sane all right. Clumly would bet ten dollars on that. He was sane but he didn't think the same as other people. He was up to something. Over and over, the past few days, Clumly had found himself going over the jail routine, as if expecting a break—he felt like a man told to lock up Houdini—or searching his brain for where he'd seen before that face he knew he had never before laid eyes on. He waited for trouble from the prisoners, but there was nothing, and he knew all the while that there would be nothing. This morning, a little surprised at himself, he'd checked the pistol he hadn't had out of its holster for God knew how long. His hand was shaking like an old, old man's.

She was saying, "The oldest one would come wake them up at three in the morning, just as drunk as could be, and he'd say, 'It's all taken care of now. He'll be a different person tomorrow.' Three in the morning. Imagine. Poor Ben has to get up at dawn to milk the cows."

"That's all over," Clumly said abruptly. "They're out of the Hodges' hands."

"It's that bad?" she asked. Her face drooped to a pattern of upside-down V's.

"Aye-up." He finished the Sanka and pushed away the cup.

She poured herself more tea and said nothing for a moment, merely moved her lips, talking to herself. He was aware that he'd cut her off curtly. Her life wasn't perfect either, God knew. At last, since life must go on, she said, "You're still keeping that madman, I suppose?"

"Still keeping him," he said. To keep her from saying more he opened the paper.

But she said, "I don't suppose he's dangerous."

"Not there in the bucket," he said.

She raised her teacup, distressed by his tone, and she touched a button on her blouse with her left hand. He watched her drink and then lower the cup again slowly, lowering her left hand to the saucer to guide the cup down. He felt sorry for her, fleetingly, and looked up at the light above the table, then down at the *Daily News*. At first, because he'd been looking at the light, it seemed that the paper was empty, no news whatever today, neither good tidings nor bad. But after a moment he could see once more, vermillion print that gradually settled to black. There was a picture of a wrecked tractor-trailer and the Thruway behind it, a hundred yards or so away. He'd heard it all on the police radio this morning. He turned to the comics and read them slowly and solemnly, word for word. Then he read the obituaries.

"Clive Paxton died," he said.

"No!" she said.

"Seventy-six."

She had heard he was ailing. He'd left a pretty penny to his sons and that poor sad daughter of his, you could bet on that. They didn't live here any more, they'd moved away to places like Florida and California and Paris France. "Poor Elizabeth," she said. Clumly made himself a note to send flowers.

He was in bed ahead of her, as always. He lay in the dark listening, his mind almost comfortably blank at last. He heard the water running in the sink, the noise she made brushing her teeth, the clatter of, perhaps, the soap dish falling, and, after a while, the flush of the toilet. She came through the darkness of the hall and opened the door very quietly, to keep from waking him in case he should be asleep. He listened to her taking out the bobby pins, dropping them softly one by one in the chipped seashell on her dresser. At last she turned down the covers on her side (he lay with his back to her) and climbed into bed. He didn't need to watch to see it all in bitter clarity: her long skinny legs, more agile than his, as ghostly white as the white silk nightie, the long, webbed feet as limber as the feet of an ape. Her lips would still be moving. Or had they stopped? He had a feeling she was looking at him with her blind eyes, as she did sometimes—watching him with every nerve in her body. He lay motionless. She drew the sheet and coverture to her bony chest and lay still on her back, her head pressed firmly into the pillow, her nose, even sharper when her eyes were out, pointing at the ceiling. She looked like a chicken in bed. He lay on his side with his hands folded, his small, close-set eyes fixed on the wallpaper a foot away, staring at it as a mouse would stare at a place where he once saw a cat. Through the springs of the mattress he could hear their two heartbeats, his own slow and awesome as the nightlong pounding of a big ship's engines on a calm sea, hers quick and light as squirrel feet. He was imagining it, he knew. She lay as motionless as a dead chicken. It wouldn't surprise him if, turning, he found that her feet were sticking in the air.

"Fred?" she said.

He thought of the rouged, naked breasts of the waitress with the coffeepot. But the image no longer stirred him. He saw himself walking along a beach where the sand was tiny grits of color, blue and green and deep red and yellow, like minute pieces from a stained-glass window. Four men who looked vaguely like Mayor Mullen sat scowling, watching him approach, with towels around their waists. He looked toward the sea and wide green sky, distressed.

It occurred to him suddenly that he was hungry. Ravenous. He thought of going down to the refrigerator, or to the cellar, where he had, if he remembered right, two cases of Carling's Beer.

"Do you hear something, Fred?" she asked softly.

There was someone in the yard. He heard it distinctly, or felt it through the walls and beams of the house and the dark packed earth below the grass. Both of them lay perfectly still. Minutes passed. Now the prowler was inside, feeling his way through the cluttered blackness from the cellar door toward the stairs that led up to the pantry. There were snakes down there, and spiders, and long, lean rats. He'd fished one out of the cistern a month ago. The prowler stood listening at the door to the pantry, head bent almost to the porcelain knob. Then nothing, not a sound for fifteen minutes. It came to him that his wife was asleep, he'd only imagined that she'd spoken to him. There was no one in the cellar, not the bearded, disfigured magician, as he'd thought, and not anyone else. In the gaunt, high-gabled wooden husk they were alone, as usual. He could just make out the darker places on the wallpaper, the crooked trail of vines and the large gray smudges, diagonally receding, a foot apart. Roses.

Hours later he awakened with a start, hungry. The night was silent. If I just had a sandwich, he thought. He could taste it. There was bologna—he could eat a whole package of it— and there was lettuce, crudely torn apart and somewhat wilted, thrust into a Baggie and tucked in the crisper drawer. And cheese, and salad dressing. Perhaps a little chicken. There was a pocket of water in his cheek and he swallowed, and he thought again of the beer. He'd have done it once, when he was younger; would have sat up in bed and slipped his feet over the side and would have gone down to stuff himself. But it was bad for you, that kind of thing. Not just because it made you fat, made your heart work harder than an old heart should, but bad in ways more insidious—the same as buying without shopping first for a reasonable bargain, or buying what you didn't need, or not buying at all, on the other hand, because your mind was too much on the column of numbers written under "Deposits" in your bank book. He'd thought all that out long ago—it might as well have been centuries—and he knew he was not going down to the refrigerator, however seductive the images coming unbidden into his head. Again the thought of the coffeepot and the waitress came sliding into his mind. Now he was angry. A man sixty-four years old needed his sleep. What was wrong with him? he wondered. But the question was not difficult. Every nerve in his body was jangling because of that prisoner. Or partly that. He'd been nervous for months, to tell the truth; the prisoner was the final straw. What he needed right now was a pill.

Before he knew he would do it he swung out of bed and then padded, jaw clenched, to the bathroom to get the sleeping pills. At the bathroom door he paused, scowling; then, furtively, he went on to the head of the stairs. Not a sound behind him. Softly, like a man drawn by voodoo, he went down, avoiding the steps that squeaked, and felt his way to the kitchen.

He ate by the light from the refrigerator door. Then, stuffed, dry of throat and as hungry as ever, he went soundlessly down the cellar steps, lighting his way with the flashlight he kept at the top of the stairs for when fuses blew. In the flashlight's dim glow the damp stone walls of the cellar were like walls of a dungeon. Drafts moved through the dark like fish. The air was moist and chilly. He thought he heard a rat scamper, but the next instant he wasn't sure. He stood for a long time with his hand on the neck of the bottle, undecided whether to open it or not, his eyes tightly focused on a cobweb. It seemed to him, in the back of his mind, that here in the cellar, if he listened hard, he could hear what was happening in every house in the city: lovers talking on livingroom couches, murderers climbing through kitchen windows, cats eating mice, old men at Doehler-Jarvis shoveling coal.

Abruptly, awake and trembling from the cold, he put the bottle back and turned to go up. When he reached the livingroom he found that his wife had gotten up, as she did sometimes when she couldn't sleep or woke up nervous. She had gotten out her sewing, a kind of dress she'd been working on, if he wasn't mistaken, for years.

"Good night," he said. He kissed her forehead.

"Good night, dear," she said.

Clumly went up.

## 2

He felt better in the morning, as he always did, at least for a little while. Not because he had slept well but because it was morning. The world had expanded, warmed, gotten back its good sense. While Esther fixed breakfast he went out to stand on the front porch in his uniform, his hands behind his back, pot belly comfortably protruding, and he sucked in the clean, cool air. He faced the round orange sun that hung just clear of the trees and housetops four blocks away, at the end of the street which began just opposite his yard, and he said, like an old king satisfied with his accomplishments, "Ah." The music of songbirds rose all around him like bubbles in a cup of ginger ale, a battle of sparrows and robins against jays. He watched Ed Wardrop start up his car and light a cigarette and pull out from the curb, and when the car turned onto La-Crosse and he saw Ed duck his head and glance over to see if he was there as usual, he nodded solemnly and waved, a little like the Pope. The younger Miss Buckland came out and called her cat.

He had papers up to his eyebrows down at the station, but they'd waited this long, he decided. They could wait one day more. It was a day for inspections, and for trying to talk with that lunatic, and this afternoon was Albert Hubbard's funeral. (Flowers for Paxton, he reminded himself.) As a man got older he spent more and more of his time at funerals, or sending out funeral flowers, or standing in the hush where old friends were laid out in their livingrooms or at Turner's or Burdett's or Bohm's.

Fred Clumly enjoyed funerals. It was a sad thing to see all one's old friends and relatives slipping away, one after the other, leaving their grown sons and daughters weeping, soberly dabbing at their eyes with their neat white hankies, the grandchildren sitting on the gravestones or standing unwillingly solemn at the side of the grave while they lowered the coffin. But it was pleasant, too, in a mysterious way he couldn't and didn't really want to find words for. There stood the whole family— three, four generations—the living testimonial to the man's having been; all dressed in their finest and at peace with one another; and there stood his business acquaintances and his friends from the church, the schoolboard he'd once been a member of, all quarrels forgotten; and there stood his friends from the Dairyman's League or Kiwanis or the Owls or the Masons. The coffin rolled silently out of the hearse, and his friends, brothers, sons took the glittering handles and lowered him slowly onto the beams across the hole and then stood back, red-faced from their life's work as truckers or farmers, or sallow-faced from the bank or grocery store or laundry. And there it was, a man's whole life drawn together at last, stilled to a charm, honored and respected, and the minister took off his black hat and prayed, and Clumly prayed, with tears in his eyes and his police cap over his fallen chest, and so, with dignity, the man's life closed, like the book in the minister's hands.

Poor Albert Hubbard. He'd inherited his nursery business from his father and he'd built it up little by little for years, and then, maybe fifteen years ago now, he'd taken in his oldest son and, soon after that, his second oldest. The youngest had moved to Syracuse. Some kind of engineer. The sons had big ideas, and it must've been hard on poor old Albert. They filled up two acres with their greenhouses, and they bought up farmland for a half-mile in either direction. They could no more pay for it than fly. It's the twentieth century, they said. They'd been away to college and learned about economics. You just keep up the interest, they said, don't you worry about the principal. Old Albert got crankier and crankier. When Clumly would stop by he'd be potching along among the bins of plants, more plants than any ten nurseries could sell, and he'd be wearing the same old felt hat he'd worn twenty-five years ago, or it looked the same, and he'd have on the same old overalls and hightop shoes and his applepicker's bib.

"Don' you worry your head about them aphids," he'd squeak, mimicking his sons, tipping his head down and looking up from under his shaggy eyebrows at Clumly. "We spray around here by the schedule, see, and if the aphids don't know what the schedule is, don't you worry, them plants is insured."

"Well, times change," Clumly would say.

"Pah! Times change! Why this next Depression's gonna make that last one look like Heaven's own feast for the blessed." He'd move down a plant, shaking his head. "Wal, mebby I'll be dead by then. I hope so."

Now he was. Soul rest in peace.

A jay walked up to the porch steps as though Clumly were not there. "Morning, young fella," Clumly said. The bird looked at him, intelligent, about to speak. Then Esther called, and Clumly went in to eat.

"You look fresh as a daisy," Esther said. Even when she spoke cheerfully, it was a whine.

"I still get around," he said. He began on his eggs.

Prowlcar 19. Kozlowski. Father had a farm out on Tinkham Road. Clean little house, clean little barn, Holstein cows and sheep and a couple of work-horses standing around the willow trees by the pond behind the barn. The old woman had expected her son to take over when the old man had died— buried alive when a pea-vine wagon turned over on him, six months ago now—another poor mortal ground under by the load—but Kozlowski had other ideas. He hated farming. Hated being tied down to the milking three-hundred-and-sixty-five days every year, hated trying to outguess the weather, hated more than anything else the everlasting tedium of setting out fenceposts, cleaning stables, unsnarling rope and old harness leather and baling twine, or mending bags, or crawling out of bed to run after the cows when they got through the fence and took off at a run through some neighbor's cornlot, no more knowing where they were going than how to spell. He was a small man, with a red face and small red hands and hair the color of dust. He hardly ever spoke. Thoughtful. He sat in the prowlcar, sheepish-looking as usual, waiting for Clumly to catch up.

Clumly locked his car door and hurried to the back drive gate where Kozlowski waited. "Morning, Stan."

Kozlowski grinned.

"Mind if I ride around?" Clumly asked. He felt exhilarated, like a man slightly drugged.

"That all you got to do?"

Clumly laughed grittily and went around the front of the car to the rider's side, patting the fenders as he passed. Kozlowski watched him get in and smiled dutifully when the door slammed shut, but he was thinking his own thoughts.

"How's it going?" Clumly said.

Kozlowski shrugged. He pulled out onto the street. The radio sputtered. He stopped for the Main Street light.

"Lot of the boys get annoyed when I come ride around with them," Clumly said. The car smelled richly of new gas. He'd just been to the pump, Clumly deduced. He sat back more and reached inside his jacket for a cigar. "They get the wrong idea, you know. Cigar?"

Kozlowski shook his head. The light changed. He started up.

Clumly chuckled. "I drove prowlcar for seventeen years. You cognizant of that?"

"No fooling," Kozlowski said.

"Yessir. Well, I was younger then. But I'll tell you one thing. We worked like the devil in those days. Eight P.M. till eight A.M. in the morning, that was my hours for I don't know how long. And the pay? Son, you couldn't get a garbage man for the pay we got then. Nine dollars a day. Just as true as I'm setting here." He opened the glove-compartment and looked inside, then closed it again.

"Garbage men make a lot of money," Kozlowski said.

A car shot past them and abruptly slowed down, no doubt noticing that they were police. Clumly leaned forward to watch the driver, then leaned back, letting it go. "Well, I kept my nose clean," Clumly said, "and I put in an hour's work for an hour's pay. I worked up through the ranks."

Kozlowski nodded.

"Life's been good to me," Clumly said. It was a good cigar. The day would be another scorcher, but the breeze coming in through Clumly's window still had the scent of morning in it, even here in the middle of town. He said: "But I miss the old days, that's the truth. I don't say I'd give up what I'm making and go back to patroling—both jobs have their remunerations. But you're freer out on patrol, I will say that. Nobody watching you all the time, keeping you honest." He shot a glance at Kozlowski.

"I don't mind it," Kozlowski said.

"Of course you don't," Clumly said heartily. He shifted in the seat, trying to get more comfortable, then closed his eyes a minute. "Well, a lot of the boys get the wrong idea," he said. "The way I figure, we do this job of ours together. A man can't run a police force if he doesn't trust his men."

Kozlowski nodded again. He turned down Jackson and crossed the one track remaining from the days when the New York Central depot used to be here in the center of town. Clumly pointed to the square brick house on the left. "Know that place? It used to be Edna's. House of ill repute."

"I've heard that," Kozlowski said.

"That's it," Clumly said. "We run her out of business a dozen times. Maybe two dozen times. Sent her up the river and I don't know what all. But she always came back, just as regular as tomorrow. It was a kind of joke around town for a good long while. Lot of people used to think it was a good thing to have a place like that, and I know cops that would turn their heads and not notice when she was set up again till sooner or later a complaint come in. They weren't crooks, you know. They weren't taking bribes, nothing like that. They just had a theory, that was all. Well, takes all kinds."

They came to the end of South Jackson and began the loop back in. Kozlowski said, "What kind were you, Chief?"

"Eh?"

"You close her down?"

Clumly inspected his cigar. "Son, I closed her *out*."

Kozlowski smiled ruefully.

"Wouldn't you done the same thing in my place?" Clumly said.

"Sure," Kozlowski said seriously. "That's my job."

"Correct," Clumly said. But he smiled ironically. He looked at the radio speaker, paying no attention. After a moment he said, "I don't know if you'd close her or not, Kozlowski. But I'll tell you this. Lot of times when things are pushing the way they are, more work to get done than an ordinary human can do in the hours he's got, a man can slide into thinking there's nothing to watch for but what he sees posted on the board. I don't mean the board's not important. What you see on that board is unusually important, that's why it's posted there. It's like—" He paused, half-closing his eyes, crafty. "It's like a farmer," he said. "When a man's got wheat to get in before the rain, he gets his wheat. But it don't mean he forgets about his milking for a while."

"Yes sir," Kozlowski said.

Clumly studied him. "Put it this way," he said. "How come you don't close down that house on Harvester?"

The blush was unmistakable and, in spite of himself, Clumly smiled again. Kozlowski waited, maybe thinking he hadn't heard right. Clumly threw the cigar out the window and folded his hands. "Turn right," he said. Kozlowski turned.

"I guess it surprises you," Clumly said happily. (There's a dance or two in the old dame yet, he thought.) "Maybe scares you a little. I imagine I'd feel the same way, if I was in your place. I imagine you wonder how the old bastard knows. You see all those papers piled up on my desk, you hear how I have to get around to the schools and make speeches to the kids about crossing the street, you see I've got worries coming out of my ears—that damned trouble with the dogs, and this plague of stealing this past two months, and now these fires, and the Force in need of men so bad it's a wonder we don't every one of us throw up our hands. Well I'll tell you something. My job is Law and Order. That's my first job, and if I can't get that one done, the rest will just have to wait. You get my meaning? If there's a law on the books, it's my job to see it's enforced. I'm *personally responsible* for every cop in my Department, and for every crook in the City of Batavia. That's my job. I'm aware as you are there are differences of opinion about some of the laws we're paid to enforce, but a cop hasn't got opinions. Don't you forget it. Some fool makes a law against planting trees and you and me will be out there, like it or not, and we'll shut down Arbor Day."

Still Kozlowski said nothing. He was passing the ice plant, closed for over a year now. There were a couple of bicycles leaning against the fence. He glanced at Clumly, and Clumly pretended not to see. "Two more blocks," Clumly said. "You know the place as well as I do, son."

Kozlowski nodded. After a minute he said, "You gonna raid her right now? In the morning?"

Clumly compressed his lips, checked for an instant. But the hunch was strong.

"You think too much, Kozlowski," he said. "It's a bad habit, for a cop. Oh, I don't blame you, you understand. Man can't help feeling uneasy sometimes in this business. But I'll tell you something. This is a democracy. You know how democracy works, son? Bunch of people get together and they decide how they want things, and they pass a law and they have 'em that way till they're sick of it, and then they pass some other law that's maybe wrong some other way. It's like a farmer," Clumly said. "Say he sets his alarm clock wrong and he gets up an hour too early, and then he sends his dog out after the cows for milking. You follow me? Well now the dog *knows* it's an hour too early, and he ain't happy about it, but he goes. Well, we're the Watchdogs of Society. We do our job or we're no use."

"Cowdogs, you mean," Kozlowski said.

"Correct," Clumly said. "Same thing."

"Shall I turn on the siren, Chief?" Kozlowski said.

Clumly scowled, annoyed, and said, "Negative." He hated a man who would sass you right out. But Kozlowski was young, another of the new ones. He'd let it pass. The car pulled over and Clumly opened his door quietly. He hung motionless an instant, no longer sure of his hunch; but his doubt passed. "You go first."

It was a low, dark-green house set back in the shadow of maple trees. The grass needed cutting, between the bare patches, and the plants were dead in the green metal boxes on the porch. There was a rusted car up on blocks to the right of the house, a legacy from some previous tenant. Weeds had grown up through the floorboards, and you could see them through the windshield like patient, brainless creatures waiting for a ride. They were people turned into thistles, maybe. The shades were drawn on all the house windows you could see from the street, and one of the windows had a pane of cardboard in it. There was a Negro child sitting on the porch roof of the house next door.

"Looks like business hasn't been good," Kozlowski said. "You remember the warrant?"

"Just ask her if you can come in," Clumly said.

"According to the law—" Kozlowski began.

Clumly flushed. They didn't need a warrant if she invited them in, and Kozlowski knew it. "Just ask her."

Kozlowski nodded and adjusted his cap. "Positive," he said. He went up on the porch, Clumly a little behind him, and rang the doorbell.

"Better knock," Clumly said. "Those doorbells never work."

Kozlowski knocked. Casually, Clumly stepped to the left of the door where she wouldn't see him at once when she opened up. Kozlowski touched his cap again as if thinking of taking it off, then changed his mind. After a long moment he knocked a second time, more firmly, then folded his red hands behind him. There wasn't a sound from inside the house, and they went on waiting, Clumbly gazing down the street toward the grocery store at the corner of Harvester and Main, where there were more Negroes. A smell of pigweed came from the end of the porch. At last, though still there had been no sound, the doorknob turned and the door opened three inches. Clumly sidled back farther along the wall.

"Yes?" she said.

Kozlowski bent toward her, apologetic as a funeral director. "It's nothing serious, ma'am. Do you mind if I come in?"

Clumly held in a smile, standing with his back against the cool wall of the house. Kozlowski would make a good cop, one of these days. She was going to let him in.

"All right," she said doubtfully. She opened the door farther, keeping behind it. Kozlowski stepped in and when he was over the threshold turned as if inviting Clumly to follow. Clumly took off his hat and stepped in behind.

"I'm sorry to bother you," Kozlowski said again. "My name's Kozlowski. This is Chief Clumly."

She looked at them, waiting. She had baggy eyes and cracks on her lips, though she was young. She was a white woman, but dark-complected. Eyes like a gypsy's. Her henna-red hair was long and loose and didn't look clean. The hair on her legs was black. She stood with one hand on the doorknob, the other clutching her robe together—quilted pink, badly faded. The livingroom behind her was gloomy and grimy, furnished like a cheap motel with low-lined over-stuffed chairs, a daybed, three standing metal ashtrays that were probably stolen from somewhere. A bus depot, maybe. On the dimestore coffee table there were battered magazines—*True Confessions, Police Gazette, Movie Life, The Astrologer*. It didn't look to Clumly like a whorehouse, and he felt a moment's panic. But this was the place and, he remembered suddenly—and smiled, cunning—he hadn't told Kozlowski which house: Kozlowski had chosen it himself. He frowned then, until his eyes were like two bullets, and tried to think what the smell was, filling the room.

"How do you do," Clumly said, extending his hand.

She ignored it. "What is this?"

"Your name Rosemary?" Clumly said.

She did not answer and at first gave no sign that he was right or wrong, merely watched him, hostile and afraid. She bit her lower lip. She had long thin teeth with space between the two in front. Then, stupidly—Poor stupid woman, Clumly thought—she looked at Kozlowski for help. "You said there'd be no trouble." Kozlowski pursed his lips and looked at the floor. She looked back at Clumly. "What is this? What do you want?"

Clumly covered his mouth with his hand, startled by his luck, and merely looked at her. So young, he thought. (It was time to pounce now: ask to see the bedrooms.) There was dirt in the cracks on her neck and below the collar line, where the sun hadn't hit her, her flesh was goosepimply and white. It came to him that the stench in the house, heavier, more concentrated around her body—a stink like rottenness, like death —was dimestore perfume.

"How old are you, Rosemary?" Clumly said.

She drew back a step, running her hand through her hair, with her left hand pulling the collar of the robe more tightly together. "Get out of here," she said. She turned her face to Kozlowski. "What does he want?"

But Kozlowski went on studying the floor, red as a beet, moving the toe of his boot along a crack, three inches, back and forth, like a boy.

Clumly went on studying her with his hand around his chin. She could have been pretty, like anyone else, if she'd wanted. "How long you been in this business, Rosemary?" he said gently.

"Get out," she said. Her black eyebrows lowered and her mouth grew taut. "Get out of my house or by Jesus I'll call—" She broke off abruptly and laughed, her voice electric.

Clumly thought about it. Her anger was queerly touching to him, and confusing. He felt he'd been here before, the same conversation. He tried to think. "Very well," he said a little vaguely, "we'll go. But we'll be back, Rosemary." He didn't move. "Young lady, if you want my advice—" He didn't finish, and couldn't. They had come to a standstill. Kozlowski knew it and wouldn't help; probably couldn't. Clumly waited, and time grew like a calm. He tried to think. Then, suddenly, she darted forward releasing the collar and letting the robe fly loose around her naked bosom, and before Clumly knew what was happening he was back inside time, she had slashed open the side of his hand with her silver fingernails and was reaching for his face. He was too startled even for anger. "That's enough!" he yelled. "Stop it!" He caught her hands, his heart pounding painfully, and simply held her as well as he could for a moment by the wrists, not knowing what to do. Then, collecting his wits, numb with the image of her nakedness, he released her and turned away quickly, ducking his head, and half-ran through the door. Kozlowski came out behind him soberly, like a man coming out of a church. His lips were pursed. The door slammed shut, then opened again. Bastards!" she yelled at them. "Sons of bitches!" She shook her fist, leaning out at them, shameless, oblivious, hurling obscenities like mud. Clumly held his chest with two hands to keep the pounding of his heart from splitting it, and he walked bent over more than usual, panting for breath. When he reached the car he fell into it and sat with his eyes shut, still holding his chest but keeping the blood from his scratched hand off his shirt. He was afraid he was having an attack. Kozlowski sat waiting, lighting a cigarette.

"A policeman's job—" Clumly said hoarsely. But a coughing fit seized him and he couldn't finish. There were people at the windows of the houses across the street. Kozlowski went on waiting till the first rock hit the side of the car. Then he switched on the ignition and pulled out into the street. He drove back through town to the station slowly, saying nothing. When he parked, Clumly got out without a word, still full of painful excitement that was almost like pleasure, and hurried in. His face was squeezed tight with humiliation, and for the life of him he could not walk upright. It wasn't that he was winded now. It was his liver or something. When he reached the door he found, to his surprise, that Kozlowski had followed him. He glanced at the man furtively, then, angry and ashamed, went on to the lavatory to wash his wounded hand, then back to his office as though Kozlowski were still out there in his car.

Finally, seated behind his desk, he knew he could no longer ignore the man's presence. He snatched his reading glasses from the drawer and irritably hung them on his ears to examine the scratch marks. Then, knowing very well what a figure he cut, he tipped his mole's nose slowly and squinted at Kozlowski.

"My badge," Kozlowski said, pushing it toward Clumly over the papers.

Clumly said nothing, and the man turned away.

"Wait a minute," Clumly said. He sucked the sore hand again.

Kozlowski waited.

Clumly closed his eyes and sat thinking, trembling all over, still sucking the hand, for a long time. He felt sick. His knees were shaking, and it wasn't just his palsy. He got up abruptly, awkwardly, to prove to himself he was still in control, and went over to stand at the window, bent-backed, and took his glasses off again and held them behind him. He changed his mind and crossed back to his desk and dropped the glasses on the papers, then returned to the window and, with gray, trembling fingers, lighted himself a cigar. Still Kozlowski waited, standing with his hat on.

"Sit down," Clumly said, gesturing without glancing over his shoulder. He heard Kozlowski move the chair a few inches and sit.

"All right," Clumly said. He began to pace, smoking, never looking at Kozlowski. "All right," he said more loudly. "Maybe I went too far. A mistake." He stood still, musing. "You know it was a mistake, and you might have said so, but you didn't." He thought about it. "Spared my feelings. That's good." He paced again. "That's very good. You could have said when we got to the car, 'Where next, Chief?'—rubbing it in, you know. But you didn't. Very good. You'll make a good cop."

"I've resigned," Kozlowski said.

"Resigned hell! I could hang you for this. You promised that little whore protection. You heard her yourself. 'You said there'd be no trouble.' You don't think I've forgotten that?"

Kozlowski lit the cigarette in his hand. "Not likely," he said. He crossed his legs.

Clumly jerked away and went back to his pacing, struggling to ignore the sass. "All right," he said. He smoked furiously, making a heavy cloud around his head. "I liked the way you got in there," he said. "I thought to myself, 'Good cop, that boy.' I like that."

Kozlowski said nothing, and Clumly glared at him, then away again, thinking. His arms and legs prickled and felt numb. He pointed at Kozlowski then and said, "You should've shut her down. That's your job. You know that." He waited, but he knew there was no answer coming. "Well all right," he said. "All right, you use your judgment. That's good. A cop needs judgment. I like that." He paced. "A lot of my men get the wrong idea. We do this job of ours together, protecting Law and Order. This is a democracy."

"Yes sir."

The interruption broke his train of thought. He was sweating. "This is a democracy," he said again, more emphatically. "We're the Watchdogs. If a man can't trust his Force, who can he trust? All right. I'm cognizant of that. Listen." He tried to think what it was he had to tell him, but the memory of his humiliation distracted him. The woman's image was burned into his mind—the youth of it, the nakedness, and the righteous indignation—and for some reason the painful image released another, his wife lying still as a dead chicken in the bed, unloved, useless. Who would mourn for her? Who would mourn for Clumly?

He went back to his desk, wincing, trying to think, and as if hoping it would help he put his glasses on again.

"Kozlowski," he said, "don't quit."

Pitiful it sounded.

The man waited, not saying what Clumly knew he would be thinking.

"Too old, that must be it," Clumly said. His chest was so full he felt like a man drowning. "Jitters," he said. "—Miller!" He squinted at the door and called more loudly, "Miller! Come in here!"

Miller came in, pushing his pencil down into his pocket, carrying his clipboard. Miller was Clumly's right-hand man.

"Miller, tell Kozlowski not to quit."

"Don't quit," Miller said. He cocked his head, grinning, looking at Clumly.

"How long you been with us, Miller?" Clumly said.

"Why, nineteen hundred seven thousand twenty-three million two and a half—" Miller talked, always, a mile a minute. His name was Dominic Sangirgonio, Miller for short.

"Stop that!" Clumly roared. He banged the desk, then clung to it.

"Long time," Miller said.

"Am I a rigid man?" Clumly demanded. "Am I a hard man to work for? Do I spy on my men, or ask the impossible? Tell him."

"Just like a father," Miller said.

"Miller, why do I drive my men? Why do I personally keep track of every job this Department does, from parking meters to criminal assault? Tell him."

"Some kind of nut." He smiled.

"Stop it," Clumly said. "This man's just tendered his resignation."

"Tendered!" Miller said, impressed.

Clumly's hand was still shaking, even when he steadied the heel on the desk—cigar ashes spattering on the papers—but for a moment longer Miller continued to watch, as if amused.

"Ok," he said finally, looking over at Kozlowski. "What happened? Old man make a fool of himself, you think?" He tipped his head and grinned again. "You'll get used to it. Honor bright. Cops are bad guys. Sometimes when you start out you forget that and pretty soon—*pow!*—you're dead, some good guy's got a knife. Like the kid Salvador we got guarding the bears. He thinks they're his friends. Gives 'em cigarettes and candy and listens to their sob stories." He laughed, but not wholeheartedly. "One of these days he'll get his block knocked off. You'd be surprised how easy it is to get your block knocked off."

"Look," Kozlowski said.

"Tomorrow. For now, put on the badge. Think it over." He reached for the badge and flipped it to Kozlowski. Kozlowski seemed to consider it. Miller said, "Shut her down, paisan. For a week or two, see? Teach the little broad some respect." Before Kozlowski could answer he bowed to Clumly and went out.

Clumly looked at the papers, and Kozlowski stood toying with the badge.

"All right," Clumly said weakly. "That's all. Things have been pushing a little, lately. Just the same, all I said in the car —" He thought about it. "We have to enforce the law," he said. "If a cop starts making exceptions—the fabric of society —" He had a funeral to go to this afternoon. The thought distracted him and he glared at Kozlowski to get his train of thought back. He said, "You ever see that man with the beard before?"

Kozlowski looked puzzled.

"In here," Clumly said. He got up, knowing it was an odd thing to do, and led Kozlowski down the hallway to the cellblock. He held the door open and pointed. "Him."

Kozlowski studied him, then shook his head.

Clumly turned back toward his office. "All right," he said. "That's all. Think it over."

Kozlowski nodded. He remembered he still had his hat on and reached up to touch it. "Yes sir," he said. He left.

Alone again, Clumly sat down and racked his brain to make out what had happened. But he didn't get time. Miller looked in almost at once. "Got time for a public relations call? Old

Lady Woodworth wants you. At her house, this afternoon, maybe."

The words would not get straight in Clumly's mind, and he strained to think. He was hungry again.

"About the robbery," Miller said. "Cops ain't doin their jobs. Gonna telephone the Gov'nah."

At last he understood. "You think it's that man we got, that Walter Boyle?"

"Not a chance." Miller turned away.

Clumly sighed, grew calmer. There was something important he'd meant to do this morning. He remembered all at once that he'd thought there was a prowler in the yard last night. He tried to think what had made him change his mind. It was possible. They'd had case after case, these past two months. A plague of them, most of them in broad daylight, ever since spring. And some of them were dangerous—the Negro boy in the red shirt who'd beaten that woman on Ellicott Avenue half to death with the handle of a mop. He was still at large. Maybe he should call his wife, see that everything was all right. Sometimes they got into your basement and stayed there for hours, waiting. He closed his eyes. Behind him, in the cellblock, the bearded lunatic was singing. His voice was high and sweet, strangely sad. He's as sane as I am, Clumly thought, and this time he was certain of it. When will he make his move?

Calmly, purposefully, Clumly got up and walked back to the cellblock. "You," he said. "Keep it down."

The bearded one smiled, all innocence, and blew him a kiss.

### 3

Ben and Vanessa Hodge were at the funeral too. They made them all, these days, like Clumly. Ben was a member of the Presbyterian Session, as Hubbard had been, and before that, a long time ago now, he'd sold milk and butter to the Hubbards. Hodge was a wide, benign man in white socks, with a face as orange as the bricks of his house and hands like rusty shovels. He gave sermons here and there, at country churches from Genesee County to the Finger Lakes, wherever someone happened to know him. He knew stories, more than an average man, and when he told them the stories would grow clearer and clearer until the moral stood out like a pearl-handled nickel-plated pistol on a stump. He didn't read much. He put in fourteen-hour days in the rush seasons of the summertime, except on Sundays, and in the winter, when he wasn't out plowing off country roads with his wired-together Farmall tractor or milking his Holsteins or forking out ensilage or manure, he lay with his face turned into the cushions of his davenport and his monumental rear end hanging over, sleeping like a bear. He made up the sermons while he worked his land or while he rode through the foothills near Olean, late at night in the summer, on his old Horex motorcycle. His voice was high and sharp, as if he was calling from across a windy wheatfield.

He stood by the casket with one hand laid over the other in front of him, looking down at the powdered, painted face, or through it into the white silk cushions or the cold dirt under the house. Vanessa was beside him, with her pink-gloved hand hanging on to the tight arm of his suitcoat and her upside-down-milkpail-shaped flowered pink hat tipped queerly above the hair that had been bright red once but was now like old cotton fluff. She was short and wide and walked the way a domino would. When they came away from the casket, Vanessa hobbling on her two gimpy legs and smiling crookedly, like an alligator, Clumly nodded to them.

"Lo there," Hodge said, loud as a plank breaking in the hush of the funeral parlor. But before they could get to Clumly, an old lady he didn't know went up to them, shaking and clutching at Vanessa with one white, liver-spotted claw.

Clumly wiped his forehead with his handkerchief (it was ninety in the shade, and though it had been cool in the mortuary when he first came in, the crowd had warmed it by now) and moved over to stand nearer Hubbard's sons. They'd be talking about Vietnam, he expected, or about unions ruining the country (which they were; he'd said to himself a hundred times). He leaned toward them a little, listening, pretending to watch the friends and relatives filing past the casket. He'd guessed wrong. They were talking about houses.

"It's that old gray house on the Lewiston Road," the older one of the brothers was saying. "Used to be the Sojda place, next to Toals'."

"On the hill," the other one said.

"That's it. With the big gray barn and the stonewall fence."

"I know the place."

"Arson, they think." The older one shook his head. He was small and lean and sharp-nosed, foreign-looking; a little like a Spaniard, or like an old-time alchemist wasted away to pure alum and sharp bits of bone. He was the brains of the nursery business. The other one was short and soft, with a purplish cast to his face and hands. Looked like he belonged in a feedstore, sitting, in the middle of winter, by the stove. There was no sign of the third son. The two older boys' wives were with them, but neither of them spoke. People said the two wives had terrible fights, at home. In public, they were like stones.

"Been a lot of arson lately," the younger one said. "Naturally, the cops never catch the ones that did it."

The older one shook his head crossly. "Beats all," he said. "Cops wouldn't catch 'em if they came in and locked themselves up."

Clumly shrank away. The floral smell which he always thought pleasant at funerals now seemed cloying. It thickened the air and made it hard for him to breathe. He fumbled for a cigar, then remembered he mustn't smoke here. When he glanced up, the younger Hubbard's wife was staring straight at him. He nodded and threw a confused, ghastly smile which he vaguely intended as consolation for the bereaved. He meant to leave and took one step, but the younger Hubbard saw him and said, "Chief Clumly," and stretched out his hand. Clumly turned, caught at the hand and shook it. "So sorry," Clumly said. "Fine man, your father."

"A blessing," the boy said. It struck Clumly that the young man's eyes were red-rimmed. He was disconcerted.

"Blessing, yes," he said. "Poor devil."

The older brother reached over sadly—as if irritably, as well—and shook Clumly's hand. "So glad you could get away," he said.

The smell of the flowers was overwhelming, and the softness of the carpet made Clumly feel unsteady. "I'm sorry," he said "Your father was—"

Both sons nodded. Their wives stood with their arms stiffly at their sides, watching.

"Hear about the fire last night?" the older one said. "The old Sojda place. Arson, according to the State Police. Right to the foundation, they say." His eyes narrowed. "I guess you people been having your hands full too."

It seemed to Clumly an accusation, and he said, "Short-handed, that's the trouble." He winced as if he'd bit into a lemon.

"I can believe it," Hubbard said sympathetically, but still he was watching Clumly narrowly, as if with disgust. "I understand you finally caught one of those housebreakers. That true?"

"Well, not a housebreaker exactly." Clumly looked down, evading the chilly eyes. "Thief, yes. One of the pros. If we can prove it." Instantly he wished he could pull his last words back.

"You can't prove it, you think?"

Clumly shrugged. "They tie your hands," he said feebly. "You get what you can on the man and you take it into court —" He concentrated. Someone was whispering behind him. He mopped his brow and pushed the handkerchief back in his pocket. "We're going through a period of transition," he said very seriously, as if addressing a visitor at the jail, or making one of those service club speeches Mayor Mullen kept getting him into. "Twenty years ago everything was different. Times are changing. Everybody moving around these days, that's part of it. Too many strange faces. It used to be when a crime was committed in a town like Batavia . . . person-to-person operation in the old days. It takes a lot more policemen now, a lot of high-price machinery, a lab no town like this can afford, and even then a lot of times you can't nail 'em. Old-fashioned rules for admitting evidence. And then the politicians get into it, with their talk about the Productive Time Factor and Public Relations, not to mention the relatives they want to give jobs . . . and yet all the citizens, the newspapers expect . . ."

Hubbard patted his shoulder. "Well, we know we're in good hands with you, Chief. Excuse me." He turned to say hello to the man behind him. The other brother had vanished. Clumly backed away. Albert Hubbard's widow was standing alone by the casket, and Clumly went to her cautiously. As he touched her elbow he realized he'd forgotten her name.

"I was sorry to hear," Clumly said. "He looks very natural." He considered. "I guess we all go sometimes," he said.

The veiled face turned toward him. He couldn't see her features behind the black netting, couldn't know for sure that it *was* Mrs. Hubbard and not some dangerous stranger. He felt like a man being spied on through a mirror.

"The flowers are beautiful," he said. "He looks very natural."

After a long time the old woman said, "Yes." He felt violent relief. The organ music started, and Clumly looked down at the corpse. The mouth was sealed forever with mortician's paint.

"He'll be missed," Chief Clumly said. He began to weep, and Mrs. Hubbard took his hand.

It wasn't until after the prayer at the cemetery that he saw Ben Hodge again. He and Vanessa were standing by the fieldstone gateposts, listening from there. The gravel cemetery drive would have been hard going for Vanessa, with those bad knees. When Clumly went up to them, Hodge said, "You still got my boys down there?"

"Slater boys? The Indians? They're there all right. We been expecting you to come down and post bail for 'em."

"Not me. I've done all I can for those boys. You can ship 'em away to Elmira, it's the only course left." He smiled unhappily.

"Blooey!" Vanessa said. "We quit."

"Listen here," Hodge said. He tapped Clumly's chest gently, as if absent-mindedly, the way his father the Congressman used to tap a neighbor's chest when he wanted his vote. "Those boys have had homes. Good homes. I don't mean just ours, which may or may not be what you'd call good. They got forty dollars a month spending money when they were at our place, and for dang little work, too. And the place they were before, over there in Byron, that woman had the patience of a saint. You wonder what gets into them."

"You heard what the younger one said to the social worker," Vanessa said. "She asked him what he wanted to be and he said—he's honest, you'll have to say that!—he said, 'I just want to hang around.' " Vanessa laughed, *mp, mp!* slapping Ben Hodge's shoulder. She was old, but when she laughed she was pretty for a moment. Bill Churchill was passing them, leaving the cemetery, and when he nodded hello she drew him into the group and told him the same story she'd just told Clumly, in the same words, and laughed, and slapped Hodge's shoulder.

"Honest!" Hodge said, "why you know what that little monkey did? The County got him a room at the Y, right after he'd decided he was fed up with us, and they gave him fifty dollars for it. For some reason they can't pay the rent direct—I don't know what the technicality is. Anyway, he spent twenty-five dollars on clothes and lost the rest of it shooting craps, and you know what that boy did? He went back to the County and told them exactly what had happened and asked for more."

They all laughed except Bill Churchill, who was outraged. "Welfare!" he said. "It's sucking the blood out of this country! How many people *are* there, I wonder, that all they want is just to 'hang around'? They can do it, too. That's what burns me. 'Gimme, gimme, gimme!' " He was still jabbing at Hodge's chest. Hodge reached out with his own, gentler tap, like a man absent-mindedly keeping time to music on Bill Churchill's tie. "It's a complicated thing, though, isn't it."

"Faw!" Churchill said.

Vanessa said, "What bothers me is the fact that those boys will buy a new shirt every day, but they'll never shell out for socks and underwear." She turned to Clumly and smiled. "They'll buy shocks—*blooey!*—" She batted away the mistake with both hands. "They'll buy *shirts,* but do you think they'll buy socks?"

Clumly shook his head.

"No!" she said, pleased with him for being alert. "Shocks," she said. "That's a good one." She laughed. "Hmpf."

Clumly laughed too and Hodge smiled sociably. Churchill excused himself and hurried down the road toward where his car was parked. Clumly and the Hodges watched people leave, most of them people Fred Clumly had never seen before, relatives from far-off places, perhaps, or friends of the family who'd moved away from Batavia years ago. The sight of so many strangers was for Clumly faintly distressing. "Times change," he said aloud, accidentally.

"Well, yes and no," Hodge said.

The Hodges started down the driveway, and Clumly went along beside them, mopping his forehead and the back of his neck. "You heard about our bearded fellow?" he said. "The one we've got locked up for defacing public property."

Hodge looked puzzled, then lighted up. "The one that wrote *love* on the Thruway? He's still in jail?"

"Yessir," Clumly said. "Order of the court. He'll be transferred over to the Veterans' Hospital as soon as it's convenient, for a mental check-up, you know. Meanwhile, he's with us." He glanced over his shoulder and leaned toward Hodge. "Between you and me, it's understood that we'll question him a little, from time to time, see if we can't find out what he's really up to."

"Ah," Hodge said.

It sounded noncommittal, merely polite, weighted with some reservation, and again Clumly felt on the spot. "Oh, I know, it looks like just another prank to a complete outsider. But there may be one or two aspects of this case you're not aware of." He gave Hodge a meaningful look.

"Hmm," Hodge said. They'd come to the Hodge truck, an old hay-green Chevy pick-up, and Hodge went around to Vanessa's side to help boost her in. Clumly followed.

"Oops!" Vanessa said. But Hodge caught her and lifted again, and after a moment she was sitting at ease, fanning herself and panting, saying "Hoo!" Even with the windows open (the key was in the ignition, too, he noticed) it would be hot as an oven in the cab of that truck. When Vanessa's door was shut, Hodge turned, found Clumly at his back, and shook his hand. "Keep up the good work," Hodge said. "Give 'em heck."

"I'll do that," Clumly said. He followed Hodge around to his side. Hodge shook hands with him again, then opened his door and climbed in. "Hot," he said, closing the door.

Clumly nodded. "Listen." He put his hands on the window-frame. Hodge waited with his fingers on the ignition key, his teeth resting on his drawn-in lower lip, and Clumly tipped his head and squinted at him. "What do you think made him burn all the papers in his billfold?"

"Him?"

"The bearded one."

Hodge gazed through the windshield and thought about it —not as seriously, Clumly saw, as he'd have had to do if he were wearing Clumly's shoes. Vanessa sat looking at them wearily, like an old woman waiting for a bus.

"What's *your* theory?" Hodge said.

"Well, I don't think he's crazy, if that's what you mean," Clumly said.

Hodge switched on the ignition and started the truck. "Well, I guess time will tell," he said.

"Here," Clumly said. "Look. Look at this." He searched through his pockets and found among his various notes to himself the folded yellow paper and shook it under Hodge's face. Hodge studied him, frowning, then took the paper, held it away a little, and looked at it. Clumly got up on the narrow strip of running board and poked in his head and looked too.

"That's what we got when we examined him," Clumly said. "Not just me. Miller was there too. Those are the answers he gave us. You can't tell *me* he's insane. Too pat. Look." Clumly leaned closer to the paper and read aloud, pointing with his finger.

MILLER: What's your name?

PRISONER: Puddin Tane.

MILLER: Look, don't be smart. It makes us irritable, and when your supper comes, no Jell-O.

CLUMLY: Do you know your social security number?

PRISONER: Pick-up-sticks shut-the-door gone-to-heaven . . .

MILLER: Come on, Chief, nobody knows their social security number.

CLUMLY: You think not? My number's 287–40–0839.

MILLER: Mister, you've committed a serious crime. You aware of that?

CLUMLY: What have you to say for yourself?

PRISONER: The Lord is my shepherd, I shall not want.

MILLER: Mine too. Praise. Now tell us who you are and where you live, and maybe I'll take it back about the Jell-O.

PRISONER: I've told you. I'm Captain Marvel.

MILLER: Right. But we got a lot of them. What are you for short?

PRISONER: I'm called the Sunlight Man.

MILLER: Good. Now we're getting places. You spread sunlight in the world, that it?

PRISONER: No.

MILLER: Are you self-employed?

PRISONER: Definitely not.

CLUMLY: Miller, this is stupid.

PRISONER: You ask the wrong questions.

MILLER: Get him out of here.

Hodge was smiling, but thoughtfully.

Clumly said, "What do you think?"

"Is this a joke?" Hodge asked. He gave the paper back.

"A joke?" Clumly exclaimed. "You can *call* it a joke, if you think it's funny. I don't, myself. I've seen wiseguys before—but this one, he can't be *broken*. He's an educated man, you can see. Could be he's a college professor." He got down off the running board. Hodge was still watching him, and Vanessa had her fingertips over her mouth, the other hand over her heart. Clumly said, "You can make them talk sense, most of them. We have our ways. But with him, nothing."

"Miller doesn't seem worried," Hodge said.

Chief Clumly dismissed it with a wave. "Miller can make mistakes too." It sounded pointlessly bitter, and he regretted saying it.

"If you want my advice, Chief," Hodge began. Clumly waited, absurdly eager to hear what Ben Hodge would advise. But Hodge thought better of whatever it was he had intended to say. Or perhaps his mind wandered.

"I think he comes from California," Clumly said.

Hodge mused on this, too. "I have a boy in California," he said. "Adopted son." Finally he nodded, noncommittal as ever, and shifted into low. "Wal, getting towards choretime," he said. "Take care of yourself, Chief." He spoke too kindly. It sounded faintly ominous to Clumly.

"Same to you," he said. He stood back, resting his hands on his hips, and watched the truck pull out onto the highway and draw away. Then, his leather shoes slipping a little on the hillside along the road, he hurried back to his car. Late, he thought. Towards choretime, in fact. His chest filled with panic. He'd wasted almost another whole day. The pile of papers on his desk was as high as ever, unless Miller had done some of the work, as he did now and then. There was a letter from the Jaycees, he remembered suddenly, that had come to him May 16th—three months ago. Something about the parking situation, wanted statistics from him, or some fool thing. He ought to have slapped them down right off:

*17 May 1966*

*Gentlemen:*
*It has come to my attention that*

Too late. Couldn't do that now. Short-handed, that's the thing. And the men available mostly new, no dedication, no sense of the dangers or difficulties. He suddenly remembered he'd agreed to speak to the Dairyman's League. When was it? Had he missed it? He bent over the car door, unlocking it, thinking again of the bearded man from California. Was he making a mountain of a molehill? He started violently. There was a dry cowplop on the seat. Kids. Jokers. But how had they gotten it there? He'd locked the door. He got out his handkerchief and mopped his forehead, trying to think. He head ached from the muggy August heat, and his shortsleeved shirt was pasted to his skin with sweat. Open window, he thought, sick at heart. Locked the door but left the window open. Must be losing my marbles.

He stood very still, looking over his shoulder toward the cemetery. He was frightened for an instant. What would they be saying about him at City Hall? Would they have heard about his crazy mistake this morning with Kozlowski?

But the cemetery stood serene in the shadow of its hemlock trees, the tombstone markers solemn and patient and indifferent to the bug-filled heat, the field flowers encroaching on the graveyard grass, indifferent to what City Hall would think, neither troubled nor amused by the joke that had been played on the Batavia Chief of Police. To the left of the cemetery, beyond the iron fence, cows and calves lay chewing in the calm, dry grass, facing toward Nelson St. John's big red barns, dreaming vaguely of grain and water. Chief Clumly screwed up his face, calmer now, and picked up the dry cowplop with two fingers and threw it in the weeds. He dusted the seat.

"Think you're smart, don't you," he said. He slid in behind the wheel and sighed. Quarter-to-four. If he hurried he could get in his talk with the Woodworth sisters. He sighed again, more deeply, sucking to get more than mere heat inside his lungs. "A funny business," he said. Poor Hubbard. An image of the casket returned to his mind, the white flowers on the lid already wilting in the cemetery's heat. There had been someone whispering behind Clumly while the minister prayed. It ruined it. What was the matter with people? Clumly gritted his teeth.

## 4

On the eleventh of July, 1966, Miss Editha Woodworth, who was said to be aged one hundred and eight and who lived

with her younger sister Octave, aged ninety-seven, the only
surviving descendants of the Reverend Burgess Woodworth,
original pastor of the First Baptist Church of Batavia, New
York, had been burgled in broad daylight, when both ladies
were at home (they were always at home) by "a wild-looking
man," as they told the police, who had gained access by
knocking out a pane of the back-porch door with a hammer
and reaching to the latch. The back porch of the Woodworth
home, like all the back porches on Ross Street, was glassed in,
and had been for fifty years. It was used, or had been long
ago, as a potting shed. It was now a clutter of old crates and
boxes, broom handles, porcelain, ancient calendars, books—
*Four Feathers; In the Name of a Lady*—so rotten from damp-
ness that they crumbled in your fingers like cake. The porch
looked out on what had once been a garden.

The Woodworth sisters could describe the burglar in detail.
So could the neighbors. He had knocked at one door after another, asking nervously for a man named Day. At the Woodworth house no one had answered his knock, though he waited
for perhaps five minutes. He could not know, of course, that
neither of the sisters could speak above a whisper, that the elder was unable to leave her chair, and that the younger moved
so slowly on her two black canes that, watching her, you could
not have told whether she was going toward the door or resting for a moment. She was standing in the middle of the parlor when the burglar came in through the kitchen, still holding
the hammer. He stopped in his tracks, and cunning Miss Octave (as everyone said) whispered, "Don't murder us, young
man. We're blind as bats. We couldn't possibly identify you
later. Just go about your business and be gone." They delivered up their handbags to him, told him where he'd find the
silverware (the second-best, however; they said nothing of the
cherrywood box tucked under the bed), and even let him
know there were oatmeal cookies in the yellow crock on the
sink. Most of their money, luckily (since there wasn't much),
was in the bank drawing interest for them. He took what he
wanted (he left the cookies) and ran away through the garden
and the back lawn of the Episcopal church, where another
neighbor saw him and shouted to him. The burglar had on a
baggy sweater and an old dirty cap, the neighbor said. His
arms were loaded with a large sack and some china and old
silver pitchers and lamps, and there were beadlike things hang-

ing out of his pockets. He was unshaven and ran awkwardly, with his head thrown forward, like a horse, the neighbor said. The Rector had seen him too. He'd been watering his hydrangeas at the time. Nobody'd seen him before in Batavia. Apparently he had a car parked somewhere, because nobody had seen him since, either. The Woodworths had insurance, luckily. And so the police had made a routine check, knowing the case hopeless and, anyway, not the kind of case that warranted an all-out effort. Perhaps the stolen goods would eventually turn up, in some junkstore in Lockport, or in a garage somewhere a year from now. They had written their reports, expressed their sympathy to the burgled ladies, and filed the case —having no choice in the matter—and they'd forgotten it.

Miss Octave Woodworth, however, had not forgotten. She was morally outraged. They hadn't so much as taken fingerprints, had even refused to take along the hammer which Miss Woodworth had left all this time on the enormous, carved walnut table and would not touch even now except with the handkerchief that had come down to her from her Great-Great-Aunt May, a Judd. She wanted an investigation.

Four o'clock. He stood gazing sullenly at the great stack of papers, sucking at the cigar with short quick puffs, hungrily, trying to get it going better than it could. He had time yet to get over to Stroh's Flower Shop, for the Paxton flowers, and then to the Woodworth sisters'. Yet he hesitated. It irritated him that there was nothing he could tell them, no way he could honestly satisfy their demand for action, and it was only partly that they were the Woodworth sisters. No matter who it was that made the complaint, Clumly would have felt the same irritation at the box he was in.

We'd have gotten that burglar twenty years ago, he was saying to himself. It's the times. What's the world coming to? They had never considered, twenty years ago, the cost of catching a criminal—the man-hours involved in the investigation. A crime was committed, you went after the man. Just like that. Not now. "As near as we can estimate," Mayor Mullen said, "every cop on your Force costs us nine dollars an hour. Nine dollars, Clumly. Think of it. That's taking account of the overhead—buildings, cars, gadgets, the whole gambit— including salaries. So I put it to you: I want time-sheets, Clumly. And I don't want you hiring a lot of office help to fig-

ure them. No sirree. I want a paying operation, and I want it
now. Here. Put it this way. Say a merchant gets robbed at his
store and he loses nine dollars. You know what that's worth in
Police Department time? One man for one hour. Period. Or
two men for a half an hour. Case closed." Mayor Mullen patted his stomach. It made sense, of course, like everything
Clumly found disagreeable in the times. You couldn't catch all
of them anyway, might as well put your time where it meant
good business. Nevertheless, it grated on him. He'd run a tight
ship, in the old days. No figuring the odds, no punching a
clock each time you started and stopped an investigation. A
man could build up pride in his work. It was a service. Do
ministers keep time-sheets, Mr. Mayor? Or schoolteachers?
And doctors? But he hadn't asked it. He had a suspicion they
did.

And so (he brooded) he would visit the Woodworth sisters,
soothe them with lies, invite them to visit the jail sometime
and look at the thief they had locked up in another connection
—Walter Boyle, if that was really his name—knowing all the
time that it wasn't Walter Boyle, he was no "wildman," a
smart old pro—and knowing too that the Woodworths
couldn't come down to the jail anyway, they never got out of
the house any more: if the sun hit the Woodworth sisters they
would shrivel up and disintegrate like corpses in a vacuum casket when you cracked the pane of glass.

The shiver of a hare-brained idea ran up Clumly's back.
Why not? he thought. The idea startled him, and he crossed
quickly to the window and bent toward it to peer out, as if
seeing if anyone had observed him thinking it. But the more
he thought about it the clearer and simpler the plan seemed,
however irregular. He'd have done it without a moment's
thought in the old days. He was Chief of Police, wasn't he?
Why not? It was four-fifteen.

Salvador handed the keys to him without even looking up
from his paperwork. Miller was nowhere in sight. Clumly hurried down the hallway, glancing over his shoulder once or
twice, to the cellblock. "You," he said. "Up on your feet." He
unlocked the cell. The thief, Boyle, looked up at him over the
top of the *Daily News* he was reading and, after a moment,
stood up. He was short and fat, slightly humpbacked, still
wearing the suit they'd arrested him in—brown trousers, black

and gray suspenders, a dark tie of uncertain color. His suitcoat was neatly folded on his pallet.

"Get your coat," Clumly said.

Boyle turned slowly, blinking his heavy-lidded eyes, and ran one hand over his thin, graying hair. He got into the coat, glanced furtively over at the others, and came out of the cell.

The bearded one grinned like a mule and closed his eyes. "God be with you."

The thief, Walter Boyle, ignored him. He held out his hands for the handcuffs automatically, and Clumly snapped them on.

On the way to the street they passed no one but Salvador, still working on his papers, the radio chattering and spitting behind him. "I've got the prisoner with me," Clumly said. "Checking an identification."

Salvador glanced up, slightly surprised, then nodded. It was a new one, no doubt, but everything was new to Salvador and would be for a long time. He was slow.

But there was another complication, it came to Clumly as he was getting into the car. He looked up at the toy-castle towers of the police station, the gaping stone archway over the porch, the barred windows to the rear. He groped with the problem, scowling fiercely as he started up the engine, and at last he saw that he'd left himself no choice. He'd have to take Walter Boyle in with him when he stopped at Stroh's for the flowers. Well, all right. He drove to Pearl Street and pulled up in front of the hydrant in front of the store.

It went off smoothly, as he'd known it would. Boyle was no troublemaker. Too slick for that. He got out docilely, walked docilely to the counter with Clumly, waited docilely while the flowers—white roses—were wrapped and boxed. They cost seven dollars, and Boyle held the box while Clumly got out his billfold. The lady behind the counter worked hastily for once, almost gave him an extra two dollars change. Through all this, Boyle said nothing, showed no surprise. Clumly felt grateful. Good man, he thought. What turned a man like Boyle to a life of crime?

At last Boyle said, speaking for the first time, "Where we going?"

"You'll find out," Clumly said. He was always stern, on principle, with prisoners. Let them learn you were human and you could end up dead in some ditch.

He turned off Washington Avenue onto Ross.

"Old Dr. Adams' place," Clumly said crisply, pointing to the right. It was a high brick house set back off the street, with round-arched windows, great heavy dentils along the roof overhang, lattice-work arbors on either side. A house of the type that was common once in Western New York and can still be seen here and there in the country—the Hodge place, for instance, out on Putnam Settlement Road—solid, unspeakably dignified with its great blunt planes of chalky orange brick, its Victorian porches, its cupola: the most beautiful architecture in the world, symbolic of virtues no longer to be found. On the wide, unmowed lawns there were tamaracks over a hundred years old, and at the end of the driveway a morose brick garage. The thief bent forward, looking back at it as they passed.

"Right there's the Richmond Library," Clumly said. He pointed, then clutched the wheel again, slowing and turning into Woodworths'.

"Ugly," Boyle observed. "The library."

Clumly scowled on principle, though it was true.

They waited on the porch for a full twenty minutes, Clumly fanning himself with his hat, Boyle standing meekly with his shackled hands folded. Maybe they're dead, Clumly thought. But they weren't, he knew. He could see nothing through the stained-glass strips at the sides of the door. The porch sloped badly, but someone had recently been working on it. There were new balusters on the railing, and one end of the porch had been jacked up and leveled. The house next door had a black and white sign standing out from the porch roof: SHADY REST. There was no more hint of life over there than here. He mopped his forehead and thought again of the flowers lying in the front seat. They'd be even hotter in the car than here. Should he bring them in with him? But he should have thought of it sooner. Octave Woodworth might appear at the door any minute now, and if she found only Boyle there, standing alone, in handcuffs, who knew? It might give her a heart attack.

"I should have brought in those flowers," Clumly said. "They'll wilt out there."

Boyle nodded.

He tried again to see through the stained glass, but it was useless. "Should have had them delivered," he said.

Again Boyle nodded. He indicated with both shackled hands

the heavy bronze knocker on the Woodworths' door, a lion's head holding a serpent in its teeth.

"They've heard us all right," Clumly said. Abruptly, before he knew he would do it, he said, "Wait here, Boyle," and hurried back to the car. He unlocked it as quickly as possible, snatched up the flowers, locked the door again, and hurried back onto the porch. "There now," he said. He was out of breath. Boyle nodded. They went on waiting. Clumly holding the flower box under his arm.

At last they heard the rattling of the chains as someone unfastened the safety latches. The main lock clicked, and the big door opened inward. "Who is it?" Octave Woodworth whispered. Her face showed the ravages of time, he saw. She looked like an old, old potato from under a sink.

"I'm Chief of Police Clumly," Clumly said. "I've brought along someone we thought you might be able to identify."

"Come right in," she whispered. "Come in."

It was the darkest entryway in the world. The walls were nearly black with age, and the full-length mirrors on each side of the door, set in oak-leaved frames that four strong men could not have carried, reflected only the dull gleams, here and there, of darkly stained wood. Clumly's figure and Boyle's, in those antique mirrors, were like two barn owls with glittering eyes. The old woman was like a raven returned from the dead. The old woman backed away from them slowly, no more than a faint silhouette in that smoky darkness. "Come with me," she whispered. She maneuvered a turn, joints creaking and clicking, and, moving tortuously on her two heavy canes, led them toward a gloomy ten-foot-high oak door that opened off the hallway to the left. "We expected you sooner," she whispered. The house smelled abandoned, full of the vague scents in an old empty cupboard.

"I'm sorry," Clumly said craftily. "It's been a difficult case."

In the parlor there was more light. They hadn't yet turned the lamps on, if they still worked, but the arched window facing to the east drew enough sun from the mostly shaded lawn to raise a glitter on the silver vases that once had held flowers, and to glint on the dim prisms of the lamps, the highly polished walnut of the mantelpiece, the ornate legs of tables and chairs. There was no hint of color anywhere. The gilt framework and the ruby glass on the lamps, the yellow-brown of the oval family portraits, the once blue or red of the velvet cushions on the rickety chairs had all sunk to black or dark gray. While Clumly introduced his prisoner to Miss Octave, the prisoner stood meekly squinting at the clutter of old china and silver on the piano table.

"I'm pleased to meet you," Miss Octave whispered.

From the darkest corner of the room came a harsher whisper. "He's not the one."

Clumly steered his prisoner toward the voice. Miss Editha Woodworth sat propped up, motionless, under a huge lugubrious oil painting of—if Clumly's eyes did not deceive him—broken columns on a hillside, or possibly horses. She sat wrapped in black blankets, among black pillows. On her head, slightly askew, sat an old black wig. Her face shone out of the darkness like a moon.

"Miss Editha," he said. "I'm glad to see you well."

"I'm not well," she whispered. "That man is not the one."

Clumly pursed his lips. The parlor was as cool as a valley between rocks, and after all his sweating he was chilly. "That's too bad," he said. "We were *afraid* we might have gotten the wrong man."

"Nincompoops," she whispered. "If Agnes were here—" (That was the oldest of the sisters, dead now for years, reduced to legend. She'd committed suicide, people said.)

"We do our best, Miss Woodworth," Clumly said.

"What?" she asked.

He realized he had fallen into whispering like one of themselves. "We do our best," he said.

She said nothing more, utterly spent, it seemed. Perhaps she had fallen asleep. He couldn't tell.

To everyone's surprise, Boyle spoke. "You're Miss Editha Woodworth?" he asked. "You write poems?"

"Why glory be!" Miss Octave whispered. "You're acquainted with Editha's verse?"

Boyle glanced uneasily at Clumly. "I've heard it mentioned," he said. Then his face became blank. "That is," he said, "no."

"How interesting!" Miss Octave whispered.

"She's a poet, all right," Clumly said, bothered by the way Boyle seemed now to have withdrawn, aloof from their awkward little ring of conversation.

"A legislator for humanity," Miss Octave said happily, a little like a tyrant. She tried to pursue the matter with Boyle, but

it was useless. At last she said, "Well do sit down. It's so seldom we get visitors here." She inched over to a chair herself and lowered herself cautiously, then laid the two canes in her lap. Clumly nodded toward the settee and handed Boyle the flower box, to be rid of the embarrassment of carrying it himself. Boyle went over to the settee while Clumly seated himself tentatively on a high-backed rocker. It must be after five, he thought, but he could not risk the rudeness of a glance at his watch. The rocker was leather, as cold and smooth as the dirt inside a cave.

"We used to have visitors," Miss Octave said. "But the new Baptist minister doesn't make calls, you know. Isn't it criminal?" She dabbed at the side of her mouth with a Kleenex.

"What's this country coming to?" Clumly said.

"That's just what I tell Editha," she said. "Poor old Mrs. Maxwell has arthritis so bad she can never leave her bed. Mine's only in my fingers, you know, though it's torment enough." She held out her hands to him. The index fingers were like knotty pieces of wood, and the hands shook. She pressed on, though the hoarse croaking was such an effort it made her eyes bulge. "Well someone said to the minister he ought to go see her, and he went over and she said, 'Pastor, I can't tell you how glad I am to see you.' 'Well don't expect to see me again,' he says, 'I don't make calls.' Now what do you think of that! He's on the City Planning Commission or whatever they call it. That's all he cares about, don't you know. He's got them to put up one of those highrise apartments—horrible!—and all that urban renewal, tearing down beautiful old buildings like the Jefferson Hotel, where President Cleveland stayed, and making everything into parking lots and I don't know what. Now he's got the congregation to agree to tearing down half of that beautiful old church of ours, going to put up an education building with a cloistered walk leading out from the church—we saw the pictures, didn't we Editha? —flimsy little thing, it makes you sick at heart! Three hundred and seventy thousand dollars it will cost, a thousand dollars from every member of the congregation! Well they won't be getting any thousand dollars from the Woodworths, we told them—I've got cataracts, don't you know, and I don't need to tell you how expensive that is."

"It's criminal," Clumly said.

"Worse than that," she said. She leaned toward him. "It's

heretic!" She spoke the word with such feeling that one saw, all at once, the Baptist minister in his coat and vest and spectacles, being burnt alive at the stake. "All to get new members, that's all they care about." She dabbed at her mouth again. "That beautiful old church means nothing to them, just new members, new members. The minister says, 'We need a new plant if we're going to appeal to new members.' A *plant*. Imagine! I said, 'A plant! Why, Sylvania's got a plant, if that's what we need. Why don't we just go borrow theirs, and we can pay the people a dollar an hour to come worship.' " Her eyes shone like needles. "Imagine," she said. "But there are all those younger people, don't you know; church architecture hasn't any meaning for them. Too dark and gloomy, they say, and smells like a wellhouse. Well we don't feel that way, do we Editha. I always try to keep Editha involved in things, don't you know. But of course she doesn't listen. Sometimes she'll just sit that way for days and I think she's dead."

"Stupid babbler," Editha said. Then, calling upstairs, it seemed: "Agnes!"

They listened a moment, but the dead Agnes said nothing.

"She'll bury us all," Octave said. "She has a strong constitution, like all the Woodworths. Good stock." She sighed, a sound like sandpaper. "Well, the younger ones don't care. They want those tiny little houses with their tiny fat chairs and those tiny little cars. I just don't want any part of it, Mr. Cooper. I like houses wih stories, places people have lived in. That settee there, the one Mr. What's-his-name is sitting on, it came down in the family from our Uncle Ferris and Aunt Margaret. They had nine children, and five of them died in one week of diphtheria."

He missed whatever it was she said next. Three fire engines went by, some blocks away, the last two hard on the tail of the first, from the sound of it, and their sirens howled along the twilight like the cranes he'd heard once crossing the sky in single file directly over the ship. When he could listen again she was saying, suddenly animated, "Wasn't it a terrible winter?"

Clumly pursed his lips. "Terrible," he ventured.

"We thought we'd die, didn't we Editha? I get the hives so bad, don't you know. We were shut up here one time for four days, right here in the city, telephone lines down and everything. I'd just get choking, don't you know, in the middle of the night, and I just gave myself up for gone. We finally got

out a message to the doctor by some children that were playing in the drifts out in front, and he came over here on foot. It
was T. Murray Steele. Such a good man, and very famous in
the medical circle, or so we hear. Not *our* circle, you know—"
she rasped out a laugh "—though he's rich, we understand.
Very active in politics too, one of *us,* where that's concerned.
He said he just couldn't understand why I wasn't dead. 'Well,
I've got a good constitution,' I says. It's so rare to find a good
doctor, these days, what with socialized medicine and the
Catholics and the rest. You wonder what this country's coming
to. Poor Editha came down with pneumonia one time—three
years ago February, wasn't it Editha? It came over her late at
night, I remember. She'd had a cold, poor thing, and my coli-
tis was so bad I could scarcely get around to wait on her—it's
so hard when you're sickly, don't you know—I suppose that
was partly what made it worse. I'd just wound this clock—I
remember as if it was yesterday—and I heard poor Editha
gagging in the second parlor. Not a doctor that would come at
that hour of the night. Except T. Murray Steele. He's known
far and wide for his medical skill, and yet out he comes in the
middle of the night, just as regular as the post office. We had
poor Editha in an oxygen tent—God's will be done!—and he
cured my bursitis the same night, as well as possible. I can't
tell you how grateful it made us. What's wrong with these
young doctors? I hear they put people in ten different rooms,
not counting the room with the magazines, and they just make
them wait. I heard of a doctor in Leroy who went away on vacation and left two poor ladies sitting in his office for days and
days. Imagine! They might have starved! I haven't been to one
of those places myself. I can't get out much, don't you know,
with these fallen arches. It's just like walking with glass inside
your shoes."

Clumly shook his head.

She fiddled with the Kleenex, looking for a place still un-
used. "Have you ever seen Editha's poetry books?" Miss Octave asked them. "There's boxes and boxes of them up in the
attic. They've never sold well, but they're lovely, you know.
She used to read her poetry all over New York State, years
ago. She's written some lovely children's pieces and of course
volumes of beautiful religious verse. She doesn't do it any
more, naturally."

She sat silent a moment, looking at the canes in her lap. At last, with an effort, she wrapped her stiff knuckles around the handles and got the canes in position to help her up. "You'll want to see where the burglar came in," she said.

"Yes, good," Clumly said. The sky was gray now, the room almost dark, but Octave Woodworth seemed no more aware of the darkness than Clumly's wife would have been. Slowly, she led them through the dining room to the kitchen and out to the back porch.

"He must have found the hammer out there in the garage," she said. "This is where he knocked out the pane of glass and reached in to unlock the door." There was plywood where the pane had been. The door was nailed shut. "We have a man who comes by to mow lawn for us. We had him nail the door, just to be on the safe side."

"Good idea," Clumly said politely.

"He's a queer," she said. Clumly glanced at her, startled, and could not tell whether or not she meant what he supposed. She said, "But he's a good worker. We're glad to have him."

Boyle stood gazing morosely into the overgrown garden, holding the flower box under his arm. The old woman, shaking like a leaf all over, noticed the direction of his gaze. "It used to be a beautiful garden. Father started it seventy years ago, and we tried to keep it up, as long as we could. But now it's gone back to Nature, as you see." She spoke the word *Nature* with hostility, as though for her it were a familiar and tolerable evil. The marble birdbath lay on its side, the base cracked, grass growing out of the opening obscenely. The brick wall at the rear of the garden hung thick with what seemed to be poison ivy—it was hard to be sure in the failing light. The tulip tree in the center of the garden was dead as a doornail, and roses overran the brick paths at liberty, with branches like the limbs of trees. In the high grass to the right of the porch, an ice-box lay on its side, with the door secured by an old rusty chain.

"He went through there," she said. She pointed to a hole yawning in the back right corner of the brick wall.

"Very helpful," Clumly said soberly. "This has all been very helpful."

She looked up at him earnestly, dim eyes loose in the dark, sunken sockets. "I hope you'll catch him, Mr. Cooper, and bring back some of our things. You'll want that hammer, I imagine, for the fingerprints."

"Yes indeed, we certainly will."

She turned back to the kitchen and brought it, still wrapped in the handkerchief, from the cupboard.

She said, "We've always been good citizens, Mr. Cooper. We don't like to trouble the police over nothing."

"I understand that," Clumly said. "This is a serious matter, as you know."

She was looking at him again, searching for something, or expecting something, he couldn't make out quite what. "That's what I said to Editha," she whispered.

"Boyle?" Clumly said.

The thief turned away from his gloomy inspection of the garden and came into the kitchen.

"You must go now, yes," Miss Octave said. "Thank you, thank you." She was looking at the flower box Boyle carried. She pulled her gaze away and started through the dining room toward the parlor. They inched along behind her.

"Say good-bye, Editha," she whispered.

In the deepening darkness there was only a vague glow of white now where Miss Editha sat. She did not answer.

"You'd vow she was dead," Miss Octave said.

"Yakety yakety yakety," Miss Editha whispered.

Miss Octave ignored it. "Think what a man like that must have in store for him," she said. "It's my belief the Lord is not as merciful as some people suppose, especially thieves. You try to lay a little pittance by, you put your money in the bank or you lend it out at a fair rate of interest, you build up a position of authority in the community, and along comes some ugly little wretch—" Her throat convulsed. "If thieves go to Heaven, then we'd be better off with no God at all. That's the truth."

Clumly patted her arm. It was dry as paper and hot as the center of a compost pile. At the front door Miss Octave whispered slyly, "Are the flowers for us, Mr. Cooper?"

Police Chief Clumly took the box from Boyle with a sigh and gave it to her.

"God bless you," she whispered. She scraped at his hand with her stiff fingers. "The Lord bless you and keep you."

From the parlor came Miss Editha's sharp whisper, "Tell them *Shoo! Go away!*"

Clumly bowed and gave the younger of the ancient sisters a wave. Then, closing his hand firmly around his prisoner's arm, he marched Boyle down to the car. There was another car parked down the street, across from the Adams place, and there was someone in it, smoking a cigarette. As he turned his own car toward Main he glanced in the rearview mirror to see if the car was following him, but it was gone. He would not think about it.

"Good people, the Woodworths," Clumly said with conviction.

Boyle looked at him.

After that, neither of them spoke. Clumly scowled and concentrated on his driving. He'd forgotten that Bank Street was one-way now, the wrong way. He caught his own reflection in the windshield, a face vague with consternation, and thought of his wife's glass eyes.

## 5

At quarter-to-eight, back in his office, Walter Boyle safely in his cell again, Clumly could not shake the feeling that someone was watching him, following him, dogging his footsteps. Salvador was off duty, Miller was nowhere to be seen; only Figlow and one of the cops off the street were in the front office. Now that darkness had fallen, the stack of papers on his desk seemed less obviously harmless. It might be true (it *was* true, of course) that he knew more about running a police department than Mullen did, but Mayor Mullen was a great believer in paperwork, and it was a bad practice to bite the hand that fed you. Figlow had given him an odd look when he'd come in with Boyle—almost a dangerously odd look, it seemed to Clumly. They'd been talking about him, probably, Figlow and Miller and Salvador and whoever had happened along. They might perhaps be talking about him now. Without exactly meaning to, merely walking around, as anyone might do, cooped up in an office, Clumly worked his way over to the door, where he could hear what Figlow and the other cop were saying. He could hear their voices distinctly, but not the words, partly because of the radio there with them, partly because the old, high-ceilinged room was full of echoes. He pressed flat against the wall and pushed his ear up against it, but it didn't help. After a moment, scowling, he stooped over toward the crack below the door. He could hear better now, but still it was not clear. He glanced around the office, though he knew there was no one there to see him, then quietly got down on his hands and knees and pressed his ear to the crack. Now the words came distinctly.

"Salami," Figlow said. "Same sandwich as yesterday and the day before."

The other cop grunted.

"I don't mean just the same kind, I mean the same exact sandwich. She sees I didn't eat it, she puts it right back in the lunchbox."

"You should throw it away, then she'd give you a fresh one."

"Hell no! I hate salami, I don't care if it's fresh or stale."

A silence. The wax paper rustled, and then he heard the sound of coffee being poured into the thermos cup.

"Just the same, fresh salami's better than stale. Stale can poison you."

"Not if you don't eat it."

"Well, just the same," the other cop said.

"You don't get the point," Figlow said. "It's a war, see? Who's gonna give in first, me or her?"

"You," the other one said.

"You wanna bet?"

"She's a woman, right? Give up, Sarge. You're beat."

Clumly got stiffly to his feet.

At his desk, he considered calling his wife. She'd be worried by now, though of course she understood a policeman couldn't be expected home the same exact minute every night, like some grocery man. But the supper would be cold, and she'd be cross. Persecuted. He put his hand on the phone, squinting, looking up at the cobweb in the corner of the room, then changed his mind. How'd that cobweb get there? he wondered. He tried to think of something to knock it down with, but there was nothing, or nothing here in the room with him. He thought, fleetingly, of knocking it down with his belt. He

Suppose Mayor Mullen had stopped by this afternoon. He did that sometimes. Miller might have talked to him—might have mentioned the business with Kozlowski, or Salvador might have mentioned his taking the thief over to Woodworths'. The Mayor would be puzzled, ask a question or two, glance in at Clumly's littered desk.

"Got to clean this mess out," he said aloud. "Matter of just settling down to it." Panic flooded his chest and he reached for a cigar. As he was just about to strike the match he became aware of the murmur of voices from the cellblock. Bearded one holding forth again. Clumly studied his cigar and noticed the scratches on the side of his hand. Now that he noticed them he could feel them again. Not a pain, exactly; a presence. Musing on the scratches, thinking nothing whatever as far as he knew, he walked slowly over to the door that opened on the hallway leading to the cells. He glanced casually to his left and saw that no one in the front office was looking, then walked on, still casually, in the direction of the cellblock. A few feet from the door, where none of the prisoners but Boyle could see him, he stopped, leaned against the wall, and lighted the cigar. Boyle looked over the paper at him, then went back to his everlasting reading.

"It's a question of point of view," the bearded prisoner explained. He would be sitting with his big white hands on his knees, that burnt, hairy face looking up at the ceiling, infinitely sad. He sounded now incredibly like one of those lawyers summing up, tyrannical and grandiose. "It's not pure madness to maintain that Society is rotten—rotten beyond all hope of redemption. Not at all! I don't hold with that view, naturally, but it's not pure madness, I give you my official word. Take a place like Watts, for instance. The evil of the ghetto is clear enough, yes?—and Los Angeles is maybe the richest city in the world. Average income of four hundred dollars a day, I read somewhere. They could do something—churches, Chamber of Commerce, businesses—but do they? Not till it explodes. And what does a city like Los Angeles do then? There are two possibilities. (Correct me if I'm wrong.) Go in with tommyguns, kill a few men, put the rioters down, place Watts under martial law. Or fiddle around—second alternative—let the fires die slowly, arrange for what's called Serious Talks. What comes of all this? If martial law stops the riot, the result is a return to the old evil, no change of any significance. Why? Because responsible officials are responsible to voters, and mostly the people of places like Watts don't vote. On the other hand, if you use Serious Talks, those Serious Talkers talk on and on, the way Serious Talkers always do, and the population keeps climbing in Watts and the responsible officials get busier and busier with the problem of houses that slide down hills, and pretty soon another explosion, more stores on fire. *Burn, baby, burn,* as the spade people say. If you happen to be a responsible citizen who feels a modicum of Christian concern for his unfortunate brothers, you try to mobilize public sentiment, you write letters, make phonecalls, talk to your fellow Elks. Result? Your wife divorces you on the grounds that you're a nut, inattentive, also impotent. Which you are, it may be. Your boss discovers you're not as efficient as a machine he can get. Your church slides into the persuasion that you're out to block the Bishops' Fund. In short, you are given good reasons for pulling your head in. Also, of course, you inevitably pick up some friends you could manage without: to wit, queers, neurotic ladies, Jewish psychiatrists, Muslim boys, and young Presbyterian assistant ministers. Those who hold this position (which I do not hold) would argue that the responsible citizen necessarily gives up. The situation is hopeless, and as a reasonable man the responsible citizen becomes indifferent. All the available options disgust him, from Ayn Rand to CORE to the Birch Society. He learns to punch the button and collect his check. In the exceptional case of the man who refuses to renounce his human dignity (as the newspapers call it), well, for him, gentlemen and friends, the outlook is by no means bright. He becomes, unwittingly, a Hell's Angel of sorts, a rebellious lunatic defying the society he lives in. There's a difference, of course. The Hell's Angel holds up no model in opposition to the society he hates. The Just Man defies society in the name of a dead cause. He is somewhat more confused than the Hell's Angel (this position would hold), but he does not recognize his confusion. In other words, in nontechnical terminology, he's crazy. Ah! As I say, I do not myself hold this opinion —or any other. I am the strawberry eater, the skylight smasher—in a word, King Solomon's cod. Meanwhile, let it be mournfully added, Watts—for all the failures of high-minded Christian citizens of the master race, or machine guns, or Talk —Watts takes care of itself, from inside, for no known reason. The people become proud, it may be. Or they overflow with foolish, sentimental emotion, and they *improve* the damn place! Life has no shame."

A long silence.

"This is called Capitalism," he said. "A deadly sickness of taste."

Abruptly, again almost before he knew what he was thinking, Clumly strode down the hall to get the cell keys.

CLUMLY: You're an intelligent man. What was your purpose, writing *love* on a busy highway?

PRISONER: The world needs more love.—Don't you think so, brother?

CLUMLY: Is that any way to get it?

PRISONER: When the spirit say paint . . .

CLUMLY: Stop talking gibberish. Listen, I'll tell you something. I don't ask these questions out of idle curiosity. I'm interested. I feel friendly toward you, generally speaking. Also, of course—

PRISONER: It's your job.

CLUMLY: Correct. You spoke of the Hell's Angels. Are you—

PRISONER: Certainly not.

CLUMLY: Maybe we're getting somewhere, finally.

PRISONER: Nonsense.

CLUMLY: Do you come from California?

PRISONER: I come from the Lord of Hosts.

CLUMLY: Don't do that. Answer my question.

PRISONER: *I've forgotten what it was.*

CLUMLY (patiently): Do you come from California?

PRISONER: Why do you keep pacing? Sit down. You make me nervous.

CLUMLY: I'll decide when it's time to sit down.

PRISONER: No you won't. You'll put it off till the last minute and then you'll fall on your ass. I had an uncle did that. It was terrible.

CLUMLY: Just answer the questions. Cigar?

PRISONER: Thank you. With pleasure. Why do you shake so?

CLUMLY: You'll shake the same way when you're sixty-four.

PRISONER: Bad for the system, no question about it. Does it worry you much? Worries the little woman, I'll bet! Good cigar, though. There are always compensations!

CLUMLY: Where do you live?

PRISONER: Big old house on LaCrosse, with a blind woman. (Pause.)

CLUMLY: What in hell are you up to? How did you find that out?

PRISONER: Startling, isn't it.

CLUMLY: Shut up.

PRISONER: Take it easy! I used to be a fortune teller. Learned lots of tricks. Are you sick of her—the blind woman?

CLUMLY: Of course not. Stop that!

PRISONER: Sorry.

CLUMLY: What do you do? Is it true that you're a college man, a student?

PRISONER: I run a business. Big desk, time cards, things like that. I worry a lot, worry myself sick. Makes me do weird things, if I may speak in confidence. Strictest confidence. Or whatever the expression is. There are certain people who know secrets about me, but I'm not yet sure who they are. I find it difficult to trust people. Sometimes I think—I can trust you, I hope?—sometimes I think of doing downright deranged things. Shall I tell you?

CLUMLY: What is this?

PRISONER (intensely): I have thoughts of spying on my boss, listening outside his window. It's insane, I know. I resist it, naturally. Nevertheless, sometimes the desire comes over me and—Christ! What's this world coming to, I wonder? Do bosses talk to their wives, do you think? Do they get phonecalls, perhaps? (Pause.) A man could crouch there in the dark outside the window, in the shrubbery, say . . .

CLUMLY: What do you want? Look, I don't want any trouble from you. I want straight answers to straight questions.

PRISONER: Negative.

CLUMLY (wildly): You sit listening, don't you! You sit in there and strain your ears to hear every word I say!

PRISONER: It's because you're my friend.

(Pause.)

Psst! (A whisper): Are you interested in metaphysics?

CLUMLY: See here—

PRISONER: I've known men would give their souls for metaphysics. (Laughs.) I know a man in Philadelphia killed by lightning in pursuit of metaphysics. I admire him for it. I'd have done the same myself, and the country be damned. (Laughs more softly.)

CLUMLY: Metaphysics! Lord!

Chief Clumly shuddered, reversed the tape, found the beginning of the examination, and carefully erased it twice. Very well. So people were talking about him, even in front of the prisoners. Well, no surprise. When he left the station (it was now almost ten) he noticed that the light was on in the Mayor's office in the City Hall down the street. He paused, scowling, his hand around his mouth, then turned back and went up the police station steps.

"Figlow, you seen Miller tonight?"

"He's been off since six, Chief."

Clumly nodded, studied the stump of his cigar, then went out again. "Funny business," he said. The darkness around him was warm as a blanket.

Metaphysics.

He hunted a long time before he located the paper—on the porch, right in front of the door. He let himself in and locked the door behind him, as usual, then waited in the darkness of the livingroom. She didn't call to him, and a light pain of fear began to build up in his chest. The house was absolutely still, and in the yard outside not a leaf was stirring. "Hello!" Clumly called.

He groped toward the kitchen, his nerves jangling, and said again, more loudly, "Hello?" He could smell her wine. His heart shook violently as he snapped on the light, but there was no one. He opened the pantry door and pulled the lightstring there, half-expecting to find she'd hanged herself. But again there was nothing. He leaned on the doorframe, gathering his wits.

He found her, three minutes later, asleep in the bed; or possibly, he thought for some reason, she was only pretending to be asleep. Her sewing was in her hands. He stood for a long time looking at her in the dim light thrown from the wall lamp in the hallway behind him, his shadow falling over her waist and hips. He was amazed at how worried he'd been at the thought that something had happened to her. And he was amazed at the joy—it was more than relief—flooding through him now as he looked down at the sly old woman lying almost motionless, only the bony chest stirring as she breathed very slowly in and out, fallen like a scrawny chicken on its back.

We're going to get through this thing, you and I, Chief Clumly thought. Whatever the bearded man was plotting—or Miller and Kozlowski and Figlow and the Mayor—Chief of Police Fred Clumly was not afraid.

He squared his jaw in the darkness. Metaphysics. Mad as a hatter—no doubt of it. And yet it was odd how the question had affected him. He could not recall off-hand what Metaphysics was—it was one of those things he'd probably understood once, long ago, had come across, say, in the days when he used to read whatever people offered him to pass the time with on the ship; or it was one of those words you heard and dismissed, knowing your limits, or knowing the thing was probably just air, an occupation for idle minds—like the words the Mayor's man Wittaker used at times, "interaction target," or something like that, and "socio-economic construct." He used them constantly, as naturally as he breathed, a little like a lunatic using words with all normal sense drained out of them. Except, when he thought about it, when Wittaker used those words of his, Clumly would turn off his mind for a moment, annoyed. The prisoner's word had a different effect: it had given a queer sort of jolt to his heart. *Yes!* Clumly had thought. There it was. Whatever it meant, spiritualistic trash for old ladies or the roaring secret of life and death, for a minute there Clumly had believed he wanted to know. *Better watch that man,* he thought. He came wide awake. What the devil had he meant by that? *Psst! Interested in—*

But all was still. All was well. The room silent and comfortable, haunted by no turbulence but the breath of his nostrils and the nostrils of his wife. The house silent. The street. Nevertheless, he had a terrible sense of things in motion, secret powers at work in the ancient plaster walls, devouring and building, and forces growing and restive in the trees, the very earth itself succinct with spirit. He had an image, culled from some old book, perhaps, or a sermon he'd heard—an image of his house taken over by owls and ravens and cormorants and bitterns, and strange shapes dancing in his cellar. And in his livingroom, thorns, and brambles. He listened to his heartbeat going *choof, kuh-choof,* and he could not get to sleep. "Dear Lord," he said, and fell silent.

Unbeknownst to Clumly or anyone else, three boys in the alley by the post office were letting the air out of people's tires with an ice pick. Elsewhere—beside the Tonawanda—a woman was digging a grave for her illegitimate child three hours old. Jim Hume was chasing his cows back through the fence some hunter had cut. There was no moon.

# II

## When the Exorcist
## Shall Go
## to the House
## of
## the Patient . . .

---

*His diademe of dyamans droppede adoun;*
*His weyes were a-wayward wroliche wrout;*
*Tynt was his tresor, tente, tour, & toun.*

—Anon., Early 14th Century

---

### 1

He came to be known as the Sunlight Man. The public was never to learn what his name really was. As for his age, he was somewhere between his late thirties and middle forties, it seemed. His forehead was high and domelike, scarred, wrin-

63

kled, drawn, right up into the hairline, and above the arc of his balding, his hair exploded like chaotic sunbeams around an Eastern tomb. At times he had (one mask among many, for stiff as the fire-blasted face was, he could wrench it into an infinite number of shapes) an elfish, impenetrable grin which suggested madness, and indeed, from all evidence, the man was certainly insane. But to speak of him as mad was like sinking to empty rhetoric. In the depths where his turbulent broodings moved, the solemn judgments of psychiatry, sociology, and the like, however sound, were frail sticks beating a subterranean sea. His skin, where not scarred, was like a baby's, though dirty, as were his clothes, and his straw-yellow beard, tangled and untrimmed, covered most of his face like a bush. He reeked as if he'd been feeding on the dead when he first came, and all the while he stayed he stank like a sewer. For all his elaborate show of indifference, for all his clowning, his playacting, his sometimes arrogant, sometimes mysteriously gentle defiance and mocking of both prisoners and guards, he sweated prodigiously, throughout his stay, from what must have been nervousness. He talked a great deal, in a way that at times made you think of a childlike rabbi or sweet, mysteriously innocent old Russian priest and at other times reminded you of an elderly archeologist in his comfortable classroom, musing and harkening back. He would roll his eyes slowly, pressing the tips of his fingers together, or he would fix his listener with a gentle, transmogrifying eye and open his arms like a man in a heavy robe. He pretended to enjoy the official opinion of the court, that he might be mad. "I am the Rock," he said thoughtfully, nodding. "I am Captain Marvel."

None of the other prisoners listened to him much when he first came, and except for young Mickey Salvador, neither did the guards. No one could help seeing that there was a kind of cleverness, even genius, in some of what he said and did. He could quote things at great length (there was no way for them to know whether he was really quoting or inventing) and he had an uncanny ability to turn any trifling remark into an abstruse speculation wherein things that were plain as day to common sense became ominous, uncertain, and formidable, like buttresses of ruined cities discovered in deep shadow at the bottom of a blue inland sea. You could not tell whether he was speaking to you or scoffing at you for your immersion in the false; whether he was wrestling with a problem of immense significance to him or indifferently displaying his hodge-podge of maniac learning. Only this much was sure (it was Miller's observation, long afterward): whatever he was up to now, in the beginning he must have gone to those books of his hungrily, hunting for something. One could see that he had bent desperately over his books late at night, night after night and day after day, prayerfully even, keeping like a hermit to his no doubt cluttered, filthy room, poring over the print as though his soul's salvation depended on it. It is unusual, to say the least, to encounter such men in a small-town jail. No wonder Chief Clumly was troubled.

There were those in Batavia who would gladly have listened to him later, would eagerly have searched out, if it weren't too late, as much as could be known of the Sunlight Man's thought, hunting down the secrets of his interwoven innocence and violence. But in the jail, at least in the beginning, he had no real audience but Clumly, as he knew. The truth was simple, at that time. First, he smelled. Second, he was an outrageously self-centered, tiresome man, however talented in his odd, unsettling way. No doubt deep down he had two or three of the usual human virtues, but it was not the business of the police to notice either virtues or defects, now that he was jailed. Their business was to keep him in his cell, feed him, and, with professional indifference, see that he stayed alive. As for his fellow prisoners, they had no time for either genius or madness. All three of his fellow prisoners had been in jail before and might have been expected to endure their confinement with some resignation; but two, the Indians, were in serious trouble, and the third, though he knew he would be found not guilty (although he was guilty), had reasons of his own for gloom.

The Sunlight Man seemed to have no sense of how the others felt. He'd never been in jail before, he said, and he apparently believed himself set apart by nature from the others—as if by that perhaps unjust and unwarranted, meaningless brand, like the mark of Cain—so that his punishment was more cruel than theirs, downright absurd, in fact. When the guard shoved him in and closed the door the Sunlight Man leaped back at the bars and clung to them, mouth gaping. Bearded, peering out with those small, close-set, wounded eyes burning deep in the ashes of his face, he looked like some pirate's minor crewman marooned for half a century, still outraged but deeply befuddled now, near despair. The Indians to his left sat unmoving on their pallets merely looking at him. The middle-aged man to his right had his back turned.

"Guard!" the Sunlight Man howled. The echo boomed at him from all around and he cringed, gorillalike, looking over his shoulder. The Indians said nothing. He gripped the bars tightly and his plump fists went white. He stood silent a moment, like a timid child, returning the calm stare of the Indians, then he began once more to howl for the guard.

At last one of the Indians said, "You get him, you'll wish you didn't, mister."

The Sunlight Man considered it, still watching for the guard, then turned his head once more to look at the Indians. They were young, teen-agers, the older one lean and muscular, with a short, flat forehead and a thin mouth. The younger one was fat, as apelike as the Sunlight Man himself, but cleaner, with downward slanting, unfocused eyes that seemed never fully opened. The two Indians were like Mutt and Jeff, like a pine tree and a mound of earth, like contrasted endocrinological types in a high-school biology book. When the new prisoner was finished looking at them, grimly and suspiciously, or so it seemed at the moment, he smiled suddenly, like a wicked child, and opened his hands like a Jewish tailor.

"But you see," he said, "I have his billfold." It hung, incontrovertible as a flat-iron, between the thumb and first finger of the man's left hand.

The Indians stared and even the humpbacked thief turned to look, and, after a silence, they all began to laugh.

When the guard came, the new prisoner handed him the billfold humbly, as if sheepishly, and explained, showing his large, perfect teeth, "Practice."

The guard said nothing. He pocketed the billfold without even checking to see that whatever money he'd had was still inside (he regretted that later, though nothing was missing), and he held out his hand again. His face was dark red, whether with rage or embarrassment you could not have guessed. Chief of Police Clumly and Captain Sangirgonio—Miller—stood watching from the hallway, with their arms folded, Clumly looking panicky and mildly outraged, pale eyes bulging, Miller grinning broadly, one eyebrow cocked. The bearded prisoner put his fingers to his lips studying the guard's outstretched, patient hand, then nodded thoughtfully and produced

from the empty air, as it seemed, a wristwatch, a pack of
Kools, a pencil, and a fifty-cent piece. The guard stuffed them
all in his pocket without glancing at them, bit his lips together,
and turned to stalk between Clumly and Miller and away
down the hall.

"He's good, you know that?" Miller said.

Clumly said, "There'll be a file on that man. You mark my
words."

Miller grinned. "Fifty bucks says you're wrong, Chief. That's
no pick-pocket there." He rubbed his hands. "We caught us a
magician."

"Negative," Clumly said. "What's a magician doing defacing
a public thoroughfare?"

Miller turned mock-solemn. "You're right, Chief. That's the
work of a pick-pocket."

Clumly scowled his disgust and went back to his office. Miller nodded admiration and farewell, and the bearded prisoner
bowed from the waist, like a Chinaman, fingertips together, his
fire-blased face like a large baked apple wrinkled and dry with
age. When Miller was gone, the new prisoner went to the back
of his cell, demonically pleased with himself, and sat down.

He'd won them all, that moment—both the police and his
fellow prisoners—and so, by some inevitable logic of his character, he had to destroy the effect. He said to both Indians, as
though they weren't worth addressing singly, "What did they
arrest *you* for?" He managed to make it sound thoroughly unfriendly, as though he wanted to know for his own safety.
When the older one answered, the bearded prisoner closed his
eyes and seemed to pay no attention—though he heard, all
right, they would find out later.

The younger one said, "Why they got *you* here?"

He leered. "Because I'm mad, friend." He stood up, threw
out his arms, tipped back his head, and lifted his thick right
leg straight out to the side so that the toe of his shoe hung,
perfectly motionless, four inches beyond the fingers of his
right hand. The baggy suitcoat opened, revealing a dirty white
shirt and no tie. It was then that he began his infuriating prattle.

"Jesus God," the older of the Indians said.

Even after the light went off, a little before midnight, the
Sunlight Man went on jabbering, playing madman. As far as
the other prisoners knew, he did not sleep a wink all night,

though for a while he was quiet. In the morning they saw him
squatting on the floor, wringing his hands, his head drawn in
between his fat, hunched shoulders, small lips pursed. He was
studying some tiny white stones on the floor. How he had smug-
gled them in no one knew. He was tricky all right. After a
long time he gathered them up and shook them in one hand
like dice and sprinkled them out again, and again sat studying
them. The thief, Walter Boyle, pretended not to notice, but the
Indians bent close to the bars.

"What you doing?" the fat younger one said.

The Sunlight Man raised one finger to his lips, commanding
silence, and went on studying the stones. At last, shaking his
head sadly, he gathered up the stones a last time and closed
them in his fist. When the fist opened again, the stones were
gone. He stood up and buttoned his suitcoat. "Casting the
spots," he said. "A mysterious business."

"What?" the older Indian said.

Once more the Sunlight Man raised one finger to his lips,
and this time he winked. "Sh!" he said. "They're listening!"

After breakfast he began to talk again, and now it was
worse than before. He was like a spoiled child insisting on attention—winking, leering, ranting, pretending to weep.

The younger Indian said suddenly, "Hey, shut up, will
you?"

"Shut up," the Sunlight Man echoed, snatching off his cap
and rolling his eyes up. "If only one could! But think of the
implications! Staggering! If I close myself in . . . if every one
of us closes himself in . . . and we can do it, of course, a simple manipulation of the switch called *Will*, what evils would be
banished! what terrifying ghosts would be laid!

"Enough. No bombast." He leaned toward the Indians, perspiration on his forehead like drops of dew on the corpse of a
mushroom.

"Take an instance. I went to a party once in Los Angeles,
through a friend of a friend. It was supposed to be for Tarzan.
Imagine the scene: a warm Saturday night and all over Southern California the smoke had begun to rise heavenward. The
summer moon was hidden, the smog was glorious—blood red
and the deep translucent brown of soy sauce. It was a holy
time. The people had all wrung out their swimsuits and they
stood now, tanned and glistening, drinking martinis in the
wide windows of the one-floor huts overlooking the freeways.

"It was in the Bel Air neighborhood, this party. The best neighborhood in the city, so exclusive that for years and years they wouldn't even let in movie stars. Clark Gable had to live in Brentwood. William Powell's three-hundred-thousand-dollar house went up just outside the gates in Westwood. But the Depression came along, and Bel Air decided to take even the money of the vulgar and crass. But I digress.

"I was greeted at the door by a lady in a hairdo that must have cost two hundred dollars, and it was almost all she had on. 'Is this the Tarzan party?' I said. 'Who?' she said. 'Here, have a glass of champagne and meet the gang.' So I did. It was wall-to-wall sofas and sliding glass doors and lampshades as big as the world. The party was in full swing, and you could've heard it to San Juan Capistrano. They introduced me as the Wolf Man. On the porch they were playing rock 'n roll, colored lights going over the orchestra, and the shriek of it all would have brought down the roof except that the roof was made of colored plastic—it had no shame. There must have been four hundred people there—dozens of 'starlets,' if you know what I mean, a lion trainer dressed in black leather, girls in leopard bikinis, press agents, camera people, a huge chimpanzee and something that looked to be a lynx but might've been a snow-leopard with its tail cut off, an old woman with glasses on a stick, waiters with name tags, a man dressed as a Canadian Mountie, and a Russian merchant seaman with steel-rimmed glasses. There were others. Who can remember! Somebody said there was a rape out by the swimming pool, but it was crowded there, there was no way to be sure. There were girls with topless swimsuits, though, and who knows what it may have led to? Nobody mentioned Tarzan all night long, and I never saw him. Well—I have never left your question, you see —how do you close in from *that?* Ah! Or are you already closed in, there? I don't mean anything complicated. No! That much pure body and maybe you're back to pure soul, *that's* what I mean. Do I make myself clear? Some people might say it was a holy event, beyond sensualism—that the whole age is a holy event. *I* don't say it. But the code you suggest, each of us locked in the cell of himself . . ." He dashed to the bars and seized them as if with pleasure. "In the ancient conflict of the Jews and the Babylonians," he said—but there he was cut off. The police came for him, to question him, and he went away between two of them, quietly, as if full of remorse for the sins of all mankind.

The older Indian stood rubbing his jaw, watching him led away, "Jesus Christ," he said.

"Shut up," the other one said.

After a long time, the older of the Indians said, "That's quite a trick, you know?"

"Aah?" the younger said.

The older one stood in the center of their cell with his lean arms stretched out and head tipped back, and he tried to lift one leg straight out to the side and hold it steady. But the knee was bent and he wobbled off balance, and it came to them both at the same time that the thing was almost impossible.

The younger one shrugged. "Practice. That's all it is."

"Yeah, I know," the older one said. He was musing.

## 2

The thief, Walter Boyle, seemed to hear nothing of what the Sunlight Man said. He sat in his cell like a creature neither alive nor dead, an ash pile which might or might not still hold some heat. He was a short man. His neck and arms and legs were sallow and thin. He did exercises every morning, slowly and methodically, combed his few wisps of graying hair with his short, square fingers, polished his thick glasses, revealing naked, for a minute or two, his protrusive, heavy-lidded eyes, than sat waiting like a hopeless and indifferent barber in a run-down shop, reading the day-old paper he'd gotten from the guard the night before. He was memorizing it, you would have thought. He seemed oblivious to the smell of the place and of his bearded neighbor, oblivious too to the man's talk, the sullen anger of the two young Indians. Boyle looked at no one, at least in the beginning, and never asked or answered questions except for a word now and then to the guards. It was as if he was busy, adding up sums in his head. At night before he went to sleep he would kneel beside his pallet for a minute, cross himself, and mumble something. He seemed to see nothing amusing or out-of-the-way in this. It was his habit. He was a fool, perhaps, as the older of the Indians—the tall one—

pronounced him, but he was not a religious crank. He was a small-time professional thief who travelled from one Western New York town to another, knocked inconspicuously on people's doors and, if he got no answer, tried the door and, if it was unlocked, went in. He took nothing but cash, impossible to identify even if he should be caught with it on him, and he never worked except by daylight. He made enough to get by and, generally speaking he was not dissatisfied. In twenty-two years he'd been arrested only four times and had never been convicted except on charges of no significance. He wouldn't be convicted on the felony charge this time either.

He was a man not easily distressed. He had a faculty for thinking nothing, when necessary, merely bathing in sensation —the rumble and clank of the trucks passing in the street outside, the noise of a television somewhere nearby, a gas station bell, voices. (It was the hottest time of year in Western New York, and the people who lived in the large, declining houses across from the jail would sit on their porches talking and drinking beer until well after sundown.) The thief heard the bearded man's chatter without noticing the words, merely catching here and there a single phrase—some blasphemous outcry—that stayed with him, briefly, as a minor irritant, like a small segment of some flat-voiced fieldbird's song, teasing him almost but not quite to curiosity. After the first day he began sometimes to glance furtively at the new prisoner, without real prejudice or even particular interest, merely as one might glance at some fat, harmless snake to see what he was doing; and then sometimes—but less often—he would glance at the Indians. He had no strong feeling about the bearded man, except for a queer sense that he'd seen him before somewhere, which in fact he had; but the Indians, especially the older one, he disliked. Why he disliked them he did not know or care, and even if you had told him what the reason was, he might not have recognized the truth. He was a painstaking, meticulous thief, a man who would never harm a soul or steal on mere impulse. They, on the other hand, were hooligans.

On the third day, sitting with his paper as usual, running his eyes along the words, he came awake to the sharp impression that the older Indian was watching him and had been doing so for a long time. He peeked between his shoulder and the pinked edge of the *Daily News* and saw that his impression had not been wrong. The Indians were in the cell beyond the bearded

man's, and the older one was lying catlike on his pallet, hands
under the side of his head, pretending to listen to the bearded
man but staring at Boyle with sleepy-looking eyes. Boyle
looked back at his paper and then, slowly, as if indifferently,
turned his back. He began to listen.

"You have to try to be realistic," the Sunlight Man was
whining quietly, as if speaking to himself, working out a problem in geometry, "it was an accident, yes. You know that and
I know that. Not to speak pompously, what is there in this
world but accident—a long, bitter chain of accidents, from al-
gae to reptiles to tortoises and rodents to man? By accident all
our poor mothers had children, and by accident some of the
children died young and the others grew up to be either policemen or outlaws. Nevertheless, where the Law is concerned—"

"You eat shit," the older of the Indians said. He stood at the
front of their cell like a red-brown grasshopper of monstrous
height, his hands on the bars. "Nothing personal, understand."
He bared his teeth in a mock-grin. The teeth were large and
even.

"I understand, certainly," the Sunlight Man said, smiling
back the exact same smile. He waved disagreement away.
"Nevertheless, as I was saying, where the Law is concerned,
there can be no fiddlefaddle about Absolute Truth. They'll
electrocute you if they can, and that's that. You're innocent
victims, that's obvious. But just the same, the jury will solemnly deliberate, the attorneys will frown their commiseration, the
judge will mournfully rap his gavel, and out you'll go like, excuse the expression, a light." He sighed profoundly, pulled off
his cap and crushed it, slowly, thoughtfully, in his hands.

"Why you doing this?" the older of the Indians said. His
voice was reedy and intense, his ape's face impassive, and
again the thief, Walter Boyle, felt revulsion. He stopped listening, but it was not as easy as usual. He named in his mind the
towns he had worked through. Portage, Castile, Perry, Warsaw, Alexander. "Warsaw," he said to himself again, almost
aloud. It was a strange name, neither pleasant nor unpleasant,
exactly; interesting. Like the town itself. An old town set in
the pocket of high wooded hills like mountains. He turned the
name over and over, worrying it until it became mere sound.
But even now he was not quite rid of the Indian's thoughtful
stare.

That night when the guard brought supper Boyle said quietly, with his round back turned to the others, "What did they do?"

The guard—young, mild-faced Mickey Salvador—said nothing for an instant, perhaps because he was a new man and didn't know whether he should answer such questions or not. Walter Boyle kept his eyes on the tin plate. "The Indians," he said testily.

At last Salvador said, "Put a couple people in the hospital, I guess." He came nearer. "It was all in the paper. They were hitchhiking, the Indians, and they tried to take over these people's car. It was a Volkswagen. Whole mess ended up in a ditch. They never got a scratch, the Indians. Drunk."

Boyle nodded. He had read about it, or anyway had passed his eyes down over it slowly and thoughtfully; remembered a picture, a snatch of headline.

"That woman dies, the thing'll end up a murder charge."

Boyle stood motionless, as if thinking about it, but in fact he had let it drop out of his mind, the vague, uncharacteristic impulse satisfied.

"She may do it, too," the guard said. "I guess she's still unconscious. It caved her head in." He added quickly, though Boyle was turning away now, "The Indians got friends, though; that's lucky for them. Older one, he lives with the son of a lawyer here in town, he's his guardian or something, I forget." He turned gruff suddenly, perhaps annoyed that he'd talked so much. "Keep it down in here." He went back up the hall. In five or ten minutes he was back again with a Lois Lane comic for the Indians. The younger one thanked him and squatted over it, reading, fat knees jutting out like a frog's.

Later, when he was drinking his coffee, Boyle glanced over at the Indians again, and again the older one was watching him, the younger one still reading. For a long moment Boyle met the boy's stare angrily, and then, as he'd done before, he turned his back. This time, however, he continued to watch furtively, past his shoulder.

The bearded man began to pace, scratching his beard and part of one rutted, leathery cheek. He stopped abruptly, put his fists on his hips, and glared at the Indians. "Can't make you see reason, can I? I tell you you're doomed, defunct, cold dead, and you go right on thinking what you'll do when you get out, wondering how you can get our friend here to let you in on his professional secrets. It's criminal!" He let his hands drop. "Youth," he said, full of contempt. "Optimism. What can wake you up?"

The older one pointed at him. "You just worry about you."

"Oh, I do," he said. "I worry plenty, believe me. But I'm not running out of time as fast as you are. It would be different if you understood exactly where you stand, if you understood what it is to be alive and how dead you are when you're dead. Forgive my talking so personal." He laughed. "I feel responsible for you. How can I explain?" Then, pompously: "Human consciousness—an overwhelming joy, a monstrous torture, the most fantastic achievement of the whole fantastic chronicle of time and space: you have it in you but you haven't opened up to it yet, and suddenly it will be too late! Horrible! What's my role? What must I do?" He squeezed his eyes shut, mock-sorrowful, and clenched his fists.

"You're crazy, mister," the Indian said. "You're really crazy as shit."

He nodded, paying no attention. He stood perfectly still for a long time, in a state like thinking, and at last Walter Boyle saw him reaching his decision—or walking into it, accepting it like a man accepting a coat held up behind his shoulders. "Listen," the Sunlight Man said. He was studying the floor, smiling craftily, like a man about to dig up the Cardiff Giant. "Your name is Slater. Vernon . . . LaVerne . . ." He paused. "Nicholas. That's it. Nicholas Slater. Vernon is your brother."

"Sure. You heard 'em saying it."

"Maybe." He leered. "You have friends, you think. An old family in town." He studied the floor still more intently. "Hodge," he said. He glanced at the Indian as if to see if he was right, but the tall boy's face showed nothing. The Sunlight Man turned away and began to walk very slowly, each step exactly as long as the last one, as though he were measuring. He pressed his hands to the sides of his head, and though he had his eyes open he did not seem to be seeing. "It's confusing," he said, "hard to pick the strands out. There are *two* of them, these Hodges. Yes! One of them is a judge, I think, and the other one is a farmer, his brother. They're married to the same woman. Is that possible?" He shook his head. "No, something wrong there. But a connection, perhaps a secret. Perhaps when they were young—" He'd lost the thread, unless he was pretending, and stood motionless, as if trying to find it. It came suddenly and violently. "*Ben* Hodge. Ben Hodge was your guardian, and he's always helped you by means of his brother the judge, because this Ben Hodge is a generous man. But you've exceeded his limits this time, he holds back his hand, and his brother the judge has some reason to dislike you. And so you're stranded. You know it. You wait for the judge to come, you make excuses for his delay, but you know he won't come. And even so you go on hoping for the best. The woman in the hospital—she's lying in a bed with a high, chromium wheel on each side, something wrong with her back —the woman in the hospital is still all right. She'll get better, you think, and your crime won't be serious." Again he stood motionless, but not straining this time. Brooding on what he knew. "She's going to die."

"Nick, baby, you better not listen to that man," the younger one said. "I'm telling you, he's out to flip you."

The older Indian ignored him. He said, "How do you do that? Who are you?"

"I don't know how I do it," the Sunlight Man said. "But I'll tell you this: you better believe me. I may make mistakes here and there—I may get infected by mistakes in *your* mind—but the images are true. The fat man surrounded by legal books, the other fat man in the farm overalls, the dead woman in the hospital. You're a child, almost, and headed for certain destruction, and nobody can save you but yourself. You better face it."

"You see that too?—the cops killing me?"

"For Christ's sake, Nick," his brother said.

But Nick Slater insisted, "Can you?"

The Sunlight Man studied him and scratched absentmindedly at his beard, smiling again. "No," he said. "Sometimes I can know things and sometimes I can't. I was in a train wreck once. Me, myself. I never dreamed it was coming."

Walter Boyle turned away, feeling sick. He'd seen a train derailed one time. While the dust and steam were still thick as fog and there were people screaming, boys in T-shirts came running and broke in the windows and scrambled among the dead and injured, looting. The memory of his horror combined with his present horror in the face of what he half believed to be magic, and he began to shake. He pressed his back against the wall and covered his eyes.

In the morning the police did not come to take the bearded

one away for more questioning. Boyle had half expected they wouldn't. They weren't supposed to be questioning him anyhow, as far as Walter Boyle could make out—both from the scraps he got from the guard who was talkative and from what he'd found in the *Daily News*. They were supposed to be merely holding him until he could be moved to the hospital for observation. Yet that wasn't what stopped them from questioning him today. The Chief had been working on him day after day, sometimes with the cop called Miller, sometimes alone, for no earthly reason, as far as Walter Boyle could see, except that the bearded man was, well, fishy, and sometimes policemen could smell a thing like that. (Boyle was now certain, by the prickle in his skin every once in a while, that he'd seen him somewhere.) If they didn't come for him today it was for one of two reasons: they had too many more important things to do, or they'd decided to leave him alone awhile, let him sweat. Boyle had seen the sweat treatment in the past. He'd seen it work when nothing else did. In fact he was convinced that if they ever got *him*, Walter Boyle, that would be the way. It was one of the reasons he'd developed his technique for getting through the hours whenever he was jailed: reading the paper over and over, disciplining himself to miss nothing, even the smallest ads, the personals, the numbers of the pages, though he'd remember almost none of it later. When the paper no longer gave him something to lean on, he would say to himself the hundreds of poems he'd memorized, for some reason no longer clear to him, in his childhood,

> These joys are free to all who live,
> The rich and poor, the great and low:
> The charms which kindness has to give,
> The smiles which friendship may bestow . . .

They got nowhere questioning the bearded man—Boyle could hear them almost clearly, in the room at the end of the hallway—and he'd seen that the sweat treatment was coming. And so they hadn't come for him today. Instead they came for Boyle.

The Chief of Police was standing at his window smoking when they led Boyle in, and he didn't bother to turn around. The room was thick with stale hamburger smell. There was a large white bag from one of those carry-out places on the Chief's desk. The policeman called Miller nodded Boyle toward a chair, and the other of the younger policemen left—at a signal from Miller, perhaps; Boyle wasn't sure. He waited, sitting bent forward. His leg tingled from the knee to the hip; it had gone to sleep while he was sitting back in his cell. It was hot and close, though not as bad as the cellblock, and the air here smelled freer. The Chief went on standing looking out, head almost hidden in the bluegray strata of smoke. Miller stood behind Boyle's back.

At last, slowly, the Chief turned and took the cigar out of his mouth. "Coffee, Boyle?" he said.

Boyle shook his head then changed his mind, made a feeble gesture with his right hand then dropped it back to the chair arm. Miller went out and came back a minute later with old cups and a percolator with the cord dangling. He was scowling as he poured the coffee. The tape recorder stood on the chief's desk, tipped up on a stack of manilla envelopes, but no one made a move to turn it on. The Chief came to his desk, sat down, sipped his coffee, or rather gulped it, hot as it was.

"Boyle, we'd like some information," he said.

Miller closed the door to the hallway leading to the cellblock, then stood nursing his coffee. He glanced at the clock over the Chief's desk, above a picture of a huge badge and some writing.

"Yes sir?" Boyle said.

"Tell us what you know about the man with the beard."

"The beard," Boyle said.

They waited.

"I never saw him before," Boyle said.

"You listen to his talk?"

Miller said, "Any talk about a jailbreak?"

Boyle shook his head. He couldn't tell which of them to look at. "I don't listen much," he said. "A lot of—" He searched his mind. "Lot of talk."

"Any talk about where he comes from?"

"Look," Miller said.

Boyle folded his hands and squinted. "He says he went to a party for Tarzan, in Los Angeles," he said dully.

The Chief looked over at Miller, who wasn't impressed. "What else?"

Boyle rubbed his chest where the sweat was dripping down inside his shirt, but he couldn't stop the itching. "He says he can read people's minds," he said. It sounded cross. He didn't believe it himself today, and he was annoyed at being pushed into saying it. More important, he felt something queer in the air, sharp and foul as the smell of something burning. Were they trying to trick him into admitting something?

Miller sighed. "How do you know that, Boyle?"

"I don't. It's just what he says. I don't know him. I never saw him before." Then, quickly, to change the subject back to safer ground: "He says he can see into the future. He told the Indians—"

They waited and he picked at his lip, trying to think what they were up to. "He told the Indians the woman they hurt will die. They believed him. I think they did." He watched his interrogators suspiciously.

Miller sipped his coffee, scowling more darkly by the minute, eyebrows lifting up and out like wings, and now Boyle was sweating all over, burning up. The Italian cop was breathing deeply, like a man in bad air, his whole chest full of anger. There was a story of some cops in Elmira who'd used hypnotism. Without quite believing it was anything like that, Boyle said suddenly, "I want a lawyer."

The Chief of Police squinted.

"Why?" Miller said. "Why did he tell the Indians the woman will die?"

"I don't know. To scare them."

Ominously, the Chief snapped his fingers and pointed at Boyle. "Maybe," he said. It was as if, suddenly, they'd made him tell them what they needed. But he knew, nervous as he was, that it couldn't be that.

"I don't know," Boyle said. "I hardly listen."

"Drink your coffee," Miller said.

The Chief's cup was empty, and he refilled it. He said, "What you think, Miller?"

Miller looked down.

The Chief scowled and lowered his eyebrows. He took a hamburger out of the bag as if unaware that he was doing it, crumpled the tissue wrapping and threw it in the wastebasket, where there were two or three such wrappings already, and bit in like a werewolf.

Miller thought for a long time. Then: "I think you got some kind of fixed idea, Chief. You know what that is?" He went over to the window suddenly and bent down to look out, holding the cup in his two hands, and his eyes searched the street as though he were expecting someone, or were afraid somebody he didn't want to see was on his way. The sunlight fell over his shoulders and down to one elbow, and when he moved his arm the light looked alive. He said, speaking fast, "It's when some little piece of nothing gets ahold of you, like lint on the brain, and you can't shake it loose."

After a minute the Chief shifted the food into his cheek and said, "You think our Sunlight Man is a little piece of nothing?"

"I think he's a magician went out on a drunk and painted a sign on the street. Or maybe he's a schoolteacher, and he's playing with us because he's afraid he'll lose his job if they find he's been in jail. Or maybe he's a rabbi. Why not? Or maybe he's King Tut come back from the dead. What's the difference who he is? I don't know what I think. What I do know is, that man has gotten you tied up in knots. Maybe he reminds you of your mother or something—and all the time the Mayor asking questions and the paper talking about Police Efficiency—"

"All right," Chief Clumly said. He dusted his hands. "I know all that."

Miller turned to point the cup at him. "Put it this way. Say I believe you. Say there's something that really stinks about this man, besides his armpits and his rotten clothes—say our Sunlight Man's planning the biggest little caper since Alonzo J. Whiteside invaded the Buffalo bank—and say you nip it in the bud. Stop whatever he's up to before it starts, and who's going to know it? What you going to say to the papers? Headline: BANK NOT HELD UP. PLANE NOT DIVERTED TO CUBA. All anybody's going to know is we never caught the kids with the mop-handles or the man with the gray coat, never could locate that pack of dogs that bit the Jensen kid. Or *him*." He turned to point the cup at Boyle. "We may as well send him home right now. We could nail him, you know damn well we could." The Chief scowled, trying to stop him, but he went on. "You know how they work, people like Boyle. Someplace not too far from here there's a quiet suburban guy whose wife thinks he's in the selling business, and he didn't come home from his last trip—he'll do that sometimes, nothing to worry her, always comes back, not the type to take up with another woman. A man with two identities. Find that nice quiet suburban house, get a history on him, and we've got this Boyle, or whatever his name is, locked up till hell freezes over. But we're running out of time. We go into court with no more case than we've got—" He stopped.

"All right," Clumly said. He was sitting very still, no expression whatever on his face. He looked from Miller to the cold cigar—he'd just now picked it up again—and kept his eyes on it.

"Just tell me one thing you've got on him, this Sunlight Man of yours."

Clumly pushed out his lower lip, then sucked it in again, and said nothing. At last, thoughtfully, he raised the cigar to his lip and lighted it. When it was going, he took another gulp of coffee.

"Ok," he said. "I'm cognizant of all that." He nodded toward Boyle. "Take him away."

Miller came over and waited while Walter Boyle stood up. As they went down the hall, Miller didn't bother to hold his arm, and at the cell he didn't bother to give him the usual shove. When he was leaving, after the cell was locked, Miller paused a moment and looked past his shoulder at the scarred and bearded man in the cell beside Boyle's. The Sunlight Man signed the air with a cross, solemnly, and Miller frowned. Then he left. Nick Slater, the older of the Indians, yelled after him, "Hey officer! Where in hell's our lawyer?" Miller ignored him.

"No lawyer," the bearded prisoner croaked softly. "No lawyer coming. Wake up child! Behold the universe."

All at once Boyle knew where it was he'd seen the man before, or rather, had it on the tip of his tongue. But again the memory darted away from his mind's grasp and sank back, little by little, into darkness.

### 3

Nick Slater awakened out of his nightmare and believed it was the cold that had made him wake up. It was well after midnight, perhaps not long before dawn. There was no sound of trucks from the street in front, no sound of voices, not even the police radio two or three rooms away, somewhere beyond the hallway that led out from the cells. It was raining. He could hear the steady, comforting hiss and for a moment it seemed to him that he could smell it. His shoulder still ached, maybe something he'd gotten in the wreck, maybe something the police had done, he could no longer remember. Though he couldn't see a thing, he knew at once that his brother was still asleep beside him, flat on his back, the way he always slept, like a dead man. His terror came over him again—a rush of car lights, the policemen—and for a second he shut his eyes.

Something made him think—the cold, perhaps—of the old woman with whom he'd spent his childhood. The old woman had braided silver hair and a face so withered and wrinkled it looked like a net. Her two half-blind eyes floated in small nets of red. He hadn't thought of her in years, yet the memory of her gazing blankly up at him from the faded yellow chair she had hardly ever left was vivid now.

And then he was thinking of Ben Hodge, remembering a trivial incident that had come to his mind repeatedly since the wreck. Ben Hodge had said, with his huge red hands hanging between his knees, the flesh around his eyes boiled-looking, now that he had his glasses off, "Everybody suffers some. Especially at your age. It's an easy thing to get pushed out of all due proportion. You're not so bad off, all things considered. Young. Smart. Got the whole world by the scruff." Always full of wisdom, Ben Hodge. Sitting there like the King of the Beggarmen on the seat of the new manure-spreader with cowshit splattered all over his back and his floppy felt hat, dangling his glasses between his two hands, getting ready to clean them when he got to it, when he finished handing down wisdom. Except that the old man was right enough, high-falutin old fart. Nick had known it all along himself. Behind Ben, that day, the birches stood out like cuts against the dark trees behind, and above the woods, like a halo around the old man's hat, the sky was streaked with orange. Nick had said, "Sure, sure, sure," and had felt disgusted with himself for saying it even as he said it. He wondered what it was in him that made him turn on even Ben Hodge. The old man had looked at his glasses, sorry to have spoken. The man seemed, that instant, like a fat, wrinkled child dressed up in grown-up clothes, as harmless as a cow, and Nick had looked down at the sharp gray stubble by the spreader tire to get hold of himself. A feeling of deadness came up through his arms. David, Ben's Negro helper, stood at the rear of the spreader, wiping his hands off on his jeans and looking toward the house. He hadn't heard or seen.

Out of the dark came the croak of the bearded man in the middle cell: "Can't sleep?"

He raised his head silently to see if he could make the man out. The light at the far end of the hallway was burning, and he could see the shaggy silhouette. "Christ," he whispered, too softly for the man to hear, and clenched his fists. The pain in his right shoulder was worse, and he remembered hitting. The grass had been wet. All his sensations had been unnaturally precise. He could feel each bead of sweat on his forehead, and he could tell the difference between the sweat and the drops of water from the grass. He could hear the man grunting and calling to his wife. He was moving, flopping about near the wreck, like a fish.

"I can't say I blame you," the bearded man said. He wasn't whispering or making any show of speaking quietly, but the infuriating voice was almost more faint than the rain. When he closed his eyes it seemed not to come from any single point but from everywhere. "It's disquieting, the thought of one's own death. And you're young, of course." He sighed, but Nick could imagine the leer. "Well, be philosophical. As a great man once said, 'The world's a hospital.' " He sighed again.

Nick said between his teeth, "Shut up, I'm warning you. I'm gonna call the friggin guard."

"No harm. But I'd help you if I could."

"Fuckhead," he whispered to himself.

"When you think about it," the voice said, infinitely weary, "the world is more like a jailhouse than like a hospital. No matter how cynical we try to be, the food is never what we secretly expected; the beds rob us of our sleep and health; the company lacks zest, not to mention how it smells; the toilets are a cruel, cold shock; and at the end of it all, instead of the justice we have a right to expect, as feeling creatures—*fzzzt!* the electric chair. If we had any sense we'd hang ourselves and be done with it."

"Do it," he thought ferociously, but still he said nothing, as though there were some faint hope of stopping the man by ignoring him. The voice stirred up in him a churning of strong confused emotion—anger and fear, but worst of all a powerful but vague longing that had no name, a feeling something like what he'd gone through at night in his childhood when he heard the train, a mile away, going through the oak-woods over at the edge of the Reservation. There was a dirt floor in Mrs. Steeprock's house, cold and smooth as the worn, worthless brown coins in her snakegrass box. He would cross to the foot-wide window in the dark and there he would see the long bloom of white light moving quickly south, up over the trees, riding the undersides of clouds. She said once, "What is it?" looking in from the kitchen where she sewed, and when he shrugged sullenly, turning away from the window again, she came to him and bent down, as if she were grieved, to study his face. He hadn't remembered that particular night for a long time. It was strange that it was still in his mind, clear as ever.

"Be that as it may," the voice said, "I have just one piece of advice for you. Break out. If you don't, I swear to heaven you're dead. And this: once you're out of this hole, don't you ever let them drag you back."

"Shut up," he whispered. "I don't need to break out. I got a lawyer."

Suddenly, unbelievably, the bearded man laughed, softly; then his laughter grew louder, though still a whisper, like the laughter of wind. The noise was frightening in the darkness. His brother lumbered awake, swearing in his half-sleep like a man grumbling something under water. When he was fully awake, Nick's brother moaned, "You again! Jesus god damn *hell!*"

The door opened at the end of the hallway, and the nearer light came on.

"Why are you doing this?" Nick hissed at the bearded man. "You got to be crazier than shit."

In the far cell he could make out the thief sitting up, fumbling for something with both hands. He found what he was after—his glasses—and put them on to look.

## 4

"Clumly," Mayor Mullen said, "have a cigar." He was expansive. A small man, noisy and quick as a blue jay—a flaming, apoplectic face—but he seemed much larger than he was, because of the size of the desk, perhaps, or because he had power over Clumly, or because he had a stubbornness about him, the same as a jay, an unshakable conviction of his own rightness that went beyond mere confidence born of his having looked through a fine-toothed comb, as he sometimes said, at the ins and outs of things. It was true, certainly, that he knew a great deal—a *working* mayor, the posters said—and had friends in high places. The glass-topped desk was completely bare, as though he never did anything, but that was because he was not a man who worked with paper: paper was for his underlings. He talked, listened, scrutinized men's tics. Famous for phonecalls, sudden trips. If he worked with books, records, letters, he did it alone, late at night, unseen by mortal eyes unless perhaps the eyes of the man called Wittaker, his amanuensis, as he said, bald hawklike man in drab brown suits, nails too perfectly manicured, on one hand a discreet bronze ring like a Czechoslovakian coin. The Mayor, thoroughly public man, had no private identity unless one counted the farm equipment store he owned but had nothing to do with any more, and had no secrets public or private except that his hair, as white as virgin snow, was dyed.

He had risen from his desk as Wittaker, wearing his hat and coat, about to leave, showed Clumly into the room, and now he came out around the desk, awkwardly past the wastebasket, holding out the cigars in one hand, reaching for Clumly's hand with the other. They were White Owls, cheaper than Clumly's own cigars, but Clumly took one. It was a bad sign when the Mayor opened with cigars. One of many bad omens It was bad to be called in in the first place—to talk about "a mutual problem," the note from Wittaker had said.

Mullen tipped his head. "How you been, Fred?" Still holding Clumly's hand.

"Fine, Walt," Clumly said.

The afternoon sunlight, breaking through the Venetian blinds to Clumly's right, made bands across the Mayor's face.

"Good," Mullen said. "That's all that matters, isn't it." He released Clumly's hand, veered away toward the center of the room, head still cocked, and rubbed his hands together. Clumly rolled the cigar between his fingers. Wittaker closed the door softly behind them, shutting out the clutter of his own, much smaller office and the closed door to the council chamber.

"Sit down," the Mayor said.

Two captain's chairs, old and nicked, faced the Mayor's desk, another stood to the right of it. It was an absurd arrangement, calculated to shatter a man's calm, because the Mayor never sat at his desk when he talked. He roamed about like a restless creature in a narrow cage, fussing with things, adjusting the blinds, studying the photographs beside the window (photographs in which he himself almost invariably appeared, inconspicuous in a second row, while men of more importance opened the racetrack, cut the tape at the western end of the New York State Thruway, or shook hands with one another, holding some solemn trophy on display). He went now to the hotplate on the waist-high cabinet where he made his coffee—a scummy glass Silex into which he spooned out Instant Nescafé.

"I'm not supposed to have to do this," he said. "Make my own coffee. That man—" He pecked with his nose toward the door Wittaker had closed as he left. "He remembers as much as he wants to remember. You know the problem. Well, good worker. Dependable. Trained sociologist, you know. Don't know what I'd do without him."

"Mmm," Clumly said.

"Cup of coffee, Fred?"

He wanted one badly, and therefore took hold of himself. "Just had one. Thanks all the same."

"Fine, fine." He screwed the lid on and put the coffee jar back in the cabinet. Except for a pair of galoshes, there was nothing else in the cabinet, as far as Chief Clumly could see. "Be right back," Mullen said. He carried the Silex out past Wittaker's office and into the hall and to the men's room to get water. He took several minutes to get back. When he had the coffee heating, he came to stand by the bookshelf under the photographs and lounged on his feet, looking at them, bent forward, hands in pockets, his back to Clumly. "Damned hot," he said. "We're supposed to get an air-conditioner in here, they passed it more than a year ago. Well, it's the old story. Corruption." He turned to wink.

"Mmm," Clumly said.

The Mayor cleared his throat and stepped to the window to the right of the pictures. (There were two windows, a wide window in the narrow wall behind his desk, a narrow window in the wide wall.) From the window where he stood he could look down on the jail or, scrooching down in his collar, up at the trees, old elms that dwarfed the City Hall.

"Well, we have a mutual problem, Fred. Speaking very frankly, I thought the best thing was to talk with you about it. I know you appreciate my position."

"Certainly," Clumly said.

He was moving again, crossing over to the Barcalounger, the coffee table, with its dusty artificial flowers and old copies of *Sports Afield* and *Life* and the *National Geographic*.

"It's about the budget." His face grew redder.

Clumly nodded, pursing his lips.

"Now I want to speak very frankly with you, man to man. As I mentioned in my letter of, I think, June fourteenth, your budget don't make sense, Fred. Now I don't know what's happening over there, and I know you have your own troubles, that's only natural, but this thing has got me, well, to speak frankly, perplexed."

"What's the problem?" Clumly said. But he knew. And it was true that the room was insufferably hot. The man's forever dancing around made it hotter.

"The problem, frankly, is communications. Between our two offices, I mean." His mouth tightened a little and he tipped his blazing head far to the left and squinted. "The problem is we don't *have* no communications. You don't answer my letters."

"Ah," Clumly said.

"Now I think you'll admit I'm not merely being petty when I say I can't win no budget for you from the skinflint council if you don't *tell* me nothing. Now I ask you, what am I to say to them? 'How much for the cops?' they want to know. Imagine how I'll look if I say to them, 'Frankly, the Chief hasn't told me nothing yet.' "

"We did submit a budget," Clumly said. He felt cross, but he kept it out of his voice.

"Well yes. Sure you did. A botch of a budget, if I may speak very frankly. You want six new motorcycles, you say to me, and what do you put under 'Justification'? 'Necessary.' Now I ask you. And BMW's you want, when Firster's been selling us Harleys for years and his brother's the County Superintendent. And what's your Justification? 'Necessary.' It won't do, Fred. It's a little thing. I don't begrudge you your fancy foreign-made motorcycles that you got to buy up in Buffalo and the local merchants be damned. But I'll tell you frankly, it's them little things that lose elections. Now listen. What am I asking you? Clumly, I'm asking you take a few minutes and write a few words about why a cop needs some motorcycle made off in Germany that's got no distributor here in Batavia. Just explain it, justify it, that's all I ask. Just answer your mail." His face was nearly purple, though his voice was controlled. His fist was closed tight. He relaxed himself, smiling. "You see my side, don't you, Fred," he said. "I wrote to you on June fourteenth, and again on the second of July, and again last week, if memory serves me right. What the devil you people doing over there with your mail?"

The coffee was boiling, and he went to it and poured two cups and brought one to Clumly whether he wanted it or not. "Sugar?" he said.

"No thanks," Clumly said.

"Funny joke I heard," the Mayor said. "It's a little off-color." He glanced at the door. "Fellow goes into a cafe and gets coffee and says to the waitress, you know how to sweeten your coffee when you ain't got no sugar? No, how? she says. Get your sweetheart to put her finger in, he says. She looks shocked and she says—" He began to laugh. "And then put it in the *coffee?* she says."

"Mmm," Clumly said.

"Well," Mullen said. He straightened up. "Well all right. Yes." He laughed again, then stopped himself. "Little joke now and then," Mayor Mullen said. He cocked his head. "Grin and bear it. Walk on the bright side. All work no play makes Jack a dull boy."

Clumly recalled the cigar in his hand and raised it to his lips, patting his pocket with his left hand for matches.

"Well all right, then," Mayor Mullen said. "I don't know what you people are doing over there, but I thought we'd both benefit from a little talk about it. A little talk don't hurt, I say." His bright little eyes bored into Clumly's nose.

"No, that's right."

"Of course the motorcycles aren't all of it. Whole budget's a problem. It runs the whole gambit. And then there's other problems. You wrote me last winter about them parking meters, the new ones we put in on the lot behind Felton's. You say they're a problem, lot of difficulty one way or another—I forget the details: take a whole different schedule than the other meters, on account of the different size coin-boxes, throws you people off your synchronization, something like that. I asked you, if you saw my letter, should we put in all new meters, all the same kind, would that be justified, or would it be cheaper in the long run to reevaluate the whole parking system, what with urban renewal making havoc of what we got? Well I waited and waited. That was way last winter. So let me speak frankly about this. Because you see *I'm* on the spot as much as you are. What's your explanation for all this? You see my problem."

Clumly sucked in on the cigar and bowed his head a moment. It was not exactly that he had no explanation. It was as though they talked different languages. Where should he begin?

Mayor Mullen turned away and put his cup on the bookshelf. He looked at the books, rubbing his jaw and frowning. A strange batch of things—God knew where he'd picked it all up. *Success in Business. The Robe.* Two volumes of an encyclopedia, a book of business law, a world almanac old as the hills, some leatherbound *Reader's Digest* condensations.

"God damn it, Fred, I'm going to level with you," Mayor Mullen said. He went purple again. "You're up to your ears and you know it. You know it and I know it and the town knows it. 'What's happened to Clumly?' people say to me. I was over at the Rotary last Wednesday afternoon, and Phil Uphill said, 'Walt, I want to ask you something? Chief Clumly been sick or something?' 'Why no, Phil, not that I know of,' I says to him. 'Well, I wondered,' he says. 'He acts funny lately. He don't get the work out,' Phil says. 'That fire on Washington, we needed that street blocked off and the police was noplace to be seen. Off chasing cats or something, I don't know what.' 'Well I don't know, Phil,' I says. 'I'll have a word with him.' 'You better, Walt,' he says, 'and that's the truth.' I says, 'One thing, sure, they mean to cooperate, you can bet your boots on that,' I says. 'But they got troubles all right. Clumly's working with a lot of new men. Big turnover there,' I says, 'and I can't believe it's Fred Clumly's fault. Maybe he sent out one of those new men and the fellow got lost. Ha ha.' Well listen now, Fred. Phil looks at me and says, 'Ain't the way *I* heard it. I heard Miller sent men and Clumly called 'em back. I heard Clumly said, if the people want to watch the place burn, let 'em watch.' "

Clumly folded his hands and said nothing. His clothes were sticking to him and his belt bit in at his shoulderblade.

"You say that, Fred?" Mayor Mullen asked.

"I may have," Clumly said. He cleared his throat. "Acting according to your instructions, you know. Time Product Factor. I don't remember the fire—what day it was—and I don't know what we were doing right then. But it's possible something more important came up. I don't know."

"More important," Mullen said. He stood staring.

"Maybe there was a wreck that afternoon, or a fight somewhere, or maybe it was the day we raided—" He checked himself. He couldn't think of a place they'd raided in a month. He tried to think when it was they'd arrested the Sunlight Man.

Mayor Mullen walked over to the Barcalounger and leaned one hand on the back, pushing it down. After a long moment he said, "You retire next year, that right, Fred?"

"October."

"Been a long career," Mullen said. "A lot of people look up to you with a whole lot of respect."

Clumly waited. The Mayor gazed at the wall where there were no pictures, absolutely blank, the wall to the left of the door as you came in. It was the wall you didn't see as you entered the room: so that when you came in you saw photographs, a window, chairs, plants on the windowsill and cabinet (dead), but when you went out you saw nothing, a dirty yellow wall as empty as a grave.

The Mayor said, "Fred, you got to put your house in order. This is no time to snap. Talking frankly to you. I think of you as a personal friend, a man I've been proud to have on my team. I mean that. Every word."

Clumly turned his head back to the desk. It gave him a crick in his neck to be constantly twisting around to follow the Mayor with his eyes wherever he roamed. The Mayor came up behind him and put his hand on his shoulder, firm.

"I'm pulling for you, Fred. Now you know I am. And every man on the Police Force is pulling for you. Yessir. But if all this keeps up, complaints keep coming, if I have to go before that City Council—" He pointed toward the Chamber—"and I have to tell them Fred Clumly's not getting the paperwork done, well . . . I hope it won't come to that. I *believe* it won't come to that." Suddenly, ferociously, he exclaimed, "More coffee, Fred?"

Clumly started, thinking for an instant of the girl Rosemary with the henna-red hair, and Kozlowski running the toe of his boot back and forth along the crack in the floor. "No no," he said. "No coffee. I'm fine. Fine."

"Suit yourself," Mullen said. Then, solemnly: "I'm glad we had this little talk."

Clumly nodded, getting up.

"Heard a funny story," Mayor Mullen said as he showed him to the door. "You'll die at this one. Lady told her three lovers whichever one brought her the most ping-pong balls could have her hand in marriage."

"I heard it," Clumly said.

"Seems the first lover went to the grocery store, and the second lover went to the sporting goods store, and the third lover went to Africa."

Clumly shaped the end of the half-smoked cigar between his thumb and first finger, his eyes tacked to it.

"Well the first lover that went to the grocery store comes back with a hundred ping-pong balls, and the second lover that went to the sporting goods store comes back with a thousand ping-pong balls, but all the one that comes back from Africa has got is two big brown bloody balls. Are these ping-pong balls? the lady says. Ping-pong balls, he says, *I* thought you said King Kong's balls!" The Mayor roared. Tears ran down his cheeks. "Well, Fred, I be seeing you," he said. "Walk on the bright side. Grin and bear it."

"Good night," Clumly said. His heels clicked loudly on the wooden floor of the long empty hallway. Behind him Mayor Mullen went on laughing, filling the corridor with quick, dusky echoes like bats.

When Clumly got back to the station, at quarter-after-six, a paper bag of hamburgers tucked under his arm, a guilty sensation like suffocation inside him, Miller was still at his desk, chin-deep in papers, and Mickey Salvador was working on the police radio speaker with a screwdriver, whistling to himself. Clumly drew off his hat. "Any excitement?" he said.

"Like a tomb," Miller said. He looked at the paper sack and, after thinking about it, grinned. "You, Chief? Any news?"

"Nothing," he said.

Miller said, "Got a minute?"

"Come on in." He opened the door to his office and went in. He sat down, motioned Miller to the chair across from him. "What's on your mind, son?" The word *son* rang oddly in his ears. They'd worked just fine together all these years, he and Miller. If he had had a son, Miller was the kind of man he'd want him to be. But he felt slightly worried in Miller's presence. He would be his replacement, if they forced him to resign. It was even possible that behind his back . . . But he checked himself. It came to him that there were things missing from the clutter on his desk. Miller had picked them up, then. Miller was helping out again, covering for him. It made him feel sick. Clumly had done the same for Miller, picked up some of his work when he was crowded. There was nothing unusual in that, no reason for Miller to sit there grinning too gently, pitying him. We all work together. You can't run a Force without mutual respect. Watchdogs. ("Cowdogs, you mean," Kozlowski had said.) He winced and opened the sack.

Miller stretched out his legs. "It's nothing much," he said. "A couple of things. One is this kid Salvador. I tried to talk to him."

"Mmm?"

He opened his hands. "I don't know. That is, nothing specific. Makes me nervous. He wants to be loved. Know what I mean?"

Clumly scowled.

"It's this. He's easygoing, gets into these long conversations with the bears. Long talk with the Indians this afternoon—kidding around with them, big friend of the family. I let him finish with 'em, and then I laid down the law—to them, not him: No more talk. One word back there in the cells and I said I'd brain the whole crowd of 'em. It's your buddy the Sunlight Man mainly. Keeps getting at the Injuns, working 'em up. So I tell them to stow it. New policy. Pretty soon I hear them back there chattering again and I go back and guess who's right up to his nose in it. Salvador."

Clumly nodded and bit into the first of the hamburgers. He was feeling guilty now about not having offered Miller one. It wasn't too late even now, but he didn't. "He'll get slugged for his trouble. After they've knocked him on his can once, he'll see reason."

"Yeah. Still—"

"You're as jumpy as I am," Clumly said. He smiled wryly.

Miller looked at the front of Clumly's desk. "It's true," he said. "Tired. Maybe I should go home and knock up the old lady or beat the dog or something." He smiled, and now he relaxed for a moment, but soon his eyes became thoughtful. "There's something in the air, you know it? It's like a smell." He tipped his head back to look at the ceiling, thinking. "You want to know the truth? I keep hearing things. Somebody digging a tunnel right under us, or some kind of prehistoric monster waking up, down under the ground, scratching to get out."

"You need a good stiff whiskey."

"You telling me?"

Clumly hunted up his pencil and wrote himself a note about Salvador. "I'll talk to him," he said.

"Yeah, good." He started to get up.

"There was something else too?"

"I guess so." He mused, then stood up, pushed his fists down into his pockets, and leaned toward Clumly. "I know how to nail our thief—Walter Boyle." He drew his right hand from his pocket and snapped his fingers.

"How?" He happened to break wind as he spoke, but not noticeably.

Miller pivoted away and went to the window. The sky was red now. "You ever hear of a paragnost, Chief?" When Clumly said nothing, he went on, "It's a guy who knows things it's impossible to know. The future, the past, what people around him are thinking."

"A mind reader."

He nodded. "Sort of. Anyhow, we got one right in our hands. Your Sunlight Man may be a lot of things, and some things he may not be, but one thing he is for sure is one of *them*. Listen." He turned suddenly and crossed to the file to the right of Clumly's desk and opened the drawer. He shuffled through the confusion of papers that lay flat in the drawer and pounced on one of the tapes. He cocked his eyebrow, reading the label on the tape, then drew the tape out and threaded it through the machine. "This is from day before yesterday," he said. He played with the buttons, running the peeping, babbling tape through the spools until he found the place he wanted. "There," he said. "Listen." They bent over the machine.

*. . . no sense of divertisement. It's a great responsibility, accepting the role of policeman. I suffer for you. Do you know why you hunt? Do you understand the Order you struggle to preserve? Alas, gentlemen, I suffer for your victims, too. The poor kid that goes through town with his muffler open, the old man that runs his cart down the center of Main, the kids that skinny-dip in the Reservoir, those Indian boys, or me, or that poor fool Benson.*

CLUMLY: *Tell us why you burned the papers in your billfold.*

PRISONER: *Because I wasn't out of matches.*

Miller flicked off the tape.

"I don't see it," Clumly said.

"Listen. Boyle told us this Sunlight Man can see things. He told us the guy predicted that woman will die—the one the Injuns put in the hospital."

"Is she dead?"

"Not yet. But she'll die. The point is, the Sunlight Man made Boyle halfway believe he really could do it, even though Boyle doesn't want to believe it. And the Indians believe it. Salvador says—"

"What are you driving at?" He broke wind again and frowned.

"Salvador says the man does it all the time, tells them things he can't possibly know."

"But *you* don't believe all that?"

"I don't know. How *can* I? There's things in this world would surprise a person. That's my honest opinion. You ever seen what a fortune teller can do with cards? I mean they tell you *facts*, not just vague stuff, some of them. Or palmists. There was one at our church one time—made your hair stand up. There may be lots of things we don't like to admit to. Flying saucers, ghosts, I don't know what. Ok, so maybe there is all that stuff and maybe not—who cares? But if some of it comes along and you can *use* it . . . this time for instance. If it's true, if it just happened to be more than a joke, say."

"Now wait a minute. Are you saying you're going to get the Sunlight Man to come here and tell us—"

"No. *Hell* no! He's told us already! Listen again." He turned back the tape and played it once more, squinting at it.

*skinny-dip in the Reservoir, those Indian boys, or me, or
that poor fool Benson*

He snapped it off.

"Benson!" Clumly said. His back crawled. Miller nodded.
Clumly said, chewing, "Hmp. Even if I accept your wild theory that he can read people's minds, how do we know it's not a
slip of the tongue—how do we know he didn't mean to say
Boyle?"

"Don't move," Miller said. He crossed to the door and went
to the outer office. He came back with his clipboard, the pencil
dangling by a string. He pushed the clipboard toward Clumly
and quoted without looking at it, "Walter Arlis Benson, 362
Maple Street, Kenmore, New York. Male. Blue eyes. Height,
5–8. Weight 190. Married. Occupation, salesman."

Clumly glanced at him.

"I talked to his wife on the phone this afternoon. He's out
of town on a trip, been out for three weeks. Doesn't know
when to expect him back. I can have her here tomorrow for
an identification."

"You told her—"

He shook his head.

"Holy smoke," Clumly said. Face drawn into a fixed wince,
he turned the tape back once again and listened. Then he got
up, lit a cigar, and went to stand in the doorway to the other
office. At last he said, "You may be right."

"A hundred dollars says yes."

He puffed at the cigar, building up smoke, shaking his head
slowly. "It's a hell of a thing. Crooks build up a system you
can't beat, and then all of a sudden—" He was uneasy. As if
talking to himself, he said, "You almost didn't tell me. You
told me the business about Salvador, and you were about to
leave. If I hadn't asked you right out if there wasn't something
else—" He was whining, he noticed.

Miller shrugged, grinning. "You gotta admit it's a crazy
damn piece of police work."

But Clumly shook his head. It was coming clearer. "When's
she due to arrive here? Who brings her—Buffalo police?"

"Who, Chief?"

"Who, who, *who!*" he roared. "The Benson woman."

"Sorry," Miller said. "Ten o'clock. With the Buffalo fuzz,
right."

Clumly came back to his desk. "Call it off," he said.

"What?"

"Call it off. You heard me. No identification, no nothing."

"For Christ's sake, Chief—" But he moved toward the door.

"And this, Miller. When they fire me and make you Chief, *then* you be Chief. Not yet."

"You mean you plan to let Boyle walk out free? Just walk out the door when you know damn well how to tie him? Boy! the State's Attorney will do cartwheels."

"I don't know what I'm gonna let Boyle do. I need to think about it."

"Let me get this straight. You think I was butting into your business, and you've decided if you can't get Boyle yourself, nobody gets him for you. That it?"

"Of course not."

"Whatever you say, boss." He raised his hands and smiled, angry.

Clumly sat down, partly because of his gas problem, and put his chin on his fists. He remembered again that Miller had taken some of the papers from the clutter on his desk, and he couldn't tell whether to be grateful or indignant. It came to him (some secondary part of his mind still grinding grist) that maybe the Sunlight Man knew Walter Boyle from somewhere. As simple as that. And if so . . . He filed it to think about later. Miller stood waiting, and Clumly sighed. "It was good thinking, Miller. I'm cognizant of that. It was a good hunch, damn good thinking. But you have to give me time. I'm not up with you yet. Whole thing's got implications I've got to think through. Sorry. No hard feelings."

Miller looked at him. "Ok. No hard feelings." He went out. There were hard feelings.

Clumly shut his eyes. The station was quiet now. If he let himself he could hear the scratching, tunneling sound, the creature waking up, or anyway feel it moving toward him, coming from the darkness outside the city limits, maybe, to smash down the door with its fingertips and have them before they knew it. Clumly snorted.

"Home," he said suddenly, aloud. It was getting late.

He ought to go out somewhere with his wife, get his work off his mind. He should take her to dinner—except that dinner would already be fixed, waiting for him. Out on the town, then. Over to Bohm's Mortuary, where Paxton was laid out.

His wife's minister was there when he got home. Clumly himself had no patience with ministers or churches, not that he had anything serious against them. He was not an atheist, simply disliked religion. Sermons left him full of a vague turmoil of questions, irritation at answers not sufficiently convincing—right answers, maybe, but answers not explained to his satisfaction. There were questions of fact—why the fish weren't killed when the other things were in Noah's flood, why Christ prevented the stoning of the adulteress but blasted the barren fig tree in a fit of pique. It was true that the questions were of no importance, no interest, even; nevertheless, he felt there were things that weren't getting said, loopholes left open, problems of contradiction and confusion. As for singing, Clumly was tone-deaf. And as for the offering, it was not clear to him that the work of the church was a thing he ought to invest in. He never went to church, except to drive his wife and pick her up after the service. But for her sake he tolerated the minister's visits. She was very religious. She got copies of *To-day* magazine in braille, which cost him plenty, and kept them piled like old telephone books on the wicker hamper in the bathroom. She gave his money not only to the church but to the Children's Home, the old-folks' home in Rochester, even a thing called the Jewish Orphans' Fund. When they were first married, she would kneel beside the bed for fifteen minutes every night to pray, moving her lips, and when she found it bothered him she had taken to praying in the bathroom before she came in. She never nagged him about his opinions, he would give her that. Indeed, the truth was, she was as fine a Christian woman as a man could know, except maybe for the drinking. At the head of their bed she had a cloth she'd laboriously embroidered before the operation, when the last of her eyesight went. A poem.

> *We thank Thee, Lord, for all Thy Care,*
> *For strength to earn, the chance to share,*
> *For laughter, song, and friendships deep*
> *And all the memories we keep.*

It did not seem to Clumly very poetic, but he was no judge.

She and the minister sat across from one another in the living-room, talking. Clumly shook the man's hand more or less politely, and exchanged a few words, then walked on in to the kitchen to get his supper from the oven. He carried the gray stew to the diningroom table and sat with his back to them where, though he couldn't help hearing what they said, he didn't have to see them. After the hamburger he felt stuffed to the throat, yet his chest was still sending up anxious signals of hunger, like a lover's. He was halfway through the meal before he realized he still had his hat and gun on. He got up, paused a moment, cautiously broke wind, then put the hat on the top shelf of the clothespress and hung the gun on the nail where it belonged. When he turned to the table again the minister was standing there in his black coat and hat, getting ready to say good-bye.

"It's so good of you to come, Reverend," she said.

"Don't you mention it," he said. He was old, emaciated, a simperer with false teeth that whistled.

"Good night, Chief," he said. He stretched out his hand.

"Good night, sir," Clumly said. He shook hands with the man, furtively broke wind again, and sat down.

"God bless you," the minister said.

"Same to you," Clumly said. He nodded as if thoughtfully, smelling gas.

Still the man hovered at his elbow. "You know," he said, "I have the strangest feeling." He smiled. His dimple flickered into sight then faded into his cheek. "I feel—" he began. He looked at the ceiling, smiling. "There's a great deal of love in this house," the minister said. "One can sense these things. So many homes, you know, have no love in them at all, poor things. An absence of the Holy Spirit." His teeth whistled sharply. She stood behind him with her head meekly tipped. She was high.

"Mmm," Clumly said. He dabbed at the stew with his bread.

"I imagine you're very busy down there at the police station these days. You look tired, to tell the truth. I can sense that too. But confident." He beamed. "I like a man of confidence."

"Gets harder every year," Clumly said. He pursed his lips.

"I imagine it *does*."

Clumly tilted his head to look at him. Like a skinny buzzard in glasses he looked, and a black hat in his claws. More gas escaped. Hurriedly Clumly went on, as if absurdly hoping to distract them. "It's a funny business, police work." He squinted. "It's the times, partly. Everything in transition. Sometimes you feel like you're flying by the seat of your pants." He felt a blush stirring in his neck. "Excuse me." Then, quickly: "I'm talking about hunches, funny feelings you get." He turned his chair a little to face the man more directly. He pointed at the minister's hat over his breast, and said like a lecturer (he had an odd sense of standing back listening to himself, dispassionate and critical, and with another fragment of his mind he waited for more trouble behind him), "We've got a man down there now, an ugly bearded fellow we picked up for a prank. Trifling little thing you'd never think about twice, nine times out of ten. But I'll tell you something. I've got a *feeling* about this man. A feeling in my belly."

The minister looked sympathetic. "The poor soul," he said.

"They want you to run a tight ship, get your paperwork done, delegate authority to the men below you, put in so much time and no more on any one certain case. Well I'll tell you something. I'm responsible. I'm directly responsible for every man in my department, and for the welfare of every man, woman, and child in the City of Batavia." Esther looked bored. He got up to pace, poking the air with his cigar, and made it to the far end of the room in the nick of time.

"A grave responsibility," the minister said.

"Correct."

She came nearer.

"Now this bearded man, he may be nothing but a tramp, for all I know. But I have this *feeling* about him. It's like a creature working up from the center of the earth, scratching and scratching. You follow me?" He could feel the pressure building up again in his abdomen, and wondered if the man would ever leave.

The minister's eyes widened a little and he drew the chair beside the table closer to where Clumly now stood and sat down.

"Well then what's my job?" Clumly said. "You see the question? The Mayor wants one thing, the men underneath me want another. You follow me?"

"Yes. Yes. Terrible." Clumly's wife, coming up behind him, put her hand on Clumly's shoulder, and the minister noticed. He smiled and showed his dimple. "But your good wife is with you."

"Mmm," Clumly said. "So here's what it comes to. If my hunch is right, the most important thing I can do is stop that man before he makes his move. But if I'm *wrong*—"

"Horrible," the minister said.

"Poor Fred," she said. "Was the stew all right?"

"Mmm," Clumly said. "Well I don't mind telling you it's giving me the shakes. The man can read minds."

"You don't say!"

"Sure as hell. Excuse me, Reverend." He squinted, listening carefully to what he was saying.

"Oh no, not at all."

"And what's more," Clumly said, "we can turn that power of his to good use. We can *harness* it. Like the atom."

"No!"

"Yessir. But *should* we? It's like voodoo. It's a moral problem." He paused, struggling to control his own problem, but also squinting at the minister to see what he thought.

The minister frowned, his whole face drawing in to give intensity to his eyes, and at last he saw it. "Like wire-tapping!" he said.

Clumly sat back and set his fist on the table. "Correct!"

The minister rubbed the bridge of his nose to a shine. At length he said, "What will you do, Chief?"

"I'm not sure yet," Clumly said, cagey. His jaw grew firmer. "I have to think it out."

The minister slid his hat onto the table and pressed his hands together. He closed his eyes and prayed, "Dear Heavenly Father, fount of all wisdom and abundant mercy, we pray Thee that Thou wilt shed Thy light on this Thy humble servant in his hour of dilemma, and that Thou wilt guide him and minister unto him and lead his steps aright in the name of Thy beloved Son, Our Saviour, Jesus Christ. Amen."

"Amen," Clumly's wife said softly, her face tipped up. It shone like the face of a saint.

"Amen," said Clumly. His jaw was set like rock.

A long silence.

"*Well,*" the minister said. "So this man can read minds!"

"That's not half of it, Reverend," Clumly said. He leaned closer. "He knows the future!"

"No!" said the minister.

"Yessir."

"Well, I'll be darned," the minister breathed.

*BARROOOM*, roared Chief Clumly's rear end. Neither his wife nor the minister batted an eye.

"That's Nature," said Clumly with a terrible smile. "Washington, Jefferson, Franklin, Lincoln—Nature is no respecter of persons. Fact."

They laughed loudly, like people at a wake.

After that he talked solemnly, pedantically, of the Sunlight Man's uncanny powers, and the more he talked the surer he was that all he was saying (and all they said, too) was nonsense. The thing was a trick. Their gullibility seemed now to Chief Clumly almost dangerous, and his responsibility weighed on him more heavily than before.

He dreamed that night that he was back at sea, standing on the bridge plotting his ship's course by the stars. It was a wooden ship that rode low in the water, perhaps because its planks were heavy as boards that have lain in the earth for years. But the sea was calm as oil in a barrel, and all was in control. The crew was restless, below and behind him, darting here and there like shadows on the deck and below the deck, or staring up at him anxiously out of their lifeboats. He knew well enough what their trouble was. Unbelievers, heretics, usurers, perverts, suicides. But he had them in control, everything in control. All was well. However, there was a storm coming, he knew by the fact that, one by one, the stars were going out. Far in the distance he could hear a mighty wind rising, a sound of sighs and wails and shrieks reverberating in the blackness, a babble of languages. "Steady on course," he said soberly. "Full speed ahead." Now the struggling winds were like groans of pain and there were thudding noises as the winds buffeted the sea, sounds like clubs banging on backs, sometimes cracking bones, an ungodly racket. It was closer now—he kept his ship steady on—exhilaration filling his chest —and the howls like agony and rage rained down on him and up from his sailors like pebbles and sand before a whirlwind. "Steady on!" he roared. And now he could see the other ship, not approaching, as he'd thought, but fleeing like a pirate toward the calmer water he saw glowing, deep red-gold, on the horizon. The captain in black was bent forward like an ape, whipping his sailors, urging them to still greater effort, and the speed of his flight made his beard whip over his shoulder. His red eyes rolled. Clumly cupped his mouth between his hands and howled, "Beware, beware, you guilty souls!" He raised his pistol, steady on, and fired. The bearded man sank like a shadow through the ship and down into the sea. It was suddenly daylight, and both ship's crews were singing. He felt serene. The round-backed old sailor at his side, bearded and scarred from many wars and many wives, was smiling. "What sea is this?" asked Clumly, with a comfortable sense of authority. The sailor looked down, inspecting its texture. He smiled again, a man perhaps not to be trusted. He said thoughtfully, "Metaphysics."

Clumly sat up in the blackness of the bedroom, wringing his hands. "What's the meaning of this?" he asked crossly. Then, understanding, he whispered to himself, "A dream. Just a damned dream!" He was hungry as the devil, and the room stunk like an outhouse. His wife slept on.

At the hospital, just then, a boy fifteen was being admitted through Emergency with multiple lacerations. He'd been drinking with his friends and had been pushed through a glass door during a fight. Later an old woman named Rohn poisoned a neighbor's dog.

## 5

On the evening of the sixth day, the police brought in a drunk-and-disorderly, an oldish man named Bob Boas. They put him in the cell beyond the thief, and he sang. The bearded man sat in a brown study, ignoring the man, only now and then throwing an irritable glance in his direction. Then something made the bearded man change. Maybe there was someone listening in the hall. Nick Slater couldn't tell from where he was, but Boyle, over in position to see, had the look of an animal being watched. The bearded man began to sing with the drunk, falsetto, waving his arms and shuffling around obscenely in his stocking feet in the cell. He called the drunk Herr Robert. The drunk—he was pale and effeminate and quick to wrath—would stop singing at this, as though the name Herr Robert had some meaning the others didn't catch. He would sink into violent, bristling gloom. Then suddenly the song would break out again by itself, like a howl of rage.

> *Mm lady come in, mmm assed for a cake,*
> *Mm assed er wat kine she'd adore,*

*Mmm "layer" she said, mmm layer I did,*
*An I don't work there any more.*

While the drunk sang, the Sunlight Man whispered to him earnestly, and after a moment the singing stopped again.

"Look out!" the Sunlight Man suddenly yelled, and he pointed to the floor at the drunk's feet. There was something there—even Nick saw it, but he didn't catch what it was. The same instant it appeared it vanished. The drunk clung to the bars, throat convulsing, then vomited. The Sunlight Man dusted his hands.

"Holy Christ," Verne said.

It was a full five minutes before it was really clear in Nick's mind that it had all been a trick, some kind of illusion. But it was amazing, just the same. Then it came to him that the most amazing thing of all was the bored calm of the thief, Walter Boyle. He lay on his pallet with his skinny legs crossed and his hands behind his head, seeing nothing.

Verne, too, noticed it. "He's something else," he said, nodding toward Boyle.

Nick sat with his chin on his fists.

"How'd they catch him—you hear?" Verne asked.

Nick shook his head.

The Sunlight Man was playing with those tiny stones of his again. It was as if he'd completely forgotten about the drunk. He was mumbling something, mumbo-jumbo of some kind. They watched him for a while.

"Must be waiting for his trial, like us," Nick's brother said, looking at Boyle again. He pursed his lips and thought about it, then nodded. Neither of them felt easy talking about the Sunlight Man or his magic. "That's what it is, he's waiting for his trial." He bit the tip of his tongue.

"Mr. Hodge defend him, you think?" Nick asked. It came out by accident, merely because it had flitted into his mind. He was wondering, really, why Will Hodge Sr had not yet come to talk to them. Had the Sunlight Man told them the truth? Will Hodge hadn't been at the hearing, even, though they'd phoned his office the first thing in the morning, after the night they were arrested. Maybe he was waiting to see if the woman would die. None of them had come, even to visit, not Will Hodge the lawyer or Luke or even Ben. Not even Vanessa.

The smell of the vomit in the end cell was terrible, but the drunk was singing again. Nick struggled to ignore it. As abruptly as it had started the singing stopped, and the bearded man yelled, "Excellent, mein herr!" and clapped his hands together smartly. The hallway door opened as if at the Sunlight Man's command, and the guard stuck his head in. "Keep it down." The one watching in the hallway said something to him, very quiet.

The bearded man bowed to the drunk. The scar tissue and the bushy beard made his eyes seem smaller than they were. The guard went out, and the drunk began talking, tortuously reasoning with the Sunlight Man, who ignored him.

Later, the drunk vomited again, this time without help from the bearded man, and the thief groaned and sat up and pressed his hands to the sides of his bald head as though he were afraid he would explode. He looked at the mess but remained expressionless, then sat with his elbows on his knees and stared at his feet.

"I'm sorry," the drunk said. He was white as a sheet, leaning against the bars between his cell and the thief's.

The thief waved the apology off almost sociably.

"S'like a sickness," the drunk said. "S'like something wrong with me. I go on the wagon for maybe two muths . . ." He closed his eyes and stood unnaturally still.

"Don't mention it," the thief said. "Happens to everybody."

"I got a daughter in high school. If she saw me now she'd be so ashamed—" He grimaced as if about to cry, but he was too sick. He gripped the bars.

"Go to sleep," the thief said. "Talk about it in the morning."

The drunk looked over at his pallet and seemed to think about whether he could make it that far. Then he leaned away from the bars and took two steps and fell toward his bed. He sprawled half on it and half off, motionless for a long time. All at once he sang out, "I use to work in Chicago, in a department store" and then, mechanically, he pulled himself onto the bed and went to sleep.

"Wages of sin," the bearded man said. "You understand what his sin is, Benson?"

The thief looked panicky for an instant, then turned away. After a while he too stretched out for sleep, and the bearded man stood with his head cocked, watching. He stood that way for a long time, a heavy-hearted tramplike figure in the dim-

ness of the cellblock. For all the clowning he'd gone through tonight, he looked miserable. Without looking at what he was doing, he began to tie and magically untie knots in the farmer's handkerchiefs he'd gotten from Salvador. What he really needed was some pigeons, he said to Nick. He talked on and on and once closed his hands and opened them again and looked up as if startled by a beating of hundreds of wings. The handkerchiefs were gone, and Nick really did see pigeons for a moment. The Sunlight Man batted the air, grieved and tired but charged with frantic energy. "Get away! Shoo! Jesus!" Feathers whirred like motors and a barndust smell bloomed through Nick's memory. Then they were gone.

"You're really something," Nick said. When he glanced at Verne he was sitting with his arms around his knees, scowling, not sure what to think.

The guard came and switched off the last of the lights, all but the end one in the hall. After that it was quiet for a long time. Nick was almost asleep, troubled by vague dreams of creatures, when the talking began.

"Don't be fooled by clever hands, sir," the Sunlight Man said. He'd be lying with the back of his head on his hands, as he always lay. "Entertainment's all very well, but the world is serious. It's exceedingly amusing, when you think about it: nothing in life is as startling or shocking or mysterious as a good magician's trick. That's what makes stagecraft deadly. Listen closely, friend. You see great marvels performed on the stage—the lady sawed in half, the fat man supported by empty air, the Hindu vanishing with the folding of a cloth—and the subtlest of poisons drifts into your brain: you think the earth dead because the sky is full of spirits, you think the hall drab because the stage is adazzle with dimestore gilt. So King Lear rages, and the audience grows meek, and tomorrow, in the gray of old groceries, the housewife will weep for Cordelia and despair for herself. They weren't fools, those old sages who called all art the Devil's work. It eats the soul."

Nick turned his head. He could make out only the outline of the high dome, the seared nose, the uncertain frizzle of beard.

"And yet one is an artist, of course. No harm in it, if one knows where one stands. Nevertheless, don't be fooled by visions of pigeons or monstrous turtles or crimson snakes. Consider this drunk, Herr Robert. American Bund. That surprises you, perhaps? Goes to meetings Wednesday nights—or would if he knew about them—puts on a black armband with a swastika, or would. And yet he's a proper citizen, you know. They'll release him in the morning. And you, on the other hand . . ."

He fell silent. Nick tried to think about it. But his body felt too wide awake, tingling with suspense. It was the kind of awakeness he'd felt just after the accident, when they were bending over the man and woman, shining their flashlights on their faces and legs, talking to them and sometimes shouting to one another across the rain-wet grass.

"It's too bad," the bearded man said pensively. "But then, of course, it's natural. Society must protect itself from whatever it thinks to be threatening it, and to Society, you seem a threat. Pity, of course. You're not much of a threat, God knows. But intelligence is not the world's strong point." He sighed. Nick's brother rolled over, struggling in his sleep, and swore.

"The thief and the drunk," the Sunlight Man said. "There's society. You find that remarkable? Ah, son, I've seen how you spy on our thief, all envy. 'A professional,' you think. 'A cool one,' you say. 'A mystery.' Poor fool. It's the glitter of the stage, the dazzling exception, mere artifice. He's a robot. It's our precious Mr. Benson who put you here, Mr. Benson who'll be your judge and jury and, if all goes well, executioner. Are you so mad as to think you've been thrown in jail because you hurt somebody? Damaged some property? Ridiculous! Listen. You're here because in the sheer ignorance of youth and defiance, with the sullenness of some sharp-eyed Injun, you disrupted prediction. I don't praise you for it. I find you mildly disgusting, to tell the truth. But I'm older, and so I allow for that. I'm sorry to see you die."

"Shut up," he said suddenly. He lay with his eyes locked open in the dark.

To his surprise, the bearded man said nothing more, and as the minute of silence stretched on into two and then three he felt what he mistook at first for relief. But gradually he realized he was no longer revolted by the senseless talk. Even at first perhaps it hadn't really been disgust he'd felt. The man's talk made him feel the way the police made him feel, treating him like an animal, torturing him for nothing. He'd wanted to kill him, the same as he'd wanted to kill the police, and at the same time he'd felt beaten before he started, as if nothing he did to the bearded man could have any effect whatever. He wasn't human. Except that that wasn't right either. With the police he felt like shutting his eyes, making himself limp. With the bearded man he felt like watching more intently, eyes as wide as when he stood in a clearing with Ben Hodge's rifle, hunting.

Before he knew he would speak, he said, "Why are you here? I mean what are you after?"

The man laughed quietly in the darkness. "A ball on an inclined plane," he said.

Nick waited.

"We're all victims of our foolishness, one way or another," the bearded man said. "The inertia of psychological patterns." He paused. "To descend to the tiresome particular, I found myself involved in an affair of the heart. With the wife of a colleague, a fellow Senator unfortunately—concerning whom I prefer to say no more. Lady's honor, you know. I've explained to them, of course, that my problem is glandular, but being fundamentally sensible people they are disinclined to trust me."

"I don't believe you," Nick said cautiously. "There never was any lady."

"Ah well, your privilege." He chuckled. "There are still vast areas of Freedom. Actually, though, you're right. I was lying. The brutal truth is, I killed a poor carry-out boy at the A&P. Backed over him while he was loading the trunk of my car. His name was Larry." The man spoke more rapidly, patting something nervously. "It was an accident," he said. "It could have happened to anyone. I simply forgot. I have a great deal on my mind—responsibilities, troubles, worries. I may be drafted at any time. The trucking firm I work for is unsound, my sister is pregnant, my housekeeper's dissatisfied with her wages. And so it was a slip-up. My mind wandered. Dear God in Heaven, *anyone* could have done it. But poor Larry, pauvre petit, poor harmless victim!" He pounded on the wall. "He lived with his mother."

Nick Slater closed his eyes.

"You believe me this time?" the bearded man asked mildly.

Nick said nothing. He felt weightless. The thing was different from teasing. He knew, without needing words for it, that there was a limit to teasing, a certain point, not quite predict-

able but nevertheless definite and final, beyond which teasing
would not go. But there was no such point with the Sunlight
Man: he could go on as long as the world endured. He didn't
care; that was the secret. Even murderers cared, had some re-
motely human feeling. The Sunlight Man was as indifferent as
a freight train driving a cow from its track.

"Blast!" the man said. Then, wearily, "All right. I see there's
no hiding it. I embezzled a large sum, it was thousands of dollars. Hundreds of thousands. I'm no piker! It bankrupt the
firm that employed me—manufacturer of cyclone fences in a
small town in northern Montana. I meant to go to Canada. It
wasn't my fault, though, the whole mess. As the Lord is my
judge. It was because of my medical expenses. I'm a dying
man, you know. That's what makes me stink. I couldn't stand
it, at first—the dying, not the smell. I was half out of my
mind, I can tell you. I'd run up to complete strangers on the
street and I'd tell them all about it. It was awful, naturally.
And the dreams I had! But then—oh bliss, sheer bliss!—I
turned to Mormonism. I wish I could give you the faintest idea
what peace, my friend, what unspeakable tranquillity . . ."

Finally he was silent.

Nick lay listening to his brother's breathing and to the stillness beyond that, smelling the sweat of the Sunlight Man and
the acrid stench of the drunk's sickness and wondering again,
cold all over, why Will Hodge had not come to bail them out.
But he would come, he insisted. The old man always came,
sooner or later. Luke would get to him, or Ben, or Ben's wife,
or maybe Luke's mother or Will Jr. He rubbed the sore shoulder and felt a sudden welming of sorrow that had nothing to
do, it seemed to him, with the bitter mockery of the man in
the next cell. What if it were true that they would send him to
the chair? But it wasn't. He wasn't guilty. He hadn't wanted to
go in the first place. "Listen," he'd said, "let's just go find us
some girls." But Verne was drunk, it had to be a joyride, and
like a fool he'd gone along. It hadn't been his fault, but just
the same when the cops had found him lying in the weeds at
the edge of the field (he could see the Volkswagen, sharp in
the starlight, smashed, the convertible roof cocked up, and he
could smell the gas and the sicksweet scent of the cigarettes of
the people who came running down from the road) one of
them had yelled, "Over here! Here's one!" and when they'd
found he wasn't hurt much, they'd jerked him up and held him

like some killer. "It wasn't my fault," he'd hollered at them, but the fat one had hit him in the chest, and when he was bent double in the grass, gasping, the man said, "Up."

He said now, suddenly, "What did you mean?"

"Sir?" the man said.

"About all that stuff. Freedom. I don't get it."

"Just joshing you. Passing the time. Try and get some sleep, son."

An hour later, when Nick woke up briefly, he heard the bearded one pacing in his cell. An image of the woman's face came to him, a white oval half-turned to him, eyebrows raised, mouth open, buck-teeth protruding like a neat little awning above the black cavern of her mouth. She was like a doll, not human. Irrelevant to the careening of the car, the whirling lights. She'd said nothing. She hadn't even screamed, as far as he knew. She had no name, no features. Nevertheless the car had lifted, in slow motion, all at once, and the Thruway sign had passed slowly to their left, and then they were gliding toward the sharply outlined wet weeds of the embankment, every water drop a precise little crystal, and the steering wheel in his left hand turned free, clutching air. "Oops!" Verne said. It was suddenly dark—the lights were smashed out—and time was hurling again. The woman without voice or features was going to die. What was her name?

At noon the next day the police let the drunk go home. The thief returned to his patient silence, sitting like a figure made out of old rags, passing his bulging eyes slowly over the words in the *Daily News*. Nick's brother dumped his dinner down the open, seatless toilet. The bearded man lay running his fingers through his beard and said nothing for hours at a stretch, merely announced once, sorrowfully, but as if to hide from them what was really in his mind, "No one writes to me. You'd think they'd at least send bills." Will Hodge had still not come. When they asked the guard if the woman in the hospital was better, he said, "You'll hear, buddy."

Nick lay looking at the thief, trying to guess what went on in his mind, but it was useless. His brother said, "He works out crossword puzzles in his head." No one answered, and after a minute Verne shook his head and said, "He's a cool one," and patted his stomach.

They were something, these old professionals. It was hard to

know what to think of them. They never got taken, they
worked out a system the cops couldn't beat and they'd get
along for years that way, some of them, and even if the cops
knew damn well what they were doing, all they could do was
bother them a little—lock them up for loitering, or arrest them
on suspicion of something. He and Verne were different. The
way they went at it it meant something, but they kept getting
caught. One time they'd gone through the coatrooms at the
First Presbyterian church and they'd gotten only six dollars, and
in half an hour flat they were sitting in the can. When they got
out on parole Luke Hodge was sitting there waiting in his
pick-up truck to take Nick home, and Luke hadn't spoken two
words to him for a week. Then it was "Go get the eggs, Slater,
if you're man enough to sneak them from under the chickens."
And once at supper: "Big man, Slater—laying all the broads,
slugging down the booze, pounding up on the little people."
He wouldn't have said that to Boyle. He'd have called him Sir
and discussed the weather with him. Luke's eyebrows went out
like a witch's and his mouth was tensed. He had one of those
headaches of his coming on, not that that excused it. Next day,
when the headache was going full blast, he'd said, "Shovel
good or you won't get your allowance." All at once it wasn't
worth the trouble and the gutter fork was right there in his
hands and he let the thing fly and Luke Hodge was spluttering
and howling and scraping the cow manure out of his ears and
eyes and mouth, yelling "Yellowleg bastard, I'll kill you!"

That'll be the day.

Then it was old Ben Hodge's place, and that was no better,
though it had seemed it at first. The old man would send him
up in the silo to get out the ensilage, and Nick would sit up
there talking to himself and singing, relaxed as he'd be if he'd
eaten some pill, full of the eerie sensation of calm that came
from saying *No more, I took all the shit from you I can* and
then shutting them out, like a door closing in the back of his
brain: concentrating on forgetting them until they were more
than forgotten, as dead as if they never were born. He would
sit listening to the echo of his singing coming back all around
him as it would at the bottom of a well, unaware that the cattle were down there waiting, totally blind to Ben Hodge's waiting, deaf as a stone to the sound of his clambering up the silo
chute—not just pretending not to hear, stone deaf—deaf to his

greeting if he gave any greeting, and blind to his huge shape
squeezing through the square concrete silo door; or if not deaf
and blind, then this, at least: no more aware than a sleeping
man of a familiar figure coming into his bedroom and closing
a window and leaving again. Ben Hodge would say nothing
and wouldn't even bear a grudge but would get out the ensilage himself, perhaps talking, until slowly, without batting an
eyelash, Nick would rise out of his waking sleep to a clean
sensation of cold and damp and the ensilage smell as sweet
and clean as the smell of cold horse piss, and he would hear
him talking, telling jokes as if nothing had happened. It was
something to watch that old man fork out ensilage. He was big
as a cow, more than two-hundred-fifty pounds, and if he'd
wanted to he could have lifted the corner of the barn. He'd
load the fork so full the ensilage would hardly go down the
chute. He was all right. When you came across him and he
didn't expect you he'd be singing at the top of his voice, or
sometimes yodeling. You could hear him some mornings a
mile away, singing to himself on the tractor. If a cow kicked
him he would knock her to her knees, but with people he was
patient. And then they'd begun to talk sometimes, late at
night, sitting in the milkhouse or in the kitchen along with
Ben's wife Vanessa, and Ben would tell him about all the boys
he'd had out here working for him in his time, and all the boys
his father the Congressman had reclaimed before him, little
shits (that wasn't Ben Hodge's word) who'd come around at
last and had farms of their own now, or good jobs at Dohler,
Sylvania, the tannery, the gypsum mines—fine men, he loved
them like sons. Verne called it bragging, because Verne was
stupid. Ben Hodge looked at you, watched you as though your
face was a part of the talk. He said, "What are you thinking?"
and it wasn't for politeness. He lived outside time, indifferent
to the wisdom of age or the rights of station, indifferent even
to that studied and fatuous indifference of people like Miss
Bunce, the probation officer, whose every gesture was a parody
of people like Hodge. So that the boys he'd brought up, and
those his father had brought up, were things that had happened; not examples or lessons, but things that had happened,
to look at, think out, and judge all over again to find out what
was true. Everything in the world was an instance for Hodge.
The swallows that nested, generation after generation, on the

beams of his falling-down garage. The dog whose leg he'd cut off with the scythe. The cow that got drunk from the soup at the bottom of the silo. The chickens, the pigs, the dead rat under the ice-box. And he, Nick Slater, would sit unspeaking, listening to it exactly as he listened to the Sunlight Man now, aware in his blood that there were no required opinions, though there were right answers, still uncertain. And the more he listened the more clearly he knew that it was true that Ben Hodge was a father to the boys he'd raised. He sweated out their troubles, cried like a woman at their weddings, lent them money and could even borrow from them, indifferent even to their idea of what he was. And beyond all that, when they went bad—when they ended up in prison or beat their wives —he went on feeling as he'd felt before, indifferent even to goodness. So that Nick had been at once awed and sickened, had come to see the world from a new ground, from inside the old man's feelings. Verne wouldn't work, the six weeks he'd lived there, and Nick had been ashamed, furious, but the old man said, "Well, well," thoughtfully, and "Well," resigned to it. Nick, when he was drunk, would talk for hours with Verne, reasoning with him, and at last to get rid of him Verne would say, "Ok, ok, I'll be better from now on, you watch." And the old man would say to Nick, "Take it easy." Late at night, when the old man came in from riding his motorcycle, he'd open the door a crack and look in at them to see that they were sleeping, and if the covers were off Verne's back, the old man would fix them, as if he was their mother.

And so he couldn't stand it. The old man asked and required nothing. He was a place to be, no more demanding or self-conscious than the land, or a bird, or somebody else's cow, not insistently kind like his wife Vanessa, who would weep when they came home drunk at night, would visit them in jail when they got into trouble, would have cocoa ready when they came in from plowing off the roads with Hodge's old tractor, and yet not professionally indifferent either, like Miss Bunce who sat listening with that prim smile, fiddling with her yellow plastic bracelet. He was wide and happy, as easy-living as a cow in a creek, and when he preached those sermons he was famous for, the people would laugh as though the walls of the church had been lifted away and the aisle were all planted in bluegrass and daisies, or they'd weep into their hankies and make out rainbows in their tears. So the responsibility that was not even demanded of Nick had overwhelmed him.

He'd said it to his brother late one night, sitting at the counter in the Palace of Sweets where the girls would come when Mancuso's Theater let out, and his brother couldn't get it, no more than he ever got anything, because Verne was an idiot—some kind of half-breed, Jim Tree used to say: half-Injun, half-shit. Verne said, grinning, showing all his square teeth, "He can't do that to you, we'll burn up the sumbitch's barn," and Nick had said, "Jesus, you got dogsick between your ears." And so it had had to be Luke he told, Ben Hodge's nephew, because Luke was twenty-two, only four years older than Nick himself, and because Luke had more or less been raised by Ben Hodge, had all the old man's ways except for things inside—and because Luke knew already. They'd stood at the corncrib at Luke's place, leaning their backs against the splintery, powder-dry, rotten gray slats of lath, and Nick had explained. It was coming on dark. They'd just finished letting the cows out. From where they stood they could see the whole valley, blue-gray miles and miles of it, clear to where the Attica Prison stood like an old-time castle, and fog was rolling in from the south. He'd said, "Take girls. You see one, a pretty one, and you know you're dressed sharp and your hair's ok, and you know you can do it. I mean you can get in her pants. It fills up your chest and you haven't got a choice, and you don't have a choice with the next one either, or the next or the next, and every time it's the same thing, the sickness feeling: you have to, she even wants you to. And what I'm telling you is, it's no different. A gas station with the lights off, standing there shining and slick in the dark—it can make you sweat. All right. Or a big car with the keys in it. I mean those things are beautiful." Luke said, "That's stupid." Dully, stating a fact. And Nick had nodded. "Just the same, I'm coming to your place. You tell your Uncle Ben you've changed your mind, you need me." Luke's face was white against the dusk of sky and trees. "You think I'm crazy too?" he said. Nick frowned. "You got no choice."

Which was true. The same thing that made it impossible for Nick to stay on with Ben Hodge made it impossible for Luke to leave him there. At Luke's, from then on, Nick could work or not, whatever he pleased. They merely waited, and when his probation was up and nothing to stop him, he would be gone.

But now his brother had screwed him up with that joyride, and the parole would be off. And so maybe he had no choice now but to jump his bail when it finally came and get moving. He had to think it out, figure where he would head for and what he would do. South America maybe. He lay watching the old professional as if the humped, calm body itself might give him some signal.

He said, glancing at Verne, "You think he likes it?—the old man?"

"Who? Likes what?" He pursed his big lips. He was sitting on the floor, looking at another of the used *Superman* comics the guard had brought.

Nick nodded toward the thief. "What he does," Nick said.

Verne said, "That old bastard, I bet you it's the same thing to him as selling shoes."

He thought about it. The bearded man leaned on the bars, stroking his beard, watching and listening to something inside his own skull.

"Sometimes I could kill him," Nick said, nodding toward the thief.

Verne grinned. "You ain't lucky enough. Only way you could kill a guy would be to fall on him out of a window."

Nick said, "Where's that lawyer?"

They'd been asking it for a week now, and they knew where he was.

"They're going to fry you," the bearded man said. "All the lawyers are dead."

"Even if she dies," Nick's brother said, "they won't give us more'n two, three years. It was manslaughter."

The bearded man opened his hands and rolled his eyes up. "Fzzzzt."

"Mister, you got a mean streak," Verne said. He shook his finger. "I mean you are a mean, mean man."

"I am the Truth," he said.

Nick's hand flashed out faster than a snake, but the man was out of reach. The man's eyes widened a little, then narrowed and almost closed. He sank into thought. You could see him falling away like a rock in the water.

## 6

It made no difference to Walter Boyle what the Indians and the bearded one said or did. Live and let live was his motto. Nevertheless, lying wide awake in the middle of the night, listening because he had no choice, he wished the whole pack of them dead. When the guard, Salvador, said once of the bearded man, "That fella's sick, you know? Christ, who needs to test him to find it out?"—Boyle had been tempted almost into talking about it. But he lit the cigarette the guard had given him and merely peered at it nearsightedly, saying neither yes nor no. He'd said, "They talk a lot. It's hard to sleep." That was all.

It hadn't been so bad in the beginning, when the Indians ignored the man's prattle. The Indians were people you wouldn't want to meet all alone at night in the city park, but they were two cells away and they didn't say much. He could put up with them for a while. And the talk was all right—like a faucet dripping, or like a pump thumping away in the basement of a house you were going over. He'd heard it before, talk like that, at bus stations and tobacco stores, at coffee shops when there was a college nearby, like in Buffalo. But when the Indians started to listen, his feelings changed. It wasn't good, giving people like that ideas. Besides, the bearded man was crazy. That pacing, for instance. And Boyle would swear—almost swear—he'd heard the bearded man crying once, sitting in pitch darkness, early in the morning. He knew pretty well what that meant. He'd had a neighbor once that had acted strange and had cried a lot, and one day he'd killed himself. He was an engineer at Boeing, sharp as a tack, people said. His wife came home about two in the morning and the radio was playing but there weren't any lights on, and she'd gone in and found him on the davenport, with the rifle on the floor— he'd fired it with his bare foot. She'd come over, all wild, and made Walter Boyle go in with her. They'd had to push the davenport over the edge at the city dump, later. She was over at his house until almost dawn, after the police left, phoning all her relatives and crying and crying and talking to Boyle's wife. He'd gone to bed.

The Sunlight Man was babbling again about freedom—sitting in the dark in a small-town jail and babbling about freedom. And they were listening, or anyway one of them was. The younger one would be asleep by now—the fat, toadlike one with the matted hair like a wet cat's.

Though it was late, there was still traffic on the street below. It was a Saturday night, the night the crowd from the racetrack was always heaviest. They'd be bumper-to-bumper for miles. He tried to focus on the sound of the traffic, but still snatches of the talk pressed through. *For most people there is no such thing as freedom, this position would hold. Not me, you understand.* Boyle was not one to call the guard. And yet the man had said he would keep them quiet—not the guard who was on duty now but the younger one, the Italian. It was a kind of promise. Boyle thought suddenly, with unusual ferocity, "They have no respect for the other person." It wasn't good for him to lose sleep this way, night after night. He'd be fifty-six in January, and the doctor had told him he must begin slowing down, try not to take his work home with him, get a hobby . . . something to relax his mind and nerves. "*Do* you have any hobbies?" the doctor had said.

Boyle had squinted, feeling naked and vulnerable with his shirt and glasses off, and the doctor had pressed, "Golf? Pinochle? Model ships? I have a brother-in-law does that, model ships." (The office looked down on the heart of Buffalo, Sheridan Drive, huge office buildings like imprisoning walls of smoky granite and brick and concrete that might have been a thousand years old. Boyle had sat looking with his hands behind his back, his shirt in one hand, miserably racking his brains for some healthful interest. Ships. He and Marguerite would go down to the docks sometimes and watch them unload the coal boats—black ships, black earth, black freight cars under the black steel scaffolding. She loved water, even here where it smelled of oil and was thick and green as cold pea soup, with something like spittle floating on the top, and pieces of paper, and rubbers. "Faraway Places" was her favorite song. She called to the gulls and waved to the people pulling out for Crystal Beach, over in Canada, across the lake. But Boyle had no feeling for ships. None. Often when he went with her he would take along a newspaper.) The doctor was studying him, smiling politely (he was a sly little Jew, around thirty: Kleiss, or Fleiss, something like that). Boyle blurted out in sudden desperation, as though he could feel his health falling away like the pigeons dipping swiftly between smoky buildings toward the street: "I memorize poetry, sometimes." He added at once nervously, for fear the doctor might misunderstand, or worse, disbelieve him:

> *The little toy dog is all covered with dust,*
> *Yet sturdy and staunch he stands;*
> *The little toy soldier is red with rust . . .*

He stopped, blushing scarlet.

"Excellent!" the doctor exclaimed, and he seemed downright delighted by it, as though it were the best cure possible. "Go on. I didn't mean to interrupt. Say the rest." He called the nurse in to hear it, but Boyle would perform no more, could only smile as he'd done (he remembered suddenly and vividly) in grade school when Mrs. Wheat called the Principal to hear him.

And so when Boyle had left the office he'd felt thirty years younger—no doubt partly because he had finally told someone his secret, and the man had not laughed. He felt as if nothing could ever worry him again as long as he lived, and he said almost aloud as he walked past the glittering, grave-cold storefronts, "Do not say that thou art weary, O my soul, do not say, 'This Life is grief, the Strife is grim. . . .' "

He had worries, nevertheless. He had always done all right, as well as most people did these days, and yet he'd never gotten ahead. Now, with his later years creeping up on him, he couldn't help thinking about the future. What would happen to them if he too should get sick, the way Marguerite had done? (She'd been employed at a bakery until two years ago, but then one morning she'd fallen downstairs—she was heavy and couldn't see her feet—and she'd broken her hip and been laid up for over a year. Even now she wasn't right.) Where would the money come from then? What would happen to the house?

There were worse things than that. Marguerite had gotten more and more to be a worrywart, these past few years. She knew he could never be positive how long he'd be away, and for a long time she'd seemed resigned to it—resigned even to his failing to phone for sometimes weeks at a time. And she knew, too, that there was nobody in this world more *safe* than he was. They'd been boyfriend and girlfriend for thirteen years before he'd popped the question. "I know Walter Benson like the back of my hand," she liked to say. (Benson was his name at home.) But lately, for all that, his extended stays seemed to worry her more and more.

"Walter I get so *worried*," she said. She sat on the top step of the green back porch, fanning herself; the cotton dress stuck to her thighs and shoulders, and there were sweat patches. He was sitting on the metal chair in the neatly clipped grass below her. He liked the baking July sun. Always had.

He looked at her, then past her. He nodded. "Gotta fix that screen door."

"Walter," she said, "you're a thousand miles away." She began to cry.

It was that that had made him decide to put in a want-ad for a boarder, someone who'd be there at night to make the place feel safer, keep prowlers away and chew the fat with her from time to time. And so now Walter Boyle had another worry. Would the man pay promptly? Would he smoke in bed and set the house afire? What were those tons of mimeographed papers lying among hamburger wrappers in the back of his car? In the back window he had a *thing* hanging, a leadlike ball with raised letters on it, like letters from some kind of printing machine.

Boyle sighed.

Marguerite would be sitting there right now, of course, worrying where on earth he was, and it was a week yet before his trial. It wasn't healthy, a man that was fifty-five years old, with a known bad ticker, lying in a drafty jail cell not getting his sleep and worried sick. And what if they should find him guilty this time? It seemed impossible, they had nothing on him, nothing that would stick. But he was worried. The man with the beard, that was the thing. Benson, he had said. Boyle shuddered.

The bearded one said now, scornfully, as if set off by something the Indian had said, "Pain! Let me tell you about pain, boy. You get inside my skin for one week, you go live for just one day with my blind, crippled mother with her 'Bruce did you this' and 'Bruce did you that'—or you talk for one hour with my poor palsied father, or watch him—pitiful!—sweeping the sewers of Dallas, Texas, with his knobby knees bumping and his shrunken head bobbing—an heir to the crown of Poland once!—then *maybe* you'll know something about pain! O Father, forgive them! They know not whom they screw."

Boyle clamped his eyes shut and pressed his hands to his ears. Still the voice ranted on, but it was faint now, and it seemed to come from behind him instead of in front. He could feel his pulse against the heels of his hands and could hear it thumping like a streetcar hitting jail joints. It frightened him. He heard the Indian laugh shortly, full of scorn. Then, for a while, it was quiet. He tried to sleep, but he couldn't for a long time. The bed was narrow and hard as a rock, and a wrinkle in his shirt, underneath him, poked into his flesh. He thought of Marguerite lying like a mountain in the middle of their queen-size bed, her mouth collapsed with the teeth out, her legs wide apart and her arms thrown out to the sides. How good it would feel to crawl up beside her, nudge her great bulk over with his back (his feet braced against the cool wall) and give himself up to that mattress! Even the fold-down seat in the Rambler would be fine compared to this. All sensation had gone out of his arms and legs now, so that he had a feeling of falling, possibly dying. To help check his fear he imagined himself stretched out in the Rambler with his shoes in the open glove-compartment and the doors of the car locked. He usually parked just off the main street of whatever little town he was passing through. Back streets made him nervous. If there was a Y.M.C.A. or a cheap hotel where he was working or in any of the towns within driving distance, he stayed there. He had seen things in his time all right. Poor people, sick people, crazy people. The world was getting worse. That was why he and Marguerite were childless. It was criminal to bring children to a world like this. But he could get along, of course, himself. When he finished for the day he would settle with a paper and would pass his eyes along the words, or he would memorize poetry by Edgar A. Guest, or would doze. At home he would sit in his yard with a bottle of orange pop (he was not a drinker) or would water the flowers or, rarely, watch television, and he could not really say he was dissatisfied.

When his wife Marguerite entered his thoughts, cutting a large mimeographed paper into tiny, irritating scraps and smiling at something he couldn't see, he realized he was asleep. "Thank God," he thought, and was awake again for an instant, but only for an instant.

After that he heard nothing at all until, hours later it seemed, the anarchist gave a kind of gasp, not loud but somehow chilling. "Go ahead," he whispered, "touch it. It's blood all right. Taste it. In remembrance of Me."

"What's he doing?" the younger Indian said. He sounded as if he'd been asleep.

"Opened up his wrist somehow," the older one said. "It's to prove how great he is."

"It's blood," the bearded one said. He sounded wild now, angry, or maybe frightened. "Taste it, go ahead."

"Is he killing himself?" the younger one said, growing interested.

The older one grunted.

"I *could*," the Sunlight Man said proudly. "I'd never bat an eye." He laughed wildly, and Boyle thought, dead sure he was right: *Faking. Why?*

They said nothing. Boyle began to sweat.

"Mother Jesus, he really is loopy, you know that? I mean somebody must've spun him around too much in the swing."

"*Free*, not loopy!" the Sunlight Man exclaimed. "Capable of gratuity!" He laughed with delight. "Also loopy, however. A difficult matter to define. A withdrawal from reason."

"Yeah, sure," the younger of the Indians said. "That's neat. Keep it up."

After a minute the bearded man's laughter changed to whimpering. "It hurts," he said. "Ow." Finally he was quiet. Now Boyle could smell the blood. He wrung his fingers.

The older one said in the thick silence, "He *is* crazy." He seemed to muse on it. In his mind, Boyle could see the older Indian lying on his back staring up into the dark, turning it over. "But also he's pretending."

In the morning they saw there was a long, clotted gash on the anarchist's left arm, from his elbow to his wrist, and there was blood spattered on his already filthy trousers. He showed it off to the guard and did his shuffling dance and gave Walter Boyle the finger. Boyle turned away.

The guard was uneasy, probably about what the Chief would say. He said, "What happened? You, Boyle, you see it?"

"I was asleep," he said.

"Since the day he was born," the Sunlight Man yelled. He clapped his hands, his elbows going out, and leered at them. "Asleep since the day he was born."

"Shut up, Mac," the guard said. He went to get the Chief and, after that, the doctor. That afternoon they took the bearded one away. When he was leaving he said, "I'll be back, my friends. If I'm not, think of me when they're strapping you into the chair."

The one called Miller said, "You. Can it."

The Chief of Police had his hand on his chin, and his eyes were narrowed to needles of icy blue.

They went out with the prisoner.


## 7

At ten-thirty that night the woman died. Nick and Verne Slater knew already by the time Luke Hodge came to tell them, the following morning. The guard had heard it on the radio and gave them the news with their breakfast. Luke stood with his hands in the pockets of his old bib-overalls and looked past them while he talked. He had a deep, resonant voice, like all the Hodges, but unlike the others he was thin, almost girlish, with big, lean ears, so that the voice was ridiculous, as though he had a loudspeaker in his chest. His ears stuck straight out from his deeply tanned, girlish face.

Verne said, "I guess that makes it worse for us?"

"Sorry," Luke said.

Nick said, "Where's your old man been? We need us a lawyer."

He pretended to know nothing about it. He lifted his eyebrows, still looking past them and reached with two fingers for the Kents in his shirt pocket. "He'll be in, probably. You know how he is. Busy all the time."

"Like shit," Nick said.

"Don't look at *me*," he said. "I didn't even know he hadn't been in." He lit the cigarette and shook out the wooden match without offering them a smoke. Verne grew sullen.

"Nobody been here at all," Verne said. "It's more than a fucking week. You'd think the whole town was in Florida having vacation. I wouldn't've minded too much for my brother. But me, I'm just a baby."

"I can see it must've been rough," Luke said. He looked at his feet, the corner of his mouth drawn back, letting smoke out.

Nick said, "How come you came now?"

"I thought you'd want to hear."

Nick nodded, squinting and snapping his fingernail lightly, again and again, at one of the polished nickel bars. "It must be unpleasant for you, having to tell us."

Luke glanced at him for a second, then away. "Not too bad," he said.

Nick smiled, fighting the fear building up inside. "No, not too bad, I guess."

"Sorry," Luke said, and this time it was not ironic. He'd pulled back inside himself; his face seemed to close up, and you might as well be standing in some other room.

Verne said, "Hey, look. Give a bastard a puff, will you?"

Luke stared right through him, deaf, and Verne looked surprised.

"It's all right," Nick said, touching Verne's arm. Then to Luke: "There's a guy says they'll give us the chair. Is that true? Can they?"

"You'll have to talk to Dad. I got no idea."

"If he shows," Nick said.

Again Luke swept his glance toward him and past, uneasy, and no doubt they were thinking the same thing. The deal was off. Ben Hodge had nothing to do with it now. There was no more question of waiting out the probation. And so Luke Hodge was out from under, it was done with.

Nick's legs were unsteady. When Luke was scraping the cow manure off, Nick had leaned back on the whitewashed stone cowbarn wall and had laughed till he could hardly see. It wasn't as if it would kill him, a little cow manure. And Luke had asked for it, he knew that himself. What about all those other times—running their asses off in the haylot to get in the bales before the rain came, or combining wheat till eleven at night because tomorrow there might be wind? But that had been back in the beginning. A lot had happened.

"Ok," Nick said, "thanks for coming by." Strange to say, he felt relieved, in a way, as if the breaking of the lifeline were not so much a failure of hope as a release into wide, calm drifting. He was on his own, with nobody to turn to. He was partly glad.

Still Luke didn't leave. He said, talking to the floor, "Take it easy. I'll tell the old man to come talk to you."

"We'd really like that," Verne said. "We really would enjoy it."

Nick said nothing, exploring the weird sensation, a pleasant numbness of emotion. He felt taller.

Then, not looking at either of them, Luke relented and handed the pack of cigarettes and the matches through the bars and turned to go.

Nick ignored it. He went and sat on the pallet, after Luke was gone, and hung his head between his knees and waited for the feeling to die. Later he said, "I'll tell you something. We got to break out." He glanced over at the thief. Boyle seemed to be paying no attention, studying his paper.

"Don't be crazy," Verne said. "Just take it easy. The old man'll fix it." After a moment, "He's done it before."

"Just keep quiet, will you?" Nick said. "There *is* no old man. Christ, don't you get *any*thing?"

"Quiet as a mouse," Verne said, eyes wide. "Watch me.— What you mean?"

It was at noon, when Salvador brought them their lunch, that they learned that the Sunlight Man had escaped. In the end cell, Boyle jerked his head around, pale, and smiled as though he were responsible for it all.

8

Short-handed. So to Kozlowski he said—Kozlowski in the act of checking out for the night—"Kozlowski, you! Hold up." The Sunlight Man stood with his hands handcuffed behind his back, his head thrown forward, chin up, beard jutting out.

"You want something, Chief?"—Kozlowski.

"Correct," he said.

And so they were in Car 19, Kozlowski at the wheel, Chief Clumly beside him, in the back seat Figlow and the prisoner. It had rained again last night, but the rain had left no coolness: a thickness of muggy air like the thickness in a cellblock.

"Vets' Hospital," said Clumly.

"Positive," Kozlowski said.

Clumly shot him a look, then let it pass. It was hell running a police department. Element of personalities. Pure hell. He said, sitting forward, screwing up his eyes, "Hell of a thing, Kozlowski. See the cut on that man's arm?" Very serious, bringing Kozlowski into it. That was the way.

Kozlowski twisted his head around; then he looked back where he was going. "Can't see it. He's sitting on it," he said.

"It's a grave indignity, having to sit on your hands," the Sunlight Man said. "Abandon fingers, all ye who enter here."

"Can't you keep that man quiet?" Clumly said.

Figlow hit him in the ear.

And so they went through the high brick gates of the Veterans' Hospital and shot up the long driveway to the hospital front door.

"Ok, buster. Out"—Figlow.

"Don't hit me"—the Sunlight Man—"I'm obeying you. Look!"

Figlow hit him.

"You wait here, Kozlowski," Clumly said. "I'll check him in, and then Figlow can stay and stand guard. Check?"

"Positive," Kozlowski said.

Clumly bit his lips. Out of patience, he shook his finger and said, "Quit that." He turned on his heel and went to the door, where Figlow was waiting with the rifle in the Sunlight Man's ribs.

"In, buster," Figlow said.

The Sunlight Man walked ahead of them and his head bobbed slowly up and down in time with his steps. And now a room with half-dead rubber plants, a black formica-topped coffee table (round) with six-month-old magazines in plastic covers and pamphlets: *Your Social Security, The Older Veteran.* An old man with no teeth, dressed in pajamas and a dirty, sagging bathrobe, stood watching, working his mouth. His hair was wiry and uncombed as blown-down wheat.

"Wait here," said Clumly.

When Clumly was back again with the room number, Figlow said, "Will somebody spell me later, Chief? I forgot my lunch."

"God damn," Clumly said. He thought a minute. "Go see if there's some kind of machine or something. You got money?" He gave Figlow fifty cents.

And so they waited, Clumly and the old man in the pajamas and bathrobe and Sunlight.

The old man said, chomping his loose lips, "Some kind of crimnul?" Squinting like a citizen.

"That's right," Clumly said.

The old man walked around them. Stood. "Dangerous?" he said.

Clumly scowled at him and decided to ignore him. He nodded the Sunlight Man to a chair and sat down across from him, the rifle pointed casually at the prisoner's head.

"He stinks," the old man said. A matter of fact. Clumly glanced at his watch.

The Sunlight Man said meekly, "Is it really necessary that I sit on my hands?"

Clumly glared at him but considered. At last, against his better judgment, he said, "Ok, up." He got up himself. When the Sunlight Man's hands were cuffed in front of him, they sat down again. Clumly glanced at his watch. "Aren't you supposed to *be* somewhere?" he said to the old man.

Nothing.

Again they waited. The Sunlight Man said, leaning closer, so that his head bumped Clumly's shoulder, "I'm sorry it's been hard on you. A lot of police get the wrong idea when they arrest me. The way I figure, we do this business together, the cops and the robbers. This is a democracy. You follow me?"

Clumly tapped the rifle barrel nervously, his heart quaking, but he couldn't make out what it was that frightened him. "No talking," he said.

The Sunlight Man nodded meekly. "I just wanted to tell you before we part that I understand your position. I have very great respect for you." He patted Clumly's knee with his cuffed-together hands. "I wish you the best. I mean that." His voice was vibrant with sincerity, but when Clumly shot him an alarmed glance, the Sunlight Man was leering at him, showing his yellow teeth. Clumly leaped up and crossed to the door to look down the hallway for Figlow. Still no sign.

"Also," the Sunlight Man said, behind him, "I want to give you something, before we part." He was standing now.

Clumly turned his head.

"First, this." He held out Clumly's wallet. Chief Clumly's heart stopped cold. When Clumly didn't reach for the wallet, the Sunlight Man dropped it on the coffee table.

The old man in pajamas pursed his loose lips and scratched his head. His eyes grew larger.

"And now this." He held out Clumly's old brass whistle.

Clumly covered his hand with his mouth. It came to him that his time had run out, but even now he could not make out what it was that was going to happen.

"This." The bullets from Figlow's rifle.

"This." His keys.

"This." His pistol.

"And this." Figlow's pistol.

"And finally, sir, this." He gave him the handcuffs.

The bearded man turned to leave.

Suddenly Clumly found his voice. "Don't try it," he roared. He aimed the pistol at the Sunlight Man's back, dead on, but the man kept walking. Clumly's heart was hammering. "Figlow!" he yelled. He tipped up the pistol and fired at the ceiling. Click. The Sunlight Man turned, smiling, scratching his hairy ear. "Ah yes," he said, "I forgot." He held out his empty hand, closed it, opened it again. There lay the bullets. Calmly, he held them out to Fred Clumly. Cunningly—a sudden flash of genius—Clumly caught hold of the bearded man's hand, squeezed with all the force he had and hurled the man clumsily to the floor. They rolled, bellowing, blowing like horses. Clumly raised his fist, murderous, to hit him in the neck, but he caught himself just in time. It was as if he'd gone crazy. He felt outraged and terrified. A whooping noise began to come from his mouth, uncontrollable. The man underneath him, staring up with bugging eyes, was the old man in the bathrobe.

*How?* Chief Clumly would ask himself later, distraught, raising his clenched fists in the blackness of his bedroom. *How did he do it?* A tortured cry as old as mankind, the awed and outraged howl of sanity's indignation: for there is more to a magician's tricks than the lightning of his hands, hands softer, gentler on your shoulder than the wind stirred by a butterfly's passing, yet surer than a knife. The great deceiver has no heart. He neither loves nor hates unless, conceivably, he loves himself. And why he comes to us again and again to amaze and mock us, no mortal man can guess.

Kozlowski jumped.

"All hell's broke loose," Figlow yelled. "Give me that radio."

"What happened?"

"The prisoner's escaped," he said, "and the boss has flipped his lid."

"You're kidding!"

"See how I'm laughing."

In a matter of minutes there were five more cars at the hospital, Kozlowski waiting at the front door, Clumly and Figlow around in back. But he must have been out already. It was only the beginning. They waited half the night, standing with their rifles in their arms on the searchlight-gray lawn, and inside, they tore the place apart. A little after midnight the Mayor arrived, and Wittaker with him.

"How in hell did he do it?" the Mayor said. "I don't believe you, Clumly! I'm talking to you frankly. I never heard such a story."

Police Chief Clumly laughed.

## 9

Two days later the lawyer had still not come to help the Indians. Eventually the court would appoint them one. But in the meantime, Boyle couldn't help but see, the thing was building up, at least in the older one. He began to pace now as badly as the Sunlight Man had done, but rapidly, and he would keep it up for hours at a stretch, until his movement was like a stirring of some sickness in Walter Boyle's blood. When they talked at all, the Indians talked of the bearded prisoner's escape. Boyle felt himself on the verge of shouting at them, but he kept himself quiet. He sat more still than ever and tried to concentrate, without even a trace of success now, on thinking nothing at all. At other times the older Indian would stand in a single position for so long you would have thought he had turned into stone. Worst of all, though, was the Indian's talk. Sometimes he spoke not to his brother but directly to Boyle, or, rather, directly at Boyle's carefully impassive back. It was as if he knew Boyle wouldn't answer and was testing how far he could be driven. "Hey, mister. How come they don't send us a lawyer? There's a law against that, isn't there? It's shit, man. What do you do when there's nobody to protect you?

Hey listen. What do *you* do?" Once he said, "I'll tell you one thing, baby. They won't keep us like this much longer, without no lawyer. I've had it. Truth. You tell your old buddy the guard."

Then something else. When the guard came in they made excuses to get him to come close. They tried it just once on the night man. He was old and tough, shrewdly and impersonally vicious. Whether you needed it or not, he shoved you hard when he put you through the door, and he'd listen to no sass. But the day man could be tricked. He would stand by the bars and answer their taunts or the irritable questions of the older one, and Walter Boyle couldn't help seeing trouble brewing. He sometimes had a confusing urge to warn the man or, better yet, say a word to the Chief when he came in, as he once in a while would do, to look the place over. He was a changed man now, that Chief. He'd been shaken by the man's escape. It had broken him—or no, much worse than that. When a man was broken he gave everything up, had no interest in struggling any more. Chief Clumly still had his fight in him, but all his power was closed like a fist around one thing, that magician. Boyle would see him in the hallway, would see the one called Miller come up to him and ask him something, holding out a sheaf of papers on a clipboard, and the Chief would turn away as though he had neither seen nor heard. "Old man's really mad," the young guard said. "He ain't hisself. I bet if you stood in his way he'd plow right through you." Far into the night the Chief's light stayed on, at the end of the hallway, and Boyle could hear him pacing pacing pacing. And something else. Sometimes he'd come out in the hallway softly, like a burglar, and go toward the door to the main office and stand there bent almost double, listening. He seemed to take on weight, as though his flesh was changing little by little into stone. One day in the cellblock the one called Miller showed the Chief that the bearded prisoner had left his little white stones, the ones he would spread on the floor and look at sometimes. Clumly rattled the stones in his hand and stared straight ahead like a railroad engine thinking. Miller said, "Maybe we should check them. Somebody in the magic trade might know something about them. You think so?" Clumly went on bouncing the stones in his hand, and then, still staring straight ahead, he pawed Miller to one side casually, slowly, like a bear, and walked with the stones in his hand back to his office. Very late the second night, a man with preternaturally white hair came in—"That would be the Mayor," Salvador said—and went into the office where Clumly was pacing, and Boyle heard them talking for almost an hour, that is, Boyle heard the Mayor talking. Clumly said nothing, and in his mind Boyle could see him sitting on the corner of his desk, scowling like a freight train, bouncing those little white stones in his hand. The Mayor came out the hallway door by mistake and stood looking at Boyle in the hallway's dimness like a cat watching an intruder in an alley, then turned on his heel and went through to the front office, and there he said: "That man's out of his mind." "You telling me," the sergeant at the desk said. "I tell you that man's *insane*," the Mayor said. "You telling me," the sergeant said.

And so, for one reason or another, Walter Boyle said nothing to the Chief, merely watched the thing build up. They were going to make a break. It was certain as Doomsday, but whenever he had a chance to warn the Chief, what he felt was only the weakening rush of anxiety that meant that this time he could still say it if he wanted; and each time he didn't, the odds that he would speak, sometime later, went down a little more. At last his trial was just three days off, and he knew that if things went right he would soon be out. He felt not relieved but more nervous than ever. The thing might blow up almost any time, and the hours between now and his escape from being involved in it took forever.

That noon the guard who was the talker said, "They're not bad kids, really." He jerked his head toward the Indians. "They sure are polite. But that woman died, you know."

Boyle nodded.

"Makes you a little sick to think about it," Salvador said. "They could get life or something. The D.A.'s dead set, I hear."

"They can't get life," Boyle said crossly. Immediately it annoyed him that he'd allowed himself to be drawn into it.

"Well, that's what people say," Mickey Salvador said.

"People are damn fools," Boyle said.

"Well, maybe," Salvador said. He looked baffled, slightly hurt.

*Ass,* Boyle thought. *Stupid ass.* "Good coffee," he said. That night he had a confused dream in which the jail caught fire and a judge whispered something to him, something he missed, and winked slyly. There were also large animals of a kind he couldn't identify, and a great many dead chickens in wooden cages. He woke up sick with exhaustion, saying to himself a poem he had not known he knew—a poem of hope. The words were full of the dream's mysterious light.

> *Tomorrow's bridge, as I look ahead,*
> *Is a rickety thing to view;*
> *Its boards are rotten, its nails are weak,*
> *Its floor would let me through. . . .*

In the morning, a Sunday, he exercised and washed and combed his hair more slowly and carefully than usual, and he never once glanced in the Indians' direction. He heard their talk and carefully did not notice the words, and when they paced—even though their shadows fell almost to the edge of his cell—he carefully did not notice that they were pacing. It was still all right, he thought. They weren't yet to the boiling point. He listened to the music of Sunday morning traffic outside, lighter than on other days, less urgent and aggressive, as if the very pavement understood six days shalt thou labor. He was going to make it, it came to him. He was going to be gone by the time their violence exploded.

But he was wrong.

After the escape, he could say nothing. He would be held as a witness if he said a word, and perhaps they would even put a picture of him in the Buffalo *Courier Express*. The big, hairless Chief of Police closed his fist around Boyle's collar and thundered at him, "Asleep hell! You'd just ate breakfast! Now you listen to me and you listen good. You tell us what you saw or by God, Walter Benson, I'll put you on ice for life. You better believe it." Boyle shook like a leaf at the old man's use of his other-life name. Yet he kept his silence praying. He could hear the crowd talking, shuffling around behind him, in the hallway. The floors and walls creaked and groaned. "I was asleep," he said meekly. The policeman jerked him closer, as powerful as a diesel crane, for all his age, and he shook him with the indifferent violence of a thrashing machine. The man's face was red, blazing with anger. Then suddenly Clumly pushed him away with all his might, and Boyle slammed against the wall so hard he believed his back was broken. "Bring in the brother again," he said. They brought in the younger brother, and the policeman hollered, "What was this man doing when it happened?" He pointed his shaking finger at Boyle, and his eyes shot fire.

"I don't know," the Indian said.

The Chief was panting like a steam engine, the Indian still as a giant toad, staring at the floor with his thumbs hooked inside his pants and a strip of brown belly showing. "But you know who opened that cell door, right?"

"No sir, I never even noticed. Never saw him before."

The Chief looked at the one called Miller. "Lock the door," he said.

Miller locked the door—the crowd was growing, beyond it —and the muscles around his eyes were tense.

"Keep back," someone said. "Everybody back."

Clumly drew out his pistol slowly and held it by the handle. After a minute he turned it around, looking at it, breathing hard, and held it by the barrel.

"I swear it," the Indian said. He was trembling. "I never saw him before in my life. I swear."

The butt of the pistol came in as swift and indifferent as a steel sledge, and the first blow broke the cheekbone.

"Take it easy," Miller whispered. "Have you gone crazy?"

The Chief's eyes were as empty as shotgun barrels. He put away the pistol. "Get them out," he said.

Unable to stop himself, Boyle hissed, "He *stayed*, for heaven's sake. He could have broke out too. What the devil do you people want?"

Nobody heard. The room was full of the smell of blood from the hallway. It was like a slaughterhouse. There was a crowd there, another crowd outside. When Miller opened the hallway door the noise of the crowd grew suddenly louder, like a sound of big motors at the opening of a hatchway, or the rumble of trainwheels between cars.

Later, in the cellblock, the Indian said, cutting through the noise of the crowd, though hardly opening his jaw—his face was swollen and nobody had bothered to look at it yet— "What made him come back?" His voice was thick. He'd been crying.

"Shut up," Boyle said.

The whole thing flooded his mind again, the scrubbed, neatly dressed lunatic—a black, new suit, a black Stetson hat with a small red feather like a lick of flame—the pistol moving back and forth in his hand. The guard clumsily hurried to unlock the cell. The lunatic said, "Out. Quick!" Then he was shouting with a dead, shrill laugh, "Behold, I am the Door!" His scarred, shrunken forehead glistened with sweat.

The older brother, the tall, thin Indian, jumped out at once, but the younger one stayed. "You're crazy!" he said. "We be dead before we get to the street." The cell door swung shut, knocking the younger brother back. There was no asking twice. They started down the hall. Something happened then, the Indian for some reason grabbed at the gun, panicked, and the gun went off, loud as a bomb in the concrete room. Then a scuffling and flailing, horrible and wet. The bearded one yelled, jumping back from the blood—his voice was like the screech of a rat burning in a furnace, to Walter Boyle—"Run for your life! You're free!"

Boyle shook violently, hurling up in secret a plea to Heaven. In his unreasoning terror he was certain they would turn back and shoot him too. He even thought he saw it happening, but he was wrong, they were running away. He waited to hear shots, but none came. The man at the desk in front sat gagged and roped (Boyle learned later), he'd never even seen who it was that had tied him there. And there was no one else to stop them. He saw the dead guard's eyes. He'd died reaching for something—reaching out toward Boyle.

*Sunday morning*, Boyle thought. *The whole place empty as a tomb.*

Walter Boyle said shakily, his hands in his pockets, staring dully at the Indian, "I was asleep." It was then that, with terrific force, the memory he'd been hunting for exploded into his mind: he *had* seen the Sunlight Man before. It must be fifteen, twenty years ago. It was in Buffalo, the first time Boyle had been arrested. *He was my lawyer,* Boyle thought. *He wasn't burned like that then. What was his name?*

Then, as if they'd guessed, they came at him out of the crowded hallway, pouring into the cellblock like water from a sluice. "You see it?" a man said. Newspaper.

"I was asleep," he whispered.

He closed his eyes, and now, mysteriously, he *was* asleep, falling away in a green sky to a nightmare of black boats, sooty workmen, black scaffolding rising out of the blackened earth, and Marguerite standing between rusty rails, fat white shoulders bare in her summer dress. As far as the eye could see there was nothing moving but the hurrying, reeling, gliding gulls, screeching rhythmically over the sluggish black water, their wide wings reaching. His chest filled with revulsion. "I didn't see it. I was asleep," he angrily whispered.

He remembered the lawyer's name. It was Taggert Hodge.

eight

# III

## Lion Emerging
## from Cage

*But fortune ys so varyaunte, and the wheele so mutable, that
there ys no constaunte abydyng. And that may be preved by
many olde cronycles . . .*

—Le Morte D'Arthur

### 1

For all their physical amplitude, the fat old man and the fatter
man in middle-age, Will Hodge Sr and Will Hodge Jr, were
diminished by the old-style sobriety of the room. The shabby
law office in which they sat—the high, dark walls of legal
books as patient and indifferent as a well gone dry or an old
philosopher writing his will, their bindings glossy and old as
the County (older than W. B. Hodge Sr by three generations,
stamped *Taggert V. Hodge, Batavia, N.Y.*), deep-toned as oil

135

paintings, cracked like bamboo, solemn and superannuated as the engraving of the Roman Colosseum hanging above the door—made Hodge and son insignificant creatures of the fleeting instant, light and brittle as a pair of Giant American Beetles on a stick moving swiftly and casually downriver. Will Hodge the elder wore wide suspenders and arm garters (his suitcoat hung on the rack by the door) and a wide tie fastened with a paper clip; his son, a gray tweed double-breasted suit which, though old, had been worthily maintained: one might easily have mistaken him for a Secretary to the Governor, or a Professor of History, or the owner of a chain of feedstores. They sat across from one another, looking at the floor and smiling as if ruefully, almost evilly, one might have thought (mistakenly), their jaws slung forward, their two large backs identically hunched below their shaggy, balding domes, shaggy eyebrows identically lowered, each man a caricature of the other, both humbler versions of the white-haired, militarily erect and awesomely fat United States Congressman who had tyrannized what was in effect the same room in another part of town before Will Hodge Jr was born. In small ways he tyrannized it yet.

Once Will Hodge Sr would have said he was immune to his father's power. The subtle trap in which he'd found himself when the old man died had all the attributes of a cage except the essential one: he did not mind it. Craftily, ruefully, squinting up from under his eyebrows at his troubled life, Will Hodge Sr recognized that the cage was there, understood it as one understands that someday one will no doubt die—that one might, if one were a twenty-year-old poet or a fool, make howling melodrama of it, but the fact would remain no more than it was, for all one's howling—an indifferent limit, a wall closing out what a man who had business to attend to had no good reason to be curious about. Thus Hodge; who by character and constitution preferred and, for all his seeming insensitivity, immensely enjoyed the useful, immediate, palpable: ruefully smiling to himself at the neatness of phrase in a null and void affidavit, ruefully grinning at the firm, responsible solidity of the newly wired-up round of a chair (the veritable image of his soul: good wire, no loop without its function, a small detail in relation to the whole but necessary, however distasteful to people inclined toward elegance, and admirable in its small way: superfluously strong: final) so that, knowing he was not his father, he had been satisfied with what he was, had cleverly revelled in it: had not built huge barns as the Congressman did—the austere gray buildings of Stony Hill Farm, each barn stern and intransigent under its sharp, high gables and neatly louvered cupolas lifting up lightning rods like safeguards against sorcery (gleaming copper, with globes of blue glass, or bluish green, like hypnotists' globes of 1900)—but had neatly, skillfully patched up the barns his father had built; had perched on beams some forty feet up from the rocky barnyard, his stubby legs clamped around the time- and hay-polished wood, shoes interlocked, big jaw slung forward (Hodge the inexorable!), ruefully grinning, driving out old pegs and driving in new: as pleased by the power and authority of his eight-pound maul as his father had been by the building of the whole estate. Hodge, Will Hodge Sr, was no carpenter, properly speaking, but a toggler. The patching he did—with baling wire, pitchfork handles, restraightened nails, whatever lay at hand—was visible at a glance and, also, visibly satisfactory. Like Hodge. His whole life was an ingenious toggle, a belated but painstaking shoring up against last year's ruin, destructions in no way his own but his to repair. (Unless his uneasy suspicion was right and the destructions were, after all, his own: effects, mysterious to him, of his limits.) Knowing he was not his father, he had long since overcome the temptation to struggle in vain to become his father. He was Hodge the immune and invulnerable, comfortable in the cage of his limitations. Or within a hair of it. For if he would have said once that he was immune to his father the Congressman's power, the power of the Image in which he, Will Hodge, had been imperfectly created, he knew better now. What the old man was unable to manage directly (and would not have wanted to manage anyhow, being a moral person) his ghost had managed indirectly: he tyrannized Hodge—if a thing so trifling was worth a big word like tyranny—through Millie his wife (or former wife), Will Jr, and Luke, his sons. Will Hodge Sr felt no indignation or regret.

His son drew in a bronchial charge of air and cleared his throat, his heart rested a little now from the short walk in from the street and up the four rubber-matted wooden steps to the office door. He was softer and more pale than Hodge Sr, not a small-town lawyer but a city one who occasionally would take a glass of whiskey. Out there it was hot, a muggy Sunday

noon in August, but in here it was comfortable, the Venetian
blinds closed against the light and the noise of St. Joseph's
church and the First Presbyterian church across from it, letting out their people, a block away. Hodge had given him already the books he'd come for, three large old canvas-bound
volumes of Genesee and Erie County maps, Will's property
left in the office from the days of their brief, unhappy partnership. He had them leaning against the door, but he made no
move yet to get out of his chair.

As always when in his father's presence, Will Jr spoke loudly, forensically raising one finger, like a man full of confidence
addressing a slow-witted jury. "Father, I stand in need of your
widely acclaimed professional assistance."

Hodge looked down, the rueful smile brightening for an instant. If he were not Hodge—dependable Hodge—if he were
his younger brother Ben or his own son Luke, he would have
been thrown into confusion by a labyrinth of conflicting, for
the most part painful, emotions. Will's voice was Hodge's
(Will Sr's) own, but the tone and the elaborate verbiage came
from Will's mother, the former Mrs. Hodge Sr, whom Hodge
had spent most of his adult lifetime pitying, hating, and—for
reasons unfathomable to him—fearing. It was she, Millie, who
had first called him "Father," with a flip and yet heart-crush-
ing scorn whose power over him he could not understand but
secretly believed, without evidence, to be justified. She accused
him of things he knew himself not guilty of (but he was
guilty), taught him every bitter grief a cunning and systematic
woman's hatred could conceive, drove him half out of his
mind with anguish until, at last, their two sons and daughter
dispersed, they had gratefully escaped each other by divorce.
Her language, that light barrage of big words that rolled effortlessly from her lightning tongue (as if not carefully
thought out beforehand to the last detail, or so Hodge Sr supposed), was meant, he knew, as cruel mockery, but what it
was she was mocking in him he could not make out; he too
knew words. But on Will Jr's tongue the words had no freight
of scorn. Sometime, somewhere, without Hodge's knowing it
was happening, Will had turned his mother's trick to his own
use: had made that antic, orbicular language the shield or bra-
vado between himself and a world he did not trust. That was a
long time ago, a thing he had long since survived and forgotten; but the habit of the tongue was there, like a scar on bark,

an occasional reminder to Hodge that Will had been moved too often in his childhood or lived too often away from his parents, with his grandparents, with his Uncle Ben, with strangers. But Hodge evaded the labyrinth. His mind walked over it as lightly and deliberately as Hodge himself had long ago walked the peaks of his father's barns. He merely smiled, conscious of his pride in Will, glad Will was here, and waited to hear what was wanted.

Will said, lowering his finger and closing his hands together, "I mean, to speak without circumlocution, Nick's in jail again. *Voilà.* The bail's completely out of reach. I suppose you knew?"

Hodge pursed his lips and lifted his eyebrows, noncommittal. It was his brother Ben's opinion that they'd done all they should for Nick.

"I could work on it, of course," Will said soberly, his forehead wrinkled as though he were debating a matter of the greatest importance to thoughtful citizens (his voice boomed, political, a compensation for the confidence he did not feel in what he was saying), "as a matter of fact, I told Luke I'd see to it. But it would be better if you did, really. They owe you favors, after all. It's out of my—ah—territory."

Hodge laughed, the snort of a bull.

"Oh, I know, I know," Will said nervously. He rolled his eyes up. "Luke should have come to you directly, *c'est vrai.* But I happened to run into him first. Louise and I stopped by the farm with the children and Luke told us about it, so—" He sighed profoundly.

"So you thought you'd make him grateful to me," Hodge said, and again snorted.

"Now Pater," Will began. But Hodge raised his hand (which was square), interrupting.

"What makes you think Luke wants him back?"

"Well of *course* he wants him back," Will said. "Because he needs him on the farm, if no better reason." Then, on second thought: "And Nick needs Luke, that's the *whole* truth of it. Nick hasn't been in trouble for a long time, living with Luke. And now suddenly this, a rather serious jam. He needs help, spiritual help, Father, and Luke's good for him." He brought down his fist on his knee.

Hodge opened the desk drawer and hunted through the mess for a pencil. There was an apple, slightly shrivelled. "All right," he said with finality but no conviction. He found the stub of a pencil at last and scribbled a note to himself on the yellow tablet. He studied the paper unhappily, sharply remembering his younger son's face, arrogant and sullen, handsome as his mother's face (except for those ears, long as an elephant's ears, and red)—quick to sneer, quick to smile, as hers was, a face as delicate as his own was blunt: his own, or Will's, or his daughter Mary Lou's—the face of Luke Hodge in whom all that was subtly wrong, for obscure reasons contemptible, in W. B. Hodge, Attorney at Law, came into enigmatic focus. (And he knew that what Will had come to do was not really necessary, had been unnecessary from before the beginning of Luke's spat with humanity, because Hodge loved his upstart son, though love was not a word with which Hodge was comfortable, any more than Luke was comfortable with it. But however unnecessary the thing might be, it was also inevitable: the trifling tyranny, again, of the Congressman's ghost.) Carefully, precisely, in order that there should be no mistake, Hodge recrossed the *t*'s and redotted the *i*'s in the scribbled note.

"I believe it was your idea that Luke take him in the first place," Hodge said, still feeling, for some reason, petulant. He couldn't say why he insisted on the point; certainly not to drive Will into a corner.

"Partly," Will said with dignity. "Partly Luke's."

(But Will was wrong. It was during the time of their partnership that it had happened, before Will had moved from Batavia to the firm where he was now, in Buffalo. Sam White had appointed Will for the defense, the case being of no importance, and Hodge had driven over to the jail with Will. He'd gone there it must be a hundred times before and since, but that time stood out in his mind even now—the gleam of the polished bars directly in the path of the morning sun, the distinct grillwork of shadows in the cell falling away toward the canvas pallet and the metal john and the boy. Nick Slater had been fifteen then, skinny and small for an Indian, and timid. He was like a captured squirrel or rabbit, standing still at the back of his cage. His elbows jutted out like cornknives, and around his round face his thick black hair was as long as a woman's; it hung level with his shoulders. He refused to talk to them, but it didn't matter. The police had arrested him for petty larceny, a grocery store. The only question was the stiffness of the sentence he would get. On the way back to the office Will had said thoughtfully, "Father, we should get that young rapscallion out of here." Hodge had said nothing. Will knew as well as he did that it wasn't that simple. "If we could only *place* him," Will said. He was sucking at the pipe he was trying out, in those days, to keep down his weight. As Hodge stopped at the Jackson Street light, Will exploded, "Luke! The kid could work for Luke!" "Hole on," Hodge had said. But he'd known already that the thing was decided. And so before he knew what hit him, Luke Hodge was a legal guardian, as his Uncle Ben had been before him again and again, and as his grandfather the Congressman had been to half the countryside before that.

A stormy business, inevitably, in which, inevitably, Will Hodge had played his miserable part. He'd stood one night six months ago now with his hands on the doorknob of Luke's back door, puffing and holding the door shut tight against his son, bracing himself with one foot on the ice-crusted wall, shouting, "Settle down, Luke! The boy will be back!" But Luke was in no mood to settle down—too furious even to realize that there were other doors he might come out, and windows. "You're God damn fucking right he'll be back," he shouted through the door. "Right back in the cell. And if he's wrecked that truck of mine he'll pay with a kidney." The pounding of Hodge's heart was a white hot maelstrom in his chest, and he couldn't push up his glasses, which had slipped down his nose, because he didn't dare let go of the icy doorknob. He was shaking all over, and he couldn't tell whether it was because of the howling winter wind or because of the way his son shot out words, danced through words the way his mother did. Hodge roared, outraged, "You sound like your mother." And instantly he regretted it, knowing that was Millie's game, forcing their son to take sides. Luke stopped pulling at the door. He said, "Get out of here. Shit on you. Beat it." His voice was ominously calm. Hodge said, not out of fear but of pity—by morning Luke's rage would have brought on a headache fierce enough to blind a horse—"I'm sorry, I shouldn't have said that." As always, the pity made it worse. Luke whispered, "Get out."

It had all been for the best, however. Late that night when

Nick Slater came back, lurching, half-skating up the driveway on foot, singing (Hodge sitting mournfully in the snowbank under the tamarack in Luke's front yard), Luke was indifferent, befuddled by some drug he'd taken for the headache, and took Nick back without a word.)

"Oh, well, all right, my idea then," Will said. "I see well enough what you're driving at." He opened his hands and ducked his head. "I admit it freely. I meddle. But look at me! How can I help myself? I'm weak!"

"No matter," Hodge said, staring into the table, sliding his lower jaw beyond his upper. The word *weak* registered in his mind and he glanced over his glasses once more and smiled. After a moment he said, "How things going up there?"

"Oh, fine," Will said, lowering his eyebrows, as embarrassed as Hodge Sr was at having asked. "I work too hard," he said then, sternly. "I chase all over hell, and when I'm home I stay in the office night after night till eleven or twelve, trying to wind up that Kleppmann case. Been on it almost a year now. And then, what little time I have left—" He lost the thread. "Debilitating," he said with a sigh.

Hodge nodded, thinking all at once of the apple in his drawer.

Abruptly, his son slapped his knee and bent forward, preparing to get up. "So you'll spring Nick Slater for us?"

The rueful smile returned. "For Nick's sake, as you say. I'll see what I can do."

Will laughed, reaching up to touch the bald place, then pressing his palms into his hams. He swung his loose weight further forward and rose like a whale. "Good. Merciful father, we thank you."

Hodge, too, was standing now. They shook hands, and as always Will hung on for a moment, still talking, holding his father's hand in both his own. "Louise sends her love. Also the kids. You've got to get up there and see us one of these days."

"I'll do that," Hodge said, pleased.

"I apologize for dragging you over from the church, making you miss the sermon. No doubt it was a six-reel thriller, as usual. But as you see, it was a matter of the greatest delicacy." He grinned and added soberly, "The *truth* is, I've been so consarned busy it was the only time I could make it."

"No trouble," Hodge said.

"It *is* trouble, and I'm sorry."

"Bosh," said Hodge.

"Just the same," Will said, "we appreciate it." He tightened his grip on Hodge's hand, and to save his knuckles Hodge returned the grip. Will said, *"Bon jour, Pater.* Take care." He twisted the hand, forcing his father to Indian wrestle. Hodge Sr grinned with his teeth clenched and stood like an iron-wheeled tractor. "Take care yourself," he said.

Will Hodge Jr released his hand suddenly and laughed. Then, puffing, he went over to the door, bent for the albums of maps, and turned to say again, "Take care." He took his hat from the rack, smiled at it, and put it on.

"Take care," Hodge said. He hooked his tingling fingers around inside his suspenders, elbows going out like ducks' wings, and, smiling as if his enormous son were some magnificent achievement of subtle wit, which he was, he walked behind Will through the outer office to the frosted-glass door which bore the neatly lettered sign, in reverse:

TAGGERT FAELEY HODGE
ATTORNEY
NO. 11 BANK ST.
BATAVIA, N. Y.

(Taggert Faeley Hodge was no longer here. He had fled in the night sixteen years ago, leaving ruins to his brother Will, and was now, the last anyone had heard, a salesman of used cars in Phoenix, Arixona.) Hodge watched his son go cautiously sideways down the steps, Will's dimpled left hand on the iron railing, the flesh white as snow beneath the curly black hair, his right arm clamped over the albums of maps like a picture-framer's vise. When Will was safely down on the sidewalk, puffing, starting out to where his Chevy wagon sat waiting with its right front wheel cocked up on the curb, Hodge closed the door and nodded thoughtfully, muttering to himself gruffly, "Monkey-business." He sighed, thinking once more of Luke the irascible, then returned to his desk and sat down to rest a minute. He remembered the apple, frowned, and opened the drawer.

## 2

It was pulpy. But Hodge had expected that. He took a second bite. He had nothing to do, nowhere to go except out to lunch and, eventually, home to the apartment. However, his horizons did not seem to him noticeably drab. He enjoyed going out, never knowing whom he might run into, and back at the apartment he was making kitchen cabinets. He did not especially enjoy looking forward to springing Nick Slater. It wasn't true—and Will knew it—that people owed him favors. The only people who owed Hodge favors, or thought they did, were sidestreet tailors, Polish grocers, farmers, Ed Bilchmann at the Camera Shop, and the second teller from the end at Mercantile Trust. But springing Nick had its pleasant side, too. He enjoyed visiting with Judge Sam White. Sam was a man who appreciated the important things: a sensible brief without rhetoric, good common sense about the problem in Asia or tapping phones, good plumbing in the house. And so maybe he'd go over this afternoon, when Sam would be in his cups. Then again, maybe not. Sometime today he had that deed to take over to Merton Bliss. He'd said he'd bring it by days ago. And maybe he could drop in to visit his brother Ben when he was out in that neck of the woods.

"Monkeybusiness," he said again.

He was sorry to have missed Warshower's sermon. There, too, was a man who understood the important things. No buck-toothed sissy like the Methodist fellow. He towered above the pulpit like a druid, when the chores were done—the hymns, the responsive reading, the half-hour prayer, the reading of the scriptures—and he spoke of the good old-fashioned puzzles—the Last Judgment, the Writing on the Wall, the Swallowing of Sodom and Gomorrah. He wrote sermons like contracts, full of firstlies, secondlies, and thirdlies, devoid of obscure allusions and rant. When a man left the church after one of those sermons he knew exactly what he'd done that was right and what he'd done that was wrong. Hodge would feel confident sometimes halfway through Sunday afternoon, in those days with Millie, before her way of twisting things could break down even Warshower's common sense. Nevertheless, the man was a comfort, his very existence satisfying in a world that incessantly demanded fine distinctions between things not worth a man's thinking about: a world of jokes to be puzzled out and laughed at in the right places (how many times, in how many grim rooms had Millie thrown back her head and white throat, and laughed while Hodge sat chuckling fierce and baffled, heavy as iron in his chair!), a world of movies from Italy which a man had no choice but to sit through, somehow outlast, like a patient horse. Warshower's very way of living, his stubborn, uncomplicated directness, was a sermon of hope to Hodge. When the Elders (Will Hodge Sr was one of them) would not put up money to get the cellar fixed at the manse, Warshower hired the work done himself and called a meeting of the congregation for a vote on whether or not they'd pay the bill. They'd taken a special offering, which came to only four dollars short, and Warshower preached on The Eye of the Needle, and prayed, as if without hope, for the people's souls. He got his four dollars. From Will Hodge Jr, as it happened, who wasn't a Presbyterian at all, but a Unitarian. Once more the subtle tyranny of the Congressman's image.

Hodge sighed. He'd forgotten to buy cabinet hinges.

He, too (but he was not thinking of this), knew the power of the image, and in a way he'd been down both his sons' roads and had found them both dead ends. Not knowing he was doing it, his mind on things more immediate—patching barn doors, calming Millie when her dander was up, milking, studying, shearing sheep, stewing over poor Tag's bad luck— he had gone down Luke's road fifteen years before Luke was born: cynical denial that the old man was what he seemed. Luke had never known the old man, knew only the sprawling farm he left, the barns, the big house, the stone fence now in disrepair, the iron gates, the dying tamaracks the old man's father had brought into Genesee from God knew where—all of them female, by some fluke, and now all withering away without issue—so for Luke the cynicism was easy. But Hodge too, or the part of his mind that wasn't busy, had managed cynicism.

He had not had to hunt far for detractors. He might have known from his father's own mouth that detractors were there to be found. He was a politician with no memory for names, and he was famous for snorting, "Names! I can barely keep track of the names of my enemies!" But for Will Hodge Sr, firmly grounded in reality, the cynicism had not worked for long. The old man was against tobacco—when he had to

smoke a pipe for a Grange League play he'd stuffed it with alfalfa and driven the audience out of the hall—but he did not
judge a man by his addictions, or countenance the suppression
of tobacco by a righteous minority. He favored the tobacco
tax, but only in hopes of discouraging nonsmokers, whom he
overestimated. He was stubborn, his detractors said. But he
would occasionally change an opinion when the other man's
reasons were better than his own; and where legitimate debate
remained after all the evidence was in he would usually grant
the point to be debatable, though he would never change his
side. He was an idealist, they said, and that was true too. He'd
never bought a lawbook in his life, had gotten along on his
father's books and had bought instead poetry, collections of es-
says and letters, speeches, books on music, palmistry, astronomy, voodoo, the Latin classics, philosophy. Off and on for
years he had tried to learn Greek. Hodge recalled it with
heaviness of heart, the way one remembers one's first disappointment in love. He would go to his father's study door and
his mother would hurry toward him from the kitchen with an
urgency she never showed at other times, her index finger over
her lips, her left hand stretching out to him in a gesture
strangely ambiguous, as though she were at once shooing him
off and drawing him toward her. In the semidarkness of the
hall her apron's whiteness was luminous against the dark of
her dress, and beside her the banister gleamed like old silver,
reflecting the snowlight beyond the front door. At his feet lay
the comfortable yellow glow from the crack beneath the study
door, but at the head of the stairs—beyond her head bending
down to him—the elderly gloom (that still went in his mind
with the dimly remembered eyeless face of his grandmother)
gave way to full darkness, and he was frightened. "Hush," his
mother would say, "your father is working." Only when he
was studying Greek were they kept from his room, he and his
brothers and even Ruth, and when he came out he'd be irritable, out of sorts. In the end, Hodge's mother had stopped it. It
was a family story. Furious for once in her life, she'd said,
"Arthur Taggert Hodge, why are you doing this? You're an
*American!*" He had stared, no doubt in disbelief, had calculated the enemy's strength and had known the better part of val-
or. "Good point," he had said, and had nodded, scowling. He
was not only an idealist but an absolutist and perfectionist, incapable of leaving unresolved such unresolvable questions as,

for instance, that of free will and necessity. Second only to the Word of God, he believed the word of Spinoza. His copy of the *Tractatus Theologico-Politicus* was underlined and marginally annotated from cover to cover (also disfigured by interlinear pencil translations: "I can read Latin," he would say, "but only the nouns"). But if he was an idealist, bookish, he knew trades, too; knew the talk of farmers at the feedmill, a farmer and feedmill philosopher himself, and the talk of shopkeepers, ministers, doctors, bankers—whose taxes he had figured, whose suits he had carried into court, and whose political opinions he heatedly debated from morning to night when he was home from Washington. It had not taken Hodge long to see what no doubt he'd been subtly aware of all his life, that those who called his father an idealist were snatching at words to express a feeling that had nothing to do with the word they happened to get hold of: the old man was in blunt truth superior, an implicit condemnation of men who were not; in short, a source of unrest. They hinted at scandals (a woman in the past, an incident with a Negro hired man, a matter of graft), but it was rubbish. The old man's secret was simple and drab: he liked his work and had a talent for it. Given the same combination of gifts but other aspirations—an aspiration, for instance, to be an operatic singer—he might have been an unexceptional man: a restless farmer, a timid seducer of hired girls, a small-town choir director, a drunkard. Or even the same gifts and the same aspirations brought together in another time and place might have stopped him. But he was lucky.

And so Hodge had toyed in the back of his mind with another kind of cynicism, and this, too, before Luke was born. He had dismissed his father's achievements as matters of no importance, blind chance. It was a matter of fact that Will himself was not cut out for the great deeds his father had done; but the case was not so clear with Ben or Tag. They were both of them, like the Old Man, visionaries, yet they could argue fine points like Jesuits, had memories for facts and figures, and they both had a way with people. But Ben had bad eyesight—a chance collision of unlucky chromosomes the night of his conception—and perhaps in fact a general weakness of sense mechanisms, so that his hold on physical reality was tentative. He was moved more by books than by life (not that Will stopped to think all this out in the dry way a novelist is forced to present it); if he revelled in Sense—in the cry of a meadowlark or the rumble of one of his big machines—there was something faintly theoretical about his revelling. His sensations, though intense, were those of a man in a museum. It was different with Tag. All he, Tag, lacked was the Old Man's invariable good luck in the conspiracy of outer events. He'd worked on a chair one time when he was six. Will Hodge Sr remembered it well. He was more Tag's father than the Old Man was himself, after all. By the time Tag came, the Congressman was old and too busy with the world to be father to a young child. It was Will, the oldest of the sons, who played with Tag, took him to work in the field with him, drove him to school, to basketball games or speech contests or dances. He'd come across him, when Tag was six, working out in the chickenhouse, putting a new wooden seat on a long-discarded kitchen chair. Will had just stood for a minute, watching unobserved. Tag worked quickly and painstakingly, as if he had figured out in advance every last detail of the job he'd set himself. He'd made a pattern with a piece of oil-stained cardboard, had drawn it onto the wood and had laboriously cut it out with the keyhole saw. He was nailing it in place now, skillfully for a child of six. Will said, thumbs hooked in his overalls bib, "You gonna be a carpenter someday, Tag?" Tag smiled with a beauty of innocence that was moving to Will. "If you want me to," he said. It wasn't fake or goody-goody in Tag. It was a quality of loving gentleness he'd been born with. In the first months of his life he was a sympathetic cryer, and throughout his childhood he was peacemaker to the family. In fact, like Ben, he was born to be a saint, gentle and unselfish —he even had the look of a saint: straight blond hair as soft as gossamer, dark blue eyes, long lashes, a quick, open smile —and unlike Ben, he saw what was there, not angels in pear trees but pears. "Little Sunshine," their father called him. Yet Tag had failed in the end, for all his innocence and goodness, had been beaten by the conspiracy of events. So the Old Man might have failed, if his luck had been bad.

It was true enough. The trouble with the theory was that the Congressman had been right about free will. It was a matter of fact, a thing not worth bothering to deny, to Will Hodge Sr, that freedom had limits, both within and without, which is to say merely that a man engaged in throwing a tantrum or a man starving is incapable of perfectly objective reason. Hodge's father had written once to his minister brother: "A passionate man may feel overwhelming pangs of guilt, but only a reasonable man, sir, can achieve the high distinction of going to Hell." Oh, the Congressman had been free, all right. Only a mind released from all passion could roll out such unashamedly grandiose prose.

That, too, his father's freedom, Hodge had no doubt been aware of long before he understood it. He'd been aware of it, perhaps, as a young man, newly married, standing between the high iron gates of Stony Hill Farm and looking up past the shaded lawn at the porch where his father sat, grossly obese, white-haired, calmly blind, surveying the universe inside his skull. When it came to the Old Man that there was someone at the gate, he called down sharply, "William, is it you?"

"Yes sir," he had answered. But he had not gone on for a moment. It was late afternoon, the shadows were long and the hills had a yellow cast, unreal, like hills in a painting. There was a smell of winter in the air, but the breeze was warm, as soft as January thawwind. The trees, the lawn, the fields, the long knolls sloping away toward the town of Alexander were all motionless and utterly silent. Signs of a change coming.

His father called, "Come up."

When he stood before the Old Man on the porch he realized that something had happened, perhaps knew even what it was, though he had no words for the thing as yet. His father, too, had perhaps read something in the weather, he imagined. He did not at first notice his youngest brother in the shadows at the end of the porch, leaning on the wall with his hands in his pockets and his face as gray as ashes. Tag was fifteen now, still pale and gentle as a girl.

Hodge said, not because he believed it but in hopes of escaping a scene with Millie, "You ought to be inside, Dad. You'll catch cold out here. A man your age—"

"Sit down," he said. He continued to stare with his blind eyes at where he knew the front fence was, and the road beyond. The snowwhite hair above his ears was brittle and uncombed, as wiry as a dog's hair, but someone—Ruth, not Millie, God knew—had trimmed the hair in his nostrils and ears. He sat as Hodge had seen him sit a thousand times—as Hodge, too, sat, and as his sons would sit—teeth closed lightly, lower jaw extended out beyond the upper, his elbows on his knees, fists locked together.

"Listen," he said. "It's come to me that I've made a mistake.

Somewhere in the course of—" He tightened his lips, concentrating. "All of us, or the times, mebby. No matter who made it. We have troubles coming. *Troubles* coming. Be ready, suffer them philosophically. Trust the Lord."

Hodge squinted, panicky. Only later would he realize that he was afraid, that moment, that he was seeing his father's first lapse into real senility. He said, hoping Millie was out of earshot, "Money troubles, Dad?"

The old man half-turned his head toward him impatiently. "Who knows what kind of troubles?" he said. "Germany."

Hodge laughed—it was like barking—and it was now that he noticed Tag standing with his hands over his face, very still.

But his father was saying, as if thinking it out for the first time, "there are always politicians. Good politicians. The people all flounder this way and that way, unsure what they want, unsure how to get it, unsure whether it's good for them, and the politician comes along to distinguish for them what they want more clearly than they want it yet, shows them the disadvantages . . ." He stopped. He'd been down that road many times. More and more he repeated himself, struggling for the old clearheadedness in a stifling attic of increasingly baffling, antiquated opinions. He turned his head more, the blind eyes staring at Will as though they could see him. "Suppose we were to have war with Hitler, and suppose Hitler were to win?" he said.

"Dad, you're stewing again," Hodge said. "Let me help you inside." Uncomfortably, he glanced again at Tag.

"Will, is that you out there?" Millie called.

Hodge jumped.

"No!" his father roared. "Not stewing. *Thinking.* Hitler could *win.* If not this one, the next one, or the next. From this point forward there'll be Hitlers for a thousand years." He thumped the porch with his cane.

"Well, we won't be here to see it," Hodge said. And then, in spite of himself: "What do you mean?"

"Will," Millie called.

"I mean America," he said. In his mouth the word was local, familiar. He might have been talking about the country. "I mean—" But the lucid moment was gone. "The devil," he grumbled.

"You think we're all Hitlers?" Hodge said, grinning, self-conscious because of his brother's presence. He had no clear idea what he meant by a Hitler; he asked it from the wish of one part of his divided mind to keep the talk going until he understood.

"I mean—righteousness," the Old Man said. "Insufficient failure—or too much failure—loss of the balanced vote. Unreason—or an excess of reason. The plots theory—"

Exasperated, Hodge said, "I was right the first time. You're not thinking, you're stewing. Let's go in."

But again he said no, and now, directly challenged, he straightened out his mind. "Listen," he said. "You believe in reason. You believe in democracy. Reflection of Natural Law, you think. But suppose people *stopped* being reasonable. Suppose they got spread too far apart to know what the balance of the country was thinking, or the balance of the world. *E pluribus unum.* Hah. Can *India* grow reasonable? China? I don't say suppose the right side goes under, I say suppose all sides are right as it seems to them and they all blur together and their beliefs grow confused and the *pluribus* becomes so complicated and, more important, so *dense* that no human mind or even group of minds can fathom the *unum*. Religion declines, and patriotism; law and justice become abstruse questions of metaphysics; the younger generation grows dangerous and irrational, shameless, selfish, anarchistic. Then someone steps up with some mad idea that's just simple enough to look sensible, simple enough that busy shoemakers can know the affairs of the world are in competent hands, they needn't concern themselves—as in Plato's *Republic*. Hah! What if?"

Millie appeared in the doorway. The Old Man turned his head, then went on, merely raising his voice a little, to avoid interruption.

"I say this: What keeps this country sailing on an even keel is not mortality or divine favor: nothing of the kind. What keeps it going is the *professionals,* the professional politicians who know that after this vote there's going to be another and another, for all the rumpus; you don't put all your inheritance on one horse, no matter how it looks in the ring. However bitter the fight may look, among the professionals nobody's hitting with all his might. *That's* what makes continuity. If the professionals fail—if the people with all their indifference and all their monstrous opinions, or their *no*-opinions . . . There are always politicians. Good politicians. The people all flounder this way and that, unsure what they want. . . ." The vague look was back. To hide his confusion he thumped the porch again.

"Dad," Tag said.

Then Hodge's mother was standing in the doorway, a little behind Millie, wringing her hands, saying: "Politics!"

Hodge said, though he would have gone on with it if the women weren't there, "Well, the world will make out."

"Will, I want to talk to you," Millie said, pushing at the screen.

He ignored her.

The Old Man studied him for a long time, or so it seemed: scrutinized his memory of him. Then he turned his head slowly and looked at Tag. Suddenly, as if discovering something— some terrible and holy secret that had slipped his mind—he smiled. He said, "Yes, no doubt you will. The world will learn. Sure as day."

Hodge could not explain, afterward, the peculiar power of that moment for him. The words were trifling, absurd if one looked them over too closely. The expression on the Old Man's face was not uplifting, not glorious, though it is true that his slightly shaking chin jutted upward and out as though he were about to fly. An image for a poster. Nevertheless, Hodge was powerfully moved, jolted as if by electric shock of love: the head ten inches from his own was suddenly gigantic, and looking into the hairy ear Hodge seemed to see past all galaxies into the void where, behold, there was light. All the rest of his life he would not be able to speak of that moment without a sharp upsurge of mysterious, perhaps childish elation, and also fear, and all the rest of his life he would be troubled, occasionally, by a new attack of that extraordinary feeling: a sense of the world transfigured, himself transformed to the pure idea of older brother in a fated house, a family destined for glory or terrible sorrow, he couldn't say which. He did not go out in pursuit of such moments. He fled them, if anything. They thrilled every fiber of his body, shifted his mind to a higher gear than it normally used (as if some door opened, as doors occasionally opened in his dreams, revealing, beyond some mundane room, vast recesses obscurely lighted and charged with warm wind and a deep red color, beautiful and alarming): he thought them dangerous, possibly mortal, like the shocking pleasure (he imagined) of falling from a roof. Or rather, to speak precisely, he for the most part thought about them nothing whatever, merely dreaded them in the back of his mind, and went on with the work at hand.

The Congressman would have done the same. Two hours before that conversation on the porch—it was this that Millie had been eager to tell him, this that had shattered his younger brother—his father had suffered a heart attack. Hodge's mother was badly shaken, Millie excited, but the Old Man, even before the doctor could make it from Alexander, was coolly talking politics. And not to evade reality. To Hodge's father, politics was more interesting than dying. Dying (if he was dying, which as it turned out he was not, yet) was merely an annoying—a disgusting—interruption.

Neither could Hodge explain even now, over thirty years later, what it was that the nations—and he himself, perhaps—were going to learn. He'd long ago quit worrying about it. The troubles had come, his father had been right enough about that—both international troubles and private—and were coming still. But they managed, Hodge and the world. If his father had discovered the formula that would quiet their unrest (and perhaps he had: he'd given a bewildering emphasis to those final words, "Sure as day"), he'd taken the secret with him to the grave. They would muddle through without it.

And so, renouncing cynicism, in the back of his mind he had taken the road Will Jr would take: emulation. Had allowed himself to be tyrannized by the Old Man's achievements. It was no one's fault—the fault of a ghost: the casual effect of time, of inevitable change, generations of Presbyterian ministers, gentleman farmers, public servants, lawyers, judges, all rising together in the apparition of one man who in his prime had a quick, deep brain and the eyes of a Moses and a voice like ricocheting thunder calling down God's wrath on Federalization. The brain was gone from the light of the sun, had shattered into its specialties in the Old Man's sons and daughter, but the eyes were still living, and the voice. Will Jr had the voice; Hodge had it himself, and Ben and Tag—in fact every one of his four brothers and almost all their sons; but you seldom heard it fully opened now, except when they laughed or, meeting at a wedding or a funeral, argued politics. It was the image, ghost, archaic (as even Will Jr knew) but still compelling, that had once made Hodge seem to himself a fool and now made him a disappointment to his elder son. He accepted it, now that the partnership was so much water gone under the bridge. For Hodge was a singularly reasonable man, as his father, despite stubbornness, had been before him. (The stiffness of the Old Man's back—exaggerated in the faded photograph which hung, thoroughly inconspicuous, centered above faded, obsolete world maps and a 1937 chart of the kings and chief ministers of the sundry nations, behind Hodge's desk—was an effect merely of time and place: a matter of style. Hodge, too, and even Will, had flaring nostrils, coarse hair in the nose and ears and curling on the backs of the fingers, but no stranger would have mistaken them for avenging angels, trumpets of Justice in days of rank corruption. The times were wrong, not incorrupt and not out of joint but subtly mellowed, decayed to ambiguity: If right and wrong were as clear as ever, they were clear chiefly on a private scale, and though God was in his Heaven yet, He had somewhat altered, had become archetypal of a new, less awesome generation of fathers: Wisdom watching the world with half-averted eyes, chewing His ancient lip thoughtfully, mildly, venturing an occasional rueful smile.)

He had nibbled the apple, pulpy as it was, to the bright black seeds. He wondered where it had come from and why he had not eaten it before. "Client," he thought. "Some farmer." And then: "Odd." If he were not Hodge—invincible Hodge!—he would have thought of Snow White, poison; or of Adam and Eve; or of love grown older. He thought: "Snow-apple," and was distinctly pleased that he still remembered the name.

Beyond the closed Venetian blinds, in the parking lot between the office and the back wall of the Methodist church, small children were playing a singing game he remembered from a long, long time ago:

> *McGregor got up and he gave her a thump,*
> *Gave her a thump, gave her a thump . . .*

Again the rueful smile came. Italian kids. He'd seen them there often, glancing over his spectacles briefly, absent-mindedly, as he passed the window with a sheaf of papers for Betty in the outer office to sort and file. But he couldn't remember having noticed before what sort of game they played. He wondered, briefly, whether Will would remember it too, and

whether he would associate the game with the long green hills
of Stony Hill Farm or with some other place, Albany, say, in
Hodge's belated law-school days, or Buffalo, or Leroy, or
Ben's place. The question entered and left his mind in a single
instant, no more than a trifling impulse of the blood, a question he would no more have asked if Will were there than he
would pause now to consider it. The world it came from was
not his world. That was his immunity to the Old Man's power,
and also it was his weakness. His mind glanced from the children playing in the parking lot to the sooty church window,
one small pane of which was broken, to the sill he'd forgotten
to fix at home. He felt himself at the edge of some unpleasant
recollection, but the instant he knew it was there it was gone,
and he was waiting again, reading the scrawled note on the
corner of his desk: *Obtain the release of Nick S.* On a smaller
sheet there was another note, in Betty's hand: *Check ins. pol.
on converted School Bus for Ben.*

Ben his brother.

Mortgaged to his ears for rolling stock already—big farm
equipment, four tractors, a pick-up truck, a station wagon, two
motorcycles, and now a school bus. His legacy from their father was one of the unluckiest; or so it seemed, from time to
time, to Will Hodge Sr. (Ben would stand in his yard at the
Other Place—as they all still called it, even now that Stony
Hill was gone—a man still handsome though grown red-faced
and heavy at fifty, his head tipped back, looking through the
lower halves of his thick, dark-tinted steel-rimmed glasses at
the newly delivered corn chopper, or the twenty-year-old
wired-together baler, and the look on his face and in his stance
was like a child's, solemn, deeply satisfied, detached as a sunlit
mystical vision from the dying tamaracks, tumble-down barns,
and the high, orange-yellow old brick house that labored in
vain to establish for Ben Hodge his spiritual limits. There were
honeybees in the walls of the house, and in the bedroom where
Ben and Vanessa slept in the Congressman's grand old walnut
bed there were coffee cans to collect the honey that dripped
down the walls from the windowsills; set squarely in the center
of the once-large kitchen was a bathroom (vented to the kitch-
en) that Ben had put in for the comfort of his (and Will
Hodge's) mother in her last year; and in the kitchen and pantry and livingroom walls there were plaster patches to recall
the time when Ben Hodge would sit up late with his twenty-

two, killing the rats his traps missed before they could nibble the sleeping old woman's fingers. Destructions unnerving, in some metaphysical way unlawful, to Hodge. For if Hodge was by temperament a mender, a servant of substance, Ben was a dreamer, a poet, an occasional visiting preacher at country churches from here to good news where. He was blind to the accelerating demolition all around him, or saw it in his own queer terms, inscrutable to all but his good wife and, perhaps, children, both his own and the numerous children he and Vanessa took in. Among them Will and Luke. (So that it had been as Hodge had expected it would be—had even, strange to say, hoped it would be: the image had been reinforced for them both, the magnificent ghost of a lost time and place revitalized, made to seem fit for a world it could never survive in except by a calculated destruction of body for soul: a world well lost for poetry, for the beauty of sleek or angular machines, big motors roaring for as long as they lasted, profligate generosity, family talk. Well lost—the barns Hodge's father had built, the trees he'd planted, the dew-white vineyard—but lost, past recovery. Lost.)

"Hah," he said.

There was someone at the door.

Quickly, slyly, he dropped the apple core in the basket by his desk.

## 3

He knew the moment he opened the door that something serious had happened and that he was, himself, in some way, accused. The two policemen he'd known for years—stooped, bald Clumly and Dominic Sangirgonio—stood on the steps suspiciously casual, solemn-faced as Chinamen, not talking, looking at him as though they did not know him. Clumly looked drained, like a man just told he will be dead before morning. His eyes were full of rage. Clumly nodded, an act of will, and gave a smile-like twitch of the colorless lips on the face as white as a grub's. The ice-blue eyes glittered. "Morning, Will," he said loudly, as though Hodge were deaf. He bristled with impatience, and Hodge had a feeling the man's mind was miles away, sorrowing, or burning after vengeance.

"Good morning," Hodge said. He slid his lower lip over his upper, instinctively cautious, like a man in a room with a lion. He had a brief, peculiarly clear sense of the motionless, deserted street, the curb where a little while ago Will Jr's Chevy had been, the sidewalk dappled with the shadows of leaves, the two men's shoes on the rubber-matted steps. At last, grimly, Hodge smiled, annoyed at that infernal sense of himself as a small boy forever ready to be guilty of forgotten crimes. But Clumly, too, was like a boy—a man of over sixty, close to retirement. He stood angrily tapping the side of his pantleg with his hat—his white, perfectly hairless head still cocked. He wore his uniform, as always. Miller, too, wore his uniform, the wide belt, the gun. He folded his arms.

"Catching up on some work?" Clumly asked ferociously, looking past Hodge into the office. He looked like a bear, bending to peer in past Hodge.

"No, not really," Hodge said, considering again. "Come in."

Clumly glanced at him, then nodded, a jerk of the head. "We won't be a minute," he said.

Hodge held the door for them, then closed it behind them. Hodge said nothing. Miller stood by the door, studiously examining the police cap; Clumly stood in the middle of the room, hands in coatpockets, scowling and looking around not as a friend but as a police professional. He asked, "What *are* you doing here on a Sunday, Will?"

"Will Jr came down," Hodge said. "He needed some maps he'd left here." He hooked his thumbs around his suspenders and stood, jaw protruding, waiting.

Clumly cocked his head, bending toward the desk to read the note on the tablet. A flush of irritation ran through Hodge, but he said nothing. Clumly read aloud, eyes glittering: "Obtain the release of Nick S." He scowled, blushing at the same time, and glanced at Miller. "You won't need this." He put down the tablet. "He's already out."

Hodge waited, and later it would seem to him that Clumly had taken a good deal longer than necessary to come out with it: he would remember that absolute stillness of Miller, standing by the door looking fixedly into his hat, and Clumly himself, touching his nose with two fingers like a man baffled by a sudden and inexplicable change in a familiar landscape, studying Hodge's jaw. He said, "He's escaped. Killed a man. You'd better come down with us."

"Poppycock!" Hodge exploded. "I don't believe it."

Again Clumly touched his nose, looking at Hodge as though he were not a man, an old friend, but some mysterious object brought back from the center of Africa or India, a contraption with no clear purpose or meaning, possibly dangerous. Under that stare, Will Hodge felt heavy as stone, freakish, sealed off from the usual flow of things as he'd been sealed off, in the old days, when his wife would turn briefly to look at him with revulsion. But Clumly, too, was transmogrified. He looked dead, as though there were no longer any intrinsic connection between the parts of his face—the round, yellowed ears, the red-veined nose, the white, sagging cheeks that lapped to the sides of his small, cleft chin like old drapery, or like dirty snow sinking into itself, or like bread-dough. The old man's shirt was blue, his tie dark green. He'd been wearing that same limp uniform it must be a month.

"Mind if I use your phone?" he said.

Hodge waved him toward it.

Clumly went around behind the desk, sliding his finger along the top as he went, and sat down heavily. He dialed, waited, looking up fiercely at the shabby rosette in the center of the ceiling, then sat forward abruptly, slightly crossing his eyes to watch the receiver, and shouted into it. "Hello, Mikhail," he said. "This is Clumly. Correct. That's right. Listen. I'm at Will Hodge's office." His eyes grew cunning. "Will Jr has been here a little while back. He's likely on his way up to Buffalo now. Tell the Thruway people if they see him, they should send him back. We need to talk to him." He listened, foxy as the devil. "That's right," he said. "Correct." He hung up the phone. He looked at Hodge again, still seething with rage but this time more as he might look at something human. Hodge was not comforted. He'd sent the State Troopers after Will, well as he knew him.

"Hell of a business," Clumly said.

Grimly, Hodge studied the man's bald dome. "Yes it is," he said.

Clumly sighed, eyes going vague, his mind far away again. "Well, let's go." He stood up.

It was only when he was standing in the parking lot—a

square like the courtyard of a dirty castle, high brick walls on three sides and most of the fourth, the air thick with the smell from the cleaners', the cinders and dirt under Hodge's shoes rutted and dented, baked hard as pottery—that the horror of the thing came over him. It seemed to him now that any fool should have seen that it would end this way, Nick Slater killing somebody merely to get out of jail, Will Jr dragged into it, and Hodge himself in some nebulous way responsible. It came to him that he hadn't even thought to ask who it was that had been killed.

He watched the black and white police car nose out into the street, the red light flashing, dappled sunlight sliding on the roof as it moved, then opened the door of his elderly Plymouth and squeezed behind the wheel. It was baking hot inside the car, and it smelled of stale cigarette smoke. He sat a moment catching his breath before painfully reaching his key toward the ignition. He ground on the starter, and at last the engine caught. "All right," Hodge said. He rolled down the window, grunting, then started for the jail.

"Blame little monkey," he said.

But he could not get rid of his extreme uneasiness. It was almost less an emotion than a physical sensation, as if the whole world had risen up against him. The heat and light of the August sun made his head ache and hurt his eyes, and the rasp of the car motor, the sporadic bumping of metal against metal somewhere up close to the left front wheel, were unnaturally loud, cutting. Nick Slater's face rose up in his mind, remarkably distinct, the hair as long as a woman's, coal black and slicked down like the hair of one of those motorcycle people at a dance. The expression on the face—the thin, wide lips, the far-apart eyes, the nostrils flared like the nostrils of a horse—was a baffling mixture of joy and terror. It was an image without background, as it first came to him, and only after concentrating a moment could Hodge draw in the rest. It was at the Fireman's Carnival, in the middle of July. Hodge had been standing with his daughter and her husband, doing nothing, taking in the noise and turbulent motion and color of the place, a Kewpie doll clutched in his two square hands, a cardboard box containing a goldfish hanging from one finger (he remembered it all very clearly now, the explosions of color in the overcast sky, the nasal shouts of the barkers and hucksters on all sides of him, the dancing girls ancient and sickly in repose, leanjawed as Baptist Sunday-school teachers with the eyes of old tigers, and above it all, mystical and hushed, mindlessly turning as if forever, the Ferris wheel: Mary Lou had said, "Ride the Ferris wheel, Dad?" "No sir," he had snorted, smiling grimly, shocked by the realization that he could do it, no one would stop him, though it would kill him). All at once some kind of commotion broke out, over by the frozen-custard truck: a crowd shouting and running, someone howling "Police!" "What's happened?" they all asked each other. "A fire," someone said, and they all passed it back. But it wasn't a fire, it was a firecracker, they learned. Some Indian had thrown one right into the crowd, and the men in the crowd had gone after him. Luckily for everybody, the police had caught him first. "There he is!" the man at Hodge's back yelled. The police had him up on the dancing girls' platform to protect him from the crowd, and in the glow of colored lights all around the platform eyes and noses were tipped up to look, and at the back of the crowd there were people jumping up and down, trying to see. "Why that's Luke's boy!" Hodge said. His son-in-law shook his head, hands in his pockets. He was six-foot-nine. "Durned if it ain't." He seemed not especially impressed. They had handcuffs on the boy. Hodge pushed through the crowd toward the platform, growling "K'out the way there, k'out the way!" in that heavy voice he'd inherited from his father the Congressman; and when he got there, puffing, still holding on to the Kewpie doll and the box with the goldfish, he heaved his great weight up the makeshift wooden steps and said, "What seems to be the trouble here?" The two policemen, sheriff's men, young fellows both of them, seemed more nervous than the boy. "I never did it, Uncle Will," the Indian said, clowning, mimicking a child. "They seen me standing there, and all it is, they *figured* I did it." But his breath stunk of beer, and his look was wild. "I'll talk to you later," Hodge said. The policemen, it turned out, were inclined to believe Nick Slater's story, if only to be rid of him. No one seemed to have seen him throw the firecracker, in any case, and if Hodge wanted to take charge of the boy, that would be fine with them. Hodge snorted with disgust, but agreed to it. Nick was in no position to go through more court trouble. Hodge had gone directly to the car with him, and there, some distance from the honking and whirring of the carnival machines, the oceanic murmur of the crowd, he had said, "Luke know you came here?" The boy sat back almost on his shoulders, his knees up over the dash. "Psshew," he said, "I thought I was one dead Redman." His smile was still wild, and he was breathing hard. He shaped a gun with his right hand and fired twice, silently, at the crowd. Hodge said sternly, "I asked you a question." Nick folded his arms, black against the white of his clean, neatly pressed shirt, and mused. At last he said, "Your Honor, I fear I must refuse to answer, on the grounds that the answer might cremate me." Hodge snorted. "Listen, though," Nick said. He looked at Hodge sideways, his face solemn now. "Thanks." Suddenly he grinned, his white teeth huge and square.

"Dang fool," Hodge said, troubled by some memory he could not make out.

A crowd had gathered around the high brownstone and concrete imitation castle set back among dying elms and maple trees. Except for the barred windows along the sides of the place, it might have been a library, or an old post office, or a school. The men from the hospital were just closing the light blue ambulance doors as Hodge drove up. He parked in front of the fire hydrant, switched off the engine, and sat watching, squinting against the brightness of the day, as they climbed into the ambulance and pulled away from the curb. A block from the jail they stopped behind the traffic waiting for a red light. He was dead then, yes.

"A man never knows from one minute to the next," Hodge said. He patted his cigarette pocket though he hadn't smoked for a month. He got out and walked up onto the lawn, watching the people. The grass on the lawn was as dry as excelsior and almost as brown. The dirt was dry as sand full in the sun. Hodge found Walt Sprague was there in the crowd, a client. Hodge started past him.

"Well hello there, Counsellor," Sprague yelled, jerking his head. He was chewing. "You come over to see the excitement, did you?"

Hodge laughed, horselike. "What happened?" he said. The people were talking all around them just loudly enough that Sprague didn't hear. Hodge repeated it. On the steps, trying to peek in, there was a queer-looking young man in a black Amish hat and clothes like a tramp's.

"They had a jailbreak, thass what they say," Sprague said. His voice was high and barren as a clay hill, and his long, burnt-dry face was folded and whiskered like a dog's. He wore a T-shirt and baggy bib-overalls. "I guess they killed somebody, too. I never seen it, myself. I was over there acrost the street getting my tractor fixed. I seen the crowd all coming around and I come right on over. Some young fellow. I seen them bring him out. I-talian, looked like. Policeman."

Hodge nodded. "Salvador," he said.

The fat woman to Sprague's left turned to look at Hodge angrily. She turned away again at once and hissed to the woman beside her, "Salvador."

"They don't train 'em right," Sprague said. "Whole town run by graft. Whole durn *country* run by graft. Dang Democrats must be out of their minds. Put a Baptist cowboy in the White House."

The angry woman turned her head again. "What you saying about Democrats?"

"I said they're crazy, ma'am," Sprague said. He touched his hatbrim. "Ain't that so, Counsellor?"

Hodge nodded absent-mindedly and started for the steps.

Clumly was at his piled-deep desk, slyly pretending to read the Sunday funnies as if he had nothing on earth to do—as if the crowd in the outer office had nothing whatsoever to do with him. He glanced up then down at the paper quickly, pretending he had not bothered to look up, and for a moment Hodge was—for no real reason, it seemed to him the next moment—furious. What the devil was Clumly up to? But Hodge kept his temper. This was no time for fury. That was one of the things you learned at Law, the ability to choose the time. He said, "They said it was Salvador."

Clumly nodded, looking up now. His eyes were ice.

"What happened?"

"Who knows? He was here alone, just one other man, at the desk. Sunday and all. Your boy knocked out the man at the desk and tied him up and got the cell door open some way or another—it was shut again when we come in—and Salvador must've pulled his gun, only he didn't have sense to use it. Your boy got hold of it, tipped it up, maybe. Anyway, he was shot up through the chin." Clumly pointed, tipping his head back. "Come look."

He got up from the desk and led Hodge to the hallway leading to the cellblock. (It was almost empty now. Two policemen, a Negro, one man in a suit, maybe from the paper.) As soon as the hall door was open Hodge caught the smell. It was like the heavy scent of cow's blood, the smell that had filled the slaughterhouse at Stony Hill. When he looked, the stuff was everywhere, sticky now, like dark paste—a wide puddle on the floor, stains on the wall, even spots on the ceiling. One of the cops—it was Clarence Pieman—and the Negro called Baltimore, were just beginning the cleaning. Hodge looked, jaw slung forward, and felt, strange to say, nothing. He was intensely aware of the sharp separation of bloodstain and wall, aware of the sharp lines in the tile, the stipple of the gray plaster, the smell; but every trace of the fierce churning of emotion that had sickened him before was gone. He felt, mainly, a keen curiosity more scientific than morbid.

"Poor devil," he said soberly, shaking his head.

He removed his glasses to polish them, then replaced them and bent forward to look more closely.

Clumly rubbed his hands. He had that vague look again, like a man with grave responsibilities who's forgotten where he is. "It must have been something," he said. "He must have stumbled around like a chicken with its head cut off."

"I was thinking that too," Hodge said.

"It must have been something for the boy, eh?" Clumly said. "Think of it!" He scowled then, musing, perhaps thinking of something else entirely. "He must have gotten blood all over him. Blood all over the gun, too." He glanced at Hodge. "Just the same, he took it with him."

"The gun?"

Clumly nodded, suddenly back to reality and dangerous. His eyes came into focus on Hodge's jaw and seemed to lock there. At last he put his hand on Hodge's arm and turned him back to the office.

"Any idea where he went?" Hodge said.

"Vanished like smoke." He touched his nose. "It's as if he had somebody out there waiting for him. We'll find him, of course. No worry about that. Have a seat."

Hodge lowered himself into the chair by the desk while, behind him, Clumly crossed to the outer office door and talked to one of the men. Hodge's chest and back and arms were pasted to his shirt. The fat he carried made him sweat more than most men. He only half-listened to the talk in the outer office, trying to adjust in his mind the irreconcilable images—the new man, Salvador, as he'd seen him last, filtering coffee through a piece of screen, and that other image, too intense for ordinary reality, the blood-spattered hallway. The man in the outer office said they had reached Mickey Salvador's family. Clumly came back, and behind him a short, middle-aged policeman with a pink face, no chin. The man leaned against the desk and crossed his shins and switched on the tape recorder. Clumly began his questions; Hodge answered mechanically.

Not even Clumly was really interested in the questions. Sometimes in the middle of a sentence he would pause to fiddle with the knobs on the police radio beside the tape recorder —reports from the State Police at the roadblocks, or men out talking, beating the bushes, circling in on nothing—and sometimes, before Hodge had answered, Clumly would change his mind and say, "No, skip it." He turned over some papers. He said abruptly "Funny thing, Will Jr's coming to see you just when he did."

"Well it's not exactly—" Hodge began.

But Clumly stood up; the question was not serious. He went to stand by the window, as though the questioning were over, but he didn't send his man away. He seemed to have forgotten.

Clumly shook his head, tapping the windowframe and looking out. "Kids," he said. "They must be something, I guess. That younger one I mean, yours. What's his name? Luke? I imagine there's times you'd like to wrung his neck."

"He's a monkey all right," Hodge said, on guard.

The man watching the tape recorder had not yet switched it off.

Hodge frowned. He tried to hear what they were saying out by the desk.

"They don't like authority," Clumly said. Now he was picking at a scab on the side of his hand. "That's what it is. All anarchists. They've gotten to the size of a man, they think they're grown-ups." He laughed. It was like laughter coming out of a stone.

"Luke's no trouble." Hodge frowned. He had no choice but to play along, see what it was about and say what was so, give the crazy old fool nothing he could blow up out of all proportion for whatever purpose he had in mind. Hodge felt queasy. Any other time he might have laughed at a policeman's trying tricks on him, trying to throw him off, if it was that. Any other time he might have enjoyed his own art in the foolish game.

But just now it made him cross and impatient. He felt, as he'd felt in his own office earlier, alien, turned to stone and put on display. And there was something more, too; some brute fact nagging at his mind like an itch.

"Now stop it, Will," Clumly said, swinging around to face him. "Luke's 'no trouble'! He's darn near a Communist, that's what people say. He's like your other boy twenty times over —the one up in Buffalo, organizing riots."

Hodge sat up. "That's slander, Clumly. One more word of that kind and I'll have you in court so fast your head will swim." His fat jaw shook.

Clumly shrank back, opening his hands to show his innocence, but his eyes were still like bullets, and his whole body had taken on an absurd, crafty look. "Now Will," he said, "take it easy." He turned to the man working the machine. "Get in there and type this up. Except the last part, wherever the questions stopped. We don't need that."

"Type it all," Hodge said.

Clumly shrugged, sly as a dragon, still mysterious, and Hodge wondered all at once if perhaps the man was merely confused and trying to keep the confusion out of sight. The other man left with the tape recorder. When the door was closed behind him, Clumly pushed his fingertips into his belt and came over to stand facing Will, squinting. "All right," he said. "What do *you* think happened?"

"What do you mean?"

"You know what I mean. The blood's in the hallway, not in the cellblock, and the cell door was shut. Why would your Indian take time to shut that door behind him, when he was breaking out? Or how'd he get out in the hall by himself? Why stop to merely knock out the man in front and tie him up, when he'd murdered the other one? How'd he disappear so quick? It's a mystery. Correct. The kind you read about." He went on squinting a moment longer at Hodge's face. But he was not up to meeting Hodge's anger, finally, too tired for that, or too busy with anger of his own, and he turned away and fished in his shirt pocket for a cigar. "All right," he said. "So somebody came here, and we need to know who." He sucked his mouth in.

"Ask them right out," Hodge said. "If either Will or Luke was here, they'll tell you."

"Correct," Clumly said. His disgust grew. He lit the cigar

and shook the match. "Because they're Hodges. Pillars of the community." The anger was building up pressure now, reddening his face. "A little extreme in their opinions, maybe"—he chuckled crossly—"but Hodges through and through. Good upbringing. Noble ideals. Solider than Uphills, even Woodworths. Some people wouldn't understand that, naturally." He laughed, as cold as a stone again, then leaned toward Hodge. "My father was a drunkard. A plumber originally, but later a professional drunkard. I used to ask myself *Why?*—all that drinking. No trouble, you understand; a *responsible* drunkard. Toward the end he wouldn't work but once a year, at Christmas. He was Santa Claus." Little by little the far-away crafty look was coming back, the pressure of rage inside him still building, and now Hodge had a feeling, wordless but sure, that he partly understood. "What was wrong with him? I used to wonder. Just a youngster, you know. He was a good enough plumber—or so people said. My mother wasn't a hard woman to live with, little too religious maybe, but not bad—not all that bad." He blew out smoke and watched it spread out in the air. Suddenly Clumly smiled without humor and snapped his eyes back onto Hodge. They were the eyes of a stranger. "His problem was metaphysical." He laughed again. Even the voice was a stranger's.

"What's gotten into you?" Hodge said sternly.

"Metaphysical." He quoted: " 'of the nature of being or essential reality. Very abstract, abstruse, or subtle: often used derogatorily of reasoning.' He had a perfectly good life, nothing wrong with it that you could see. Just the same, he got to be a drunkard." He sucked at the cigar and again blew out smoke, his grub's face compressed tight. His hand trembled, holding out the cigar. "They arrested him for theft once. I use to visit him at the jail. 'Mr. Hodge will take care of me,' he said. Tipped his eyes to heaven. And Mr. Hodge did. God bless the Hodges. Made a speech that would've made statues weep. Your old man that was. He was good, yes. Pure magic. My old mother standing there, hanging on to his coattails and my father blowing his nose and crying—they were like sticks, my mother and father, and *your* father, by Heaven, he was big as a room, and his head thrown back like he thought there was somebody painting his picture. 'God bless you,' my old mother said, and I said the same myself—I was ten or eleven—'Dear God, bless Mr. Hodge!' " He spat at the wastebasket and

sucked again at the cigar. It seemed to dawn on him at last
that all he was saying was pointless—plain mad, in fact. He
cast about, panicky, it seemed to Hodge, as if hunting for
some way back that would not make his wandering off too noticeable. Abruptly, he clenched his fists. "I'll tell you how it is,
Will. If I thought your father might've opened that cell door
I'd put him on the carpet, same as you, same as your boys. No
faith, you know? No faith at all. That's what they pay me
for."

Hodge said nothing.

Clumly nodded, fingertips still trembling, calming himself
by will. "Listen, forget it. You see how it is. We never had a
jailbreak in thirty years, now we get one it has to be complicated with . . . I don't know which way's up, I even use the
forms they give you for times like this." Then he was angry
again, the blood rushing up in his neck. "Shoot. You know
how to do my job better than me—take it, Hodge. Maybe you
do. Everybody else does, they think. I keep a clean office, pretty well, whatever people say. *I* know what the talk is. I never
drink, that's one thing I can say. Their criticizing goes off of
me like water." His face was shaking.

He turned to the door before the knock came. "Come in."

Hodge pursed his lips.

Miller said, "Hodge boys are here. Both of 'em. And Salvador's mother."

Clumly puffed at the cigar, still trembling, looking at the
floor. "She been to the morgue?"

Miller nodded. "She wants to talk to you."

"Send her in."

Miller went out, and Hodge started to follow, but Clumly
stopped him. "You stay, Will. You want my job, this might be
good experience." He leered.

Mrs. Salvador came in.

Hodge had probably seen her before; he thought he had.
Hundreds of times, it might be—sitting on some run-down
porch on Liberty Street, or South Jackson, the old Italian section, talking with some woman exactly like her except slightly
fatter or slighter thinner, the same cheap clothes, dark, limp,
her hair as black as midnight, garlic coming out of her pores
like soap from a sponge. They talked lightning Italian, paused
suddenly to laugh, called out fiercely to their children in the

street, who merely shrugged or showed no sign at all of having heard, and behind the younger women, protected by them as by battlements, there would be an old one with iron-gray hair, rocking slowly back and forth, saying nothing. When they were young they were beautiful, and then they got married and moved in with Mama and got mean, and then they got fat. When they came to his office for legal advice—tax troubles, some lawsuit, or to ask timidly about an annulment—they grew mysteriously smaller, more childlike, and Hodge, for all his plowhorse dignity, was distressed.

He had expected her to come in weeping, but she was not, and it came to him that Salvador's face must have been blown to smithereens: it wasn't time yet for grief. Her eyes were violent. She settled them on Clumly first, then turned her head slowly toward Hodge.

"You his lawyer?" she said. "The Indian?"

("Like ice," he would say later, again and again.) The voice shocked him.

"Mr. Hodge is the boy's guardian," Clumly said.

"No, Luke's the boy's guardian," Hodge said at once, defensively. Immediately he was annoyed at his pettiness. "Luke's my son."

"I pray to the Virgin your son may burn in hell." Dark as her skin was, the flush of her cheeks showed clearly.

Hodge said nothing.

"This is a terrible tragedy, Mrs. Salvador," Clumly said. He tipped his head toward her. "Won't you sit down?" The color was draining out of him again.

The woman ignored him. As though he were not in the room, she said to Hodge, spitting, "I know you people, you do-gooders with your fat bellies and your fat smiles, helping killers get out of jail so they can kill some more. You *stupid!* I see you in the newspaper, how you smile for the camera when you just got Frank Cirotti out of jail, you get some foolish old woman to say Frank he's not guilty when everybody knows he's guilty, yes!—so now maybe sometime pretty soon he can rape some poor little kid."

"Mrs. Salvador," Clumly said. But he was enjoying it.

Light came off her skin like shocks. "So now you're happy, yeah. You got my boy dead with all your helping crooks. How many people you think you killed so far? You. You're like poison."

"Now wait," he said. A pain like a small lump of flame closed off his throat, and before he could get back his voice, the woman had turned like wheeling fire and was gone. The room still rang.

Hodge sat down, and still he couldn't speak. *Justice,* he thought. *Hah!*

Clumly gave him a glass of water, and he sipped it. It helped.

"I can see why you want my job," Clumly said, squinting at him as he would at a mouse in a cage. "I wouldn't want yours!"

"I never said I wanted your job, Clumly," he said.

"Mebby you didn't," Clumly said.

Hodge scowled, aware that something was going by him.

"You care to stay while I talk to your boys, Will?" Clumly said then. Though the voice was gentle, the eyes glittered more brightly than ever, as though the woman had thrown new coal on the fire inside him.

"Lord no!" Hodge said. He got up, quickly for a man of his proportions, and hurried toward the door.

Clumly leaned against his desk and puffed at the cigar, musing. *"Ciao,"* he said.

Hodge left.

He paused on the steps to adjust to the breathless heat outside, heat so intense that it made the hairs on your arms curl. Two policemen were busy dispersing the crowd, or trying to. There Clumly caught him again.

"Hodge! Wait a minute! I forgot something."

Hodge turned, sagging, and Clumly ducked back inside for a moment. A reporter from the *Daily News* drew Hodge over to the side of the steps to ask questions. "I can't tell you a thing," Hodge said. "I'm sorry." The man persisted, a stupid fellow, as it seemed to Hodge; his eyes and voice were slow, and here in the rush of events he seemed out of place, like an old Ford truck on a racetrack. He had a permanently startled look, like a sheep aware of thunder. "I'm sorry," Hodge said again. The man—Bob Swift, his name was—asked about the Indians and Hodge grew angry.

Then Clumly was back to thrust a picture in front of him. "You know this man, Hodge?"

"No," Hodge said.

"Look again," Clumly said.

Slowly and deliberately, steadying himself against the as yet unintelligible howling of indefinite memories, Hodge took the police photograph between his thick first finger and thumb and studied it. Then he knew. The burn-scarred, crassly bearded face was the wreck of the eldest brother's life, and the gentle eyes looking out through that monstrous corruption of flesh were to Hodge like tokens brought back from the dead as a sign. But Hodge stood on legs like pillars, and for all the roiling blast of his emotions, his mind was like a stovelid. He pursed his lips. "Who is this?" he said when he could speak.

"You don't know him?" Clumly said.

"Do you?"

Clumly squinted at him, judging, then shook his head. "It's the prisoner that got away," he said. "We call him the Sunlight Man."

"Yes," Hodge said. "I heard on television."

"All right, just wanted to check." Clumly went on watching him, but Hodge showed nothing. At last the Chief took back the picture, nodded, turned, went in.

Hodge walked mechanically to his car. No one in the crowd could have guessed. Calmly, deliberately, his lips pursed, he drove out of sight of the police station before he gave way to his grief.

## 4

"To tell the truth, I've come for advice," Clumly said.

The Judge stood with his head tipped, one white hand closed around his pipe, the other around his whiskey. The drapes of his study were closed, as usual, and the room was dark with legal books, old leather chairs, a typing desk with black oilcloth draped over the machine and part of the messy stack of papers—perhaps the local history he was said to be writing. On the large desk by the draped window there were more such papers, yellow with age; above them a skeletal, globelike thing that put you in mind of sorcery. "Legal advice?" he said.

Clumly shook his head. "No, not exactly."

The Judge closed the door and went soundlessly to his chair. "Sit down," he said.

They sat.

At length Clumly said, "I made a bad mistake this morning."

The Judge waited.

"I lost control. Hit a boy with a gun." He looked for some sign, though he knew better. The Judge went on smoking, withdrawing into his yellow clouds, as he always did on such occasions. "I've been pressed lately. I imagine you've heard. I don't know what it is, exactly. Sometimes I think . . ." He stopped to work it out and remained silent for a long time. "I've been thinking I ought to resign,'' he said, at last.

The Judge said nothing.

"My health's bad," Clumly said. "My mind seems to wander. It's not working right." Panic seized him for a moment, then passed. "No, that's not it. I can work all right. It's worse than that. You get old and you get impatient with things. Roadblocks. People in the way, making everything harder than it is. My men, for instance—the pay they get. You can't keep a police department going if the city won't pay. But I tell 'em what I need, I spell it out for them, and—nothing. Irrelevant questions, forms, I don't know what.

"And then, judgment. Man works for years, he learns certain things, learns to get certain hunches, you might call it, he knows he can trust. But they don't let him work from his hunches, y' see. Pretty soon the hunches get confused.

"No, that's not it either." Again he fell silent.

"Well, this impatience. Talk about that. Men aren't properly trained, they start running their job their own way, you can't count on 'em. Things get out of hand, and you do all you can to get it all straightened out but all the time there's new troubles coming behind you—kids robbing the meters, for instance, or drunken drivers, or somebody turning in false alarms, and old ladies groaning about this and that—pretty soon you're out of patience and without meaning to you've broken somebody's jaw."

The Judge said mildly, "You broke the Indian's jaw?"

"Mmm," Clumly said, nodding slowly. He knew he had not told the Judge it was the Indian. "He saw that man come in and let him out. He could've said."

"You knew though, in any case."

"Correct. Yes. But he could have said. That's it, right there. It's not real problems, it's the lack of cooperation, you might say. The general nuisance. All the same, it was a bad mistake, letting go. Bad for morale, for one thing. And for another thing, it's dangerous. The whole fabric of Society—"

He mused.

The Judge smoked on.

"We get so many of 'em, in and out down there at the police station, we begin to stop noticing they're people. When you think about it—" He paused again, all at once remembering the prostitute, Rosemary, on Harvester Avenue. That was what had gone wrong, all right. Because of Kozlowski, it might be, he had seen that she was human. "It makes your blood run cold," he said.

The Judge said, "Sometimes a man needs to be cold-blooded."

Clumly frowned, considering.

"When I was young," Clumly said, "there was a man, a Chief of Police here in Batavia, by the name of Poole. They had a parade for him when he retired. It was something, really something. You may remember it. You see, they kept it a surprise from him. He goes down to the station, the last day, and he works all day and the men don't so much as mention that he's retiring today, unless he brings it up. He felt bad enough about that, all right. But then when he goes out through the front door that last afternoon, wham! There they are! 'Surprise!' they all yell, 'Surprise! Surprise!' And then the drum majorettes start dancing and twirling their sticks and the Batavia Junior-Senior High School Band begins to play, and St. Joseph's Drum and Bugle Corps, and the people are all singing

> *For he's a jolly good fellow*
> *For he's a jolly good fellow*
> *For he's a jolly good fellow*
> *Which nobody can . . ."*

Clumly cleared his throat. The room was blurred. "I don't want anything like that, of course," he said, blushing. "That's not what I'm saying. All I'm saying is, when I step down I want people to know—a few people, anyway—I want 'em to know I was a man that did the best he could. He made mistakes, but he fulfulled his responsibilities as best he could."

"Fulfilled," the Judge said.

"Correct. That's what I said."

"You got the boy a doctor?" the Judge asked.

Clumly nodded. "We transferred him over to Vets. He's there now. I realize you can't hide a thing like that. I wouldn't want to, come right down to it. If a man can't do the job——"

The Judge set down his pipe. Clumly waited, but for a long time the old man merely thought about it. At last he reached his decision, or so it seemed, and leaned forward. "A singular ambition, distinctly American," he said. He chuckled silently. "A Retirement Day parade." Then he stood up and drank from the glass as if it were water.

Clumly said, "You'll use your influence?—on the other matter, not the parade. As for that——"

Again the Judge chuckled. Experimentally he said, "Surprise!" He chuckled again.

Clumly had made another mistake, he could see. Again blood prickled up his neck.

But the Judge said, "Go in peace, Clumly. You'll have worse news than this is, the next time I see you. That's my prediction."

Clumly bowed his head, compressing his lips.

The Judge put his hand on Clumly's arm. "Cheer up, your lot's no worse than mine, in the end. You get plenty of fresh air——" He waved in the direction of the curtained windows. "—and you haven't got woman troubles."

Chief Clumly glanced at him in perplexity.

The Judge put a finger to his lips. "As for the advice you wanted," said the Judge, "I will say nothing at this time. That reminds me, though, I've got an article you might like to read. Tell me what you think."

"An article," Clumly said, uneasy.

The Judge hunted through the papers on his desk and at last found it. It had been cut from the magazine it came in and was held together with a paper clip. "Ah yes," the Judge said. "Here." He held it out.

"Thank you," Clumly said. He glanced at the title, "Policework and Alienation."

"Don't thank me yet," the Judge said, and smiled.

And so they parted.

## 5

Second only to William Hodge Sr, Merton Bliss was the bluntest man in the whole of Genesee County. He was shingling the wellhouse roof when Hodge drove up, late that afternoon. The sagging barn behind him was black with age, sunk in brightly blooming burdocks. Bliss pushed back his cap with the side of his hand then drew it back to where it was in the first place, as if his object were merely to let in some air, and sat on his irontoed shoes smiling like a halfwit. He was an odd-looking man. His nose was so narrow and flat at the sides it looked like he'd ironed it. Hodge pulled into the shadow of the wellhouse and looked up. "That how you observe the Sabbath?" he said. Meant to be a joke.

Merton considered it, looking up at the visor of his cap. "Idle hand is the Devil's instrument," he said. When he smiled, his mouth made a sharp and narrow V. "I hear that boy of yours killed somebody now."

"Hah," Hodge said. The feeling that his life was in ruins welled back. He opened the car door, swallowing, and slid his briefcase across the seat toward him. "We did what we could for those boys," he said, evading the center of his grief. "There was no way we could know it would come to this."

"Always does," Merton said. He had the clearest Western –New York twang in all Western New York—*a*'s that stretched for a rod or more, and *r*'s as rich as elderberries. "It's in their blood, them Indians. Bill Covert had one of 'm— it must be some forty years ago now. He was a goll-ding good worker, so Bill put up with him, don't you know. But he was trouble, nothin but trouble. He use to set traps in the milkhouse for Bill—just foolin, of course. Old Bill, he'd walk in with a pail in each hand and when he stepped through the door he'd trip a lever the boy had, and by golly a great big ten-by-ten beam would come dropping on his head. *Aye*-uh. And then another time when Bill was climbing up the mow and he was no more'n a foot from the top of the ladder, why all of a sudden *whooey* down he went sir, tail over tincup. The Indian boy'd sawed that ladder more'n nine-tenths through. He had a sister, Bill did. That poor girl was drove halfway crazy by that goll-ding Indian. One night around the middle of Feb-

ruary, it was so cold you had to fold your blankets with a
hammer, that poor girl went out to that brick johnny they had
behind the house, and that Indian boy snuck out behind her,
and the minute she'd just got comfortable he hauled off and
threw a pail of water at the door. Well it froze in two seconds.
Sealed her up just as tight as a bankvault, and then he went
back for more water and did it again. By golly, Hodge, it took
us a week and four days to break her out. That's God's own
truth." Once more he looked at the visor of his cap, solemn.

"Hah," Hodge said. He opened the briefcase, resting it
against his huge stomach and looking down as well as he could
by pulling in his chin. "I brought that deed by, Merton."

"I thank you kindly. Them Indians of yours are the worst I
ever seen though. That's the truth. They'd be trouble no matter what, but living with that son of yours, why it's lucky they
didn't scalp that man instead of jest blowing his head off. That
Luke. I was driving down the road behind Hobe Dart one time
—you know how Hobe drives, bat out of Hades and more'n
half-sound-asleep at the wheel—well Hobe swerved over in the
left-hand lane, not watching where he's going, and as luck
would have it there's Luke bearing down on him ninety miles
an hour in that semi truck of Paxton's. Man, I thought, there's
a wreck for sure, and I just pulled on out in the field. Damn
lucky I did. How they missed each other I never will know,
but by golly they did it—why that whole goll-ding semi was up
on two wheels! Whooey! Whooey! Well they no more missed
each other than that son of yours throws on his air brakes and
goes scootin off the road maybe sixty miles an hour and he
drives in a circle around Brumsteads' barn and then—
*whoomm!*—he's away after Hobe and I thought he's going to
kill him. I just set there in the field with Eleanor, and I says to
her, 'Eleanor, that Hodge boy's crazy.' I guess Hobe got away.
I hope he did. What's the matter that boy of yours, I wonder?"

Hodge said nothing, his chest full of dynamite. He was only
half-listening. It was Tag who'd let out the Indian. He was
through denying it to himself. What was he to do? As for
Luke—

*Luke's young,* he could have said. And there was all that
trouble he and Millie had had. That was hard on a boy, no
question. And the trouble when he and Will Jr broke up, when
they couldn't see eye to eye on anything—"Damn country
shyster," Will Jr had said: but had apologized later, more hurt

at having said it than Hodge had been at having had it said.
And then Luke's troubles in college after that, and then all the
trouble with Mary Lou's husband . . .

As though he were reading Hodge's mind, Merton said,
"And then that son-in-law yours. Lordy. I've said to Eleanor a
hundred times, Something funny bout that boy. You go look
at where he lives. The downstairs all more or less straightened
up and clean, as much as you can hope for in a house with
nine little kids, but on that second story, not a sign of a shade or a
curtain on the windows, old clothes piled up to the ceiling almost, and in one of those bedrooms—you know it's a fact as
well as I do—that boy's got old motorcycle parts. I said to
Eleanor, 'He's not right upstairs.' Heh. I'd throw him out if I
was Ben. What's Ben want him there for anyways, big good-
for-nothin boy like that? Why he don't even carry insurance
on his like, man with nine little kids. Don't you worry how I
know. They'd be out in the cold if it wasn't for Will Jr. *He's*
the one buys their insurance for'm. That son-in-law yours, all
he wants to do in this livelong world is go huntin with that
yappin little beagle of his—it bites, too; I been bit by it myself
—or go riding around out on one of them six, seven motorcycles. Rides in the hill-climbs, way I heard. Man with nine little
kids and a wife. Lord. And then down in the cellar he does
mechanic work. Why it's criminal! I bet you that house must
be a hundred and fifty years old. Worth a fortune if Ben fixed
it up. Must have twenty-five rooms in it, ain't that right? But
that brother of yours just lets it slide, rents out the best half to
that son-in-law yours for no more'n forty-five dollars a month,
big old house, and lets him do mechanic's work down-cellar.
Shoot! I been by there at night, every light in the whole goll-
ding house is on—must cost five hundred dollars a month just
to light—and I hear those motorcycle motors down-cellar, and
you look up there and it looks like the whole doggone house is
on fire, just a great big blue cloud of that gasoline smoke all
around it as thick as a fog. It's poisoning the place. And with
nine little kids! Seems to me like somebody'd *talk* to him."

He could have explained. Mary Lou and her husband were
good tenants for Ben. They didn't complain when the well
went dry or a crack opened up in the old brick wall, and they
didn't object to the wasps in the attic or the honeybees that
lived in the bricks around the chimney. They fixed their own
plumbing every time it went out, which was time after time,

and put up with the leaks where the rain came in, and jacked
up the floors when they sagged. Their boys helped out with the
farm work, and if their father was lazy—which maybe he was
and maybe he wasn't—he was a downright genius with motors,
and that was a fact. He could tear down one of Ben Hodge's
tractors in an hour and a half and put it together again—
whether it was one of the new ones with the latest gadgets or
some old Farmall or John Deere twenty years old—so that it
was better when he got finished than when it was bought.

All right.

No reason Will Hodge should defend himself against Merton Bliss or Mickey Salvador's mother or anybody else. "Never complain, never explain," Millie used to say. Something
she'd learned from a man she'd had an affair with once. Rich
man, she thought. Lived with a wife and their one sickly
daughter in a great big house in Amherst. Millie had told
Hodge many a time about all the books her lover read, all the
companies he had, how he couldn't take a job because he was
so "wealthy"—her word, not Hodge's—that if he earned any
more his taxes would run him bankrupt. Hah! "You think I'm
lying?" she'd said. "I think you're a little misled," was how he
put it. It progressed. She flaunted the thing, as she always
flaunted those affairs of hers, knowing how deeply Will Hodge
was shocked. On an impulse, he'd hired a detective, it cost him
two hundred dollars. And he'd proved beyond any shadow of
a doubt that the man was exactly what Will Hodge had
guessed, a fraud. And what did she say to that? "You *monster!*" she said. He saw for a fact he was a monster.

Now, his wide chest bubbling with violent confusion, he was
sick to death of it. Sick of being blamed for things, the faults
of his sons, the crime of an Indian he hardly knew, the waste
that teemed and rumbled around his brother. Blamed by all of
them. Blamed by himself.

"Well I guess it'll cost me plenty, talking to you the way I
am," Bliss said. "That's how it is. A man gets too old for just
sitting around with his mouth shut. Your father would turn in
his grave if he saw it, old family place been sold to niggers,
and Ben's place turned to a motorcycle shop, that son of yours
tearing down the Brumsteads' wooden fences and the other
son up there in Buffalo working with the Communists. Ding!
Well, you just figure up your bill and I'll pay it. Man can't
beat his attorney, Lord knows. I'm just tired, that's why it gets

my dander up. Seems like the whole darn world must be tired. Vietnam there, all them little yellow fish-head devils in the woods making traps for our boys out of poisonous snakes and nails with pee on them, the way I hear, and these people back at home having marches in praise of the Vietnams. And De Gaulle over there making friends with the Russians, no more grateful for all we been doing for him than a mad dog with the rabbies, and the English no better with all their talk, pure Communists theirselves, just playing in the enemy's hands. Well shoot. You can't ask for common sense, Lord knows. It's never been and it never will be. But when I think how it's going I get sick to my stomach. Truth. Some the best families in Western New York going downhill by tail over tincup. And nobody cares. It makes you sick. How much this cost me, your work?"

"Fourteen dollars," Hodge said.

"Fourteen dollars." He rolled his eyes up.

"Don't you fool yourself," Hodge said. "You're getting a dang good bargain." Angrily, he wiped the sweat from his forehead.

"Lord knows," he said. "You could just as easy have said five hundred dollars. I never could stop you." He looked toward the house, the veranda dark and cool in the shadow of the maples. "I guess you want it now."

"Any time," Hodge said, meaning yes. He slid his lower jaw beyond his upper and smiled, businesslike, his eyebrows drawn in toward the wide, dented bridge of his nose.

Bliss turned around and got onto his hands and knees and felt behind him with the toe of his shoe for the ladder. As he made his way down he said, "Justice. What a world." He stopped to scratch his armpit.

Hodge went on smiling like a man about to be shot. He stood with his legs planted wide apart, his head tipped forward as if for balance, his folded arms resting on his monumental belly.

At the kitchen door, handing him the check, Merton Bliss said, "Hottest summer I ever seen. It's a hundred and ten by the thermometer on the barn. So hot in the goll-dern chicken-house the shells won't harden. That's the truth. Franny Buckenmeyer filled up that silo of his with some hay ensilage, and the weather got so hot it just turned into ashes. You drive by in your car and you can see it. Ashes blowing from the top of

the silo and scattering over the pastures till they're whiter than
snow. Fact. And the milk! The cows lie out in the sun all day
and when you put your hands on their tits you got to use
gloves, that's how hot they git. The milk comes out powder.
You ask anybody. All the water's just boiled right away. This
last two weeks we been shippin our milk in paper boxes.
That's the truth."

Hodge held out his hand and Bliss read the check over,
blew on the ink, then gave it to him.

"No hard feelings, Will?" Bliss said. He smiled.

Hodge read the check.

"Too bad Eleanor ain't here. She'll be sorry she missed you.
She's off somewhere hellin around for the fool Red Cross."

"G'day, Merton," Hodge said.

"So long, Will. See here, I'm sorry about that boy."

Hodge said nothing, outwardly calm as a tree.

"Sometimes these things'll just happen," Bliss said. "It's just
Nature. Nothin you can do about it. It's like the time Glen
Westbrook slept out on his porch all night. You heard about
that. Woke up in the mornin and his wooden leg had been
chewed off clean at the stump. Beavers had got it. That's Nature." He shook his head. "But I'll tell you something." He
poked Hodge's belly. "Say a word to that boy of yours. Thing
about a lawyer, he makes his money getting people off on
some technicality, and pretty soon he don't *know* there's a right
and wrong. And that's the truth."

Hodge swallowed.

"No hard feelings," Bliss said.

"G'day," Hodge said. Like a dazed horse he went toward his
car.

He drove by Brumsteads'. The white board fence had been
broken down and run over on both sides of the barn. So it was
true about Luke. He drove on down Putnam Settlement Road
toward his brother's place. At the crest of the hill he could
look across the valley past the slow green creek and the meadowland with Queen Anne's lace and wild mustard and daisies
scattered through it, and he could see on the crest of the farther hill the square wooden silo, the paintless barn with its
rusted tin roofs, the tamarack trees, the house. Ben's. His grief
welmed up in him again and threatened to overcome him. The
air grew less breathless, and the shadows of the yellow-green
apple trees of the side-hill orchard intensified his sorrow. Poor

Ben. Maybe he'd stop and say hello, and then visit his daughter Mary Lou, in the front part of Ben's house. Could he manage it? Apple pie came into his mind. Pale country pie, with crusts as flaky as the day is long. Mary Lou made the best apple pies in New York State.

Tears came in a rush and he pulled to the side of the road until it was over.

## 6

They sat in Ben's bright yellow kitchen. (Mary Lou wasn't home, in the front part, and there was no pie, but there were cookies.) Outside the window, to Will Hodge Sr's left, the yard was like a lot outside Walt Mullen's farm machinery store. To Will Hodge's eye every detail outside was unnaturally distinct, the way things look in your childhood or after a death in the house. There was a big red self-propelled combine parked under the tallest of the tamaracks, beside it a yellow self-unloading wagon of newly combined wheat, beyond that a rusty corn chopper, two old tractors, a Gravely lawn mower, the school bus Ben had bought from the Alexander Central system, Ben's motorcycle, the truck. There were also two bicycles leaning on a tree, and a teeter-totter on a sawhorse. Beyond the machinery and toys, the hillside sloped toward pastureland, the broad valley, the basswood-shaded farther hill. The basswoods were yellow-green where the sun struck them, its light breaking in wide shafts through glodes in the overcast sky. It was beautiful, sad and unreal, where the sunlight struck. You felt as though life would be different there, the air lighter and cooler, the silence more profound.

They could see that his eyes were red, but they didn't speak of it. He had known he could trust them to wait for a sign from him.

Ben's kitchen was close and crowded. Once it had been huge, built in the days of another kind of farm life, when there were thrashing crews to be fed in August, and hay crews in June and July, maple-syrup crews in the early spring, and in the winter, woodcutters who'd come in from their week in the black-oak and maple and pine woods a mile south of the house and would be full of tall tales of their week in the cabin, their faces bright red and greasy from the cold and the diet of fatty pork. The woodshed would be wet with the snow of their boots. But now the kitchen had been broken up, a large square right in the center of it sealed off to make a downstairs bathroom for the Old Woman, the last year she lived. The wide iron woodstove was gone, replaced by a small, more efficient stove run on butane. The wide wooden table was gone, too, replaced by scalloped aluminum and formica, cluttered always with Ben Hodge's bills and books and equipment manuals, and with Vanessa's papers from school. The kitchen walls were littered with more papers—calendars, more bills, papers for taxes— tacked or tucked wherever they could be, from armlevel almost to the ceiling.

Ben said, "It's terrible, all right." He polished his tinted glasses.

Will Hodge nodded, emptied of emotion, and, wanting a cigarette, took another cookie.

The Negro boy who worked for Ben sat stirring his coffee, the spoon going around and around mechanically. You never knew what he was thinking or how much he heard. His round, coal-black face hung forward from his slumped shoulders, and his eyes might as well have been the kind a taxidermist uses, yellow-brown and devoid of any hint of depth.

"Poor devil," Ben said, shaking his head, thinking.

"Well, Salvador never felt a thing at least," Will said. "Dead instantly, doctor says."

The Negro boy sipped his coffee, looking at nothing.

Ben nodded, but he had been thinking of Clumly, not Salvador. He said, "We saw Fred Clumly at Al Hubbard's funeral. Worn to a frazzle. It's funny he didn't mention that bearded fellow to you—the one he calls the Sunlight Man. It was all he could talk about when we saw him."

They looked at each other, frowning, then looked away. Ben knew Will had left something out, Will could see. Will slid his lower jaw forward and said nothing.

"Poor devil," Ben said again, accepting Will's silence. He put his glasses back on, brushed a crumb from his cheek, then leaned his red, stiff hands on the edge of the table. "He's having kind of a time of it, I've heard. Who knows. Maybe it scares him to think it might've been that Sunlight Man that came and let Nick out of jail. It's bad enough letting a prison-

er escape. Whole lot worse if he comes walking back in afterward and lets out another one."

"Mmm," Will said. Excitement was building up in him, dull
and slow in its beginning. That was it, all right. Ben had put
his finger on it. Will said, "So he tries to fool people into
thinking Will Jr—"

"I wouldn't go that far," Ben said, not understanding what
he'd caught in Will's voice, merely knowing there was something there. "Put yourself in Clumly's place. Even if he does
think that bearded man did it, that's not your business, far as
Clumly's concerned." He spoke a little too slowly, casting
around for what was wrong. "He comes to your office and
finds out that just by coincidence Will Jr's been there that
morning. That might not be odd, some other time, but it's true
Will Jr's been a friend to the boy. You and I may be sure Will
Jr wouldn't go and set a prisoner free, and maybe Clumly's
pretty much the same opinion. Just the same, there it is, here
he was in town on a Sunday morning, and alone, too, family
not with him. It's queer enough that he can't overlook it, whatever his opinion is. Clumly's a policeman. He can't afford to
trust his private opinions." But Ben was not convinced himself
of what he was saying.

Will nodded guiltily.

They could hear Vanessa starting down the stairs, on the far
side of the bathroom in the kitchen. Will leaned forward and
poked the tabletop with one finger. He said, keeping himself
very calm, "He's covering himself, that's what he's doing. He
let that little Redskin out just as sure as if he opened the cell
door himself. He let . . . the bearded one . . . slip through his
fingers. . . ." He lost track of what he was saying and had to
concentrate, leaning over and covering his eyes with one hand.
"That was bad enough all by itself," he said then, "but it's a
whole lot worse if it was just the beginning, if the one that got
away was—a maniac." He bit his lip, listening to the silence.
He said then, fiercely, "Clumly's hiding the connection. Covering himself."

"Well, maybe," Ben said. He didn't like the conversation, it
was clear. He knew Will too well. Will was aware that he'd
spoken much too loudly.

Vanessa appeared at the foot of the stairs, sweating and
puffing hard. "Will!" she said. "I thought that was your voice."
She was pleased, smiling her crooked alligator smile.

"Afternoon, Vanessa," Will said still more loudly.

"Well what have you heard?" she said. "What a horrible thing!" She came over and, though it was bad for her, took two cookies. "Mmp!" she said. *Grick, grick.* She was a loud chewer.

Again he told his story, all but the picture. The truth came clearer and clearer as he told it, as though it were Ben who was telling it. Vanessa sat now squeezed between the table and the bathroom wall, hands leaning on the edge of the table, exactly as her husband's were, except when she reached to the cookie plate. Her cotton-colored hair flew around her head like fire.

"We saw him at Hubbard's funeral, you know," she said, meaning Clumly. "He acted odd, we thought."

"So Ben was saying."

"I can tell you I know just how he feels," she said. She sighed, thinking of herself, and took a bite. "I remember how Eva Thompson was, toward the end. It was such a sad thing. She was a wonderful teacher before she got old. But then she got to falling asleep in her classes, and the children were just too much for her. So baffled she used to look sometimes! Poor dear. And she smelled, everyone said." She paused to chew. Then: "Terrible."

"Fred Clumly's hardly to that point," Ben said. He sounded annoyed.

"Oh, I don't mean *that*," Vanessa said. "But he *was* peculiar, at the cemetery. And you know as well as I do what people say." She compressed her lips, then licked.

They said nothing. All four sat considering the tabletop, and Ben seemed as sunk into his thoughts as the Negro boy. Outside, the sky had turned greenish golden now. Storm weather. The tamaracks on the lawn looked darker, and space had taken on a new intensity, like space in a three-dimensional slide viewer. Ben's Holsteins were standing by the barn door at the foot of the slope. It was choretime.

Vanessa said, "The poor Paxtons!"

Even before he had made the adjustment or knew that the subject had suddenly changed, Will Hodge started inwardly, feeling the connection before he knew he was seeing it. That was all years behind them, the Paxton trouble, but for Will Hodge the misery of that time was still alive, however far buried under layers of days. Even now he would sometimes awaken in a sweat, as he'd done then, though his brother Tag's bills were long since paid, and Kathleen Paxton long since hidden away. He never saw the Paxtons any more. Almost no one saw them, for that matter, except Vanessa. Vanessa Hodge saw everyone: she had a hide like an elephant, and she could not tolerate bad blood, broken friendships. So that for all Clive Paxton's dislike for the Hodges, Vanessa had kept touch. She would talk for hours on the telephone with Elizabeth Paxton —not regularly, not more than twice or three times a year, but regularly enough. And at the time of old Paxton's first stroke she had gone to the house with her sympathy and some beans. It was a wonder to Will Hodge Sr that it hadn't killed the old man. But no doubt she had wept and held his hand and overwhelmed him. Her emotions were like a child's, as swift and intense and as innocent, however absurd; as irrational as the emotions of a sheep.

Ben was cleaning his glasses again. The conversation was painful to him, too.

"Elizabeth says there wasn't any will. Clive was superstitious about it, she says. It was as if as long as he hadn't had a will drawn up he didn't believe he could die. And after all those attacks! I imagine you heard how they found him."

"Well now," Ben said.

But Vanessa was a freight train, once she got started. She even forgot to eat. "He was sitting at his desk in the study. Sitting bolt-upright, with his eyes open. He's been practically living in his study, this past year. He couldn't go up and down stairs any more, so he slept in his study on the couch and took his meals there, off a TV tray—so Elizabeth says. They had an oxygen tent right there for him, and all those things they use. She had a terrible time getting him to eat anything, he was so sick. But he still kept busy. He was working on his memoirs—all those trips they used to take through the Genesee Valley, the interesting characters they'd met, and so on. And he still kept his diary. Clive had a record of every day of his life, except for his time in the hospital. But the entries got shorter and shorter, the last few days. And the last night—" She shook her head and rubbed her fingers together. "He seemed to know he was going. On the last page he was just writing 'The End,' Elizabeth said. It was an awful scribble. If only he'd had the sense to write a will!"

Will Hodge scowled. She made it sound like a soap opera.

Ben cleared his throat.

"Poor Elizabeth," she said. "He was sitting in his pajamas and bathrobe, bolt-upright behind his desk. He was so shrivelled his face was like a skull. He was like a child in a grown-up's red bathrobe, she says. How awful it must have been for her, coming in on him like that! Well, there's sure to be trouble enough! It never was a happy family, Heaven knows, and you can be sure there'll be a court case over the money. And how on earth they'll manage to look after Kathleen—"

Will Hodge snorted.

"I wonder if Taggert knows," she said.

Again no one answered. A pain forked up through Will's belly and chest. Even if he did know, what was he to do? Kathleen wouldn't know him—she no longer recognized anyone, as far as they could tell. And the family had no love for him. Even his relationship with the rest of the Hodges was touch and go. It came to him in a flash that Tag *did* know. *That's the reason for all this. He knows. Half out of his mind.* He gave an involuntary jerk, and they looked at him. He made himself calm.

Before Will Hodge was fully aware that he'd stopped thinking about his brother, he found himself toying cautiously, as if at arm's length, with a new idea. Clumly would be at the funeral. Fred Clumly made them all. It was one of his oddities. A man could see him there. Why it was that Hodge wanted to see him, watch him from a distance, was not clear to him; nevertheless, he felt the desire rising like a madness. He felt again the sting of the Salvador woman's accusation and felt again the urge he'd felt then to defend himself, for once in his life take some bull by the horns, strike out, be rid of confusion. Tag, Luke, Will Jr. He saw him fixing the chair in the chickenhouse, hair light as down. The child's face was a blur. With surprising clarity he saw himself standing in the crowd as he imagined Ben and Vanessa had stood at the cemetery, observing the wrinkled grubwhite policeman at the side of the grave, police cap resting on his belly. It was like an image from the Devil, dreamlike, full of some unhealthy pleasure. So he'd felt —it must be three weeks ago now—sitting by the road in his car late at night, with fog spreading out from the marsh between the tarpaper house and the woods, his car full of the stink of old cigarettes, as he watched for the sordid lover of his client's wife to come creeping to the house. He saw Tag sitting at the desk across from his own, feet up, expensive shoes polished like dark brown piano wood. Kathleen had a desk to the left of his. She worked on income tax forms. Will closed his eyes tight.

"Well," Ben said loudly, in a tone that might have been Will Hodge's own, except that Ben's voice was musical, like a voice that might come from a big silver cup, and Will's was like the voice of an empty barn at night, "time to milk the cows." He stood up. Though the Negro didn't move, his eyes came partway to life.

Will got up too. "I'd better get back to town. Thanks for the coffee." His knees were weak.

Now Vanessa got up, awkwardly, as always. She almost knocked Will's cup from the table. "Pooh!" she said. The near-accident upset her.

"Let's go, boss," Ben said. The Negro got up. And now, all standing, they were embarrassed. A calf bawled, down by the barn.

"What on earth made them do it?" Vanessa said. "Why did they have to *kill?*" Her eyes filled with tears, and she took one last cookie for comfort.

Ben mused.

Will, too, understood what she meant. It was fear, no doubt, that made them kill the guard. Not malice, exactly—but more like malice than what went before, the wreck of the Volkswagen. What next? And where would Nick Slater run? And Tag? He almost slipped and said it.

"They were such *strange* boys," Vanessa said, weeping. "Nick especially. You never knew what he was thinking."

"Time will tell," Ben said.

Will Hodge looked at his vest-pocket watch. The numbers, even the hands, were too blurry to read. The face was all gray. "I better run," he said. A whisper. He stepped back to reach behind the Negro to shake his brother's hand. It was an awkward handshake. It wasn't Ben Hodge's nature to shake hands, nor Will's either, for that matter, which was why Ben was looking at him.

"It's just awful," Vanessa said. "You keep wondering—" She limped to the sink with her cup, lips clamped together with grief, and turned the water on. The pump started up in the cellar, thudding like a heart.

"He won't show his face around here," Will Hodge said. "He'd be ashamed."

"Well, we still have some of his clothes," Vanessa said. Ben mused on it, still watching.

The clock struck in the livingroom. Quarter-to-seven.

Will Sr began hunting for his hat and found it, after a moment, on the dish-drainer. "Well, take care," he said. Then, with his hat on, a cookie in his hand, his eyes set thoughtfully on some point in space, he left.

## 7

The idea grew in Will Hodge's mind—or fixation, maybe— as he wound his way up the Creek Road toward Batavia. "The old monkey," he said aloud, but not quite crossly now. The Chief of Police had been sly, no denying that, and Will Hodge had been fooled. It wouldn't have hit him in a hundred years that all Clumly's suspicions of Will Jr and Luke were mere smoke in his eyes, the old man knew as well as he knew his own name who it was that had come and pulled out the floor from under him—from under Clumly. Except that he didn't know the name, and mustn't find out. It was sly and also ridiculous. How long could he hope to keep people confused by a fool trick like that? Except that Clumly was hardly even thinking about that, of course. Stalling for time, snatching at straws. Hodge slid his huge jaw forward and drew his eyebrows down. "Well you've snatched the wrong straw this time," he said. Hodge the avenger. If Walt Cook's dog had run out at him he might have run over him and never looked back. He sat erect as a walrus behind the wheel, his hands stretched out straight in front of him to steer—the spitting image of his father the Congressman, forty-odd years ago, driving his family to church in the great leather Phaeton. His horses were faster than the horses of his neighbors, huge dapple-grays with murderous checkreins and crotches white with nervous sweat. When he passed some neighbor in his country buggy, drawn along by the team he would plow with on weekdays, the Congressman would lift his beaver hat and boom, "Morning to you, Luther!" or whatever the name was, and, "Good morning

there, Mrs. So-and-so!" And then, to his family, "Firm sup-
porters," he would say. "The salt of the earth." Taggert was
only a baby then, a face like an angel's, a smile like all springtime, clean and sweet as an orchard full of apple blossoms.
He'd be sitting on Ruth's lap looking up at the blue and white
sky as though he knew what his proper dominion was, their
mother beside him—a redhead, most beautiful woman in the
world, it had seemed to Will Hodge—and the three older
brothers, Ben and Art Jr and Will himself, the oldest, would
be sitting in the soft leather-cushioned back seat, half-asleep
from the whirr of the hard-rubber tires. The horses cut the
spring breeze like axes. They had the whole world before
them. They commanded it as easily as the green stony hillsides
commanded the Tonawanda Valley, or the Phaeton commanded the high-crowned dirt highway that fell away before them
as yellow as a road in a picturebook. But subtly, so subtly that
no one had noticed the thing as it happened, the might of the
Hodges had sifted between their fingers. Betrayed by life itself.
The richest farm country in New York State had mysteriously
grayed: the land had quit; stone fences had fallen into disrepair; the Guernsey dairies—best dairies in the world—had begun to give way to Holstein dairies, quantity over quality; and
then price supports came, and the hard-kernel wheat that grew
nowhere else in America as it grew in New York State was
swallowed up in the indifferent bins of Government to mold
and fester as though it were common wheat. Then at night the
wooden-wheeled milktrucks from Buffalo pulled over into the
weeds and stopped, and the drivers got out at riflepoint, and
bent-backed farmers in bib-overalls, with red farmers' handkerchiefs over their noses, yanked out the bungs of the milk-
tanks and the milk went back to the land. "It's criminal! Monstrous!" said Hodge's father. But he knew who they were, and
he made not so much as a gesture toward naming their names.
And then—Hodge's father a blind old man now, baffled and
lost—then came machines. The holy silence of the steam age
passed, the enormous steam tractors that moved along on their
ridged iron wheels with no sound but the bending of the grass,
the slap of a beltseam striking the pulley, an occasional hiss
like the sigh of a dinosaur dying. Instead of all that came the
roar and clatter and pop of gas engines. He'd mowed hay—
Will Hodge—with the quiet team, no sound in his ears but the
creak of the harness and the clicking of the sicklebar. But now

he careened on a high gas tractor with spiked iron wheels, and
the sound in his ears was like mountains falling in. There was
no more use for thrashing gangs, or those big thrashers' meals,
or the talk. There were combines, balers, cutting-boxes; the
time was coming when a farmer could work his land all alone,
as solitary as the last living man in the world. So that not only
had the land gone bad, the heart had gone out of it, too. Only
Ben had stuck with it, that world that had seemed to lie splen-
didly before them. Ben the mystic. Art Jr, inheritor of the old
man's gift for tinkering, had become an electrician, a supervi-
sor now at Niagara Electric: a good man, gentle, not a mystical
bone in his great square body, with opinions as straight and severe as wires, a sad man, however unbent and unbroken,
weighed down by his whalish wife and family as cruelly as a
man pinned under a tree. And their sister Ruth, inheritor of
the Old Man's gift for organizing, had run away with a tele-
typist, a union organizer as full of rage as an iron stove: who
had baited them all, in his younger days, scorned all their Upstate Republican opinions, knew curious facts and doubtful figures, could cut like a knife—a man no more willing than a
knife to hear reason and who felt no need to, omniscient as
God—but drew older, for all he could do to prevent it (for all
his two-hundred-dollar suits, that sharp handsome face that
made the Hodges in the room seem as blunt as old turnips, for
all his knowledge of baseball and football, or the grayblue
Porsche or the pointed shoes) grew older in time, and even
mellow, so that the last years of Will Hodge's mother's life, he
would come to visit her, more welcome even than her sons by
blood, for he understood women as no Hodge could, not even
the Congressman himself, and more welcome for other reasons
too: because he came by choice, by an act of will, a decision
of kindness, and if they too were kind it was the kindness of
nature: only in staying away could they have acted by choice.
The hundredth lamb. Also, he loved her. Now Ruth had a
nursery school, the best in Rochester. As for Taggert, the child
with the angelic face, the most brilliant of the lot, a mind as
wide as the Congressman's, one would have said, if he only
could have gotten himself collected, and a heart no less gentle
than his father's was—he was gone, for all practical purposes
dead. (His fire-blasted face rose up again in Hodge's mind and
shocked him cold.) Tag had half-ruined the practice their
father had left them—it had taken Will Hodge ten years to re-

build it—and had fled the state, could never return, must
waste his mind and all his learning as a janitor in a public
school, or a salesman of used cars, or a peddler. Lord be with
us. There had been no way to help him, and it wasn't safe to
try, Will Hodge had found. He'd come back just once, to hide
in Will Hodge's house and see his children, and before Will
Hodge was aware of what was happening his brother Tag had
vanished with his boys, taking Will Hodge's car. He'd mailed
back the keys from Cleveland. Not that Hodge blamed him.
"You'd have done the same thing yourself," Ben had said, and
Hodge had thought about it. He wasn't sure one way or the
other. In any case, Tag had been their hope, or at any rate so
it seemed now to Hodge, and Tag had failed them, or rather,
life had failed Tag. His malpractice was no matter of choice.
Poor devil had been driven half out of his mind and, hard as
he worked (except that that wasn't quite right either), it
wasn't enough. His wife was a sick woman, losing her mind,
and because he was Tag—inheritor of the Old Man's vanity,
too—he could not tell them about it, ask for help like an ordinary man. Millie had said—Will Hodge Sr's wife had said—oh
a thousand times she must have said it: "You knew. You *must*
have known." And the truth was, Hodge had known. "You *destroyed* him," she said. Her face shone with twenty-five years'
worth of hate, a face as beautiful and cold as a diamond on a
drill-bit, and Hodge said, "Faugh." He had destroyed him.
Yes. Had helped, or not helped against it. But Tag had little
by little rebuilt what he could from his rubble. He'd remarried,
brought up his children, transplanted to Phoenix; a cartoon of
their father's identity. He'd even borrowed the Old Man's
name. Poor devil. Christ forgive us.

"Paxton's dead," he said as though his brother were there in
the car with him.

But Tag would know by now. Millie still kept touch, that is,
wrote to him, though she never got a letter back—fond of Tag
because Tag was an ally, a fellow destroyer of the Congressman's image, whether he wanted to be or not. She'd have written; maybe it was that that had brought him here. What was *he*
thinking—that great, corrupted mountain of political and private craft, lying there staring with empty sockets at his coffin
lid? *The world will learn. Sure as day. But not from me.*

Hodge grunted. "Well, poor Paxton," he said aloud. He
thought of Clumly.

There was a sharp, ugly smell in the downstairs hall, and he paused a moment, scowling. "Something burning," he said. The smell was so thick it was impossible to know where it came from. "Hang," he said fiercely. "I must've left the kettle on."

He caught hold of the railing and went up the carpeted stairs to his apartment as quickly as he could pull his weight along, then hunted in the dimness of the hallway for his key. Puffing, still muttering angrily to himself, he got the door open and went in. But there was nothing on the stove in the kitchen. He stood scowling, jaw protruding, still holding the key in his hand. The sky beyond the kitchen window was darkened now —there was a shower of a rain building up—and it threw a green cast across the gray of the floor and the pale blue of the kitchen walls. "Must be downstairs," he said. He pocketed the key and hurried back down, puffing, slapping his hand on the railing as he went. Mrs. Palazzo's door was open. He stuck his head in and called to her. No answer. He called again. He wiped away the sweat that was dripping into his eyes. The smell was intense here, and he was afraid to wait longer. He went down the long hallway, calling "Hello?" ahead of him and came to the kitchen-dinette. That was it, all right. The saucepan on the stove was bright red and collapsing, the bottom melting into the burner. "Holy Crimus," he said. He turned off the burner and went to the sink for a towel and caught hold of the melting handle to pull away the saucepan. "Consarned devil of a thing," he said to himself. "Where the heck did that woman go?" The back door was open. He went over to close it, reflected for a moment, then stepped out onto the porch to look around. No sign of her. Smell of ozone in the air. Lights were on in the back windows of the houses on the next street. He went back into the house, muttering, and began to look through the rooms, snapping on the lights. His heart was racing now, and he was sweating rivers. The TV was on in the front parlor, but the sound was turned off. On the coffeecart there was a kitchen glass with wine in it. "Darned strange," he said, lowering his eyebrows until his eyes looked like caves. Suddenly he was afraid. The house was dangerously quiet. He shuddered. He left the room at once and went across the yard to the next-door neighbors.

No one had seen her. But in the warmth of the toy-cluttered livingroom, with his neighbor on the lumpy yellow couch with a bottle of beer on his stomach—Joe something, Hodge had forgotten the name—the panic he'd felt seemed childish. "I just wondered if she might have come over here and got talking," Hodge said.

"Nope," his neighbor said.

The wife said, holding a baby in her arms, "Why don't you try Faners? That's probably where she is." Her hair was black and stringy.

Hodge nodded. "Thanks. I'll try there." He watched Ed Sullivan waving his unfriendly arm at the glittering curtain. "Ladies and gentlemen—"

The wife said something and he missed the name of the performer, but it was a man, tall, with a fat face. He smiled and bowed all around and began to yell. He looked insane, and it made Hodge shiver.

"Want a beer?" Joe said.

"No thanks. I better run along."

A boy with huge eyes and a dimple peeked from behind the ironing board piled high with clothes. He had a blond crewcut, and at first it looked as if his head had been shaved. Hodge nodded, said his thanks again, and went out.

The Faners, on the other side, had not seen her either. She probably went to the corner store, they said. She was probably right in the middle of cooking and she found she was missing something—cinnamon, you know, or salt, or something—so she ran to the store. Got talking. That's probably what happened. Hodge saw that they were right. The truth was that the grim business down at the police station had shaken him about as badly as a man could be shaken—the blood in the hallway, and Clumly's strange behavior, and then that Salvador woman throwing all the blame on him. He saw the picture in his mind again, more clear than the porch where he stood.

"You want me to come over with you, Will?" Bob Faner said, standing at the door. He looked up at the gathering clouds.

"No, no," Hodge said. "Don't trouble. I just thought I'd check. I'm sure everything's all right."

Faner looked at him and smiled vaguely, still willing. He was tall, silver-haired. Looked a little like a minister.

"Thanks again," Hodge said.

"No trouble at all, Will," he said. "If you need me just say the word." He laughed. He was a good man, Faner. A dentist.

And so he returned. He entered the front door muttering crossly, annoyed that he'd gotten himself upset, and he went up the front stairs slowly this time and paused at the top for a full minute to catch his breath and quiet his jangling nerves. He opened his door. "Dang monkeybusiness," he said to himself. He snapped on the light. The real point, it came to him in a rush of anger, was that Clumly's tomfoolery was dangerous. If he did get hold of Tag . . . Who could know for sure what that Tag was capable of? Who knew what Nick himself might do, for that matter? He was a scared boy now. Again Hodge was shaken by a rush of mingled terror and guilt, as if every word the dead policeman's mother had said were true. He made himself coffee at the kitchen sink, using hot water from the faucet, and started for the bedroom with it to change his clothes. Still the house was unnaturally quiet, as if hiding something. Through the livingroom window he saw a flash of far-away lightning. A shiver ran low on his back, between his shoulders. When he pushed open the bedroom door, the light from behind him broke across open dresser drawers and clothes strewn all over the floor.

"My God!" he said. The coffeecup rattled on the saucer in his hand. He put the cup down on the dresser quickly, without even stopping to snap on the light, and went for the phone beside the bed. There was no dial tone. It was cut. Hodge wiped his forehead with the back of his sleeve. He was shaking and his hands were hot. When he looked back toward the lighted doorway he saw Mrs. Palazzo, like a propped-up doll, sitting against the darkness of the wall with her head tipped onto her shoulder. Her dead eyes shone.

*But not from me,* they said.

And now the house was full of noise, a roar like wind in a cavern, and he smelled her blood.

"Tag," he whispered. "Tag! *For the love of God!*"

# IV

## Mama

---

*The story seems to begin with the creation of mankind by the goddess Mama.*

—A. Leo Oppenheim, Ancient Mesopotamia

It was late afternoon. Every line of the enormous willow trees on each side of the road, every rut and tuft of grass and weedy pile of round gray stones on the hillside pastures, every crack and shingle on the black barn standing severe as the angel of death on the nearest of the hills—on its roadward side the sharp white warning: *Chew Red Man Tobacco*—was unnaturally precise, as though time and motion had stopped and the world were a corpse. Nothing moved but the truck, its shadow flying beside it like a monstrous owl hunting, dropping for an instant where gullies fell away below the road, briefly rising where the macadam skirted a knoll, dangerously swift. The light on the hills was green. There was a storm coming.

Under her wide black brand-new hat, Millie Hodge sat erect

and rigid as a stake, on principle showing no sign of leaning when the antique truck hurled into a curve—the right wheels spitting up gravel from the shoulder to strike at the floorboards like rattlesnakes at a pane of glass, the shuddering truckfenders barely missing the white triangular concrete posts —merely tensed the muscles of the arm lying flat on the window to the right of her and braced her left foot more firmly on the littered red rubber mat, her left leg a shaft of iron below the relaxed right leg crossing the left at the shin, the right foot casually tapping air with the deadly precision of a clock. Even if he were to roll the truck over the embankment into the Tonawanda, brown-green and motionless in August, thick as bad soup and faintly smelling of city sewage and horse- and cow- and pig-manure from the outer edges of Buffalo and the heart of Batavia and the villages, barnyards, hundred back pastures it slid down through—even if he were to slam the truck into a concrete abutment—she'd be outside the reach of her son's childish anger, invulnerable even if he killed her, which he would not. Not on purpose. The narrow macadam road straightened out, falling away through an arch of darkening basswood trees toward the railroad underpass where long ago she had stood every Monday and Wednesday evening waiting for a lift to Batavia. Luke slowed a little, not bothering to pretend he had not sped up to scare her on the curve, then stepped on the accelerator again for the approach to the underpass and the hairpin curve just beyond. It was a blind curve, and if they came on some lumbering piece of farm equipment there they would be done for: he was not the expert driver he liked to think. She was afraid, all right. If shouting at him would have stopped him, she would have shouted; but it wouldn't, and she did not waste her shouts or curses or tears on nothing. It was a cunning she had been born with, to know what she could do and couldn't and when helpless to keep it hidden, watch and wait; or a natural cunning refined after fifty-two years into an art. She was a bitch. She made no bones about it. (So Millie Hodge, teeth clenched, her hat pinned firmly to her head, the wind snapping strands of her tightly pinned hair.) Bitchiness was her strength and beauty and hope of salvation. Luke's bitchiness was inept and sentimental by comparison, mere callow petulance. He had no philosophy. He took it on faith that the curve would be free, that the truck would not be smashed to atoms against some cleat-

track diesel tractor or buried under crazily tilting wings in the
iron womb of a baler. She herself never made such mistakes,
had not made them even when she was young.

But the curve was free, and the truck rushed on, past Webb's
and Burkmeister's and Ford's and Mahoney's, the motor
screaming like a buzz-saw cutting through ironwood, the rat-
tles from every hinge and bolt filling the cab with a noise like
chattering leaden bells or wasps stirred up to rage. She did not
need to look at her son to know that his jaw was tightly set,
his witch's eyebrows slightly drawn in, his gray eyes glinting,
unblinking, like a madman's. *Little bastard,* she thought; and
even though his troubles were unreal, mere play troubles, neurotic phantoms, she was sorry for him; coldly, objectively, but
also bitterly sorry that he had to be young, if only for a time,
and idiotic. His temper fits gave him splitting headaches—histamine headaches, according to the doctor in Rochester. (He'd
diagnosed it even before he'd heard the symptoms, or so he
claimed later, from no more than a glance at Luke's painfully
flawless handwriting. He was a cocky man, the doctor, red-
and round-faced as a wino, and ugly, sitting with his legs
apart, soft hand lovingly laid on his crotch.) They were half-
day-long sieges of pain that would fill up Luke's skull, more
fierce than the fiercest hangover, until he could see, hear, think
of nothing but the dry fire in his brain, and at last he would
faint. He'd been born unlucky: he had an enormous tolerance
for pain.

But he would not lose consciousness now, while he was driving. If the headache were that far along he would long ago
have forgotten his anger, would have forgotten even what
steering wheels were for; he would be clinging to her hand, his
eyes clamped shut, beyond even praying that he might pass
out, merely waiting for it, and she, Millie Hodge, with heart
painstakingly fashioned of ice, knowing herself beyond any
trace of ordinary motherly hate or love (crushed tight, until
time if it moved all around her had nothing left to do with
her), would be wishing with every nerve in her body that the
burning brain were hers, not his. Not because he was her son
and not for duty or charity or guilt. She'd been through it
many times, a thing far worse for her than for him because
Luke knew nothing, in that last hour, while her mind rushed
on over thoughts as precise and sharp as the rods of an iron
fence: had been through it and out of it to the light again,

forced into the shabby role for which she had not the faintest desire and from which she drew, she devoutly believed, no satisfaction (she knew what satisfaction was, knew where she would prefer to be)—the role of God or archetypal mother or stone at the center of the universe—because by senseless accident she had borne sons. *I exist. No one else. You will not find me sitting around on my can like some widow, or whining for the love of my children.*

Half a mile from the old place he began to slow down, and the feeling of dread that had been waiting far back in her mind, closed off like a room ghoulishly sealed up after the death of a child, opened suddenly to her consciousness. Already they were passing the century-old stone wall half-buried in woodbine and purple nightshade, and pear and apple and cherry orchard, the remains of the vineyard now grown up to thistle and ragweed and Queen Anne's lace. They came to where the tamaracks stretched dead limbs across the road, throwing parallel arched shadows like the bones of a fish—the truck moving quietly now, and slowly—and she knew he was going to stop. *Damn him to hell,* she thought. As always in the light of a late afternoon before a storm, the place was unreal, a scene from some greenish, dimly remembered childhood dream that hovered between the hope of escape and nightmare. She compressed her lips, the rush of strong, indefinite emotions channeling efficiently into anger. She said, "Why are you stopping?"

He ignored her. "Stony Hill Farm," he said. He smiled, lugubrious, and as always when he smiled the center of his forehead pinched down and the outer ends of his eyebrows lifted, making him look more than ever evil, witchlike (but artificially so: she had watched him practice it in front of their oval bedroom mirror as a child, and later, when Luke was in his teens, she had watched him put it on for girls, poor adorable Werther, born for woe—with ears sticking out like Dumbo's) so that for an instant her anger became mingled pity and disgust. He said: "The dear old homestead of the Hodges. Will you look at that!" His voice was thin and intense. The headache was bad now, she knew, and she thought, *Good.* But the easy spite brought no pleasure. He had never lived there, and his reasons for wanting to have lived there or to live there now, claim Stony Hill for his barony, were repulsive to her;

nevertheless his grief and indignation were as real as if their cause were real. Somehow, God knew how, she was to blame, and his anger was just. She felt a sudden, sharp desire to be somewhere thousands of miles away—in some German university lecture hall, or walking in London early in the morning, or sitting on worn old steps in Rome, with her shoes off, a scent of sewage and flowers in the air.

"I said, look," he said. All righteousness.

As if casually, she turned her head.

Nothing she saw shocked her. She had expected and grown used to it long ago. She had planned it, in a way, or so it seemed to her now—as to him. She had perhaps begun planning the destruction of Stony Hill years before she knew she was going to get it from the Hodges and sell it for trash. Though she knew there were people living there—the Negroes Will Jr had found for her when she wanted to sell it—it looked abandoned, the wind-wrecked remains of a farm no longer fit for an Arab to pitch his tent on, or a shepherd to put up his sheep in. Only a small patch of the wide, sloping lawn was mowed, a square directly in front of the balustered and pillared porch. The rest of it, to the left and right and rising beyond the deeply shadowed walnut trees to the nearest of the barns, was grown up like fallow pasture except for, here and there, a burnt-out black patch where it looked as if some dragon had recently lain. The globes she remembered on the lightning rods of the three barns visible from the driveway gate were gone now, the rods themselves crooked or broken off. The high, square silo was precariously tilted, and patches of siding were missing from the barn walls. But the house was worse. The pillars on the front porch were gouged as if by woodpeckers, there were squares of cardboard in some of the windows, nothing was painted, nothing any longer upright. A wide new door had been neatly sawed into the side of the house, the wooden frame left unpainted, and over the gap hung a Sears Roebuck aluminum screen with a large italic *M*. There were toys lying here and there in the grass, half hidden —a mud-caked bicycle, a rust- and oil-blackened wagon—on the porch steps a naked, headless doll. In the shelter of the wide old walnut trees there was a black Cadillac with a heavily pitted chrome visor.

"It must give you great satisfaction," Luke said.

Her anger rose sharply, but she said, "You'll never know the half of it." She sounded calm and collected. *A place for doleful creatures, a dance of satyrs.*

He shifted into low and the truck jerked forward. He was squinting badly, and, precisely though Millie Hodge understood the familiar chaos of her emotions, there was nothing she could do against the touch of nausea rising and growing inside her like ugly weather. It was unreasonable that she should be asked to regret for his sake what had nothing whatever to do with him, nothing even to do with his father, little as Luke might understand that; and unreasonable that merely because she was there she should be asked, required, to endure his childish and confused vengeance for wrongs in which she had no part. He was a baby, a twenty-two-year-old baby: the slightest cut, the slightest affront, and home he came howling to mother, the source of all grief. *I'm sick of it*, she thought, but even as she thought it she knew it was rhetoric.

(She had waited in the livingroom, pretending to read the novel that had come from an old friend, male, that afternoon, knowing Luke would be purposely late and carefully not worrying when the time they had agreed on came, but worrying in spite of that, growing angrier with the passing of each of the minutes she had known would pass, because Luke was childish—she could never be sure *how* childish—and because she, Millie Hodge, self-regarding bitch, as she described herself, invincible to all reasonable and honest attacks, had been forced again into the silly and degrading role of poor suffering Mama. He had been betrayed by his Indian boy; he'd broken out of jail. The minute she'd heard it—Ben Hodge had told her, stopping by with some of that honey from his bedroom wall (inedible, as always, yellow-gray and specked with unidentifiable pieces, wings maybe)—she had known she was in for trouble. Within half an hour—Ben Hodge was barely out the door—Luke had called, asking if she'd come to supper. "Why Luke!" she'd said coyly, well aware that the girlish act repelled him, but not aware until later just why she'd turned it on. Luke had ignored it. So far he was only upset, he hadn't yet distorted the Indian boy's trifling betrayal of Luke's ridiculous faith into something cosmic, unavengeable except on his mother. Or at any rate—since he'd called, after all—he had only just now begun to distort it. There was a pause, after she'd accepted—no sound but the inevitable humming and

clicking of Luke's country line—and she had said sympathetically, "Ben was here. He says Nick's broken out of jail." Luke
had said, "Yeah. Bastard." That was all. But she had known
(waiting like Whistler's Mother in the livingroom) what
Luke's irritation would lead to. When he arrived not in the car
but in the pick-up truck—but at least, thank God, it wasn't the
semi—she knew he was angrier than she'd expected, and she'd
taken a quick Miltown before going out to him. She'd said
only, "Hail the late Mr. Hodge!" "Car wouldn't start," he'd
said. She'd said, "No, I imagine.")

They had crossed Route 20 and were climbing the Attica
hills, toward Luke's farm overlooking the Attica Prison.

She said, half by accident, "Beautiful time of day."

"I hadn't noticed," he said.

"Well do notice. Don't be a philistine."

"Oh, I come by it naturally enough." He stared fiercely
ahead, fists clenched on the steering wheel; and almost without
thinking, as lightly and quickly as she'd have swatted a fly, she
said: "Not on *my* side." Instantly she saw she'd cut deep, and
she realized what she'd realized before and conveniently forgotten a thousand times, that Luke could cut, but he couldn't
take it—or no, worse: he couldn't even cut; would say merely
childishly snippy things so far from the mark that they carried
no sting, then would wither at just one word from her because
she knew every sore spot he had, all sixteen hundred and six
of them and all with one name: Father.

"You," he said, choking, "what would *you* know?"

"Skip it," she said. He was speeding up though, taking the
curves too fast already—the cars on the lower road, half a
mile down, had their lights on, and the sky, the creek far below them, the dirt road ahead of them were gray, the hills,
stretching away toward the town of Wyoming, black. In studied slow-motion she got out a cigarette and lit it. "Why do we
put up with each other?" she thought. But the time wasn't
right for saying it. "It's turning out to be one hell of a date,"
she said.

"Stop it," he hissed.

*I exist; and nothing else. No one sees me.*

(Seven-thirty, according to her watch. If she hadn't had to
come hold Luke's hand she'd be riding up the Thruway now
with Sol Ravitz, to the lecture at Buffalo U. She'd be sitting
laughing and smoking and talking, telling him he hadn't the

faintest idea what Plato meant by imitation, because Sol liked being attacked head-on—and because it was true, he really was all confused about Plato—and she would feel unnaturally alert, alive, both her body and her mind; would be conscious —as though she were balanced on a tightrope—of the distance between himself and her and the distance between herself and the door on her side: conscious that she smelled good, that when he glanced over at her she was pretty, so that sooner or later it would occur to even Solomon Ravitz that perhaps after the lecture and the drinks, coming home along the Niagara River or driving through the park, they might stop for a little; she might not take offense. She thought, *I have my world.* They had come, in her mind, to where blue-white lights splayed over the Thruway, impersonal and stark as the lights at the prison, to their left and right the outlines of tall buildings, the lights on the far-off office windows as precise and clean-cut as stars. The night air would be thick and warm, tinged with the smell of the chemical plants a mile away, and with the city all around them, the cold lights on the pavement, the car would be cozier than ever, the conversation full of overtones Sol would not yet be catching. "It's absurd to trace art to ritual," she said. "It's as silly as saying sex began as religion." He glanced at her, smiling. It came to her that what she was saying was truer than she'd realized at first. "Art and sex are very much alike," she said. "I suppose the similarity is the reason for Freud's mistake." "What I like about you is your humility," he said. She blew smoke at him and laughed. When she reached to the ashtray to scrape off her cigarette her hand was less than four inches from his, and she concentrated on the flutter of excitement she felt, wondering if he too felt it now and whether he ever felt it any more with his fat, stupid wife. It was impossible that he should, she knew. Perhaps he was not repelled by her, as she had been repelled for God knew how long, living out her best years with Hodge. But the thrill was dead, inevitably; created to die from before the beginning, like all illusions, and impossible to revive except feebly, momentarily, when one happened to be made jealous. "Love is revolt," someone had told her—Stanley Burrish, when they met in San Francisco three years ago—and it was true. A flight from the humdrum, from reality: you shucked off all you had been before and the world that went with it, you became the enemy of the universe and imagined your lover to be another just like you, and so for a moment the two of you were free, lifted out of all ordinary dullness, out of the old vulnerability, became godlike or childlike or a little of both, and the world, no longer a fence around you, was beautiful. So that love was doomed, the new world sickened like the old. Move on. She stood in a white dress waiting at the underpass, half a mile from the paintless tenant-house where her father sat on the porch staring, spitting sometimes, his mouth sunk until the tip of his nose almost touched his chin, cracks of black dust encircling his neck, a ne'er-do-well, but no worse than her mother who whined and cried and peopled the yard with worthless Jewels, the boys doomed to tenant-farming like their father, or to factory work, or to working as guards at the Attica Prison, the girls doomed to whining and childbirth and sour old age: but not Millie, waiting in a white dress, standing erect and dignified (she was sixteen), as casual and as wide awake as a lynx. She knew the lights of the Hodge Pierce Arrow the minute they appeared at the top of the hill, and she put her hand out awkwardly, as though she did not know how to hitchhike. She waited until they had already seen her before she smiled as if with pleased surprise. More often than not it would be Ben, and he would tip his cap grandly, like his father at election time, and say, "Millie Jewel!" as though he too were surprised. Ben was a year older than she was, in Millie's opinion the most beautiful boy on earth. He drove with his left hand clinging to the windshield post, all the windows wide open, the leather top roaring behind her ears, his right hand not closed on the steering wheel but walking it with his fingertips. He would say, "Where tonight?" "To class," she would say, and he would smile, kind, as though there were a sweet, sad secret between them, and she would think, terribly moved, *Oh Ben, Ben!* but would stay where she was, pressed to her door, erect and polite, smiling.

One night she said, "Where are *you* going, Ben? There a track meet tonight?"

He glanced at her, thoughtful, then grinned. "A practice, sort of."

"I hear you're very good," she said.

He laughed. "People lie. I'm miserable, but the others are even worse."

"I wish I could see you sometime," she said. (She had seen him many times, in fact—watching from the end of the foot-

ball field. He had powerful shoulders and powerful legs and a waist like a girl's. When he stabbed the pole in the box and twisted upward, his bare feet pointed like a diver's, rising smoothly, as if in slow motion, his dark hair would fly over his face and stay there until he was above the bar, turning and arching over, quick, like a fish leaping, and then when he snapped back his head and shoulders, his hair would fall into place again, as though the whole trick were not missing the bar but preserving one's grooming. She had seen him flip off balance once and drop flailing into the sawdust, and she had seen that when he got up he was limping and one leg was bleeding, spiked. She had wanted desperately to run to him, but she had been afraid. She had covered her eyes, sick, and that night, walking alone in the pasture, she had cried, and had called in the darkness courageously, "Ben! Oh, Ben, Ben!")

Ben said, "Believe me, you're not missing a thing." Then, quickly, as though the talk made him nervous: "How's class?"

"It's awful," Millie said. She added at once, because she'd let out more emotion than she'd meant to, "But no doubt it will improve my character. I'm going to be much, much nicer once I learn French. You wait and see."

He laughed. After a minute he said, "Why French, though?"

Her cheeks burned and she wanted to say something withering, but she could only say, defiantly, "Why not?"

He smiled as if from infinitely above her. "Everybody who's anybody speaks French, right? And you want to be anybody." He shook his head.

"Anybody but who I am," she said, confused. Again she knew she ought to lighten it, but she couldn't seem to think clearly. Ben looked at her as if studying her features closely for the first time.

At last he said, his voice strangely like his father's all at once, "You're a nice girl, Millie."

She thought her heart would break. "No I'm not," she said. "I'm a bitch."

He said nothing. The Hodges didn't use words like that. The mistake reawakened her to the abyss between them: she might as well have decided to fall in love with a statue of King Edward. She remembered—this time with more horror than usual—the victory party her father had taken her to at Stony

Hill. There were lanterns along both sides of the road and over the gates and hanging from the huge dark trees in the yard. On long white tables beside the driveway there were cider barrels and paper cups—the first paper cups she'd ever seen—and wherever you looked there were women in beautiful long colored dresses and men with suits on. Even the boys had suits—Ben, Art Jr, Taggert, and the oldest, the funny one, Will—suits from Washington, D.C., her father told her, and their sister had a full-length gown (it was pink), like the grown-ups. Their father the Congressman stood on the porch, white-headed and terrifying, as big as a house, shaking hands and offering sweet cider toasts and laughing like a railroad engine. And *her* father—oh honey-sweet balls of Christ!—stood spitting tobacco, his striped Sunday pants tied on with a rope, his hair sticking up like the bright blue bristles of a burdock.

She said, "Excuse my French."

Ben laughed. "No harm. I know how you feel."

"You don't," she said. "You really don't know at all."

"Don't be too sure," he said, smiling. It was merely a pose, and he knew it as well as she did. Nevertheless, she was flattered and excited. He was so handsome she thought she might die of a heart attack.

They'd come almost to Batavia, to make things worse, and she was feeling the sensation like homesickness that always came when she knew her ride with Ben was almost over. The rolling hills were cleanly outlined and oddly close in the moonlight. It was late May, a scent of orchards in the breeze.

He said, "I was lying before."

"What do you mean? About what?" Her mind plunged into confusion. She felt shaky with guilt, about to hear her worse fears about herself put into words.

He walked his finger up the steering wheel for the turn leading into the railroad crossing. "About track practice," he said. "There really isn't one tonight. But I knew you'd need a ride to town."

"Why, Ben!" she said. Her reeling thoughts fell into sense, as though she were thinking clearly all at once, and more swiftly than ever before. She said, "Why, thank you!"

He laughed. "There, I feel better. Would you like me to pick you up, after?"

*He loves me,* she thought. *Could he?*

Her heart was beating so hard it hurt. "Well—if it's really

no trouble . . ." She pressed her fingertips to her chest to calm the beating, thinking, *If this is love, give me aspirin.* She said, "I really would be pleased, Ben."

"Then I'll be there," he said.

They jounced across the tracks and had half a mile of city streets to pass before they reached the school and the night class, half a mile with nothing to say because they'd gone as far as either of them dared. She sat primly erect, her hands folded (her mother's voice: "Don't you ride with no stranger. Your father's out of his mind, that's all, girl your age running all over the county in the dead of night. Oh what are we comin to! Lord have mercy! And I sweat and I slave and a daughter of mine known far and wide as walking the streets in the dead of night! Your father's out of his mind, he's lost and damned, and us confounded!"). Ben walked his fingers on the wheel and studied each passing tree as if watching for a squirrel, and he whistled "Jesse James." He was safely around the corner, out of sight, and Millie was standing clutching her notebook on the high-school steps, when she began, helplessly, to laugh.)

Luke was scowling at her, irritated by the smile, and she felt old. But he said nothing, turned to look out his window and down the dark hill falling away toward the lights of the prison. His protruding ears were elephantine when you saw him from behind. How sad for a would-be Romantic hero, she thought, and smiled again, detached and wearily fond, as though she were looking at her son from beyond the grave. They turned off the dirt road onto the narrow bumpy driveway that lifted them past the cowbarn and chickenhouse and the parked tractor-trailer to the weedy yard and the house. He stopped the pick-up beside the gas pump, beside the old car, and turned off the motor but left the lights on, shining into the cluttered garage. Unreal. Like looking into a cave by torchlight, or knowing the thoughts of a horse. With the junk out of it, the garage would be wide enough for three good-sized cars, but Luke kept open only space enough for his Chevy coupe, no space for the truck or for tractors. There was an old wooden hammermill—it had been here when his father had bought the place for him—or rather when he'd seized it by foreclosure (Will Hodge Sr was a whiz at that)—huge stacks of half-rotten burlap bags, piled-up used lumber, balls of string, baling wire, axe-handles, rusted milkcans, oil barrels, boxes of bolts, an electric fan for the cowbarn, old radios, frocks, boots, an acetylene torch, bedsprings—the ones the Runians had died on. Here, as at Ben's place, there were swallows' nests on the beams. The whole garage, in fact, showed Ben's fine hand—as though working those summers for his Uncle Ben, Luke Hodge had learned to scorn all his sober, potching father represented, had turned with sudden violence on his father's deliberate, painstaking life of ugly, neat repair: repainted banisters, plugged up holes, jacked up floors, wired up chairs, new lintels for sagging doorways. No doubt it was because of his Uncle Ben, too, that Luke had gotten the Indian. All their lives Ben and Vanessa had been taking in strays—from prison, from the Children's Home, from friends with troubles. And so Luke must do it too, of course. Pass on the kindness, emulate the hero. (It had not occurred to her before. She had taken Luke's own explanation, that Will Jr had badgered him into it. But she knew she was right: it wasn't his brother's fault but his Uncle Ben's; and she was sorrier for him than ever: as always, she'd been there before him.)

She said, "What was he arrested for this time?"

He went on staring into the garage. "Who?"

"Nick, of course."

The corner of his mouth drew back. "Who cares? I come home and they call me up and they tell me he's there, him and his brother. Tried to steal a car from somebody, ended up killing this woman."

"They were drunk?"

"Naturally. Somebody gave the little bastard some booze and he went out helling it up with his brother."

"His brother must be crazy. How old is he?"

Luke shook his head, the muscles of his face tense. "It's not just his brother. It's both of them. He's worse, for Christ's sake."

"Do you really think so?" It was too much to hope for. Luke was a sentimental idiot, and Nick Slater was officially in his keeping.

Luke didn't seem to have heard her.

She said, "Well, you mustn't think about it. It will all come out in the wash. Father will think of—" She paused, distracted by her having slipped into calling him "Father," as though nothing had happened.

Luke groped with his left hand for the lightswitch, found it, and turned the truck lights off. "Let's go in," he said. "I need a fucking pill."

There was a gentle south wind and a flickering of lightning to the west. The air was weighted, the storm much closer now. When she glanced over at the house it looked eerie in this light, as if made not of wood and stone but of strange jewels —of jasper and sapphire and chalcedony and emerald. She shuddered. She jerked at the door-handle until it caught, then forced the door open with her shoulder. When she was down, she saw that Luke had made no move to open his door, sat pressing the heels of his hands to his forehead. She remembered his fierce rage earlier, utterly forgotten now, on his side, at least, as though it were not himself but someone else whose life she had mysteriously ruined—as though he were a four-year-old again, and she his gentle and innocent mother. She thought: *Jesus' nuts.* (Sol Ravitz would be sitting in the lecture hall, his big left hand wrapped around his pipe, pretending he was not still smoking, here where smoking was forbidden, his kingly bald head tipped back as if with arrogance, knees up on the seat in front of him. When the speaker came out—she couldn't even recall who was speaking tonight—Sol would close his hand tightly over the pipebowl, smothering the pipe, and would applaud by slapping his knee with his long right puddingsoft hand with hairybacked fingers. In the row in front of him—Sol would be in the very last row—some college student would be elbowing another discreetly, saying, "You know who that is, the bald one? That's Ravitz, on TV." And Millie, if she were there, would poke him in the ribs and say, "You have been spotted." Ah, how he would grin!) She reached up her hand. "Can I help you down, Luke?" After a moment he slid toward her. "Thank you." There was anger in his voice, but now it was not anger directed toward her. Thinking of Sol, but standing here under the eaves of Luke's garage, giving her son her shoulder to lean on like some long-suffering, docile old mother—aware that whatever was between them, whether his anger or his crippled love, was meaningless, pointless, a time to get through because it was there—she felt a cruel urge to laugh. She stood here for the moment nameless, a human presence, nothing more; a kind of ghost; not out of charity or duty or guilt but because she stood here. "By the virtue of the fact," as Sol would say. Who knew nothing of the virtue of pure fact, fact prior to words, shocking and unnatural.

"I'm all right," he said, shaking her hand loose. He started ahead of her through the darkness of the garage toward the steps into the kitchen. She waited until he had the door open and the light on, then picked her way through the trash. When she reached the kitchen he was already in the bathroom taking a pill, playing his own physician, as usual. He came back at last and went over to the green wooden table and sat down. It wouldn't take long, but it would hold him only for a while. She took off her hat and hung it on the back of one of the green wooden chairs. Then she too sat down. She took her mirror from her purse and once more settled her red-brown hair (but before the rinse it was white as snow). It was soft to the touch. She noted the fact with satisfaction. She lit a new cigarette.

"I'm sorry to be doing this to you," he said. Already the pill was beginning to take effect.

Two steaks lay still wrapped in white butcher paper, oozing blood, on a grease-blackened cookie sheet on the table. It was what he always gave her when he invited her out. It was as if it were all he'd ever heard of. "Shall I put on a barbecue fire?" she said.

"I'll manage," he said. A whine.

"Fine and dandy."

He went on just standing. She wished he would offer her a drink, but she could get by. He would remember when the pain was eased a little more. Outside, the wind was howling now, making the pines moan, a kind of mindless choral singing. He would have to make his fire inside the garage. A clap of thunder shook the walls and lightning filled up the windows. The rain came hard and all at once. In a matter of seconds it was as though it had been raining for hours.

"It must give you great satisfaction," he had said, and she: "You'll never know the half of it." That wasn't exactly true. He would never know the particulars, but sooner or later he would know how it was, when he grew past imagining himself unique and, more ludicrous yet, tragic. What did he do up here nights, alone? Wander from room to room, no doubt, looking at the garbage that had been in the house when his father got it for him, turn the things over in his hands—broken candlesticks, pewter pitchers, books with clumsy old-fashioned engravings, rickety tables, chamber pots, letters—imagining they carried the history not of the Runians whom no one

remembered any more (two old sisters, fat and colorless, with
growths on their necks and arms and legs and protruding
through the cheap cotton-print dresses that covered their loose,
fallen bellies, the last of what might have been despite all evidence some noble old line, or the last except for the dull-wit-
ted nephew who had smashed their skulls with a ball-peen
hammer, imagining the mattresses or cookie jars or the upright
piano to be crammed with a king's ransom in old dollar bills:
finding instead for all his trouble and perhaps grief (because
the nephew had lived with his aunts as a child) nothing but
dust, pressed roses, and corset hooks, so that after he'd buried
his aunts like dead calves in the manure pile—trueborn country boy—and washed the caked blood from his hands and
arms, he'd been too disappointed to run away, too sunk in angry gloom and disgust to talk sense to the Baptist minister
when he came to call, and was waiting there still when two
days later the sheriff came, and was waiting yet, hands folded
on his knees, a mile from here, in the prison)—the history not
of the Runians but of Luke Hodge, Esq., and his ancestors, a
fallen splendor. He was twenty-two and tortured by headaches,
not lucky like his brother or his mother, both of whose nervous troubles showed up in the form of rectal bleeding. So he
had to be excused, for now. He would come to his senses,
eventually. It was a time to be gotten through.

God help us to wise old age.

She had stood on the rock ledge overlooking the quarry, her
hands folded behind her back, Ben standing beside her, his
hands in his pockets. In the glassy water the reflection of the
moon was as clean and distinct as the moon itself, but off to
the right, where the hills rose more sharply and there were lo-
custs and skeletal crabapple trees, there was fog moving in,
coming onto the water slowly, tentatively, like a skater trying
the thickness of ice on a pond. Millie was cold; she'd left her
sweater in the car, but she knew it might be dangerous to admit she was chilly. He might give her his sweater, and then
again he might snap at the chance to take her home. She knew
well enough that Ben felt guilty, bringing her here. All night
she had sensed that there was something troubling his mind.
She would know later that she had guessed at once what the
trouble was, but she had not yet admitted that she knew.

After a long time he said, "It's beautiful, isn't it."

She nodded, knowing he was watching her though pretending not to. "I like it that you like pretty things," she said. She looked toward her shoes, for a moment, embarrassed and conscious that her embarrassment was attractive to him. There was a light wind that picked at her collar and unfurled her skirt, and she knew that that too was good. He slid his hands out of his pockets and folded his arms, and she let her hands drop casually to her sides. Sooner than she had imagined he would dare, he closed his right hand around her left. The reflection of the moon grew sharper.

"It makes you want to make speeches," he said, "or say poetry or something."

"What does?"

He waved toward the water and she laughed.

"I heard you speak, Ben," she said. He had been in the VFW contest. He was the best of them all but his brother Tag had beaten him. All the Hodges had beautiful voices, deep and resonant as their father's, and they looked on a platform as if they'd been born there. Ben talked as if softly, though it filled all the room, and thoughtfully, as if he were letting you hear him think it out for the first time, speeches filled with fine images and pleasant ways of saying things and sudden connections that made your heart beat faster for a minute, so that people leaned forward, here and there in the audience, exactly the way they might lean forward when the pole-vault bar was at eleven feet, higher than any Batavian had in those days ever gone. He was beautiful, splendid, or so she believed; but Tag, four years or more younger than he was, had wild yellow curls and light blue eyes: he could do amazing things with his face and voice, a comedian; he could make you laugh when all your family had just been drownded in a cistern, her mother said. He won not because he was better than Ben but because for a boy of fourteen he was a genius. His speech said nothing, it was out of a library book.

She said again, because he hadn't answered, "I went to the contest and heard you."

He nodded. "I saw you."

"Ben," she said, "tell me what's the matter."

After a long time he said, "Millie, I'm in love with you."

She turned to face him, taking his other hand, dead serious for all her excitement. "Is that so bad?"

He met her eyes, saying nothing, and she thought over and over, like a command, *Ben, kiss me. Ben!* Then suddenly he took her in his arms, and he kissed her lips and cheek and throat, so that she could say it out loud at last, "Oh Ben, my dear, dear Ben!"—or absurdly believed she could, imagining herself unique and, more ludicrous yet, tragic (an error which not even over thirty years later, unconsciously pressing the back of her hand to her forehead, sitting in her son's kitchen, could she fully accept, she knew, for what it was)—and "Ben, I love you, I've waited so long for you to kiss me." His hand came to her armpit gentle, then went to her waist and inside her blouse and brassiere to close on her breast, all his beautiful timidity replaced by a beautiful boldness, and she wanted to scream. Now she was not cold but burning up, saying, "Do what you want with me, anything!" (and saying mentally thirty years later, a word picked up from Solomon Ravitz, *Oy*). He began to take away his hand and she clung to his arm, trying to keep him from it. "Ben, what's the matter?"

He was biting his lips together. "Millie, forgive me."

"For what?" She was frightened, knowing already, having known for hours. "I don't *mind,* Ben. I love you."

But his hand was gone and he had stepped back and stood now with his fist against his forehead. And already she was beginning to hate him, feeling tricked and befouled, seeing him not as tall and splendid but as a hulking baby, sentimental and stupid. "Ben," she said gently, *"why?"*

"I was lying," he said. "How can I explain? I don't love you, it was just that I thought I could get you. From the first time I gave you a ride to town, or even before that, when I would drive past your yard and you'd be sitting on the stump watching the kids, looking pretty, dressed like some kind of hobo's kid. People said—" He stopped and ran his hands through his hair, then slid his hands back into his pockets. He looked sullen, distant.

"Said what?"

"People said you were 'possible.' "

It was as if he had hit her in the stomach. There was nothing she could say: it was as if some kind of skin had been peeled from her eyes and she was seeing the world for the first time as it was. The fog had covered the moon's reflection in the water, but even so every blade of grass, every stipple in the wide flat rock they stood on, every indefinite shadow in the fog was as definite as a razor cut.

She said angrily, "Then why did you stop?" She had not

known what it was she would say, but the moment she said it, something came clear in her mind, not yet risen to her consciousness but there in the darkness waiting, never to be lost.

"How could I?" he said. "It wasn't true. You're good. Kind . . . gentle . . ."

"I *am* a whore," she said. "That is, I'm willing."

"Millie, don't talk that way. You know what you are."

"You're afraid," she said.

"That's not true." He laughed angrily.

She snatched his arms, caught up in something she didn't understand; not love, now. Not desire. "Ben, make love to me. Do it! What difference can it make? I'm Millie Jewel. Have you forgotten? Old Clarence Jewel's daughter. What in hell's the difference!"

He looked at her calmly, pitying her, Christ on the mountain. "You read too much," he said.

She felt crushed, and in the same motion of the mind she was in love with him again, because it was true, he'd seen through what she hadn't seen through herself: she was playing sentimental poor-girl. And she loved him, too, and more than ever, because his tongue was quick. She too had a lightning tongue: he was making a mistake, she knew how to make him happy.

She said, "Ben, how do you know you don't love me? I excite you, you know it. And you think of me at night, the same as I do of you."

He looked at the fog on the water, not thinking about it, she suspected; he had thought about it already. She went on waiting, and at last he looked at her forehead and kept his gaze there as though she had something written on it. "I think of a few minutes with you, not a whole lifetime. I don't know you."

"You do," she said. She opened her arms. "Look."

But he only looked away. "Maybe you're right." He took her hand then (a thing she could not understand even now, squinting at the rain washing down Luke's window) and started back to the car with her. When they got there he opened the door for her, closed it behind her gently, and walked around the front, oddly smiling. He cranked the engine and came around to his side without a word and pulled out onto the road.

"You feel virtuous, don't you," she said irritably.

He nodded.

After a while she said to soften it, though she was lying, "I do too."

When they passed Stony Hill Farm the study lights were on. His father up working, as always, at three a.m. She wondered if Ben was going to get hell when he finally got home. *She* was, you betcha. Her mother would come to the door in her slip, or maybe, if her mother was really angry, her father would come in his gray long johns. Yes, that was how it would be tonight. They would try to whip her, and she would fight back, an old ritual, stupid and boring and almost without passion, the children peeking out from their bedroom like red-eyed mice; it would go on and on and on until at last she began to cry in disgust, and as though a switch had been snapped, it would be over. She began to feel a little sick, anticipating it. She might have years left before she escaped it. Except that one of these nights she would leave. She had thought of it often, and once with frightening clarity, a few nights ago, standing over the well drinking from the red and white tin dipper. As though it were actually happening she had seen herself climbing out her window to the slippery porch roof, dropping her bundle to the dirt yard as softly as possible, swinging over the eaves-trough to the loose porch post as she'd done a thousand times in play, snatching up the bundle without stopping to look back (the house all dark, no sound but the dripping of the cistern pipe and the rattle her father made when he slept) and running for the highway.

Ben sat with his head tipped, thinking, his fingers light on the steering wheel. His lower jaw was pushed forward in that funny way all the Hodge boys had, like their father, a look humorously rueful. It came to her that she had lost him, and almost before she knew what she was thinking she slid over beside him and pressed her head to his shoulder as if sleepily. She'd never been more wide awake in her life. Her left breast still tingled from his touch, and all that he had said ran through her mind, distinct and frightening now, like words in a dream. *I think of a few minutes with you.* She had lolled through daydreams of living as his wife at Stony Hill (it never entered her mind that they might live anywhere else), but she too had thought chiefly of minutes—the few minutes when she saw him next, the few minutes when finally he would make love to her. In her bed, in the dark, she had thought—with an intense sensation of mingled dread, joy, and guilt—of Ben Hodge's secret parts, a quasi-mystical vision compounded of all she had ever seen or guessed, the small naked organs of her little brothers, the hairy erection pictured on a card Sonny Wall had shown her once, the awesome rod and stones on Mr. Kistner's bull. But she saw now, leaning on his shoulder, not visions but lost reality: she would have been a good wife to him, would have borne him sweet children, supported him through troubles, listened to his talk. She would have been a lady, refined and beautiful, all at her ease and never even lifting her voice—like his mother.

It came to her—and she knew it was final—that, one way or another, she would marry a Hodge.

She said as if sleepily, moving her cheek on his arm, "You know, I really don't understand you. What made you stop?"

"Honor," he said.

She laughed, patting his arm. "How dear." She peeked up at him and saw that he was smiling. She said: "What would you do if I took off all my clothes right now?"

"Probably run the car into a tree," he said. A second later he said, startled, "Darn you, I think you'd do it!"

"Nope," she said, smiling. "I've made a great decision."

He crinkled his neck to look at her. "You're going to be a nun."

"Mmm, something like that." She thought about it. "Something very much like that." Then: "Ben, honey, how old is your brother Will?"

He looked at her again, squinting. "Why?"

She kissed his muscle.

It was always the same. By the time they'd finished dessert and coffee, the pain was beginning to overwhelm the pills and Luke was irascible again, baiting her, nagging her as though he did not know as well as she did why they went through these scenes. She could almost wish the bad part would come on him at once, so that the whole thing might be over sooner. She got herself a glass of bourbon from the diningroom cabinet, carried it to the kitchen for ice, stirred it in slowly, knowing he was waiting at the fireplace impatiently, eager to be digging at her again, make her see clearly once and for all that all her life and all her thoughts were hollow sham. That was the bitterest part of it. He was bright. They might have said things to each other. And was it from living with Ben, too, that he'd

learned that awful righteousness? He could never forgive her
for "cheating" on his father. His word, not hers. A child's
word. "Selfish bitch," he'd called her once, he who knew nothing of selfishness or bitchery, no more than he knew of self-
lessness or whatever the opposite of bitchery was (sophro-
syne?), knew only his own colossal ego, too self-centered even
to understand why he couldn't simply dismiss her as evil and
forget it. Sweet Christ how she hated him! But no. No more
than she hated his father. It was past that. Caught in impossibilities, but knowing, at least, why she hated the part of herself
she hated and why she could not escape, ever, for all the grinning cow-catchers and whistling boats and twinkling propellers
in Christendom. *Ah, Christendom!* she thought.

When she reached the livingroom with the drink he was
staring at the door as if he'd been staring at it all the time she
was gone, and maybe he had. "Luke," she said quickly, before
he could speak, "you really should think of getting rid of this
place. You know you're not cut out to be a farmer."

"You'd like that, wouldn't you?"

"My dear child, I don't give a damn one way or the other,
and that's God's truth."

"God's truth," he sneered. He leaned forward in his chair
and pressed his hands to the sides of his head. He was handsome, with his ears covered. All the Hodge features cut fine,
for once: a face triangular as an elf's, a chin square and strong
but small, compared to the others, cheekbones as high as the
Indian boy's. The firelight flickered on his hair and shoulder
and gleamed, bright red, on his shoe. She listened to the pouring rain, another huge shudder of thunder.

"I just think you ought to try graduate school," she said at
last, crisply. "I know you're convinced they have nothing to
teach you, but who knows? maybe you'd find someone who's
almost as clever as you are." It was a stupid thing to say. He
was right to ignore it. She crossed her feet on the hassock and
sipped her drink. At length she said, flip, "You know I'm
right, Luke. Farming's impossible. It's been impossible for
years, unless you're the Bell Telephone Company. Try something where you've got a chance."

"Sure," he said, looking down, grinning horribly.

She sighed.

She felt stifled in his junk-filled house with its high, dark
ceilings, gloomy wallpaper, threadbare floral rugs. A place for

dying, a house for sick old women, not a twenty-two-year-old boy. But maybe it was right. Her son was a sick old woman, not a boy. (He'd come home in the middle of his first semester of grad school at Syracuse—a history major—and had refused to go back. Because of the headaches, he'd told his father, and probably it was the truth, or partly the truth. Pressure could bring the headaches on, they'd found out later from the specialist. He'd moved into his father's apartment—it was not long after their divorce—just two weeks after she'd sold Stony Hill—and had settled down to a life of drinking gin and ice and reaching mysteries and playing his ridiculous banjo. Will had put up with it for a while, as Will put up with everything, potching at the sinktrap with a loose old pipewrench, humming his one tuneless, fragmentary song as though the banjo were not going, refilling the ice-trays which Luke left empty, and going nearsightedly over the papers (talking to himself, scoffing, grumbling) he brought home every night from the office. He had never asked what Luke's plans were. (No one had told her that, but she knew him.) Had merely waited, enduring it because that was his way—Will Hodge had patience where other people had blood, she'd once told him—and eventually Luke's brother Will Jr had said, "Luke, boy, you ought to try your hand at farming. *C'est vrai!* Great emoluments of the spiritual variety in toiling close to Nature." And so his father had gotten him a farm, had foreclosed on the man who'd bought it, with Will's help, from the Runian estate.)

They sat in silence until Luke could no longer stand it. He said, "The cops had me down for questioning this afternoon. D'you hear?"

She glanced at him, then looked into her drink.

"They think I'm the one that let him out, either me or Will. Because we're bad guys." He laughed palely.

"What are you talking about?"

"Somebody let him out, that's all, and they think it was one of us."

"Was it?"

"Why not? Think how easy it would've been. Either one of us could have gone up to Salvador, with a note from Dad, say, or maybe Judge White—*he* wouldn't know what their writing looked like. Or we could've just said we wanted to talk to him, away from the other prisoners. He'd have opened up. Hodges, you know. Grand old Hodges. And it's the kind of thing you'd expect from me or Will. Antisocial. Revolutionary. Dirty Commies."

"Stop it," she snapped.

"Why?"

"It's sentimental tripe. Speech-making. You sound like somebody on TV, full of self-pity. It's childish."

He leaned forward, glaring, and for a moment he couldn't speak. The room filled with the sound of the rain, a rattle like a river going by. He said at last, quietly, driving the words out by intense pressure, "What did you expect us to be? Are *you* a grown-up? Is Dad? How do you think it was all those years, listening to you two bitch, the same old sentences over and over, neither one listening for a second to the other, like a couple of deaf idiots shouting at each other in the dark? Every word he said was moronic, according to you, and any fool could see what *you* said was moronic, not that the Old Man didn't trouble to point it out. And you were the people we were supposed to listen to!—take orders from! Jesus, I'd sit there in the living room hearing you blather at each other out in the kitchen, the Old Man sitting there fuming at the table with his bib tucked under his chin like a baby's, and you slamming around at the sink saying clever clever things like some brat to her mean old papa. Talk about childish! And then you'd go to bed and he'd come in in his stupid damn nightdress and beg you like a kid that can't have candy, and you'd sit there wide-eyed like an outraged little virgin. By God it was an education! Prepared us for the world, that's a fact. The great university, for instance, where the stupidest people you ever saw in your life get to *teach* you. You don't know what it's like. You're so stupid you believe them—or some of them, which is dumber than believing all of them. It's the truth. Listen." He suddenly stood up, as if afraid she would cut him off. "They're like chickens, big fat stupid chickens. They come examine your brain like chickens inspecting the inside of a clock. I had an English teacher, he had us buy an anthology and then he got a different one, and every question he ever asked, the answer was there in that other book. There wasn't one single thing he knew! Not one! But Jesus what a show that horse's ass put on. He had all the gestures. He knew how to make his eyes light up just like a human being. And oh was he kind—to fat, dumb girls. And he would lecture on what trouble they used to have getting the snow cleared off the sidewalks at Hahvid. Yeah. With diagrams on the board. And another one. He taught us how to find symbols in novels. Like this blue parachute that comes down in *Lord of the Flies*. 'Blue,' he'd say. 'What does *blue* make you think of?' He looked like Dylan Thomas, but with yellow hair and pink cheeks. He was in Counter-Intelligence during the War, which is why the fucking War took so long. 'Blue,' he would say. 'Think now. Blue.' Some fat dumb girl with blue pimples would say, 'The Virgin Mary?' and he'd say 'That's it! *That's IT!*' Sweet Jesus please us! One class I was in, the lady brought in a *World Book* salesman. I swear to God. He took half an hour giving his pitch to the whole fucking class. And then the math classes. That was worse. Man would spend an hour writing out on the board the same explanations you could get in the book, except the book was faster and clearer, and he knew it. He cut class maybe twenty-some times in one lousy semester. But history! Jesus!"

"Stop it," she said.

"Let me finish." He was leaning on the mantelpiece now, pressing his hands to the sides of his head. "Everyplace you looked, *children*. You'd see them in the cafeteria primping and preening and puk-puk-padokking, speech-making at each other, some of them, the rest of them nodding, very solemn, as if it were all *oh so interesting*, talking about books nobody past the age of twelve would read all the way through except to punish himself, yammering about Communism and Capitalism and Christianity and the Good Lay, and back in the dorm all the baby professors would do imitations, learning the gestures and the Right Quotations, prattling about Tillich and Bishop Pike and Mr. Fromm, and relaxing their minds in the great American way with talk about baseball and football and cunts, and the brave stupid ones would talk about defending freedom in Vietnam and the cowardly stupid ones would talk about How We Had No Business There, and if you fled to where the intellectuals weren't, it was as bad as anywhere else, cooks, bartenders, ushers at the show, talking talking talking, or standing around like mutes because they hadn't even the brains for *their* kind of talk, not human, kids, not even grade-school age yet, big as they were, or the med-students, the real true anti-intellectuals, with their contests over how many girls they could screw, parties where everybody screwed everybody, eight, nine in a bed. Fun? Christ's hair. But they were great stuff, they thought—all of them, med-school children, bartender children, professor children—they were all somebody; thought they were cops. If a movie came that was supposed to be Art they all sat solemn and said *Look at the Art;* if it was supposed to be funny they all went Ha-ha, if it was supposed to be sad they made crying noises; if they were church types they preached at you, if they were atheist types they preached harder than the others. They kept falling in love, and it was like one huge chorus going up in the park, a thousand voices all howling 'She's different!' But I was ready for it all. I understood. They were children, horse's prick children dressing up. And I was one too, right—the grouchy one that wants to play some other game, because he can't play this one—but say what you like, at least I wasn't fooled. There *are* no grownups. There are only children and dead people. So I quit. *Bon soir, mes enfants.* For which I thank you."

"Are you finished?" she said.

He laughed. "Am I finished. Eschatologically speaking, I am finished."

The glass was empty, and she went to the kitchen to refill it. When she came back he was sitting bent double, his eyes clamped shut. She was glad he was in pain.

She said, "Even raving Communists believe in something."

"All foolish people believe in something."

"Did you let him out?"

He sat perfectly still, the tips of his fingers white with the pressure he was exerting against his temples.

"Did you?"

Still he didn't speak. She waited. He said then, "No. I'd have given my life for him. That's the truth, lady. Fuck it up if you want."

She sighed and closed her eyes, disgusted, then drank, watching him over the top of her glass. *"Why?"*

He turned his head from side to side slowly. "Because he was there."

"You didn't even like him."

He said nothing, and she realized he hadn't heard. "You didn't even like him," she said again.

There was only the rattle of the rain. He drew his head up slowly, his mouth twisted, eyes wide open, and she put down her glass quickly and crossed to him. He was unconscious when she reached him. "Luke," she said gently, emotionlessly. She eased him out of the chair onto the floor, then went to the bedroom for blankets and a pillow. When she had the blankets over him and the pillow under his head, she rose again and went to finish her drink. She stood in front of the window with it, looking out into the darkness. Lightning flashed, and the landscape stood out like a bad memory, then sank once more into darkness. She could see her reflection in the window, and though she knew what it was, it frightened her. The Indian boy was out there somewhere, terrified and dangerous, and she had nothing with which to defend herself. Where would he have gone? On an impulse, she went to the telephone in the kitchen and lifted the receiver. The line was dead.

It came to her then that Nick Slater's brother was still in jail. They'd been arrested at the same time, and if the brother had escaped with him, she surely would have heard. Was it possible then that it really was Will Jr who'd helped him escape? But she knew it wasn't. Who, then? And where was he now?

"Millie, don't be a fool," she said aloud. "Keep your famous wits."

She gathered up the dishes and filled the sink with hot water and soap. The house was full of creaking noises, thumps, scrapings. It made her skin crawl. She closed her eyes, listening, close to tears, and all at once she remembered something. Her father stood in the church doorway, smiling and holding out his arms to her. She ran to him, still crying. She had believed he had forgotten her, had driven home without her, but now he was here, red-faced and beaming, beautiful to her child-eyes, though his pants were baggy, his shirt unpressed, and when she reached him he caught her and lifted her up to hug her, laughing. "Poor baby," he said, "my poor, pretty little girl." And she'd been overwhelmed with the joyful knowledge that her father loved her and she was pretty. She tried to think what had made the memory come, but now again she was hearing the ancient creaking of the house, the rain rattling in the grass and rumbling in the downspout. "Forgive me," she said earnestly, hardly knowing what she meant. She thought she heard Luke moan, and she went over to the door into the livingroom to look in. He lay as before, but she was terrified. A second ago, she was somehow absolutely sure, there had been someone with him in the room.

It was not mere nerves. After half an hour of kneeling on

the floor beside Luke, almost not breathing, she was still dead
certain that there was someone here in the house. There were
perhaps sounds of movement in the adjoining room, or somewhere upstairs, but in the noise of the storm mere sound
meant nothing. The creaking of the floor, the slamming once
of a door upstairs, meant no more than wind. What was definite was the smell. It was subtle, but it was as surely there as
the fireplace or the full-length windows that showed her only
her own drawn face. Her terror had calmed to a numbness
now. She tried to think. She was afraid to go to the phone and
call the police. (She had now forgotten that it was dead.) The
intruders might be standing, listening, behind the nearest door.
And she was afraid, too, to run out for help and leave Luke
alone. At least she wasn't in immediate danger. They knew she
was here. It was her return from the kitchen that had made
him—them perhaps—flee from the room. Perhaps what she
ought to do was stretch out on the couch and sleep, let them
take what they wanted and go. But it was impossible. What
she really ought to do was get a drink. She thought about it
for a long time—there was still no definite sound of their
movement in the rooms around her—then got up and started
toward the kitchen. She moved slowly, talking to herself as she
walked—in order to let them know, if they were there, that
she was coming. No telling what they might do if she were to
startle them. She paused at the kitchen door to say "What was
I after? Oh yes, a drink." *Oyez, oyez, oy* came senselessly into
her mind. She took a deep breath and went in. The room was
empty. She went to the refrigerator, got out the ice-tray, and
dropped four cubes into a glass. She filled the glass nearly to
the top with bourbon and, after a moment's reflection, decided
to carry back both the glass and the bottle to the living room.
She amazed herself. Her hand was absolutely steady, and despite the whiskey she'd drunk already, earlier tonight, her
mind was as clear and sharp as a day in winter. Because of
Luke, she thought. If it had happened at her place and she
were all alone, she might have been half-crazy with fear. But
he lay there unconscious and vulnerable, defenseless as a baby.
If they were to kill him, murder him in his sleep like some
poor sick animal . . . She thought, *Am I really afraid of
that?*

She frowned, leaning on the sink, with the bourbon bottle in
one hand, the glass in the other, ice-cold against her palm and

fingers. And still she would swear it was not because she was his instinct-ridden Mama, though it somehow had something to do with his being her son. And not because she loved him, either. She knew what she loved. She loved strength, a body like Ben Hodge had had once, taller than Will's, and quick and graceful: strength that had something to do with beauty (not the stocky power and indifference to height that had moved up and down the barn roofs at Stony Hill, shouldering easily a tarpaper roll or a bundle of sunlit shingles: not that) and something to do, more important, with freedom. When a leak appeared in the cowbarn roof or the chickenhouse roof or the roof of the towering, square wooden silo, it was a law of Will Hodge's existence that it must be patched, even if the barn was not used any more and never would be. It was not a law for her. There was something fine about a roof that let the sunlight in through a thousand chinks, or a buckled wall, a concrete foundation splitting open to the roots of trees. For she, Millie Hodge, put her money on sunshine, the restless power of the hay pushing outward, and slow, invincible roots. All her life she'd been breaking down roofs and walls—intransigent gray Presbyterian stone, the brittle beams of dry legalism, vows and rules and meticulous codes—exploding them as a white shoot cracks a stone, though she was a woman, held down revoltingly to earth. "Look!" she'd said. They were leaning on the railing. The falls roared like thunder, and the earth shook. "That's the Bridal Veil," Will said, pointing. She was as angry as the river, repelled by his pettiness and pedantry, his flight from the furious truth of the place to the name of a paltry trickle. Without bothering to answer she pointed again, forcing Luke to see what she saw, the tons on tons of hurtling water at the heart of it all, and Luke said, "I want to go home." Will was grinning, with his jaw slung out, "Hah," he said. "Don't be a sissy," she said. But Will took his hand.

How strange that all that should come back to her now, when any moment the intruders might come, murder them both! Yet not strange, either. For though her chest was calm, as though it had found out some way to survive with her heart turned stone, the storm was raging as the Niagara had raged, howling and plummeting down like the dead through time. "God is physical," she'd announced once to Warshower, after one of those incredible sermons of his. "The trouble with all your sermons," she'd said, "is that you've never wrestled with a bear, only with angels. How can you lose?" He was baffled, of course. No doubt he'd believed she was crazy.

It came to her suddenly that Luke's shotgun would be standing in the woodshed. She took two steps toward the door, then changed her mind. They were men, and Nick Slater, at least, had had experience with guns. She'd be dead before she knew what hit her. She raised the glass and half-emptied it, then started back to the livingroom, not bothering, this time, to talk to herself, but clicking her heels down firmly to make a noise.

They were seated, waiting for her, and for an instant, as if all this time they had been drilling secretly at the base of her mind, terror went through her like an underground shock and she felt blasted out of her reason. But only for an instant.

"Hello," she said. She gave them a smile she knew to be brilliant, baffling them, she hoped, smashing their outlaw defenses.

Nick Slater stared, his yellow face pale. He was soaking wet and sitting close to the fire. It was Nick, she knew, who'd killed the guard, but it was the other one that frightened her. He had a black thing over his face—a cut-off stocking, it looked like. It came down to below his nose and over the moustache to the beard. His clothes, like Nick's, were soaking wet. A dark blue suit, too large.

She stopped, looking at him. "That's quite a get-up," she said.

"It is, yes." He had a mincing way of talking, a thin, reedy voice that sounded like an affectation. Something about him made her think at once of Will, her ex-husband, and the next instant she knew what it was. The suit he was wearing was Will's. It even smelled of him, or so she imagined.

"How did you get here?" she said. And still she felt unnaturally calm, turned to ice.

"The question, my dear," the bearded man said, "is how we are going to get out."

"I'm afraid that's *your* problem," Millie said, and smiled fiercely again.

"You're mistaken," he said. "Sit down."

She pretended not to hear. "Where did you get that suit?"

"You may sit down," he said.

Suddenly Nick Slater covered his face with his hands. "Sit down," he said. "I'm telling you."

And now, finally, the multitude of her sorceries and enchantments failed her, and without knowing why, she was afraid. She moved back numbly toward the couch and sat on the edge of it. After a moment she lowered the bottle and the glass to the rug. "Why are you doing this?" she brought out. The stocking over his eyes made it impossible for her to know where he was looking.

"Im not sure," he said. "It's an interesting question."

They sat very still for a long time, listening to the storm. At last the bearded man said, "Get some clothes. You'll catch pneumonia."

Nick got up and went over to the doorway, toward the stairs.

"Did you kill him?" she asked. "My husband?"

"Are you hoping I did?"

"I'm asking."

"He wasn't there to kill," he said in that same high effeminate voice. "Just empty clothes. Curious, isn't it? He'd been eaten up from the inside out, as far as we could tell. Left only his clothes."

The smell that came from him was overwhelming.

"Do you mind if I smoke?" she said.

"Very much." He nodded as he spoke. "I want you to suffer. No smoking, no nothing."

"And Luke?" She tipped her head toward where he lay.

"I don't know him yet. Perhaps he'll be human."

She reached for her drink.

"Put it down," he said.

She ignored him, and suddenly—out of empty air, it seemed to her—the man had conjured a gun. Her heart stopped cold.

"Put it down, Madam. We're going to make you a saint."

"You're insane," she whispered.

"Not yet." The pale lips smiled. "These things take time."

# V

## Hunting
## Wild Asses

*Ach, unsre Taten selbst so gut als unsre Leiden,*
*Sie Hemmen unsres Lebens Gang.*

—Goethe

### 1

Chief Clumly ate in his office that night, and as he ate, alone for the first time in hours, he looked over the article Judge White had made him take. It was not the kind of thing he'd have read past a sentence or two, normally, and it wasn't an easy thing to get through or with the radio on in the outer office. But he read attentively, straining to catch any possible hint of why the Judge had made him take it. It was conceivable that the Judge had merely thought he'd be interested, but Clumly did not read as though he believed it could be that. He had the shade pulled and the office door locked, and he sat hunched forward, spectacles low on his nose, left hand reaching blindly to the white bag of hamburgers and Sanka from Critic's, and

227

when the writer made allusions he couldn't catch he felt panicky. He'd have worse news the next time he came, the Judge had said. Was the article a clue? Flies buzzed, up by the lightglobe. The fan on the cabinet moved back and forth slowly, hardly stirring the muggy air.

*"Policework and Alienation.*

"Insofar as we view the whole matter abstractly, nothing in the world, not even abject poverty, is more degrading and, ultimately, dehumanizing—at least in potential—than police work. Against the poor unlucky policeman all the physical and spiritual forces of the universe seem to conspire. It has always been so—though it was less so in simpler societies, including our own fifty years ago, than it is in America today. And no doubt it will always remain so, for all the labors of psychologists, sociologists, criminologists, and so on, and for all the honest effort of those most directly involved in the problem— law-enforcement agencies themselves. The subject is a difficult one to treat frankly without appearing to sink into petty faultfinding or name-calling or, worse, melodrama, and, worse yet, cheap exposé. But the subject is worthy of attention. Police work has so often been sentimentalized, both by those who make policemen old-fashioned heroes and by those who would soften and domesticate them into weary, hard-working custodians and clerks—and the qualities of the police mind have so often been polished and ornamented, much as coffins are, and made to seem not only tolerable but downright commodious—that it behooves us to take stock of what police work does to the human body and soul.

"We could speak, if we were seeking dramatic effect, of that paradox so frequently pointed out by psychologists and sociologists who have interested themselves in the policeman: 'The defender of peace is a trained killer.' The phrase is not altogether unjust, for all its mercantile ring. One cannot watch the training of a police rookie without realizing, perhaps with some horror, the extent to which his profession removes him from the ordinary run of humanity. The targets on a police firing range are not innocent circles or *x*'s but silhouettes of men, and the familiar saw of police training, 'Never draw your gun unless you're prepared to use it,' is not mere air. More than one man has died needlessly in demonstration of the truth in that saw, both criminals who should not have been drawn on, and policemen who drew and were not ready to shoot or, stymied by their partisanship with the human race, failed to shoot in time. Among psychologists there is no debate as to whether or not the loaded gun the policeman carries with him constantly has any effect on the structure of his personality. It does, and the effect tends to be bad. The plain truth seems to be that the men who go into police work are society's needful sacrifice for order.

"But to focus on the gun the policeman wears is to miss the complexity of the problem. A gun is, after all, a tool, and can be used, like a shovel or a frying pan, in more ways than one. It need not kill, and it need not give the man who wears it nightmares or result in his estrangement from his wife. All that goes into the selection and training of a modern policeman is designed to minimize the likelihood of the tool's destruction of the man. The forced-choice questionnaires he fills out when he first applies are designed to rule out any man not a good deal more stable and mature than the common human run, and the training he goes through—unlike the training of, say, a soldier—emphasizes not the efficient use of the power society has given him, but the responsibility involved. There is no denying the powerful symbolic significance of the gun at his hip, but it is not just in the policeman's mind that the symbol burns: in the darkness at the bottom of consciousness, the man who passes the policeman on the street knows as well as the policeman himself that the gun is there. And it is in the relationship, or rather the gap, between the policeman and the rest of mankind that the trouble has its genesis.

"Though every man wants law and order, at least up to a point, most men want it mainly to keep other people in line, not themselves. Nobody wants his child run over; nevertheless, nothing is more infuriating for a man with serious business in the world than hearing behind him, as he hurries his car through congested traffic toward his office (late through no fault of his own) the yawl, like the yawl of a big angry cat, of a siren. That is indeed, the least of it. One doesn't last a day in police work if one wears one's feeling on one's sleeve; and the man who takes very little personally, who with mild eyes and a stern jaw accepts all abuse, threats, mockeries with the indifference of a man born deaf and blind—who puts insult away as quickly and lightly as he drops his ball-point pen back into his pocket—that man grows tougher yet with experience. Often the lamb turns tiger when he comes before the judge;

and often those who howl loudest at the time of arrest, on the other hand—who call down on the poor policeman's head the most terrible curses, and take the lowest view of his generation and lineage—are the same men who, when the trial comes up or the fine has been paid, are most generous with their forgiveness of what seems to them, even now, the policeman's small-mindedness. Remembering this, the policeman learns such patience as would shame old Job. He learns to stand lightly in the present moment, at once committed and detached, like a true philosopher or like an old-time Christian who knows this world no home, but a wilderness. So much the better, some opine. Only young lovers and elderly fools mistake the moment's passions for equal in value to the ups and downs, the larger illuminations, of a total action. What is police work, some may inquire, but a new approach to old-fashioned *caritas* —the heart's concern with, not simply some part of the cosmic bog, but the whole? Ah, true! The ability to rise out of one's narrow cell of time and place—to behold and admire not simply some particular woman or campaign or golden vase but the total order into which all particulars must necessarily fit— is not only the beginning but the true end, both the purpose and the method, of wisdom. But alas, *caritas* has never in this world had much charity in it. The man who loves with a pure heart, who loves his friend for the virtues he embodies, does not love his friend very much—as women understand. Thus saints love mankind but do not much care for men. The man deeply mired in cupidity, who so greatly enjoys, say, lemon drops that he walks in front of trains without seeing them, all his wits curled up around the sour-sweet sensation in his mouth, is no doubt a poor miserable unfortunate who deserves our pity here and, hereafter, hell. But the man who leaps past the mere lemon drop to the glory of God there figured forth —that is to say, the man whose eye is on the larger order of the universe, both the lemon drop and the freight train he stops to watch rush past—is more pitiable yet, from a certain point of view, and richly deserves the eternal tedium of Heaven.

"So it is with policemen. Detached from mankind—thrust back with sharp insults or, simply, blank stares by those whose activities he indifferently impedes—fawned over by fools who, in an analogous situation, cannot walk past a sleeping dog without calling to it and holding out their fingers—smiled at by children who tomorrow will frown or fawn, like their parents—the policeman little by little slides away from whatever comfortable humanity he may once have shared with his neighbors. Every stranger is a potential excuse-maker or gratuity artist, if not an outright enemy, and every friend is a potential favor-seeker. Men of some stature in the community, who might conceivably make good their threats to 'break you for this,' as the saying goes, are tin cans on the social watchdog's tail. Men of no stature are merely a quiet annoyance. The policeman resists this inevitable tendency of his thought, if only because human beings are by nature social creatures, even policemen; nevertheless, the subtle pressure toward cynicism is everlastingly there. It is of course primarily for this reason that police departments hire family men, when possible. The bachelor policeman inevitably turns more and more for friendship to others of his own Jesuitical kind, that is, fellow policemen; and out of such friendships, out of membership in that proud and exclusive club, he draws precisely the confidence and security, almost bigotry, which, in a man with a gun, can be dangerous. In your truly Protestant department, where after his day of professionally indifferent justice (strained, bent, dented here and there by the age-old hammerings of low pay and temptation always too ready-at-hand, by anger, boredom, and the despair which comes with dealing out more justice than any policeman gets), the man of the force goes home to a wife who involves him, as soon as he crosses his threshold, in excuse-making and bribery and pointless anger of his own; and lest he begin to slide into a comfortable self-hatred, a schizophrenic separation of the policeman in him and the tawdry man, she kisses him on the cheek and, sooner or later, unmans him in his bed.

"But either way, bachelor or married, the policeman is lucky if he does not eventually (however subtly) go mad. It begins in disengagement. It is not the man but the uniform that makes the arrests, takes the insults or the fawning or (most common of all) the averted faces, the stares that pass through him. Like a man in a hypnotic trance, he moves not by his own power but by the force of a thing outside himself, his badge. Like the hypnotist's subject, and like a true schizophrenic, he must regularly deny to himself—far below the level of conscious assertion—that the voice with which he speaks is his own. Standing with his foot on the bumper of a reckless driver's car, writing down the license, he no more writes, himself, than the hypnotist's subject raises the arm he has been told he cannot raise: it is the Law that writes. It is the Law that bangs, like God on Armageddon day, at the debtor's barbican, or holds up one glove to impatient traffic at an intersection, or dispassionately—for all the pounding of the policeman's heart—fires a bullet through the murderer's head, or pulls the power switch at Sing Sing.

"All men, admittedly, play artificial roles. A doctor is not the same man when he's wearing his stethoscope that he is when he sits at the breakfast table across from his wife, reading his paper and picking with the tip of his fork at the yolks of his eggs. But here, for the most part anyway, the professional and the common mortal can live comfortably and harmoniously together. If a doctor withdraws from his humanity —closes off his emotions, for instance, while performing an operation—he does it in the *name* of his humanity. Only small children hate a doctor when they require his ministries, and sometimes even the most recalcitrant children can be persuaded. For the policemen, whom only small children love with a pure heart (and the recalcitrant among them are not quickly persuaded), there is no such pride and pleasure. He can be proud that he is, as he is frequently told, 'an efficient, modern machine'; he can be proud that he is indispensable to civilization—however little the word may in fact mean to—as Plato says—a man of silver. He may be proud, when he looks in a mirror, to see that his tie is straight and his shirt neatly pressed, as the tie and shirt of the silver imitation of a man should be. But he cannot take much pleasure—any more than his nearest analogues, the artist and the saint—in his everyday communion with good, plain men. He meets the world and gets along with it by means of a conjuring trick inside his brain.

"His situation, we are sorry to say, is worse nowadays than it used to be, and worse in large cities than in smaller towns or in the country. The cop on the beat—an old-fashioned curiosity as impractical and inefficient today as the hand-crank butter churn or the medieval gisarme—could come to know his neighborhood, protect it and be protected by it: he could be as well liked as the grocer or mailman or launderer. (His position was not merely a function of his walking unarmed except for a nightstick.) He could usually stop a riot before it was thought of—or so most authorities on crime now believe. And if trouble did start, whatever its nature, he knew at once whom to look for, whom to let pass and proceed about his business, as one uninvolved. The cop on the beat had another advantage, more subtle and yet even more important: he need not be bored. As he made his way down the streets assigned to him he could talk with people or fall away into the abstruse speculations of a soul turned inward, whichever he pleased. If the day was quiet, he could bask in the quiet, speaking casually of this and that, or he could praise the Lord by eyes rolled up and over. Not so the man in the prowlcar. There is no quiet for him, but a steady hiss from his radio, like horsemeat frying or seas rolling through bones and grits, or like snakes and steam contending with the feet of the damned. Or else voices come in with that nightlong leak of trivialities—addresses, names, every once in a while some cautious little joke—whereby the soul of man is overthrown. Alas, he has neither the peace and isolation of the Gnostic, sweating in the prison of his flesh but dreaming nevertheless grand dreams, nor the fitful joy to be had from the earthly communion of, loosely, saints. In comparison to the casual turning of the head and a pleasant Good-morning, there is a certain offensive obviousness about pulling over to a curb in a car with a silver-throated siren and a big red light like a basilisk's eye, and calling out to the man who stands on the sidewalk waiting for his bus. The man in the prowlcar is thus cut off both from outer reality and inner, from communion with men and from communion with himself. No message comes over his radio directing him to a corner where he will find a man whose conversation would be worth gold and silver and all one's best linen. Outer reality is represented by boys who have just knocked down old ladies, by prowlers, reckless drivers, exhibitionists, peeping-toms.

"The man in the car, for his sanity's sake, becomes something of a diner-hopper, and since he cannot hear his radio while sitting with whomever he finds there to talk to, the radio which he of course must hear if he's to go where he's needed in the large patrol area one prowlcar covers, he learns to live not only with the isolation of the new man of silver but also with guilt.

"There, ironically enough, is the cruz of it: guilt. The policeman cannot be perfectly sure he is doing his best for the department that has won from him his loyalty (it is interesting that in police slang, headquarters is known as 'the house'); he cannot be sure he is doing the best he might for his family (the pay is bad, there are risks, and the work wrecks one's nerves); and to the extent that his original selection and training have done their job, the old civilized man within him cannot always be perfectly content that the job is civilized.

"Yet for all that, we might note, the man on patrol has it better than the man who must work with prisoners. The voice at the other end of the prowlcar radio is not sullen or hostile, and though prowlcars have their distinctive smell—the same smell as school buses or taxicabs or any other vehicle regularly and without any trace of affection serviced and stored in a large garage—at least prowlcars do not, like cellblocks, stink. Patrolmen grow increasingly mechanical, with experience, withdrawing to something like a permanent state of light trance. Guards, forced by their circumstances to make a sharper distinction between *us* and *them*, may grow brutish. The prevalence of alcoholism, marital failure, neurosis, and psychosis among guards is notorious. This is particularly noticeable among guards in large prisons; but every city or country jail provides its instances. Indeed, taken as a general class, cellblock policemen are the graphic symbol of what has been called the power-failure of civilization, the black gap between Actual and Ideal. In the lumbering old Leviathan, they are the heartbeat that misses. The fault is not theirs, nor yet ours either. An occurrence more than a fault: a necessary waste of human spirit."

The article was signed "A. Taggert Hodge, Phoenix, 1959." A mistake of some kind. The Congressman had been dead by then, and Phoenix pointed to Taggert Faeley, the youngest of the Hodges.

Clumly frowned. The Judge was right; it was all very interesting, though not true. What would Will Sr say if you showed him that? Clumly smiled. But he would not show him, naturally; he was not completely heartless.

He frowned again. He folded the article and dropped it into the wastebasket, then on second thought retrieved it and put it in his drawer and locked it there. The whole thing was disgusting, unbalanced maybe, and yet it was just true enough to make a man stop and think. He closed his eyes.

Chief Clumly himself was not one of those people the article talked about; he could state it for a fact. He was changed very little, all things considered, from what he'd been as a young man, standing on the ship with the smell of the ocean in his nose and his heart beating lightly. Merely older, heavier of heart. Who could escape it? Neither was Miller or Kozlowski or even Figlow the kind of man young Hodge imagined cops to be. (Clumly knew his men. That was what he was paid for.) Every one of them had joined up, originally, by accident, with no serious intention of remaining in the work very long. Kozlowski, for one, was mildly scornful of, and mildly amused by, the uniform he wore. He scolded jaywalkers with a severity he secretly found comic, and now and then, with an unexpected, momentarily baffling smile, he let them know it. Once, when he'd found children throwing bricks at a blind horse in an East Main Street field, he'd reacted with indignation which —it was plain to see, or anyway plain to Clumly, watching and listening to the talk at the station—had nothing to do with his function as preserver of the peace. He would have done he same and would have felt the same if he had seen the thing while driving a tractor between two fields on a neighbor's farm. It was not the crime he reacted to, but the stupidity and cruelty of the thing. As he would have chased heifers that had broken through a fence, he'd chased the three boys down in his prowlcar, penned them in at the corner of the Sylvania fence, leaped out red-faced with rage and, exactly as he'd have done if he were not a policeman, delivered them to the station. The only real tie he felt with the police department he served was his general, and not especially intense, liking for the men he worked with—a tie no different from the one he had felt with the baseball team he played on, back in high school. He watched Chief Clumly (Clumly saw) with remote fascination partly because he was different from the others—a narrow-minded, stiff-hearted old man, a mystery. He observed as a city man might observe a cow with the wuthers. He had no expectation of being in this business long, and so while he was here he would see what he could see. Ah, Kozlowski!

Miller, too, had joined up, originally, by accident. He'd grown up in Batavia, among the Northern Italians on the better side of town, not among the Sicilians that he too looked down on. (Clumly's race on his mother's father's side.) He had a ruddy face like an Anglo-Saxon and brown hair, and he was taller than most of Batavia's Sicilians grew. He'd served with the Marines in World War II, a young man at the time, broad-shouldered and grinning and innocent. Clumly had heard it all until he might as well have been there. Miller hated the Japs in the same abstract way he hated the cowmen who fenced off their waterholes in the Luke Short novels he was always reading. He was a first-rate Marine in the same way he'd been a first-rate football player before and was a first-rate volleyball player in the South Pacific: he enjoyed fighting, though before the fight started, in the time of waiting, he was afraid. Once the landing was on, or the jungle fight, the fear dropped away and he fought like a man in a War picture —and was even conscious that that was how it was. Only once did it occur to him that they really might kill him, when he was dragging his boots through a marsh between trees at dusk, and people were being hit around him, the same as in a landing except that that night, in the dimness and confusion, he couldn't tell even vaguely where the shots were coming from. He was hit three times in the stomach, and as he sank into the snake-grass, losing consciousness, sinking, in fact, into the deepest and calmest blackness he had ever experienced in his life, he had believed at last in death. They'd sent him home and he'd married a girl he'd gone with most of his life—a Protestant, and so, with a shrug, because his parents were the kind who would bite their lips and weep a little and forgive it, he too became a Protestant, a Methodist like his wife, whatever that meant. To support her, he'd taken a temporary job, as he'd thought at the time, as a cop.

Even now, middle-aged, he looked like the man on a Marines poster, at least when he had his uniform on. When he sat at home in his undershirt, barefoot, watching TV—Clumly had visited now and then—you saw that his arms and shoulders were not as thick as they'd once been, that his chest had sunk, and that his trunk was wider all around, though not exactly fat. His normal tone of voice was friendly teasing, even when he asked his wife Jackie for a shirt or asked his sons if they'd finished their homework. He was the same with, for instance, the mailman if he saw him on a Saturday morning: "You're late with the bills again, ain't you?" he'd say, as if belligerently; but then when the mailman's moment of uncertainty had passed, or had stretched out long enough, Miller would grin, abruptly and warmly, and cock his eyebrows, and he and the mailman would laugh. Clumly, watching (having stopped

by for some reason), would feel proud of Miller. Yes. He told
no long, involved jokes like the Mayor's, but he was fond of
short quick jokes, old as the hills, and he used them over and
over, whenever they would fit. *The kid wanted a watch for
Christmas, so we let 'im.* With his teasing and his jokes and his
comically monstrous threats he ruled his wife and four boys
like a tyrant. They loved and feared him. He was a father, but
almost not part of the family. When the belligerent, jovially
teasing voice would not work, it was hard for him to speak.
He would sit by the TV, in his private circle of gray-blue light,
watching wrestling or some old detective movie, and his wife
and boys would play Password or Chinese Checkers or Mo-
nopoly in the yellower light of the dining room at his back.
Sometimes, on a sudden impulse his family did not dare resist
and, in any case, rarely wanted to resist, he would take them
all to a drive-in movie or a stock-car race or a hockey game.
And sometimes, with that same mock-belligerence, he would
announce to Jackie that they were going to the VFW Hall to
dance.

Miller's family was not fooled by his boyish manner. They
knew him earnest and just and restless—a first-class mechanic,
typist, square-dancer, home-workshop carpenter, radio repair-
man, you name it. Without talking about it, he lived by rule
—a tight rule he'd perhaps never troubled to think out but
would never, come hell or high water, slip from. He drank
with the others at the VFW Hall, but no man could say he had
ever seen Miller drunk, not even high. He drove his car fast,
eyes glinting over the high cheekbones, nose like an axe; but
he drove with the precision of a professional racer. It seemed,
in fact, that he never even laughed except by choice. Looking
into his eyes, you seemed to see there the lingering images of a
thousand bad moments he had calmly come through: an
eight-year-old boy on Chandler Place who'd been hanged by
his playmates, a farmer's wife, out on Ellicott Street Road,
stabbed twice with a pitchfork, and other scenes no less terrible, though not as striking: head-on collisions, fires and the
Tonawanda's floods, children run over and crippled or killed,
violence, drunkenness, sickness. Once, before the time of the
Creek Road overpass, a man who had two children in his car
had tried to outrun Miller's siren by crashing through the
crossing gates. The train hit them broadside, and the car exploded like a bomb. Miller could tell about the things he'd

seen with a kind of detachment, almost light-heartedness, that would have made you think, if you did not know him, that his emotions ran no deeper than rainwater washing down a street. But it wasn't so. He was as shocked by such things as Clumly was himself. Maybe more so. The images ate at his generous heart and at times tinged his mock-belligerent cheerfulness with alum. Once in a while, after one of his jokes, he would forget to throw in the open, boyish smile. At such times he seemed much older than he was. Since the beginning, he'd had it in the back of his mind that one of these days he'd get out of police work; but the images he carried with him had made him put it off, year by year—so Clumly guessed—until one day it had come clear to him that, for better or worse, he was going to die a cop.

In Miller there was not an ounce of what young Hodge, in his article, had called "schizophrenia." He acted in his own right, as surely as Kozlowski did, and unlike Kozlowski he acted out of more than a native feeling for right: he believed law important and valuable, not simply in theory—Miller was no theorist—but in his blood and bones. In his blood and bones he believed in boxing and wrestling but hated a street brawl which had no rules. His whole body tensed with joy to the clatter and slam of a stock-car race, but with speeders he was a tormenter out of hell. He used his uniform as he used his voice, as an unself-conscious assertion of lawful authority. His virtue and defect was that he thought he knew better than other men, in the same way that he knew better than his wife and sons; and, generally speaking, the truth was that he did. He accepted the responsibility laid on him like a mantle by both nature and society, if Hodge's article was right, and, overworked, forever lonely—for all the good humor in his disposition—he preserved his good health by the voluntary self-abandonment of watching television or dancing at the VFW Hall or building mahogany knickknack shelves—he had literally hundreds of them—in his basement. And Clumly knew one thing more. Miller was superstitious. Where he got it, who could say?— some spark of true religion, maybe, in a generally indifferent Catholic childhood; or perhaps it was simply a snatch at absolute control by a soul uncommonly conscientious but imperfectly informed on the ins and outs of time and space, struggling through a labyrinthine universe full of surprises. He had the kind of superstition which runs not to avoiding black cats, walking around ladders, or carrying talismans, but to nervous presentiment and an obscure sense of the stirrings of omens and portents. He distrusted this tendency he had: he jokingly denied it and mocked what he saw of it in others. He was the first to scoff at talk of flying saucers, or prowling ghosts, or healing by faith: nevertheless, he read whatever happened into his hands on such subjects, and he frequently glanced at his horoscope in the *Daily News*, scoffed to the others at what he read, and, if any of it seemed to come true, took what he no doubt imagined was merely casual note of the fact. He'd been the first to mock Clumly's indefinite hunch about the Sunlight Man and had found good reason for laughing it off as an old man's nervousness. Nevertheless, he too had waited uneasily, had commented over and over that the weather was wrong for the time of year (in some way he could not pinpoint), and, when finally the old man's hunch had proved right, Miller had felt, you would have sworn, a peculiar relief. The feeling had not lasted. He was troubled now by dreams which he could not remember afterward and which, in retrospect, did not seem to have been dreams at all, but something else. So he'd told Figlow, Clumly listening at the keyhole. "Beats all, the way the boss knew all along," he said, grinning thoughtfully. "Shit," Figlow said. "Pure guessing."

Figlow, too, believed he knew better than other men, including Clumly. Their stupidity sometimes astounded him and at other times merely filled him with mild disgust. When a man came in to pay eighty dollars' worth of parking tickets—such things happened sometimes—he was incredulous. "It's crazy," he would say, shaking his head. He had a wife he could barely stand the sight of: she ran up bills and actually seemed not to understand that with a charge account you still, sooner or later, had to pay. She worked as a waitress at The Red Ozier, and he suspected, without any real evidence, that she had lovers. He suspected his daughter, too. She was fifteen. By accident he had found out she was taking the pill.

Yet Figlow, too, had good in him as well as evil. He wanted no trouble in the world and generally made none himself if he could help it. He was a stubby little man with bushy eyebrows and coal-black hair and very little chin. The men called him "Shorty," and though he hated the name he accepted it with no overt complaint, exactly as he accepted, day after day, the salami sandwich in his lunchpail, neither fighting the thing nor submitting to it. He wanted peace not because, given peace, there were things he would like to do. He took it for its own sake, on the grounds (Clumly guessed) that the easiest way of life is the best. He was not brave, especially, yet not cowardly either: his awareness that the gun was there on his hip made up for the shortness of stature which, before he'd joined the Police Force, had inclined him to leave trouble alone whenever possible. He'd had plenty of that swallowing of pride, in his former life. He had a slight heart murmur, which had kept him out of the Korean War, and so he'd worked as a cook in a tavern-diner. He'd suffered the usual brainless complaints of diner patrons, no two of whom meant the same thing by "rare" or "medium" when they ordered a T-bone steak, and along with that the eternal nagging of the owner's wife, a short-tempered middle-aged Irish lady who blamed her flare-ups, afterward, on the fact that she was a redhead, which she was not. But even with the gun adding inches to his stature, he was not out-and-out vicious, merely impatient. What made an offender behave as he did was a matter of indifference to Figlow. Breaking laws was moronic, whatever the motive; and, what was more, law-breaking meant more dull, petty work on Figlow's desk. He accepted the work without comment, nevertheless, just as he accepted his daughter's whoring around, if it was that. In the back of his mind, only Clumly knew, he carried, like a secret treasure in a small boy's trouser pocket, the idea of someday throwing the whole thing over and going to Mexico, alone.

Not much of a figure, another Police Chief might have said of him. But not all men are fit to be heroes, any more than all men have the face and stride to carry off the role of the moustached villain. Clumly could say for Figlow, at least, that he was the first after Miller to see with perfect clarity that the Chief of Police had—as Figlow put it directly to Clumly an hour after the pistol-whipping of the Indian boy—a screw loose. It was no mere manner of speaking; it was a judgment. And, to his credit, whether his motives, ultimately, were right or wrong, Figlow could be trusted to make no trouble; he would simply watch him and wait patiently, skeptical of the future, as always, but hoping for the best.

Clumly wadded up the hamburger papers and threw them in the basket. Was it possible, he wondered, for a man to lose his grip and know it, recognize every step of it? But he knew, all right.

Then Will Hodge's call came in, reporting the murder.

## 2

"Hooligans," said Clumly. "That's what it'll be. There's been a lot of that lately. Miller, put every man you've got on these teen-ager devils. I want this town cleaned up." He clenched his fist.

"Hah!" Will Hodge said. "Hooligans my hat!"

Clumly looked flustered—head tipped down, eyes like little beads. You might have thought he'd shot her himself. Miller was expressionless, reserving judgment. "It's sweeping the country, this hooliganism," Clumly said. "Juvenile crime's up sixteen per cent over August of last year. I was reading about it."

Hodge snorted again, angry now. "Why, hang it all, Clumly, they took nothing but clothes. What the devil do these teen-age burglars want with clothes—and clothes of a man my size?"

They moved back, getting out of the way of the police photographer. The officer at the door shouted at the people in the livingroom, moving them back to let the ambulance men in. A man from the *News* took a picture over the policeman's shoulder.

The ambulance people were soaked to the skin, for the rain had come now. It was pouring down like Niagara Falls, and the wind howled like a pack of dogs out of Hades. Something was slamming out in the back yard, a loose garage window, a fence slat. Inside the room it was hot and smoky.

"Keep those people out of here," Clumly said. He jerked his head toward Hodge. "I got no time to stand here and argue with you, Hodge. We got sixteen burglaries this past three weeks. One of them the boy beat a woman half to death with a mop."

"He take *clothes?*" Hodge said.

Miller scowled, concentrating on Hodge. There was something out of whack.

"Damn good market for clothes," Clumly said fiercely. "Also television sets, typewriters, electric toothbrushes. They take what they can sell."

The ambulance men put the stretcher down and hunkered a moment, waiting for Rideout to finish. At last the doctor got up and closed his medical bag. He said, "She's been dead for hours, six or seven, I'd say. I can give you a definite estimate after the autopsy."

"That's fine," Clumly said. "Send in your report in the morning."

Miller looked at him.

"Or whenever you get it," Clumly corrected himself. "The sooner the better." He wiped sweat from his neck, then he crossed to the door, bent-backed, rubbing his hands. "This is what I think," he said to the room in general, turning to face them all. "They were going through the draws there"—he pointed at the drawers—"and she walked in on them. Heard them from downstairs, where she was watching TV." He squinted. "First she thought it was Hodge, you know, but she hadn't heard him come in: that was funny. She thought about it, went on listening, and after a minute she went over to the foot of the stairs." He took a few steps to suggest to them how it was, reached out for an imaginary door, opened it, and tipped his head up. "She called to them. They couldn't hear, because of the television—or, no, she'd turned down the sound on that. They heard, and they tried to work faster. She came up to the apartment. She opened the door with her key and called again. They dropped everything. Kept still. Waited. They heard her coming toward the bedroom, and the one who had the gun took it out from his belt and wrapped it in the blanket and pointed it. Then suddenly there she was in the doorway." He showed how she'd looked. *"Blam!"* He clutched his heart. "Then they beat it, out down the stairs and through the back door and away through the gardens and neighbors' back yards." Clumly stopped, reflecting, and looked from one to another of them for reactions. At last he said, "That how you see it, Miller?"

Miller rubbed his jaw. "It could be," he said doubtfully. "With a ballistics test—" He stopped. It was impossible that Clumly hadn't leaped to the same conclusion he had, whatever he might say to Hodge and the papers.

"Check," Clumly said. He glanced down at the ambulance men. "Take it away."

The two men lifted the body onto the stretcher and carried it out.

Miller said, speaking before he'd thought: "Except for the phone. That doesn't fit. I never heard of a burglar cutting a telephone wire."

"I'm cognizant of that," Clumly snapped. He shot a glance of what seemed pure malice at Hodge and said no more. Miller said nothing. Clumly turned to the man at the door. "Tell the paper 'No comment at this time.' " Then, turning back again: "Hodge, that agreeable with you?"

"Why?" Hodge said. "What's the reason for it?"

"Because I advise it. You can do what you want, you know. It's mere advice."

Hodge looked at the corner of the room and reached no decision. He had something booming in his mind, you could see. He knew something. Miller saw Clumly's mind filing it for thinking over later.

"Ok," Clumly said, "let's get out of here." To the policeman at the door: "Don't let anybody in. And nobody out there in the back yard, either." He turned his iron mask of a face to Miller. "Miller, get Hodge's description of the clothes and anything else that's missing. Check the bathroom, especially the razor. And check—" He turned again to Hodge. "What would you do if you came in here and you wanted to get rid of some clothes?"

"There's a furnace," Hodge said. "Old coal-type."

"Check the furnace. Keep every ash. The Troopers'll run it through the lab for us. They're likely to end up in on this thing with us anyway. Maybe the F.B.I. One thing more." His eyes grew crafty. "That new man, Kozlowski. I'm assigning him to you to help with this thing. Good head on him." He pointed at his forehead. "Ok. Keep in touch." Clumly saluted, official. Miller half-heartedly returned it. Starting for the door he said over his shoulder, "I want these hooligans nailed, men. Society has a right to be protected from these lawless little hoodlums."

"Is he crazy?" Hodge said.

Miller said softly, not meaning Clumly to hear it, "You never know, with him. Might be something up his sleeve."

Clumly's pinpoint eyes burned more brightly. *Up his sleeve.*

He was reminded of the cracked magician. So was Hodge. Both men kept it to themselves, for their separate reasons.

At the station only the light in the front room was on, and the light in the hallway. Figlow was at the desk, reading a paperback. He straightened up as Chief Clumly came in, but it was too late to hide the book. He saluted and Clumly made a vague pass at the visor of his cap. "Any business?" Clumly said.

"Somebody slashed some tires," Figlow said.

Clumly dismissed it with a wave.

"It was at the fire house," Figlow said. "Firetruck tires. Right across the damn street from us. Uphill's ready to hang us."

Clumly dragged his hat off wearily. "Anybody see them?"

Figlow shook his head. "Clarence Pieman was closest, Car 26. I sent him over to see what he could do." He was looking at the top of the door, not meeting Clumly's eyes, and his mouth showed more than the usual measure of disgust.

"And?"

"They slashed his tires."

Clumly closed his fists. Pure hell was what he put up with. Nobody knew. A god damn comedy. When he had himself in control he got out a cigar and banged the end of it on the top of the rail, then licked the tip.

"Anything else?"

"Man from the Dairyman's League called, said to remind you of a speech there, week from the thirteenth of this month. I put a note on your desk. And let's see. D.A.'s been on the phone. Wants to talk to you."

"It'll keep," Clumly said.

"I do' know. It was pretty near ten when he called. He wouldn't call that late if it wasn't important. Been after you all day."

"Love of Christ, can't he see we're busy? Nobody tell him about the break?"

"Yessir, I told him, and the day man had told him already." He lit a cigarette.

"Well what'd he say to it?"

Figlow looked down at his book, then answered without taking the cigarette from his mouth. "He sent his congratulations. Still wants to talk to you."

Clumly lit the cigar.

Figlow said, "Salvador's mother called. Wants to talk to you too. And then the Mayor called. Real het up. He says you should call him right away."

Clumly pointed his cigar at him. "You tell the Mayor—"

"Yessir. But he says you should call him."

"Ok, that's enough. Put a note on the board for Kozlowski. Tell him come see me first thing in the morning."

"Yessir."

"And call my wife. Tell her I'll be home in an hour."

"Yessir."

He turned toward the door of his office, but Figlow said, "Sir?" Clumly waited, bent over and scowling. "Any luck?" Figlow asked. "You know who did it?"

Clumly considered, his molish face squeezed shut. "I'll tell you one thing," he said. He considered further and changed his mind. He shook his head once, with a jerk, then went into his office and snapped on the light.

He had plenty to do, but he stood at the window and smoked, bent over like a beetle on its hind legs. "It's a funny business," he said aloud. What should he talk about to the Dairymen? Thank God he hadn't missed it! *Crime and Automation. The Minimum Wage and the Juvenile Delinquent.* He'd done those already. Change a word here and there, talk of automated farming. . . . The light was on in the Mayor's office. Time was running out on him. The Sunlight Man's phrase. There was a new bundle of letters on the desk. He knew all right what the D.A.'s call would be about. Walter Boyle was due for trial in the morning, and as things stood now it was a blowout. Miller was right, they could convict him if they wanted, since the Sunlight Man had given them something to go on. And if by magic, well, according to a piece he'd seen in the *Reader's Digest* once, there were police departments in big cities like New York that used people like the Sunlight Man all the time. Why not? No different from tricking a man into confessing things you had never found out he'd done.

But all that was beside the point.

It was not so much that it smelled of voodoo, for him, at least. It didn't. The Sunlight Man knew Boyle because there was some kind of connection. It was the connection, not just the convictions, you had to get hold of. A man had to *know*, understand the whole thing. No short-cuts. He had to get to the truth, the *whole* truth. . . . Or was he fooling himself? Suppose it was impossible to get to the truth.

He felt uneasy, exactly the way he'd felt when he was standing with Kozlowski, talking with the whore they'd cajoled into letting them in. "Too old for this work," he said aloud. "Old head's giving out." It was true, but it wasn't the point. He was responsible for every man, woman, and child in the city of Batavia—*that* was it. But he shook his head. It was not. All had something to do with Mayor Mullen's Time-Product-Factor. Boyle's case didn't *warrant* throwing out the larger possibilities. That was the thing. (Is that true? he wondered. He went on testing it.) You might throw away concern for the whole picture when you went after someone like the Sunlight Man, someone dangerous. But a man like Boyle . . . "The Truth-Product-Factor," he said aloud. His brain felt wider for an instant, and his heart jumped. *The Time and Truth Factors.* Name of a speech. He covered his eyes with one hand. "Yes, fine," he said. "Hell."

Sure as day, his days were numbered. Let Boyle go, let the teenage hoods keep on beating up women in their beds, let that damned pile of mail on his desk keep building, and he was finished—no big testimonial dinner, no parade, no pension, no gold watch. A jailbreak in a town like Batavia! The love of God! And a jailbreak he'd almost expected right from the beginning. Suddenly, reaching his decision, he crossed to his desk and picked up the phone. The number was on the card Scotch-taped to the desktop, beneath the papers. He pushed the papers away to see it, then dialed.

It was the D.A.'s wife who answered. He was asleep. But when she heard who it was that was calling she said she'd get him.

The D.A. said, "God damn it all, Clumly, I never heard such a thing. Why the fucking trial's *tomorrow*."

Clumly scraped the ash from his cigar into the green glass tray and waited.

"Well ok," the D.A. said. "Ok, ok, ok. What have you got?"

"Suppose we had to get it by *wire-tapping?*" He bent lower over the phone, looking down his nose with sly, glinting eyes like a rat's.

"Sweet Christ, Clumly, come off it, will you? It's one o'clock in the morning."

"Correct. One o'clock in the morning."

"Ok ok. Wait a minute. I gotta light a cigarette." There was a pause. "Ok. I don't care if you got it by sleeping with his mother. Now let me have it."

Clumly was sweating. His decision had been clear. But he couldn't remember now why he'd come to it. A pain began to feel its way out from his abdomen into his groin and stomach, and he racked his brains for a way to stall, think it through again. "I can't," he thought, and by accident said it aloud.

"What?"

"I can't go along with that," Clumly said soberly. He bit his lip and checked an absurd urge to giggle.

"You what?"

He repeated it. "It's invasion of privacy," he said. "You see that piece in the *Saturday Evening Post?*"

Silence at the other end. He felt as if he were falling, tumbling slowly head over heels, nauseous, and he wanted to howl. *A cop hasn't got opinions,* he'd said to Kozlowski. But it was a lie. Kozlowski understood. He wished Kozlowski were here, something to fix on, get steady by, like the lines of a chair when you were drunk.

Then the howling came, but not from Clumly. The D.A. was swearing like a maniac, cursing him up one side and down the other. Clumly hung up.

He sat shaking, with his fingertips pressed to his eyes, the sickness spreading all through him now, like something green and rotten, a primeval sea seeping up in a burnt-out field. You're digging your own grave, Clumly. For a principle you can't even get clear. Right. And who's to decide when holding out for the Whole Truth is warranted by the Truth-Product-Factor? Ha! You. Certainly. *The State of New York versus Clumly.* Called also God. "You want my job, take it," he said aloud. They would. Nothing could save him except— He opened his eyes. The Sunlight Man. The old feeling came over him again, the absolute, irrational certainty that the bearded man was the sum total of all Clumly had been fighting all his life. Scrape together the Sunlight Man's secrets, and you'd have in your hands a collection of horrors, it might be, that would knock a common mortal on his hiney. The pain was suddenly lighter. He'd beat them yet. What could they do to the Police Chief who'd brought down the Sunlight Man?

He relit the cold cigar hurriedly and got up to go around his desk to the filing cabinet. He jerked the drawer open. Mess. Have to clean all this up, get organized. Part of the file was in the manilla envelope, where it belonged, but some of the tapes from their examinations of the prisoner were mixed in with other things, and he couldn't lay his hand on the picture until he tried the drawer below. He called for Figlow, and after a minute he came in.

"Take this," Clumly said. "Get a copy to the F.B.I. if they haven't been sent one. Have 'em check the print file. Rush it."

"Yessir." He started to leave.

"One thing more." He sucked at his cigar, crafty, waiting for the butterflies to settle. "This stuff on the desk." He jerked his thumb toward it. "Get it out of here."

"It's mail, sir. What shall I do with it?"

"Who knows? Give it to the Boy Scouts. Send it to the Mayor and let him draw pictures on it."

Figlow was wincing, his hand closed lightly around his tie, fiddling with it.

"Oh hell," Clumly said. "Then leave it where it is." He gestured toward his visor, still holding the cigar, and Figlow returned the salute. As Figlow reached the door Clumly stopped him. "Word from Miller?"

"Nothing much. A question for you. Wants to know if you want pawnshops checked for the clothes."

"Certainly."

Figlow shrugged, but he put off leaving. "You think it was kids, then?" he asked.

"Epidemic of it," Clumly said. "You know that yourself. A sign of the times." He pushed the drawer shut and leaned on it. "What's the matter, don't you read the papers? All over the world there's kids gone wild. Sweden for instance. Juvenile Delinquency's tripled in the past fifteen years . . . main age of offenders is fourteen. Thefts, burglary, willful destruction of property, the same as Batavia. And the same kind of truck. Clothes, office equipment, things like that. Or they vandalize public telephones, park benches, schoolrooms, playgrounds, bus seats. Police can't solve but a third of the cases. Talk about car thefts! Thirty thousand cars in the past five years— in five years a fifty per cent increase. And why? Well I'll tell you what the article says—a piece in *Look*. Urbanization, the rapid growth of towns. Unemployment. Parents have been raised in the country or in towns like Batavia use to be, and they got small-town or country values, but the kids want to live the way city kids live, or the way they think they do. They think cities take toughness, and so pretty soon the kids are at war with the parents, as well as with everybody else. Psychologist's opinion. I recommend you read it."

"And that's what it was tonight, eh?" He was so incredulous he took the cigarette out of his mouth.

Clumly waved. "All over the world, Figlow. Even in Russia and China, where the cops outnumber the people. Take Leningrad. The vodka sales went up thirty per cent in the past five years, almost all the increase to juveniles. When the cops ask the drunk-and-disorderlies why they did it, over sixty per cent of them say it was 'for kicks.' Little thing, you thinking? You thinking, Anybody can get stoned? Fifty-eight per cent of the criminal offenses in Leningrad this year were committed by drunken kids. And what are the offenses? They steal clothes and office equipment and household gadgets. It was all in the paper. Or they wreck public telephones and park benches and schoolrooms and playgrounds and bus seats. But the reason's different in Russia, you understand. Capitalist liquor sellers." He laughed like a murderer. "Or you take London."

Figlow said, "But this shooting tonight, I don't know." Then, detaching himself, replacing the cigarette, "Maybe you're right."

Clumly scowled and went over to the window. The light was off in the Mayor's office now. He sucked at the cigar. Then he turned to study Figlow with small icy eyes. "Right," he echoed. He laughed. "You think I'm crazy? He cut that telephone wire to give himself two, three extra minutes—the time it would take a man to run to a phone at his neighbor's. That's no panicky kid, Figlow. When they check that bullet, they'll find it's from Salvador's gun." He turned back to the window as though he were finished.

Figlow said, "So it was him."

Clumly grunted. "Who else goes in and out of locked doors like they were nothing? It was locked when Hodge got there, according to Hodge—I don't think Hodge has realized the importance of that just yet."

"How?" Figlow said quietly. "How did he do it?"

Clumly looked up past the firehouse roof at the clouds. The roof tiles gleamed from the rain. "I'm not sure," he said. "But

I'll tell you my guess. My guess is, he opened the door with Will Hodge's key."

"Is it possible?"

"Who knows what's possible?" He looked at his watch. "I'd better go home. Poor wife will be out of her head."

In the car he thought: *Hodge's key*. It had hardly seemed worth considering until Figlow had asked. But now it seemed beyond speculation. It was *not* possible, but that was irrelevant. It wasn't possible, either, for a man who stunk like a backed-up sewer to sneak up on a cop who was sitting at his desk and bind him and gag him and blindfold him and never leave so much as an impression of who the assailant was, though the cop had smelled him often.

"So he'd bathed and changed," he said aloud.

That too was incredible. Bathed where? At the Y.M.C.A.? The sink in some church? He'd have to have washed his clothes, too. Or changed them. Where?

When he stopped for the light at North Lyon Street it came to him that he wasn't alone in the car. There was someone crouched in the back seat behind him. Slowly and carefully, heart burning in his throat, he jerked around to look. There was no one. The boy and girl in the car beside his were looking at him, solemn. He pulled the visor of his cap lower and set his jaw firmly. "Little hooligans," he said. When the light changed the couple took off fast. He thought of switching on the siren and hauling them in. But this was where he turned, thank God. They couldn't see him any more. In the rear-view mirror the lights of Main Street, though the stores had been closed for hours now, fell away yellow, blue, green, white, like the eyes of watchful dragons.

When he reached the end of his driveway he was afraid to open the garage doors. He didn't even fight it. Some fights were worth the trouble and some were not. He left the car sitting where it was, locked up, and went up on the porch. He was afraid to look for the newspaper. Why should he? He bent toward the door to listen. The house was all dark. A car came around the Oak Street corner and very slowly passed his house. His heart was hammering. It was the Mayor! But it wasn't. He slipped the key into the lock and opened the door just wide enough that he could slip his hand in and flick on the light.

"Is that you, Fred?"

She was sitting on the couch waiting up for him, working on that sewing she'd been at all these years. It must be every thing she did on it she had to undo and do over. Her glass eyes glittered.

"Just me," he said. The strength had gone out of his legs. He sat down quickly on the arm of the couch, the door still open behind him.

"You look sick," she said. She got up and came toward him. He would have sworn the glass eyes could see.

"Be quiet," he said. "Listen."

It was only the rain starting up again, whispering in the leaves. He saw once more the glittering eyes of the dead woman sitting by the wall.

"Just tired," he said.

"Let me fix you a nice cup of tea," she said.

"Yes, do," he said. One final shudder went down his back and it was over, he felt all right. "I'll come with you," he said. Halfway across the room he remembered that the door was still open and went back to close it. Though both of them had been here in the room all the time, his fear was back. He was convinced that someone had slipped in, invisible, and was somewhere in the house.

"You're jumpy," she said. She had turned as if to look at him. She stood, tipped and lean as a beanpole, bony hands folded like a singer's, prepared to be frightened.

"No, no," he said. Then, with conviction: "Everything's fine. Tired as a dog, that's all." He gave a laugh.

"Good," she said. "You had me worried."

He took a deep breath, then unbuckled his holster belt and hung it in the clothespress, where it belonged. He followed her into the kitchen, rubbing his hands as he walked. The muscles of his face were frozen to a cheerful smile.

*3*

The Sunlight Man had gone upstairs. To sleep, they imagined; but they were wrong. While Nick Slater sat at the living-room window, shoulders hunched, brain numb, watching the storm as he would have watched some foreign movie without subtitles, full of dark scenes of ominous import, monstrous faces, branches of trees like scratches on a sky from which all life had sunk away, his two hands lightly closed around the gun, the Sunlight Man was overhead in the front bedroom, sitting in blackness like a Biblecover, thinking.

He could not see the vanity mirror he knew stood solemn and indifferent before him like a messenger with news already known, no longer a matter of sorrow, much less shock. Let it be as it was. He felt like a man come back from the dead to find the world less than he had one time imagined but not for that reason drab; more glowing than before. "Millie," he said, perhaps aloud. Not fondly, not with horror either, merely as one might try out a word in an unfamiliar language, torturing it toward sense. He had not seen her for a long time and had not known he had any particular feeling for her; his brother's wife, simply; a sword in his brother's side but not in his, a matter of sad indifference. "So get rid of her," he'd said easily when Will Hodge sat suffering in the chair by the bookshelf, wooden-faced as an Indian but boiling within with grief and outrage, some latter-day Hrothgar, mighty and patient and beyond all human counsel. Will said nothing, merely moved his hand a little as if toward his face, then thought better of it. He had said, "It's up to you, Will. Anybody else would." But he had not felt quite as callous as that. He knew his brother. What would have been for himself or Ben or Art Jr a matter of snapping the fingers was for Will a case of vast difficulty and subtlety, a labyrinthine question of justice. *Was I wrong? Was she wrong? Where is the guilt?* And though the question was absurd, the asking was noble, and Taggert Hodge had looked away, understanding his uselessness. He might have laughed, measuring his brother's troubles against his own; but to each man God gives the test he can endure.

> No man who has passed a month in the death cells
> believes in capital punishment
> No man who has passed a month in the death cells
> believes in cages for beasts

And so, confronting her face to face, finding that the leftward veer of her chin, the way she held her glass, stood with one strong foot thrown forward, weight squared and balanced like a fencing master's—finding that above all the music in her voice, however deadly to a man armed only with a shield of wood—rekindled the past more violently than Batavia's streets or the stink of its water or the hellish heat that lay on it in August like a dying beast—he had been shocked to a sudden pain of love or anguish or something between, a vacuum of feeling between two fires: an intense upsurge of memory and hopeless desire.

But he was calm now, beyond his first rage and love-hate to reflection and the abstract knowledge of his fear. The feeling he'd experienced long ago in his father's house was back, yet strangely not inside him: it had gone out to penetrate and shine in things external—in Millie, in the boy he had not known except as a child of three or four, in the Indian boy he had found in jail, of whom he had heard in the letters that Millie had written neither for his sake nor for hers but because he was a source of torment to Will. The feeling had gone out into objects as well, they were alive as if with his memory of them, though he'd never seen them before in his life: the swaybacked couch, the rug, the cheap old andirons and scuttle by the fireplace, in ashtrays, magazines, pieces of paper—a glow as if of brute sensation, shining in one thing more and in another less, he could not tell why. And he felt, as he had felt in his childhood, that there were things he knew, great mysteries, a knowledge too deep for the power of memory to pull down or dredge up, a light moving through subterranean passages, drawing to a focus around God knew what queer images—crosses, circles, his mad wife's eyes?—something outside the limits of his mind.

He had felt then for a moment that he knew. She was looking at something, her eyes fixed with a stare like an eagle's, and now he too seemed to see, not so much an image as a center of pain, like an iron just brought blinding white from the forge. And then, drawing back, he had fixed his eyes not on what she was seeing but on her.

"Poor bitch," he whispered when she fled.

The doctor said nothing. A gentle spring breeze came in off the patio of the therapy cottage, but no sound came with it.

Beyond the walls of the hospital grounds there would be traffic moving, business as usual, but not here. *Wherever she may be . . .* The grass was smooth and clean as only grass officially kept can be. Like her mind, officially kept in the neat regulations of her madness. The doctor said, "These treatments—" He paused, studied Taggert's face, decided to continue. "They're a distressing sight, as you can see." Taggert Hodge nodded. "You understand the principle, of course. But until you've seen one . . ." He smiled. "Good though, those boys of mine. You saw their reactions. Like lightning!" He snapped his fingers. "They have to be of course, but it's impressive just the same. The first time I saw it—I was interning; I remember as if it was yesterday—I just plain couldn't believe it. Well, takes time, of course. What it comes down to, you know, is you have to think like a madman. They're just as quick thinkers as anybody else, understand. Quicker. You get so you can think like them, and then you've got to go *beyond* that. You've got to control them, lead them where you want them to go, block them. Take chess now. A simple game, compared to this. You've got hours to think out every move—and just as many conditions as we have to deal with here—and even if you lose, what is it? A game. But every move *we* screw up—" He glanced at Hodge again, then smiled. "But we don't."

Hodge nodded, doubtful. The man was tall and heavy, with slow, shallow eyes, a dark brown suit. He did not look like a chess player. "She recognize me?" Hodge said.

"Hard to say," the doctor said. He was evading some long explanation. Then: "Ah. I think they're coming back. Have a seat?"

Hodge sat down again. It was a comfortable room. It didn't smell lived-in. This time, walking between the two attendants, Kathleen did not even glance at him: neither did she glance at the doctor. It came to him that it was from the doctor she'd tried to run, to Taggert Hodge she was as indifferent as to the walls, the stale smell of flowers. His heart shrank around the recognition. She was haggard; once beautiful. Her eyes, once dazzling with Irish humor and gentleness, were dazed now, the eyes of a sleepwalker. She walked slowly, lightly, as though all substance had drained out of her with her sanity. "And in her looks . . ." What was the line? He clung to the question as to the arms of his chair.

*And in her looks, which from that time infus'd*
*Sweetness into my heart, unfelt before,*
*And into all things from her Aire inspir'd . . .*

Now the doctor was speaking to her. It was as if Hodge were no longer in the room. "You think you're going to get well now, or is it going to be back to the asylum with you?"

She stared at him, and the corner of her mouth trembled. At last she said, "Where's . . . where's my brother?"

"He's in the kitchen." He indicated the direction with a jerk of his head.

"He shouldn't be here." She glanced at Hodge, then away. "I'll send him out. He has to obey me, and if I say—"

"You're wrong," he said. "You have to obey him. He's supposed to keep an eye on you. Don't you know who's God around here?"

She bristled, then calmed herself. "I'm God," she said.

The attendants laughed, and Hodge narrowed his eyes. He was beginning to sweat.

"You?" the doctor said. He drew back a little, incredulous. She nodded.

Instantly, he moved toward her a little. "Kneel down."

She shook her head. "No. *You* kneel."

"All right boys," the doctor said, "show her who's God."

They seized her roughly, as though she were a criminal, and forced her to her knees. Her face worked, full of rage. "Now listen," she whispered.

"Kneel!" he said.

"You're not supposed to use force against me."

"Don't be silly. I'm the boss."

The dark-haired attendant said, "She's on her knees."

The doctor nodded as if immensely pleased with himself. "Now." He folded his arms. "What are you doing?"

Her face worked violently. It was the face of an old woman, and Hodge closed his eyes for an instant.

"What are you doing to God?" the doctor said.

*"Please!"*

"All right, let her up."

She got up slowly. They gave her freedom enough to raise her hands to her face. "There are conditions under—" she said.

He shook his head. "Who's boss here?"

"You do what I say," she whispered, "and there are conditions under which we can make conditions under for dealing—"

"There are no conditions."

Kathleen drew in a deep breath, eyes blank for a moment. She touched her hair, trying to smooth it. "I am the Creator," she said patiently. "If you don't do what I say then what can we—"

"Who kneeled in front of whom?"

"I will have to destroy you," she said.

Again he shook his head. "You can't destroy me because I'm God."

"No, I'm God. Have you no faith?" The hand moving on the hair had lost meaning. It worked like a machine.

"No," he said, "I'm God."

She was squinting. "Well, I happen to be a better thinker and more—more of a leader than you of human beings and I think what I am and I realize I'm God, and I see what you are and—" She stopped, and Hodge could feel her panic in his chest. "You are and I under conditions—" She stopped again.

The doctor half-turned away from her. "Show her again, boys. There's no point trying to argue with a crazy woman."

The dark-haired attendant said, "Kneel to God."

Again she looked at Hodge. "Tag," she said.

But the attendants were forcing her down. She tried to scratch at their wrists, but they held her arms too tightly and her nails closed on air.

"Take it easy on her," the doctor said. And then, to Kathleen: "Make it easy for yourself."

"Why does God have to cry for Tag?" the shorter attendant said.

She got her hand free for an instant and struck at him, but again he caught her wrist.

"Why does God have to cry for Tag?" he asked again.

"That's true," the doctor said. "I hadn't thought of it." He bent over her. "That's true, what he says."

"You're not supposed to use force—you're not boss."

"Who's God?" he said.

"I am God. *Nomine matris . . .*"

"Why don't you get up then?"

"Well, I'll push them away." She tried. "Tell them to get away," she said angrily.

"All right boys, get away."

The attendants released her and stepped back. Hodge waited, the back of his neck tingling. Suddenly, as though she were perfectly sane, Kathleen laughed. "That was a mistake," she said. "I should have pushed them away, I should have obliterated them."

Now, crazily, they were all laughing. "Obliterate, yeah!" the shorter attendant said.

"Obliterate, that's it," the doctor said. "But you're absolutely helpless."

After it was over the doctor said, "So now you've seen it."

Hodge shook his head, still shaky. "It's a hell of a thing." His brother-in-law was leaning on his arm against the door-frame.

"Not too pretty, no," the doctor admitted. "But you see how it is. Reality's damned unpretty to Kathleen. You have to drive her to the admissions one by one."

"You wonder if it's worth it," Hodge said.

Her brother glanced at him, thinking the same, it seemed.

"Of course it's worth it," the doctor snorted.

Hodge nodded, but the man's voice made something ring far back in his mind. It was the game again, he realized the next instant. "Tell me something," Hodge said as if thoughtfully, "do you really believe you're God?"

The man smiled. "Easy boy," he said. He closed his hand for a moment around Taggert's arm.

When the doctor was gone her brother said, "We've got to get her out of here, Tag. It doesn't work."

"You're crazy," Hodge said. "It's only been six weeks."

The mild eyes looked at him, swollen behind the thick glasses. "Aren't we all?—crazy, I mean?"

He stared at the place where he knew his burnt face would be staring back at him out of the darkness of the mirror, and his mind played over and through the past and the present and lived in neither.

*Purity, cleanliness, contentment, patience, devotedness, self-denial, above all, silence.*

But they had moved her, in spite of him. They had the money, not he. He had pleaded, argued, had even once caught Robert, the oldest, by the lapels of his damned high-yeller suitcoat, prepared to hurl him through the wall. The Professor had sat with his thin legs crossed, as always, tapping the tip of his moustache with one finger, passing no judgment. He agreed with Hodge, but he was the old lady's slave. "Virtuous love," Sir Thomas Malory called it. *Knight-prisoner, in the ninth year of the reign of Edward Fourth.* If the old lady wanted Kathleen burned alive, the Professor would have offered his matches. But so it was with all of them, wasn't it? Virtuous love. For love of Kathleen the brothers, miserable neurotics themselves, evaded the father whose rule was otherwise in all respects absolute and absolutely corrupt. For love of Kathleen the brothers leaped from cure to cure, as if they were the psychotics, not she. For love of Kathleen the old man hated Hodge like death, her husband, in his mind her destroyer. And as for Hodge,

He stood in the school hallway, leaning on his broom, and he looked at the child who reminded him of the pictures of Kathleen when she was a child, watched her so hungrily, with such brute anguish that if anyone had noticed they'd have locked him up on the spot for dangerous. Perhaps not that bad, quite. He was capable of looking down, capable of smiling with kindly middle-aged-janitor indifference when she passed, walking like music, a drop of sweat beside her nose.

"Possessed," Helene Burns had said. The mathematics teacher.

He had explained to her lightly how it was with him, and she had seen, for all his light-heartedness, how it was. There were very few of them there that he could talk to; she was the chief one. Recently divorced. That was why he appealed to her, he knew. He had been happy in his marriage, she had been miserable. Into his wounded animal love for a creature beyond either love or hate, translated into a present eternity, she projected what her marriage might have been; and his loss of what had seemed invulnerable was the objectification of her loss of what never was.

She understood, too, his restless arrogance, the disgust he felt for teachers, principals, Education professors at the University, parents who were riding high in the world, who spoke kindly, condescendingly to him as though his fallen condition were of course a punishment for sins. (And yet he was lying to himself, he knew; they did not scorn him but merely passed by, oblivious even to the fact that he scorned them. Insiders.)

"It's temporary, Tag," she said. "You'll be on your feet

soon, you watch." He slept with her sometimes—that was before the accident—and often he would lie with his hands behind his head and listen with egoistic pleasure to her analyses
of his condition. She had a throaty, New York Jewish voice,
eyes like a piece of sculpture out of Syria. "You were the one
with the smarts," she said, smiling, nodding, toying with how it
must have been. "Also the schmertz. And the baby of the family, that's what did it."

He was not fooled by his pleasure. As indifferent to that as
he was to almost everything, in those days. Everything but his
sons. As if saying to himself, "Very well, you too like flattery."
He could have been bored by his vulgar humanness, but he
was beyond it. She said once: "The magic tricks are interesting, though. They're the key, if you want my opinion." At her
apartment, the light on in the kitchen, visible from the bedroom where they lay. On the record player a Broadway musical.

"I don't," he said, "—want your opinion—" and grinned in
the half-light falling from the doorway.

"Yes you do," she said casually. He did not protest. "The
way I figure, you were always quick, and people made a big
fuss about it, and pretty soon it was a game. The quickness I
mean. You learned all this stuff, but you didn't really understand it. Like a quiz-kid or something. You just skittered on it,
like a waterbug. A thin film of sense. And they all said 'Ooh!
Aah!' That's how it was."

He frowned.

She said, "Too bad."

For a long time they were both silent, and then she said
again, as if to herself, "Too bad." She put her arms behind her
head, making her breasts rise.

"I need a cigarette," he said.

After a minute she sat up as if to get them, but looked at
him. "Hurt your feelings, Tag?"

He shook his head. "Mere truth. A butterfly's wing."

She slid out of bed then and went to the dresser for the cigarettes She lit one for each of them.

"What started you on the magic tricks?"

"I don't know."

"Your father, I think."

Hodge grinned, then nodded. "Started me on everything. He

was—" He had hunted a moment for appropriate words, then let it go. "A forceful personality, as they say."

"A casket for everything he loved."

And that too was true, it had seemed to him, but he caught the truth lightly, half-evading it as he caught it, the way you catch a fast pitch that will break the bones of your hand if you take it straight on. "He was beautiful," he said. "Which is nothing much, in a way, I guess. Not uncommon. But he was."

Helene nodded. "I thank God my father was somewhat a klutz. He let me be."

"You're pretty," he said. He was tempted to quote her Sappho; but that was for Kathleen. Now it seemed to him that it wasn't true—was too easy—blaming their failure on the Congressman. Directly under her eyes he palmed the cigarette, made it reappear, palmed it, made it appear, and continued to do it, over and over, mechanical. He watched his painfully won skill dispassionately, with artist's pleasure, as though he were not the magician but only the assistant, a dutiful instrument. "It was once commonly maintained that Beauty, Goodness, and Truth were subsistent entities," he said. "That is, that they are properties which attach to existent particulars, but which might without absurdity be supposed to attach to nothing." He saw the words cut into the wall in precise, ornamental calligraphs.

"Here we go," she said. She smiled politely. It pleased her to be loved by a man who was clever, though she was not interested.

"I'm serious," he said and saw it in italic. "As long as the world was solidly theistic, the absolutes were plausible; when it got fashionable to speak of the death of God, people began to talk as though Beauty, Goodness, and Truth were psychological effects—probably base ones. For instance, beauty is described as the sense of relief experienced by 'living tissue'— that's jargon for mind and soul—when it's able to adjust present experience and remembered attitudes, in other words, is able to stop worrying. Some people didn't believe this account . . ."

She was leaning on her elbow, watching the cigarette slowly appear and disappear in his hand, her lips drawn to a half-pout half-smile, eyebrows lowered with concentration; but she was thinking neither of what he was saying nor of what his magician's hand was doing: remembering something out of her own life, or planning where she would eat tomorrow night, or making a list. Her breasts were like a young girl's, firm and small, and they would rise surprisingly to his touch. He knew that by the simple flicking of a switch he could understand her, move into her experience if only for a moment: it was exactly what he was trying to tell her. He had seen such things, and it was not true that they had to be destructive. On the contrary, that was the greatest of heresies. His father, busy at his work, looked up from his desk, recognized him, smiled. Even if it was only for a moment, it was complete. Politics ceased to exist for him that moment; and as for the small boy in knickers—the casualty of Christmas past—the high, polished, formal room, the crossed flags behind the desk, the littered filing cabinets, the books—all came down to a homely familiarity, mere frame around the Congressman's face. He had thought at first that he was special to his father, like Benjamin in the Bible, but it wasn't so, he learned later. To the old man, all that stirred was special—the geese flying over the capital building, for instance.

> (Look! he'd said, and hunkered in solemn attire
> to lift his son, like any God or farmer,
> and pointed. Over the capitol dome, to the west,
> a wing of one-and-many geese went sliding,
>
> honking south like old Model T's redeemed,
> gone glorious. Oh, not for the lesson in it,
> not for the high-falutin falling mind
> organizing itself to swim or fly
>
> with ease searching out the dire vacuity:
> not for that: for thisness: twenty-four geese
> enroute from swamp to swamp, encountering a dome
> at twilight, passing and touching an unseen mark;
>
> they freeze, fall out of time and into thought,
> an idiograph in the blood of man and son.
> No image. The pure idea of holiness.
> His mother said when they told of their vision, "Ah!")

That was how it was. When they were together at supper—the big room bright, the table as loaded with his mother's old china serving dishes as a table would be at the Grange Hall, the four brothers and their tanned, boyish sister contending

busily, passionately for truth and mashed potatoes and applesauce—the old man, white hair streaming, saw them all,
reached out with his heart and mind and knew them. He made
them more themselves than they normally were, not in the
sense that he forced them to some identity of his own choos-
ing: he *looked* at them, guessed out what went unsaid and
made them clearer to themselves and also surer. Not always.
He too could be abstracted, sunk inward to his own considerations. His white hair lay like dirty cotton on the collar of his
coal-black formal suit, his liver-spotted white hands lay on his
belly like the hands of a man in his coffin, his chin protruded
like a snowplow blade, and his eyes grew calm as stones in the
bed of a stream. For hours he wouldn't move a finger,
wouldn't even sniff. After such spells he was a hurricane of energy and joy. A manipulator, an orator, a writer of bills and
crafty epigrams. They had not minded his periods of remote-
ness. One intense moment is longer than a thousand years.
And the moments when his concern for them turned on were
dependably frequent. He became a knower of gestures, a pure
imagination. He knew a man's character by becoming it, like
the flagae who lurk in the mirrors of the Hindu. When strangers came to the house he would sit tense with concentration in
his chair, huge old gentle hippopotamus with shaggy brows, tie
askew, and before the talk was over he would know the man
and would know, besides, the road to the man's conversion.
Not that he sat in judgment, ticking off rights and wrongs.
There was nothing in him of righteousness, hard doctrine. To
think that a man's opinions were wrong was for him no more
to think less of the man than to think that a tree planted in the
wrong place was wicked and pernicious. He was impatient
with men who refused to stop speaking platitudes, but it was
against his faith in life to suppose such stubbornness proved
stupidity. He was a work of art, and living with him was like
living in the presence of art. The absolutes of human intuition
took on the weight and form of reality. The Good became, in
his presence, an aquastor, an ethereal form made as visible
and tangible as an angel standing on a stone. It was impossible
to say afterward, "There are no angels." At worst one must
say—Taggert Hodge must say—*Dear God, where are the
angels?*

And so (he remembered, floating in the dark), knowing he

could reach out with a simple question and know her, be translated in an instant to the beach in her mind, or the list she was making, or the fear she was toying with, and knowing, on the other hand, that he could reach out with his hand and touch her breast, make it rise to him, and knowing, finally, that she was not hearing a word he said, Hodge had gone on talking, struggling to tease his feeling into knowledge. He burned more delicate calligraphs into the clay-dead bedroom wall. "The difference between knowing and understanding may be obscure at first—the distinction between 'whatness' and 'thisness'—but it's one we commonly recognize in ordinary speech. All men acknowledge that no human being can 'know' another one: I can know your name, your age, your classifications. But understanding is beyond the brain's analysis. When I say I understand you I mean we're the same. Imagination."

"It's chilly," she said. "You notice?"

He stopped the motion of his hand, the cigarette half concealed, half showing. If she had looked she would have known how the trick was done.

"You're right," he said. They hung motionless in the vacuum between the light in the kitchen and the darkness beyond the window of the bedroom.

> *The cicadas continue uninterrupted.*
> *With a vain emptiness the virgins return to their homes*
> *With a vain exasperation*
> *The ephèbe has gone back to his dwelling,*
> *The djassban has hammered and hammered,*
> *The gentleman of fifty has reflected*
> *That it is perhaps just as well.*

"Shall I turn up the heat?" he asked.

"Yes, do."

"I love you," he said thoughtfully and falsely, though it was true.

"You love your wife," she said.

He nodded. *The truth is larger than you think.*

The child in the hallway full of hollowly resounding clicks and thuds and voices studied him soberly, seeing what use he was. "Do you have any children?" she said.

"Two boys," he said.

She turned it over in her mind. "I have a brother," she said. "I don't like boys."

"Hold off judgment," he said. "There's good in everything."
It wasn't true, it came to him, that she looked like Kathleen.

## OHM
*In the beginning was the wod, and the wod was with gord,
and the wod was gord*

He remembered his brothers walking the peak of the barn
roof, Ben and Will. His heart stirred with panic and cried out
in secret, Be careful! But he went on standing, as if casually,
his hand lightly resting on Kathleen's arm, and made himself
go on watching until his heart was calm with probability: they
had not fallen yet; they would not fall. It did not frighten him
to walk there himself: he got joy in it, positive that he would
not fall or that if he fell he would catch himself or if not,
would not die, or if he died would not mind dying. He knew
the feel of the slippery new cedar shingles under the rubber
soles of your shoes, the comfortable tension at the ankles, the
warm wind through your shirt. You could see everything, up
there. The hills falling away to Alexander, the railroad track
cutting through the fields a half-mile back of the house, the
rails gleaming like newly sheared tin, ties black and neat as a
logical argument fully understood, the woods in the distance
yellowgreen with spring, like the grass in the cemetery, and
above the woods a sky of mottled clouds as pure and venera-
ble as his father's stone. His emotion went out and made an
aerialist's net around the barn, and he stood stock-still, like a
pole supporting a guy wire. Ben stood up slowly, with a bundle
of shingles on his shoulder, saw that his younger brother was
watching, and waved. All balance, alert to the gentlest stirrings
of the breeze, Taggert raised his arm, waving back.

Kathleen said, "Could *we* go up there?"

"We'd better not," he said. His heart slammed. "Our good
clothes," he began.

But she was running toward the ladder, her yellow dress
sharp against the gray surroundings, her red hair flying behind
her. "Come on, sissy!"

He laughed and followed. She reached the roof, in her
stockingfeet now, and went easily and lightly from the ladder
onto the shingles. Ben stood perfectly motionless, watching,
smiling as if with certain reservations. Will scowled. "You'll
get slivers in your feet," Tag called up to her, but she laughed.

He swung around past the prongs of the ladder onto the roof and started up behind her, quick and careful. It felt good. He was not afraid for himself, and he was able to believe that she too was being careful and would be safe. She walked the peak like a tightrope-walker, her outline sharp as an open razor-cut against the sky. He went up the roof at an angle to catch up. "Now be careful, there," Will said. Ben stood under his shingles like a boulder. She came to the end of the barn, where the square wooden silo went up to the steeply pitched silo roof, ten feet above. She looked back, throwing a smile, then started up the silo braces toward the top. He looked down without meaning to. The roof fell shimmering away then abruptly broke off, and his gaze plummeted on down to the small round rocks far below in the barnyard, fenceposts like toothpicks, hoof-prints filled with water reflecting the sky.

"You're far enough," he said. "Why do you have to go farther?"

She kept climbing. "To see if I fall, silly!"

He could reach up now and catch her foot if he wanted, but he was afraid to. It might make her fall. But in secret he knew that it wasn't what he was afraid of. She might kick at him, purposely, viciously—except without quite knowing that she meant it to be vicious—and it would be he who fell. He couldn't tell whether the fear was right or wrong; but he didn't catch her foot. It was not because he believed her all goodness that he loved her. He had known all his life that nothing could be all goodness. Counterbalanced against the iron is the sweet lyre-playing. "Wait for me!" he called.

"You two be careful!" Will shouted. Ben was still.

She was clinging to the eave, struggling to get up over it, and though she smiled, twisting her head to look down past her shoulder, her face was white.

"Let me help," he said. "You can't do it alone."

She waited, clinging to the rusted eavetrough with her elbows, the silo brace with one foot. He steadied himself below her and bent his head so she could stand on his shoulders. When she was up, he swung up after her. And now at last, thank God, she'd had enough. Getting up over the overhang had scared her, and she sat against the roof-pitch bracing her feet on the trough and looked around her, going no higher. "Thanks," she said. He reached out slowly, all balance, to touch her hair. "Crazy little bitch," he said. They could see for miles from here, down to where the foothills rose blue in the south. "I wish," she began. She lifted her hand as if to touch his but thought better of it. "I wish I could be a seabird who with halcyons skims the surf-flowers of the sea."

He smiled. "Alcman of Sparta."

Kathleen pouted. "Pedant."

Now, on the barn roof below them, Ben was moving again, walking slowly down the pitch with the shingles. "Dang little monkeys," Will said.

They had not fallen, that time. That was as much as you could ask.

> *Und in den Nächten fällt die schwere Erde*
> *aus allen Sternen in die Einsamkeit.*

Pedant.
pedant.
Jadis, si je me souviens bien, ma vie était un festin où s'ouvraient tous les coeurs, où tous les vins coulaient.

> (But all shall fall, and all shall pass,
>   As well a lion as an ass)

Very well then,
let us go visit the insane.

We mount the stamped-out steps of the city bus
with humility, knowing our gall,
and more or less pure of heart as three old Jews
(a balding, middle-aged man and his two thin sons,
pedants in plastic spectacles, each one bearing,
timidly, his meaningless, cheap token).
A growl, a belch of gasoline,
and deathless Aphrodite stirs on her way,
descends to the city limits, drawn down not
in a chariot pulled by sparrows, grandiose gold
sinking aslant the burnt-out factory chimneys, the heavy air
trembling at the heart to the pulse of countless wingbeats,
but laboring stop by stop, as she always comes.
              (Now in this season for me
          there is no rest;
              out of the lead-cold sky,

a Thracian north wind blowing,
            dark and pitiless . . .)
In the hallway, a shuffle of attendants,
a lady reading a magazine, who is well
except in that at night there are Indians on her roof,
a minor irritation: it throws off her sewing.
(Let us beware of these innocent distractions.)

She comes in view,
the one to whom we throw our love
like coins into a pit. She will not see back.
The tall red-headed boy who looks like her
smiles kindly, old, sick-hearted before his time,
addresses her as "Mother." The younger stares.
*He* knows where it's at, reality:
Her face is modeling clay, her eyes are stones,
her nightgown hangs like dusk on her winter skin.

(Stones, too, can speak their secret names.
*My lips are stricken to silence, under-*
*neath my skin the tenuous flame suffuses;*
*nothing shows in front of my eyes, my ears are*
*muted in thunder.)*

> *Und sie schwiegen weil die Scheidewände*
> *weggenommen sind aus ihrem Sinn,*
> *und die Stunden, da man sie verstände,*
> *heben an und gehen hin.*

All that is not for us. We keep
our vigil, heads bowed, waiting
for a sign that the trance is done,
knowing we may be wrong in waiting.
It may be, we know, that the tomb we watch
is empty, in which case we are fools.
But we are resigned. We do not ask
to be treated with dignity. There is no rest.

Some tale of an Irish saint . . .

> *And so at dusk he watched her in her garden,*
> *touching her roses, hands more light than dew,*
> *and where her fingers passed, the blooms would awaken*
> *shimmering like grass the moon shines through.*

*the choice of the blooms she clipped and threw in the air,*
*and there they floated, weightless, at twelve feet,*
*and formed a crucifix. And he in fear*
*retreated from the place. He could not compete.*

Well, so.

He no longer knew, then, where his sons were, or Kathleen. God's holy fire had reduced, as it sometimes will, to a burning house. He'd come flying home as soon as he'd heard that she'd escaped, and he'd known from fifteen blocks away, by the glow in the sky, what it was he would find, though he'd fought belief until the image was there in front of him, past contradiction: the windows of his house were full of wheeling fire. It was not to save anyone that he went in; it was to die. But he was overcome too quickly, too close to the door—something exploded—and so they'd drawn him out, burning. He could not hunt them after that, imprisoned as he was in the hospital; but his brothers-in-law knew where they were, though they wouldn't admit it. Every gesture gave them away. "You're not well, old boy," they said. He understood. *Virtuous love.* "All in good time," they said. He understood.

It was not impossible that he was mad. He had earned it, if he was. It felt like the rage of a madman, at times. Kathleen's three brothers stood around his bed like dangerous angels, one on the left side, one on the right, one leaning on his elbows at the foot, penning him in. His anger made the room crackle like burning boards, but the three brothers, deaf to the fire around them, went on setting out their words of consolation and counsel like spear-headed pikes of an iron fence. He lived by regulations. He must not think, worry, feel. Those were the rules. At certain times he must eat. He must not smoke.

"They're not *my* rules," he said. "Where are my sons?"

"Dead," they told him at last.

He did not believe them. He knew well enough where his sons were. With the old man. The old man had tried from the beginning to shackle them. Not satisfied with having produced a psychotic daughter and three neurotic sons, he had to destroy his daughter's sons as well. Except that he too worked for love, of course. Not virtuous but tyrannical. Bue love, however twisted. (Nothing passes belief when a god's intention wills it.) So once old Paxton had tried to shackle Kathleen, but they had outwitted him, healthy love overwhelming sick, if only for the moment. They had eloped, and the old man's rage could not touch them—howled around them, burnt up walls, melted the very steel of the furnace that held them; but they were serene, watched over by shadows from a seven-times-mightier deity. For the moment. While Kathleen held all the threads in hand the brothers were more loyal to her than to their father. They lied to him (timidly, mouths no doubt shaking), feebly and, in view of their feebleness, bravely blocking the old devil's cruel pursuit. But the father had ruled for a long time, and for all her arrogance Kathleen, too, was weak. One by one she had allowed the threads to slip; their courage had collapsed, and now it was to him, Taggert Hodge, that they timidly lied, lips trembling. He must steal back his sons, as he had stolen them back before. And so he had bided his time, watching the lying brothers, listening to the crackle of their funeral fire around them, and had obeyed, for the moment, their laws.

Jadis, si je me souviens, bien, ma vie était un festin . . .

He had come to Batavia, and had looked, incredulous, at the graves of his sons. Around the slopes of the cemetery where the graves lay, flower-strewn, there was an iron fence, and beyond the fence a deafening sound of fire. He lay in the grass sobbing.

He saw (jadis, si je me souviens Ben) his brother Ben, who did not know him. It was not surprising, all in all. He was much changed. They passed without a word, Ben politely lowering his eyes as if it were an everyday affair to meet a man brought back from the dead, a face half-rotted in the grave. Ah, Ben! Once loved. Fat, gentle, confident. Ben.

> *Keep walking, former brother.*
> *Go through the Lydian land, past the tomb of Alyattes,*
> *the grave of Gyges and the pillar of Megastrys,*
> *the monument of Atys, son of Alyattes,*
> *big chief, and point your paunch against the sun's setting.*

Taggert had stood with his hands in his pockets, head bowed, staring at the sidewalk, trying to make out whether or not he still had it in him to love his second-eldest brother. Coming out of the cracks in the sidewalk around him he saw—or at any rate powerfully imagined he saw—fire.

"Then I have gone mad," he said.

But it was not necessarily true. A memory too terrible to bear may fill the mind without unhinging it. He did not believe

the fire, merely saw it. When he began to believe it, that would
be something else.

His brother was out of sight now, and a blow of anguish
came. He thought, standing with his hands in his pockets, his
monstrous face drawn up in a squint, "I love him then. Good."
He raised his right hand to scratch at his beard and trudged
back toward the center of town, winking to himself as he
walked and saying to himself, over and over, "Good." He understood that the winking, the muttering, would seem madness
to an outsider. It made him smile. The flames of the sun licked
down at him, and all the trees were parched. An illusion, he
understood.

"I'm as sane as you are," he said. "Note, sirs, my deport-
ment." He was full of an anguish of love and hexameters. He
decided to go see her father.

"Wait up!" he shouted.

The boy stopped running and glanced at him.

"Where's the fire, son?" he said. He roared with laughter.
The boy backed away a little, and instantly, to show what perfect control he had, Hodge turned sober, pressed his hands together, elbows out, fingers up, like a man praying, and walked
on.

Nevertheless, it was not necessarily true that he was insane.

But Clumly was insane. You could see it in his nose.

> Old Man Clumly
> Won't go far,
> Fucks his wife with a
> Wrecking bar.
> Two little eyes as
> Red as blood
> Little limp penis
> Brown as mud!
> Live like you should, boys,
> Don't you sass!
> Hell's a-smoulder
> Up his ass!

He was sweating. It wasn't true even that he hated Clumly.
And not necessarily true that Clumly was mad. What he felt
about Clumly,

It was hard to say. He had known him long ago, in the days
when Clumly was in his prime, not Chief yet: an officious,

sharp-eyed, sharp-witted little man, not yet gone fat. He did push-ups in those days; his arms and chest were as solid as truck tires, and that was how his talk was, too, steaming with dangerous conviction. When he talked about the Communists the veins in his temples would pump. You would see him at church, sitting in his heavy, black wool coat, arms folded over his chest, solid and out-of-place as a cannonball. When the minister prayed—it was Dr. MacClean, in those days—Clumly would sit with his head erect, stubbornly not bowing. Taggert Hodge, sitting in the pew where his family had sat for a hundred years, felt violated. He was religious, like all his family. It was not a matter of pride with him, and much less righteousness. He had lived with his father, had seen the works of love, and therefore knew in his very blood that God was huge and unkillable and good, a pressure of history laying to earth one by one all the barriers the piddling creature had lifted up —the walls between races, colors, creeds, and continents. The hymns they sang brought tears into his eyes. They were the essence of his past (the long, singing rides home from town in the buggy and later the Pierce Arrow) and they were the essence of his culture's past, as well. It did not trouble him that he could not believe, as his mother and perhaps his father did, in the literal resurrection of the dead, the virgin birth, and the rest. He believed in the joy of life, the banquet of the blessed on earth. He believed that life in the world was a highway, and all the traffic lights were stuck on green. More than believed it: knew it was true by the open sign of his father's life and many more lives like it. Clumly, beady-eyed, bald as a snake, was ominous. His brother Will would not discuss it. "Judge not that ye be not judged," he said. As for Ben, "Well, yes and no," he said, as always. Ruth said piously, "You never know what's happening in the other person's mind." His father glanced at her, smiling with one corner of his mouth, having something he might have said, but was silent. What he said, later, was (smiling again), "How do you see so good with your eyes shut, boy?"

He'd had dealings with Clumly afterward, when he was in law. Not often, luckily. "A man of principle," people said, which was to say as inflexible as a chunk of steel, with a heart so cold that if you touched it you'd stick as your fingers stick to iron at twenty below zero. Taggert Hodge had had a client who'd gotten a little drunk and taken a danceband home to his house on the south side of town for a party. The neighbors complained—the band was right out on the front porch blatting away like Resurrection Morning—and when Clumly and his crew came to raid they had their police dogs with them. Hodge's client was incensed. "The principle of it," he said later; but that night it was not abstract words but a principle leaping in his blood. He came reeling down off his porch like a madman, swinging a four-foot two-by-four at the nearest of the dogs. Clumly drew his gun. Luckily, the man was shocked sober and quit. Because, though there was no proving it now, Clumly was going to shoot him. Hodge saw the man's eyes telling the story and knew it was true. There are such men. You knew it a long time before you ever met one. Hodge had met many since then—a Professor of Education, when Hodge was working on his high-school credential, trying to start over in a new profession; a Hollywood actor of TV bit parts he'd met in Los Angeles; a man who ran a bookstore in St. Louis. Or Old Man Paxton.

But Clumly had changed in the years Hodge had been gone. He was a puzzle now. Capable, it might be, of things more monstrous than anything he could have dreamed of before; yet modified, too, like a Hegelian thesis generating its own antithesis. It was not that he had mellowed: there was not a hint of that in him. If his arms and belly were flabby it was not because he'd gone soft inside. The opposite. All that had gone into fiber before had drawn inward, leaving flaccidity outside, solid granite at the core. Touching his arm was like touching the flesh of a thing newly dead, but if you weighed him you'd find he weighed tons. He was, like all his kind, an iron fence; but the fence was not square and neat, it was a labyrinth; and Hodge, in Clumly's presence, felt a mysterious temptation to try his luck in its wanderings. He might have asked Will or Ben about him, if things stood otherwise. Might have asked the thief in the next cell, Walter Benson, what he knew. He'd been tempted, in fact. He had a feeling, almost a conviction, that Benson had recognized him. If it was true, there was nothing to lose. But without deciding to say nothing, he had said nothing. He had merely waited, playing his deadly serious games, watching with a morbid curiosity he himself could not understand, and then the feeling had come that it was time to get out, and effortlessly, almost without plan, he'd gotten out.

It was another of those mysteries of luck, as if all he'd read into the Babylonian rituals was true.

He could hear her walking, downstairs. If the Indian had fallen asleep she'd have the gun. It did not frighten him, and not because she would not shoot. No one would shoot more quickly and lightly or forget the error more easily when she learned who it was that she'd killed. He felt no fear because he was feeling, just now, nothing. His emotions had all gone out of him into the darkness around him, making it heavy and charged as thunder-weather, more a presence in the room than he was himself. He was trembling, but not with feeling; growing abstract. The house around him seemed to pitch and yaw very slowly, and the rain was still falling like floods coming down off the backs of mountains, settling in thick torrents of mud where a man might find God only knew what—huge eggs of unnatural production, hatching quickly in all this angry heat, strange creatures crawling out of them, howling on the hills. Of all this he was only half-aware.

It's sorrow that changes a man. But there was no sorrow in the life of the Chief of Police. That was his crime. There was only order, lifted against the world like rusty chickenwire to keep out a smell of cows.

(He heard her take a step on the stairs and stop, listening upward.)

There were only Clumly's ancient codes, the tortuous carvings on his tablets. Only in brass or stone can codes be maintained; and even so, the wind nibbles at the edges of the runes, and the rain beats down, taking its microscopic, dusty bites. Thou shalt not commit adultery, for instance. Why? Is love a thing so timid, withered by a breath? (I have watched leaf-shadows play over ladies' knees and the white of their thighs. I did not find them less clean for the leaves' affection.) The Sexual Revolution, they called it. The New Morality. But it was older, in principle, than time. King David murdered because his age could not know it. For better or worse, the new age was coming, or the age-old principle coming to life. Not an end to marriage and family but a new beginning, an end to old tyrannies, a beginning of agreement. The truth is always larger than you think. That was what he would have liked to say to Clumly. I've seen how they live, this underground culture you hate. Gentle people with mild eyes, who can fix their hearts as firmly as you or I. They close their hands on what they love by choice, not lashed to life like bloated, black, drowned sailors to a spar. They share their flesh like food. And when they choose, at last—when they resolve—it's with a finality that humbles us, reveals to us what we are. No doubt it was just as well that he could not say it. One knew well enough there was no breaking down those doors, double-locked and night-locked and chained. Let time unfold the arguments, since it would.

She was coming up the stairs now, stealthy. There was no doubt of it then. She had the gun. Though still he felt nothing, the air around him sickened. Was he to be responsible for the world? The sour smell of the cellblock was behind them, and the policeman full of rules he only dimly understood walked trembling ahead of the Indian boy who tiptoed though there was no need, his flat face twisted up like twisted iron, a rage of rules. And a rule said to the policeman, "Duck and turn!" and another howled to the Indian, "Get the gun!" The room exploded and fire leaped out of the walls, and the policeman fell back, thrashing and gurgling. They began to run, stepping lightly through the flames. It was not his fault. He could construct a fault, but not one he believed. He was not the one who had englished the tottering world off course, slammed home this debauchery of laws to crucify the living heart and nail the dead in place with a stake of ash.

Nor was it his fault that Millie was coming down the hallway with a tread absurdly light to attack his trance. Like a man asleep, he stood up, or part of him stood up, and moved without a sound toward the door. (*Erxias, where is all this useless army gathering to go?*) She stood outside the door, motionless, listening for his breathing. The doorknob turned, so noisily, as it seemed to him, that it might have wick'd the dead. He stood across the room in the absolute blackness and watched himself watching the doorknob. Then a breeze came. The door was opening. He slipped the gun from her hand so lightly, he knew by practice, that she would not know for a moment that it was gone. "The tigress strikes," he whispered, the same instant.

She started back and realized the gun was gone.

"La bête féroce," he whispered. "Do not think I cannot guess why you have come." He began a wild patter of lunatic talk, patting her cheek, tousling her hair, hissing, howling,

whining. She did not realize until too late that she was naked
to the waist. A lightning flash filled the room and revealed his
face. She screamed, though an instant before, crazily, she had
been willing; almost willing. The Sunlight Man lifted his arm
to hide his ugliness and backed away. He shook with anger
and believed for a moment in the fire breaking out at his feet.

"Keep it down in there," Clumly said.

Kathleen's father stood at his shoulder, dead.

<u>4</u>

Ed Tank slid out of his prowlcar and hurried to the barn
door. There he stopped, bent forward, listening. Hearing nothing, he drew his pistol and went in. A tangle of old rope, a
harrow that had not been used in years, two old woodstoves
leaned against the wall for storage; otherwise nothing. He
could take in the whole barn at a glance—there had been no
hay in the mows for a long time. Light came through holes in
the roof. He came out again and went around the side, and
there, sitting against an old barrel, was what he was after.

He saw at once that it was not the Sunlight Man but somebody else, a short young man wearing a heavy black coat and
a black Amish hat, though the morning was already hot. His
beard was small and scraggly. The young man nodded, curiously polite and remote. Ed Tank put the gun in its holster.

"What you doing here?"

"Just resting."

It might be true. There was a battered metal suitcase by his
leg. He might be some kind of tramp just passing through.
Tank scowled and scratched his stomach. "You better come
with me."

"Ever you say," he said. He leaned forward and rose to his
feet. He bent over for the suitcase. The hem of the black coat
came almost to the ground.

"What's your name?" Tank said.

"Freeman," he said. He smiled and held out his hand as if
to shake.

Tank ignored it, then thought perhaps he shouldn't have.

Might be a harmless nut, one of those halfwits you heard about, wandering around from place to place. There were birds on the fence, he didn't know what kind, watching them.

"What's yours?" the young man said.

"Mine?"

"Your name."

He studied him. At last he said, "Officer Tank."

"Ah!" the boy said. Again he held out his hand, and this time, thinking he must be crazy as he did it, Tank accepted the handshake.

"Am I bothering someone?" the boy said.

"You'll find out down at headquarters." He moved guiltily toward the car and the boy came, as if voluntarily, beside him. The sun was still low but it had lost its redness. Houses and trees stood out clean and sharp and sounds were very clear— the bell-like ring of a milkcan cover being knocked off the can, the sound of a compressor starting up. Tank reported in. Then he started up the motor, backed away from the barn, and turned toward the crumling-asphalt street.

"Law Street," the boy said, seeing the sign. He smiled.

Tank said, "You live around hereabouts?"

"New Jersey," the boy said. "I'm just visiting."

"Who?"

"Oh, nobody special. Just visiting. Nice country."

Miller bounced the empty flowerseed packet up and down in his palm. Tank leaned against the door with his arms folded. "How many of these you take?" Miller said.

"I don't know," the boy said. He sat with his arms around the hat in his lap. "As I say, I was hungry."

"Mmm," Miller said.

"Did I break some particular law?" the boy said as if concerned.

Miller looked at him, thinking about other things. At last he said, "Not any law that's written down."

"Ah," the boy said. He nodded. "An unwritten law." He did not smile.

"How old are you?" Miller said.

"Twenty-four. How old are you?"

"Pretty old." He dropped the package in the wastebasket. "You're just passing through, right?"

The boy nodded.

"Good. Keep passing and we'll forget about this."

"Keep passing?" He showed nothing at first. Then little by little a look of incredulity came. He tipped his head. "Excuse me, are you saying I must go, whether I prefer to go or not?"

"I'm advising—"

"I don't understand. It seems to me—" He opened his hands to show his amazement. "Why in the world should I leave?"

"Look, take it easy on us, will you? Just vanish."

Head tipped, he stared fixedly at Miller. "I'm sorry about your unwritten law, but that's your bag, it seems to me. Since I'm thoroughly inoffensive and a great respecter of law, and since I'm not ready just yet to move away from here—"

Ed Tank broke in, "What if everybody started eating morning-glory seeds?"

The boy shrugged. "It might be a good thing. I'm no philosopher, but it seems to me like you people could use some. Meaning no offense. Pretty colors, funny shapes—" He gestured.

"It looks like we'll have to lock him up," Miller said.

"For what?" the boy said.

"We'll think of something."

The boy shrugged sadly, resigned to it already.

Ed Tank said, "A person doesn't have a right to destroy his own mind."

The boy smiled hopelessly.

Miller said, "Suppose you start pushing this stuff. Pretty soon we got kids all over town that are hooked on it, maybe dead, some of 'em."

"That's fantastic," the boy said. "Why compared to plain beer—" He saw it was hopeless. "I was hungry. I told you that. Even if I knew the stuff was psychedelic, as long as there's no law—"

"Do you realize what you're doing to your *mind*?" Miller said.

The boy sighed. "Your information's bad. But I'm no converter. Two thousand years of wrong information—"

"Ok, book him," Miller said.

The boy sighed. He put on the black hat to show his sorrow.

5

Clumly avoided the trial. There was no need for him there, though he usually went in cases like Boyle's, to make sure there were no slip-ups. But Miller could handle it if anybody could. The jury might send Walter Boyle up to Attica on the strength of nothing more than Miller's grin. Miller could win them like a child. He sat solemn-faced as a girl in church. His shoulders and chest and arms and legs were the kind that gave you confidence in American law enforcement, yet his eyes were mild: he would not maltreat your son when he broke a school window. And Boyle, on the other hand, looked so much like a thief that if you saw him in the movies, sneaking into a house, you'd have laughed. His eyes roved constantly, full of fear and suspicion and malice, and he sat with his head ducked, the hump on his back almost higher than the round, graying head. He wrung his fingers and sat with one toe on the other, and once in a while he would jerk, looking over his shoulder. When he was agitated, a tic came over him, a spasmodic smile of fright that went up his left cheek. All right. That was damn near all they had on him, that was the truth.

Always the grim fact remained that no one had seen what he did in the houses he knocked at and entered; it was impossible to prove that he had not stood just inside the partly opened door, waiting for some answer to his call. And impossible to prove that the money in his car was not his own.

"Circumstantial," the defense would say. And would make his point with homely illustrations—the same illustrations he'd been inspired to use last time and the time before, it might be, but skillfully, feeling presented, nonetheless, like comforting poems he'd committed to memory years ago. And Boyle would probably go free.

He hadn't wanted to see it, so he'd stayed away. There was another reason, too. Miller had said this morning in Clumly's office, in front of Kozlowski, "It's all right here, Chief, the case against Benson. You sure you won't change your mind?"

Clumly had taken the folder from him and had looked at it. More mere circumstance, that was true, but such a weight of it that it might wake up even Sam White. Correlations of Benson's absences from home and burglaries in a neat semicircle around Buffalo. An old record of minor offenses by Benson, from the days of his apprenticeship. And three larceny arrests, no convictions, against Walter Boyle.

"You've been busy," Clumly said.

Miller waited.

He shook his head. "It won't stand up anyway, Miller. A good defense—"

"It might."

"The answer's no."

"I could take it to the D.A. myself, you realize."

"You could. It's up to you."

"For Christ's sake, boss. Be reasonable."

"No." He flushed. "I don't choose to be reasonable. I'm sick of it."

Miller said, "They'll eventually get your head for this."

"Maybe," he said.

"They'll get you sure as hell."

He grinned without humor, and his white face squeezed like a fist around his secret, his one way out. "Maybe," he said again.

But when Miller left, Clumly did not feel sure of him. It might be he *would* take it to the D.A. Or it might be that even if Miller kept quiet, the D.A. would find some way to make him speak on the stand. Clumly himself had as much as told him last night on the phone that they had more on Boyle than they'd given him. And so he hadn't wanted to watch.

When Miller went out, Kozlowski said, "What's all that?"

"That's the Future," Clumly said. "It's the next five hundred years."

Kozlowski studied him.

Clumly said, looking at the floor, "Well, never mind." And then: "We're doing some shifting around, that's what I called you for. You're to work under Miller now. Cops-and-robbers stuff."

"Yes sir."

He seemed neither pleased nor displeased. A puzzling man. It was that, the bafflement that came of talking with a man without visible emotions, that urged Clumly on.

"Listen, I'll tell you a story," he said. "Five years ago we had a series of armed robberies. Crook named Roy-something, turned out. Over on the East Side. Negro fellow. Little Polish grocery stores, barbershops, beauty parlors run in one room of somebody's house—that kind of thing. There was a drugstore down there, and we decided to stake it. Dirty little place, not making a dollar—same as all those little places, poor neighborhood, druggist not doing well enough to hire a helper or need one. You follow me? Well this drugstore had a little balcony along the wall over the front door, looked down on the counters full of the usual bottles with faded labels, displays of stale candy, toothbrushes, fillum, combs—you get the picture. We put a man up there in the balcony to wait. Well, we were lucky, it only took three days. Negro came in, pulled his gun on the druggist, and our man up there in the balcony shot him through the head. What you say to that?"

Kozlowski said nothing.

"It was absolutely legal, you know. Thief had a drawn gun. All right. So the cop shot him in the head."

"A little extreme, maybe," Kozlowski said. But he was thinking his own thoughts, not planning to argue it.

Clumly poked him in the chest. "You would've shot him in the leg, right?" He laughed scornfully. "You ever see how fast a crook can turn around and shoot? It's adrenaline, they tell me. He goes in there and he's scared—you ever try pulling a gun on a druggist?—scared as hell he is, all the juices pumping up in him till he's not in control any more, got a demon in him: damn near can't miss. It's the fear in him, see? It's taken over his body. Quick as a magician he can turn around and put a bullet between your eyes. That's no lie, son. You saw the blood in there." He pointed toward the hallway where Salvador had died. "You want to end up like that?"

"Ok," Kozlowski said. "Maybe so."

"I don't say the kid was bad, the thief. I don't say he deserved to die. Jesus no! It was terrible! But what if the cop had yelled and the gun had gone off in that boy's hand and killed the druggist?" He waited, bent toward Kozlowski, and he could feel his face twitching.

At last Kozlowski said, "Ok. I see your point." He ran his finger and thumb along his shoulder strap and thought about it. He'd reddened a little. He said, "Yeah, I guess it was right." He was not exactly convinced, but convinced enough.

Clumly turned away abruptly to keep his twitching face from Kozlowski's eyes. "Right!" he hissed. "You crazy bastard, the kid was only sixteen years old."

Kozlowski said nothing.

Clumly said, "I fired that son of a bitch, Kozlowski. I shut down that man's *life*." (It was a lie.)

Clumly put his hat on. "Ok," he said, "come with me."

All right. Good to have company nevertheless. Face of reddish stone, impassive as a priest's: yessir, nosir. I was righteous as you when I was young, Kozlowski. Believe it! Oh yes, they're always full of virtue, the fatassed littlechinned young. A conspiracy of Nature, a mystery: three- and four-year-olds with that incredible *in*nocence—over there on the sidewalk, looking blue-eyed up at the cop car, smiling, waving with pleasure at the old fat cop with the green cigar: Hi, Mr. Policeman! Hi hi hi! Beautiful. Zap. Full of mysterious trust that fills the best of their parents and teachers with alarm, with grief for them because the world will change them, and with baffled shame because parents and teachers can't hope to prevent it, and even the best must contribute to it in ways they will not recognize themselves. (Bill Tenny at the corner with his whistle between his teeth, loose, holding up a hand to let the children cross: grinning at them, talking with them—kids who later will grow sullen in the presence of a cop, or defiant, or obsequious-friendly. Observes his boss with the green cigar and comes erect, all dutiful cop, stretching out a distance between them by his change. A salute. *'Lo Bill. Good morning Chief.* Transformed. What was the word? Changeling. So they too would come erect with years. *Good morning Miss Brown.* The squealing schoolyard transmogrified to the half-solemnity of the high-school lawn.) We watch the change and we mutter against it with pride. But the change will be incomplete, we think. They will be better than us. We look up at them out of our yellow-eyed, senile ignorance, reduced to wrinkled, toothless elders, smiling, waving at their brassy youth with pleasure like a kid's: Hi hi. And join the conspiracy, from bafflement: yes: we're the world, there's no denying it: we're old: and whatever it is that the world has done to them, it was us, we did it, whatever it was. So we fall to lies: Young people, harrump, you see what a mess the older generation has left you. Herkapf. Be stout of heart! Arise and do better! And they believe it, oh yes. They are *going* to do better! Who could *believe* what fools we were? They will tolerate us, as we tolerated our idiot fathers before us. Correct. And they will fix all this. Right. Well you're mistaken, Kozlowski. All your reasons for righteousness will come down on your head like broken beams, and nevertheless you'll go on, because that's the law, son. That's THE LAW.

"Pull over here at the corner," Clumly said. "Here's where we'll start." He handed one of the Sunlight Man pictures to Kozlowski.

"You really think somebody will recognize him?"

"No idea," he said. He believed there was no hope, in fact. But you couldn't just sit around and wait. Miller's men would have the pawnshops covered by noon, and there would be answers by then from the State Police lab and the F.B.I.—worthless answers, Clumly had a hunch. At any rate, he wasn't going to sit in his office writing letters and thinking about the trial. "Put it this way," he said, "what makes a man write *love* in the middle of the street?"

"God knows."

"Correct. Our job is to find out. Where'd he get his paint? What did he say to the man he got it from? Follow me? How did he look—Nervous? Happy? Batty as a bedbug? How'd he get where we found him Walk? Hitchhike? Let's go."

But no one had seen him, the whole length of Main Street. They pulled the police car in at the Miss Batavia Diner for lunch.

"It's like chasing a ghost," Clumly said. Beads of sweat stood out around his forehead like jewels.

Kozlowski nodded. They radioed in. No news yet from anybody. They ate.

"What's this?" Clumly said.

It was afternoon now—still no news, except that the F.B.I. had reported. No record on the man. It was just as he'd expected. The Sunlight Man had been too smart for them. He'd done things, all right, and had bigger things ready, but they no more had any record on him than they'd had on Alonzo J. Whiteside that day fifty years ago when he finally made the mistake of walking into a bank too close to home. Clumly and Kozlowski had covered both sides of Main Street now and all the stores on Liberty Street and Ellicott and Jackson. They were on Harvester, heading back toward Main, when the funeral procession turning in to the stone-walled cemetery blocked their path.

"Somebody's funeral," Kozlowski said.

"Oh yes. Yes," Clumly said. "I know what it is." He snatched his hat off and held it to his chest. "The funeral for Paxton. Pull over to the curb, we'll pay our last respects."

Kozlowski pulled over as though it were a perfectly reasonable command, and they got out. Still with his cap in his hand, Chief Clumly started up the sidewalk. Kozlowski hung back a moment, radioing in.

They stood with heads bowed in the large crowd, waiting for the men from Bohm's to get the hearse backed up to the grave and the casket out. It was cool here in the perpetual shade of the maple trees. Beams of sunlight broke through the eaves in threads, dappling the grass, lighting up one part of a name on a glossy granite marker. The new-mown grass smelled sweet. The Harvester Avenue cemetery was older than the one to the east of town, where Hubbard had been buried, and it was larger, three blocks long and at least a block deep —it was hard to say exactly how deep: the hills and trees threw you off, and then there was the irregular back boundary of what looked from here (deceptively) like woods.

"He was a fine man," Clumly said out of the corner of his mouth. "Did a lot for this town. Kept people working when everything else except the G.L.F. was shut dead. Those are his sons, those three over there by the lilac bush, other side of the grave. That's his wife in the wheelchair. Wears that veil all the time, not just funerals. Got a birthmark down the side of her face. They had a daughter, too. Snuck her away to an asylum when her husband left her. It's a story. I'll tell you about it sometime. Over there mopping his forehead, that's Professor Combs. Old friend of the family, used to take care of their money for'm, but they say there was something between him and the wife, and the Old Man found out—Clive Paxton, that is—and the Professor moved away to Utica or somewhere. Back now to pay his respects, must be. Funny world."

The priests came over from their Cadillac, blessing the crowd.

"They were Catholics," Clumly said. "Used to be Catholics were beaten from the start in a place like Batavia, but Clive Paxton broke that. Now half the richest men in town are Catholics. Bought up all the fine old houses from the families that used to have the money—and pretty well wrecked them. Tear big holes in them for picture windows, cut the trees off the lawns, paint 'em red, that kind of thing. Not that I'm say-

ing all Catholics are like that." (Kozlowski was a Catholic.)
"Just the way these ones happened to be. You follow me?"

The casket was in place. The graveside prayer began, and
some of the older people kneeled in the grass. Not Clumly.
But he held his cap across his heart. Ben and Vanessa Hodge
were back by the cemetery gates, with their heads bowed.
Someone in the crowd behind Clumly was talking. He turned
and glared, and the woman stopped, looking startled. Beyond
her, Will Hodge stood watching him.

Clumly walked bent over beside the wheelchair, offering his
sympathy. (Kozlowski came behind him.) "He'll be missed,"
he said.

"He'll be hated more than ever," Mrs. Paxton said. She
raised the veil a little with one gloved hand and dabbed at her
eyes with the other. "He left no will, you know."

"I heard that," Clumly said. He glanced at the tall young
man pushing the wheelchair, the eldest of her sons. There
were stories he'd been in and out of insane asylums himself.
His brothers were beside him.

"The boys will be at one another's throats over it. They'll
have it in the courts for years." She'd always spoken bluntly in
front of her sons. She had a cruel streak, like her husband.

"Well," Clumly said. But he could think of no way to finish.

"I always thought he'd die by violence," she said. "Sometimes I thought I'd be the murderer myself. It shows what
fools we are. It's disgusting to die sitting up at one's desk in
one's bathrobe, writing one minute, dead the next. I wanted
something better for him."

Chief Clumly touched his chin with two fingers, reflecting,
and glanced again at the sons. They still seemed oblivious to
their mother's talk. They wore expensive-looking clothes, almost identical glasses, as if to emphasize the resemblance
among them—the chubby bloodless faces, sharply cleft chins,
pale eyes that rarely blinked. But one was balding and had
dark hair where hair remained, the other two were redheads.

"Sometimes I thought one of the boys would kill him, and
then when Kathleen went mad I was sure it would be her.
Then again sometimes I thought it would be those union people, and then during the War I thought it might be one of your
people, or someone from the Government. I'd be glad, I said
to myself. He was a dreadful man, and he deserved it. He de-

stroyed us all—turned his sons into robots and drove his poor daughter mad and chased the only friends he ever had out of town from pure jealousy, and then me. Oh God!" The fist in her lap clenched.

Professor Combs said, walking on the other side of her, "Now Elizabeth. Don't strain."

Clumly said, "I'm glad you could make it for the funeral, Professor."

Combs nodded solemnly, as always when he didn't hear. He was deaf as a post.

She caught Clumly's hand. "All those years I was sure he'd be murdered, and I was glad of it. But I was lying to myself. He was a strong man, so brave and merciless—as merciless to himself as to anyone else—but with a streak of gentleness, too, or weakness at least. I must have loved him. But that morning —I'll never forget it—when I walked into his study and saw him, the scales dropped from my eyes. Horrible! To think that a human being should come to this! He was all shrunken and horrid, with dirt in all his wrinkles, and the quilted red robe he had on was forty years old. He must have thought he was still imposing in it. He always wore it, anyway. But sunlight in the morning shows things as they are: it was faded and threadbare in that hard, steady light: as ruined as the dead thing inside it. I saw everything, that morning, as clear as something you see in your childhood: like a vision of death. I felt like Lazarus awakened from the dead, stretching his eyes open, looking around him in amazement and disgust. Yes! His old rolltop desk was gray with age, all pockmarked: it made me think of bone that's been lying on a hillside for years and years; and the plush of his chair was stiff with age, like bristles—I don't know what. The room was dirty, and my husband was dirty— not that we keep a messy house. It went farther than that. In that drab, dusty sunlight it was dirty with age and uselessness, like the paper walls of an empty trunk in the attic. I was sick at heart. I felt as if I'd suddenly seen the world with Kathleen's eyes, not that I'd gone mad but that at last I'd seen things as they are, so that the rest of the world would have to judge me mad, the world that hadn't yet seen, or refused to admit it. If only you police could have shot him, back in black-market days, when he was still astonished by his luck and all that money he made, and full of excitement and life. He was devil-may-care, in those days. He'd never even bother to take the keys from the car, never bother to lock a door or turn on a light when he went down a hallway. That all changed, later. It was as if he knew what it was he'd become —a man made of old dry rags, vulnerable to fire and damp. I was sick. 'Clive?' I said, but not because I thought he was alive. It was as if I thought he'd been dead so long now he might not be too dead this morning to answer. Who can say why I called? Because I felt like a person in a stage play, perhaps. A great moment of drama. It *did* feel like that, I remember. I was conscious of it. God help us, I played it to the hilt. Stuffed rags, all of us. Big Raggedy Anns gone gray from being left on the porch. God forgive us. You should have seen me. I stretched out my arm to the window—" She showed how she'd done it, the back of her right glove theatrically on her forehead. "—and I sank almost to my knees. I thought I would faint, but the breeze coming in revived me a little, though it wasn't a cool breeze: an August breeze. I crossed myself. 'He's gone!' I said. Horrible, isn't it? I kneeled by that window a full ten minutes before I went over to the body to close the eyes. But I'm grateful, in the end. After a lifetime of delusion, I began to live on the morning of August twenty-third of this year, when I found my husband dead, exactly like a horse or like a starling on the lawn." She raised her head triumphantly, gave Clumly's hand a squeeze, and released him. A dozen people had gathered around and were waiting to speak to her, but perhaps they hadn't been listening. They were talking now among themselves.

Clumly said, "What did you do then?"

"Then?" She seemed to study him crossly, though he couldn't be certain. The veil obscured her expression.

"After you closed his eyes."

"I've no idea," she said. "I think you've missed my point."

"No no," Clumly said, "it's very interesting, yes. But what did you do then?"

She made no effort. "I've no idea," she said.

"Ah well, not surprising," Clumly said. He considered the caning of the chairback behind her shoulder, the bloodless fingers of her son, the curling hairs on the backs of the fingers, the wide gold wedding band. "At times like these . . ." he began. He let it trail off.

Elizabeth Paxton leaned forward in her wheelchair. "Why are you questioning me?"

It caught him off guard, and he could think of no answer. He merely stared more intently than before at the eldest son's fingers. It came to him that her eyes were not the only ones boring into him, there was someone else, staring at him from behind. He turned slowly, holding his cap in his two hands, and saw Will Hodge.

"Afternoon, Will," he said.

"Hah!" Hodge said, and reached out to shake his hand.

"Why *were* you questioning her?" Kozlowski said, as they went toward the car.

"Later," Clumly said.

Ben and Vanessa were beside the police car waiting for them, Vanessa with her pink nylon glove around Ben Hodge's arm. "Yoo-hoo!" she was calling, and both of them were waving, getting him to hurry.

"They're calling for you on the radio," Ben said, when they were closer.

Kozlowski leaned into a trot and went around to the driver's side and answered.

"Any developments?" Ben said. He stood with his weight on his heels, leaning back a little, giving the impression that he did not mean to butt in. But it did not occur to them to move away out of earshot of the radio.

"I don't know," Clumly said.

Kozlowski handed him the mike. There was news now. The pawnshop check had turned up nothing, as Clumly had expected. The Boyle trial would not be wound up until tomorrow, but it was not too early to predict that the whole thing was hopeless. The D.A. had been by. And one thing more. A car had been reported missing.

"Go ahead," Clumly said. He glanced at Ben Hodge.

"It was taken from a garage two houses away from the jail," Wilbur Haynes said dryly over the radio.

"Find it," Clumly said.

"We did," Haynes said. "It was right back where they took it from. In the man's garage."

Clumly chewed it awhile. "Ok," he said. "How far's it been?"

"Man's not sure exactly. Forty miles, he thinks."

"Blood?"

"Not a sign."

"Christ. Ok, don't let anybody touch it. Is Miller handy?"

"He went out. He got a phonecall."

"You know who it was?"

"Not sure. It sounded like the Mayor."

"Mmm," Clumly said. The order he'd meant to give slipped his mind for a moment. "He head for City Hall, you happen to notice?"

"I didn't watch, Chief. Sorry. I can phone and see."

"Forget it. I'll talk to him later." At last he remembered. "Get vitas on the Paxton boys. Clive Paxton's sons. Everything down to the color of their underwear. Find out where they were when he died."

"Something up?"

"Hell no, I'm just curious about 'em. Gonna sell them a bridge."

"Yessir."

"That's all. Ten-four."

"Ten-four."

"Correct. So long."

He handed the mike to Kozlowski, though he himself was nearer to the hook. He turned to Ben Hodge. "Some business," he said.

Hodge nodded sympathetically. "Well, you were right, your hunch about him."

"Correct. Lot of good it did."

Vanessa shook her head sadly. "Esther says it's got you half sick. I can see it's so."

"I still manage," Clumly said. He hunted for a cigar. He was out. "At least he was able to steal a car without murdering somebody. I had a feeling we were going to find some farmer . . ."

"Thank goodness for that," Vanessa said.

Clumly nodded. "Well, so long, Ben, Vanessa."

They nodded and wished him luck. Kozlowski started up. The sunlight had yellowed now, as it always did late on a summer afternoon. It made the trees seem taller, their colors richer, and gave a new sharpness to the lines of the Richmond mausoleum and the iron urns beside its gate. It was as though all the world were alive with spirit: in the woods beyond the graveyard there might have been satyrs and dancing nymphs, or at least parked cars.

"Where to?" Kozlowski said.

"Just drive," Clumly said.

"You serious?"

Clumly turned to squint at him, scowling. "Does it seem to you I'm a playful man, Kozlowski?"

"You're serious," he said.

They drove.

At last Kozlowski said, "You got a theory, haven't you."

"No," he said. "Stop at Deans', I need a cigar."

Kozlowski nodded and, when they came to the drugstore, pulled over.

Then afterward, smoking, sitting on the middle of his back in the seat, Chief Clumly said, "I got hundreds of theories, Kozlowski. I believe them all. Some of them I believe in the morning, some in the afternoon, and some of them I believe when it's late at night. You follow me?"

He opened his hands on the steering wheel, a kind of shrug.

"It ever occur to you that a cop's just like a philosopher, Kozlowski?" He leaned forward a little to look at him.

"No," Kozlowski said.

Chief Clumly sighed. "It's occurred to me sometimes," he said, petulant. "A cop's just like a philosopher, and a robber's just like—" Imagination failed him.

They drove in silence. Then Kozlowski said, "Like a magician."

Clumly shot a glance at him to see if he was mocking. "You serious?" he said. "Is that supposed to mean something?"

"Only in the late afternoon," Kozlowski said.

Clumly frowned and thought about it. "You're a good man to work with, Kozlowski. You make a man think."

Kozlowski sighed.

*Cops and Robbers, or Philosophers and Magicians.* That was good. A title for a speech.

"You're kidding," Chief Clumly said suddenly. "That's pure nonsense, no meaning at all." He squinted at him, watching for a sign. The young man's face was a mask.

## 6

Miller stood in the high, dry grass of the bank watching. The car looked as if it had grown there. It was up to its door-handles in silt, and it was seaweed green all over, even the windshield and windows. Willowtrees hung motionless and unreal behind and above it, their tops reddened by the setting sun. Beyond the willows stood the crumbling stone walls of what had been, long ago, a flourmill feedstore and carriage shop. Beyond that you could see a little of the black brick of the box factory. Borsian, of the State Police, stood with his foot up on a rock, his right arm leaning on his knee. "How long the fucking thing been here, you think?"

Miller shook his head.

Borsian said, "Current must've brought it down, that's all I can figure."

Miller nodded. If the current had brought it, it had done it a long time ago. Fifteen, twenty years. There were tin cans, tires, a snarl of old barb wire on the creekbed around it; mostly they weren't as green. The creek was down to nothing—a trickle along one side, here and there a muddy, isolated pool. Inside the car there were two skeletons with bullet-holes in their heads. All the windows of the car were closed and there were no holes in them except the one in back that the three boys who had found the skeletons had made.

## 7

He was getting home earlier tonight, not for lack of work down at headquarters but for plain lack of strength. He had a couple of hours yet before sunset, to sit in the overgrown garden with the paper or to pace back and forth on the porch, making up his speech for the Dairyman's League. But Esther's minister was there again. Two nights almost in a row. Was the man after money? Clumly nodded his greeting, then took off his gunbelt and hat and put them away. Then he said, "I'll be out in the garden," and went out through the kitchen and back entryway. When he reached the bench in the garden he realized the minister had followed him out.

"Beautiful retreat you have here," the minister said. "So restful and serene."

"We like it," Clumly said.

Weedpatch. The lilacs along the fence had taken over completely, so that the tulips and crocuses he'd planted five years ago—it was over a thousand bulbs he'd put in—were as shaded now as a worm down in under a rock. He hadn't sprayed the roses once all year: there was hardly a leaf left on them. And the hollyhocks he'd had such a devil of a time getting started had taken over every corner of the garden now and were spreading out into the vacant lot behind it. In the shadow of the weeds there would be lizards and sleeping snakes.

"Nothing like Nature to take a man's mind off his troubles," the minister said. He came over to stand beside the bench. He said, "How *are* you, Fred?"

"Just fine, fine." It came to him that the man had come out here to tell him something. Instantly he felt as he would feel in the office of the Mayor.

"Every man needs a place like this to retreat to," the minister said. "It's like Eden. Do you mind if I sit down?"

Clumly made room and the man in black sat down. He took off his glasses to polish them on his handkerchief, and he beamed toward the sunset as he did it. His dimple showed. *"Well,"* he said. "I've been thinking over our talk."

He leaned his elbows on his knees and tipped his head, waiting.

"Our talk about, so to speak, the Sunlight Man. The magician, and wire-tapping."

"I remember," Clumly said. "Yes."

He began to speak rapidly, smiling all the while with pleasure, like a satisfied crow. The faster he talked, the more his false teeth whistled. "It goes right to the heart of our modern predicament, doesn't it. Especially with respect to the church in the modern world. Perhaps I don't express myself clearly, but I'll try to explain. You're a good man, Chief Clumly, but you never go to church."

Clumly straightened up a little.

"Now now," the minister said quickly, patting Clumly's knee, "don't misunderstand me! I'm not canvassing for members. Nothing like it. God bless you! I'm here to talk to you, as one thinking man to another, because your remarks the other night interested me, and to tell you the truth, a man in my profession can sometimes find himself starved, truly *starved*, for good talk."

Clumly leaned over his knees again tolerantly (the man was lying) and pursed his lips as a sign that he was listening.

"The church has always considered itself responsible for the welfare of the world, the *spiritual* welfare, that is. Yes good. Now in *what*, we might ask ourselves, does that responsibility consist? And to what extent are we *equipped* for our responsibility?"

"Mmm," Clumly said. He nodded.

"It was once a fact of life in our society, that the decision-making forces in the community were in general people of the church—I don't mean just legislators and judges and the like, I mean decision-making forces on every level. That situation has altered, if I'm not mistaken, particularly in the larger cities, and the presence of people like yourself in a town like Batavia —please understand I have no grudge in this, we're talking as one thinking man to another, nothing more or less—the existence of people like yourself in small towns is an indication that the prevalent condition in the larger cities can spread. Now the question is, is this good or not good?"

Clumly tipped his head and considered. He got out a cigar.

"There's one very serious difficulty in religion, you know. It can result in megalomania, as I call it. Are you familiar with my colleague Reverend Warshower, the Presbyterian? A good man, a *fine* man in many respects. But a touch of megalomania, all the same. A very righteous man. The Presbyterians usually are. Don't you think that may have certain dangers in it—political and social, I mean?"

Clumly thought. "I may not be following you, exactly," he said.

"Precisely. Let me try to explain. Don't you think it's just possible that we, as a nation, have perhaps been crippled for world affairs by a slightly excessive sense of righteousness? I mean Asia, for instance. A very difficult matter. It's very possible, I think, that we really do involve ourselves in Asia's problems for Asia's sake. And yet sometimes . . . You see, a megalomaniac, as psychologists tell us, is a man who has done a good deal of repressing—pretending to himself that he does not actually feel what he actually feels if you see what I mean. He feels very powerful through his rectitude, but in fact, hidden in his heart . . . evil." He smiled as though evil were a great delight to him. "Or take social problems. The white and the Negro. Isn't it just possible that the racist's view of the Negro as a person may be nothing other than a megalomaniac projection—that is to say, a feeling of righteousness in one's superiority to a person onto whom one has projected all one has had to repress to become what one has become. I mean: our civilization is built on work, and to do well in it we must repress our desire to loll about. We project, so to speak, this repression into the inherent nature (as we think) of the Negro. We say he's lazy by very birth." He paused for comment.

"Mmm," Clumly said.

"But you see, if there's an ounce of truth in all this I'm saying, our religion—our puritan ethic in one form or another, is at the heart of the American *problem*."

"I see," Clumly said.

"It's a discouraging thought for a man of the cloth, you can imagine." He looked at the setting sun.

"It would be, yes." Clumly remembered the cigar and lit it.

"And what it comes to, of course, is this: if the church is truly to be responsible for the spiritual welfare of the world, its business must be to hunt down and expose the evil in people's hearts. *Or,* our business is to contend against the very megalomania we tend to induce, if you follow my reasoning. Our business is to point the finger, so to speak, at pious hypocrisy—not simple hypocrisy of the usual sort but a psychological kind, a sort of lie in the soul."

"Yes, I see," Clumly said. "I'm with you."

*"Precisely,"* he said. "But what a terrible dilemma! What of the invasion of privacy? What of our wire-tapping of the *heart?* In short, what of—as you say—our voodoo? We pry into men's souls. It's our stock in trade!"

Clumly nodded, a trifle startled. It was an interesting question. He stood up, studying the cigar. "What's *your* opinion?" he said.

"My opinion," the minister said, "is that I am responsible. I recognize the megalomania in myself, and I recognize that I must make perfectly sure that my motives are as pure as possible. But ultimately, when I find what we might call sin, I must act against it. I can see no reasonable alternative."

"You may be right," Clumly said. "I'll have to think about it."

"For instance." He smiled. In the gathering dusk his smile seemed ghostly now, perhaps a little mournful. "If I discover a man who in my best judgment is destroying himself and those near and dear to him, whether that man is a member of my congregation or not, I believe it is my responsibility to worm my way into his thought. Am I right, do you think?"

"It's a question," Clumly said.

"God bless you, so it is!"

The minister stood up and began to pace slowly, with exaggeratedly long steps, back and forth in front of the bench. "A man, say, who, with the best intentions, has so thoroughly thrown himself into his work that he's forgotten what worries may be torturing his wife. A man who, by his very diligence, has begun to set people around him to talking and fretting against him, people who might, potentially . . . Hypothetical, of course. But possible, barely. I suspect I should make myself his demon."

Clumly stood watching him. "Maybe you should."

He stopped pacing. "It's difficult to know, isn't it. By what right? I ask myself. All very well for the prophet to tell David, 'Thou art the man.' He had God's voice buzzing there in his ear. But the voice of reason is not necessarily the voice of God, is it?"

Abruptly, surprising himself, Clumly said, "What are you getting at?"

Again he smiled whitely. "Conversation," he said. "You've no idea how starved a man . . . one thinking man . . . hard to express."

Clumly said, "Well, it's getting dark." Then: "Would you care to have supper with us? I assume Esther—"

"No thank you," he said. He seemed alarmed.

Clumly smiled, puzzled. "Whatever you like."

They studied each other in the reflected red of the sunset. Abruptly, the minister shook Clumly's hand, then put his hat on, ready to leave. "You'll excuse me to your wife, I hope. I really must run."

"Certainly, yes."

The minister nodded and smiled one last time, funereal, and started across the grass to the side of the house.

"You had a nice talk with Reverend Willby?" Esther said.

"Very interesting, yes."

"He's such a kind man," she said.

"Mmm. Interesting." He looked up briefly, watching her chase her stew around the plate with her bread. Like all blind faces, her face had a look of unspeakable weariness, despair. "This past couple weeks has been hard on you," he said.

"Oh, don't think about me."

"Well, it won't last forever," he said cheerfully, though he didn't feel cheerful.

"I hope not," she said.

He drew his Sanka toward him and sucked at the edge.

She reached for her teacup.

"To the left," he said.

She found it and leaned forward, raising the cup to her lips. Clumly said, "Any interesting mail?"

She lowered the cup a little. "I'm sorry. I forgot to look."

"That's not like you," he said.

She laughed, glass eyes staring, and he was distressed.

"Why are you laughing?" he asked. It came out a little sharp.

She said nothing for a moment, her face fallen to despair again. "You're right, it's not like me to forget the mail. I'll go get it."

"No no, I'll do it." He got up.

There was nothing. An electric bill, a second notice from the water company, a letter from Esther's younger sister. "There's a letter from your sister," he said. "Shall I read it to you?"

She said nothing, and he read it in an interested voice. Half-way through he realized she wasn't listening—in fact she was talking to herself. He went on with the letter. When it was over and she'd made no response, he said, "Aren't you feeling well, Esther?"

She smiled. "Just tired."

"We'll get us a good night's sleep," he said.

She got up to clear the dishes and, after a moment's thought, Clumly got up too. He patted her shoulder. "I'll help with the dishes," he said.

"No, don't bother. Please. No trouble at all. Really."

He stood in the kitchen doorway rubbing his nose. What was wrong? But he knew, yes, now that he thought about it. The Sunlight Man again. She was worried, that was all it was. She'd picked it up from him. He would have to be careful. To-morrow he'd bring her flowers.

Later, in the bathroom, looking at the braille *Today's,* he had a sudden suspicion that the copies were old; she'd allowed her subscription to run out. The image of the minister's smile came back to him, and then the black, narrow back hurrying across the yard to the side of the house.

Just as he was crawling into bed his usual nighttime fears came over him more powerfully than ever. He was absolutely certain that there was someone in the house. So certain, in fact, that he drew his trousers on over his pajamas and got into his slippers and bathrobe and went downstairs to investigate. She lay sleeping like a log, as far as Clumly could tell as he left. He stood in the darkness of the livingroom, listening with all his ears, but there was nothing. He looked out at the lawn. There too, nothing. And yet the crawling of his skin was not to be denied. Something was very wrong. Where?

Miller had talked with the Mayor this afternoon. About what? They might have sat there for hours in the Mayor's office, swapping stories, perhaps, and then slipping back to business. One could guess pretty well what business it was. Then finally they'd have parted, and after his laughter at his own last joke, the Mayor would have returned to his office, abruptly sober, grim, and would have gotten his suitcoat from the closet next to Wittaker's office. . . . If only there was some way of knowing how much time a man still had! But forget it. Drive as fast as possible down the road to the Sunlight Man, the rest would take care of itself, more or less. He would go back to his bed.

But the sky was very light, the night air warm, the street completely deserted beyond the window out of which Clumly stood peering. What was happening over on Ellicott Avenue now, at the Mayor's house? The hunger to be sure grew into an ache in his abdomen, and sweat prickled on his chest. He remembered with revulsion the Sunlight Man's words in one of the examinations: "I have thoughts of spying on my boss, listening outside his window." The man was a devil! He knew your desires before you knew them yourself, or maybe it was that he created them. The devil. Insane, the whole business insane. He'd go up to his bed. Lord yes.

But he'd been wrong, it came to him. The street was *not* deserted. Directly in front of his house, in the dappled shadows under the maple trees, by the sidewalk, there was a car—not hidden, though not out in the glare of the streetlamp either—impossible to miss except by a trick of one's vision. It was not the car of anyone he knew, but he knew in the back of his neck that he'd seen it before. After a moment it came to him. It was the car he'd seen parked down the block on Ross Street, when he'd gone with Boyle to the Woodworths'. He drew back from the window and collected his thoughts. "All right then," he said aloud, and he walked quickly to the clothespress where his hat and pistol hung. He fastened the belt around the outside of his bathrobe and started back for the front door. Just as he was passing it, the telephone rang. He jumped. He let it ring again—he stood with his head cocked, looking at it—and then, full of dread, he lifted the receiver. "Yes?" he said.

"Good evening."

He could not recognize the voice. After a moment:

"This is a friend of yours. You'll realize who in a moment. We have things to talk over. Problems. I should like to arrange—"

"You!" Clumly whispered. He felt again throughout his body the half-superstitious alarm he'd felt in the waiting room at the hospital as the man held out toward him his own wallet, his whistle, the bullets, the keys. . . .

"That's right. Your friend. I should like to arrange a meeting."

"Where *are* you?"

"Always the wrong questions." For an instant the voice itself was recognizable, but then it was once more a voice he had never heard before, not a disguised voice, he would have sworn, but the voice of some other man. The Sunlight Man said, "We have problems, both of us, which we must reason out. Your world is tumbling around your ears, and as for me—"

"How'd you get into Will Hodge's apartment?"

"As for me, my situation is as difficult as your own. I propose that we talk. Negotiate, so to speak."

"Tell me where you are."

"Sorry. Come to the sanctuary of the Presbyterian church at midnight tomorrow night. Be alone."

"Why there?" Clumly said, "—why midnight?"

"Because it amuses me."

"All right, all right. Tell me just one thing. . . ."

The line went dead.

He dialed the operator on the absurd chance the call could be traced. As he hung up he remembered the car and crossed quickly to the window. The car was pulling away just as he looked out. He drew his revolver, on some impulse, but hesitated and slipped it back into its holster. "What the devil?" he said. He rubbed his head. Had the person in the car made the phonecall?—tapped in from right outside his house?

Behind him the door to the stairway opened, and when he turned Esther was standing there, listening in his direction. She had her eyes out. "What's wrong?" she said.

"Nothing," he said gruffly. "Everything's all right. Go to bed."

"You had your gun out," she said.

He shivered. "It's all right," he said. Then, gently: "Everything's all right."

*Very well then, I'll meet with you, my "friend." And yes, I'll come alone. It's irregular, I'm cognizant of that. But I'll find you out, and sooner or later I'll nail you. I give you my word.*

Chief Clumly felt mysteriously calm. Also, he felt ravenously hungry. This time he did nothing to resist the urge. He made himself ham and tomato sandwiches in the kitchen, then carried them down cellar with him. There he sat in the half-dark, silent as a huge block of ice, chewing solemnly, and drank two bottles of beer.

tated and slipped it back into his holster. "Wait the devil," he said. He rubbed his head. That the person in the car make the phone call"—tapped in front of her outside his house?

Behind him the door to the stairway opened, and when he turned Rachael was standing there, leaning in the doorway. She had her eyes out. "What's wrong?" she said.

"Nothing," he said gently. "Everything's all right. Go to bed."

"You had your gun out," she said.

He answered, "It's all right," he said. "Then, ready. Everything's all right."

"Very well then I'll meet with you, too." "Friends," she went to sleep, and we'll see us later I'll find you. I'll see you tomorrow.

Carol Christy felt in relief forty calm. Now, he felt very hungry. The time he did nothing to reach the trunk. He made himself ham and potato sandwiches in the kitchen, then opened them down cellar with him. Then, sat in the right desk sitting in a huge block of ice, chewing solemnly, and drank two bottles of beer.

# VI

## Esther

*1*

of release. Sometimes she can hardly remember, and she is
confused by dreams. It was very much like a dream, and now
it has been a long time since the operation failed. There was a
round greenish light and the shape of a head (perhaps) bending toward her, the doctor's head it must have been, but she
couldn't see his features, perhaps she had never been able to
see people's features, she was confused about that—saw only
light with colors in it, and shapes of people and forms like objects in a fire—but after the operation she would see things
clearly: "We can never know for sure about these things,"
they said; "there's a very good chance." So she fell from the
round greenish light into darkness and the operation that was
going to make her well at last, released from all bungling and
stumbling and confusion and released from pain—the operation began, and failed. "Esther," he said, "my dear, dear Esther," and she understood that it was even harder for him than
for her: they must live out their lives like two people in a dun-

geon, and for her the dungeon was blindness, and she could rail against it and hate it and scorn it and eventually learn to tolerate it, but for him the dungeon was his wife. "I'm so sorry," she said. He said, "No no no. Don't say that. You act as if it was your fault." It was not, that was true. But just the same she was his dungeon and he would not be free till she was dead, and since she was younger than he was, and since women live longer, he would not be released until the day he stepped into his grave. "I'm sorry," she said. Well, she'd loved him. She'd wanted to die, and one night when he'd been kinder than ever before to her, more gentle than anyone had ever been, so that the moment when the climax came was like fire exploding through all the room (it was September; she smelled burning leaves and there was a taste of winter in everything: the time of year when her mother would sit at the window, depressed, looking out without hope as though winter were all that remained for her—and rightly, yes, because all her life she must live in September or the memory of it or the fear of September) she, Esther, got up quietly when he was asleep, and put her clothes on, full of sweet pity for herself, and walked out on the lawn of the house they had lived in then, by the creek, and walked quiet and unseen as a druid to the footbridge and stood there believing she would drown herself, free him, but not yet, in a minute or two, not yet. The wooden railing was cold and damp and she could smell the water below her, and she could hear it, though it moved quietly, a sound as sweet and gentle as the pity for herself that filled her heart. In a minute, she thought. She could not tell how it was or how far below her. The air was warm but it had the smell of winter and burning leaves in it and . . .

*Who listens to such stuff? I will not think. Won't think. . .*
*Words.* Will not. Won't.
*Dear God prevent*

(She stood in the darkness and smell of winter and burning leaves, her long blind hands clenching the splintering and yet soft wood of the railing, blind eyes looking down at the brown-green sluggish Tonawanda that she did not know then must be brown-green and sluggish as witches' brew, for in her mind at least there was dignity yet, and romance and poetry and revenge: she would slip into the moonlit water as silently as a mossy stone and be carried away without grief or remorse and without even fear except for, of course, the first shock, like the shock of the ice-cold water around her body, biting at the white of her thighs and invading the funereal and elegant black dress, transforming cloth to the indifferent murderous lead that would drag her downward and soon, before she knew what was happening (she who had planned it) swallow her alive. *Not yet,* she thought. Her blind hands clung like roots to the damp-softened wood of the railing, and she thought, clinging, *Let me die.* Her life was, she thought, an indignity, and it made his life an indignity as well: and though she could not change it, neither by urgent smiling and cheerfulness nor by flight from him, because she knew he would pursue her, not from need or love or even duty but from his lack of any reasonable argument against it, she could end it: she could raise her fists to the sun and say: *It's not good enough.* But not yet. Her life was a fall from light to darkness and a brainless hope for light that would never come, but she had at least this: she knew that her hope was brainless, she could refuse to be deluded, refuse to hope. That much at least. She was moved by the beauty of the idea of dying, the clear moonlight water closing above her, her pale corpse drifting through enchanted groves by the Tonawanda Creek to the Genesee River and in time the Atlantic, possibly, and behind her the healthy sorrow of release. (But the water was green, she was able to suspect, and she would be found, black, bloated, absurd, in the slime at the edge of some farmer's pasture; and perhaps there was no moon that night after all.) *Not yet,* she thought, and waited a fraction of a second too long and discovered that the thing was impossible. And years afterward, sitting at the supper table, her husband reading aloud to her a piece from the paper about a girl who had thrown herself into the creek and been found two days later on the Cole farm, she would understand what dignity she had missed. But she had returned to the house, with her jaw set, and had found him asleep as if nothing had happened, and two or three days later she'd said with half-conscious malevolence that she would kill herself, she was a burden on him, and he had said "No! Please! Please!" She had felt like a whore, or like some medieval saint split down the middle between lust for evil and the longing for good. She wanted to sacrifice, be crucified for him, for in a part of her heart she was innocent and childlike and pure as beryl, but the other part of her laughed at that and said *Esther, you stick with me and we'll make us a life.* Well, what could she do? She had given in.)

*I did what I could, I was a better wife than some.* There were times when it seemed to her that they were happy, more happy than anyone she knew. She would sit in the truck at the Indian Reservation and smile fondly to herself while he talked his ridiculous pidgin English to some fat drunken Indian she could smell from fifteen feet away. "Buyum vanillum," he would say —selling Watkins products then—and the Indian would say "What the hell is 'vanillum'?" *But my dear good Clumly would not understand, for, whatever his other virtues, his greatest virtue was tenacity, especially when the idea he was clinging to was wrong.* But they liked him, understood him, by some clear and infallible instinct knew that he was not looking down or milking them of whatever he could get but merely bungling: "N'yas-kah-weh-noh-gah-gweh-goh," he would say at the door, and they would answer in ancient Seneca and not laugh in his face, and when his truck mired up to the axles in some yard set deep in the woods they would take off their shirts and come grunt him and hoist him up to hard ground again, and they'd laugh and they'd slap each other's shoulders and they would shake her hand and, if they were drunk, would kiss her. She was young, still able to charm without intention. Then old Mrs. Blue-eyes.

*She was old, and her granddaughter was blonde, they said. We always went into her cabin when he sold to her, and that night the granddaughter was there. She was home from college. She moved as silently as any of them, but her smell was the smell of a white girl from the city. "I want you meet my grandaughter," Mrs. Blue-eyes said, and the girl stood before me and I said, "Hello." "Clara is her name," Mrs. Blue-eyes said, and I said, "What a pretty name." The old woman said, "Her eyes are blue, like all my children, so therefore she is white." "Let me look at you," I said, and she came a step closer. The instant my fingers touched her cheek I knew she was beautiful, and as I moved my fingertips over her forehead and down past her eyes and the wings of her nose to her mouth, I became afraid. "How do you like college?" I said. "I enjoy it very much," she said. And I thought, Do you pity me? Do I disgust you? I had seen the line of her mouth, and though it was a gentle mouth there was pity in it, disgust. I said when we were*

*driving home, "She's a beautiful girl." He said, "Oh, so-so." It
was the first time he'd lied to me, as far as I could tell.*

Enough. That was not what she'd started out to say.

We were happy, much of the time, she'd meant to say.

*Were we?*

*Well, we made do.* She was glad to say, he was always a
man who loved work. Jobs that would have bored another
man were exciting to him. Even the bakery truck. He would
calculate ways of speeding up the loading, ways of rearranging
the bakery goods he carried so that everything was conveniently in reach. He would think about it nights, and when he
solved some trifling problem, he was radiant. She thanked
God. How lucky I was, I thought, to have a husband like him.
There were times when I felt less than human, and studying
my face with my fingertips in the dark, I knew I was no longer
pretty—if I had ever been pretty. Uglier than ever then, to
speak plain. But it was not as great a disaster for me as for
many women: my husband was not that kind. He loved his
work, sat fascinated beside the radio listening to Drew Pearson
or Lowell Thomas or Gabriel Heatter, or sat with some magazine, grunting with surprise or interest or irritation, and it
seemed to me that he was better than other men, more mature,
a rock.

She would hear them in the evening, she sitting on the back
step in a holy spell of peace and silence, when he was working
in the garden, and some neighbor was telling him some dirty
story. His laughter was merely polite, a little embarrassed, annoyed. On Saturday nights their neighbors to the left would sit
up drinking late, and when she and Fred were in bed half-asleep the neighbors would begin to shout, and they would call
each other names it made your heart race, and sometimes he
would beat her. "Dear God," Esther would cry in her heart, "I
thank you! Watch over my precious, good husband who hasn't
the sense to watch over himself, and make him happy." He
seemed to be happy. He was so wise, so considerate of others,
it used to make her cry. *"There's a very good chance that if
you have children," the doctor said, "they'll be afflicted." Blind,
he meant; half-blind at birth and, by twenty, blind as bats.*
They had wanted children. It had seemed a kind of payment
life owed for what they'd suffered. She was ashamed. Once
again it was all her fault; her weakness—some ugly burnt-out
thing in her blood—was once again an invisible wall raised

more around his life than hers. He accepted it, with such terrible kindness that she was robbed of any right to anger—the
rage that had been building in her all day, since the doctor had
told her—anger that for sanity's sake she had to vent on him
because there was no one else, had no possible outlet—and so
she raged at him, unthinkably cruel, stark mad, in fact.

*Why do I do this? Over and over and over the same old
ground. So much love, so much happiness.*

("But perhaps, in spite of all you say, he drove you to it,"
Reverend Willby said. His voice seemed sly. Then is nothing
good? Is nothing honest? "I don't say that, my child, not at all.
But isn't it *interesting*, after all, that all his loyalty and patience and kindness should inspire in you no self-confidence!
Think of the love of our Heavenly Father. As I said in my sermon, just the Sunday before last, what freedom, what confidence we feel when we know in our hearts that the Lord is our
shepherd, He loves us and forgives us and cherishes us as we
cherish our children! My child, my child, I *believe* you when
you say that your husband is kind and patient and good, but I
*cannot* believe you when you hint that he is beyond all the
sticky unpleasantness of our common human nature. Surely
we must not forget, dear lady, that there is *pleasure* in our
self-sacrifice. Our kindness has been tainted with masochism
since the world began, and it is not to our best interest to forget it. Think better of yourself, my dear Mrs. Clumly. No man
was ever perfect but Jesus Christ. Do you think it doesn't give
you pleasure—if only a drop of pleasure—tell me that you are
unworthy of being alive? And, on the other hand, do you think
I don't find some touch of pleasure in suggesting that your
husband is less than he seems—no better than yourself, in
fact? Perhaps worse?" She had not believed him but she had
felt better afterward, riding home in the taxi. Reverend Willby
had no idea what human goodness was, and no more religion
than a fly. She sat smiling to herself like a crafty witch, as
though she had just avenged herself—though in fact she'd said
nothing to the minister, of course: had nodded her thanks, as
if thoughtfully, and had retired timidly, ashamed of herself for
having turned to a man she had no reason to trust. And yet
her anguish had been urgent, so terrible lately that she was
afraid of the approach of September. She had been right to
ask for help, merely wrong in imagining that anyone could
give it. When the cab driver opened the door he reached in

and caught her arm and threw her off balance a little, so that she bumped the door with the side of her head. *Let go!* she cried inside her mind, *get your hands off!* but she said nothing, paid him timidly and allowed him to lead her up on her porch, where she said, "Thank you, you're very kind," and gave him a quarter and hoped he would swallow it and choke. "No trouble, Ma'am," the driver said. *You don't know,* she said in her mind. *You'll never dream!* Blindman's tears seeped down her cheek, more horrible, she believed, than tears from the dead.)
*I told him he smelled old, and it was true, but he should have defended himself.* She told him that when he made love to her the stink of his breath made her sick. She had told him that he was like an animal and that when friends came to the house she was ashamed of him. She told him he was stupid and that all their friends knew it. "They mention it to me," she said, "they ask how I stand it." "You're angry and upset," he said. "We mustn't say harsh things and then tomorrow——" "I'll say what I please," she said. "For years I've said only what *you* please," she said to him. "I'm sick of it. You stink. I don't want to live with you. I just walk into a room where you've been sitting, filling the air with your stink . . . I don't want to live at all!" Sobs. "Esther," he said, "my poor, poor dear——" She locked the bedroom door that night and wouldn't let him in, and he slept on the couch. But in the middle of the night she went down and asked him to come up where he belonged, but he was grieving and wouldn't come—it had come to his poor slow wits, finally, that though all she had said she had said in rage, and the words had nothing to do with the rage, they were incidentally true. He had committed no crime, the crime was, as usual, life itself, the immemorial curse, and she had raged at him because life itself is impossible to seize in one's two bare hands and choke. But though he was innocent, he smelled. That was true. "I'm sorry," she said. "I love you, Freddy." "Just go to bed," he said. When she got up the next morning he had already fixed himself breakfast and washed the dishes and left the house, and she sat and wept. That time too she wanted to die, and she said to herself with conviction, *I am going to kill myself,* but she was afraid. She wanted to be even with him, balance the score once for all, but it was impossible, so impossible that she began to laugh as though her mind had slipped: "How can you balance the score with a policeman?—with the Law?" she said, and laughed and cried. It

was he who had wanted children—both of them had, but he more than she—and because she could not give them to him she had turned on him in rage, and now to punish him for her rage she was thinking, like a maniac, of killing herself. It was life she wanted to settle with. She wanted to smash through this bungling idiotic darkness into peace, but the hope was pure madness. There is a moral to this: The operation inevitably fails.

*Mother would sit by the window and her fingers would move slowly over her upper lip, where there was colorless hair like the peachfuzz on the cheek of a boy (I could not see it under her fingers but in the fingertips of my own hand I had the memory of it) and I would smell the burning leaves, but I could not see what it was she looked at—outside the window it was too bright, a wide whiteness like the heart of a fire with vague shapes being consumed in it like kings with melting crowns burning up on a pyre: I put my arm around her and said, "I love you, Mommy." She said nothing. My father said, "She can't hear you, Essie. Go and play." When winter came she would be well again, but would watch me as though she were about to go away on a long long journey and never come back, or would come back only when I was grown and we had forgotten one another. It was I who went. The train wound up through the Catskill Mountains where the air smelled of oil and beyond the spackled train window the world swam with blue. I cried, and at night I was cold. There was no one with me on the train because my father couldn't leave the milking and the wheat harvest, and my mother had to feed thrashers. I wanted to write to them and tell them I loved them and wanted to come home, but I had nothing to write with and no paper but the note my father had printed, bending down to it, squinting through the thick gray glasses that made his eyes seem larger than chickens' eggs. I had a dream, I remember— a kind of waking dream—in which my mother seemed to speak to me very clearly, saying "Essie, can you make us some tea?" I started and looked all around me; the voice had been clear as could be; but there was only the half-empty car swaying on the mountains' turns, and vague faces like objects in a fire, and rainbows at the edges of my glasses.*

*I did not like Batavia—the funny way the people talked, the bright red brick streets that a half-blind child could barely cross without falling, the stores where no one knew your name or, for that matter, cared, and in winter the snow drifts where sighted children squealed and played and blind children floundered and grimly pretended to laugh. And as for the Blind School itself, a horror! It was not their fault. The halls were long, and for what seemed a long time I could never remember where they went: the light that came in through the windows at the ends was gray, filtered through the shade of elms, and whatever direction you looked—north, south, east, west—the light was the same. I walked slowly, keeping to the wall, running my fingertips along the cool, smooth, painted cement, and the others ran past me, shouting (it seemed to me) angrily, and sometimes bumped me. I stood once by a door beneath a high wooden arch—I could just make it out in the dimness of the place—and I couldn't remember where the door went. A boy came through it, holding his hands out toward me, a boy no older than myself, I think, and I watched as he came closer and closer, and I couldn't speak. He bumped into me and jerked his head toward me, a face without eyes or nose or mouth, as far as I could see in that murderous light, and he held my arm tightly, as if to keep me from getting away, and with his free hand ran his fingers over my cheeks and eyes; then he released me as though I were a thing not alive, and he went around me, silent and indifferent, and felt his way on down the hall. Every night I prayed that my father would let me come home again, not because the people were unkind to me—it was not that—and the other children all prayed the same. I didn't want to learn braille: my fingertips were stupid, every form felt exactly the same to me, and the very idea of reading a coarse page of scattered bumps seemed as hopeless as reading the stipple of a plaster wall. I did not believe I needed to learn. At home I sat in the front row of the one-room schoolhouse where I went, and if I concentrated I could see what the teacher printed on the blackboard. I had listened carefully, and at home, sitting with my mother at the diningroom table, I had worked carefully, painfully, with the books I brought home from school. I was getting better, I thought. But in the Blind School they put me in the next to the last row, and the room was dimmer than our schoolroom at home, and sometimes I could not see the teacher. I felt sick, as if I were sinking in quicksand or endlessly falling through empty space, and I said to the teacher one day, "I can see, Miss Ford. Please, please. I can see." She took my hand—she*

*was an old woman, kind—and bent her face to me, gentle. She
had no eyes or nose or mouth.*

*You can see what sort of dreams I have.*

"It would be inhuman," I said. "One has no right to bring
blind children into the world."

*He said nothing, puffing away at his cigar, and I knew that in
his deep, dim-witted way he was mulling it over.*

"Freddy," I said, "for heaven sakes!"

"I don't know," he said and reached to touch my hand.

"Suppose your parents had had the choice—suppose their doctor had known and had warned them. Would you want—"

"Don't ask," I said.

"Now Esther that's foolish," he said. "We all have our handi-
caps. Nobody's life is perfect." *Cross as a bear. It was all so
simple, so right and obvious and true: I am happy ninety-eight
per cent of the time, as Mother was, and I let the two per cent
poison the rest. And so he is good, yes; the minister's talk of
how no one but God is perfect is just like atheism, like denying there's sunshine because you've lost your sight.*

*How incredible, though, that faith in life! No wonder if some-
times one envies him—and sometimes almost hates him.
Heavy-minded, ponderously reasonable, he muses on the fit-
ness of unreasonable things, and drops like old wood clothes-
pins to a basket the pros and cons of giving a child a life devoid of vision.* "A lot of them make great musicians," he said.
*I laughed. Freddy can't tell high from low on a piano.*

"Well," he said, getting up, "I'll leave it to you. That's only
fair."

*I did not want it left to me, and it was not fair.*

*I wanted—what?*

*No, words again. Large gestures.*

*I wanted to be beautiful.*

*I wanted to be loved for myself alone, as God loves even
giraffes.*

*There is a moral to this. There is no such thing in this world
as love. Until the day we go to Heaven, there is only childish
infatuation and jealousy, duty, despair.*

*A sickly moral, admittedly, but better than endless burning.*

*I wanted him to make me feel pretty. Isn't that sad?*

"I am not myself today," Esther said.

## 2

She awakened to find the bed empty, as usual, and the weight of wordless, irrational unhappiness still over her. She sat up and waited to be completely awake, then turned and reached her legs down, long and thin and white, she could guess; more dreadful than her darkest fears. She began immediately to move her lips, resuming her endless dialogue with her soul. It was a long time since Clumly had made love to her. It was because he was getting old, he said, but she knew it was more than that. They'd been, generally, morning lovers, in that glowing first age now endlessly receding like her memory of sight. She would awaken to the gentleness of his hand on her breast—she'd had pretty breasts once, though they were small—his leg lying lightly over hers, his penis growing against her hip, and she would turn to him, still half-asleep, and smile, and he would kiss her, just a peck, and climb up on top of her, and she would part her legs and close around him like a fist. But something had happened, and now she lay waiting through the months like an etherized patient for what would never come. Her waiting disgusted her and made her feel ashamed: she was old, her desire was to her obscene. Her very womanhood, all she could offer him once, as it seemed to her, had become a revolting imposition. He had learned to get up and go downstairs before she awakened, and she, if she awakened too soon, had learned to pretend to be asleep until he made his escape. After they were up and dressed it was better, almost exhilarating, a trap avoided. When he was gone finally, she felt relief. Relief for his freedom, not just her own. She would begin her chores, endlessly talking to herself without uttering a sound, watering the ivy and the dining-room ferns—one finger in the dirt to find the level of the water—dusting, sweeping, mopping, waxing; she would talk on the phone to the boy at Loblaws' Market or to Vanessa Hodge or to the Superintendent of the Methodist Sunday school where, sometimes, she taught (she'd taught there regularly once, but she'd had discipline problems); she would fix her lunch—a braunschweiger sandwich and a glass of wine—and would begin down the long, drab corridor of afternoon.

It is easier to bear a cross than to be one. She still sometimes thought, but without real interest or hope, of suicide. And at times, strange to say, she suffered acutely from jealousy. When she met a young woman, she could sometimes not resist the temptation to ask to touch her face. Even if the girl was plain, Esther would tell herself she was pretty and would wonder if her husband did too. She knew he was not that kind of man, and yet for all her certainty, the fear was there. How she longed to release him, or at very least show him some proof of her gratitude! She was unable even to say the words any more, because her voice, which had once been soft and sweet, had grown harder now.

She always spent almost the whole of the afternoon preparing supper for Clumly, always stew, but she had many varieties of stew, and sometimes soup for a first course, with side dishes of frozen peas or stringbeans or spinach. When she tried to make steaks or some kind of roast she burned her fingers. While she cooked she had a little wine. Not much, just enough to bring a feeling of warmth.

And so she made do, today as on other days. Something was wrong down at the police station, that was the trouble. She could always tell. He blamed himself for that young policeman's murder, of course. That was like him. And he blamed himself for the escape of that insane magician, and that too was natural, though it was not his fault. If there were only anything she could do!

At five-thirty, when she had supper ready, her husband had not yet come home. He was late almost every night, these days. She stirred the stew irritably and turned the burner off under it. She had no right to feel irritable, of course. He wasn't staying down there for the fun of it. He might have phoned, though. That was like him, letting her worry and fret. If she told him afterward that he'd worried her sick he would behave as though that were merely her problem—as though there wasn't a reason in the world for her to have worried, even now, right after two murders in Batavia, when everyone in town was worried sick and the papers were full of it, people told her. "Everything's fine," he would say to her. He would talk cheerfully of this and that, or would settle with his newspaper and after a while read the obituaries aloud. Sometimes she was ready to believe he did it on purpose, to make her miserable. But that was thinking negatively. It was of course necessary to guard against thoughts like that. To keep her mind busy she examined the question of what to have for dessert. "Canned peaches," she said. She went down the cellar stairs and moved easily through the darkness to the shelves of canned fruit, took a jar from the section where the peaches were, and started back up. She heard something and paused for an instant. Rat, perhaps. "Filthy cave of a place," she said. Her foot bumped something and she bent over. Empty beer bottles. She went chilly for a moment, then dismissed it. She continued up into the house and locked the cellar door behind her, as usual. (She had no strong feeling about locking doors, herself. It was one of her husband's rules.) She put the peaches away in the refrig and went in to the livingroom to turn on the television to listen to the news. There was nothing interesting. They hadn't yet caught the magician.

At six-thirty the phone rang. It was Fred.

"Esther," he said, "I won't be home until late tonight, maybe even early in the morning."

"Is something wrong?" she said.

"No no, everything's fine."

She said, "I had your supper all ready."

"I'm sorry. You have yours and put a little away for me, I'll warm it up when I get home."

"You sound tired," she said. It crossed her mind that he did not sound tired. He sounded full of excitement.

"Well, yes, tired," he said. "You'll be all right?"

"Try not to be longer than you need to," she said.

"That's fine," he said, "don't worry about a thing." He hung up. As soon as the receiver was on its hook she was wearied by the thought of spending the whole evening here alone, fretting. She went to the kitchen to have a little wine and halfway through her second glass she decided she would go out.

It was very pleasant out at this time of day, which was why she had decided against calling a taxi. It was beginning to cool. The sun was no doubt fairly low by now. Sounds carried more clearly than at other times, the way they would carry across a lake. She listened to the shouts of a group of boys a block or so away, playing flies and grounders, if she wasn't mistaken, and the sound of a hose spraying grass a house or two from where she walked. She could hear traffic moving, far in the distance. She walked quickly, though she was not in a hurry.

The sidewalk on LaCrosse was old and broken, and here and there it buckled abruptly, throwing one slightly off balance. At Oak Street she turned right, toward the center of town, but before she reached Main Street she cautiously crossed the street and took the cut-through to Ellicott and then Washington. Here the air felt closer—the close-set houses and the trees impeded the breeze—and sounds took on a new density: her footsteps came back to her from all directions at once, from the walls of old houses, the windows and old metal signs of walk-down grocery stores and beauty shops, from parked cars, from thick old hedges clipped at the level of one's waist. No one spoke to her. She thought of calling on the new organist at the Methodist church; she lived here somewhere on this street. But she couldn't think which house it was. Now she was hearing, far away, the noise of a drum and bugle corps or, possibly, a band. Coming from the high-school athletic field, probably. The school was right at the end of this street, where Washington ran into Ross.

Car brakes screeched beside her and she jumped, but it was all right. She was still on the sidewalk, it was not for her that he had stopped. The driver called, "You want a rrr-rrr—want a *rride*, Mrs. C-C-Clumly?" She recognized the voice. Ed Burlington. "No thank you, Ed," she answered, and gave him a little wave. She leaned toward the sound of the car's idling motor. "How have you been?" She'd had him in Sunday school when he was still in the grades. He was out of high school now, surely. A good boy, very serious. He'd been an Eagle Scout, when he was in high school—Fred had read her the piece about it—and she'd felt as proud of him as she'd have been if she were his mother. She hadn't bumped into him for, it must be, three years or so. She moved off the sidewalk a step, cautiously, toward him.

"J-j-ust ff-fine, Mrs. Clumly. I got a g-g-reat j-j-j-job, I work for the puh-paper."

"Wonderful," she said.

He said, "Are you sure you don't w-w-want a rrr-ride?"

She shook her head. "No thank you, Ed. I need exercise."

He said nothing for a moment, but he didn't leave yet. At last: "They didn't th-th-THINK I couldddd-*do* it, at ff-first, because of mmy handicap. B-but the writing p-p-p-p-p-part I do vvv, uh, vvv, uh, the writing p-p-p-p—part I do vvv, uh, vvv*very* well."

"I'm *sure* you do," she said.

"I see your husband all the t-t-t-t-ime, Mrs. Clumly. I didn't get to do the mmmmMURDERS, b-b-b-but I dddd, uh, ddddd, uh,—I dddd, uh, b-b-ut I ddddd—"

She was fleetingly conscious of a difficulty about how to ar-range her face as she waited for him to slam through the *d* into his word. Should she help? A thousand times she'd won-dered that, when she was waiting for an answer from him in Sunday school. She could feel the uneasiness of the whole class growing, could feel the teacherly smile on her face going frozen, her mind backing off from the pain of watching it, and she could feel, too, the rising force of his effort, a hint of stubbornness and anger coming into the struggle as it be-came, as if *because* of the stubbornness and anger, impossible. At last, as if in rage against all the observers of his tongue's anguish, Ed Burlington would clap his hands or stamp his foot, and the word would burst into daylight, like spirit through recalcitrant clay. And so it was now:

"DID get to write on the Woodworth robbery!"

She touched the ends of her fingers together. "The Wood-worths? I didn't hear!"

"Oh y-y-yes. They were robbed one-one day b-b-b-by a wwwwwwwild l-l-l-looking m-m-man. I wwwwrote it up."

"My goodness," she said. Fred must have skipped reading it to her on purpose, sheltering her. She thought instantly of the bearded man who'd broken out of jail. "Did they catch the robber?" she asked.

"N-n-n-never dddd, uh, did."

"My goodness," she said. It came to her that she was going to visit the Woodworths. "Well it's so good to see you, Eddie," she said.

"Same t-t-t-t-, uh, same t-t-twice OVER," he said.

She gave him her little wave. The sound of the car envel-oped her, a roar like some kind of animal's, with a queer clicking noise in it, and then, as though a part of the sound, the half-pleasant smell of exhaust rose up around her. She gave her little wave again. Then, cautiously, she turned around and got herself back onto the sidewalk.

"It's right on my way," she said to herself. "It's only three more blocks to Ross Street. I ought to have dropped in on them long ago, for that matter. How lonely it must be for

them!" She lined herself up with the edge of the sidewalk and
began her quick march east.

The wallpaper had a peculiar softness, a sort of weakness
about it, like cardboard that has gotten wet and then dried out.
The wooden floor of the entryway was oddly dry under your
feet, like the floor of a granary that has had nothing in it for
years but a few old sacks, a rusty shovel, an old-fashioned
wood-and-tin bagger. That was what the smell of the house
made you think of, too: an abandoned barn. It used to be that
at the Woodworth house you would be greeted by a beautiful
and mighty scent of crabapple jelly or applesauce or pumpkin
pie, but there was not so much as a trace of a cooking smell
now. It was as if they had given up eating entirely, and perhaps they really had: Octave's hand was as small as a child's
and as meatless and dry as a limp glove with sticks in it.

"What a pleasant surprise!" Octave Woodworth said. Her
full name was Octave Thanet Woodworth. She had been
named for a famous lady novelist. Her father the minister had
been a radical in his day, although a Baptist, and had greatly
admired Octave Thanet's opinions—so much so, in fact, that
he had invited her to the house when she was passing through
on a lecture tour one time. (It was toward the end of Miss
Thanet's life, Octave had told Esther, when Miss Thanet
weighed more than two hundred pounds and had a wooden leg
and carried a pistol.) It was because of Miss Thanet that Editha, the older of the Woodworth sisters, had become a lady of
letters.

"Won't you come in!" Octave said. "Editha will be so
pleased."

They passed through the entryway into the hushed parlor.
Octave held Esther Clumly's arm to guide her through the
maze of wobbly tables, umbrella stands, lamps, bric-a-brac.
The smell of decay was stronger here, a smell that reminded
you, to tell the truth, of the air in a bathroom where an elderly
person has recently moved his bowels.

"Editha, dear, look who's come to see us!"

Esther smiled and waited with her bony hands folded, nodding politely in the direction toward which Octave Woodworth
seemed to have spoken. She had a distinct impression that the
room they stood in was absolutely dark, or that Editha Wood-

worth was behind a screen, so that the smile and nod could not possibly be perceived.

There was no answer from Editha.

"She hardly ever speaks any more, don't you know," Miss Octave said. "She's more than nine-tenths dead, poor thing. She's a hundred and eight years old, and you know how it is after all that time. I really don't know why she hangs on. But that's how the Woodworths have always been. Agnes lived to a hundred and four or it may have been a hundred and five, the records weren't clear, don't you know. She was just like Editha, hardly said a word, those last few years, except that she used to curse, poor thing. My! Father would have turned in his grave! We used to tell people she wasn't right in the head when she started her cursing. Such language! You wonder where on earth she learned it. 'Agnes is not herself,' we'd say to people when they heard her doing it, but oh she was an imp. 'I am *so* myself,' she'd say. 'It's *you* people. *You're* the crazy ones.' She used to take off all her clothes, don't you know, and sit on an upside-down pail in the livingroom. It was a terrible problem. In the end we had to lock her up in there, even if it made her break things, because if we didn't, you know, she'd come walking right out where we had company and not a stitch of clothes on. I thank the Lord Editha don't curse, at least. And of course we're lucky that she can't get around very well, or undress herself. All things considered, she's a very good girl, aren't you Editha."

Editha said nothing.

"*Well*," Miss Octave said. "Won't you sit down. Let me get you some tea." She guided Esther to a wobbly little chair with a velvet cushion and forced her to sit.

"Yes, thank you," Esther said.

But as soon as Esther Clumly was seated, Miss Octave turned and began shuffling very slowly toward (presumably) the kitchen. "I won't be a minute," she said. "You and Editha have a nice talk while I get the tea."

"Yes, good," Esther said. "That will be nice."

She sat silent then, listening to the slowly retreating footsteps, the creaking of the floor. There was no other sound. The house was sealed like a tomb from all sounds outside, and if Miss Editha was alive or even present in the room, she gave no sign of it. There was not even a stirring of drapes or an occasional whisper of paper stirring on a table, for the house was breathless, no window open anywhere. She felt buried alive. She tried to think whether or not she ought to say something, and the question stirred a flurry of nervous excitement in her like the excitement which comes when one looks down over a cliff. She had said she would talk—had said it would be *nice!* —and if Miss Editha had been listening she would be laughing now with old-womanish disgust at the hypocrisy of it. But what if there were no Miss Editha? Suppose it were Miss Octave's senile joke, and Esther sat facing an empty chair, or a china statue? She cleared her throat. No response. She heard Miss Octave turn a faucet on in the kitchen. She let it run for a long, long time.

Do you have much pain, Miss Editha? she thought of saying. But it was a terrible question, and she did not want to hear its answer.

I hear you had a burglar, she might say.

They went on waiting.

Then—sooner than Esther had expected—Miss Octave's footsteps came shuffling toward the parlor where they sat. As soon as Esther tasted the tea she knew the reason: Miss Octave had made it with hot water from the faucet. It tasted powerfully of chlorine, and it was anything but hot. Miss Octave sat down, not across from her but beside her, as though they were watching at Miss Editha's laying-out.

"I hear you had a burglar," Esther said.

"Yes we did. The police won't do a thing for us, don't you know. I suspect they don't believe it ever happened. They came and fooled around for an hour or two and asked questions and made me walk around with them, with these poor broken arches, don't you know, just like red-hot nails in your shoes, and one of them must have owned a cat, I think, because after they left I had my allergy for three days. It was terrible. The doctor came over and he said he couldn't think what kept me alive. Dr. Steele, you know. A wonderful doctor. He's one of us, one of the Conservatives. It's so good to know there are a few of us left. But of course they're all leaving the profession, don't you know, because of Medicare. They can't do their work when the Government interferes. So much paperwork, you know, when you have the Government getting in the way of things, and of course the Government tells them how much they can charge, and it's so little they simply can't make it any more—they're all poorer than church-mice, since Medicare. Isn't it criminal? But that's the way the world's been going since that *Madman* was President, Franklin Roosevelt, you know. He was a Communist Sympathizer, you know. Editha and I just stopped listening to the radio entirely, when we saw what was happening—except for Edgar Bergen and Charley McCarthy. What ever happened to them, I wonder? Television, I suppose. Charley McCarthy was actually a kind of puppet, and I suppose you can't do a thing like that on television. Still, it wouldn't have mattered to Editha and me. We've been more than half-blind for years, and we'd never have known the difference, no more than you would, Esther. There ought to be special television programs for blind people, don't you think?"

"That's an idea," Esther said. She gave a tinkling little laugh.

"We don't like television, ourselves," Octave said. "We don't own one, in fact. We had one for a week, a year and a half ago, when the Maxwells went to Florida, but we didn't care for it. Of course the world is changing, it's something we have to recognize. There's a great many more Jews and Communists and Catholics and Nigroes now. The burglar we had happened to be a Nigro. Did I tell you?"

"No." She was surprised. It had become almost a matter of fact in Esther's mind that the burglar was the bearded one.

Miss Octave said, "Yes. He happened to be Nigro. You could tell by his voice."

"That's odd," Esther said. "I don't think when Ed Burlington told me about it he mentioned—"

"Well, no, perhaps not. We gave the police the best description we could, don't you know, but there was no point in mentioning that the man was a Nigro. The Woodworths have always tried not to be too prejudiced. Of course the Scripture does tell us—"

"I had no idea," Esther said.

"Well, they never caught him, of course. Your husband came and visited—brought some flowers, too. Do thank him for us. But he didn't really investigate. None of them did. You're familiar with A. Conan Doyle, I imagine?"

"I can't imagine why he didn't," Esther said.

The old lady sighed. "Well, these days, what with all those politicians . . . The Mayor's a Communist, you know."

"Is he?"

"Oh yes. The family's been Communist for years. Well, times are changing. It's something we have to face. I suppose they resent us at City Hall. The Woodworths have always been very civic-minded, don't you know, and sometimes we've just felt we had to put our foot down. Doesn't do any good, of course. When Father was alive—" She let it trail off.

Esther said, "I'm sure my husband did the best he could, Miss Woodworth. You've no idea the kind of pressure a man in his position is under."

"That's so, no doubt. I suppose they have spies everywhere."

"Oh yes," Esther said, surprising herself and, to tell the truth, feeling wickedly delighted. *"Every*where!"

Miss Octave seemed to think about it. At last, with a deep sigh she said, "Such a good man, isn't he. With all the troubles he has to put up with, never knowing which of his best friends may be a Government spy, he still has time to bring flowers to two poor old ladies."

Exactly as though she believed every word of it, Esther was smitten by a sense of great sorrow and loss. "He is good, yes," she said. "He's a wonderful person." Her voice was unsteady.

Miss Octave did not miss it. She laid her tiny hand on Esther's arm. "How lucky you are, Mrs. Cooper. How very happy you must be!"

The irrational sorrow was now out of all control. She could only say, "Yes, very happy."

Then they were silent. The pause grew and became one with the mindless silence of the house until, from the heart of this mystical hush, Miss Editha spoke: "Take me potty."

"Oh dear," Miss Octave said.

Esther half-rose from her chair, preparing to retreat.

Miss Editha whispered again: "Potty." A voice full of terror.

"You needn't go," Miss Octave said, withdrawing her hand from Esther's arm. "I'll just help her to the potty and then we'll have some more nice tea."

"Potty," Editha said. Now she was crying.

Esther sat down again, rigid as stone. She heard the noises of Miss Octave struggling to drag Miss Editha's wheelchair toward the hallway, where the bathroom was.

"Won't take a minute," Miss Octave whispered gaily.

It seemed to take hours: the long painful struggle to the hallway door, the struggle from there to the door of the bathroom, the fierce battle of whispers and grunts and whimpers as she got Miss Editha out of the wheelchair and ready. Finally, alone, Miss Octave came back. "Now I'll fix the tea," she said. "Editha will be there for a long, long time, poor thing. And then after I've cleaned her and brought her back in here she'll be convinced she never went and she'll want me to take her back again. It's a burden, you can see. And of course she can never really *do* anything, if you know what I mean." She leaned closer. "Just little black marbles."

"I think, actually——" Esther said.

"No no, you stay right there. I'll run get the tea."

Esther sighed.

Suddenly there came from the bathroom a kind of bumping noise, and they both caught their breath. Miss Editha had fallen.

"God *damn* her," Miss Octave whispered. "She *always* does that. She does it to get attention!"

"Let me help you," Esther said.

They could hear her calling to them, a kind of whispered moan of rage.

"Oh well, don't you know," Miss Octave began. But she was confused, and still Miss Editha was calling.

At last, full of revulsion and grief of a kind large and vague, as if for all humanity (but it was not: she knew what she was grieving for), Esther got up and groped her way ahead of Miss Octave to the bathroom. The smell was overpowering, unspeakable, violent, and the old lady's moaning was wound inextricably into the smell. Esther Clumly felt her way toward the noise, walking bent over, both arms out, reaching, and came at last upon a cold, wet, bony knee pointing up at the ceiling from near the floor. She felt up the body toward the head, awkwardly but quickly, and at last found the elderly poetess's arm and shoulder. "Let me help you," Esther said.

Behind her Miss Octave whispered clearly, like some Eastern priestess pronouncing the terrible secret, "She'll outlive us all. Don't pity her. She's indestructible."

It was dark out now, the way Esther Clumly liked it best. She could tell by feel when it was dark. Main Street east of the business section was solemn and full to overflowing with night-sounds as crystal-clear and clean as the taste of a glass of white wine from the refrigerator. She passed the iron fence of the Children's Home, and, straining her ears, she caught the pleasant sounds of their playing inside the big house. One of Batavia's mansions, in the old days. People said it was falling to ruins now, huge ugly cracks in the white brick walls, the fire escapes gone rusty and crooked with age. Through the wrought-iron posts of the fence she discovered stiff grass almost waist-high. Poor children, she thought. And poor Miss Octave, poor Miss Editha, poor Ed Burlington, poor Fred, poor Esther. Once May Brumstead had run the Children's Home, the kindest, sweetest woman who ever lived. She'd been a singer once. The sweetest singer in the world. She'd studied in New York, and Lily Pons was a friend of hers. She'd given her life for those children, and when she was there it really had been a home, whatever it was now. She was as round and soft as a pigeon, and her voice was exactly like the gentle *coo-roo* of the pigeons in Esther's father's hayloft, long, long ago. It would be good to give one's life for a worthy cause, find satisfaction. And it was terrible, oh, *terrible,* to be, instead, a Cause for other people.

I was a person of talent, Esther Clumly was saying to herself. I could carry a tune when I was very young, or so my father used to say, and I was a quick learner. I could have written poetry, like Editha. Fred used to say I talked just like a poet, and I did. "How beautiful it is," I would say, standing with him on the hill looking down on the gravel plant stretched out gray and mysterious in the dusk "It's like fog gently drifting on the breast of a quiet sea." He'd squeezed my hand. "You're like a poet, Esther," he would say. But I lost that. Why? It made me feel odd, I guess, trying to talk that way. There were people who would laugh and say cruel things. That girl. What was her name? She had white-blonde hair, and she was a cousin of Fred's, no more than a child, sixteen or so, and I was in my twenties. I said, "On a day like this you feel God's very close." She said, "We better look busy." She was right though. I felt foolish, and the reason was that the thing I'd said was silly, whatever Fred might think, and perhaps it was after that that I began to see that all the pretty things I had always thought and said were horribly horribly silly. I wanted to *do* something, change beautiful hollow words into actions. I remember thinking, if only I could see, so that I could paint. But I couldn't see, and so I tried to take music lessons—as my mother had wanted me to do. But it was too late, and, worse than that, there was something the same about pretty words and music. I wanted to be

Horrible

*Dear God I want*

(She saw herself squatting in the garden, turning over a chip of earth-smeared brick. She wanted to be a piece of dirty brick, or an old wooden crate, or one of those tumbledown barns on her father's farm. The foolish blind woman stands up now, vague face crafty, rubbing the dirty brick between her fingers and thumb. A saint, ha ha ha. Full of visions of joy forever lost, the steep green hillsides of Liberty, N.Y., the noise of the waterfall, the thrill of running in an open field, head thrown back, hair flying, beyond the fence six cows and a bobcalf watching with bored curiosity. One grew up, in spite of everything, and life became self-betrayal.)

Words. More empty, pretty words.

Self-betrayal.

Tulips.

Steam shovel.

It's interesting, when you think about it. All love poems talk about the lady's eyes. It's impossible to write a love poem without speaking of eyes. Eyes are the windows of the soul; something like that. A poem, if I remember. Then a woman without eyes cannot be loved. Her soul is sealed up like a vicious dog chained in a cellar, and little by little it goes mad, or loses spirit and eventually dies, and lucky to escape, at that. My only hope must be giving my love to others, and I've failed. At the Sunday school, when Ed Burlington was there, I couldn't control them. "Make them love you," they said. But they missed the point. Then I tried to help out at the Blind School after that, and there I was worse, because the children were as rowdy as any other children, still stupidly happy, or so it seemed to me. And then too, of course, all that self-pity of mine. Surely no one in the world has ever been more sick with self-pity. A dungeon worse even than blindness, inescapable. The very wish to escape turns into self-pity, and so the shovel I try to escape with turns out to make the dungeon room smaller and smaller.

Stop this this instant.

Yes, certainly. I meant to. Any minute now.

But still she was moving her lips as she walked through the center of town, past the stores, the movie theaters, the solemn stone and granite banks where her footsteps came back to her more sharply than elsewhere, and the noise of passing cars took on a harsher, more insistent growl.

As she was passing the police station she frowned and her lips stopped moving and she stopped to think. Then, abruptly, she turned up the walk to go in. Why not? She would stay for just a moment. A nice surprise.

As she touched the door it opened away from her as if by itself, and she was startled.

"Well look who!" a cheerful voice boomed at her. Miller, she realized after an instant. "Hey Shorty! Look what the cat dragged in." Again he laughed, and Esther felt, suddenly, like Esther the Queen. She heard Figlow coming around his desk to greet her. Behind him the police radio was crackling and spitting as usual, and overhead the old-fashioned fan was mumbling softly. The room smelled of smoke and linseed oil —the oil on the floor.

"Hello there, Mrs. Clumly. Long time no see," Figlow said. He took her hand and squeezed it, like a gentleman. "To whatta we owe the occasion of this honor?"

"I thought I'd just drop in and say hello," she said. "I was passing by, you know. Is Fred in?"

"The boss?" Miller said. "He went home."

She could imagine him smiling at her, winking perhaps.

"Home?" she said.

"Yuh, home," Miller said. "Six-thirty and *pazooey!* he's out." He talked very fast and it made her a little confused.

"Well, when he *called*," she said. She smiled uncomfortably. "He said he might be—late."

"You see the ole man around, Figbar?" Miller said.

"Gee I'm sure he went home," Figlow said.

"I see," she said. He'd changed his mind then. What a fool she'd been. When he found the house empty he'd be worried sick. She should have *known* better. "Well, I guess there's nothing for me to do but—"

"Hole up," Miller said, "lemme see'f I can getcha ride. Eh pisan!" He was calling beyond Figlow to someone else. The one he called to came toward them.

"My kid," Miller said. He sounded proud, and again she

was filled with a kind of warmth. "Thomasa, meet the boss's old lady." He laughed, and a young, strong hand took hers.

"I'm very pleased to meet you," the boy said. He was sixteen or so, and his voice was very nice, very refined.

"Name's Tommy," Miller said, "but we call him Einstein. He's smart, see? Gets it on Jackie's side—his mother's."

They both laughed, and Esther smiled tentatively, feeling shy, then abruptly joined the laughter.

"Got him down here to help with some papers and stuff. You won't tell, eh? Big secret, see. We get behind as all hell, and the hurrier we go the behinder we get, like they say in Pennsylvania. So we figured we'd bring down Tom. Call him a consultant."

"I'm glad to meet you," Esther said. "Fred's mentioned you often." It wasn't true.

"Thank you," he said.

"Hey listen, drive Mrs. Clumly home for me, will you? Take the prowlcar."

He did something with keys.

Figlow was turning away, going back to his work. "It's good to see you, Mrs. Clumly," he said. "Long time."

"It's good to see you too, Sergeant Figlow," she said.

"There you go," Miller said. "And hey, baby, *please,* watch the stop-signs, for the citizens' sake?"

"No siren?" the boy said. She had a feeling they were joking, but she couldn't be sure.

"Not if you can help it," Miller said.

They laughed. Then the boy took her arm and turned her gently toward the door. He smelled of shaving lotion, and she would have liked to put her fingertips to his face to see what he looked like. She believed he must be handsome. At the top step he squeezed her arm lightly, and she'd already responded, stepping down, before it struck her that he must have guided blind people before—he knew the signals. No wonder his father was proud of him. Such a *good* boy, he was. She felt tears coming.

"It's really nice out," he said.

"Yes it is," she said. "I wonder what time it is?"

"Oh, nine, nine-thirty maybe."

She nodded, thinking in horror, *that* late?

At the sidewalk he said, "Here's the car. Excuse the cigarette holes in the seat."

Esther laughed. She really did feel like a queen.

She had no idea where they were going. She always lost all sense of direction in a car. She knew only that he drove as beautifully as he did everything else—drove like his father, in fact. She'd ridden with Miller now and then and had always liked the feeling. When Fred drove, you were sure you would go through the windshield any minute, unless you went through the back of the seat first, when he started up. Even her worry about what Fred would be thinking, sitting in the house alone at this hour, did not prevent her from enjoying the smooth comfort of Tommy's driving.

After a moment he began to talk. "I certainly admire your husband," he said. "Dad does too. He says your husband's the finest police chief in New York State."

"Why thank you," she said.

"It's true." He sounded serious, troubled. "It's getting hard to keep up with police work in a town like Batavia. Dad says it's darn near impossible to operate except in the big cities, with things changing the way they are. And of course the big cities have plenty of problems of their own."

She thought about it. At last she ventured, "Changing?"

"Well, technology, you know? Bureaucracy. I guess that sounds silly—big words always do."

Why yes, she thought. Yes. Like poems. He *is* very bright.

"Anyway, you just don't have the equipment in a town like this, and yet law enforcement is as complicated in a little town as in a city, in a way. I mean, the State puts the same demands on a town as on a city. It's the same as the grocery business. —I used to work for Perkowski, in the grocery store. They make laws for grocers, health laws and things, they make you put in open-top freezer cases and then they make you take 'em out and put in a different model, because there's a possibility of gas escaping from the old model or something like that, and the corner grocer has to go along with it just as if he could afford it. Or farming. I talked to a guy once. It was really something. On a dairy farm they have these milk inspectors, and they made a rule that all the dairy farmers had to put in Pyrex tubing that took the milk from the barn to the milkhouse. It cost thousands of dollars to install—I don't remember how much he said, exactly. And then they discovered there was no way of cleaning the things—though actually that was stupid too, of course: in chem labs they clean tubing with steam, but the State's never heard of that, I guess. Anyway, they found there was no way of cleaning the tubing, so they made the farmers rip it all out. Naturally, you couldn't sell the stuff, once the State had come out against it. All over New York State there are barns with Pyrex tubing hanging on the wall like old harness leather. Just one thing after another like that. No wonder all the small businesses break down. At Perkowski's grocery they have to pay the same wage as Loblaws' pays, and yet all Perk's got working for him any more is his own family. Isn't it crazy? Buck-sixty an hour they pay. When I left there they hired a Negro kid named Ronald for ninety cents an hour, the same as I got, and if you ever saw the inside of Perk's house you know darn well he's paying more than he can afford to, even at that. So along comes the minimum, and the kid's out of work and Perk's doing one more man's work alone. It's the same down at the station, only worse. Perk can at least go out of business when he wants. You can't very well put a police station out of business. It makes you think you ought to go into politics."

She thought about it. Yes.

"What do you plan to go into?" she said.

"Ministry, I guess."

"That's very good. Your mother must—"

"It's Dad, really. Or, really, it's my own thing. But Dad's funny. Big brute like that, used to be a Marine, looks like he oughtta be a prize fighter. But he's a funny guy, really. He thinks nowadays—" He let it pass away.

"You like your father very much, don't you."

"He's a good man."

"I'm so happy for you," she said. She could not hold back tears.

"Well," he said, but again he retreated, and her heart went out to him.

"What were you going to say?" she said.

"He really would like to be a minister himself. You know how it is. He's sorry for those guys he takes in—old drunks and kids mostly—and yet he has to take them in, naturally. He even has to realize that in a way they can be dangerous. You may understand why some tough little hood feels the way he does about a cop, but it doesn't mean it's safe to turn your back on him or let him think you're his friend."

"That must be hard, yes."

"And then the few real criminals you can catch these days, the judges let them off. Or the laws do, I mean."

"That's too bad," she said sadly.

"Well, win a couple, lose a couple," he said.

"Yes, that's so," she said.

"It's a funny world," he said.

He sounded, that instant, exactly like Fred. It was Fred's favorite expression, in fact: It's a funny world. Had the boy learned it from his father, and his father from Fred? She felt sadder and sadder. Furtively she wiped her cheek with the back of her right hand.

For a moment there was silence.

"Where are we?" she said.

"Ellicott," he said. "I thought I'd go up to North and then down Oak."

She nodded. It wasn't the shortest way, but even her hurry to get home did not prevent her from feeling glad that the ride would be longer.

"Hey," he said suddenly, "there's his car." He was slowing down.

"Whose?" she said.

"Your husband's," he said. "The Chief's. It's parked." He brought his own car to a stop, very gently, and then began backing up.

"Is he in it?" she asked.

"I don't see him. Wonder what he's doing?"

"Where are we?" she said. An uneasiness began to rise in her, a kind of premonition. Was he all right? Six-thirty, they'd said. That was when he'd left. It came to her now, finally, that it had been six-thirty when he'd called to say he'd be late.

The boy said, "I don't know. In front of a house, lot of trees. I can't see the number."

"He's not in the car?"

"Nope. Funny, isn't it."

They mused. There was a pain in her throat, as though her heart were lodged there and hurting.

"Well, I guess I may as well take you on home." But he didn't start up. The motor went off.

"Do you see something?" she said. She strained her ears.

"He's behind us, up the street aways, standing in some bushes."

Now she was shaking. "What do you suppose—"

"He's just standing there in the shadows. He doesn't look at us. I don't know if he's even noticed we're here."

"What bushes? What kind of house?"

"The bushes under the front window. He's listening or something. It's a big white house with shutters."

"Oh," she said.

"Oh-oh," the boy said. "There's somebody coming to the door, opening it. He's turned the light on."

"Does he see him?"

"Not yet. No, the Chief's ducked down, he's out of sight. The man's turning. Thinks he made a mistake."

"We'd better leave," she said. He was starting the car already.

"Funny," he said. "It's the Mayor's place." The car started forward with a jerk.

# VII

## The Dialogue
## on Wood
## and Stone

---

### 1

The Oliver Cleatrac howled and popped and whined and Ben Hodge sang, plowing up, the way it looked from where he sat, a field as big as the world. It was close to eleven at night; he plowed by the lights on the tractor. Where the hill rimmed, ahead of him, it looked like the edge of the flat earth; beyond it stretched immeasurable sky, in the center of it, poised like a dancer on one foot, towering Orion. The steel cleats slipped along at each side of him, gleaming and quiet as flowing oil, and against the light of the dashboard gauges the gloved fists closed on the left- and right-wheel brake handles, thumbs pointing upward, were huge and solid as churches. He came to the rim of the hill and dipped over, and the roar of the tractor lightened for a moment then steadied again, urging the five plows onward, hammering like a fast, steel and diesel-fuel heart in the tractor chest. He could see from here the security lights around Jim Hume's barns and silos, beyond that the silver of the highway and the shaggy back of the woods. As he neared the lane fence a paintless and dented panel truck moved into the aura of his headlights. Merton Bliss.

Hodge stopped singing. The night went gloomy. When he came to the lane he pulled back hard on the left-wheel brake, pivoting sharply, tipped the plow out of the ground the same instant, and heaved in the clutch. He shut down the motor. Even idling it was too loud to talk above. He was deaf for a moment. Then he began to hear, faintly, the sound of frogs. He pressed the sides of his head, popping his ears open, and suddenly the sound of frogs, of light wind passing through the weeds, a sound of ducks far away were clear and pure. Bliss stood leaning on the fence in his loose bib-overalls.

"Od do," Hodge said.

"Evening. Yer workin late."

"Just ketchin up," Hodge said. He leaned his forearms on the wheelbrake handles. It would take Merton Bliss a long time to get to what he'd come for.

"How's the wife?" Hodge said.

"She's fine, jest fine. Little spell of asthma this last few weeks. You can count on it, this time of year." He talked about her asthma, told one of his stories, shook his head as if he too could barely believe it. They talked then of politics, in the age-old style of Western New York farmers, arguing shades of a point of view no longer remembered, much less believed, in most of the world; spoke, sorrowful and incredulous, of all that was falling apart in the world; to Bliss an outrage, a matter of plots and stupidity; to Hodge a subtle mystery. It was against his faith that the bulk of humanity was stupid or indifferent or selfish. Why the world was going as it was he could not fathom, but he could not think it was treachery. "Well yes, but then again," Hodge said. He leaned into his right shoulder, pointing his huge gloved fist at his neighbor's chest.

They spoke of Hodge's sermon at the Bethany church.

"You make 'em sit up and take notice," Bliss said, "and that's the truth."

Which was good, coming from Bliss. He too knew storytelling.

Hodge was having a hard time lately getting pulpits to speak

in. It's the ministers, he said. Bliss nodded, understanding. It
was good to have a man you could speak to about it.

"They don't preach the old way," Bliss said. "It's all full of
reasoning, don't you know. There's too much of that in the
world, that's my opinion. You listen to one of those ministers,
it's all like multiplying fractions. It makes your head ache."

"That's the truth," said Hodge. He said, "Been working out
a sermon about punishing." He slid his jaw forward, thinking.
"I was thinking of telling the stories of some people that were
stoned to death, in old Greek times, and what they were
stoned for, and then some stories about people that were
burned, and then some about hanging and electrocuting. I
thought I'd mention what we do to people that write obscene
books, and just mention some things you find written in the
Bible, or in Shakespeare. I've been toying with it."

Bliss shook his head. "You can't get away from it though.
Evil is evil. A man has a child—"

"That may be," Hodge said. "I don't know."

They talked about next year's crops, about the Cleatrac.

"That boy Luke," Bliss said.

Hodge grinned. "Seems to me you got it in for that boy,
some reason."

"Ding right," he said. "That boy's owed me twenty-four dollars for going on a year. I sold him a ewe."

"That's too much for a ewe," Hodge said.

"Mebby so, but he took the price."

"You'll burn in hell, Merton Bliss, and that's God's truth."
He grinned.

"Wal I'll tell you, though. I went over to his house, place all
lit up like Santa was coming, and that boy wouldn't come to
the door."

"He's not well," Hodge said. "Passes out sometimes." The
night's gloom came back.

"Not this time, by gol. I could see him setting there, and his
mother too. They never batted an eyelash." He pushed his
head forward over the fence. "Gol ding, let me tell you. I went
home all right, but I got to thinkin, and this mornin I went
over to his mother's place, going to lay it on the line. Wal,
whattia think?"

Hodge waited.

"Not there. Wasn't nobody there. I looked all around, and

pretty soon I just happened to notice that cellar door was open. You want to know something, Hodge? There's somebody been living there."

"No," he said.

"Wal I know what it could be, all right. People know pretty well how it is with her. No offense to your family. Just the same, it's mighty ding strange, somebody living in a divorced woman's cellar. You got to admit it."

Hodge nodded.

"I was you, I'd look into it. That's all I've got to say."

Hodge took it in, no longer meeting Bliss's eyes. "What kind of things were down there?" he said.

"Canned food, some little boxes with padlocks, shoes."

"I'll look into it," he said. "Could be she doesn't know."

"Could be," Bliss said doubtfully.

"Well, thanks for letting me know," Hodge said.

"Sure thing. Just thought it's my duty, being a friend of the family and that." He drew back a little, preparing to leave.

"Thanks," Hodge said.

"Sure thing."

If there was something he'd come to borrow, he forgot to say.

Someone in the cellar. It had happened once before, the last time Tag had slipped back. It had been Will's house then. Hodge ground on the starter and the Cleatrac exploded to life. He shoved in the clutch, shifted to third, and went clattering down the headland. At the furrow he pivoted left and dropped the plows. It must be midnight by now. The headlights inched forward toward the wide black silence and the stars. He could hear behind him, or thought he could, the whisper of the mollboards turning the black, firm earth, exposing old arrowheads, it might be, or pottery shards, or bits of murdered Indians' skulls. He plowed on, silent. A crop of spring wheat to get in.

## 2

The Sunlight Man worked in haste, sawing, hammering, knotting, wiring at the bench in Luke Hodge's garage. The pistol lay on the vise, where he could snatch it up in an instant. "Ridiculous," he said to himself aloud once. But he could not let himself think about that. It was, for some reason not clear to him, necessary. He had meant to go to Ben, had instead gone to Clumly—had at any rate set up a meeting with Clumly. It was, he could only explain, necessary. What he must say he could not say to a brother; it must be to the coldly reasonable unreason of officialdom. It did not require all this lunatic equipment, of course. (The formless clutter of Luke's garage was changing, little by little, to a clutter of toggled magician's devices: false boxes, a bomb made of fertilizer and flour, a crudely fashioned thing of leather and cloth which, released in a dimly lit room, would be unmistakably a bird.) With a part of his mind he was resolved to go straight to the heart of the matter when he met with Clumly. Another part insisted upon preparation for jokes, the laughter of despair. He might not use them, he thought. But he understood he was fooling himself. He would use them. His prisoners were in the cellar, Millie gagged, full of bitchery and rage, Luke passive and despairing as himself, Nick silent as a snake, sunk into his mind. He would not think about them. The thought of Millie's naked breasts, sharply revealed in the lightning flash, filled him with an obscene and bestial hunger that mocked his grief and disgusted him. In the gas chambers, no doubt, they copulated. But he would not. Nor would it be a gas chamber for him. He would make himself plain, knowing all along that what he had to say could never be plain to Clumly's kind, and then, the absurd gesture finished, he would be gone without leaving a trace. Why he must make the gesture he did not know. He would make it, and afterward, "silence, exile, cunning." He could escape easily enough. In Luke's truck, perhaps; property of Paxton Corp.; a fitting irony. It was Kathleen's father he'd have said it to, if destiny had allowed it.

The Old Man, not old then, stared at him with mindless eyes, comfortable in the leather chair, the magazine—Taggert's magazine—closed indifferently over his finger.

"I'll make you a proposition," he said.

"You didn't like the article?"

He ignored it. "I'll put you on your feet. I owe you that. I'll make an honest man of you, and you annul the marriage."

"Bluntly spoken," Hodge said.

"And I'll assume all hospital expenses."

"Because you owe her that."

That, too, he ignored. "Take it or leave it."

"And if I leave it?"

"You'll take worse."

"I believe it," he said. "I know your history. Just the same, I think I'll chance it."

Paxton leaned forward, put the magazine on the chair-arm with distaste, and stood up. "I won't debate my history with you."

"Of course not," Hodge said. "Even if you won, it would be vulgar, and a man like you can't afford vulgarity. That's for old families." A nasty cut. He'd been a master of the nasty cut in those days. "But then, no need for debate. I know why you work as you do, the rationalizations. A thousand old saws in defense of shooting an organizer through the head. To the victor belong the spoils. He who hesitates is lost. Finders keepers losers weepers. In Rome do as the Romans do. Let sleeping dogs lie—you being, in this case, the sleeper. And above all, It's a Free Country."

"I should like to leave now."

Hodge remained in front of the door, leaning on his arm. "Shouldn't you, though. To push buttons, pull strings. A man of influence."

Paxton stood waiting, patient. He had curly gray hair around his ears; the rest was black.

"You don't care to debate it, naturally. I must defend all points of view myself, my own antagonist. It's my training, however. The defense insists, ladies and gentlemen of the jury—"

"You're unbalanced." He showed, as usual, no sign of emotion.

"Yes. The defense insists that this gargantua you see before you has his reasons. This cyclops. This grendel. He was poor in his youth. He suffered much. He saw those around him— his fellow poor—tossed blindly on the current of their uncertain emotions, saw them reach out in all directions, undecided, feeble. It came into his mind that a man must have a purpose —some single, undeviating, divinely inexorable purpose. Purity of heart. He must get power, seize it come hell or high water and cling to it. And he has done so. Whom has he opposed? The kind of people he has known since childhood— working people, businessmen unsure of their positions, the weak, the scatterbrained. He has prevailed, and there can be only one reason: he was right. He has done much good. He has given men jobs when there were no jobs to be had. That is a fact. I ask, I implore, I demand that this man be given justice!"

Paxton closed his hand around his lapel and looked at the floor. "You're making a fool of yourself."

Only then was Hodge furious. For all his power over men, over his family, even over Kathleen, Paxton was not worth the opposition of a Hodge. He was not cunning enough to know viciousness when he heard it, so idiotic that he believed in full confidence that his antique saws were parries. He had no brain, had not even physical strength in which Hodge might spark some fire to answer his own. He had nothing but his monstrous righteousness. His daughter had married against her father's choice, and now, going mad, must be saved from her demonic husband—a man known to be dishonest in business (what wonder if the poor child raved, set fires to curtains?).

Hodge said, "Are you really blind to it?—that it's you who drove her mad?"

"I will not discuss it."

"No, of course. Will merely correct it. Find her a pretty garden, perhaps. Buy her keepers."

"Mr. Hodge, I have engagements. I'll see you in court."

Hodge calmed himself. He could understand the Old Man's side. That was the horror. So one understood Germany, or the Chinese Communists, or Africa. The clear head's burden. Thus by abstraction he fought the urge to murder his father-in-law, because she loved him. He stepped back from the door, letting him through. "I'll see you in hell," he said calmly.

The Old Man nodded—a strange thing, now that Hodge thought about it. Soberly nodded as if to say, "That's so."

He'd been working faster and faster, as if in flight from the memory burning in his head.

From the magazine, too, he had debts. They were slight, compared to the rest. They were among the debts he had meant to pay off, because Mollman was a friend of sorts, a former classmate, and besides that, a rare printer, the kind who took on obscure magazines from faith in them, gave honest prices and did a first-rate printing job. He even made a go of it—the riskiest business in the world, not even a business, as a matter of fact. No arty little journal really paid. You supported them by sweat and begging and living off the hog's toes. So Hodge had planned to pay, the same way others paid, by sacrifice. But he had not gotten to it; never would. Whatever bills came, month by month, he threw out with the trash. He would read them, pay up, when his ship came in. So he'd told himself. But his ship was sunk. He admitted that now. He would have to start all over, maybe Argentina. He must not think about it. *Deadly Opinions,* he'd called it. A subscription list of two hundred, mostly unpaid. He had somewhere card-catalogs of names, a bundle of unreturned manuscripts, packets of galley proof.

He would think about the weather.

The night was pleasant.

*that time of night when the troublesome cares of humanity drift from our hearts and on seas of luxury streaming in gold we swim together, and make for a shore that is nowhere*

> *(To the white-mantled maidens*
> *of Tanagra I sing my sweet lays,*
> *I am the pride of my city*
> *for my conversational singing)*

Greater love hath no man than this: than he give up his head for his beloved.

"That's enough," he said. He thought of striking his hand with the hammer.

"I need a drink," he said. That, at least, was true, but he did not stop working.

The inability to act, except absurdly. Familiar plague of his existence. He'd been doing it, walking the same circle, round and round, since before the time . . .

It was not true that he himself was blameless. Had the Old Man sensed that, for all the sharp-steel brutality of his mind?

In the beginning, before he knew that the sickness was serious, he had been unfaithful to her in his thought. She'd made demands, was forever interrupting his work, insisted on knowing everywhere he went, constantly spoke of his scuffed shoes, his untrimmed hair. She complained that he was getting fat.

"You're *sick,*" he said, lashing out viciously, and she answered that he was the sick one, and made him believe it. They would have terrible fights, frequently about her father. Then it would all be as it had been before, for a while. He would notice the beauty of her walk, would sit on the bed

watching her fix her face for a party, and he would reach out
to touch her when she passed. Then it would happen again,
and he would endure it for a time, withdrawing to his
thoughts. Sometimes she would go rigid with anger, would talk
gibberish; and he, though he held her, soothed her, assured her
of his love, would be full of secret hate. The Old Man had
started it perhaps, but he himself had pushed it along. He had
drawn back into his mind, and when she beat him with her
fists, ludicrously futile, he had endured her violence with
scorn. What she said of him was cruel and false, and because
it was painful he had developed defenses. There were plenty of
people who did not find him fat, ugly, stupid, malicious, whatever it was she accused him of at the moment. They became
his battlements against her. He began to long with all his heart
to be rid of her, not to be with some other woman—her cruelty made him hate all her kind—but merely to be free, to prove
himself in some battle worth the trouble. And at the same
time, precisely because he was no longer able to believe in any
of them, he wanted to couple with every woman he saw. It
was true, he would see later, that he was sick. He would realize with a shock of horror why it was that he'd been able to
win her so easily from her father: it was no victory, the same
regime.

But he had not known that yet and would not make it out
until too late, after he had won by destroying her, had sapped
her mind because he would not learn what his father's life
taught: *stop, listen, wait.*

It takes strength to listen and wait, and neither one of us
was strong. To desire too much, to think oneself unfit—

Not a circle, a spiral inward *(introversion)* to a madness of
cool objectivity.

*Nothing passes belief when a god's intention*

We weren't ready yet, either of us; we loved each other and
were at war for fear that we didn't deserve what we took.
Withdrew by separate paths. You forward to madness, and as
for me—

*Deadly Opinions.* He had meant it to be ironic, but the title
told the truth. Thoughts of a mind half god, half goat. *It was
like that, yes.* He had written once.

> *Burning nights and days in his sullen grove,*
> *Funereal as onyx, hind legs splayed,*

*Sick and omnivorous, the ruptured goat*
*Participates in the antics of the brain.*

*His monstrous groin cries out to mount the wind*
*As the mind cries out for subtleties worth thought*
*And the heart for a sacrifice as thick as time:*
*Hunger and surfeit gathered in one red heat.*

*His eyes are blank as stones. He has no name,*
*No physics for his rage. Collects his force,*
*Attacks and painfully couples; then, alone,*
*Broods once more on anger; finally dies.*

*I am unhinged by that fierce unholy image:*
*Fed up with gentleness, and sick with thought,*
*I will tear down my kingdom hedge by hedge,*
*Make war on the scree-gashed mountains, lord the night!*

*I turn to life! In every glittering maid*
*I'll plant my burning wrath till the last flame*
*That cracks my chest is spent away to head*
*And the parched ribcage cools to easy dying.*

*I'll learn to mock responsibilities,*
*These cold whereases capping the living well*
*That churns, beneath the ground, by fiercer laws.*
*I'll have no truck with words. Discretion. Guilt.*

*I'll put on joy, or something brother to joy;*
*Butt down the delicate gates I've helped to firm.*
*I'll turn blind eyes on tears, stone ears on sighs,*
*No more the pale good friend. A mindless storm.*

*For I have cause! I've proved what reason is—*
*Paid with contempt, indifference. Honored laws*
*I do not need; made peace with foolishness*
*That steals my hurtling-downhill time and laughs.*

*I too have blood to burn. I know the case*
*Of those I am of use to. A human voice*
*Making the time pass, keeping the night outdoors.*
*No more! Go hire pale virgins in my place!*

*Virgins. Who smile, who weep, who ask to be loved.*
*I am no raging goat (nor meant to be):*
*A kindly ass in glasses, lightly moved,*
*Sniffing back tears at the movies tenderly.*

*Or worse. A ruptured goat with a thinking head,*
*Aware that maidens fall betrayed not by*
*My pagan code but out of their own dumb need*
*As I fall headwards, raging thoughtfully.*

*Where is the man, while body and head make war?*
*Holy Abstraction, catch us up as we fall!*
*Turn us to saints. Distract us out of earth*
*To love of things celestial and unreal!*

*Make me the singer of lovers' agonies,*
*No victim now, pale comforter to victims,*
*Some kindly grandmother with inward eyes*
*Forgiving harmless fools for slight destructions.*

*Make me the mindless brute in Plato's cell,*
*Walled from sense, bereft of the flesh's curse:*
*Teach me the trick of granite, burning yet still,*
*A seeming rest in a tumbling universe.*

Such was his betrayal. Infinitely subtle compared to her
father's, and for that reason more deadly. There was no atone-
ment for it, no court to hear his confession or defense.

He stood, hands on hips, surveying his work, and saw that it
would do. He began to load it into Luke Hodge's car. When he
was finished he rubbed his hands and nodded. "Poor old bastard," he said.

> *When God made Clumly*
> *He was old and sick,*
> *Where he should've put 'is head*
> *He put his prick.*

He made a quick trip to the cellar to check his prisoners,
then started for his meeting. "Poor lunatics," he said, sinking
toward grief.

## 3

The front door of the church was unlocked. Clumly had
had a hunch it might be. He looked all around with the great-

est possible care and saw no one. The corner of Liberty and Main was gray and deserted, full of dead, pale light from the streetlamps, the fluorescent nightlights of the appliance store across the street, the floodlights reaching up like hopeless prayers toward the steeple of St. Joseph's, across Main. Farther along toward the center of town the gray took on a pinkish cast, only faintly satanic, from the neons burning like flares above commercial doorways as dark as coal bins. A long, glittering car passed, heading west on Main, and after a moment a semi heading in the opposite direction pulled up at the light, which had turned red now, and waited. The light changed; the truck made a hissing noise like a sigh and started up. Quickly, Chief Clumly opened the arched door just enough to let himself in, glanced over his shoulder one last time, threw down his cigar, suppressed an annoying yawn, and ducked into the cool, funereal darkness of the vestibule. He pulled the door shut behind him and stood bent over, hands clasped, small eyes peering into the blackness, listening. There was not a sound, but he could feel the maniac's presence and, what was more, could smell it. The church reeked. He moved the tips of his fingers to the handle of his pistol and started toward the sanctuary door, only a pale gleam of wood in the almost perfect darkness. He was sick with weariness; he hadn't been up so late in years. The floor creaked with every step he made. Twice he turned abruptly, believing there was a man behind him on the stairway that led up to the balcony and, beyond that, the steeple. At the sanctuary door he paused to listen again. His head ached. Still nothing. It was lighter here, the smell even stronger. The sanctuary walls were gray—they would be white by daylight—and held a faint glow of uncertain color that came filtered through the stained-glass windows along the side. As his eyes got used to the semidarkness he found he could make out the pulpit and font, the crenellations of the wall behind, the carved symbols on the panels of the elevated choir loft. On the minister's tiered dais stood three high-backed chairs, old and dignified, and hanging above the chairs an elaborately ornamented lamp, not burning tonight although it was a symbol, Clumly had somewhere heard, of some kind of everlasting fire. Suddenly something burst into motion right under his nose—a bat, he thought as his alarm subsided—or perhaps some kind of bird. Before he knew what that fierce whirring was he had lifted his hand to his face, ducking back, and had let out a whispered cry; but immediately he saw the thing flying along the right wall and knew it was nothing supernatural. He reached down once more to touch the pistol. The pistol was gone.

"You're right on time," someone said the same instant. A deep voice full of anger like a glow of red light inside the skin. The high arched ceiling, the walls of wood and rock like plaster, the sea of gleaming pews falling away toward the altar made the voice seem even deeper, perhaps—and nearer—than it was. Clumly reached inside his coat and clicked on the small, flat tape recorder he'd tucked there, then smiled craftily, though his heart pounded, and took two more steps, his head cocked to listen for any hint of a footstep, the rustle of a curtain, some sign of where the man stood hidden. The skin of his arms prickled and all his body felt hot. At last he saw what he was looking for. In the central altar chair something moved, a darkness more intense than the darkness of the chair itself. It was only a slight movement, at the start, no more than a heart's intuition of movement, like a stirring of some creature millennia old in a mountain of Siberian ice. But the intuition grew, and now he was moving forward toward the altar, raising his arms with grim and macabre dignity, half Miltonic dream of Lucifer, half whitefaced mechanical man in drab, once-black, moth-eaten clothes, responding with tin emotions to the demand of a drive in a museum of horrors. Incredibly, he must have been sitting there all the time. Yet here, a hundred feet away from where he sat, the pistol was gone.

Clumly clenched his fists and made himself calm. "So you came," he said. He continued slowly down the aisle to the front pew, center, stood musing a moment with his right hand clinging to his left, then slipped into the pew and lowered himself cautiously onto the polished wood of the seat. It came to him all at once that for all his panic, he was really terribly tired, hardly able to keep his eyes open. It had been a long time since he'd stayed up all night. He clenched his jaw and squeezed his eyes shut, then opened them again, trying to bring himself wide awake. Should he mention the pistol at once? Suppose the madman had brought him here for the purpose of murdering him. It was foolhardy, coming here without telling a soul at the police station what he was doing. But necessary. How else could he get what he had to get on the Sunlight Man? Correct. How slowly his mind worked! It seemed to creak as it moved, like his bones. Now that he thought of it, he wasn't sure the Sunlight Man had answered him. "So you came," Clumly said again. He ventured a crafty smile. After a moment he forced his eyes open and saw that the man was at the pulpit now, hands closed on the corners, gazing down on him with, it seemed, compassion. He was well dressed, almost elegant, the beard neatly trimmed, the grayish blond hair curling around his ears like the locks of an angel of ambiguous allegiance. Clumly let his eyes fall shut again. It was not so much that he was sleepy as that his eyes were tired. Yes. Still, thank God he'd had the presence of mind to bring the tape recorder. He was in no shape to catch any subtleties, that was for sure.

"You look tired, Fred."

Thus began the remarkable dialogue Batavia Chief of Police Fred Clumly would play over and over later, with confused feelings of bafflement and rage and sorrow. The Sunlight Man leaned on the pulpit. Clumly pressed his knees together and sat back in the pew and closed his eyes. It was not that he was going to sleep. He sat tense as a tiger poised to spring, every nerve alert—though he was tired, yes, that was true. It was in-human, having to stay wide awake at such an hour. If nothing but his personal safety depended on his keeping his guard up, then strange to say he would have slept: when you were sixty-four years old and dead with weariness it didn't matter any more. But there was no telling what dangers he had been chosen (so to speak) to protect the people from. And so there could be no question of his drifting off to sleep. The Sunlight Man's voice receded.

"*Are* you?" the Sunlight Man asked sharply.

Only later, sitting bent over the tape recorder in his attic, would he know what had gone before.

CLUMLY: So you came. (*Long pause.*) So you *came.*

SUNLIGHT (*angrily*): What are you fiddling with, there inside your shirt?

Ah yes, of course. I might have known. Very well, just as you please. (*He laughs. Then, soberly, his anger suppressed now:*) As I said on the phone, we have problems to talk about. As you know, I let one of your prisoners out. I'm afraid I didn't anticipate the complications his . . . enthusiasm . . . would introduce. (*Laughs grimly. Pause.*) We now have on our hands, you and I, two murders. I thought it might be help-

ful if we could come to an understanding of our rather different positions. I respect you, you see. But I'm in fundamental disagreement with your philosophy of life. I thought if our two stands were clearer, perhaps ... Are you listening? *(Enraged:)—Are* you?

CLUMLY: Yes yes! What?

SUNLIGHT *(after a long pause, in control again):* My feelings about murder are ambivalent. It's antisocial, granted. But then, society itself can be murderous. I'm an authority on that. Let me tell you about ancient Mesopotamia.

CLUMLY: What?

SUNLIGHT *(in the voice of a lecturer):* You're familiar, I suppose, with the conflict of the Old Testament Jews and the Babylonians? Our whole culture is a product of the Jewish point of view, and we tend to take their side without bothering to reflect. But the Babylonians were an interesting people. Consider their ideas about the gods—"sticks and stones," the Jews used to call them. What do *you* think of when you think of God?

CLUMLY: Why, I think ... *(Pause.)* This is very irregular!

SUNLIGHT: Yes.

CLUMLY: I think of *(pause)* a spirit.

SUNLIGHT: Excellent! Exactly! That's the *Jewish* point of view. But the Babylonians saw the matter quite differently, if I'm not mistaken. All the evidence we have—fragments, representations, clay replicas, even literary evidence—indicates that the Babylonian gods were conceived as actually residing in their images, effective only within the substance of their images. As ineffective without the physical image as a radio wave without a radio to receive it. You follow me, I take it. You see how clearly I explain things. A talent I have. Very well then. The images. Excuse me, but I must expand on this. You'll soon see the reason. All right. The gods. They were made of rock or of precious wood and covered with fine garments and plated with gold. For eyes they had precious stones—sometimes really magnificent stones—huge rubies, emeralds, diamonds, sapphires. Dressed very much, I might mention, in the style of Mesopotamian kings. Distinctly. A point which gains importance when we observe that their temples were arranged and adorned exactly in the manner of the kings' palaces—with one significant exception, of which I may speak, if I remember, sometime later. They were not kings, however. To modern eyes some of them looked like artistic representations of certain human ideals—the dignity of old age, the innocence of youth, the technical struggles of the craftsman, and so forth— or sometimes they looked like representations of ideals beyond human understanding: Anu, the Sumerian sky god, for instance, was misanthropic, and Enlil (or Illil, as some texts say), the underworld god, was totally indifferent to man. Curious? As for gods reflecting aspects of the human condition, some were perfectly clear and reasonable in meaning—some were representative of the grace and majesty of femininity, for instance—but others were baffling, for example the bull-shaped son of Samas, with idiot's eyes and a crown of unbelievable splendor. What were such creatures worshipped for? we ask. What the devil did they mean? But of course we don't ask it very seriously, coming, as we do, from the Judeo-Christian line. We appreciate the noble mystery of whirlwind-voiced Jehovah, all-powerful, all-knowing, as irresistible and unknowable as the universe itself, a God in whom, as in the universe itself, the ends meet and all seeming contradictions form an order, or so we prayerfully trust—an order merely too vast for human understanding. He he he! *(Soberly:)* We appreciate even the Eastern Buddhas, in whom confusion is resolved to an unearthly smile, that is to say, a renunciation of substance and all the Manyness which clings to it—the exultant pale smile of victory that comes from withdrawal from this world of mutual conflict into the oneness of flawless spirit. The East and West come together at least in this: they are both of them rational, succinct with the dignity of mind's separation from matter. But the ancient Middle, that's something else!

Listen! Consider with your soft Judeo-Christian eyes the flat absurdity of the Mesopotamian gods. They're *man*-sized. Think of it! Not huge and awe-inspiring, like the greatest of the Buddhas in China or the forests of India. And neither can we excuse them as we excuse the manettes, the household images, the icons of sensible societies: our small images of holiness are not worshipped as holy in themselves, they are symbolic reminders of the larger, grander Buddhas of the forest, or humble symbols of the unspeakable, itself by no means humble. The Mesopotamian gods, on the other hand, reside in their images, and the images are nothing more, nothing less, than dolls. Hacked out by men, dressed, painted, adorned by human hands. They play house. They eat breakfast, dinner, supper—served by their priests. They are undressed every night, put to bed with their wives, re-dressed in the morning. They go to parties, they ride into battle on gilded litters, they even ride horses and occasionally go out, with the help of priests, on hunts! Fantastic. Imbecilic! Surely the people who worship them must be insane! No wonder the Old Testament prophets pour out the acid of their derision on the idol and its maker. Who but a halfwit Mesopotamian, some blundering antique Arab, would believe it! And yet think of this: the religion survived for thousands of years, it was embraced by some of the greatest generals who have ever fought on the face of the earth, and some of the greatest poets, magicians, statesmen, artists, and, above all, architects. Were they all doubters? Were they all fools in one huge area of their experience? Unbelievable!

*(A pause. He calms himself, then continues.)* Consider the feast of the gods. We have a number of cuneiform descriptions, luckily. A table was brought in and placed before the image, then water for washing was offered in a bowl. A number of liquid and semiliquid dishes in appropriate serving vessels were placed on the table in a prescribed arrangement, and containers with beverages were set out. Next, specific cuts of meat were served as a main dish. Finally, fruit was brought in in what one of the texts takes the trouble to describe as a beautiful arrangement, thus adding an aesthetic touch comparable to the Egyptian use of flowers on such occasions. Musicians performed, and the cella was fumigated. Fumigation was not to be considered a religious act but—an important detail —a table custom to dispel the odor of food. Eventually, the table was cleared and removed and water in a bowl again offered to the image for cleansing of the fingers. Having been presented to the image, the dishes from the god's meal were sent to the king for his consumption. Always and only to the king, you understand—except in one case, as far as we know. Never mind. Clearly the food offered to the deity was considered blessed by contact with the divine and capable of transferring that blessing to the person who was to eat it. Baffling, isn't it! Come now, you must admit that the whole thing's incredible.

*(No answer. On the foreground of the tape there is a sound of regular, heavy breathing. Chief of Police Fred Clumly is asleep.)*

Very well then, baffling. And yet from all indications they

were a serious people. The greatest mercantile civilization of thought, creators of the most beautiful cities—perhaps the only truly beautiful cities—the world has ever seen. Yet a spiritual civilization as well. Only in the short-lived Middle Ages —speaking relatively—was religion more central to the whole life of a people. They were the founders of astrology, and, indirectly, of astronomy. They were the cornerstone of alchemy, the fathers of all modern science. What gifted madmen, then. Yet their gods were wood and stone. How can we explain it?

Mercantile. *(Slyly:)* An important detail. They were lovers of substance—fine cloth, gold, precious stones, the very land itself. The first great agriculturists, remember. While the Hebrews moved from place to place with their sheep, turning green meadows into enormous deserts, indifferent as any intellectual to earth, the Mesopotamian peoples studied it, toyed with it, experimented with it as elaborately as they experimented with, for instance, sex.—They were also the inventors of all the great perversions. No doubt one can explain it geographically—the Mesopotamian peoples had better land than the Hebrews—but that misses the point. Whichever came first, the chickens or the egg, the Assyrians, Sumerians, and Babylonians loved substance in every form—they explored their flesh, tabulated the movements of the planets, studied the chemical components of matter, followed the seasons and made the finest calendars of the ancient world. Became the first great jewellers, the first great goldsmiths, weaponsmiths, architects, artists. Cities of hanging gardens and magnificent towers, devoid of slums—compare miserable Jerusalem or Rome or Athens, or London and Paris in the fourteenth century!—not because they had any love for the poor but because they had a love for *things,* brute matter—unsullied cities, aesthetic creations. And yet they were lovers of spirit too. Their alchemy and astrology was religious to the core, a celebration of the essential holiness of matter itself. They bought and sold by the horoscope, farmed according to the omens, catalogued the organs of living things for their simultaneous physical and spiritual meanings. My God! In a word, with everything they did they asserted a fundamental co-existence, without conflict, of body and spirit, both of which were of ultimate worth. And as for the connection between body and spirit, they ignored it. It was by its very essence mysterious. They cared only that the health of one depended upon the health of the other, God knew how. When their battles went badly, they chopped their battle-gods to bits and made themselves new gods. Well might the Children of Israel mock!

Duality. Listen. Suppose an ancient Mesopotamian came to us now, having read all our books but remembering his own culture. What would he say to the problems that enrage us?

Sex. Think only of the usual case, as though there were not a vast Kloot's Congress of sexual miseries in the modern world —as though there actually were, these days, such a thing as the usual case. A man falls in love, marries, has children, and so progresses through troublesome ages to the troublesome age of thirty. In the hypothetical usual case he feels a certain trifling longing for experience with women he is not married to —because a wife is a great responsibility, and that very sense of liberation, escape from parents, norms, old chains, which made sex an adventure when he married his wife, has become for him now a jailhouse. You'll surely understand, married as you are to a blind woman, a skinny stick of a creature. How exciting it must have been for you at first, copulating with a lovely freak, a violation of Nature! But violations, like other people, have their heartaches, desires, requirements, and, with love or without, one must satisfy. That's the law of the Jews. One must make the life one has imposed upon a woman not unbearable. Did you notice, at thirty, that all the women in the world are beautiful, Clumly? There are statistics on such things. It is not an unusual predicament. The answer of the ancient Jews was simple: Having made a vow, a commitment, one must live by it. One might marry more than one—it was the usual practice of ancient civilizations—but one did not leave any of one's wives forlorn. One studiously did one's job: one acted as though the love, once real, was real. Not Babylon! Marriage was a union of estates. In other words, the marriage vow was practical, it had nothing to do with love. Both husband and wife might experiment, flirt and, for that matter, copulate as they pleased. The whole culture was behind it. "Satisfaction" was left to mysterious instinct, and any lawlessness whatever was allowable. The only law was that husband and wife, estate and estate, should remain everlastingly allied. And so, for thousands of years, the Babylonians survived. And felt no great guilt. A Jewish product, guilt. You will say it's against man's grain, because, like any honest Jew, you are a

capitalist: man's pride, confidence, is a function of his knowledge that *this* and *this* he possesses. But I say, with the Babylonian, Faddle! One must possess—so Sholokhov tells us, the
greatest of all Russian novelists. But it is not important that he
actually possess exactly what he possesses on paper and not
something else. What man needs to possess is what he actually
posesses, whatever the paper may say.

Put case:

If a Don Cossack had exclusive possession of his horse in
the sense that he alone was responsible for its care and feeding, it would be irrelevant to him who happened to carry the
ownership papers. Yes! Sufficient that his actual possession is
secure and perpetual. So with women. What does it matter
that the woman you love is another man's wife? What matters,
in our culture, is that she cannot commit herself utterly to
you. If the culture understood that marriage was convenience,
that a wife's sole responsibility to her husband was to give him
her money and lands, and that her emotions were her own, her
lover a matter of her own satisfaction, there would be no trouble—no problem from without. It's the error of the culture
which destroys. I see you understand me, since I speak, as
usual, so clearly.

So the Babylonians understood that a man must be physically and spiritually prosperous, and that the two had no necessary relationship. What has this to do with the gods? you say. I
say this:

The Babylonian gods were, to ordinary perception, brute objects. Their physicality had no rational connection with their
spirituality. Witness. For the ancient Jews, as for the Greeks,
feeding the gods was a rational matter: it was the *scent* of the
food which appealed to gods, they being less substantial than
we are. So in Homer the emphasis on the smell of the offering.
But in Mesopotamian culture, the smell was *purged!* The cella
were fumigated, cleansed of all scent. In short, nothing ordinarily human was offered to the gods. It would be impolite,
grotesque, and above all, irrelevant. What was offered was
nothing more or less than an act, absolutely symbolic—if you
wish. There was the world of matter and the world of spirit,
and the connection between the two was totally mysterious,
which is to say, holy. Were they wrong? Can you define the relationship between love and sex? *(Pause.) Can* you?

*(Regular breathing on the tape.)*

Or take politics. In politics the Babylonian would assert a close but mystical connection between rulers and the mumbling gods. He would make governing, laws, contracts, and the rest merely *practical matters,* but he would finally leave the welfare of the state to the ruler's intuition—aided, of course, by the diviner's reading of omens. I grant you, it's obvious that the system didn't work in ancient Mesopotamia—but compare the failure of Israel, where law was wholly rational, as no one has shown more clearly than Spinoza, in his *Tractatus Theologico-Politicus,* or whatever it's called. I forget, for certain reasons. Just the same, the principle that a ruler's great freedom and great responsibility make possible great wisdom, an ability to act flexibly, moment by moment, not on a basis of hard and fast principles but on a basis of action and intuitive reaction —is worth thinking about. But I'm getting off the track. I was saying *(Pause.)* I was saying . . . Ah! In ancient Mesopotamian politics, exactly as in ancient Mesopotamian religion, there's a sharp distinction between the practical, that is, the physical, and the spiritual. The king rules, establishes simple laws and so on, but he judges by what we would call whim— though it isn't whim, of course: it's the whole complex of his experience and intuition as a man trained and culturally established as finally responsible. You see problems in that, I imagine.

*(No answer.)*

For God's sake, *listen* to me. Do you see problems in that? CLUMLY: Problems.

SUNLIGHT *(impatiently):* Good. That's better. Well you're right, yes. I'm glad you pointed it out. Very interesting. Yes. It's a system which can only work when the total population is small, and the troubles are trifling. A very good point. But the problem is not that the system is wrong, it's that the mind of man is limited. Beyond a certain point, intuition can no more deal with the world than intellect can. We're doomed, in other words. Do you follow me?—wake up!!

CLUMLY: Doomed! *(He sighs.)*

SUNLIGHT: Don't go to sleep. You have no idea how little time we have, you and I.

CLUMLY: I'm not—

SUNLIGHT: You were, you were! I try like the devil to ignore it, but there it is, you were asleep. Well, all right. No time to go over it all again. Besides, you have your tape. But try to stay awake.

CLUMLY: This is all . . . What are you doing? What the devil are you up to, bringing me here, ranting and raving, acting as—

SUNLIGHT: Try to have faith.

CLUMLY: Faith!

SUNLIGHT *(speaking rapidly):* We're wasting time. I wanted to talk to you about social progress.

CLUMLY: You wanted—

SUNLIGHT: Yes. All right. Take social progress. Listen now. Listen closely. One of the most remarkable differences between the Babylonian and the Hebrew mind is that the Babylonian places no value whatever on individual human life. Got that? Individual. Human. *Life.* Every Babylonian lives his life as fully as he can, but to the culture he is, himself, nothing, a unit, merely part of a physical and spiritual system. An atom. An instance. Compare Israel's overwhelming concern with the individual accomplishment, the family name, the old man's blessing. So what would the Babylonian say about civil rights? Pah, he would say. In other words, civil rights must work themselves out on their own, he would say—proceed by inevitable natural process at the usual gross natural cost in human lives. A sickness cures itself. So in physical medicine. The Babylonians *had* no science of medicine, at least nothing we'd recognize. Medicine is a half-Greek, half-Judeo-Christian product, that is, half result of pagan hedonism, half result of the Judeo-Christian notion of a reasonable God. But I'm obscuring what I mean, losing the thread again. I was saying . . .

Listen, I used to be involved with civil rights. Right up to my ears. I was in CORE in San Francisco when they decided to segregate it. That's right. Man named Breely—Bill Breely. Dapper guy, handsome, big boss. Had these white guys, half-crazy they were, I swear it—big pasty-faced white guy named Schroeder or something. Breely would yell at the bastard: "Where those circulars, Schroeder?" and snap his fingers. "I'm sorry, Bill," he'd say. Cry almost. "The press broke down and we—" Wrings his hands. Close to tears. "That's enough there, Schroeder. I want those circulars, hear me?" And this Schroeder would cringe like a person whose penis you've cut off with a knife. "I'll try Bill. Honest. I'll try, I'll try!" Loved it. Both of 'em. Old Breely say: "Difference between you and me, you whites, is *you* are the sons of *Masters* and *I* am the son of *slaves*. Yeah!" Half the whites in that room were Ukrainian, second-generation. Christ. Black Power they wanted, the black ones—most—and they got it. Had this meeting, going to segregate the CORE. It was a meeting right out of the Hitler days. You get to speak once if you're against segregation, but Breely and his crew can talk as much as they please. "I *know* you," they say. Man Jesus they wise. "You a *social* worker, see? You 'on't know it, mothuh, but I seen you kind *befo'*, seen you *plenny* times, *yeah*." "I've never done social work in my life," you say. "Shut up, hear? You ain't be *reckanized*." A lady there. Speech therapist she was, talked like her tongue was in sideways. "I go in a wite neighborhood, baby, I'm *dead*, hear me? They gwine *kill* me, hear?" All the people: "Yeah." They scared, man. They scare theirselves good, full of pipedreams and idiot novels. Yeah. "Man I'm *dead*, I go were the wites are. Alla time talkin *trash*, man: We gwine *hep* you, nigger. Why they gwine *kill* me, dad, that's wat they gwine do." Time to vote, Bill Breely gets up and he reads us from a book about lynchings—a piece about some Negro they strung up down South, cut his feet off, then legs and arms and head, all the usual. *Then* we take the vote! I could tell you stories . . . Man named Gonzales, or something like that—we thought he was an idiot—rolled his eyes, never talked, wore old jeans all the time, old motorcycle cap—one time he got mad all at once and came out with this stream of high-falutin young writer's talk, and *then* we knew him! He *hated*, man! He played idiot in front of whites because if he didn't he would tell them the truth, he wanted their balls to hang up from the rear-view mirror in his car. Ok, I said. Black Power. Don't tell me any stuff about political power, the Might of the Vote, all that razz-matazz. It means guns and knives and fists and BBB. Ok. Man from Durham North Carolina was with us, a Negro that was human. They scared that man out of the cause. All right. So where do you go when CORE and SNCC and the rest go out for your blood? If you're Schroeder you love it—"Yeah Bill! Cut me lower! *Lower!*" But if it's not what you're after, if what you really want is mere plain civil rights, what do you do when they come at you with a gun? You wring your hands and sweat, that's what. But I'll tell you the word from Babylon. Let it go. Cool it. Forget it. They want Power, let 'em have it. Go after the whites with violence and you'll get vio-

lence back, and more and more until finally they drive it
through your skull that your violence won't work, you're back
where you started and then some. I'll make it clearer. I'm saying there's nothing you can do: try brotherhood and their
hatred will eat you alive. Be understanding when they say
they're out to kill you and—surprise!—they'll come and kill
you. So this: all your grand American responsibility is trash:
what will happen will happen. Make laws that're practical, like
the marriage of estates, and if you find anybody that believes
in your laws, make 'em cops for defending the black and white
estates, but don't hope, don't love: don't expect and don't give.
Hate as freely as you love, by inclination. Wait and let progress happen when it can, because it will, if the gods will it, and
if not, then it will not. Listen!
    *(Pause.)*
    I'll tell you the truth. I didn't live in San Francisco, I lived
in St. Louis. This is true. I was lying. I'm sorry. I drove a diaper truck in St. Louis. One night I was going home late, driving my truck through Forest Park, and all of a sudden, near
the art museum where the statue is, there was a woman right
there in my headlights, waving at me, trying to stop me, and
there was blood running down her face. I jerked the wheel to
miss her and hit the brakes the same minute. "I been robbed,"
she yells. "A nigger boy—he ran down toward the golfcourse."
I let her in, and then we took off in the direction he'd run.
"Get him!" she says. And so forth. I swung the truck out onto
the grass of the golfcourse so that the headlights splayed out
over the fairway and there he was, running down the hill. I
went after him. I realize this may be a little distasteful to a
person like yourself, but there's no avoiding it. I have to tell
you the truth. Murder will out. I went after him. He tried to
zig-zag, slipping and falling down sometimes, but he couldn't
get away. The lady was leaning forward, her face almost
pressed to the windshield—I'll never forget it, that white,
white skin with the black-looking blood, and behind us the
stink of the dirty diapers, and the kid zig-zagging, yelling
"Please! Hey man, please!" Then suddenly it was like he gave
up. Jesus! I saw him throw the purse, as if he didn't want it
wrecked, and he held his hands out toward me—he was running backwards—and I hit him. You hear what I'm saying? I
ran that boy down!
CLUMLY *(a whisper):* Now wait—

SUNLIGHT: I stopped the truck as soon as the bump came, and I backed away and turned around to shine the lights toward the place where he'd thrown the purse. There it was, sharp black against the white of the dew on the grass. I got out and got it and I gave it to the lady. She reached out for it, and her hands were shaking like she'd gone crazy. "Thank you," she said. I'll never forget it. It was as if she'd lost her mind. Well, I drove her back as far as the Jefferson Memorial—she'd been heading someplace on Delmar, I remember—and I let her out. She didn't say anything. Just walked away holding the purse in her two hands like it was her dead baby and she'd lost her mind. I was laughing. Not because I was crazy, you understand. I wasn't. I laughed because I'd done what she wanted and the poor bitch woman couldn't stand it. I drove back and I picked up the boy. He was alive, so I took him home with me and made a place for him in the cellar. He was unconscious, mostly, but now and then he'd come to. Both his legs were broken, that's all it was. I put splints on him, and I went up and made him some soup, and then I gave him some whiskey to knock him out again. I don't drink, myself, but I always keep some around for times like that. After that I locked the cellar door and went up to my bed. I'd hear him moaning sometimes, but it wasn't too bad. The next day he was better, well enough to yell for the police and things like that. I had to whip him a little with a chain, but I managed to control him. So ok. I kept him down there for two years. He never saw daylight. No windows. I put some straw down there for him—

CLUMLY: Now wait a minute. This is—

SUNLIGHT: Just listen. You can talk in a minute. I put *straw* down there for him, and once in a while I would clean the place up. He got thin, of course. A lot of times he wouldn't eat. He was stubborn, you know. It was only natural. But after the first three months or so he came around a little, even though he did leave his food sometimes. It got so when I'd come down to feed him or clean the place or just have a look at him, he'd act almost glad to see me. He'd even talk. At first all he did was swear, but after a while he got to crying and whining and things, acting like a human, and I liked him. He couldn't help seeing it, of course. What the devil! Imagine what it's like, living in a cellar, a captive, no better than a dog! All right. "Look, boy," I said, "you're here for life, you understand? You might as well make the best of it." He was half-crazy by this time, and a lot of times I had to say a thing over and over before he would get it. Still, he did get it, eventually. He began to make the best of it. One morning he said, "Hey. What's happening outside?" He was twelve or thirteen at this time. (I never knew how old he was exactly. I never asked.) "Oh, war," I said. "Riots. Troubles." "Yeah," he said. "Yeah." I began to tell him about outside. I told him something had happened to the sun and the whole world was dark now. The Government was working on it, I said, but the prospect wasn't good. All the crops dying, not even any grass growing. Just dirt where there used to be grass. The trees all dead. People starving by the thousands. There weren't any dogs or cats left, I told him. They'd been eaten long ago. But he didn't need to worry. I had another six months' worth of food in the freezer. He was grateful to me. He said once, "Why you keeping me here?" It was winter now. I told him the cold was a result of the sun's being out, and of course he believed me. Well, I sat down on the door sill—he never bothered to try to push past me any more—and I looked at him, all compassion. I lit my pipe. "Son," I said, "I'll tell you the truth. It was a hell of a thing that night in the park, the night I ran you down. I must've lost my head. Anyway, I couldn't just leave you there to die, so I went back for you, and I healed you as well as I could." (Actually, the legs had never healed right. He kept fighting the splints or something, so now the legs were all twisted. He could hardly walk.) "The trouble was," I said, "after I'd healed you, how could I go to the police and tell them what I'd done?" The boy said, "Yeah." He understood about policemen. "But then a new problem came up," I said. "There was the sun problem. The Government shot a rocket at the sun, for some scientific purpose too complicated for me to explain, and somehow—I don't pretend to understand it—the sun went out." He believed me. That's strange, you'll say. But remember, he had no one but me. I was reality. Alone! "Well," I said, "when all the dogs and cats were eaten the Government passed a law that we should eat felons. That means you," I said. "Robbers, murderers, disturbers of the peace." He believed that too. "It also meant me. If I turned you in, we'd both be cooked and eaten." He was very impressed. As for me—I won't deny it—I was deeply moved, horrified. I too believed it. We wept.

Thus we continued for many years. We became the closest

of friends, though also we were enemies. And then one day— horrible! horrible!—I forgot to lock his door. He didn't leave. In fact he may not even have noticed, I've no idea. But I was excited—almost feverish. And that night I left his door unlocked again, but this time on purpose. I left it unlocked for months and months, and still he stayed, a creature of habit. Only natural. It was as if I had him chained to the wall. Spring came, and it got warmer. I told him the Government had discovered a way of making heat by some atomic process. But I knew I was finished. Sooner or later he would venture out of the cellar and into the street. I waited for it. We went on talking, night after night, and I went on leaving the door unlocked. I didn't know whether I wanted him to stay or wanted him to leave. I merely waited, tortured by anxiety, sweating, terrorized by nightmares. And so, inevitably, it happened. He came out of the cellar. He must have known for weeks that he could do it if he wanted. What agony he must have undergone! Nevertheless, at last he came out. Picture it. A creature crawling on hands and knees, unspeakably grotesque! His beard hung down like an emperor's—he must have been eighteen or nineteen by now—and his eyes had grown enormous, like the eyes of a fish who's spent all his life in some cavern, looking at darkness. Slowly, tentatively, he crawled from his prison to the cellar stairs, all his body awake to the memory of the whippings I'd given him long ago. Up he went, step by step, an agony of guilt. At the top of the stairs he found the entryway, the door leading out to the garden, and in the door's glass pane he saw—God forgive him!—sunlight! Fantastic! He couldn't believe it! His wits reeled! He was nauseous! Perhaps he fainted, fell away into madness. But there was no turning back! Perhaps hours passed, or perhaps he went back to his cellar, shaking like a leaf, and did not come out until two days later. In any case, out he came, at last, and he saw that beyond any shadow of doubt, the sun was still burning. He crawled onto the sidewalk and called out to passersby for explanation. They ignored him, fled from him. Nevertheless, the sun was burning. Eventually he attracted the attention of a child and asked his questions and learned the truth. I had lied. All his life had been a lie, for years and years! The pity of it! Christ! So then tell me. What would *you* have done, Clumly? What?

CLUMLY: You're mad!

SUNLIGHT: No, sane. What would you have done?

CLUMLY: I would have killed you.

SUNLIGHT: Yes!

*(Long pause.)*

CLUMLY What are you up to? What does all this mean?

SUNLIGHT: Yes! What meaning?

*(Long pause.)*

CLUMLY: I don't believe you. The whole thing's a lie.

SUNLIGHT: Yes. No.

*(Long pause.)*

CLUMLY: I'm old. I'm tired. What are you talking about?

SUNLIGHT: He returned to the cellar.

*(Long pause.)*

CLUMLY: Incredible!

SUNLIGHT: Yes. He was a philosopher.

CLUMLY: You're mad.

SUNLIGHT: He died three weeks later.

*(Long pause.)*

CLUMLY: I don't know what to say.

SUNLIGHT: No. Nor I.

*(Long pause.)*

CLUMLY: Does all this have to do with civil rights? Or with
. . . Babylonia?

SUNLIGHT: Babylon.

CLUMLY: Yes of course. I *meant* to say Babylon.

*(A pause of two full minutes.)*

SUNLIGHT: He'd misunderstood reality, and so he died. And
so I say this. Suppose you're wrong. You ask me what my answer is to America's problems—psychological, social, political.
I have none. I do not deny that we ought, theoretically, to continue fighting, labor on, struggle for improvement. But I doubt
that anything in all our system is in tune with, keyed to, reality. How can one fight for what he doesn't believe in for a moment?

CLUMLY: You make things too complicated. Law and
Order. . .

SUNLIGHT: Bullshit! That boy I freed from your jailhouse was
an *Indian*. Do you know what it's like to grow up on a Reservation? I don't mean pity him. I don't mean sob. I mean your
laws are irrelevant, stupid, inhuman. I mean you support civilization by a kind of averaging. All crimes are equal, because
you define the crime, not the criminal. It's effective, I admit it.
But it has nothing to do with reality. There is good and evil in

the world, but they have nothing to do with your courts. I know better than anyone, believe me! I have been the victim. But that's in the past. Assault and battery is always the same, no matter who does the assaulting and battering. That's your Jewish law. Well I reject your law!

CLUMLY: Nevertheless, we have two murders . . .

SUNLIGHT: By panic, yes.

CLUMLY: What has this to do—

SUNLIGHT: Very good! I judged you right.

CLUMLY: This is a democracy. Bunch of people get together and they decide how they want things, and they pass a law and they have 'em that way till they're sick of it, and then they pass some other law—

SUNLIGHT: But that's insane.

CLUMLY: Well—

SUNLIGHT: Have you *really* missed the point? Listen! How can you act for what you don't believe in? And don't tell me "That's democracy." Don't take me for a fool. If I accepted democracy I'd put up with the majority opinion until I could muster the voting power to change it. But I don't! Who in his right mind does? Take a look at the world! Are the demonstrators accepting majority opinion? Are they setting up an alternative? A demonstrator is a Hell's Angel without brains. Or put it this way. You say accept majority opinion, work lawfully to change it. Suppose the majority favors anarchism, or suppose the majority goes Nazi. Will you quietly pass pamphlets soberly arguing for a change of opinion? It comes to this: I say the world you support is foul, and, personally, I opt out. I don't say I can beat you. I'm not interested in beating you. I say only that the will of the gods is with *me*. Your side will win, eventually. You've got the votes. But meanwhile I will kill you. The gods will rumble on, indifferent to your theories, and your house will in due time fall around your ears.

CLUMLY: You've got no feeling. You don't care about people.

SUNLIGHT: Ha! Madness! I care about *every single case*. You care about nothing but the *average*. I love justice, you love law. I'm Babylonian, and you, you're one of the Jews. I can't cover every single case, I have no *concern* about covering cases, so I cover by whim whatever cases fall into my lap—the Indian boy, the Negro thief, for instance—and I leave the rest to process. But you, you cover *all* the cases—by blanketing them, by blurring all human distinctions.

CLUMLY: That's unfair. We're closer than you think!
*(Reconsidering:)* That is—

SUNLIGHT: Yes, true. I've said so all along. You are my
friend. Yet my enemy. "The greatest good for the greatest
number." In Germany ten people out of a hundred were Jews.
Suppose it were forty, or forty-nine! Still they'd be the smaller
number. I say your rule's insane. Can you really think number
has anything whatever to do with truth?

CLUMLY: I can't understand you. You seem such a *moral* person, and yet—

SUNLIGHT: I make murder possible. Yes! I watch a man I
have talked with shot down, and afterward I don't show a sign
of remorse. Not a sign! Am I twitching? wringing my hands? I
watch an old woman shot dead for merely entering a room,
and I don't even say to you "excuse me." It baffles you.

CLUMLY *(stubbornly):* You're insane.

SUNLIGHT: Say it with conviction.

CLUMLY: You're insane!

SUNLIGHT: Exactly. Just the same, they're puzzling, aren't
they, those man-sized gods of wood and stone. Who eat and
drink and sleep and hunt, who show no visible sign that they
are gods and who are, for all that, certainly gods.

CLUMLY: That may be. I don't know about such things. It
seems all muddled. But I'll tell you this. Give yourself up,
bring the Indian back—

SUNLIGHT: Impossible. The request is absurd!

CLUMLY: You're a lunatic.

SUNLIGHT: You are a bore.

*(Sound of an explosion.)*


### 4


The pulpit seemed to blow up in the Sunlight Man's hands.
When the smoke cleared, he was gone. There seemed no question of his having ducked to right or left, or having sunk
through the floor. The oldest trick in the world, and one of the
simplest, you may say if you know. Nevertheless, Fred Clumly
blinked, wide awake now, sick with futility. He got up at last,
reaching into his coat absently to turn off the tape recorder,

and stepped out into the aisle like a man publicly chastised. He stood squinting for a long time, rubbing his jaw, and then at last he went up the carpeted steps onto the dais. His skin still crawled. The smoke had left a scent that mingled now with the Sunlight Man's stench, a faint pungency like that left where a cherry bomb has gone off. Aside from that, nothing. Not a trace. Beyond the stained-glass windows the sky was gathering the first gray of dawn. His ears were still ringing with the sound of the explosion. He touched the pulpit. Black dust came off on his fingers. The man was still here, it came to him —crouched somewhere close by—and he wanted to speak to him, to show he was not fooled. "Next time, then," he thought. He would see that he was not sleepy next time. He would not be so easy to fool. On the pulpit, where the Bible should be, he found a box elaborately wrapped in a small iron chain. He listened. It did not seem a bomb.

He walked down the aisle toward the vestibule, then over to the door and out onto the street, the queer, chained box under his arm. It was cold out, but still summery. It would be hot again tomorrow. There was no one on the street, not a car in sight except one, parked halfway down the block, beyond the Lutheran church. He walked to his own car, got in, started it. It was almost five in the morning when he got home. He lay down on the couch, instead of going up to his bed, and fell asleep at once. He dreamed of being buried alive and woke up freezing cold and furious. It was seven now. Esther was fixing his breakfast in the kitchen. He gritted his teeth and went slowly, painfully upstairs and went to bed. Half-asleep he realized what it was that the box contained. It would be—he clenched his fists—his stolen pistol.

# VIII

## The Kleppmann
## File

*This know also, that in the last days perilous times shall come.*
        —II Timothy 3:1

## 1

Will Hodge Jr sat with the seat pushed back as far as it would
go, fists squared on the steering wheel, shoulders and belly
monumental, trousers drawn up a trifle to preserve the press,
revealing lean bare shins as white as milk. He drove with authority and grace, head back, jaw thrown forward: an Assyri-
an king. He surveyed the city as though it belonged to him and
he to it. The tall buildings threw angular shadows over the
pavement, dignified and impersonal, as was fitting. He was
home. During the absurd session at the police station, he'd
been tormented by confused emotions, among them a momen-

tary sense, unusual with him, that there was deep meaning in all of this. There was no specific cause behind this feeling he had, as far as he could tell—not his father's storming past him without a word as he and Luke stood waiting for their turn with the Police Chief, not Clumly's ridiculous accusations (not even Clumly took them seriously: a stall, an evasion, an explosion of senseless energy in what seemed for the moment a senseless universe), not the feeling of accomplishment Will Jr had had as he exploded Clumly's ludicrous theories one by one, not Luke's shame and indignation, not even the smell of the dead policeman's blood. Perhaps simply this: sitting in Clumly's office, soberly reasoning with a half-senile country cop on a case that would never have come up in a city like Buffalo, he had felt a burst of pleasure in his having escaped all that, having fled that cave of miscalculation and inevitable embarrassment that had once been his prison—the discomfiture summed up for him in his partnership with a small-town, old-fashioned attorney, Will Hodge Sr. It was almost frightening, when you thought about it. His father had been dealing with tax cases all his life and yet, compared to a first-rate tax man, knew nothing: his client was a helpless victim, and neither the client nor the lawyer was so much as aware of it. Will Jr knew it for a fact. He himself, as attorney for a small corporation—Flemming Construction, of North Tonawanda—had automatically been made an official of the company, a position in fact no more meaningful than, say, Head Custodian, but an "official," nevertheless. So that when the Government had slapped a twenty-thousand-dollar fine on all responsible officials for the company's failure to pay its taxes, Will Jr, though he had known nothing about the evasion of payment, had been held to be liable, like the others. Some of them, too, had known nothing about the thing. "There's nothing you can do," his father had said; "buy them off. Pay them ten thousand." And he would have done it except that at lunch with Lou Solomon he had gotten, between two puffs from Solomon's leather-covered pipe, a specialist's opinion. "Show cause why you shouldn't be considered a 'responsible official.' Stop by after lunch and I'll show you what to do." Obvious, and yet even he himself had missed it. It was a grand old ideal, the Jack-of-all-trades attorney, but like all grand old ideals, it didn't work. He'd been amazed when his father had told him, long ago, that he couldn't afford to run his office in Batavia if he didn't get seven dollars an hour for every case. Here in Buffalo, with Hawley, Hawley & Poacher, it was forty-five an hour. But the difference was important. Here they didn't make mistakes, or anyway not obvious mistakes. Tax specialists, litigation specialists, labor specialists, merger specialists, the work. A murderous overhead—ten dollars a foot for office space, someone had said—and murderous hours, if you were the type who cared about the client's pocketbook, but it was worth it, you could hold up your head.

Sitting in that small-town police station with that small-town chief, smelling the pungency of his small-town green cigar and hearing the twang of small-town reporters in the hallway—and more than that, yes: sitting in that green-treed town he'd more or less grown up in and loved the way he loved his own arms and legs—he had felt released: he had grown up, had finally broken free of the myth, the old hunger for the ancient south (or whatever the line was)—broken out of Eden, anyhow, released his childish clutch on the impossible: it was a transition place, an evolutionary stage he and his kind had broken out of for the world coming in: the city.

He drove to the office instead of home, moved his station wagon in and out of the Sunday afternoon traffic with confidence as ample as his belly, jaw thrown forward with comfortable superiority, and he looked up with satisfaction at the towering buildings of darkening concrete and brick, their upper reaches bright where the falling sunlight struck, their lower windows full, like abstracted eyes, with the reflected glory of neon and blue-gray smoke and the shining roofs of passing cars. He slowed with majestic benevolence for a brown dog wandering out in the street; stopped for the light when it was only yellow; and passing the old Methodist church he felt a warmth rushing up through his heart as though he were himself responsible for the lighted windows, the small pleasant crowd of idlers on the concrete steps preparing for the evening service.

There was a parking space waiting. There always was on a Sunday evening. He pulled his station wagon into it, got out and locked the doors. He bought a *Buffalo Evening News* with the air of a patron of the arts, though Louise would have a copy at the house already, and he unfolded it with the detached curiosity of a stockbroker as he let himself into the M&T lobby. He signed in, gave his usual polite greeting to the attendant-and-elevator-boy, and rode to the fourteenth floor. The old man—the "boy"—stared at the buttons Will Jr might have pushed for himself if things were done that way in the M&T Building, and Will Jr bowed his head and pretended to read. The old man had gray hair, huge spots on his neck, long spotted ears. One of the wrinkled hands folded behind him was missing two fingers. "Poor old Sam," Will Jr thought, though he was unsure of the name, and shook his head. The elevator hung in space a moment, then settled level with the fourteenth floor, and when the door opened Will Jr stepped out. He observed that his shoes still shone like mirrors. He let himself into Hawley, Hawley & Poacher, allowed the door to click shut behind him, and walked to the seventh door on the left, his office, and turned on the lights. He phoned his wife.

"You'll be late then?" she said. Her tone was an accusation.

"Something's come up," he said. "I'll hurry, love. I give you my solemn assurance." He smiled into the phone.

"Ok," she said. After a moment: "Can you say hello to Danny?"

Will Jr wiped the sweat from his upper lip and smiled again. "Sure thing," he said, "put him on."

Then his son's voice. "Hi."

"Hoddy do-dee?" Will Jr said. A silence. "You doing everything your mommy tells you, honey?"

After a long silence the boy said, "Hi."

The sweat was there again. Nevertheless he said jovially, "You and Sister been having lots of fun?" Then: "Is Mommy still there, honey?"

Again the boy said, "Hi."

He said, "Can I talk to your mommy again, Danny?"

He heard the child say, forming the words carefully, "He wants to talk to you," and then Louise was on again, and then Maddie, his six-year-old daughter. She said, "Hi, Daddy." He could see her, standing with her blond head tipped, both hands on the telephone receiver.

"Hi!" he said.

"Bowser got out without his muzzle, Daddy," she said.

Will scowled. "Did Mommy get him back?"

"We had to chase him, and we were by the store and we got some Spook."

"How nice!" he said.

"Danny spilled his," she said. "He cried and cried."

"I should think so," he said warmly. "That must have been *something!*" He laughed. Then: "Well, bye-bye, honey. I'll see you soon."

"I miss you, Daddy," she said.

"I miss you too, honey," he said. "Give Mommy a big kiss for me. Bye-bye."

He heard her hang up.

He replaced the receiver and leaned back in his padded swivel chair and covered his eyes with one hand. He was back in Buffalo, back in the old grind. He reached in his coat-pocket for the roll of Tums. *C'est la vie,* he thought. He sat forward. As he was reaching for the new collection form he'd been working on, he thought again of the little white stones Clumly had shown him, and his hand paused in mid-air. For the twentieth time, it seemed to him, the memory had almost come, but again it sank back and he could not catch what it was. He concentrated on the image that seemed to have released it, the hairless Chief with the green cigar in one hand, the stones in the other, his small eyes glittering. "What are these stones, Will? You seen them before?" Will had almost told him. It had been right on the tip of his tongue and perhaps if he had not pushed himself, if he'd been able to speak without thinking, it would have come out. But then the memory of half-memory was gone, and he was baffled. "I don't know," he had said. "They remind me of something, but—" Clumly was watching him, and even Clumly, no doubt, could see he was telling the truth. "If you remember, call me," Clumly said. There was a hellish intensity in Clumly's look. "I'll do that," Will said. "I'll call," and went on trying to remember. He drew the collection form toward him and fished in his inside coat-pocket for his pen. On the desk just beside the form lay a thick manilla folder with the neatly typed heading, *Kleppmann.* Organs inside his belly closed around the name and, once again, he felt sweat on his lip.

The Tums never helped, really, and he knew he was deluding himself in pretending to imagine they gave temporary relief, but he had no choice, he was a man mercilessly driven, as it seemed to him, both from without and from within. Day after day, whether he was at home or off on one of his innumerable trips, he worked lunatic hours, often from eight in the morning until midnight, and when he asked himself why—

there were many in the firm who felt no such compulsions—he could find no adequate reason, or, rather, found too many.

He had not meant to get into legal collection: all the force of his past, all the force of his personal kindness, stood against the paltry business of debtor chasing. He had dreamed of going into politics, at first, which was almost the whole reason he had gone in with his father when he passed his Bar exams. Genesee County was small enough that a man could get a toe-hold, and the family was known there, known both personally and politically. And so Will Jr had gone to Batavia full of joy, in the rich sunlight of his idealism and personal ambition.

That was done with, shot down not by any campaign of his own but by what he'd learned campaigning for his father.

They'd bought a house in the country, fifteen miles from the office. It was a place two hundred and fifty years old, made of fieldstone, with beautiful chimneys at each end and a view of, you would have said, Paradise. It had a windmill and barns and a creek running through, and there were sugar maples on the wide, sloping lawn. The barns, made of native oak, were in good repair. They could live there all their lives, if they wanted. They could return to it between sessions at Albany or—who knew?—maybe Washington someday, just as Will Jr's grandfather had returned year after year to Stony Hill. It was June when he took Louise there. He stood with Madeline on his shoulders—Danny was not yet born at the time—and he held Louise's hand tightly in his own.

"It's beautiful, Willie," she said, eyes bright as the morning.

They had the place fixed up by fall; his father's campaign for County Judge was winding up. But September and October are the saddening of the year in Western New York. In the morning the air snaps and there's a smell of winter; at noon it warms to a kind of false hope—gray corn in the fields, gray expanses of frost-bitten grass. Wasps, stir in the eaves, preparing for their sleep until spring. The shaggy, toothless old people who come out from the County Farm every spring to work as hired men or to beg put on their sweaters and overcoats and put their belongings in grocery bags with string handles and begin their trudge along the high-crowned gray dirt roads, going in. The evening slides in cold, and birds fly south. The Indians leave too, old men and boys who come out for the summer to do handywork or man the gypsum quarries, tanneries, trucking lines, construction jobs; they shrink back into the Reservation.

Will Jr, full of nervous energy and troubled thought, went calling for his father, wrote speeches for him, attended country banquets. No one in Genesee County had ever worked harder for public office, but the omens were bad. The blunt truth was that Will Sr was not good at it. Loving his father, loving his virtues and defects alike, he had not until now seen his father with the eyes of an outsider. Now he had to. The truth was that Will Hodge Sr did not have an open, engaging smile. When the Congressman smiled, in the old days, the room grew brighter, the very crops improved: his huge white teeth shone like enormous square pearls, and even a man who opposed him was softened. Uncle Ben had that smile, and Uncle Tag had had it—a smile as easy and natural and gentle as a child's. They could smile at themselves as quickly as at anything else, and yet, however sunny their dispositions, their minds raced smoothly on, ingenious and just. They were invulnerable. They made you think of airline pilots or acrobats or millionaires. You felt safe. But Will Hodge Sr's smile was rueful. It was as if he saw impossibilities at every turn. He would do his best to administer justice wisely, he promised, and there was no doubt whatever that he told the truth—yet you felt uneasy. And there were other troubles, more palpable. When Will Jr's Uncle Taggert had fled, Will Sr had soberly covered the losses, had worked himself hard paying the debts a dollar on the dollar. Nonetheless, he was tainted by the event. There were even insinuations that Will Sr had cut corners in his own right. There was no question, if one saw the case with the eyes of God, that Will Hodge Sr was a better man than his opponent. But the case would not be judged by the eyes of God.

Louise said (they were kneeling on the carpet in the living-room, working with tinker toys Madeline was too small to work—they frustrated her to tears of wrath—and the record player was on in the background, Spanish music that neither of them liked, though they wanted to like it, because friends did. The sun had set half an hour ago, and the sky was lifeless, as if the world had stopped turning and time was running down), "Will he win, Willie, do you think?"

Will Jr scowled, tugging at the lodged tinker toy. It seemed to him that the room smelled of urine, and he wondered why a child three years old was not trained. "Win?" he said. *"Hell no!"*

Madeline looked up at him.

They ignored her.

Louise put her hand on his shoulder. "Well," she said, "maybe next time. Plenty of people—"

"Never," he said. He let the tinker toy fall to the carpet and, helping himself with the arm of the couch, stood up. He went over to the window and stood rubbing his groin absentmindedly, looking out at autumn.

"Well, one great politician is enough for one family," she said.

Misunderstanding her "one great politician," imagining she was talking about his own future, he said thoughtfully, "Politics is a dirty business. I wouldn't have believed it." Madeline was watching him again, her small face narrow and blank as a skull. He said, "I'm going for a walk." He went to the door and fled.

It seemed to him remarkable, that night, that he should have thought this place his home. But an understandable error, yes. His hope, his foolish innocence had projected itself on the world and filled it with beauty the world had, itself, no interest in. Chemistry, he thought. Point of view. To a rabbit running for its life from a dog, the world was a white blur of terror. To a cow ruminating in a field, the world was a vast green comfortable stasis, and then at evening, when choretime came, the world was a great swollenness. Hah! Will Jr, in this depression, looked around him. Leafless trees sharp black against the gray of the sky, black barns angular and empty. (Why had he wanted a place with barns? Was he going to raise sheep for the wild dogs to feed on? Pigs to die in the August heat? Chickens, maybe, to escape their coops and hide their eggs and hatch baby chicks for cats to kill and disease to cripple and weasels to suck?) "Rat race," he thought.

He thought of walking through the fields, down toward the swollen creek. But the ground was mushy from last night's rain, and the wet grass would ruin his shoes. He walked around the yard, the lighted house solemn and distant as the moon, it seemed to him now. He decided to walk on the road. It was dark. The moon was hidden behind invisible clouds, but the dirt road itself gave off a kind of light, as though the earth he awkwardly walked on, the road uneven with pebbles, was alive, like himself, and full of useless energy, an outreaching of love toward nothing satisfactory. The lights in the farmhouses perched on the hills ahead of him were as far away as stars.

It was not his father's failure that made him angry, it was his own. He had smiled when he did not feel like smiling, had shook hands when the muscles of his hands were limp with weariness and he felt only revulsion for the hand reaching out to his. He had not kissed babies, but he had cooed at them as he stupidly cooed at his own child, and if someone who saw through him, someone maliciously cruel and shameless, had raised some baby for his kiss, he would have kissed it. "Filth," he thought. He was not fit for it, and for that matter politics was not fit for him. He'd been betrayed by the memory of a dead man.

He remembered the evenings in his grandfather's livingroom at Stony Hill. He was no longer active in politics by that time, but people still came to him to ask his advice, get his "moral support" for their campaigns. The phrase had seemed curious and impressive to Will Jr once. He'd had some idea that the word *moral* was serious—that his grandfather was an anchor of goodness and stability, and the man who won his approval was a proved man of justice, Christian, one who would serve his state or county selflessly and wisely and do it good.

But the world the Old Man had created at Stony Hill was different from the world where he worked, doggedly honest but out of place, in the end. Stony Hill Farm, inside its stone walls, was as self-contained and self-perpetuating, even as serene—or so it had seemed to Will Jr's childish eyes—as Heaven itself. It was a garden for idealism, where there was painting and poetry and card tricks, and sober worship on Sunday evenings; where neighbors got together and spoke thoughtfully of the Future of the United States, and of taxes and balanced trade and the troubles in Europe. It made you want to be a minister.

All mere illusion, he knew now. Mere entertainment. But if there was no God, there was no Devil either. So much for absolutes, then. So much for politics. He would throw it all up and go—where?

That was the point he'd come to, that night on his angry walk. He stopped. He was standing on a high hill where he could look down on all the Wyoming Valley—the lights of the village far in the distance, the nearer lights of farmhouses going out one by one, like Einstein's furthermost stars. "A man should try to be a father," he said aloud. "Make the best of things. Not improve the world so much as make it tolerable for his children." Immediately, he scowled. It didn't sound convincing. He loved his daughter: going in to her crib at night when she lay there asleep and vulnerable he felt himself almost at the point of tears. But the fact remained, she would not obey or respect him. When he played with her he often ended up hurting her. He was a big man, and clumsy, and the more inexpressible his emotions became the more he felt the need to burst through the isolating walls by sheer muscle. He'd broken Maddie's arm once. He was bouncing her on the bed —a foolish thing to do, he knew at the time, but she liked it, and he felt joyful, dropping her to the mattress and catching her as she bounced up to his arms again with a child-laugh like bells—and suddenly Louise was there, reaching out, crying "Willie, stop it! You'll break her neck!" He missed his rhythm and the child fell with her arm tucked under her, and when he snatched her up her eyes rolled up out of sight and her body went stiff and he knew beyond any shadow of a doubt—though he was wrong, thank God—that she was dead. He ran to the garage with her, threw open the car door, and lay her down in the seat and drove—it must have been at speeds of ninety and more—to the hospital in Batavia. "Never again, dear God," he'd said, and if she was dead, as he thought, he swore he would kill himself. But by the time they reached the hospital she'd come to again, and when the doctor looked her over in the Emergency Room he said she'd only broken her arm. Not even a break, in fact. A minute crack. Will Jr seldom rough-housed with Maddie now. But he could no more talk with his daughter than with Louise, could only hug her until she cried out in alarm, or shake her hand so hard it made her eyes widen. It would be the same with his son (the son still unborn, almost undreamt-of, the night of his walk), and it was the same with his brother, his father, his sister—the same as it would be two years later in Buffalo, when he would accidentally push his good friend through a window at the Unitarian church. And it had been the same with Ben Jr, before he was killed, and with all Will Jr had ever known and loved. And so his speech to himself that night rang hollow: *Make the best of things.* He stood watching the farm-house lights go out one by one, and he imagined the stars going out one by one, and he thought, *Where will I go? What will I do?* and answered, *Nowhere. Nothing.*

The air had been hushed a moment ago. Breathless. Now it was stirring, and it came to him that it was going to rain again tonight. He was miles from home. He turned back and began walking hurriedly, and then as the wind mounted and the trees began creaking above the road, he began to run. He became irrationally frightened, almost terrified. When he reached the house he was wet to the skin and the wind was howling like a banshee in the trees, and he was breathing so hard it was as if his throat was afire.

Louise said, "Willie!" bending to him, white, and he gasped, "It's all right. I made it. Everything's all right!" The next morning he ended the partnership.

It was that same year that his father had broken with his mother.

Will Jr removed his hands from his eyes and sat brooding, staring at the drab yellow walls of his office. There were no books here. He had no need of them in his specialty. When he had a research job to do for HOME—Housing Opportunities Made Equal—one of his numerous social causes, he could go to the firm's research library on the sixteenth floor. Or when the State assigned him a defense. It took no great reading to deal with the usual humdrum debtor or even with professional skips—a man like Kleppmann, for instance.

But he had not come here to think about Kleppmann, and he wouldn't.

Nevertheless, he was thinking about Kleppmann. Or rather, everything he thought had Kleppmann inside it like a cancer, the worm in whatever ripe apple-sweet thought he could summon from the cellar of his mind. Someday, chances were, R. V. Kleppmann would kill him, and Will was afraid. He reached out abruptly and turned the file over to keep himself from staring at the name.

"I should go home," he thought. "What am I accomplishing, sitting here twiddling my fingers? Nothing." He laughed sour-ly. *"Eh bien.* I submit to you then, Counsellor, you damn well ought to go home." He did not stir.

## 2

"Rat race," he thought.

"*Perdu.*"

But it wasn't just himself. Something had gone wrong with all of them—his father and mother, his brother Luke, his sister, the times in general. It was no good fretting and whining about it, but just the same it was there, a fact. Somehow one had to escape it.

A specialist in collections. Who would have thought it!

They could have found no one less suited for the work—an idealist, sentimental, generous, fond of good music and books (he was a member of the Columbia Record Club and three different book clubs). He loved movies. He sang in the church choir—the Unitarian church four blocks from his house. He'd even tried cello lessons, six months ago now—had sat up late squinting heartsick at the page and clumsily laboring like an anxious dinosaur in glasses, Louise knitting in the semidarkness behind him. The cello would help him relax, he had said. In his childhood, living on Uncle Ben's farm, he'd spent hours playing "Danny Boy" and "Old Man River," playing and singing at the top of his voice. But it hadn't relaxed him, of course. The opposite. He didn't have time to practice, and going to his lesson unprepared made the sweat run down him in rivers. When he did get to practice, on the other hand, he felt guilty because he was using up time he should properly have spent with his family. Just the same, a strange man to be hunting down debtors, seizing bank accounts, property, wages, getting judgments from the courts. Three or four days a week at least he was off on the road somewhere, hunting through documents in Albany, chasing down stocks in New York or Pittsburgh or Kansas City, investigating the debtor's associates and family. He, Will Hodge Jr, who had hated travel all his life and could get airsick merely by watching a big plane land.

There had been a kind of cruel inevitability about his becoming what he'd become. He was by nature a man who worked feverishly at whatever he did. It was that that had decided them on putting him into collection. The workload there was heavy and also vital, and the man who had done the job before him had been even less suited for the work, apparently than Will. There were accounts six months old that hadn't even been acted upon, and some of them were accounts with the firm's most important clients. *Mercantile Trust* had collection accounts worth hundreds of thousands. To goof on them meant more than losing those accounts: it could mean losing their merger cases too—their tax cases, their suits, and on across the board. And so, much as he hated the work, he had thrown himself into it. He had tried at first to do everything in person—writing letters, pursuing examinations, chasing, demanding, seizing. It was all very well to throw injunctions around, seize property, put a man out of work by taking his wages and inconveniencing his employer, but one did not have to do it impersonally, brutally, so it had seemed to Will at the start. But then he'd begun to hear their stories, had begun to see what incredible lengths they'd go to, even under oath, to hide their unlawful nesteggs. He'd been fooled again and again and again, so that eventually whenever at the end of it all it appeared that he had for once been dealing with an honest man, he could not be sure at all of his opinion. *Don't fool around*, became his motto, *slap a judgment on him!* He had begun to develop forms, convenient sheets which could be filled out by any secretary, so that judgments rolled off his assembly line like new refrigerators. It had altered his life. He'd been annoyed, in the old days, by those signs in corner grocery stores: *No Credit*— that is, No Belief. Now he understood the feeling. *No Checks Cashed. No Installment Sales. Cash Is King.* He saw how even his own family robbed him—his sister, his mother (he'd lent her the money for her car; he would never see a cent of it), even his wife, bringing out dresses she said she'd sewn herself but had really bought that morning and hadn't even bothered to take the tags out of. Dominus! All right then. He would put up with their thievery, because they were his flesh and blood, but he need not stew about the others. Predictably, he'd become good at his work. He turned out the work so efficiently that his department expanded, in fact almost tripled its output. He made, now, very few mistakes about people. The few mistakes he did make were his errors in thinking honest debtors to be dishonest, but he did not let those errors trouble his sleep. It was only to be expected that there would be, here and there, an honest man (a fool, more like, given the harsh realities), but if you judged all men thieves you had statistics on your side. As for all his former nonsense about justice and goodness and the Legal Ground of the American Way of Life, well, this:

He'd been appointed by the State to serve as defense counsel. The boy was a hoodlum. Tall, curly-headed, with thick, sneering lips. All his life he'd been a troublemaker. The police knew him well. He was standing in a bar when two policemen arrived in answer to a call from the bartender, a complaint about some minor disturbance which was over by the time the police got there. The two cops went to the bar where the boy was standing and talked to the bartender. The boy said, reportedly, "Beat it, fuzz, you're not wanted here." One of the cops told him to mind his own business, and the boy, without further provocation, elbowed the cop in the stomach hard and said, reportedly, "Go fuck yourself." He was promptly arrested, taken to the car, and shoved into the back seat. There, according to the boy's version, one of the cops said, "You're a wiseguy, ain't you," and struck him. The boy struck the cop with his handcuffed wrists. He was charged with and tried for disturbing the peace and resisting arrest.

Will Hodge Jr had spent forty-some hours researching the case—digging up witnesses, questioning the boy, the cops, then ten bystanders he could locate. What he learned, beyond any shadow of a doubt, was that the boy belonged in prison, all right, but the State had no case. The Buffalo ordinance against obscene language in a tavern did not qualify as disturbance of the peace, and beating a cop without any intention to escape did not qualify as resisting arrest. And so Will had won, ultimately. Had sweated out the ordeal of the trial, had awakened in the middle of the night with his heart pounding so badly he was afraid he was going to die, asking himself in terror *Should I have objected? Did I ask the right question?* But had won. A stupid and pointless victory of technicalities. And a victory, worse yet, that accomplished nothing but a return to the status quo—like all legal victories: a kind of high-falutin auto mechanics, a perpetual repairing of broken parts, bent fenders, leaky tubes. Poets, for instance made poems that might—if the poet was lucky and talented and careful—endure for a thousand years. But what was it that a lawyer made, preparing a brief of, say, four hundred closely reasoned, meticulously researched, precisely stated pages? Did the poet put in any more of his heart's blood, his brain's electricity, torment of soul? At

best the lawyer established a precedent: a man sentenced to
life in prison instead of the chair because of "extenuating emo-
tional circumstances." At best. *Where will I go?* he had asked
himself. *What will I do? Nowhere. Nothing.*

And one of these days, Mr. Kleppmann would put a bullet
through his head. Why did he go on with it? He could teach.
He'd talked with Louise about it. He could get a credential,
shuck the salary—a piddling salary anyhow, all things considered—and shuck the house in Kenmore—yes, no alternative
to that—but eventually teachers could afford to buy houses
too. He could drop the rat race, break free. As simple as that!
And yet he was not going to drop it. He'd go on and on until
he managed to destroy himself. From ego, must be. From a
vague sense of his own image, not clear to him yet, but there,
final, however unrealized inside his head: a shadowy higher
ground toward which, instinctively, he must go on witlessly
fleeing. An image of himself as—was it that?—a blind old man
enthroned in his livingroom, speaking with neighbors of balanced trade and income taxes and the troubles in Asia? The
Congressman through the looking-glass, then, turned inside out,
gone dark.

But if it was ego that drove him, why was he not a professional skip, like Kleppmann—a man who moved from city to
city setting up paper businesses, borrowing on them, vanishing
as if in smoke. What could be more satisfying if it was ego,
nothing more?

But that, too, he had an answer for. The Congressman's
ideas were no longer viable, his faith was as empty and dead
as his estate, yet they'd left their mark on Will Hodge Jr as on
all of them. The American dream turned nightmare. They
were not such fools—or anyway Will Jr was no longer such a
fool—as to pursue the dream, but at least, with the impossible
ideal in mind, he could hate the forces that denied it. Nothing
short of hate could explain his continuing pursuit of a man he
knew had the power—and the indifference—to kill him. It was
no fantasy. His evidence wouldn't stand up in court, but he
had evidence that R. V. Kleppmann had arranged the murder
of a private detective in Madison, Wisconsin. The man had
been found shot through the head, sitting on a public toilet.

It gave Will Jr nightmares, and when first he'd learned he
had seemed to see Kleppmann on every dark streetcorner, in
every alley, in every airport crowd. Once, pulling up at an in-

teresection, he'd looked over at the man in the car beside him
and had imagined in stark terror that the ghostly white face in
the car next to his own—as white as a tangle of potato sprouts
in a dark cellar—was Kleppmann's, the pipe in the man's hand
a revolver. And once, getting into the M&T elevator, finding
another man ahead of him, with his face hidden in his newspaper, Will had thought—heart pounding in his chest—that
when the door closed the newspaper would be lowered and he
would be meeting Kleppmann's eyes. Wrong, of course.
Kleppmann was not a man to do his own exterminating. Nevertheless, Will had gotten out his almost forgotten Army .38
and now carried it with him wherever he went, tucked into his
briefcase. The nightmares continued, but little by little his daylight fears had withdrawn. Almost casually he seized the few
trifling Kleppmann stocks or accounts he could locate—here
fifty dollars, there seventy—stocks and accounts left, as if with
malicious scorn, to mock him. He had, all told, ninety thousand to collect for Mercantile—God knew how many more
debts the man had for some other poor collector to chase. But
as for Kleppmann's large accounts, Will Hodge was always a
few hours or a few minutes too late. To Will's certain knowledge, the man had pulled in a hundred and sixty thousand dollars since March, but always, as soon as Will could trace the
stuff, it was gone, had vanished to thin air. It was as if the
man had someone right here in the office keeping tabs. It was
not beyond the realm of possibility. It had come to this, to tell
the truth: whenever June, Will's secretary, came into the room
behind him, the hair on the back of his neck began to tingle
with alarm. Louise said, "You're going to have a breakdown,
Will. I mean it!"

"This is stupid," Will said aloud. "I should go home." He
leaned toward his desk, about to rise. That same instant, a
door slammed, maybe the front door of the office. Will Jr
jerked so violently that he almost fell off his swivel chair. He
caught himself, splashing out with both hands toward the
glossy desk on one side, the rolling typewriter table on the other, and got to his feet as quickly as he could manage.

"Who's there?" he called.

His voice resounded in the dark hallway. No one answered.

Hurriedly, breathing in huge gulps, heart hammering, he
went back in to his desk, moving his arms at his sides like a
man swimming. He bent to his briefcase for the gun. When he

had it in his hand he went back to the door and called again. After his shout, the silence seemed deeper than before. He went cautiously down the hallway, panting, and snapped on the light. All the office doors were closed. Through the high window at the end of the hallway he could see the dark windows of the office building opposite the M&T and he could feel in his blood the abyss falling away toward the street.

Behind him, in his own office, the phone rang. He started violently again and almost fired the gun. The phone rang a second time; he went to it.

Louise said, "Will?"

"It's me," he said. He struggled for breath.

"Will," she said, "do you know what *time* it is?"

"I'm sorry," he said. "I got involved and—"

"Are you alone?" she asked.

"Who in hell would be here with me?"

She said nothing.

At last he said, speaking carefully, to hide his fright from her, "I'm just packing up to leave. I'll be home in twenty minutes."

The phone clicked; she'd hung up.

Then, crazily, he wondered: *"Was* it Louise?" He closed his eyes tight for a moment, then opened them. If it wasn't Louise, then whoever had been inside one of those closed offices would be gone. What kind of people was he dealing with?

When he reached home she was still angry.

He said casually, "Did you phone me, at the office?"

She stared at him. "What's the matter with you? Of course I did." Her squint came.

"It's all right," he said. "All I meant was—" He could think of nothing to say. "Kids asleep?" he asked.

"Well what do you think? It's almost midnight."

Hours later, just as he was going to sleep, he thought again of the small white stones which the Chief of Police had held out to him. He remembered now. He had seen them twenty-five years ago. They'd been kept, in those days, in the locked drawer of his Grandfather Hodge's desk. The effect of the memory was shattering, and he heaved himself up onto one elbow. With the sharp recollection of the stones there came, in terrible soul-crushing clarity, the desk itself—polished walnut that had seemed to burn with an inner light—the walnut captain's chair where the Old Man always sat, the notebooks, the Bible, the legal books, the wide, clean window looking out on a world now utterly vanished—expanses where trees grew taller than any trees grow now, where fences stood out in precise detail and flowers were sharp particulars—a world where, for all the offices of the banjo clock and for all the gloomy intimations of the boggy, squitchy painting hanging on the study wall, a sailing vessel sinking in an eerie light, there was Space stretching out endlessly from the center of his child's brain, but no hint yet of the antique serpent, the old destroyer, Time.

The stones had gone to his Uncle Taggert, it came to him. He was the only one who'd followed the Old Man's interest in the occult. In horror, he realized that he knew the bearded creature in Clumly's photograph. There was no possibility of mistake, much as he was changed. "Has it brought him to this?" he thought. "But what are we to do?" He saw again the malevolence in Clumly's eyes.

"Louise," he whispered.

She was asleep. All the street was asleep. He held his breath to listen to her breathing.

3

He awakened stiff and miserable, the covers tangled around his knees, the rest of his huge hairy body exposed to the morning chill. A patch of hair on the side of his head had been pressed the wrong way against the sheet and stuck up now, rigid and cold, as if it had been starched. He evaded the question that had troubled his sleep all night. His wife, too, had the covers off, but she'd pushed them away on purpose. She lay on her side, facing him, naked breasts softly, comfortably resting on the frame of her right arm, her left hand under the pillow just under his neck. He got up on one elbow and slid his jaw forward, studying her as though she were a stranger. Beside his own enormous bulk she was childlike and pitifully vulnerable, he thought, and his heart went out to her—or went out, rather, to all of them—Louise, Uncle Tag, his father and mother, his memory of himself as a child. Her hair was thinning a little on top, and the precise hairs rising from the white of her scalp made him think of the wax figure he'd seen once at Sutro's in San Francisco, a self-portrait of a Japanese wax artist the hairs of whose head were, alas, all too literally numbered. With a detachment faintly disturbing to him he observed that Louise was still pretty, even in the morning, even with her dark, naturally curly hair slightly matted, a little coarse-looking, and her skin blotchy with sleep and the slowing of the blood. The trouble was that he did not feel drawn, stirred, interested. It was the dreams he'd had, that was it. Nightmares which began in a world radiant with a beauty organized and harmonious and full of light, like naked women to the eyes of an adolescent. The hills in his dreams shone as Louise had shone when he was first in love with her, or as the world had shone when he was still in love with the world: full of springtime sunlight, the hope of mysteries, when there were angels perched among the apples and plums and pears. But the dream world kept going monstrous, as life had done. Nothing shone for him that way any more, outside mere dreams. Not because of sins of commission or sins of omission, not because he had tasted the knowledge of good and evil, but because he was what he was, merely a man. His half-mad uncle would understand.

He lay back and closed his eyes. He'd been through all that before, without the dreams. It was exactly what made this Buffalo rat race so monstrous and, at the same time, so neurotically satisfying. One was born to a world luminescent with mother-and-father love, a mere upsurge of animal instinct never meant to be translated into idea, vision, and yet inevitably translated by the very nature of that terrible accident Man. One projected onto the indifferent breezes—onto the indifferent greens or the softness of snow—the absurdities of one's human temperament—beauty, holiness, truth. One made of sticks and stones and rivers and mountains the grandiose affirmation of human heads. Thus the writer to the Hebrews on the subject of Faith: an outreaching of the mind beyond what it immediately possesses. Self-transcendence. But the reach did not imply the existence of the thing reached for. One knew it even as one reached.

But that too he had been through before. It was one thing to know that "first love," or one's first idea of God, or one's first shock of reaction to a work of art is mere chemistry, a trick of the universe on its victim. It was another to be able to resist.

He'd talked with Ben Jr, long ago—it was the year before Ben Jr died—about painting. They were up in the Musicians Union Hall, waiting for Ben Sr to come pick them up in his truck and drive them home. The Civic Orchestra had just rehearsed. It was late, half-past eleven or so. Main Street, below where they sat looking out, was dark and quiet.

Will had said, "I wish *I* could paint sometimes, a night like this."

Ben stood tall and gloomy, the French horn still cradled in his arm, blond hair vague in the darkness. "I don't know," he said. "I can't see it. Tonight, anyway."

Will scoffed. " 'See it.' Talk about grand affectations! 'I can't see it.' "

Ben said nothing, and after a moment Will said guiltily, "Forget it."

Ben put his long shoe up on the windowledge and looked at the mouthpiece of the horn. "Something happens to your eyes," he said. "Sometimes you decide you're going to paint, and you work and work, and—nothing. You ever stop to think how many artists take drugs, or get drunk, or screw around with women—abandon their families?"

"Well."

"There's a reason. The world is *not* beautiful. Tonight, say. I look out and it's nothing but junk. Like the orchestra tonight. Everything sounded out of tune; Civic Orchestra's always out of tune, we all realize that, but sometimes your ear does things to it, it all starts swinging. Same with painting. Sometimes you look at some hills or something and you get out your paints and everything you do is right—you could give the paints to a cow and it would be right, or anyway great, something you could fix. It's inspiration. When you've got it, everything's terrific, and when you haven't, the world is all worms."

Will thought about it. "I need a beer," he said, then laughed abruptly. "If you got painting you'd be in a different mood, pretty soon."

Ben laughed, too, hollow and terrible, and a year later when the news came that Ben Hodge Jr was dead in Korea, Will Jr would hear that laugh again, like a comment from beyond the grave. That night, lunging drunkenly along the bank of the Tonawanda Creek, flailing his arms and crying, Will Jr though he did not believe in prayer had prayed that when the machine gun caught him Ben Jr had been seeing like an artist, the waters alive. Will had fallen then, his feet tangled in a roll of rusty barbed wire, and had gone to sleep, the whole world wheeling around his drunkenness, and while he slept he had a dream in which Ben Jr came to him and said, "Everything will be all right." He sat wide awake in the wet grass, the wire cutting into the calves of his legs, and in the place where Ben Jr had been standing there was nothing. He got up, cold sober, and made a small pile of stones. Then he went home.

The room was full of sunlight around him, and Louise had gotten up. He must have slept, then. He would be late for work. But he still resisted the effort of will that would throw his legs over the side and hoist his head up into the room. He could hear Danny and Madeline chattering happily, down in the breakfast room, and now and then Louise's voice commanding them to eat. The voices blended with the sunlight and the dancing motes, and the sunlight blended with the walls, the yellow maple of the highboy, the covers no longer in a tangle around his knees but drawn up over him and gently tucked in around his shoulders. *Everything is going to be all right.* No sooner were the words established in his mind than his belly closed tight and sour around the thought of his uncle. Tell Clumly what he knew was out of the question, obviously. Should he go to his father? Uncle Ben? Should he hunt Uncle Tag himself? His mind worked quickly and efficiently, raising up obstacles. The emotions that might have given him some signal would not stir.

He got up, groaning with pain, drew on his bathrobe and padded into the bathroom. He got the roll of Tums from the medicine chest, then sat down on the toilet. His bowels burned like hot bricks moving down, and when he looked, afterward, there was blood. Well, he would live. He'd lived this long. He brushed his teeth and shaved.

If a man were really wise he would not merely wait for the waters of inspiration to move, he thought; he would freeze his heart against their moving. He would refuse to be deluded. *A gritty, corpuscular universe, a grating of stiff and angular machines. Beware the colored lights that turn mere stagecraft into dinosaurs and singing rivers from the morning of the earth. Beware of chemistry, counsellor! What man not born a witch can tell the pastures of Paradise from the devil's green illusions? Take the narrower view. I am not a man unaffected by*

*chemistry, but I have at least this: I can try to withstand my
poisons.*

### 4

"Mr. Kleppmann, I believe?" Will had said, extending his
hand. He was aloof, official, for he knew nothing yet of R. V.
Kleppmann: another debtor, merely. It was Will's place to be
polite, his business to be cold, a functionary, invulnerable to
any wedge of fellow-feeling.

"Good day, sir," Kleppmann said. He was tall, well kept,
with a face large and emotionless, a precise gray moustache,
small and yet oddly protruding eyes adorned with neat, low-
hanging gold-rimmed glasses of the sort seen in Czechoslo-
vakia, say, or Russia. His manners those of a prince.

"Have a chair, Mr. Kleppmann." Will Jr pointed with three
fingers, palm up.

"Thank you."

Will remained standing after Kleppmann sat down. He
stood over his desk, his arms folded over his upper belly, his
lips pursed judicially, and after a moment he began, formal,
"As you know, I think, it is my unpleasant duty to ask you to
answer a few questions this morning, for the purpose of ascer-
taining, so to speak, the whereabouts of any holdings which
might be applied to the satisfaction of your present obligations
to my client."

Kleppmann nodded. He was a man of sixty or so. It was
difficult to believe, from the looks of him, that he was not a
man of the highest integrity.

Will cleared his throat. "We may as well proceed at once," he
said. "As you know, I presume, I'm obliged to examine you
under oath." He corrected himself, oddly flustered, 'That is
to say, *you* will be under oath, if I make myself clear."

Kleppmann sighed. "Just as you say. Yes."

"We may as well proceed at once." It struck him that he'd
used exactly that phrase a few seconds before. A bad beginning.
He irritably switched on the tape.

Well, a grim ordeal. Seated, holding his hat in his hands like
a supplicant, Kleppmann had managed to make Will Jr crawl.

He was brilliant, that was all there was to it. He had a trace of
an accent. In a soft voice, speaking in short, perfect sentences
now and then punctuated by the involuntary sighs of a man
ground under by adverse fortune, he told his tragic story. He'd
been born into a wealthy family of Polish Jews, clothiers
originally, but that was long before his time: his father was an
art speculator, a man who bought up the work of promising
young painters, sculptors, and ceramicists all over the world,
particularly those in Paris, then waited, to put it politely, for
their stock to rise. In point of fact he did not merely twiddle his
thumbs, watching the market. His method was difficult to explain in a few words, Kleppmann said, but it went something
like this. One must understand, first, that the world is amply
stocked with art collectors who know nothing whatever about
art, who buy for fashion's sake or on speculation, but lack
Kleppmann Sr's eye. And one must understand, second, that
a Miró which sells for an unheard-of price automatically raises
the value of all other Mirós. The elder Kleppmann's system
was this: he sold paintings in groups, each group including one
work—a blue Picasso, for instance—worth plenty. He gave
away the Picasso for a song but jacked up the prices of the
works by unknowns—and thus jacked up the value of other
works by those painters, including, of course, the paintings in
his own collection.

"It might seem," Kleppmann said, "a dubious kind of business." His sad eyes half-closed. "But there are virtues in it, or
so it seems to me. It's a help to the artist, certainly—it can
sometimes mean the difference between life and death. And
it's not as if my father was—" He hunted for the word. "Indifferent. He had a superb eye. But I'm not speaking to the point,
I'm afraid. I'm sorry."

The old man was murdered by the Nazis, and Kleppmann,
just beginning to make his mark as a classicist, was arrested,
along with his mother and sister, and sent to concentration
camp. He showed Will Jr the tattoo. He was there for three
years. Both his mother and sister vanished and he had never
been able to learn what had become of them. By a kind of
fluke, a story too long to go into, he'd been released at the end
of three years, his freedom bought for him by the United
States Government, part of a project at that time to rescue in-
carcerated Jewish intellectuals. He'd come over penniless and,
on top of that, physically and mentally sick. He waved two fin-

gers, like a rabbi, dismissing it. "To make a long story short, I gradually improved. In 1952 I returned to Europe to hunt for my mother and sister and reclaim what I could of what we'd had before. It was futile. I married while I was there, however. A countess, beautiful, sensitive, well-off. We returned to this country and I tried to get back into teaching, but, unluckily, I was not up to it. I suffered a relapse of my former mental illness, and I spent from 1953 to 1961 in a private hospital on Long Island. When it was over we hadn't much more than the clothes on our backs." He sighed.

"I'm sorry," Will Jr said.

"Life goes on." Again he gave his despairing rabbinical wave. "We interested friends in a project. We borrowed money, and in September of 1963 we began, as you know, our hosiery factory here in Buffalo. An odd choice you may say. So it is. But my wife has connections in that line, and it seemed to us best. Luck was against us. We had labor troubles, legal difficulties, a terrible accident for which we were unjustly held liable—you have, I imagine, the record of all this. Things went from bad to worse, the pressure brought on a return of my old complaint, and, in short, we were forced to bankruptcy. I give you merely the outline. I could mention other troubles, but they will not be helpful, I'm afraid."

"Have you stocks? securities of any kind?" He could not look at the man as he asked it.

"Nothing."

"Household valuables, perhaps?"

Kleppmann smiled wanly. "You must visit us and see."

Will Jr rubbed his upper lip with the inside of his finger. "Yes, I must, actually. It's part of—"

"Yes of course."

Kleppmann reached up to his face, brought his hand up under his glasses, and pressed the tips of his fingers to his eyes.

"Are you all right?" Will Jr asked.

"Yes, thank you," Kleppmann said.

The questioning went on, useless. It was perfectly clear that the whole story was true. At last Will Jr switched off the tape. "I'm sorry to have caused—" he began.

"No harm, Mr. Hodge. I perfectly understand." Kleppmann rose sadly from his chair and held out his hand.

Will shook it. "Thank you for coming."

"My pleasure," Kleppmann said. Then, with dignity, he withdrew.

The second examination was even more painful than the first. It was at Kleppmann's place. A splendid house, but Kleppmann did not own it. He did not own the paintings either, he owned only the statuary, inexpensive plaster imitations of Renaissance masterpieces. That day Will spoke with Kleppmann's wife.

She was tall, as tall as Will Jr himself, and thin, and elegant as glass. She had a clear voice, far-apart blazing eyes, a thick accent—Austrian, he thought. She walked slowly through the house with him, nodding with distant politeness when he praised the view of the garden from the second floor, admired the luxurious carpet (he felt like a peasant beside her, his bulging briefcase an old sack of beets). In the master bedroom he stood at the foot of the largest bed he had ever seen, with magnificent posts of hand-carved myrtle, and he said, "Good heavens! What a beautiful bed!"

She smiled, looking straight at him, and the openness of her smile was like a girl's. "Yes," she said. "Ours, I'm afraid."

The frank, almost amused admission of what their business together was made Will Jr blush. And it was more than merely her admission. She was fifty-eight, but she looked perhaps forty, and when she smiled, standing in the sunlit room with the enormous bed, the handsome white shades and purple drapes, her bosom full and perfect, Will Jr's heart sped up.

They walked down the second-floor hallway the same way they'd come, and the memory of her smile molested his thoughts. He felt more than ever like some public executioner. As if reading his mind, she stopped at the landing and put her hand lightly on the ball of the newel post. "You know about my husband's health, don't you, Mr. Hodge?"

He nodded. "He told me, yes. I hope from now on he'll be better. I sincerely hope."

Her eyes narrowed just perceptibly, and a hint of the smile returned, ironic this time. "My husband is dying of cancer."

It shook him to the soles of his shoes and he touched the banister for support. "I'm sorry," he said.

She looked at him, her eyes gentle now, as though he, not she, were the one to be comforted. As if speaking to herself, she said, "I shouldn't have told you. It can only make it harder —your job."

"Sometimes—" Will Jr began.

She touched his arm. "Don't say it," she said very gently. "We understand."

His final examination of the Kleppmanns—together this time—was scheduled for a Thursday morning, two days after his visit to the house. Will Jr reached his office at seven in the morning, when the city was still asleep, the streets empty except for the winos sitting against walls, the pigeons, and the blowing papers. He had work to catch up on, he'd told himself. But it was a lie. He had come to pace and slam his fist into his hand and agonize. Nine o'clock came. The Kleppmanns were late. He ate Tums like candy, but still it was as if he'd drunk gasoline and swallowed a match. Nine-thirty. Still no Kleppmanns. At quarter-to-ten he was so sick at his stomach he believed he would have to go home for the day. June, his secretary, lectured him about seeing a doctor. He stood at the window, looking out at the tops of the buildings, ignoring her. Suddenly, he slammed his fist on the windowledge. "Damn them!" He bellowed it out so loudly that Ray Polsby ran in from his office next door. June sat with her mouth open, her fists at her collarbone.

"What's the matter?" Polsby said.

Will snatched his coat from the back of the door and stormed out.

The house was stripped clean when he got there. Even the old silver doorknobs were gone. He learned from the neighbors that it was Mayflower that had moved them out, and he immediately phoned the company to get them to stop the truck. The truck was in Utica by now, they said. It would cost him a hundred dollars to bring it back. Will Jr paid. He seized what he could legally seize, auctioned it off, and so collected twenty thousand dollars. It still left a long way to go.

## 5

I can try to withstand my poisons.

Danny's and Madeline's voices came from outside now, and when he pulled back the plastic curtain he found he could see them, in the driveway almost directly below him. They'd finished their breakfast, then, and she'd sent them out to play. He rinsed the shaving cream off his face, put on scented aftershave, patted the skin dry on the towel, and hurried to his room to dress. He was later to work than he'd been in months, and strange to say, it gave him a kind of satisfaction, almost elation. It was like playing hookey, like the times when he and Ben Jr had casually walked away during noon recess and had gone down the long hillside where the town of Alexander lay, and had stripped and gone into the creek. It had been very fine, the warm silty creek with the willows hanging over it. It was in weather just like this that they would go, a steamy morning after an August rain.

Today was— He thought a moment. Monday. He remembered all at once that this afternoon he had a flight to Chicago, chasing an account on the Cobb file. His stomach gave a quarter-turn. He felt in the pocket of his suitcoat—still hanging in the closet where Louise had put it—and found the Tums. Then he got into his shoes, a tortuous business, hooked his suspenders and hunted for cufflinks. He found in the mess two silver ones that matched, and as he was putting them on, gazing absent-mindedly at the odds and ends in the plastic box, he thought again of the little white stones Chief Clumly had asked him about. He looked at his watch. Ten-after-nine. He would call Uncle Ben from the office. He got out his suitcoat and was just in the act of putting it on—taking a deep breath, catching the cuffs of his shirt under his fingertips—when Louise screamed, downstairs. He bounded down, his mouth gaping open, and met Louise running up to meet him. She held out the paper.

"Will," she said, "look! Someone was murdered in your father's apartment!"

He thought it some lunatic joke, at first, though he knew at the same time that it was not. He took the paper from her, his mouth still open, heavy eyebrows drawn down, and read. "Mrs. Palazzo!" he said. He said it as if with relief.

Louise said, "Will, this is terrible! Why didn't he phone us last night?"

He went on reading, walking on down the stairs now, scowling. The back door slammed and the four-year-old, Danny, came tentatively toward him, silently clapping his hands together. "Coogie?" he said.

"Don't talk baby-talk, Danny," Louise said. "Go away and play. We're busy."

Still silently clapping, unpersuaded, the small boy watched his father moving toward him, oblivious as a tide. "Coogie?" he said. The same instant Will ran into him with the side of his leg and knocked him just enough off balance to make him fall. Danny began crying furiously, and Will looked down at him with undisguised rage. "Damn it all, Danny," he roared. But Louise broke in sharply, extending and spreading her fingers apart at her sides as if in agony, and Will gave in quickly. "Daddy's sorry, Danny," he said. The crying turned to screaming. "Danny, Daddy *said* he was sorry."

"Oh, *Will!*" Louise complained.

He tried to look back at the paper. "Well I don't see *you* doing anything about it."

"That's all we do around this house. Fight, fight, fight. When I married you—"

"I'm sorry," Will shouted.

He stormed out to the car, carrying the paper. He backed out of the garage too fast, beside himself with anger, and almost slammed into the side door's concrete stoop. Madeline came running from the back yard, arms out to him. "Daddy, let me kiss you good-bye!" she wailed. A phase she'd been in for it must be almost a year now. He understood very well how it was for her: he remembered his own acute sorrow, in his childhood, when his mother or father left, and at times he pitied her fiercely. But he was repelled now, too. Because the love he had tried to cling to as a child, the family he'd tried to bind together by the sheer force of his childish hunger, had been done for already, in his case, and was done for already in hers. She must sooner or later be betrayed, heart-broken, however sweet the Judas kiss he gave her. But he opened the door for her and accepted her kiss. "Be good," he said. She looked at him sadly, as if she knew he'd betrayed her. Abruptly, on an impulse, he slipped his left hand under her armpit and lifted her off the ground and shook her hard, meaning it for love. She caught hold of his arm with both hands, accepting the shaking. He put her down, disgusted with himself, the infernal complexity of things. In the house Danny was still crying, and Louise was yelling at him.

"Good-bye, Maddie," Will said severely.

"Good-bye," she said.

Louise appeared at the door, holding Danny's hand in one hand, Will's suitcase in the other. "You *taking* this?" she said.

He got out to take it from her. "I'm sorry," he said.

"Sorry, sorry, sorry!" she said. "You're always sorry."

He bent his head and backed away a step. She caught his wrist.

"God damn it, Will," she said.

"I'm sorry," he said, and winced as the word fell out. Nevertheless, he kissed her, Maddie and Danny standing there watching with solemn faces. In the middle of the kiss the thought of Mrs. Kleppmann crossed his mind, that sudden, beautiful smile, and with the image his weakness and helplessness were transformed to a pleasant feeling of cruelty. As simple as that, he thought. He was closer to the Kleppmanns—closer to both of them, to tell the truth—than to Louise or Maddie or Danny.

He tightened the one-armed hug. It would leave another bruise, no doubt. "Bye," he said. He carried the suitcase to the car.

# IX

---

"Like a robber,
I shall
proceed
according to
my will."

---

*We have hitherto considered only two possibilities: that the received opinion may be false, and some other opinion, consequently, true; or that, the received opinion being true, a conflict with the opposite error is essential to a clear apprehension and deep feeling of its truth. But there is a commoner case than either of these; when the conflicting doctrines, instead of being one true and the other false, share the truth between them. . . .*

—John Stuart Mill

## 1

*[The Judge in his Chamber, smoking. Enter Fire Chief, pulling at suspenders, sweating.]*

FIRE CHIEF: Ah! Caught you!

JUDGE: So you have. Good afternoon.

FIRE CHIEF: Hardest damn man in the world to get hold of, that's the truth. We been looking high and low for you all morning. You ever seen such weather? *(Wipes his forehead and neck.)* Kills you in the end. Never mind! You heard about the business at the church?

JUDGE: Church?

FIRE CHIEF: So you haven't. Somebody set it on fire—around midnight, we figure. Or they tried to. Put these holes in the floor behind the pulpit and packed chemicals in, plain fertilizer, the way it looks—ammonium nitrate—and rigged up this contraption so you could stamp on a board and blow it all up, but they figured wrong, looks like; just noise and smoke and barely enough heat to singe the rug. Janitor found it, six-thirty this morning. Smelled something, he said, and he went to look and there it was. Called the police, naturally, and they came and looked around and said "Hmm! Hmm!"—but you know how it is with them, if nobody's killed they don't worry their heads, just file it under "Trouble."

JUDGE: Which church?

FIRE CHIEF: Presbyterian. I thought I mentioned. *(He wipes his neck again.)*

JUDGE: I should have guessed.

FIRE CHIEF: Guessed? You know something then?

JUDGE: If somebody sees a vision, you can guess it's one of the Catholic churches. Man gets out of his wheelchair and walks, it's a Baptist church. But when lightning strikes a pulpit, that's Presbyterian.

FIRE CHIEF: I see you're in a good humor. The police—

JUDGE: Unlike some, yes.

FIRE CHIEF: —wanted us to come look, so we went.

JUDGE: And found?

FIRE CHIEF: Just what I told you. It's an old coal miner's trick —use it in strip mining instead of dynamite, to blow off the side walls along the bed. If they'd packed it right, they could've blown that church right to heaven. Ha Ha Ha. Never mind, that's not what I came to say; you're a busy man. We have been having a lot of trouble with these arson cases. No cooperation from the cops—not on that or on anything else, matter of fact. Couple months ago I took the bull by the horns and sent some boys of mine over to Albany, the State's got a course they give there, all about arson investigating. I put 'em right on it this morning, first thing, told 'em "Anything you need, you just sign for it. I'm up to here. Charge the Department." You want to hear what they found so far?—Sir?

JUDGE: I'm listening.

FIRE CHIEF: They found a cigar.

JUDGE: I see.

FIRE CHIEF: You may not know it, but a cigar can be just like a fingerprint, at least this one. So they tell me. Found it right outside the door, and it got there since the rain. Now maybe the fellow that smoked it went in and maybe he just set on the steps there and smoked it, but you gotta admit it's interesting. It's not as if a lot of people sit on the steps of the Presbyterian church and smoke cigars. I'll tell you something else. It's a more or less expensive cigar, kind not too many people smoke, made by a company called Dunhill. You heard of them?

*(Pause.)*

JUDGE: Go ahead. I see the point.

FIRE CHIEF: Right. We checked the drugstores, just to make sure, and Marshall's Newsstand. It's dead certain.

*(Pause.)*

JUDGE: Clumly.

FIRE CHIEF: That's right.

*(Long pause.)*

JUDGE: You got Clumly's explanation?

FIRE CHIEF: No, sir. But never mind. What would we know that we don't know already? Assuming he didn't set the fire himself, which I suppose we can assume—though I haven't ruled that out either, in fact—it appears he went there because he'd gotten a tip, or else because he saw something, or was out investigating on his own. However you read it, it adds up to one thing: Clumly's not working by the rules. And that kind of man, in Clumly's job— You see why I came to you.

JUDGE: My hands are tied.

FIRE CHIEF *(bending forward, speaking rapidly)*: I don't be-lieve that. You've put people out before, just a word here and there to the right people; the old buzzards that run this town—

JUDGE: Not any more. That was the old days. I've made peo-ple and unmade them, and so did my father and grandfather. But times change, Mr. Uphill. There are no more powers, principalities, gods, demigods. No more wizards, kings. And even if I could—

FIRE CHIEF: There you are. That's what I thought, you don't want to. You realize what he's *like* these days? You realize what kind of trouble he makes? Ask anybody! For his own sake help us get him out. Think of it, a crazy man running the police department! It's no good. No good. What about the poor devil's wife?

Look, I call them when we got some big fire and Fred Clumly sends away his boys on a picnic. He won't work with us. Won't work with anybody, not even his own men. He's dangerous, that's the truth. Just like a rattlesnake. All right, I know what his argument is: can't do everything, first things first. But never mind. Suppose *I* said that—"Sorry Mrs. Block, we're working on a fire on North Street right now, we'll be over soon as we're finished." I'd never last a minute! No sir! A fire starts in Batavia and we put it out, that's *it*. You just do it, whether it's possible or not. Can't do it yourself, you call in help from Attica.

JUDGE: In the last days great cities shall be consumed.

FIRE CHIEF: Maybe so, I don't know about last days. But there ain't gonna be no cities consumed while *I'm* the Fire Chief.

JUDGE: Commendable.

FIRE CHIEF: Maybe. *(Flustered:)* I'm not a man of words, I guess you know. So. But get rid of him. And once he's out of the police department—

JUDGE: Not yet. Sometime later, perhaps.

FIRE CHIEF: If you won't—

JUDGE: You'll manage it yourselves, you and Mullen and the rest.

FIRE CHIEF: I thought if *you* would take care of it—

JUDGE: Not at this time. As I say, I'm doubtful that I could in any case. But I'll say this. When he comes to talk I'll mention the problem.

FIRE CHIEF: You're expecting him?

JUDGE: Not definitely, but I have lines out, so to speak. Your family's well?

FIRE CHIEF: Well. Yes. As far as I know. Times like these . . . Fine, I believe. Yes. Lines?

JUDGE: Good-day, then.

FIRE CHIEF: Yes. *(He moves toward the door.)*

JUDGE *(aside, scraping his moustache with two fingers):* Righteous old fool! There are fires and fires, Mr.

Uphill! And you, sir, can be replaced by a tidal wave.

FIRE CHIEF *(at the door):* Your Honor. I ought to explain—

JUDGE: No need.

FIRE CHIEF: I don't mean to offend you. I've got my duty to the City, you know.

JUDGE: Of course.

FIRE CHIEF: I've always been very grateful for whatever favors—

JUDGE: Certainly.

FIRE CHIEF: Good. That has to be clear. I assume this disagreement—

JUDGE: Don't mention it! A trifle! Glad you could drop by, Phil.

FIRE CHIEF: Good-bye, then.

JUDGE: Good-day. Don't forget your hat.

FIRE CHIEF: I have it. I don't often forget things, as you know. Well, never mind.

[*Exit Fire Chief. The Judge draws back with a sigh into his smoke. The desk he has leaned his elbows on is reduced by his withdrawal to an object, or, rather, to an assembly of objects —pencils, an open ink bottle, papers, books, magazines. Among the magazines a stack of five with bright covers: Hodge's folly. The shadow of a blowing curtain reaches toward them, misses, reaches again. A sound of retreating footsteps on the stairs.*]

## 2

Chief of Police Fred Clumly suffered a sleep full of troublesome dreams, agitations, old memories. When he turned his head on the pillow he felt his thoughts tumbling from the left side of his head to his right, reappearing there as seemingly new, unrelated dreams and agitations. He had stepped through a familiar door and had emerged in a strange place, and now he'd gotten turned around somehow, had lost his bearings. At odd twistings of the maze he encountered his wife—naked, at one point, with an ecstatic smile which repelled him—but in general he encountered only strangers with muffled chins and with hats drawn low, who spoke to each other with voices as muffled and unrecognizable as their faces. Once he caught sight of the waitress in the magazine picture, sitting at her window high above the street, smiling. It was snowing. The buildings—he was in a city of some sort, not Batavia but some large, dark city where there were chemical plants, or tanneries —the buildings were heavily draped in snow, and there was snow like sifted flour on the sidewalks, treacherous stuff to walk in. He was in a great hurry, though he could not remember what his appointment was, and there was something in the way of his getting wherever it was he had to get. Once a tree fell slowly and solemnly in his path (the crowd drew back, unconcerned, as if they'd been forewarned that the tree would fall). Another time a truck plunged slowly and solemnly over the curb directly in front of him and there, without a sound, turned over, like an elephant falling dead with a heart attack. He came to a peculiar, elaborately wrought concrete portal— columns on each side, statuary (armless figures in attitudes of greed, agony, debauched pleasure: a naked leering fat man, at his feet young girls, also naked, looking up with expressions of mingled delight and disgust—in all this nothing shocking, Clumly felt, nothing out of the ordinary), around the bases of the statues bits of broken glass, a hubcap, a bleeding hand. From a window, a naked, emaciated old woman without a face extended a ticket to Clumly. He took it and tipped his hat. The woman was his wife. He started down the steps; cold, wet stone slabs on which rats scampered. "Terrible place," Clumly said without either delight or distaste. The fat man beside him nodded curtly. "Terrible." A public official of some kind, here merely to inspect, like Clumly. A bearded man in a high black hat. "Don't I know you from somewhere?" Clumly said. The official smiled, and Clumly saw that the mouth had no teeth in it. Her jerked himself awake.

"Incredible," Clumly said. "Horrible!"

It was light out now, time he should be getting up, but he closed his eyes and allowed himself to drift back into sleep. The dream seemed to continue, but it was another dream. He seemed to be standing in a public dancehall—in colored lights above the stage the enormous legend THE FAT PEOPLE'S PLEASURE CLUB. All the people were fat and naked, pinkish and bluish in the mysterious light, and all the men were alive, all the women dead. This did not seem strange. Some of the couples were dancing, the men straining and heaving, dragging around their dead partners. Here and there a man stood kicking the body of his partner, or beating the body with a club. "This won't do," Clumly said. But someone was clutching at him, dragging him toward the floor, stripping his clothes from his back like skin as she pulled him along. "All right," he said irritably. He could think of no reason to refuse, though it gave him no pleasure. "It's time," she said. She gave him a loaf of bread. "You're supposed to feed me. It's *time*," she repeated, cross. "What's the matter with you?" He opened his eyes and, half awake half asleep, saw the staring, scrawny hen's face of his wife.

"Wake up, Fred," she said, "it's almost ten. They want you on the phone."

The room beyond her gray face was toneless and drab.

"A minute," he said. He struggled to clear the images out of his brain, but against the undertow of his weariness his effort was paltry. "Later," he said. He scowled, forcing himself to think. "Tell them—" He let himself relax.

"Well all right, Fred," she said doubtfully. He heard her drawing away.

"Half an hour," he said.

She gave no answer. The door closed and he felt himself sinking, a little sickeningly, as though it were the earth itself that was falling toward sleep. If he dreamed, this time, he could not remember it later. He knew only that all at once he was wide awake, though lying with his eyes closed. Were the stories true? Had the man really kept a Negro boy locked in his cellar all that time? Impossible! And yet Clumly had half-believed it—half-believed it yet. The image of the horrified white woman leaning toward the windshield, the image of the purse in the grass—convincing. He would telephone St. Louis. And then San Francisco. Yet clearly *both* stories couldn't be true. Was one of them a lie, a joke? Both? It came to him that what was convincing was less the details than the mockery, the godlike indifference of the man. What in the world could make a man so indifferent? Was *that* the lie, after all? The dreams came back into Clumly's mind and shocked him. *He insists on calling me his friend,* Clumly thought. He was suddenly angry, but in the same motion of his mind he felt himself drawing back, spying on himself—it was as if he crouched at the foot of his own rumpled bed peeking at himself, or sat on the red asbestos shingled porch roof outside his window, peering suspiciously in. *What makes me so angry, then?* he thought. But there was no time, always no time, always the pressure of events: trouble at the station, they wouldn't have phoned him otherwise, and something else—he struggled to remember, then placed it: some unlikely story Esther had told him when he came up to bed, or when she got up, it wasn't clear: a visitor last night, some weird message on a paper airplane. Was that, too, just a dream? But the message was there on the dresser, waiting: he must meet the Sunlight Man again this afternoon. He wouldn't do it, of course. His foolishness was over; he'd send in Miller and Kozlowski to arrest him, and any talk they had from now on would be down at the station. Anything else would be asking for disaster. No question.

But if he did decide to meet the Sunlight Man this afternoon, which he wouldn't, he had work to do first. He got out of bed and called down to Esther. While she worked on his breakfast, he looked over the mysteriously delivered note—a map and instructions—then stuffed it in his pocket with the other slips of paper and carried the box wrapped in chains out to the garage, where he had a hacksaw. When he'd sawed the chain through and sawed off the lock he opened the box and found another inside it, wrapped in binding twine, old and dirty, wound round and round and repeatedly knotted—it would have taken an ordinary man a good hour to tie up—and when he'd cut the twine and sawed the second lock he found the pistol. It was still loaded. He hurried back into the house.

Esther said absently while he ate, "Miss Buckland phoned. She noticed you weren't out on the porch this morning, and she wondered if you were all right."

"Mmm," Clumly said.

Esther talked on, mere words, as if her mind were far away, but he scarcely heard her. Nothing was secret, a town like this. Had anyone seen him outside the Mayor's house, bent to the windowsill? A chill went through him. *Have to watch that,* he thought. He'd known at the time it was not quite sane, and he'd known very well that he'd hear nothing. And yet it had been oddly exhilarating, to tell the truth. The absolute silence of the street, the surprising distance of lawn between the shelter of shrubs along the sidewalk and the shelter of bushes below Mayor Mullen's window. He'd felt alive, more awake than he'd felt in years, and bending over the hose faucet projecting from the stone foundation of the house—a smell of mint all around him, the earth a little soggy beneath his shoes, lilac leaves scratching at his ear and cheek—he had felt, all at once, indestructible, as if it no longer mattered that if he was caught he would be ruined. There was nothing on earth that could ruin him. It was like standing lightly balanced on the prow of the S. S. *Carolina,* looking down, far down, at his perfect shadow on a sea as smooth as glass. He remembered the time he'd gone off the road in his breadtruck, years ago, and had broken through the guardrail and plunged into the Tonawanda Creek. As the car settled slowly he'd thought "I'm a goner!" and he had felt, to his astonishment and delight, no fear—it was only later he'd felt fear, and even then not real terror: a kind of memory of fear that he might have felt. It had been just like that, crouched outside Mayor Mullen's window, listening to the subdued, tinny noise of the Mayor's television. The news. *The murderer reportedly took the nurses from the room one by one, threatening them with a knife.* He listened with the indifferent curiosity of a visiting Martian. And then for some reason the Mayor was at the door—not because of any sound from Clumly but from some mysterious jungle intuition that someone was there, spying. But looking straight at where Clumly crouched, the Mayor could not see him, and he did not trust his jungle feeling, and he looked the other way, then cleared his throat and went back inside. Clumly had smiled. He had crouched there for fifteen minutes, and now it was as if he'd forgotten why he'd come. When the Mayor and his wife talked, Clumly scarcely bothered to listen. He bathed in the feeling of leaves against his face, the ache of his cramped knees, the smell of mint and moist earth. It was something that had happened outside time and space, or so it had seemed then. But time and space were always there, reaffirmed like shrubs and flowers every spring, like birds flitting down to the night crawlers on the lawn with every sunrise. Nothing went unseen. He could almost remember, in fact, that someone had seen him—that he had felt eyes watching him critically, perhaps amused or scornful. He said, breaking into his wife's vague monologue, "Who phoned?"

She paused. After a moment: "Miss Buckland."

"No, from the station."

"Oh. It was Miller. He says Mayor Mullen—"

"All right," Clumly said. He spoke too quickly, unwilling to hear how much Esther knew. He wiped his mouth and stood up. "I'll be late again tonight," he said.

"Very late?"

"No telling."

Esther sighed. "Be careful," she said.

As he stepped out onto the porch he saw the fat old lawyer, Will Hodge Sr, just getting out of his car to mail a letter at the box on the corner. Clumly knew at once that something was fishy. "Morning, Will," Clumly said.

Will Hodge nodded and waved. When he'd dropped the letter he returned to his car and switched on the motor. Clumly had come down the steps now. The morning was already too warm, stuffy as an overheated room in some cheap hotel far from home. Will Hodge said, "Getting a late start, aren't you?"

"Little bit," Clumly said. He covered his chin with his hand and watched Hodge pull away from the curb, the rattling old car smooth and dutiful as a lawyer's reasoning; he drove toward Lyon Street. Clumly shook his head, denying the butterflies under his belt, and went toward the garage.

When he slipped the key into the lock on his office door he found the door already open. The Mayor stood with his arm on the file cabinet, waiting. Back in the cells there was commotion, Miller chewing someone out, and boys' voices, someone crying.

"All right, Clumly," the Mayor said, straightening up, "what the devil do you mean?" His face was red as fire, the jaw muscles tight.

"Mean?" Clumly said. He took his cap off slowly, turned half-away from the Mayor, and hung the cap on the rack.

"I've been waiting down here for two hours. I'm a busy man."

"I'm sorry," Clumly said. "The men will tell you—"

"The men have told me as much as I want to hear. You're in trouble, Clumly. You think about that."

Clumly moved over to the window to look out, scowling. The Mayor said behind him, "I asked you over to my office for a friendly chat. Gave you every opportunity. Result? *No* result! All right, what's the matter over here, I ask myself. Who's throwing a monkeywrench in the works? Somebody's not doing his job, I say to myself. By God, it's time for a look-see. I come over and I sit here for two whole hours, a busy man, and where are you—"

"If all you've got on your mind—" Clumly started.

"Fred, you hear me out. I've got plenty on my mind." He was pacing now. "I've got murder—two murders—on my mind. Thievery. Prowlers out there in my own goddamn yard. Found the footprints. Right. No kid's footprints, either. Are you aware this thing's cast a horror over the whole entire city of Batavia? People can't sleep! I get phonecalls from morning to night, and your man out at the desk—well, ask him! And what are you doing? Have you got so much as a shred of a clue?"

His head came suddenly to Clumly's shoulder. The face had gone gray. "Right outside my window, you hear? Right outside my own window!"

"We've been doing—" He paused, compressing his lips, tempted to smile.

The Mayor looked startled. But he said: "And now I get a call from the District Attorney. You won't cooperate, he says. 'Walt,' he says, 'what the devil's come over Fred Clumly?' You had a man here, he says, and you had him dead to rights, but you let him slip through your fingers. I talk to Miller. 'Yes it's true,' he says, 'we could've nailed him.' Course he doesn't come out with it quite like that. Out of pity, you know; sorry to see the Old Man losing his grip. But push him a little, he admits it. You let the man off. Why?" He jerked his head away. After a moment: "Because the man's your friend, *that's* why. You had him dead to rights, but it turns out the man was your friend."

"That's ridiculous," Clumly said.

"Is it? *Is* it? You were seen out walking the streets with him."

It was a great stroke, the Mayor seemed to think. He beamed malevolently.

Clumly sneered. "Idiotic," he said. "You tend to your business, I'll tend to mine."

"Oh I will," Mayor Mullen said, "I promise you. And my business is you." His face was red again now, the ashen look gone completely. "I'm here to tell you you're in for a formal investigation. You understand that? I give you until tomorrow morning to give me your explanation for all this fol-de-rol—in writing."

Clumly nodded, touching the sash of the window though he felt no need to steady himself.

"In writing," the Mayor said again.

Clumly nodded. Then: "How long will this take?"

"What take?"

"The investigation."

The Mayor sneered, trembling a little with anger. "Not long, you'll see. A day, two days . . ."

Clumly nodded. The Mayor walked away. With his hand on the doorknob he stopped and considered a moment, perhaps getting control of himself.

"Listen," Mayor Mullen said then, forcing himself. "I'm sorry, you hear? I'm God damned sorry about this."

Clumly nodded. It came to him that he was rattling the little white stones in his pocket, pleasantly clicking them together.

"You've been a good cop," Mayor Mullen said, "and God knows I'm sorry we couldn't—"

Once again Clumly nodded. "You have to do your duty," he said. And again he almost smiled but forced a scowl. He looked out the window. Across the street they were washing the firetrucks. They often did that in hot weather. Uphill supervising it, very official. A couple of men stood talking to Uphill, looking over something on a clipboard. The firetrucks shone like Christmas tree balls in his childhood. (He would go swimming with his cousins, hot days like this. He would hold his hand up and let himself sink, showing the others how deep it was, and he would bend his knees and crouch to make them think it was over their heads.)

"Yes," Mayor Mullen said, grim all at once, "my duty."

Clumly hardly heard him. It was as though he too were across the street or farther, miles and centuries away. "So long, Walt," he said. The Mayor said something more, and Clumly said nothing. He thought of the dreams he'd had and fell deeper into reverie Now he distinctly remembered the door he'd gone through: the front door at Woodworths', but the door as it had been long ago, when he was younger.

Poor old hags. No wonder no minister came to call on them! What did they do when there was no one there to visit? Not talk, probably; that was too laborious, and the older one would hear nothing. And not walk from room to room; too painful. They sat, then. Silent, patient as corpses. What would the old buzzard Willby say to that—the cop of the soul?

Prying into their secret thoughts for their own good, would he find anything there at all? Memories of swimming or dancing or worshipping in pretty-ribboned hats a hundred years ago? Shadows, more likely. Indefinite sorrow and hate. Thank God it was Willby's responsibility, not his own. —Except that they were Baptists, not Willby's responsibility but that of the man who made no calls. Someone else's responsibility then; some neighbor. Merciless God! The Reverend Woodworth, dead for half a century now, was remembered as a great caller on the poor and enfeebled—there was a plaque on the Baptist church lawn that told about it. Yet he too had had his building programs, his politics, not to mention his precious collections of paintings and silver and Seneca artifacts, now gone black, crumbling to dust.

> *Clumly! Clumly! Where are the Woodworth sisters?*
> *Am I their keeper?*

He shuddered. They came across the ocean from England and Scotland or over from Holland and up from Pennsylvania, and they cajoled the Indians, sometimes shot them, took the woods and the sloping meadowland and made an Eden out of it—and then moved on. And those who were guiltless of the cruel invasion came in behind them and bought from the Holland Land Office with honest cash, nursed what remained of the Indian nations, the old ones, the drunk and spineless, too sick of body and soul for defiance, much less flight, and they possessed the milk-and-honey land and were known for high-born saints.

> *We're marching to Zion*
> *Beautiful, beautiful Zion*
> *We're marching upward to Zion-n-n*
> *The beautiful city of God.*

Mormons, Shakers, Spiritualists, and Millerites; Covenanters and Brotherhooders and the Monroe County Lambs. And then came the Children of Physical Culture, and they too had their holy saints (Macfadden by name) and shrines and hymns:

> *A band of good fellows are we,*
> *In this helpful club of P. C.*
> *We pursue here our health*
> *And our troubles they melt.*

> *And orders we get to be slim or be fat.*
> *Our consultant does guide us each day*
> *The masseur rubs our toxins away.*
> *And we all stick together*
> *And we don't care whether*
> *The world is now round or is flat.*

And there was money, O! and empire! Old Eastman's house
with its twenty-eight bathrooms and pipe organ, and the houses up and down from it on East Avenue—more Kodak profits,
or Bausch & Lomb, Hickey-Freeman, Adler Brothers, Stein-
Block, or profits from Sibley Lindsay and Curr's Department
Store. All that was in Clumly's father's day, had been not his
life but his model for life—no lord, Clumly's father, but a dutiful servant who understood greatness by the complexity of its
plumbing.

That was how it was in Western New York, in the Genesee
Valley, where a longshoreman like Fingy Conners could get to
president of Buffalo's fanciest boating club, rise from the dead
as surely as Jemima Wilkinson did in the Year of Grace, 1776,
becoming the Publick Universal Friend (so Fred Clumly's
grandfather spoke, gray of beard and pale of eye, himself mysteriously no baron, no saint, a dutiful servant in plumbing, a
keeper of other men's sanctity) or as Joseph Smith rose from
death-in-life to holiness in Palmyra, or like what's-his-name
Harris, prophet. Something about the land, or the York State
land as it used to be—the near horizons lifting up their high-
angled screens between folded valleys, the days full of clouds
forever drifting, ominous and beckoning, sliding past green-
gray summits and throwing their strange shapes over the tilted
fields, sunny elms inexorably darkened by the march of shadow from the straight-edged slopes. "Stand up and seize," the
land said; "or rise and prophesy, cock your ears to the invisible." At the edge of dark woodlots facing on swamps where no
mortal trespasser could ever be expected, there were signs
KEEP OUT: THIS MEANS YOU.

Was he another of them, this Sunlight Man—called, driven
—spooked, more like—a man compelled to speak out, having
nothing to say? It was possible. A terrible thought, that after
God's withdrawal into silence the ancient mechanisms which
made prophets arise should continue working, like machines
left on in an abandoned factory: so that bearded wild men

strode forth as before, howling, to any who would hear, their inarticulate warning.

"A master criminal," Clumly said. "Prophet of the Devil."

*Clumly! Clumly! Where is my Devil's prophet?*

"Sh!"

*I'll tell you something. A man can't run a universe if he doesn't trust his men. I'll tell you something. My job is Law and Order. That's my first job, and if I can't get that one done, the rest will just have to wait. You get my meaning? I'll tell you something:*

He sat at his desk, chin on his fists, musing.

"You ok, Chief?" Miller said.

He waved it away, a slight movement of his right hand.

"You need a rest," Miller said. "How long since you took a vacation?"

"Too late for that." He spoke without interest. "What's the Word?" He smiled.

Miller shook his head, then sat down across from him. "Nothing on the Indian or the Palazzo woman. We went out to the Reservation, combed it. Talked to the old man, Chief Bailey, and he let us in. Nothing. Checked out the places the Indian might head for—lady he use to live with, in Byron, couple high-school girlfriends we found out about from his brother, the Hodge places. Nothing suspicious. Little run-in with Will Hodge's ex-wife. Kid's sick as usual. Gets headaches —really something I guess. Anyway, she wanted us out of there, you could see, so we scrammed. It was true about the headaches. The kids looked dead. It's all in the report."

"You look around?" Clumly said. He hardly bothered to listen to the answer.

"Combed the place pretty good. Clean, looks like."

"The Indian wouldn't go there," Clumly said.

"No, or anyplace else, from the looks of it."

Clumly nodded.

*Where is my murderous Indian?*

Miller looked up at the corner of the ceiling and drew out a cigarette. "You asked for a check on the Paxton boys—what they've done with themselves, where they were when the old man had his heart attack. We got it for you. There on your desk." He leaned forward and pointed to the folder. Clumly picked it up. "Nothing there," Miller said. "Oldest was out at some dude ranch, Colorado. Other two in New York. They're small-time brokers, set up by the old man about fifteen years ago."

"Right after their sister went bats," Clumly said.

"Some connection, you think?"

"You're sure the brothers were right where they say they were, August twenty-second?"

"The night the old man died. Right."

"The sister?"

"Hospital in Palo Alto called Twin Pines."

Clumly struck at it instinctively. "California?"

Miller lowered his eyebrows, studying him. "California, yeah."

But Clumly was in a hurry now. "That where she's been all along? I heard she was in Clifton. I thought—" He tried to think where he'd gotten that. Old gossip? Had Elizabeth Paxton said it?

"They move her around," Miller said. "They had her in Phoenix for a while, later Detroit, St. Louis, place near Louisville . . ."

"Why?"

"They don't say."

"They don't say! Well Jesus, Miller, *make* them say!"

He opened his hands. "What are you up to?"

"Come off it, Miller. You know what I'm up to. You also know I'm not telling you. I tell you what I'm thinking and I leave you no choice, you'd have to interfere. You follow me?"

"No."

He fished one of the small white stones from his pocket, studied it a moment, then handed it across to Miller. "Find out what this is for me."

"Yessir. State Police can do that in their lab, I guess."

"Maybe. Maybe not. Find out." He skimmed the folder on the Paxton brothers, lighting the cigar as he did so. It was true. Nothing there. His eyes narrowed. "I don't believe it, the part about the dude ranch. Listen. Phone 'em up. Get a description of Paxton, and after that—" He paused, letting the idea swell up through his belly and chest. "Phone up the place in Palo Alto. Find out when she left."

"Left?" Miller echoed. He rubbed his ear.

"She's here, Miller. Right under our noses someplace. Get

ahold of Will Hodge's son—the fat one, the lawyer. Get him back down here."

"I'm lost," Miller said. He was also skeptical, annoyed.

"Correct. Me too, it could be."

"But why should it be connected? What signs are there?"

Clumly drew himself up, and the muscles of his face squeezed inward around his eyes. "Everything's always connected, Miller. There can't be order otherwise. It's all some kind of Design." He stretched his fingers as if holding an invisible ball. "It's all one pattern. Find out the connections and *bam!* everything's plain!"

Miller said, "That's crazy as hell."

"That may be," Clumly said. His jaw tensed. "That may be." At last he said, "Ok, Miller, what else?"

"Well, plenty of troubles one kind or another." He was still thinking about the other things, Clumly's hunches, but with an effort he brought himself back. "Damn jewelry store robbery. You heard about that."

"What?" Clumly said.

"Jewelry store. Francis and Mead. Christ, Chief, you don't even know about it? All morning we—"

"I got here late. And then Mullen was here . . ."

"Well ok. We went over it with a fine-toothed comb. Nothing. Professional job, out of town, most likely. Just unlocked the back door and walked in and unlocked the safe. Couple hundred thousand, it looks like, but they haven't yet figured the loss exactly. Must've happened a little after midnight."

"A little after midnight," Clumly said. Then: "Nothing at all?"

"Not a trace."

Clumly shook his head. "Anybody hurt?"

"Not this time."

"It's like trying to get hold of the Devil," Clumly said.

Miller looked doubtful.

At last Clumly said, "Ok. That all?"

"Just about. Some funny business at the Presbyterian church—a firebug, maybe religious nut. We're checking it out. Other than that just the usual minor stuff. Couple of bar fights, lady that thought she heard a prowler."

"Where?"

"Over on Ellicott, by the Mayor's." Clumly gave no sign, and Miller went on. "And we picked up some kids last night.

Four of 'em. Good families. Parents had no idea. The usual. Garage of bikes. Torn apart and reassembled. Been talking this morning to the Goddamned parents. Oldest kid's twelve, youngest one eight. Couple of 'em—"

"Throw the book at them," Clumly said.

"Well, sure. But you know how it is."

"Makes no difference," Clumly said "At a time like this it's important we set an example. Discourage . . ."

Miller nodded. "I know. I thought about that. But if you talk to 'em you'll see that possibly, this time—"

"You want to let 'em go?" His voice shook.

Miller thought about it. "It depends," he said. "You know how it is. It's like you said to Kozlowski, you have to use your judgment."

Clumly sat forward. "He told you that?"

Miller glanced at him, then grinned. "What's eating you, boss? I overheard it, that's all." He jerked his thumb toward the door. "I was standing right out there and I heard you telling it. What's it matter?"

Clumly thought about it. He pressed his fingertips to his eyes and once more the memory of his dreams came back, and then something else, the footprints outside Mayor Muller's window. At last he said, "Ok. Do what you think. Anything else?"

"That's about it," Miller said. He stretched his neck, getting a crick out, then swung his hands to his knees and got up. "Out at the Reservation we heard Will Hodge was there before us—the old man. Asked a lot of questions, the Indians said."

"Funny business," Clumly said. He pursed his lips, studying the cigar. "He was out in front of my house this morning. He'd been sitting there. Had his motor off. When I came out he got out as if he'd stopped to mail a letter."

Miller folded his arms and looked down at him, musing. At last: "Any ideas?"

Clumly said, "A lot of ideas."

For a minute neither of them spoke, both of them conscious of something dangerous hanging between them: not a danger that some truth would be opened to the light, some admission pass between them, and not a danger from without, though that was part of it—the outside danger hanging there as surely as the dust specks dancing in the shaft of light that fell from Clumly's window to the worn, oiled boards of the office floor

—but more than that, an obscure and secret threat to their mutual past as much as to present or future. At last Clumly said, "All right. What?"

Miller met his eyes. "It was you outside the Mayor's house, standing in the bushes."

Clumly squinted.

"Why?" Miller asked.

"I don't know."

"Ok," Miller said. He looked down. "I thought it was that." Then: "What did he want this morning?"

"I'm going to be investigated."

Miller said nothing.

"There'll be questions," Clumly said. He compressed his lips.

"Can I help?" It sounded reserved.

"Too late for that," Clumly said. "I think I can beat them." He did not, suddenly; but he was indifferent to that, for the moment.

Miller glanced at him, uneasy, then away. He said, "You want some advice?"

Clumly felt a sudden, absurd leap of hope, and his face showed it. But the sensation of freedom passed instantly, or rather gave way to a different freedom, and his jaw grew stubborn. He shook his head.

"I was afraid of that too," Miller said. He was going to say —Clumly could see it in his eyes—*How long do you think we can cover for you?* But that was not Miller's way. He too took an obstinate look, and after a moment he came over to the desk. He lifted the folders and manilla envelopes from the stack of papers, revealing, beneath them, a dozen neatly typed letters. He said quietly, "If you don't mind, sign these before you go."

"Who wrote them?" Clumly said. "What are they?"

"They're mail," Miller said. "Me and Einstein been working on it, a little. Einstein's my son. Good writer."

Clumly looked at them. The top one began,

YOUR HONOR:
I sincerely regret that pressing duties have necessitated my postponing immediate answer to your questions concerning the budget submitted to you 12 May 1966. I shall seek to reply to your question point by point . . . .

Clumly said, "You expect me to sign these things?"

Miller took a deep breath. "You better, boss," he said. He turned away. Halfway to the door he paused, then turned back slowly. "Listen. No more poking around like a crazy old woman. You keep this up you'll hang us all." Miller turned his back.

He'd felt panicky, knowing how much there was to do, yet he sat reading the letters over and over, imagining the writing of them—Miller and his son running over his mail, wincing maybe, or maybe laughing, who could tell? like a couple of ladies at the laundry sorting undershorts. The letters were not his voice, nobody would be fooled; but that was not all. The letters were his responsibility, a stupid responsibility he should never have been saddled with in the first place and should never bend to now. And yet he would bend, he knew that. It was merely a question of time, of aging endurance.

It was twelve-fifteen when the call from Marsh Niemeyer came. A prattler, one of those farmers who worked like the devil when alone in the field or the cowbarn and then talked on and on as though he could never get enough when some neighbor came around or he met some friend at church or made a phonecall. He said at length, "Well, Chief, what I called for was, we're printing up the programs for the program. Ha ha ha."

"I see," Clumly said.

"Well we wondered what the title of your speech was going to be. It's next Wednesday, you know. Y'see we have to tell the printer—" He explained in detail.

Clumly said, "I thought I'd talk on Law and Order."

"Law and Order," Niemeyer said. He sounded doubtful. "Did you have a title?"

"Law and Order," Clumly said. He smiled with considered malice.

"Good," Niemeyer said. "That's good. Direct, no running around Robin Hood's barn."

Clumly nodded at the phone. "That's about it."

The man talked on, and Clumly waited for it to end. His mind wandered vaguely to the Babylonian puppets, and he frowned. There was a connection, but he couldn't make it out exactly. *Ladies and gentlemen, my subject tonight . . . No. As the salesman said to the farmer's daughter . . .* He thought suddenly, with a shiver of mysterious anger, *King Kong's balls.* And then: *But seriously, folks . . .*

"Well thanks," Niemeyer said. "It's something to think about."

"Mmm," Clumly said.

*A touch of megalomania. Don't you think that may have certain dangers in it—political and social, I mean?* Who had said that? The Sunlight Man? *Refuses to renounce his human dignity . . . a Hell's Angel of sorts, a rebellious lunatic . . .*

The phone in his hand was dead.

*Salvador's funeral,* he thought. He looked down, startled, at his watch. *Where is my servant Mickey Salvador?*

At the desk he said, "Where's Kozlowski?"

"Having lunch, sir."

"Where?"

"I dunno. Polkadot, probably."

He hurried out to the street and made for his car.

---

**3**

---

"We're in an age of violent change, Kozlowski," Clumly said.

Kozlowski nodded, winding spaghetti around his fork with the help of his spoon. His face was redder than usual, as though it embarrassed him to be caught eating lunch with the Chief. But there was hardly anyone else there—a teen-ager with longish hair and his collar turned up, sitting at the counter to Clumly's left, and around the corner a workman of some sort, maybe a welder, with thick glasses and thicker bubbles of glass in the middle. The waitress was telling the workman that he and his wife were tearing that poor boy apart. "Say it's true," the workman said, "let's say I'm willing to grant that." He pointed at her with his fork. "You think you and I had it better when we were kids? I give him the best home I can. It's up to him too." The waitress waved it off scornfully and turned to Clumly. "What's yours?" she said.

He pointed toward Kozlowski's spaghetti. "One of those and a cup of Sanka."

"No Sanka."

"Root-beer."

She turned away.

"Violent change," he said again. "Im not against the future. Not for a minute, no sir! What I ask is, who's conserving the values of the past? Who?"

Kozlowski shook his head and glanced at the waitress.

"It's all very well to say the old order changes giving way to the new, or whatever the saying is, but where's the new? *That's* the question!"

Kozlowski poked the forkful into his mouth.

The man in thick glasses said, "A man has to look out for himself. If my parents are to blame for the way I turned out, then it must go back to Adam, for God's sake, and who's responsible for *him?*"

"All right," Clumly said, "so take—" He leaned closer to Kozlowski. "Take the Sunlight Man. A dangerous criminal, right?"

"Right."

"But how dangerous nobody knows, because we don't know who he is, right?"

He nodded, poking in a forkful.

"So Miller and the boys may bring him in for the minor counts, but as for his *real* crimes—"

"Good thinking," Kozlowski said.

Clumly scowled at him. "What side you *on*, Kozlowski?"

Clumly's spaghetti came, and Kozlowski was spared the inconvenience of answering. Clumly took a mouthful and leaned toward him again. "All right," he said, "what would you say if I told you I have a chance of meeting with this man alone, and talking? Suppose I knew how I could follow him around, but I had to do it all on my own. Well?"

Kozlowski said, "I'd say it was a crazy idea." He chewed.

Clumly grinned. "Ah! Crazy. Why?"

Now, for just a moment, Kozlowski looked at him. "Because sooner or later the chances are he'd kill you. Even if killing's not his usual way, what choice would he have, some cop following him around, pushing him in a corner?"

"And yet the other way we may never find out—"

Kozlowski said nothing.

"Well?" Clumly said.

"No difference. The reason you have what's called a 'force'

is when the cops outnumber the robbers fewer people get killed." Still looking straight ahead, as if Clumly were merely some irritating stranger, Kozlowski began on his coffee.

"Suppose I told you——" Clumly whispered.

Now a muscle began to twitch in Kozlowski's cheek. He set down the coffee and waited.

Clumly changed his mind. "Suppose I told you I know for a fact that this Sunlight Man once ran someone down in St. Louis, Missouri—ran him down with a diaper truck, in cold blood, and then picked him up off the grass and locked him up in a grimy cellar. He was crippled for life."

"How?"

"How do I know? Because——" He studied Kozlowski's eyes, then changed his mind. "I know, that's all. Never mind how."

"You'll get killed," Kozlowski said. "And you'll deserve it. Start busting out on your own like that, acting like a vigilante . . ."

Chief Clumly's small eyes glinted. "I've tried your way. You're forgetting something. I'm responsible for this town, you follow that? Responsible! It's like a king. I don't mean I'm comparing myself to a king, you understand, but it's *like* a king. If a king's laws get tangled up and his knights all fail him, he's got to do the job himself. They're *his* people. He's responsible. Or take God—not that I compare myself to God, understand. If the world gets all messed up He's got to fix it however He can, that's His job."

Kozlowski shook his head and rolled his eyes up.

"This spaghetti's all grease," Clumly said. "Hey, Miss!"

"You gonna arrest her, boss?" Kozlowski said.

Clumly ignored it. When the girl came he said, "This spaghetti's all grease."

She looked at the plate. "You get what you pay for."

He pushed the plate away. He said suddenly, "Listen, Kozlowski, come to the funeral with me this afternoon. For Salvador."

He shook his head. "Miller said——"

"Forget it! Is Miller the Chief?"

"Look. We all been by there, paid our respects. You can't just shut down the police department for a funeral."

"True. But I want you there, see?" He added, crafty-looking, "I've got a hunch."

Kozlowski sighed. Clumly had finished his root-beer now,

and they both got down off their stools. The waitress looked at Clumly's check. "Ninety cents," she said. He paid her and she rang it up. Kozlowski paid nothing. Clumly thought about it.

At the door, Clumly squinted at him and said, "You got some deal cooked up between you, you and her? How come no charge?"

Kozlowski blushed. "What kind of deal could we have?"

"I don't know," Clumly said. He thought: *book-making, petty extortion, prostitution, health code, fire code . . .* "I don't know," he said again. "You're a riddle, Kozlowski." He grinned, watchful.

Kozlowski looked up at the sky and slid his cap on. It must be a hundred out now. The sheen of wax on the police car top was blinding.

"You drive," Clumly said. "We'll stop by afterward and pick up my car again." He closed his hand around the little white stones in his pocket.

Kozlowski got in, switched on the ignition, and waited while Clumly came around the front to his side.

For all the heat, it was a good funeral, one of the best he'd seen. Almost all the people there were Italian, and most of them he didn't know. Nobody talked. They stood motionless in their dark suits, even the children motionless, and when they bowed or knelt or crossed themselves—all but the half-dozen Protestants there—they did it together, as though by a single impulse in their hearts. Everyone wept, including Clumly, and even Kozlowski had water in his eyes. Beside the open grave the priest spoke English, sadly, with Italian feeling.

"God lift this boy to Heaven," he said. He wrung his hands. "And forgive him his sins. He had much, much good in him, as you know, Lord, and what faults he may have had were the faults of any mortal child on the threshold, only the threshold, of his manhood. Even to our limited mortal sight it seemed only a day or two ago that he laughed and played on the sidewalk in front of his mama's house, and only a matter of hours ago that he distinguished himself as a football player in our high school. He was gentle and kindly, and he gave his life for the defense of peace and justice. Have mercy on his spirit, and give comfort to his mother and his brothers and sisters who have lost him in all the great beauty of his youth. When they came home to the house now suddenly emptied, You be there in his stead. When they hear a young voice they mistake for his, in that first tragic instant, You be there to give them peace." He shifted to Latin, or maybe Italian.

An untimely end, but the funeral was fitting, and all the dignity of Mickey Salvador's life was there—his mother, weeping, the younger children, the relatives heavy of body and heart, the school friends. *We all go sometimes,* Clumly thought. At last, whatever tensions, uncertainties, joys and sorrows warred in the heart, law and order were restored, and there was peace.

He looked out at the field where cows lay weary from the heat and two dogs stood sniffing a fencepost. *Life goes on,* he thought. It was beautiful. He gave himself up to the pleasure of weeping.

When he wiped his eyes the first thing he saw was the enormous back of Will Hodge Sr, moving toward the cemetery gate. *Poor devil,* Clumly thought, remembering the scene with Salvador's mother in Clumly's own office. Well, they'd made up now. She walked beside him. That was odd, he thought the next minute. Unsettling. Hodge turned to glance back, and his eyes fell instantly, as if he'd meant them to, on Clumly.

But he got no time just then to think about it. There was a commotion over at the edge of the crowd, an argument perhaps, or a purse lost, or some accident. He pressed toward the place, Kozlowski just behind him. When he got there the small crowd fell away to give him room. There was an old Italian woman sitting on the ground, her legs splayed out, skirt hiked up to reveal the terrible gray of her thighs above the rolled stocking-tops. A boy was pulling at her, trying to help her to her feet. She was blind and seemed dazed. When Clumly bent over her she drew back as if alarmed, saying something in Italian "—*uno stormo d'uccelli.*"

"What?" Clumly said. He glanced at the boy for help.

"Storm of birds," the boy said. In answer to Clumly's look of bafflement he merely shrugged. He was so thin he looked made out of sticks.

"*Voli di colombi,*" she said.

"Flights of pigeons," the boy said dully, looking down.

"What's this mean?" Clumly said, but no one answered. The crowd drew nearer to listen.

"*La morte,*" she said.

"Death," said the boy.

She was speaking directly—unmistakably—to Clumly. She began to whisper, and the boy went on translating, quick, toneless, indifferent. "Some will die for uncontrol and animalness and for cruel mastering. Some for violent kindness."

She touched Clumly's face—her hands ice-cold—and said a word which the boy did not translate. She repeated it. *"Disanimata."*

"What does it mean?" Clumly said.

The boy looked blank and sullen.

The others would not say either.

"Let me help you up," Clumly said. He took her two hands. "All right you people, make room there." Kozlowski put his hands under her armpits.

He had an hour yet before it was time to leave for his appointment with the Sunlight Man.

"You're home early," Esther said. "You said you were going to be late."

He nodded. "Work to do. See I'm not disturbed."

Without another word he proceeded up the stairs to the second floor and then on to the third. Here the house was above the shade of the trees, and the bare, unfurnished rooms were full of light. He got out the tape recorder from the closet where he'd left it, threaded the tape in, and bolted the door behind him. He straightened up and got a cigar out, then stood at the high, narrow window to smoke and listen. He felt again the heavy-hearted weariness he'd felt last night in the church, but he felt something else now, too. A kind of joy, almost the kind of joy he'd felt years ago, going over and over a letter from his nearly blind sweetheart, on the ship. His head was clear now, as it always was up here where he could look out on half the city. As the tape spoke he cocked his head and bent nearer.

*He'd misunderstood reality, and so he died. And so I say this. Suppose you're wrong.*

Clumly snapped off the tape and stood thinking a moment, bent-backed as a beetle, his hand around his jaw.

Downstairs the telephone rang. Esther called, "Yoo hoo! Telephone, Fred!"

He bent lower and unplugged the tape recorder, then stood motionless, squinting, enclosing himself in silence.

# X

## Poetry and
## Life

*That some Elephants have not only written whole sentences, as Ælian ocularly testifieth, but have also spoken, as Oppianus delivereth, and Christophorus à Costa particularly relateth (although it sound like that of Achilles' Horse in Homer), we do not conceive impossible.*

—Sir Thomas Browne

## 1

Walter Boyle (or Benson) had a round face and round, surprised-looking eyes like a rabbit's. Now, as he drove home to Buffalo, sitting far forward in his seat, as always, and clinging to the steering wheel with both hands, his eyes looked rounder and more surprised than ever. He was frightened and, for the first time in years, tormented by something he could even recognize himself as guilt. If he consciously tried to think back to the murder of the guard, his mind would shy away stubbornly, like a horse avoiding a bridge; nevertheless, the memory repeatedly came back, around unsuspected corners, and though his thought recoiled the way you would draw back your hand from a snake you'd mistaken for a vine, he could not escape reliving that moment—the dead guard's hand reaching out to him—over and over. He had always known that there is violence in the world, he'd seen minor examples. But he had never fully grasped what he had known. It was equally impossible for Boyle (or Benson) to grasp the magician's return to the jail to free an Indian who meant nothing to him, as far as you could see, or meant worse than nothing, an irritation. Insane, that was all there was to it. But Boyle was not convinced or comforted. He had not really grasped that there was madness in the world. Worst of all, though, was the pistol-whipping of the Indian who had stayed. Boyle had a certain respect for the police. He feared and disliked them, but he feared and disliked them less than do many citizens. He understood their rules and, as a professional, worked not so much against those rules as around and under and up inbetween them. But there were no rules behind the pistol-whipping. It was more insanity. And neither was there any rule to explain their calling him *Benson*, showing they were onto him, yet letting him off scot-free. The world was topsy-turvy, and Boyle was afraid of it. He felt that he was being tailed, that any moment or any day now the whole thing—whatever that meant—would blow up in his face. He dreaded meeting his wife or neighbors or what-was-his-name, the roomer. He felt, though the trial was behind him, accused, and felt everyone knew it. He, Walter Boyle, it seemed to him now (or seemed to some gloomy, befuddled alley of his mind), was personally responsible for the magician's return and so, in effect, for the murder. He could have listened more carefully to the conversation of the magician and the Indian; he could have told the police more than he'd told them, or warned them about the break he had known was coming. And after it was over and the police were asking angry questions, their faces bright red, he could have told them at least who it was that had let the Indian out. It was his error—his refusal to answer them—that had led to the pistol-whipping.

Not that he consciously thought all this out or believed it. Boyle thought nothing. Nevertheless, he was a changed man, for whether or not he was able to think about it, he had seen the caves of Hell. All his life he had been a decent man, exactly like the best of his neighbors. A good American. He took pride in his work, as other men do, and pride, too—though he did not flaunt it publicly—in his judgments, his feelings, even his comfortable shape, size, and visage. He worked hard and earned money and kept hold of it—he was the farthest thing from a profligate. He knew the value of food, and, like anyone, he frequently ate too much; he took considerable pleasure in making love to his wife when he was able, once a month or so; he was never fanatic, and if he felt himself slipping into an extreme point of view he would check himself at once, relax every nerve; he had a healthy American's envy of people slightly better off than himself. And though he said little, he was not by any means a milquetoast; indeed, he was as capable as anyone of manly fury. But for all his common decency, he now knew himself guilty; in fact, past pardon. He suffered and hunted for words. The world was full of danger, and something terrible was in store for him.

Half a block short of the driveway leading to the old barn in North Tonawanda where he always made his change, Boyle stopped the car and sat looking around him, making sure he was not being watched. There was no one. He started up again, drove down the driveway between high weeds, stopped to unlock the barn door, then drove the Rambler in. Inside, everything was in order. The Ford sat dusty and discarded-looking except for the clothes hanging behind the side window —Benson's. Boyle undressed, down to his underwear and socks, removed the money from his billfold and put the billfold in the Rambler glove compartment. He stood a moment between the two cars, facing the closed barn door and rubbing his hands absent-mindedly, savoring the queer sensation of being neither Boyle nor Benson. At last he locked the Rambler and unlocked the Ford, dressed in the Benson clothes, took the Benson wallet from the glove compartment of the Ford, filled it with the money that linked his two natures, and put on his wedding ring. He opened the barn door, started up the Ford, backed out, got out again and locked the barn door behind him.

Even now he dreaded going home. On an impulse very unnatural for him, against all his rules, he parked his car in a downtown lot, thirty cents an hour, and got out to walk. He

had no intention, at first, of walking all the way home from here—it was nearly two miles—but he started out, by accident, in the general direction of home.

Though the afternoon was in fact pleasant, somewhere in the seventies, Benson felt chilly. He felt so cold, and the light breeze seemed to him so piercing, that he shivered in his thin suit and walked as fast as he could. He thought about the people he'd seen in the jail—the Indian boy with his jaw broken, the cracked magician, the drunks, the teen-aged hoodlums the police had brought in after the escape—and, hardly aware that he was doing it, he began to compare them with the hustling Buffalo people all around him. As he passed department stores, wide, brightly lit office-supply stores, bookstores, tobacco shops, ladies' shops, he was struck by the wolfish, but at the same time trim and prosperous, look of all these well-fed, neatly dressed customers and salespeople. There was nothing like this back in jail. These people too looked cross and impatient, but they looked busy, at least, and satisfied that their business was the most important business to be done. He passed an air-conditioned shoestore (a waft of chillier air swept across him), and beyond the double-width glass doors he caught a glimpse of a tan young man with a bright, false smile squeezing a cheap, too-small shoe on a fat woman's bloated foot. It was not the shoesalesman's business that the shoe was mere paper or that on that huge gray foot it was ridiculous. They were both cheats, the shoe man and the lady. (The thought flickered up momentarily and died.)

He passed an old woman with a gray, smashed face and above it a hat of shiny dark blue with light blue flowers on it. Benson's guilt increased.

The taxi drivers with their golfer's shirts and dirty-yellow imitation bandsmen's hats looked equally fat and satisfied, and so did the hotel doormen with their padded coats and buttons down their backs and gold epaulettes on their shoulders. He looked at fat, darksuited businessmen, gloomy as Indians, graying at the temples, hurrying along in small shoes that shone on the sidewalk like tinted steel, and it seemed to him that they were grimly satisfied with their lives of hard bargains and tricky deals. Like wolves, all of them, the same as the people in the jail, but these were the wolves who made it. Even the women. He could have been afraid of them, if he'd let himself. They walked in tight clothes that shone like knives,

and their soft, pretty faces or square, blunt faces knew just
how to get what they wanted, some by a pretense of helplessness, some by a sweet false gaiety, some by foxy irony or bellowing or crying or endless timid whining. It was not a street,
it was a battlefield, and though they might smile from time to
time, Walter Benson was not fooled; they were at war, and every man-woman-child of them was fighting for himself. If
some of the salesmen were polite, they were polite because
that would make the sale. If it worked just as well, they'd have
gladly cracked open the customer's jaw with a pistol. If he,
Benson, were to step through the low revolving door and
snatch the woman in the green dress, the young one picking
through the used-looking talcum bottles on the counter, and
hurl her to the floor and smash her head against the marble
tile (or whatever it was), not a one of them would lift a finger
to save her. They would scream, duck down, look out for
Number One. A sobering thought. It filled his chest with a
coldness.

He came into the scruffier section now; the department
stores and banks and expensive shops had fallen away behind
him; ahead of him lay the hunting grounds of less powerful
thieves, shoemakers working at basement windows, a medical
supply store with Maidenform corsets and bras in the window,
a body shop with a red and yellow sign, YOU WRECK 'EM I FIX
'EM. He passed two painters working on the front of a beauty
salon. Their sleeves were rolled up on their lean brown arms
and showed their swollen veins. One of them was swearing.
The sign over his head said CHARLES OF PARIS, and there was a
picture of a lady with bright blue hair. Charles of Paris would
pay those painters through the nose, and Charles' customers
would pay, after that, because it wasn't enough, just getting
along, just making ends meet, paying the bills: a man had to
get ahead, retire to the country, a cottage on Silver Lake. He
passed a restaurant where people were eating hamburgers in a
quick, nervous, wolfish way as though they had important
work and could only spare a minute. Some of the people eating were old men who sat alone and had their hats on. By the
window sat a man with lifted eyebrows, pouting lips, and a
fixed stare; he seemed to be struggling to remember something.
In the back of his mind Walter Benson had a feeling he was to
blame for all this, too. He walked still more quickly, lost in

reverie, and before he knew it he was hurrying down McKinley, his own street.

He slowed down, suddenly remembering his weak heart—his bad ticker as he put it to himself, a phrase less frightening to him. His dread of meeting his wife washed over him again. He'd been away a long time, this time. He could hardly blame her if Marguerite was cross with him, driven past the limits of her patience. What had never entered his mind before came absolutely clear to him now: it wasn't a kindness he'd done her, bringing that roomer in; it was more work, more worry. Why hadn't he thought of that?

He walked on toward his house, still a block away, and as he walked he hunted through his suitcoat pockets without the faintest idea what it was he was hunting. In his inside coatpocket he came upon *The Pocket Book of Favorite Poems.* Finding it gave him a just barely perceptible touch of comfort. Even so, walking up to his own front porch he felt more like Walter Boyle than like Walter Benson. He glanced over his shoulder, then went up the steps and tried the door. It was locked.

That was something he could not possibly have expected. Marguerite never went out any more, not since she'd broken her hip that time. Had she fallen down again? He tried the doorbell. No answer. He went over to the window behind the porch swing-chair and peered in, but except for the familiar old brown overstuffed chairs and davenport, the mantelshelf with the pictures of her family on it, the standing lamps, and the television, the artificial flowers, there was nothing. It was as if she'd died. The thought alarmed him, and he went around to the side door, where he had a key beside the meter.

Inside, everything was as usual, except that Marguerite was gone. The plants in the kitchen, in clay pots set on old kitchen dishes, were in perfect health; the linoleum shone as usual; everything was clean and excessively neat. Only one trifling irregularity caught his eye, a paperback book on the kitchen table, *Castro's Revolution.* It was not the kind of thing she would read. The roomer, then, Benson decided. Leaning over it, he noticed that there was a newspaper clipping in it for a bookmark. He opened the book and, because the print of both the clipping and the book itself was very small, carried it to the window beside the washing machine where he could see.

The clipping was about a Negro church being bombed. As for the book, the pages were cluttered with underlining, and along the margin at one point there was a wild, vertical bar in bright red ink.

Walter Benson blinked his protruding eyes and pursed his lips and read through it twice. Then he closed the book on his finger and stared up at the wall as if half-expecting a voice to come out of the wall and explain. At last, glancing over his shoulder again, he put the book down exactly where he'd found it and went over to the refrigerator to get himself an Orange Crush. It came to him that she might be in the back yard, working over her flowers, say, so he carried the pop with him to the back door and out onto the porch. She was not there either. The lawn hammock was there, though, and all at once it looked inviting. He went down the rickety steps and across the lawn and got cautiously into the hammock, where he lay on his round back, arms hanging out on either side, almost relaxed though he was still not easy about her being away. Benson closed his eyes.

Here in the back yard it was like being in the middle of the forest, miles from civilization. True, he could see the back yards of all the people on this side of the block, or if not the yards then the trees and garage roofs; and true, he could hear the traffic of the city, the roar of an occasional jet overhead, the televisions a little ways off; but this was, nevertheless, *his* yard, and even though he could be seen by anyone who bothered to look from a nearby yard or some upstairs window, he felt private here: he felt he was himself. He caught the scent of a barbecue and felt, one moment, pleased by it, the next, restless again. Suppose something had happened to her? Suppose she'd been murdered in her bed, or no (he had looked in her bed), lured out of the house and murdered in the street. He wondered for the hundredth time whether the police had worked out, finally, what he'd failed to tell him, that it was no one else but the Sunlight Man who'd come to let the Indian out. Could it be he was planning some terrible murder and needed the Indian's help? The murder of Benson himself?

He found himself worrying as badly as he'd worried all that time in the jail. It was dangerous for him. The doctor had said so. For his ticker's sake if for no other reason, he had to get himself out of this state. He took a drink from the pop bottle, then closed his eyes and lay with his arms hanging over the sides of the hammock as before. But comfortable as the hammock was, good as it was to be drinking Orange Crush again in his own back yard, he could not drive away his heavy dread. He drew the pocket book of poetry from his inside suit pocket and opened it where it opened easiest, from many past readings. The poem began to affect him even before he began to read.

> *O friend, my bosom said,*
> *Through thee alone the sky is arched.*
> *Through thee the rose is red;*
> *All things through thee take nobler form,*
> *And look beyond the earth,*
> *The mill-round of our fate appears*
> *A sun-path in thy worth.*
> *Me too thy nobleness has taught*
> *To master my despair;*
> *The fountains of my hidden life*
> *Are through thy friendship fair.*

Walter Benson read it again and again, and gradually the world around him was transmuted. All that had been, a moment ago, grim and dangerous and too heavy to bear seemed now mere passing illusion, and what was real was, he thought, the arched sky and the rose and the sun-path, whatever that might be. Tears brimmed up in his eyes.

Something stirred, nearby. He hid the book quickly and glanced around. It was only the Springers' dog, so he drew out the book again, cautiously, and reread the poem twice, until he'd gotten back his former emotion. His eyes filled once again with tears, and it grieved him to remember what harsh thoughts he had thought about the people he'd passed on his long walk home. He, Walter Benson, was as much a sinner as any of them, he knew. He'd been looking merely at the outer husks, forgetting the inner fountains, as one of his poems said. He read one more time the poem about friendship and suddenly, ardently, Benson wished he had a friend so he could mail the poem to him.

He closed his eyes and gave out a tiny whimper, profoundly at peace with the world, if only for the moment, and two minutes later the pop bottle dropped almost soundlessly from his fingers onto the lawn.

It was dark when Benson awakened. At first he couldn't tell what it was that had made him wake up. The cold, maybe. Then he saw the car in the driveway. It took him a moment to recognize it. It was the roomer's car. He remembered the name now: Ollie Nuper. Marguerite and Mr. Nuper were just in the process of opening the door on the back porch—he young and wild-haired and gangly, she old and crippled and fat—and Mr. Nuper had his arm around her, helping her through the door. They turned the back-porch light on. Walter Benson half sat up in the hammock and was just about to shout his greeting when an incredible thing happened. They kissed. He could not believe his eyes, but there was no mistake: they kissed each other as if with youthful passion, she throwing her fat legs apart, he pressing hard against her. Benson felt himself going pale, his hands as cold as ice. *I'll kill them!* he thought. They parted then, and Marguerite laughed. Benson was sick with anguish. "It's an outrage!" he whispered to himself. He meant to leap from the hammock and run up to them, but he continued to sit in complete silence, holding his breath, watching. The back door closed and the kitchen light went on. A moment later, the porch light went off. He whimpered, "Has she no *shame?*" Then he thought, "I dreamed it! It's nothing but a dream! I was asleep!" It came to him that he'd said that before. And yet perhaps it really had been a dream. There was no other explanation.

He got out of the hammock without a sound and began to move slowly, furtively, toward the house.

## 2

It was a night Walter Benson would never forget. Though a professional thief, he was, in point of fact, a perfect innocent, a babe in the woods. He had heard there were people like Ollie Nuper in the world (had heard once of a rich doctor somewhere in Florida who had a huge bedroom done all in red, with paintings of naked people on the walls, and mirrors all around the ceiling) but he had not actually believed it. Who would?

When he reached the back porch the door was locked and

the kitchen light was off. They'd gone on into the livingroom. Without a sound, and having not the slightest idea what he really meant to do, Benson opened his jackknife and flipped the doorlatch. He went in, closed the door softly behind him, put the knife away, and stood listening. Mr. Nuper and Marguerite were talking and giggling. They'd been drinking.

"You're insatiable," Marguerite was saying. "I never *knew* such a man!"

Mr. Nuper mumbled something, maybe kissing her or burying his face in her bosom.

Benson curled his lips, but whether with rage or disgust or grief he could not have said. The door to the livingroom was closed. It had no latch, though; he could press it open half an inch and peek in. She was letting Mr. Nuper undress her. She held her fat arms out to the side and had her head tipped up, and Mr. Nuper danced around her like a drunken tailor, unhooking, unbuttoning, unzipping, giving kisses and pats to her bulges as he danced. He was not at all handsome, not at all what one supposes such people ought to be. He had a nose like a sheep's, with hardly any space from the flesh between his nostrils to the pink of his upper lip. His ears stuck out, his limpid brown eyes were close together, his teeth were full of silver. He was short. His arms and legs were thin and his head was the size of a ten dollar jack-o'-lantern. Benson allowed the door to come shut and leaned against the wall. He ought to have acted immediately. It was too late now, he thought.

When he heard them going upstairs he roused himself and tiptoed into the livingroom where their clothes lay on the rug. He stood at the foot of the stairs rubbing his face with both hands, trying to get his thoughts straightened out, growing more befuddled every minute until finally it seemed to him that he had driven her to it, or worse, that she had endured him all these years only because she'd known nothing any better; he was, beyond any shadow of a doubt, a miserable person, a freak who ought to have been mercifully killed at birth.

They were having a wonderful time up there, making not only the bedsprings but the whole house, as it seemed to Benson, squeak and creak and sway. He went cautiously up the steps and bent his ear toward the door.

"Tell me what you're doing to me," Marguerite said.

Benson clapped his hands over his ears and hissed with rage. They didn't hear him.

It came to him suddenly, with perfect clarity, as though someone right there in the hallway with him had whispered it into his good ear, that even if he himself was partly responsible, it was nevertheless a terrible thing they were doing to him. A terrible crime! He had feelings, didn't he? And there was his health! They ought to have thought about that! He would kill them! It was what anyone would do! He closed his hand around the jackknife in his pocket. The blade would be too short. But he'd find something. Yes! It was the natural thing! The right thing! He would tear out a post from the banister and go in there and stove their heads in!

But immediately he thought of a great many complications. Nuper was younger and probably stronger than he was, and perhaps, if the whole truth were known, Marguerite was just pretending to enjoy it. Some kind of blackmail, say. Also, his picture would be in the paper if he murdered them, and someone would see it and remember Walter Boyle. Also, it was really his own fault in the first place. His own stupid fault—yes! Tears suddenly welled up into his eyes. Here he was, fifty-six years old, and his whole life was a waste: long, wasted nights sleeping in the Rambler in some unheard-of little town, wasted weeks sleeping in a jail, poring over some newspaper he didn't care about one bit, and he was getting on in years now—for what? all for what?—and what would they do with no social security coming in? He thought of his father, wasting away on some desert island or some flophouse in Chicago or wherever it was he'd gone when he disappeared, and his poor mother wasting away in the poor folks' home, and his poor sister wasting away with that brute of a husband the bus driver, who would beat her every Saturday night and walk out on her and the four little children and come back again Tuesday morning, sure as doom. He sat down on the top step to cry but then thought better of it: there was not a sound coming from the bedroom now. The small, familiar pain came over his ticker.

The bed creaked. Somebody was sitting up.

Mr. Nuper said as if sadly, "I can't stay any longer, love. Pamphlets to deliver."

"Must you?" she asked. A groan of satisfaction.

A sound of kissing. "Forgive me, dearest."

Giggles.

The sense of what they were saying broke into Benson's

mind and his eyes widened with alarm. He got downstairs and out of sight just in the nick of time, before Mr. Nuper came padding barenaked out to the hall and down the stairs behind him. Benson fled to the kitchen and stood there clenching and unclenching his fists, wondering why the devil he'd run away. It was his house, wasn't it? It was his wife, too, in fact. He heard Mr. Nuper dressing in the living room, whistling to himself under his breath and then having another drink. Again just in the nick of time Walter Benson got out the back door and down on the lawn, out of sight, before Mr. Nuper came into the kitchen. As he crouched at the foot of the steps, waiting, Benson's hand accidentally fell upon a dew-wet two-by-four he'd forgotten to put away a month or two ago when he was fixing the back-porch steps, His heart raced. He lifted it up—it swung easily, a little like a baseball bat—and he ducked behind the spirea to wait for Mr. Nuper. When the man reached the bottom step Benson would leap out behind him and *blam!* He clenched his teeth and held his breath, smiling.

At last the back door opened. Peeking up through the leaves, Benson could see him coming toward the steps with a box on his shoulder—no doubt the pamphlets he'd mentioned to Marguerite. Benson kept absolutely still, almost painfully alert. He could smell the rich earth under his shoes, the spirea like violent perfume, and he could hear sounds as much as a mile away—a garbage-can lid grating down onto the can, a motorcycle out on the highway, a man's voice calling a dog. Louder than thunder, it seemed to him, was the soft footfall of Ollie Nuper coming down the steps, momentarily passing out of sight behind the spirea. Walter Benson knew now that he was going to do it, he actually was, and he felt a ghastly joy. When Nuper reached the bottom step, Benson waited only a fraction of a second more, then leaped out behind him, bringing down the club with all his might. But at the last quarter-second he pulled back and swerved the club to one side so that it missed, and Benson, in confusion, ducked back into hiding. Nuper had shifted the box to his head; the blow would have had no effect. Benson panted. He wanted to cry and pound on the earth.

Nuper, moving on, oblivious to it all, put the box in the back seat of his car, reaching it in through the open left-rear window. Then, instead of getting in at once, he walked around behind the garage. Benson could hear him urinating against

the garage wall. The sound went on and on. Suddenly, on a lunatic impulse, Benson dropped the two-by-four, darted over to
the car, and, for fear the door might give him away, squeezed
in through the window and huddled, panting hard, behind the
driver's seat. Only then, with his knees pushing into his chest,
did he realize his predicament. He had nothing to fight with,
and Nuper would certainly discover him here the moment he
reached in for the box. He raised up his head, like a madman
newly come to his senses, and he meant to climb out the same
way he'd come in; but Nuper was coming now. Benson ducked
down again so quickly that he scratched his ear on a spring
coming out through the back of the driver's seat. Nuper
opened the door, making the light go on, and slid in, still whistling to himself. He started up the engine.

## 3

In point of fact, Benson need not have worried. Ollie Nuper
was exceedingly drunk, in the first place, and in the second
place, the box of pamphlets was a ruse, a device for escaping
Marguerite and moving on to further adventures. It was true
(as Benson would later learn) that Nuper was a distributor of
pamphlets, an organizer, a devout radical—a Communist, in
fact—willing to lend his talents to any cause he believed to be
worthy—and whatever one might finally think of him, he had
his most definite, most righteous beliefs.

His chief belief was that most people are not merely foolish
or short-sighted or lacking in imagination but consciously and
viciously hypocritical. His father was the manager of a savings
and loan association in New York, an aging junior executive
who kept a house he couldn't afford on Long Island and a cottage he shared with two other people on Lake George. He'd
spent a lifetime smiling politely in the general direction of the
people he detested, including, some of the time, his son; and
though he loved his wife he was not always strictly faithful.
Both he and his wife had thought at first that they were very
lucky to get a bookish, nervously intelligent son: Ollie was
going to go far, his father said. Later, though, the father grew
less sure of this. All through school and even through his un-

dergraduate years at the University of Connecticut, Ollie Nuper had no friends. It was the usual story. He'd learned to read before he went into grade school, but he hadn't learned to play. When other first-graders stood in the playground watching the older children play kickball and dodgeball and steal-the-sticks, learning the mystical secret of play by watching other people do it, Ollie Nuper, full of six-year-old righteousness which both his parents and his teachers admired, retreated to books. When he did play, he cheated or got into fights which he always lost. He was not completely antisocial, however. He discovered very quickly that he could gain at least a kind of admiration by knowing things before other people did, and he had a not too-surprising knack for guessing what the people around him were about to want to know. In high school he became an authority on sex, a distributor of obscene slides, a notorious drinker, a smoker of marijuana. Despite all this, his marks were excellent. In college he suddenly matured. He became a coffee-house poet, an unwed father, so to speak, and a follower of Trotsky. He tried the twelve-string guitar, for a time, but people told him he had no ear. (This enraged him. Not so much the fact that people said it to him, though that hurt, of course, as the fact that he really did have no ear. He became, because of this, a confirmed atheist and wrote long, closely reasoned letters to famous ministers, among them Bishop Pike. None of the ministers answered him, but the letters were for a short time widely circulated at the University of Connecticut, and some were passed around even at M.I.T.) In graduate school—Brooklyn College, where he majored in philosophy—he at last came into his own. He discovered the doctrine of hypocrisy, and discovered, best of all, that if he was neurotic it was emphatically not his fault. It was not even his father's fault, in fact. It was the fault of America, of Capitalism, of White Anglo-Saxon Protestantism. Of "the Western Crime."

He dropped out of school; volunteered for the Peace Corps but didn't get in; burned his draft card; marched to Mississippi and came home profoundly disillusioned with Negroes; moved to Buffalo, N.Y., where according to a friend there were going to be riots any day. The cliché might have gone on and on except for the accident of his moving in with the Bensons.

He himself could not have told you how or why it happened, but one night, sitting in the kitchen, drinking bourbon and telling his tragic story to Mrs. Walter Benson (old enough to be his mother), he'd found himself making sexual advances. She had not exactly returned them, but she had not exactly rejected them either. She had said, "I'm so confused!"—but she had not looked confused. In the morning, looking down at her with pity and disgust (her false teeth were crooked), Ollie Nuper had been unable either to flee in revulsion or confess to her that she was revolting to him. Looking at himself in the bathroom mirror he had said to himself, in abject misery, "Well, you're not so pretty yourself." The girl he'd lived with at U. Conn. had hit it on the head. "Your face isn't really so *ugly*," she had said, "it's just, well, *silly*." And so now the great hater of hypocrisy had fallen into a life of gloomy hypocrisy. He spent hours waiting on Marguerite Benson—taking her shopping or off to movies he himself couldn't stand, talking with her politely about Thorstein Veblen and Bertrand Russell and Karl Marx (her false teeth clicking all the while she talked), swivving her night after night with a look of wild rapture on his face and a prayer that it soon be over in his head. It was worse by far than any marriage, God knew, and he hoped America would burn in Hell for bringing him to this.

Who would believe what he went through? He took her to Niagara Falls and sat, lodged in all that traffic, with his arm around her, watching as much as it was possible to see of the colored lights on the water and mist. He soothed her when she cried about how she'd betrayed her husband and he repeated over and over that it was their passion that had done it (not even she believed that, he knew, but it comforted her to hear it; it made her feel younger). He told her—surely he was out of his mind!—that if she drove him from her he would kill himself. With an ice pick. He even took her to the sooty, stinking wharf to watch the sooty, stinking ships come in from Detroit. He wondered where the devil her husband was, why the devil he didn't come home and free him but the answer was obvious, of course. He'd left for good. He'd seen his chance and he'd grabbed it. Pow! Like that. And that was what Ollie Nuper should do, no question about it! But he couldn't. A man should be honest, face right up to what he'd done and call a spade a spade. Or jump off a bridge.

Besides, in the back of his mind he knew it was all going to turn out all right. Things always did. Also, there was a girl

named Gretchen Niehaus who, when he told her what trouble
he was in, told him that he had the most beautiful, most generous soul she had ever been privileged to meet. She was a paint-
er, twenty-eight years old (seven years older than Ollie was), a
loyal member of the Party. That was where he'd met her. She
lived in a trailer on Grand Island, and any time he could make
it, she said—even if only for a cup of tea—she would be
grateful. She was golden brown except for her breasts and
hips, which were white as snow, and if he liked, she said, he
could tie her up with clothesline.

Of all this, Walter Benson was not yet aware. He huddled
on the floor of the car, out of sight, with his left hand over the
back of his head and his right hand inching back and forth under the seat, hunting for some weapon. A wrench, a screwdriver, anything. His fingers closed around some sort of spraycan.
Dear God! It would do! He closed his eyes thankfully and
gave himself up to the sensation of hurtling through space.
Under his hand the floor was filthy, like the space behind a refrigerator that has stood for a long time in an old, old house.

# 4

It seemed to Walter Benson that they'd been driving for
hours when, finally, the car slowed almost to a stop and pulled
off the road into what felt like a new-plowed field with innumerable stones in it, or bricks, or possibly treestumps. With his
ear pressed flat to the floor he heard the clutch thump in, the
bump of the gear going into neutral, the louder thump of the
clutch being released. Then the motor went off, and the night
was suddenly still. They were in the country. He could hear
crickets and a kind of whispering noise, a pump somewhere, it
might be. The car door opened and the overhead light went
on, filling him again with momentary panic. But Nuper got out
immediately and slammed the door shut behind him. Benson
lifted his head a little and drew the spraycan up close to his
chest, prepared to spray whatever was in it directly into Nuper's eyes the moment he reached through the window or
opened the door. But nothing happened. Nuper's footsteps

were going away, very quiet on the unpaved ground, yet loud as heartbeats in Walter Benson's ears. He raised his head to look out.

The car was parked in a ruined orchard. Nuper was already out of sight in the darkness, but Benson could still hear him. He was going toward what appeared to be an abandoned farmhouse. Quickly, before the man could come back, Benson squeezed his chest and belly through the window and dropped, with what seemed in his own ears a terrific racket, to the ground. He lay perfectly still, listening. Nuper continued on his way.

The grass was full of the scent of apples. Benson felt around in front of him and found three that were large and hard as rocks except for the small bruised places where they'd hit when they fell. He dropped them into his suitcoat pockets where he could get at them quickly if he needed to throw them, then got part way up and rubbed his cramped knees and rump. He scowled, wondering whether or not he should follow the roomer and, after a moment, without reaching any decision, began to follow. Apples lay everywhere and he had to scuff his feet a little to keep from twisting his ankles on them, but at last he came out into the open, where the yard around the farmhouse began.

The house had apparently been empty for years. Decay and neglect hung over everything. Pieces of the tin sheeting on the roof were bent back, no doubt the work of a storm, and some of the weather boarding had been wrenched off the walls. The front porch had rotted away and broken down, and nothing was left of the steps except the supports on which they'd once rested. Some of the windows were boarded up, some merely gaped, devoid of glass—perhaps children had torn the boarding off. When he poked his head over the sill he could see nothing definite except the two gaping windows on the next wall, but he had an impression of old wallpaper and bare floors, no furniture. There was no sign anywhere of Ollie Nuper.

Then, rounding the front corner of the house, he saw the trailer parked right up against the side wall like a small animal huddling up to the dead carcass of its dam. The trailer was as dark as the house, yet he sensed that it was lived in. He crept closer, crouching so near to the ground he was almost on hands and knees. He heard a woman's voice say softly, "Is that you, Ollie?" And then Nuper's voice: "It's me. I let myself in." A light came on in the trailer window. A candle. "Mmmmm!" the woman said. Walter Benson puckered his lips, then pressed his good ear tight to the warm tin wall of the trailer.

He listened to them for half an hour, only drawing his ear away now and then from disgust or to clean out the wax with his finger. It was outrageous that the man could come here from doing what he'd done with Marguerite and do it all over again with another woman. Worse yet, he talked and talked about it, telling this second woman how the first one disgusted him, how ashamed and miserable he was. Were there others beside this one, and did he say these same things about Marguerite to them?

The night was hot and there was a low, monotonous whistling of some bird out in the bushes grown up around the dilapidated barn, east of the house and trailer. From time to time distant sheet lightning lit up the barn and what was left of what had once been a garden. Thunder rolled, far away, and a black cloud covered nearly a quarter of the sky. He could hear cocks crowing, far, far in the distance. He felt as sullen and thundery as the night.

Suddenly he straightened up like a man who has reached a decision, turned on his heel, and stalked, almost without any effort at secretiveness, to the ruined barn. There would surely be something there that you could kill a person with. "It was a terrible crime they did to me," he said to himself. The woman in the trailer was now as guilty as the roomer. "I admit I was partly responsible myself. Let them send me to the electric chair. I don't care what they do. It was a terrible crime, that's all." Almost instantly, as though fate had left it there waiting for him, there sprang to his hand a wide, rusty fork-like thing without a handle. It would do. It had one, two, three, four, broken-one, five tines. Gripping it tightly in two hands, bringing it down with all one's force . . . *Horrible!* he thought. He was pleased.

He stepped out of the barn again and started back toward the now silent trailer. Were they asleep, then? Well, all right, he would kill them in their sleep. He was not a vindictive man. He felt very excited. The black cloud had grown and was spread over the whole sky, and now forked lightning lit up the yard and outlined the metal trailer and the house with its crumbling porch, and thunder rolled directly overhead. H slowed his walk, listening. The birds were silent. The leave began to rustle and a breeze stirred Benson's hair, what littl he had. He paused irresolute for a moment and not full aware what it was that had distracted him from his purpose An instant later large, warm drops began to fall, drumming o the burdock leaves behind him and the roof of the house i front of him. There was a brilliant flash of pure white al around him and then a terrible silence. Before he could coun three a violent roar exploded directly over him and went roll ing along the sky, and then came hurtling rain. He threw dow the fork and ran back to the barn, clutching at his collar an trying to cover his face with his elbows. *I'll do it after th storm,* he thought. He huddled against the wall inside th barn. He was already soaked to the skin, and the barn seeme no help. He looked up. There was no roof, not even so muc as a beam. Rain poured down on him like a punishment fron Heaven. The world went white again and the thunder struc and rolled away, and he was terrified. He remembered how hi mother had hidden under the bed whenever it thundered Wind lashed the trees and made the barn walls shudder an sway. *This is no joke,* he thought. And now, suddenly, he wa horrified by the magnitude of the crime he had meant to con mit.

For fear that the barn would collapse on top of him, he fle across the lawn and around the trailer to the front of th house and climbed in one of the open windows. Here th storm was noisier than ever, but at least the rain could not ge at him, part of the house roof still held. The draft goin through here, not to mention the wetness of his clothes, woul give him a case of pneumonia, no doubt, but better pneumoni than be buried alive under the barn. And this, dear God! wa what he had come to, a man fifty-six years old, with a know bad heart. (He seized the word boldly, like a penance, an seized it again.) A known bad heart! He had brought it o himself, all of it. There was no question about that. None And were there people dying somewhere in the night becaus of him, because of Walter Benson? Horrible! he thought. H covered his face with his hands and crouched in the corner sick with the burden of his wickedness. "Asleep since the da he was born," the Sunlight Man had said. How true! Preciou Mother of God, how true! He would call the police first thin, in the morning and tell them all he knew. As for Ollie Nuper . . .

The lightning flashed again and the thunder boomed, but Walter Benson was tremendously at peace, weeping with joy and terror. "Bless them," he whispered, thinking of the man and woman in the trailer. "Praise God," he whispered. He thought of the Indian boy with the broken jaw and whispered, "Bless him too, and God be with him, and with all of us! While we obey His commands we are at peace!"

When he awakened in the morning he had the beginning of a very bad cold and the roomer's car was gone from the orchard. The road was full of mudpuddles. It was a long way home. He stood hugging himself and shivering and working his throat. "The Lord is just," he thought hopefully, sick at heart. "Praise the Lord."

He shuddered once, so violently that he nearly fell down, then climbed out through the window and started toward the road. His *Pocket Book of Favorite Poems* was ruined, but Walter Benson was never at a loss for poetry. He swung his thin arms to keep the blood moving and tipped his face up and straightened his humpback as much as possible, and recited aloud to himself as he walked:

> *"These joys are free to all who live,*
> *The rich and poor, the great and low:*
> *The charms which kindness has to give,*
> *The smiles which friendship may bestow,*
> *The honor of a well-spent life,*
> *The glory of a purpose true,*
> *High courage in the stress of strife,*
> *And peace when every task is through . . ."*

The blue morning ahead of him danced with sunlight.

in the morning, and told them all he knew. As for Mr. [Harper.]

The light-room flared again and the thunder throbbed, but Walter Penson was tremendously at home, stopping with the and pressed them tight. He absorbed the shining of the man and woman at the railer "Praise God," he whispered. He thought of the [fading] day with the broken law and winced. Bless him too, and shod be with him, read with all of us. While we obey Him commands we are at peace.

When he was at his post in the car, must be had the pleasure of a new bird cold and the injured car was gone from the car stand. The road was full of indescribable. It was a long, wet bottom. He stood hanging himself, and shivering and wringing his hands. "The Lord is nigh," he thought hopefully, each at heart. "I had [a] dream."

He knocked once, so presently that he nearly fell down, then climbed out through the window and started toward the road. His feet trod softly. Service began, was ended, but Walter Penson was away at a tree-top again. He swung himself away to keep the blood moving and tried his foot up and straightened out his limb, and, as much as possible, and reeled and stood as much as he could stop.

"There is" are the last words with him
The chief amusement, the sweet and long,
be saw the church which seems to him so plain
once The walkers well from in the other person
loose The church he could read the
acts The sight of a perspective sun
In the In a prayer for the hope or such
seeks and hope that before where every break through.

The like seen are stained of him dressed with children
once in all the minutes
beller to see, to the story
while in remember [a] son that he
hog I am sure, with a sad end
the silk blocked upon her to manage
L.
last the remote are grass
each there is where

# XI

## The Dialogue
## of
## Houses

*If, then, any one would enter into the secret life, real character, and true condition of persons and things, so as to know the absolute truth concerning them, he must first get mentally still. . . .*

—Dr. L. W. De Laurence, Lama, Yoghee, Adept and Magician by Alchymy and Fire

### *1*

The Sunlight Man could not afford to waste more than a few hours on sleep. It was four in the morning when he got in. Roosters were already beginning to crow, though the sky was black. His prisoners in the cellar were asleep upright, sagging in the ropes that tied them. The gray light falling on their necks and shoulders from the bare cellar bulbs, the blackness of earth and rock wall behind them, gave them the look of the closed-off, uncommunicating dead. Luke hung with his head fallen forward, shoulders drawn inward as if he'd passed out while in agony. In the darker shadows to his right, the Indian hung in the same position, but with his back to the stairs and his shoulders slumped, relaxed. Millie Hodge, on the other side of Luke, slept with her head fallen back and to one side, and at last she showed her age. The gag biting into her mouth and cheeks was wet with spittle, and at the edges of the gag her

441

gray face was discolored by a dark bruise. Two lines of black, like rainwater stains on a white wall, ran down from the corners of her eyes. The roots of her hair were silver. The Sunlight Man smiled, unconsciously cringing a little, showing his teeth. "O blynde world, O blynde entencioun!" he murmured in the hollow dimness. He raised his hand in blessing, like the Pope.

> "How often falleth al the efect contraire
> Of surquidrie and foul presumpcioun,
> For kaught is proud, and kaught is debonaire!
> This Mrs. Hodge is clomben on the staire,
> And litel weneth that she moot descenden;
> But alday faileth thing that fooles wenden!"

He looked again at Luke, but for all his gleeful bitterness, he could not mock him. His arms and shoulders were thick as a man's, the iron-toed shoes, rising out of the water on the cellar floor, enormous; but his face (the Sunlight Man observed, moving closer, stirring the sluggish lake) was like that of a suffering child, some ravished half-wit virgin. The Sunlight Man stood pigeon-toed, with bent knees, wringing his fingers. "I find no fault in him," he said, and grotesquely rolled up his eyes.

He saw then that Nick Slater's eyes were open, watching, shiny as a rat's. After a moment the Sunlight Man went over to him and, without a word, untied him. The boy made no move either to resist or to help. His legs were unsteady, and he opened and closed his two hands slowly to get back his circulation. The Sunlight Man helped him through the water to the stairs, still without a word of explanation, and left the others as they were. He began the slow climb, supporting Nick as he would an invalid. Upstairs at last, he whispered with a leer, "You see why I had to do this to you, my boy." He cocked his head, eyebrows lifted. Then he sat Nick down in the kitchen to put salve on the boy's sore wrists and ankles, and to wash his feet—bluewhite from the dirty, cold seepage in the cellar—and wrap them in hot towels. "I suppose I can trust you to stand guard, now that I'm back?" he said. Nick Slater said nothing, merely stared, puzzled and full of hostility. "If anything happens," the Sunlight Man said, "don't stir, don't even think; just wake me. If I find I can't trust you—" He pointed to the cellar, smiling. Still Nick said nothing, but it was answer enough, at the moment, for the Sunlight Man. He had a great deal to do before afternoon if he was to meet again with Clumly. First, he must sleep.

As a rule he was a man who could snatch more sleep in an hour than most men could in three. He knew the art of what had been called in his father's day "concentration." But not this morning. He was of many minds, as excited, as tangled in his wits, and as full of daring schemes as a young man in love. Not even he could say why, nor did he ask. "A new lease on life," the expression went. Why he should get a new lease on life from teasing, perplexing, confounding an old man who sat half-asleep, witless and innocent as an ancient bull with a ring through its nose—who could tell? Nevertheless, he felt like a man reborn. If his head was filled with images of fire, his heart, for all its churning excitement, was precariously serene. Somewhere even now Clumly would be sitting with his hands around his nose, his tiny bullet-eyes half-shut, listening with all his poor clumsy wits to the Sunlight Man's grand tirade, or walking back and forth in a locked bedroom, puffing fiercely at his green cigar, going through in his mind all the subtle twists of the Tale of the Negro in the Cellar.

And so now, like a man on the verge of embarking on some shrewd course of action for the good of all humanity, the Sunlight Man lay huddled in his bed, still in his clothes, his hands pressed between his thighs, his knees drawn nearly to his chin, trying to concentrate on sleep but racing all the while from scheme to scheme, from one dazzling trick to another, plotting grand gestures and cadences, concocting metaphors and puzzling allusions, a splendid, unheard-of entertainment. Half-waking, half-sleeping, he would laugh sometimes at things he couldn't make sense of a moment later. When at last he was more asleep than awake, the Indian sitting stock-still at the window, he had curious, frightening dreams.

He was in, perhaps, the Paxton Dairy. (Paxton had never owned a dairy.) All around him lay white perfection: clean walls, clean floors, huge snow-white trucks, a sound and smell of ice-cold water churning. There were stainless steel tubs and milkcans on clean concrete ramps, and corrugated stainless steel doors that rolled open and shut with a sound like faraway thunder. Kathleen, perhaps—perhaps someone else— was at the desk in the office, writing. He noticed with only a

part of his mind, for someone was explaining, pointing into a
vat which had no water in it, no visible bottom, that the enemy came from down there. Taggert knew who the enemy was,
but he could not bring it to mind for a moment. Then, momentarily, everything was clear. The girl at the desk (her red
hair falling forward softly, hiding her face and most of the
summer-sky blue of her blouse) was named Prosperinga. She'd
been captured by a man called Plato, a business rival of Paxton's, who'd risen up out of the underworld when the girl was
working there alone. He'd kept her prisoner all winter but had
for some reason released her in the spring. The problem was
to board up the hole, because fall was near. Taggert Hodge,
called in to help, made a careful sketch of his plan while the
man at his elbow admired the sketch and whispered of the awful difficulty.

When he looked up from the paper it was winter and all the
windows were broken. Snow was blowing in, and the milkcans
were cracked down the side like frozen eggs. He was alarmed
at first, then remembered he was not the man they thought,
but a secret agent. He smiled, crumpled the paper, and
dropped it on the floor. Hurrying away, he took the wrong
door and found himself in what appeared to be an old country
kitchen converted into some kind of hospital room. On the
kitchen table, under an operating light, the attendants had
stretched her out naked and had given her ether. She was
beautiful, skin as white as marble, and they could not resist
passing their hands lightly over her breasts and belly and legs.

"See here," he said. They stopped at once and dropped their hands to their sides, looking sullen. "Have I got to be everywhere at once?" he said. But from under a small table on wheels, with bottles on it, and scissors and tubing, someone whispered to him and reached up his hand in dreadful supplication. Crossly, he turned to do what he could for the poor hopeless devil—there were wormholes in the arm—and he heard his attendants climbing up onto the operating table behind him. His younger son's hand reached out to him from a basket of clothes by an aluminum ironing board. Suddenly he smelled smoke. He glanced around in alarm and saw cracks appearing in the walls, and small, quick tongues of flame. He shouted in rage at the attendants crawling over her body like spidermonkeys, and with the shout he awakened himself. The Indian boy stood over him, holding the pistol, and he could not tell—perhaps Nick Slater could not tell either—whether Nick was there to defend him or to kill him. Wide awake but confused and sick, Hodge met the boy's eyes. At last Nick lowered the gun.

"You were shouting," Nick said dully.

Taggert nodded and swallowed.

"Dream, I guess," Nick said. He turned away and limped back to his watching without a sound. Hodge, after a moment, returned to his nightmares. He was thinking as he drifted off, *I must try to explain to him.* Nick had said nothing, had not even showed surprise, when Hodge had tied him up in the basement with the others. Perhaps he'd assumed it was simply more madness, and then again perhaps he'd understood. There was no sign whatever of what he thought, if anything, in his flat, dark face. The likelihood, perhaps, was that he showed nothing because he was still watching and waiting. One of these days—one of these hours—he would stop that watching and act. Then Taggert Hodge, too, must watch and wait. But he put it off now and slept. "Let me tell you why I had to tie you up," he said reasonably and kindly in his dream. The explanation he gave was involved, incredibly subtle, and though it was thrillingly lucid at the time, he could not remember it later.

At eight-thirty, when Nick Slater touched his shoulder to wake him, he sat up on one elbow, blinking, licking the dryness from his mouth. The room around him was still sick with the atmosphere of his dreams. "All right, I'm up," he said.

"You can turn in." The boy nodded, but he didn't withdraw. Taggert brought him into focus. "Well?"

"We should get out," Nick said accusingly. "We can't stay here like this."

"Soon," Taggert said. "We'll go when it's right."

The boy shook his head. His face was drawn with fear and lack of sleep. "It's too dangerous. There was somebody here last night. Knocked for a long time. Scared me to shit."

"You kill him?"

The eyes narrowed—Nick had been tied in the cellar at the time—but he said nothing.

Taggert sat up and swung his feet over the side. His head ached and the inside of his mouth was dry, as if he'd been drinking all night. There were bubbles of panic—only partly the aftertaste of his nightmares—stirring in his chest. He observed that Nick had cleaned and polished his shoes. Even in the deathhouse his shoes would be clean and polished.

"A curious pair, aren't we," Taggert said. "Rise up and follow me, and I will make you harpooners of men." He leered.

The boy went on watching him, looking at the scar tissue, not his eyes.

Hodge said, "What will you do when I get you out of this?"

"I don't know."

"Turn on me, I suppose." Hodge nodded, indifferent. "That would be natural." He tried to think about it, knowing it was impossible; his mind was not yet willing. "Or turn on yourself. Yes. That's more like it. Destroy your freedom by burning it up. I knew a young fellow that did that once. Name of Ike or something. He was locked on this island with his father, people say, and no escape. But the father was crafty, and he figured out a way to make eagle's wings that a person could fly with." He closed his eyes, faking a smile, raising his arms like wings. "Well, never mind. A story."

Nick said, totally ignoring the act, "What *you* going to do?"

He shook his head. After a long time he said, "Watch you, I suppose. See where it leads."

The boy took it in and, after a second, to Hodge's surprise, nodded. Hodge was shocked, filled with pity. It had never occurred to him that sooner or later the boy might understand that they were caught in an experiment, and no one was in control.

Nick said, "I'd like to be out of here. Someplace else."

"Not yet, love," Hodge said. He thought again of Clumly, bent squinting over the tape, and then he was remembering Old Man Paxton, bent over the letter Kathleen had sent to the newspaper. It was a mad letter—she said she'd been captured by Communists—and Paxton could not make out how to deal with it. When his children went wrong it was his habit to slap them, bark out some brilliant cruelty, and return them to his image of what they were; but he had now no slap fierce enough, no cruelty that could reach her. In the wide, sunlit room with the enormous fieldstone fireplace that had never been lit for fear it would confound the heating system, he sat like a coiled snake uncertain where to strike. "I'll get you for this," he said. Hodge smiled, thrilled with hate, and said, "You're as crazy as she is, then?" But afterward Clive Paxton walked in his garden, scrutinizing his lilacs and althea for minute flaws, giving orders, critically turning loose earth with his foot. And the precision in his madness filled Hodge with awe. Paxton did not say later, "I lost control when we talked this morning. "He was no more able to apologize than to complain or compliment. He stood—but this was long before—stood at the gate of his huge truckbarn as the diesels came out in a chalk-white fire of headlights, and would not stir from their path but forced them to swerve and creep like monstrous lions cowering past the whip. *He ruled from terror,* Hodge thought. *Any psychiatrist would say so: the tyranny of the insecure.* At the age of fifty-one he'd established a boys' camp, had risked bankruptcy for it, stamping his troubled image into the Catskill Mountains: a huge stone lodge, a chapel, cabins, a long white dock and boathouses. And there he dealt out contests and awards, branding boys as successes or failures, stamping out hearts and souls in his own tigerish image. And now, meeting Nick Slater's noncommittal, unblinking gaze, he thought: *I've loosed another Paxton on the world.*

Or was it that he himself was the dangerous beast? Who had triumphed, after all, old man or son-in-law?

"Better get some sleep, my boy," he said.

The Indian lowered his head—not so much a nod, it seemed, as a gesture requesting blessing. Solemnly, Hodge made a sign of the cross in the air.

*And they shall be afraid; pangs and sorrows shall take hold of them; they shall be in pain as a woman that travaileth; they shall be amazed at one another; their faces shall be as flames.*

Hodge said, "Thy will be done." But he thought of Clumly, servant of law, and anxiety flared through his chest. He had to hurry, he would be late and, worse, unprepared.

## 2

He worked furiously, forcing Luke to help, since Nick was still asleep. Luke said nothing for a long time, merely obeyed, cutting rope, painting, sawing. His wrists were red and sore from the tight bonds, and he breathed by a kind of heavy sighing, like a man sick to death with sorrow. The Sunlight Man struggled to ignore it. Out of odds and ends—bits of wood, rope, wire, an old tarpaulin—the Sunlight Man's huge, absurd contraption took shape.

"What is it?" Luke said. His voice was full of pressure, the light, fast beating of his heart.

"Prop for a happening," the Sunlight Man said. He went on with his work.

Luke said. "There are no happenings. When things seem to happen it's illusion."

"Prop for an illusion," he said. "Hand me the pliers."

Mechanically, fingers trembling, Luke obeyed.

"What's it all for?" Luke said after a while. It was like a sob, yet he labored at making it mere talk. "You make all these doo-dads, you go out and hold up some stupid store—"

"Nonsense. I don't hold up stores."

"Well, whatever." A whisper. "Just the same, what's the point?"

"What's the point of anything, you mean. Ah! That's very philosophical."

"Right, be a cynic." Luke let it go, choked by emotion.

Taggert Hodge frowned, cross and threatened but tempted as well, and at last, because Luke had his father's eyes, his father's voice, something even of his father's plodding goodness (however bent, dented by the batterings of his mother's uncommon, unsensible wit and, worse yet, by experience too full of ambiguities for common sense to cope with)—because of all that but also because he could not endure the sight of such pain—he put down the pliers and turned around to lean on the workbench, folding his arms and lowering his bearded chin onto his chest. He said, "As a matter of fact, I do have answers to certain questions. Small ones. What was yours?" He spoke as if with scorn, but by accident.

"Nothing."

They looked together at the clutter filling the garage. Beyond the open back door there were burdocks, motionless in the sunlight, their white and blue flowers singing with honeybees. The leaves were unnaturally large and their shaded stems were thick, fed by the sewer and not cut back in years.

Luke said, "My question is, Why do sinners' ways prosper?" A whisper of rage.

The Sunlight Man forced a smile. "Another illusion. Nothing prospers but the soul. The universe is a great machine gun, and all things physical are riddled sooner or later with bleeding holes. You're bombarded by atoms, colors, smells, textures; torn apart by ancient ideas, appeals for compassion; you twist, writhe, try to make sense of things, you force your riddled world into order, but it collapses, riddled as fast as you build, and you build it all over again. You put up bird-houses and cities, for instance, but cats eat the birds and cyclones eat the cities, and nothing is left but the fruitless searching, which is otherwise called the soul."

Luke stood silent, throat and temples swelling.

"I'm serious, my boy," he said. "Don't be fooled by rhetoric. Even a master of illusion must have his defenses. Witness our Saviour."

"You just talk," Luke whispered. "You duck out of everything with talk."

"Well, yes, perhaps. But I've also acted, from time to time. There has to be a convenient opening for action."

"Yes. Like finding Nick in jail, so you could turn him into a killer."

"No, I freed him."

"It was vicious and you know it. Or I hope you do. Maybe you really meant to free him, but you didn't know him. *That's* for sure. Anyone who knew him would have guessed. We tried —me, my father, Uncle Ben. You wouldn't understand. It was no use, anyway. Jail was the only hope left; maybe it would show him." He gulped for air. "But there you were, believing in nothing, grabbing whatever little kick came along, exactly like the rest—an 'existentialist,' as my mother calls herself. There is no past, only the present; no future either, only the future-present. You know what I'm saying. You didn't know him from Adam, you had no idea what direction he'd been heading before you came, and you set him 'free,' you say, like some new Jesus, as if anything might be possible if you said it was—as if a falling rock could change its mind and go upward at your command."

The Sunlight Man moved only his eyes to study him. Luke's jaw was tight, his speech thick and quiet, forced out by the lightning-fast pounding of his heart.

"Are you *afraid* of me?" he said.

Luke nodded.

"Why?"

"Because—" He changed his mind. With square Hodge fingers he touched his raw left forearm, looking at the floor.

"Because I'm crazy, you were going to say."

"The way you walk—like you weren't human, like something imitating the way human beings walk. And when you talk . . . all show. You have no feelings. You shuffle, and yet your feet don't make any noise. A creature like you would kill in a wink if the mood came over it. How can we know what you think? If there were people from outer space—"

"Or inner space."

"There. You make a point of speaking without talking. 'Inner space.' " His lips shook.

The Sunlight Man pursed his lips and looked up at the rafters. There were swallows' nests. He remembered the swallows' nests at Stony Hill. They were everywhere there—in the cowbarn, the garage, the smokehouse, even the wellhouse. Art Jr had knocked one down once, when he was twelve or so, and Will had put it up again—the eternal repairer—with old rags and bits of mud, and he'd put the baby birds back in. The mother, knowing his heart, had accepted his work. It was the kind of thing Luke too would do, you had a feeling, though he might not do it as well. For all his sharp tongue, his whining misery, his wrath, he too had eyes of the kind that must look sometimes at swallows. Like Kathleen. They would go out at dusk, the two of them, to watch the swallows' sharp-winged, arrowtailed flight against the sun's setting, a lovely fragrance of new-mown alfalfa scattered across the farm. *Blessed is he that has seen these things and goes under the ground.*

Luke was turning away, and Taggert Hodge saw that he should not have let it pass—"speaking without talking." He nodded, pretending he'd been thinking about it. "It's true, yes," he said as if just discovering it. "I avoid plain speech, communication. It's interesting, now you mention it. I also do it when I talk to myself. I apologize."

Luke said nothing.

"Suppose I say I do believe in the past? Suppose I say I once walked and talked like you?"

"But you don't say it. You say 'suppose.' If you said it, it would be asking me to wonder what happened, what turns a human being into a monster. It would be talking as if we were both human. You can't."

He looked at the side of Luke's jaw, and again he was tempted. But he said, ironic and tentative, "What made you decide to speak to me so frankly, my dear boy? It's very strange, you know."

"It was an impulse."

"But you'd been thinking about it. Brooding on it, in fact. That's how impulses begin, as St. Augustine tells us. Suggestion, delectation . . ."

"Maybe."

The Sunlight Man squinted. "Hunting for soft places in the dragon's belly?"

"I'd expect you to think that."

"I don't, necessarily. Generally speaking, I think nothing." He picked at his lip, unwilling to go farther until the uneasiness in his chest calmed down and he was sure of his voice. "What I think—" He paused once more. "As a matter of fact, I think you've made me a symbol. You've brooded too much, connected me with your mother and father and your childish frustration. I'm the enemy, inhuman. I mock your hot desires for things you scorn. Wife, children, house in the country, profession, even decency."

Luke looked away, compressing his lips.

*So you're one of us*, the Sunlight Man thought. He continued in a rush—"If I mock you, you suspect I may be right. You think what you love is probably not worth loving, no lasting significance, no derring-do, no bizzazz. And so you'll test me, poke at me, turn me over and maybe in time you'll assume me."

Luke made no response.

The Sunlight Man leaned toward him, sly. "You're toying with making me into an example for your life." He smiled like a wolf. "You'll grow a beard, stop washing your face and hands and first thing you know you'll be learning to walk without noise, like one of us devils."

"You're paranoid."

The Sunlight Man unfolded his arms and turned back to the bench. "And you, O child of midnight, are a liar."

It was almost a minute before Luke said quietly, "You're wrong. You teach me to admire stupid people and arrogant bastards who do no harm—unlike you."

"Hold these wires," the Sunlight Man said.

Luke obeyed.

The Sunlight Man said, "I believe in the past, and I once walked and talked like you. God's truth. But I don't want you to wonder about me. Let whosoever is without sin cast the first crumb." In the filings on the bench he traced the word *Youth,* then smiled, showing teeth.

Luke said, "You haven't understood. I was offering help." His voice was quieter than before.

The Sunlight Man stood very still. At last he said softly and violently, "With what, boy? With *love?* Is *Love* your weapon?

> *Down pour'd the heavy rain*
> *Over the new-reap'd grain;*
> *And Misery's increase*
> *Is Mercy, Pity, Peace."*

It seemed pure, inexplicable rage, and Luke Hodge was hurled back into his cage of misery and confounded.

The Sunlight Man went back to his work. He wouldn't say anything more.

## 3

In the milkhouse, where he was supposed to be washing the milking machines, Ben Hodge's boy David was playing complicated rhythms on the milkcan covers. The farm around the milkhouse lay as quiet as a picture in a magazine, but because of the music it seemed nevertheless alive and sentient, like motionless stone imperceptibly trembling with a dance of atoms, or like a sleeping head full of dreams. Ben Hodge, greasing his corn-chopper on the hill behind the house, paused and squinted. Vanessa was in the kitchen cutting rhubarb into a burnt-black saucepan for lunch. She was breathing hard, as usual, and the gray curls at her temples were dark with sweat. Her paring knife stopped moving and she listened to the rhythms moving out from the milkhouse through breathless air to the hills and valleys and woods. Once she'd labored out to him when he was playing the milkcan covers, and the moment she'd touched the door he'd stopped. It was a shame, she felt, that he only played when alone, hiding his candle under a bushel. "Whooey!" she'd said, hand on her thudding heart (the walk to the milkhouse had tired her). He'd merely stared back with blank, deferential eyes, a trace of a smile at the corners of his mouth. She could not get him to play. He was a giant, standing black as coal in the white, low-ceilinged room, his glistening bare shoulders solid as a horse's rump. He lay his hands on his hips and looked down at her with indifferent friendliness. And so she knew better, now, than to go and interrupt him. Besides, the heat out there would wilt her like lettuce. Well, she was grateful that the boy was so happy. She wished *she* could sometimes be as happy as that. She was grateful that they had happened to find him, so that now, working in the murderous heat, she could be uplifted by that wordless, glorious music of praise, forget herself for a moment and join him in spirit. She looked out the high, round-arched kitchen window at the brown grass of the lawn. She wiped her forehead with her arm. *Poor Elizabeth,* she thought. *Poor Will —poor Fred Clumly—poor Esther—poor Mrs. Palazzo—the poor, poor Salvadors.* She must get to her letter-writing this afternoon.

Sometimes the music was slow and thoughtful, sometimes wild with excitement.

*Poor Vanessa,* she thought, and smiled with a startled look. "Poor silly lummox," she said to herself, "it's from *loneliness* that he drums."

The music fell away to silence, then after a moment began again, rapid and light.

Ben Hodge, still listening, went on now with his work. In the valley below him, beyond the house and barns, beyond the tamaracks—in the yellowgreen valley that thousands of years ago had been a glacial river, graveyard of fantastic beasts—his black and white cows were sitting in the shade of the maple trees at the corner of the pasture. They too were the Negro's instruments. He would stand in the cowbarn, when he thought he was alone, and would lightly drum on the cows' backs and sides, getting sharp, thin notes from their upright hipbones, hollow, deep sounds from the hide around their lungs. He played tractors, too, and water pipes, old boards, stone walls; if he thought no one was there, he even tapdanced music out of the caked, yellow lime behind the gutters.

A blackbird whistled, and again Ben Hodge looked up. It came a second time, a clean pure note on the crest of the drumbeat. There was a light breeze here on the hill, and a sound from across the lane of rustling corn leaves. All at once an idea for a sermon came: David playing for mad King Saul. *The whole world is a kind of music, and everything living plays its part, either in tune or out of tune. Now when a man is out of tune . . .*

He thought again of his brother Tag, and his face drew up to wince. Guilt rushed over him. What was there he could do? It came to him suddenly then that it was *not* because he was in tune with the world that the Negro boy played or the blackbird whistled or he, Ben Hodge, made up sermons. And not because he was in tune once more that Saul came out of his madness or Taggert came home. *We're more like organ pipes, then,* he thought. *Somebody pushes the right key and we're filled with sudden music and can't say why.*

*"so Saul was refreshed, and was well. . . ."* . .

*And the bitterness is, there are pipes and pipes—some pipes sweet and melodious, and others that tremble and howl like the Day of Doom. But either way, somebody pushes an unseen key.*

*(But a man is different from a cow: he ruminates by a different set of laws, and asks himself why.)* . .

*Not organ pipes, then, or tractors, waterpipes, boards, stone walls; not even the slime of the earth. A man is the player and the instrument in one, and, most of the time he's the composer, note by note.*

There came into his mind the beginning of a new way of telling the story of Saul and the harper: "There was a king full of wrath and vindictiveness, the Bible says, and he was what you'd call a man with a demon in him. He was a powerful king, and whatever tune he called, why, the people danced to it. Well sir, there was a harper in that land, and though the Bible doesn't record it, he was deaf. . . ."

But all the while, the Negro boy in the milkhouse played on, wincing from the effort, baring his teeth, his eyes clamped shut. His arms ached, and the sweat ran off him in rivers. The sounds shooting out from his fingertips and palms and knuckles and the heels of his hands were like things alive, like birds or bats, and they flew to the cinderblock walls and struggled and escaped.

And until he stopped, the mindless, sullen air was full of wings.

### *4*

The paper in Clumly's trembling fingers shook so badly he couldn't read it. He didn't need to. He'd gone over it a hundred times at least since the stranger had delivered it to Esther last night. (She whimpered with fright as she told it.) He'd come up on the porch just a little after midnight—she was certain of the time, or thought she was—when Clumly was hearing the monologue of the Sunlight Man at the Presbyterian church, and he'd knocked sharply, as only a policeman would knock, or an agent of the German Gestapo in one of those movies. She'd gotten on her robe and slippers and turned off the radio and hurried down. "Who is it?" she'd said. The deepest voice she'd ever heard had answered quietly, "Message for Chief of Police Fred Clumly, ma'am. My name's Warner. Open your door an inch and I'll slip my card in." She opened the door and groped for the card and pretended to study it in the pitch-dark room. "All right," she said, and opened the door somewhat wider. She had an impression (it was hard to know how she formed her impressions) of a huge man in a coat. He was tall, at any rate. His voice seemed to come from at least two feet above her, which would make him at least seven feet, eight inches tall. And one other thing was certain, too. He had a sickening smell. It was like hoofrot, she said, or like burning flesh. It was like a cancer smell and like a sewer on a hot, wet day. He smelled like a goat, like an outhouse, like fire and brimstone. She was frightened, half-convinced she was confronting some monstrous apparition. But when he spoke again his voice partly allayed her fears. "You have to sign for it ma'am," he said. She took the pencil and pad he placed in her hands and signed where he showed her she must sign. The smell made her feel faint. At last he said, "Good. That will do. Here's the message." He handed her a paper airplane. Clumly had scowled furiously, sitting up in bed, hearing the nightmarish account. "You must have made a mistake about the time," he said. But she wasn't mistaken. She'd been sewing and listening to the midnight news on the radio when he came—she couldn't sleep—and after he left she'd checked the clock. It had occurred to Clumly that perhaps his own watch had been wrong, perhaps the man had tricked him into going late to his appointment. But his watch was right now. He remembered all at once the Sunlight Man's first words last night: *You're right on time*. And so it seemed certain, it had not been midnight at all when he entered the church. (If anything was certain, it was certain that the Sunlight Man would lie.) "Well, thank you," he'd said to his wife. Then, reassuringly: "You did the right thing." He'd waited until she had left the room, then unfolded the paper airplane. It was a map, drawn by, one would have sworn, a child. A kind of pirate's treasure map. Some roads, a railroad—DL&W—some words along the bottom, badly spelled.

He stood now, in the murderous heat, pressing the map against the semaphore post to steady it enough that he could read it. He hadn't much farther to go. He glanced at his watch. It was five after three. In ten minutes he was supposed to be there. He had no way of knowing whether he'd recognize the place of the appointment when he finally got there, and no way of knowing that the Sunlight Man would be waiting. But he had no choice. That is, he had chosen.

He trudged on, trying not to think. His ankles ached from turning and twisting on the cinders and stones of the railroad bed, and the raw place on his left foot, from a cinder he'd gotten inside his shoe and not stopped to take out until much too late, was stinging now. His brown police shirt was soaking wet —it couldn't have been wetter if he'd jumped in the creek that wandered in and out along the railroad embankment—and his crotch was chafed and raw. His ears would be blistered by sunset. He had burdock leaves hanging out of his hat now to shade his ears and neck, but he hadn't thought of it until the sun had already done its work. The heat was incredible. Had the devil *known* it would be like this? The woods to his left stood motionless, wilting and steaming in the heat. To the right he looked down on fields and pastures where cows lay unmoving beside dried-up creekbeds or stood huddled in the shade of locust groves. The rails of the track gleamed blindingly, and Clumly had no sunglasses with him. When he closed his eyes and gently pressed the lids to soothe them he saw the rails in red-vermillion, as bright as the arc of a welding torch. The world stretching out all around him was enormous—dry, hot, dull, and, above all, indifferent as the Sunlight Man's wooden gods. It did queer things to his mind. He felt like a man out walking against his will on some desolate mountainside. He could see for miles, behind him, in front of him, and off to the right—piles of smooth round stones, white as bone in the sunlight; smoothly nibbled pasture; here and there a lacy grove that gave no particular shade; a solitary pine tree; a row of dead elms; overhead, blue sky, white clouds, the sun burning down like a pure white, sightless eye. As far as one could see in any direction, there was scarcely a house or a barn. In all this silence and emptiness, the slightest tricks of his mind took on ludicrous importance. A song came into his head and refused to leave:

> Old Molly Hare,
> What you doin' there?
> Sittin' in the fireplace
> Smoking my cigar.

It was the only verse he knew.

And this, even more infuriating: when he'd first come up onto the tracks, miles ago now—he'd parked on the Creek Road and climbed up where the Little Tonawanda went under the railroad bridge—he'd watched a freight train pass. It had entered his mind that one might put a bullet on the tracks, the train would fire it. It was a foolish thought, a child's whimsical reflection that would have entered and left almost unnoticed at any other time. But now as he walked through the seemingly endless afternoon he could not get the idiotic thought out of his head. He tried to distract himself with memories of the days long ago when he'd stood on the deck of the *Carolina*, soaking up heat like this but smelling the water and getting, now and then, a tingle of spray. "That was the life," he said aloud. But to no avail. He had to do it, and at last, craftily, looking all around him first—he bent over, slipped a bullet from his belt, and placed it on the track. Then he hurried on. He felt relieved, and the relief, like everything else, was exaggerated. He felt, crazily, like a new man entirely. Then he began to believe he was being followed. It became for him almost a certainty. He even thought he caught a glimpse, once, of a man with snow white hair peeking out from behind a tree.

Then Clumly stopped, and his fists closed tight. The place he'd been told to come stood directly in front of him, a hundred yards down the track. "Idiot!" he thought in a rage. The Sunlight Man's map had made one omission: it did not include the Francis Road. Incredibly, Clumly had not noticed. He had walked miles to a point that he could have reached by car. He touched the burning-hot handle of his revolver and for a moment found he was thinking, with perfect seriousness, of murder. He got hold of himself.

He took a breath and walked nearer, with exaggerated caution, to the preposterous place of meeting. It was a tent. It was square, with a pointed roof—an old tarpaulin which had been furnished with a wooden floor and had been painted white, as gleaming white as sugar. On the white there were painted symbols of glittering red, blue, and yellow, and purple. Over the door there was a picture of a lion's head, vaguely Egyptian. Strangest of all—and most ridiculous—the tent was not on the ground. It hung suspended from the railroad trestle, directly in the path of any train that might come. The log-chain that held it up had been painted bright yellow.

Fifteen feet from the tent, Clumly stopped and stood rubbing his nose.

"Ridiculous," he whispered. "What am I doing here? Ridiculous!"

Then he caught the smell. There was no question about it. Inside the tent he would find the Sunlight Man. The tent-flap opened and a dirty rope ladder dropped slowly down. Clumly studied it, studied the tent. For a long time nothing happened. At last, behind him, the Sunlight Man said, "Shall we go up?" Clumly whirled and reached for his revolver in a single motion, but the revolver was, naturally, gone. The Sunlight Man bowed. He had on the same drab black suit he'd had on at the church last night, but today he had added to his costume an enormous turban. Clumly's gaze went to the clasp on the turban and remained there. The clasp was a police badge. He did not need to touch his shirt to know it was his own.

The Sunlight Man bowed again.

After a moment, heart quaking, Clumly moved, half-stumbling, toward the ladder. When he clambered inside—the tent both swinging and turning now—he found that whoever had thrown down the ladder was gone.

SUNLIGHT: You find our tent curious?

CLUMLY *(coughing)*: The tent-flap . . . if you would . . . some air!

SUNLIGHT: Ah, yes, One forgets. It's a bit of a trial to be cooped up this way with a man who carries my curse. Air then. Better.

CLUMLY: Thank you.

SUNLIGHT: Haven't you wondered about that smell? Have you tried to identify it?

CLUMLY: At times. I've wondered about how it comes and goes. You take it off and put it on like a coat.

SUNLIGHT: That's interesting, yes. Fascinating! But we must hurry along. You were asking about the tent.

CLUMLY: No, *you* were.

SUNLIGHT *(speaking rapidly)*: Have some manners, you old fool. Be civilized! Good manners are all that stand between you and Kingdom Come. Don't forget it! We're here in truce, not peace. Just once in the history of the world I want to see cop and robber understand who they are, what they're doing it for, before they come out blasting. I want you to know my position, sir, so that if you kill me it's not with that tiresome leer of self-righteousness. But I warn you well, I too can be driven to righteousness. Mock me, abandon the decent forms, and I'll shoot you. I think I may be serious.

CLUMLY: I'll be careful.

*(The Sunlight Man laughs.)*

CLUMLY: Are you all right?

SUNLIGHT: Well enough. I thank you for asking.

CLUMLY: No trouble. No trouble at all.

SUNLIGHT: You're very kind.

CLUMLY: I try . . . *(Pause.)* This is a funny sort of tent.

SUNLIGHT: Bless you! You *are* kind! What drives a man like you to a life of decency? *(He laughs again.)*

CLUMLY: Well—

SUNLIGHT: Enough. *Sh!* The tent. We're on the track—excuse the pun. Our time is limited. Precisely limited, as a matter of fact, because the afternoon freight . . . Are you getting all this? Does the tape recorder work inside your shirt? Have you listened over to what I said last night? Did you pick it up?

CLUMLY: It came out fine, yes.

SUNLIGHT: You make me nervous, keeping it inside your shirt. Get it out where it can work right. The microphone— *(Sounds of the tape recorder being shifted; a sharp bumping noise from the microphone.)* Good. There. You won't run out of time and miss the end?

CLUMLY: No danger. You see, there are three separate—

SUNLIGHT: Enough, enough! Don't tell me the details. You've no idea how sharply our time is limited. I wanted to tell you about the tent, explain all the symbols. No time for that now. On the wall there behind you, those are Babylonian figures for the twelve houses—astrological houses. I wanted to explain, but you got me off on . . . what was I saying?

CLUMLY: I got you off.

SUNLIGHT: Astrology. Yes. No doubt you laugh at astrology, like everybody now. The same as they laugh at religion. They do. Don't fool yourself! The arrogance! If only we had more time! If only you hadn't . . . *(Calms himself.)* All right. This much: if religion is scorned in America—and everywhere else in the modern world—it's because nobody understands its terms any more, nobody can penetrate the distinction between religion and mere theology. So with astrology. People look at it now, with their incredible modern arrogance, and they ask precisely the wrong questions, look precisely in the wrong direction, and when astrology gives them no answers they scorn it, mock it for childish superstition, and, worst of all, foist it off on the stupidest people in the culture, the devout of the drugstores—old ladies, gamblers, uneducated halfwit housewives thirsting for adventure. Well they're wrong, and if my lips shake as I say it, I apologize. I hate this modern slime, I make no bones about it! Centuries of labor by serious men, ah, *brilliant* men, shrugged off by a pimply, pasty-faced age which conceives itself—

CLUMLY: The wrong questions?

SUNLIGHT: Such questions as *Does it work?*, yes. Such questions as *How does it work?* Modern. Interesting and valuable questions, perhaps, but irrelevant if your concern is with whether a thing makes sense. What did the ancient astrologers *do?* In other words what did they *think* their usefulness was? Did they predict? No! They tabulated and afterward by study of their tables they advised the king on what the gods seemed to be saying. There was no guarantee that what the gods seemed to be saying was true—no guarantee whatever of the prediction. They did not ask *why* albinos tended in those days —as they do today—to be born in certain months, or why Virgos (as we would say) are flighty. They were statisticians. They filled up enormous libraries with statistics on human character in relation to the seasons, and they discovered in their statistics profound patterns. They discovered, for instance, that axe murderers have, invariably, certain physical features in common—blue veins in the forehead, among other things—the very same discovery made in Germany thirty years ago from a wholly different direction, endocrinology. All right. They were students of fate, mind-readers of the gods. If they read dimly, they knew it; it was natural, after all, because the minds of men and the minds of gods have very little in common. In modern language, the order of the conscious human mind and the order of the universe are dissimilar, as far apart as the particles of an atom. Nevertheless, for students of human character there are no more valuable books on earth than the books of ancient Mesopotamia and India and Egypt. Fact! But enough! I've run on too long, our time is running out. Let this suffice: we are here to speak of houses, the twelve houses of the sun, and of how the world turns now, and of omen-watching, the art of divination.

CLUMLY: For *my* part—

SUNLIGHT: Let us make a distinction. Omen-watching, divination, has nothing whatever to do with magic. Divination is man's attempt to find out what the universe is doing. Magic is man's ridiculous attempt to make the gods behave as mortals. Divination asserts passivity, not for spiritual fulfillment, as in the Far East, but for practical and spiritual life. After divination one acts *with* the gods. You discover which way things are flowing, and you swim in the same direction. You allow yourself to be possessed. Soldiers understand it. The so-called heroes of our modern wars especially. A man runs up a hill with a machine-gun, gives up his will to live, his desire to escape: he has a sudden, overwhelming and mysterious sense that he has become the hill, the night sky, the pillbox he's attacking. The machine-gun fires of its own volition—he ducks, spins, turns as the gods reach down to duck him, spin him, turn him. A fact of experience. A question for science, possibly, but not to the man with the machine-gun: for him it's a thing done, sensual act: he's one with God. Race-car drivers know. The mind grows large and irrational, one suddenly knows things impossible to know. In extreme cases— Don't shut off your mind when I say this, sir. Resist. In extreme cases, a man can remember the future. We hate that. Naturally. We are embarrassed by the bearded professors who brood on the mysteries of parapsychology. But every scientist who's studied the evidence has been forced to agree: it's real. And every man who's discovered and worked at his own psychic quirks knows certainly, beyond any question, that he does indeed know more than he can know. I could tell you experiences myself . . . But I'm off my schedule. See how my hand shakes! *Mukil res lemutti,* stay far from me! *(He begins to speak more softly, more rapidly than ever.)* I'm talking about luck. Do you believe in it, Clumly? Luck? They have words for it in Old Babylonian, Sumerian, the rest. Mysterious words for mysterious ideas. *Istaru,* the blueprint already complete for all Time and Space. And *simtu,* personal fate. No escaping it. No more hope for escape than you have, hanging in a tent with a madman in the path of a freight train, a madman holding the policeman's gun, pointing it straight at the policeman's forehead. There's only luck, good luck or bad, the friendly or unfriendly spirit that stood at your side when your *simtu* was designed, and stands there yet, and changes nothing. Changes only the *quality* of the thing. You understand me?

CLUMLY: In all this heat—

SUNLIGHT: You whine too much. A sign that your luck is bad. You won't act with the universe, you'll be acted upon by it, like a log in a buzzsaw.

CLUMLY: Your ideas about luck—

SUNLIGHT: I know. Difficult the first time through. But no time to explain. You have the tape. Study it. Is the machine all right? Are you getting all this?

CLUMLY: As far as I can tell—

SUNLIGHT: Listen! Was that a train whistle?

CLUMLY: I don't know. I didn't hear—

*(The Sunlight Man laughs.)*

SUNLIGHT: See how I'm sweating! My luck is bad too, as you see. What were we saying?

CLUMLY: The tape recorder?

SUNLIGHT: No, no. Christ! What help are you? If Socrates had had—But wait! Now I have it. Luck! Good luck is nothing but being in shape to act with the universe when the universe says, "Now!" What is personal responsibility, then? The Babylonian would say it consists, first, in stubbornly maintaining one's freedom to act—in my case, evasion of the police, you see—and, second, in jumping when the Spirit says, "Jump!" You never know, of course, that the gods will speak. There's an old Mesopotamian story, very famous—it's one of the Naram-Sin legends; survives not only in texts from Nineveh and Harran but in Old Babylonian too. Story of a king who waited and waited for some word from the gods but got nothing, absolute silence, no matter what form of divination he tried. "Very well," said the king. "Has a lion ever performed extispicy? Has a wolf ever asked advice from any interpreter of dreams? Like a robber, I shall proceed according to my will!" Ah, *then* they spoke! They smashed that poor devil like an ant! You see the point. You never know when the gods may speak, you never know what your luck is. You can only wait, and if they say act, act.

CLUMLY: But all this—

SUNLIGHT: Exactly! What has all this to do with the ancient Hebrews? A brilliant question! According to the Jews, a man is responsible for obeying laws, performing his duties. According to the Babylonians, the greatest responsibility is to remain absolutely free. Very well, let us think about that. Take sex.

CLUMLY: Excuse me. What time is that train due?

SUNLIGHT: Were you going somewhere?

CLUMLY: I was merely thinking—

SUNLIGHT: Take sex. In the sexual sphere, from the ancient Babylonian point of view, one must never marry, or else one must maintain one's sexual independence in marriage. To the Jew, of course, that notion seems monstrous. But let us consider it. The Jewish point of view has not been an unmitigated boon, after all. You've heard about mad medieval nuns and monks turned rapist. You've heard about queens murdered one after another by husbands with a roving eye. And you know as well as I do the way we live now. The Playboy philosophy. The Ginsberg terror. Perhaps the Babylonians were right. Is their answer possible? Is the sexual revolution you read about—all those West Coast surfers and beatniks and Berkeley students, fornicating fourteen-year-olds in Los Angeles—or in Syracuse, if we dare tell the truth, and in Johnson's Forks, Missouri, and Batavia, New York—is the sexual revolution a step in the right direction or madness?

It's possible, I say—I've no time for details—but in our culture possible only for superior people. The woman's problem is greater than the man's in one respect: she carries the more-than-merely-cultural shame of menstruation. You don't need that explained. Every animal has some measure of distaste for mess. It tells lions where one has been, if nothing else. For the male, on the other hand, the central problem is that he can't invariably achieve an erection. When the honeymoon's over, the first storm of infatuation, his potency depends heavily on his feeling of at least equality with his partner—among other things. If intercourse is a job, strictly a familial function, or a pitying gift or an embarrassment or a thing of no mystery, then sex is poisoned for the male. And both male and female must contend with the family instinct by which each seeks to entrap and control the other. You follow all this?

CLUMLY: I—

SUNLIGHT: What are the necessary rules, then? Simple, of course. First of all, both male and female must be *practically*, that is to say, functionally protected from their own weakness by the total culture—at least insofar as possible. It's not enough that males and females understand each other's problems. Through analysis say. Excessive rationality about sex leads to duty and guilt and to unintuitive sex. The proper place of intellect, then, is to establish the cultural norms—build the highway, so to speak, down which lovers can unthinkingly speed. Excuse my manner. I was a college professor once. I was saying . . .

Yes. Now it's back.

The "superior people" I mentioned, then, are not superior intellectually but superior by cultural gift: they are the accidental product of the right homes. And the sexual revolution is a step in the wrong direction—an anti-puritanism which has only disastrous results. For one thing, a loss of mystery, and heightened guilt of a new, strictly psychological kind. Sex is pure *kick*—a violent kick—at the age of fourteen. It points not home to itself but away to new kicks—LSD, murder, suicide. But it remains a possibility that the wrong step, the sexual revolution, might yet be transformed by accident of history to a mediate step toward a right step. The revolution leads away from ancient Israel. It does not lead home to Babylon, but it may make Babylon once again a live option.

There still remain problems, no one denies it. There's mismatched desire, the familial instinct, the difficulties of the insecure, dominant male or female, so on. So it was in ancient Babylon. I could tell you horror stories. Sodom and Gomorrah, the lunacy of Belshazzar in the Jewish temples . . . No time. But granting the innate imperfection of the species, some cultural premises are better than others. O ponder the end of the man God chose as the last just man on earth—the wine-sot patriarch, fucking his daughters in his tent! Don't be shocked. The story is religious. So this: Babylon is fallen, but so is Israel. Sexual independence remains a high value from which our culture—and every modern culture—seems blocked.

Take social and political implications. Here the Babylonian imperative that one remain free raised even more difficult problems, as you can see. Socially, one must at once maintain one's ethnic identity and yet spurn any ethnic identification—white, black, Irish, Jewish, so forth. Compare the Babylonian and the Israelite ways of assimilating the foreign. The Babylonian asked nothing but token acceptance of ruler and gods. Israel demanded circumcision and total transformation. Neither worked, but for special reasons. Rome proved later the wisdom of the ancient Babylonian choice, though Babylon itself was overcome by the furious stubbornness of Jews not yet gone soft, true fire-eaters—if you'll forgive it. As for Israel, the system failed because it had, built into it, a contradiction of the nature of man—an assertion that a man can renounce himself. We cannot "love one another," to quote a philosopher, by renouncing self and becoming the other. The only way people can love one another is by simultaneously knowing themselves and coming to personal, intuitive knowledge of those who are different. That's impossible now. The population's too large, by now, and our heritage is against it. Armed truce—that is, democracy—becomes the only apparent hope —a false hope. Truce has always meant regrouping. Ask any general. And so ultimately social problems must be resolved by the annihilation of all minorities. How the annihilation is accomplished is an irrelevant detail, a matter of aesthetics. One answer, the Rightist answer, is "Kill them now." Another is "Intermarry," an answer which destroys the individual social unit as surely as State religion destroys the citizen.

Nevertheless, you will say to me, we should do what we can, and your theory, Mr. Sunlight, does offer certain hopes. Recognizing the distinction between body and spirit in social affairs—recognizing that the exact nature of the connection between the two is mystical and unimportant, an idle speculation —we might put emphasis on each culture's understanding of itself—an unsentimental understanding of both virtues and defects, and we might minimize concern with the other culture as foil. If individuals want to intermarry, let them. If minority groups want to borrow majority values, even ridiculous values, let them. But let every man know, moment by moment, who he is. It is true (you would grant) that knowing who you are can sometimes entail hatred of the man who is *not* you and whose identity requires a modification of your own. Well, we must simply put up with that, you will say. Stress cultural pride, as modern Irishmen, Jews, or Welshmen in America do, and as for bigotry, the flip side of cultural pride, make laws against it. Ah yes! I answer. But the gods are indifferent to the beauty of your having been born Czechoslovakian or French or Bantu or Greek. Babylon has fallen, and Troy has fallen, and no trace remains of the work of the greatest of sculptors.

Then farewell politics! The waves of Asian history roll toward waves of American history and strike, crash together and blend and subside to a trough where new waves will crash and merge and subside millennia hence. In the valleys at the bottom of the sea, layer on layer, sunken treasure ships. *Istaru!* Food of the gods!

CLUMLY: Can you honestly say you've got no feeling whatever for your country?

SUNLIGHT: I have no feeling for anything. I am waiting.

CLUMLY: To act.

SUNLIGHT: Exactly!

CLUMLY: Completely free.

SUNLIGHT: Yes, free!

(*Abruptly, rapidly, as if shocked by what he is saying*): I'll tell you the truth. I wasn't always free, as I am now. I've given myself to many causes. In Albuquerque, New Mexico, I used to put out a newsletter for Krebiozen. I believed in it implicitly, and as an ophthalmologist—hah! you see, my profession's slipped out!—I knew for certain that the AMA was rotten to the core. I attacked them brutally, brilliantly, in issue after issue. I told about their shocking tactics against Medicare—the banquets for doctors' wives, for instance, where the wives were given a speech that was an absolute tissue of lies, a speech that ended with outrageous rhetoric, more moving than any account of a lynching, and the final line: DO YOU WANT THAT KIND OF WORLD FOR YOUR DAUGHTERS AND SONS? I showed them why the doctors and their wives were hit in separate meetings which took pace at the same time and where each was asked for a family pledge; I specified times and places, named names. And lest any man make the foolish mistake of thinking the AMA was a merely systematic evil in which the participating doctors had no part, I set down in cold print, with facts and figures, the inhuman collusion of doctors and hospital administrations—the kind of collusion which results in thousands of deaths per week throughout this country: Negroes left to die in hospital waitingrooms, indigents not admitted or inadequately treated, outpatient cases not followed up because of bills unpaid at discharge. Every word I said was true. I'd seen things myself that would make your hair turn white. In Filer, Idaho, there was an Indian family that drove two hundred miles to the nearest hospital with a child who had peanuts down her windpipe. The hospital refused to admit them, and the child died. I was there on a fishing trip. I could do nothing! Enough. You've heard such stories. You refuse to believe them, or you think them exceptional. Insanity! You refuse to see what's right there in front of your eyes! Read the magazines! You think they exaggerate? I give you my word as a professional doctor, they hear *nothing,* they print a mere tenth of the horror. One story in a hundred! I tell you, read the magazines and tremble! So all I said was true, my attack on the profession was wholly just, my facts and figures unassailable. However, I was wrong about Krebiozen, and I became a laughingstock.

I had another cause, later. A student of mine who opposed the war in Vietnam and marched against it was subpoenaed by the House Un-American Activities Committee. Being young and foolish, and knowing he was right, he rejected the possibility of taking the Fifth Amendment, or the First, or the First and Ninth and Fourteenth, or any other of the usual options, and instead he made a speech. They crucified him, needless to say, and I attacked them masterfully in a series of articles for the *Oregonian.* I became a target for the Rightists—they burned my house and drove my wife from me, poor child. It turned out in the end that, though I was certainly right, my student was, as it happened, a Communist.

Another time I fought the professional Educationists, the

most dangerous, wasteful, and thoroughly ignorant single group in America. They creamed me, of course. I got twenty-seven of them fired, before I was through, but in the end they creamed me. If I'd had time I'd have gotten them all, every one. But one never has time, finally, and in any case they weren't really the heart of the matter, I realized later. If the public wants cheap and worthless education—not schooling but a sop for the public conscience—someone will come to provide it. And so I became, at last, an anarchist. In Houston, Texas, I dynamited the F.B.I. building. This was in October, 1964. I did it at night, killed only an elderly burglar who was there. I had not yet entered my violent period, you see.

But the most spectacular cause in my whole career—I'm telling you the truth—was Muntz TV. I was out of work, owing to various financial reversals, and I was living in the basement of a fraternity house at Harvard—unknown to the fraternity, of course. One of the boys in the fraternity had an old red car, in terrible condition. One day he came home and the car had been repainted—quite handsomely: green and yellow and blue, I think. Across the side it said MUNTZ TV. I was impressed. It seemed a beautiful thing, a kind of symbol of the American way: a poor, battered car in need of paint, a great corporation in need of advertising. I resolved to work for them, support what was best in our heritage. I went to their main office—the only office they had in Cambridge, Mass., as it turned out. A first-floor office on a scruffy street—I forget the name. An office that had clearly been many things in its time, one fly-by-night outfit after another. Muntz would be different, of course. TV was new, at this time, and the Muntz TV, with its miraculous single knob, was destined to make that scruffy street a place of prosperity. I was sure of it. I went in. Everything in the office was on wheels—desks, chairs, filing cabinets, everything—but of course it didn't occur to me that it was all designed for get-away. I was broken in, taught the virtues of the set and, in short, made a salesman. Then came meetings. Daily. Sales meetings. Selling Muntz TV's was a religion. First we sang the Muntz TV hymns—"The Muntz riders in the sky"—things like that. Then came confession and inspiration. A salesman would stand up, wringing his hands and trembling. He'd lost a sale. He had both the man and the woman convinced, the lady even had her pen out to sign the check. But then the man said, "Lovey, maybe we ought to

think this over. Why don't we talk about it and—" The salesman telling the story bowed his head. "I lost the sale." We
were silent. Shocked and grieved. Then up stood Ace. The
bold and swift-tongued Ace. He was our leader, the Ace of
Aces. A little Italian with a smile like a spider's. "Ridiculous
mistake," he hissed. "Don't make it again. Now look, the minute the man starts talkin, you just say, 'I'm sarry, I don't think
I can take a check.' Zap. You got 'em. 'You can't take my
check? Why of course you can take my check!' " Smiles.
Leers. "Now lissen," says Ace. He ducks his head half into his
collar and out again and rolls his eyes. "The customuh," he
says—he squeezes his fist together—"the customuh is . . . a
fly. He's a mos*qu*ito. You push him into the corner little by little and then you—*squash* 'im!" Cheers! Applause! Blessed be
God. Those TV's had a half-life of maybe two months. And
when your set went *pow* and you took it to the store, no store.
As soon as I found out, I was furious, of course. Betrayed
again! I thought about it for three days and I made up my
mind, and the next meeting I went to I took a Browning auto-
matic. I was going to kill every one of them, clean them out.
But I was too late, when I got to the meeting the store was
empty, they'd all lit out. Well, needless to say, I didn't give up.
It took me three years, but one by one I tracked them down
and shot them.

CLUMLY: You didn't!

SUNLIGHT: Certainly. Some of them I shot in their beds. Some
I shot as they came out their doors, kissing their wives good-
bye. One of them I got when he was mailing a letter. A couple
of them I shot on the BMT. Caused quite a stir, to tell the
truth. It was my last serious encounter with American business. Listen!

CLUMLY *(alarmed):* The train!

SUNLIGHT: Yes.

CLUMLY: But aren't you going to—

SUNLIGHT: No. I'm staying.

CLUMLY: For the love of God!

SUNLIGHT: But you can go. I excuse you.

*(Sound of a train approaching, still a quarter-mile off.)*

CLUMLY: I can't allow this. I must order you, in the name of
the law . . .

SUNLIGHT: There *is* no law.

*(Boom of a diesel engine whistle, not far off.)*

CLUMLY *(shouting. The train seems almost on top of them):* I beg you. Come with me!

SUNLIGHT *(loudly, a little pompously):* I care about nothing! Pooh.

CLUMLY: Then I'm going. Maybe I can stop it yet. I can't be responsible for—

*(He breaks off. Crunch of cinders as he jumps, holding the tape recorder. Sound of Clumly shouting wildly. The train lurches and shudders near, the engineer trying to stop it in time. Clumly's shout comes through clearly now: "Stop the train! Stop the train!" And now there are other voices too, a young man shouting from the distance, a booming, congressional-sounding voice yelling "Stop! Stop!" Sounds of the train stopping. The voices grow wilder, with hope in them now, and with the train's last shudder a chorus of hysterical cheers, joined by the engineer and fireman. In the foreground, Clumly, howling: "Thank God! Thank God!")*

VOICE: What the devil's going on here?

CLUMLY: No time to explain right now. There's a madman inside that tent. Stay back! He may be dangerous.

*(Sound of a car pulling up.)*

RURAL VOICE *(distant):* What seems to be the trouble, folks?

*(Several at once, in confusion, tell him what they know.)*

ENGINEER: Well, someone do something. I've got a schedule.

CLUMLY: You people stay back. I'll try to reason with him. *(Crunch of his footsteps in the gravel.)* You in there! *(No answer.)* Come out! We've got to let this train through. *(No answer.)* All right, Sunlight, I'm coming up. Do you hear me? *(No answer.)* Will somebody hold this damn machine? *(Background noise.)*

RURAL VOICE *(distant):* That's a brave policeman, men. He'll get himself a citation for this. I'll write to the Gov'nor myself. *(Bystanders comment on the policeman's courage.)* You, up on the bridge, you with the camera! Get a picture!

SECOND VOICE *(distant):* Yes sir! I'm getting it.

THIRD VOICE: There, he made it. He's got his head and chest in the tent now.

FIRST VOICE: He's looking back at us.

THIRD VOICE: Looks sick.

SECOND VOICE *(distant):* Is he all right?

*(Pause. Puzzled murmurings from the bystanders. Crunch of Clumly's approaching footsteps.)*

CLUMLY *(too softly to hear clearly):* He's gone.

FIRST VOICE: What?

CLUMLY: He's gone.

FOURTH VOICE *(a young man):* Impossible!

CLUMLY: Look for yourself.

THIRD VOICE *(aggressively):* How do we know he was in there at all?

CLUMLY: Think what you like. I'll take that tape recorder.

FOURTH VOICE: Yessir. Of course.

RURAL VOICE *(distant):* I'm sorry, officer. But look here. I got my car. Can I take you somewheres?

CLUMLY: I'll walk, thanks. I'm parked down this way.

RURAL VOICE *(distant):* Well, ever you say. It's a gol-danged disappointment, man can see.

CLUMLY: Ha. *(Crunch of his footsteps. Behind him, silence. The engineer calls his crew and puts them to work getting the tent out of the way.)*

RURAL VOICE *(distant):* Officer!

*(Clumly stops. Waits.)*

Even if it turned out bad after all, I want you to know folks is going to be impressed by your courage, that's the truth. They won't forget it. You know who I am, sir?

*(Clumly waits.)*

Young man, take this here over to the officer. Good. Fine boy. Well, I better be getting on. God be with you, friends. G'day. *(Sound of car starting up, backing away, pulling out onto the road. Footsteps as the young man draws near.)*

YOUNG MAN: Sir, the man said to give you—

CLUMLY *(infinitely weary):* Thank you.

YOUNG MAN: What is it, you think?

CLUMLY *(absently, sunk in thought):* It looks like a box with a chain around it.

*(Switches off the tape.)*

# XII

## A Mother's Love

*But if ye bite and devour one another, take heed that ye be not consumed one of another.*

—Galatians 5:15

### 1

The morning of the room and the yard beyond the round-arched windows lay to the left of her, stiff as old knees, violated in the night but uncomplaining: it might have been any of a hundred mornings, as though Millie's life were all played out but not yet over—she might put herself where she pleased in time, like a needle on an endlessly repetitious record; or, at any rate, she had seen before a thousand times this graygreen dawn after autumn rain, a presence in the room, or the memory of a presence, old, blind, despairing, a relative out of a tintype in the attic, *Memento mori, Millie my maid,* who sat in the room, hands folded on his cane, his wide tie drooping on his scorch-yellow shirt, his lumpy shoes toeing inward wearily, fingers the color of piano keys: and it was a part of his weariness that his substance did not interfere any more than a stranger's—that Coleridge poem—with her undevout vision of the chair behind him or the threadbare rug beneath his heavy shoes: not a ghost, exactly, or a dream either, but the heaviness of the morning brought down to the not quite invisible figure of a man because once on such a morning he'd been there, as if by way of explanation, sitting opposite the couch where, after she'd left Will Hodge in anger, she had slept. "Well, well," he had said. "Good morning," she had said. He had smiled with vast and weary scorn, then had raised himself, slow and ponderous as an elephant waking from a dream of swamps, and had shuffled out of the room. It had come to her that she had wanted him to tell her something, heaven knew what. But the Congressman was gone and would not return, she understood, would lie in his coffin with that same weary scorn, and she would be, as she had always been, on her own. She could endure it. Waking another day and year to look out at another autumn morning after rain, not at the wide lawn of Stony Hill Farm or the scratchy, truck-rutted lawn at her son's, but at city streets where pieces of newspaper lay and early morning trucks muttered irritably in the alley behind the pizza parlor and the grocery store next door, her lover gone down now, no longer romantic and mighty in an aura of wine but heavy and woppish, a tradesman tending to his business, she would see the Old Man again or would remember him or would remember the day as though all other days were illusion and only this—weariness, violation, despair—were real. She knew well enough, on days like this, where the truth lay. It was the physical pattern in the carpet, where the blueblack lines intersected the brown and where figures of roses showed their threads; in the broken putty on the windowpanes, in the angular shadows inside the glass of a doorknob, in the infinite complexity of lines in the bark of trees, in the dust in the sunbeams: substance calling beyond itself to substance. And coming to life was an act of will, an act of waking up, putting substance to some human use for the moment. Poor Luke! Who knew nothing of all this—a saint, merely. Mad as a hatter. (She remembered the sound of their hammering, high above her, Will and Ben, balanced on the comb of the barn, stripping off shingles black with age and soft as the deadmen embedded in the bottom of the Tonawanda Creek, replacing them with goldenbrown cedar richly scented and light as wings; and for all her weariness she would open her eyes and look up at where they crouched, enormous and light as bumblebees, or walked the comb with a bundle of shingles on one shoulder, solemn as Noahs at work on another antique, preposterous ark.) She lay still, moving only her eyes, her substance one with the pointless substance of the room and the morning outside. What time was it? Early, she was sure. Not eight. Then, wide awake, she remembered that this morning was dangerous. Luke lay exactly as he'd lain last night, dead looking, inert body and soul from his heavy drugs. Nick and the bearded stranger were nowhere in sight.

It was no dream, she realized suddenly. He'd had her half-naked before she knew what was happening—prattling at her, poking her, tickling her roughly, and like smoke her blouse and brassiere were gone—but then the lightning struck: she saw again now, as clearly as before, the fire-blasted face, the close-set, startled eyes, the arm rising to shield his ugliness. His shadow, black on the lightning-white wall, showed every hair distinct. *Poor bastard,* she thought, filled with pity and disgust, for she saw now his shame and pain as well as her fear. And then all at once the joy of victory ran through her: she could defeat him, body and soul. His sleight of hand could not make thin air of the pain if, opening her arms to him, she stabbed a knee into his nuts. She could do it. She'd thought of it before, not just once, not just with one man; had calculated the jab and had resisted, plunging to victory in her mind. Or like the Basque shepherds, she could bite. Or she could defeat him more subtly and terribly, by pain worse than physical pain, pick his bones and snap them in her jaws, destroy him with the image of his own ruined face.

She half-imagined, half-dreamed of getting up, dressing in purple and red, a golden plastic bracelet on her wrist set with precious-looking stones, and going softly to him with poisoned tea in a golden cup. Her mind cleared, and she was afraid for a moment, then calm again. *Yes,* she thought. So once in Jeff Peters' apartment in Hartsdale she'd lain in the bluewhite stillness of a January morning, waiting for Jeff to come back, poor Luke's beloved idol, his history teacher ("How can we do this?" Jeff had said; "it's unthinkable!" and they had laughed);

and because she had found he had other women—and despite the fact that it did not matter in the least to her—she had lain on top of the covers smiling, planning the terrible vengeance that, in the end, she had not taken. But it was different now, not justice merely, and not merely justice for herself. She felt warm, relaxed. She might seem to them as vulnerable as any bird, defenseless as a swallow, but she could pick the flesh of kings, the belly-meat of captains if she chose. She opened her eyes again and saw that it was later; she seemed to have dozed.

She sat up as quietly as possible, and still there was no sound. Perhaps they really had left, it came to her. Vanished like nightmares. She rose to her feet and listened. No sound but the steady dripping from the corner of the house; no motion but the pendulum of the clock. Through her stocking feet the carpet felt stiff as the bristles of some animal in a field, long dead. They were gone. She felt mysteriously lucky. It was the way she'd sometimes felt after a night of abandon, when she'd thrown all caution to the winds and made love to some man beneath her husband's nose—in the kitchen, once, when Will had gone into his cluttered, rabbinical study to work on some papers—and, not caring whether or not she was caught, she had miraculously not been caught. It was as if the universe was in conspiracy with her, which perhaps it was: for there was a law, surely, against men like Will Hodge, or against the conspiracy of Will and Ben and all their plodding, wooden-hearted kind. She was, at any rate, no sneaking pleasure thief: she made no bones about it, confronted the world with as much boldness as her lover of the moment allowed her. A natural force, unconstrained, and not merely ignorant either; prepared for the worst—and sometimes it had come—and she had survived. They were the cosmic outlaws, not she: they lurked in shrubbery, spying in (so Will Jr had told her, Will Sr pursuing an adultery case for a client who wanted a divorce; and Ben had gone with him and they'd parked Will's car at the edge of the woods where they could watch the house, and there they'd sat all night, waiting, their eyes shining like the eyes of murderers. Will Jr had refused to be a party to it: "For Christ's sake hire a detective!" he'd said); but no shrubbery for her, no lurking and spying; her lines and life were free, or as free as was possible, she being a woman. That was what was so dreadful in Luke's stupidity. For him all doors were open, he might have been anything—a man, not a woman—yet he chose to cower, to cringe and hiss, to hide under rocks, though he might have struck down the sun if he'd had the heart.

He still had not moved, and looking at the awful immobility of his wristbone she had a moment's panic. She quickly overcame it. Better off if he *was* dead, she thought, safely knowing him alive.

She strained to hear any faintest intimation of movement that would tell her they were still here, but there was nothing. At last she walked toward the diningroom door, still in her stocking feet, and pressed it open. There was only the glitter of the china closet, the heavy old buffet, the lamps and bric-a-brac of the dead Runians. She closed the door again, still listening, then turned toward the kitchen.

Nick Slater sat at the table absolutely silent, motionless except for the fingers turning a cigarette around and around, rolling the ends to points. The pistol lay on the table beside his elbow. He raised his eyes to her.

When she was calm she said, "Where's your friend?"

"He left."

She waited a long time, but he was volunteering nothing.

"For good?" she asked.

He shook his head.

"He took Luke's truck?"

But when she looked out over the cellar door she saw Luke's pick-up truck still there, and up the hill, in the semi-dark beyond the open barn door she could see the rear end of the semi. Luke's coupe was still here too, standing by the gas pump beyond the garage.

She said, "How long will he be gone?"

Nick looked back at the cigarette, and she knew now that nothing she said would make him talk to her. "You should get out," she said slyly. "You'd have a better chance alone. A man like that stands out like a sore thumb. Everyone who sees him . . ." She folded her arms to keep her fingers from trembling and looked out toward the road. There were pines where the road and the driveway met, and she had walked there once with her brother Gil, who long after that had killed himself, the best of her brothers. She said abruptly, firmly, "Nick you must turn yourself in."

Nothing.

"Nick, listen to me," she said, "I'm going to call the police.

I have to. For Luke's sake, and Ben's. I *have* to. You see that, don't you?"

She waited a full minute, or pretended to. Waiting had nothing to do with it. If she moved toward the phone his hand would move toward the gun, and if she drove him to it, he would kill her. It was incredible: not terrifying but quietly beyond understanding; she was not waiting for Nick's reaction but for insight, a parting of the veil. She asked sharply, "What are you thinking?"

He said nothing.

"*You* make the phonecall," she said. It came to her that the phone was probably not fixed yet. But she said, "I hear when you give yourself up of your own free will they go easy on you."

He was turning the cigarette again, his eyebrows lowered so that between the flat of his forehead and the flat of his cheekbones his eyes were like the slits in a medieval helmet. It came to her that she needed a cigarette terribly, and she turned to open the cupboard over the sink where Luke kept his.

Nick said softly, "I killed somebody last night." The voice seemed to come from very close, as if from inside her. She waited, frozen.

"Three people, that makes," he said. "The first one completely by accident, the lady in the car. Then the next one a little less by accident. I didn't know I would do it, but then when it was done I knew I did it, so that it was different from the other. I knew I had a choice, but I only knew afterward for sure. Then last night the third one, only just barely by accident. We heard her coming, and I knew I had the gun and maybe I'd kill her, and I knew I better not, it was bad enough already, but I was thinking, What would it feel like?—wondering if I really could do it on purpose, and he said, 'You shoot off that gun, boy, and you'll have the whole city on top of us,' and I was wrapping it up in the blanket from the bed and all at once she was there and I knew she was going to scream and I had it aimed at her wrapped inside the blanket and I squeezed. I wondered if the blanket would slow the bullet down, but the way she jerked it must have hit her hard." He broke the cigarette in half and dry tobacco fell from the center, spattered on the tabletop and lay still. He said, "And all the time he was standing there watching me, pulling at his beard with his hand."

"Jesus," she said.

He sat holding the cigarette ends in front of him, nothing moving now, not even his eyes. His shoulders sagged and the neck of the white shirt he'd taken from Luke's drawer was open to show his collarbone and a small brown medal on a chain. The clothes they'd had before, the Sunlight Man had burned. "It was him that said about the three," he said, "first the lady in the car by accident and then the guard and then last night. We walked out of the house like we owned it and went to where the car was parked—"

"What car?" she said.

"—and he got in and didn't say a word, just drove off like nobody would think of stopping us, and when we were in the country he said about the three."

"You've got to get away from him," she said. This time it was no trick. "He'll destroy you."

He shook his head.

"Call the police," she said. "He'll be back soon. You have to do it now, before he comes." Then: "Call Ben. Tell *him* what happened." But the phone would be dead. If she let herself, she could laugh.

"He'd said he'd come back, when they took him out of the jail. I never gave it a thought, but he did."

"Because he's crazy," she said. "Would you have done it?"

"I don't know if he's crazy." He thought about it. "Ben Hodge would sit and talk with us, tell us all this shit and we would try to do better for a little while, but he give up on us. *I* would've given up on us."

"You should call the police."

He shook his head again. "Go sit in the livingroom," he said. He glanced up, almost apologetic, but then his face hardened, took on a sullen, bloated look. "Go on."

She turned away.

She stood at the window staring out at the drab, hot morning, waiting for some sound from Nick Slater in the kitchen, waiting for the bearded man to return, waiting for Luke to come to. A strange indifference had come over her. She knew for certain now that the phone was still dead—from the storm last night, possibly; or maybe they'd cut the wires. She'd tried it half an hour ago, when Nick ran out in the garage for a moment, startled by some sound there. But the phone was not her only hope. One scheme after another passed idly through her mind, and she watched them pass like images in a dream but remained aloof from them, abstracted. She was afraid, but it seemed more than mere fear. She felt withdrawn the way schizophrenics are withdrawn, indifferent to how it came out. She imagined herself darting out the livingroom door and around the house, across the thirty feet of lawn to the locust grove and then up the narrow, shaded road to the nearest neighbor's; but she was sure she would not make it. She would turn to look back and the boy would be there, aiming the pistol at her, eyebrows lowered, as if lost in thought, conscious that this time it was on purpose, and to their mutual surprise he would fire and she would fall, faintly astonished. She imagined herself darting to the semi, to the pick-up, to the car; she saw herself hunting for the keys, finding the ignition empty, or turning the ignition on and grinding on the starter to no avail, and he came toward her with his eyebrows lowered, lost in thought, aiming the pistol at her head. She saw herself waiting at the livingroom door with the flimsy poker from the fireplace, and when he came through she struck and he fell, but the gun was still in his hand and he turned to look up at her and raised the pistol slowly, and, as in a nightmare, she could not move. It seemed to her that she'd been through it all before many times. She remembered standing in her room as a girl, looking out over the porch roof toward the yard in front and the well and the highway beyond, thinking how easy it would be and knowing she would not do it, at least not yet. She could hear the thump of the iron on the ironing board downstairs, and now and then her father's racking cough. Instead, she had said in her mind again and again, "I need to talk to you, Will. It's important. Please." She could imagine how it would be, his look of distress and then the rueful smile meant to hide the distress. She knew exactly how it would be, but she could not get up her nerve for it. And then one night, amazed at herself, she had heard herself actually saying it: "Will, I need to talk to you." It was apple-picking time, and she had come to buy apples from them. He stood in his picker's bib beside the two-wheeled handcart loaded high with apples, and darkness was coming on. The others were down at the house. You could hear the sorter rumbling, and now and then you could catch their voices. The smell of the apples was beautiful, and she had ridden on the cart when she was a child and her father was here to help with the work, and she too had climbed the pointed ladder and felt its gentle give against the boughs. Tears came, and she felt one going down her cheek, and whether or not they were honest tears she could not have said herself. He looked at her, his squarish lips pursed, his coarse dark hair falling over his forehead, already beginning to recede. "Here now," he said. "Now wait a minute!" He fumbled under the picker's bib for his blue and white farmer's handkerchief and held it out to her. "Millie," he said. He thought about it, then clumsily laid his hand on her arm. "What's the trouble?" she said: "I'm pregnant." Suddenly she was sobbing, turning away from him in terrible shame, only partly a device. "Good Lord!" he said. Full of concern, for whatever else he might be he was a good man, compassionate, quick to forgive a fall. "What can I do?" he said. "How can I help you?" "You don't understand," she said, "I'm pregnant by your *brother*." "No!" he said. He did not even ask which one. He knew well enough that Ben had been driving her to town night after night, that he had walked with her at times. After a moment he said, almost a whisper, "I'm sorry, Millie." Then: "Have you told him?" She nodded. He said, "Does he . . . That is, are his intentions—" She shook her head. He stood blunt-faced and miserable, huge hands buried in the picker's bib. "He denies it," she whispered. His face grew stern. She had not judged him wrong. "I'll talk to him," he said. But she shook her head. "No, please. I beg you. If he doesn't want me, I don't want to burden him. Please, I'm serious." And then, excitedly, "If I had dreamed you'd take it this way—I mean, think it was your duty to speak to him—oh, please, please, Will! I beg you!" And so he had asked, befuddled, "But then, what—?" She wiped her eyes and calmed her grief. "I just had to tell someone," she said. "It's such a terrible thing . . . all alone. And when I saw you here, and knew I could say—I'm sorry. Forgive me. Perhaps someone—" He waited, wringing his hands inside the bib. She sniffed and said, "I can find someone. I'm not ugly. Am I?" She looked at him. "Oh, Millie," he said. "Poor, dear Millie! Lord *knows* you're not ugly! If there's anything in the world . . ."

She stood in the bedroom, hers, not her husband's, looking out over the bare branches of the new orchard toward the old one where it all had started, gnarled and blasted trees bent like ancient cripples over the snow, icicles like old men's beards hanging from the dying branches, and thought: *I will leave in the spring*. But she would not leave, she knew. It was all a stupid play.

He sat half-dozing beside her, beginning to snore, and she poked him with her elbow and hissed, "Pretend to be amused." He glared. They were so far from the stage she could barely make out the expressions of the actors. He had said they were lucky to get seats at all, and perhaps it was true; he hadn't the imagination for a lie. Nevertheless, she suspected he'd gotten these seats because he was cheap.

"If you'd read the play maybe you could follow it," she whispered.

"Hah!" he said. "I can follow it all right."

She cringed and put her finger to her mouth. "Sh!"

The people in front of them turned to look. She smiled.

It was a new play called *The Devils*, the first New York production, and even if it was not good (it was brilliant, in fact), anyone else would have been grateful for the chance to see it. Not Hodge. He would rather sit with his Rotary pals, listening to some perfectly asinine speech, or play checkers with the judge with the long red nose, staying down the hall from them at the Washington Hotel (another outrage), or talk about Thomas Dewey with some black elevator boy.

Afterward they went to the restaurant Jeff Peters had recommended, a French place, expensive, with superb wine, and Hodge ate salad with thousand-island dressing. She was boiling mad now—even the dressing seemed a personal affront. "All right," she said, "so you think you followed it. What did you *get* out of it."

"A lot of yammer," he said. He stared at his plate. "A lot of righteousness."

She exploded. "Righteousness! For the love of God, Will, that was the point!—the righteousness of those who suppress life!"

"You talk like a book," he said.

"That would naturally bother you."

He chewed and held his peace. He ate with his head low, eyelids lowered, as though she had over the years destroyed whatever there might have been in him, just as he had destroyed whatever there might have been in her. His suitcoat hung open, and she could see his wide, gray and white suspenders. A terrible sorrow welled up in her. She pitied him as much as she hated him, and pitied herself as well. "Well," she said, "it's an interesting play historically."

"Hah," he said.

She put down her fork. "What do you mean, 'Hah'?"

"Nothing," he said. "Nothing."

"That's largely how it was, you know," she said. She leaned forward. "For centuries people with stupid theories have been murdering people who try to just live, enjoy life, seize the day and make the most of it. Priest, politicians. Truth is mostly in the sewer. *You* wouldn't understand, of course."

"I understand all right," he said.

She heard her laugh outside her like crystal ringing. "Really!" she said. "You wouldn't know a symbol from a cider barrel!"

"That's different," he said. "You weren't talking about symbols."

"What did I say? Repeat exactly what I said."

"You said—" He pursed his lips crossly. "You said people with theories don't understand people who have a different theory."

"No. You see? You can't even repeat what I said! No wonder you leave trials to other people!"

"In substance, what you said—"

"*You* tell *me* about substance!" She stabbed her fork into her steak.

He said no more. She had beaten him, as always. She bit her lower lip to hide the trembling, and her eyes were filled with tears, so that the candles were a blur of yellow and white.

In the car he said, "I didn't mean to spoil your evening."

"Never mind," she said. "The trouble is, you keep trying to control how I think, as though I were a child. It's insidious."

"I apologize," he said flatly.

He took a wrong turn on the way back to the hotel. She rode with her eyes clenched tightly shut—she could have told him the turn, could easily have directed him anywhere in the city—but she was still full of sorrow over forcing him again to admit his stupidity; and it pleased her to see him go wrong, see him knowing he could not get anywhere without her. That night, standing at the window of their hotel room—Hodge in bed already, sleeping with his head under the pillow to close off the light—she had a frighteningly strong urge to jump. How he did it she would never know, but the truth was that by every gesture, every glance, he made her feel worthless, brainless, obscene. She could make a laughingstock of him, turn all his sober arguments to the jabbering of a monkey; her very appearance made him clownlike, bumpkinish; and yet his wordless righteousness, more insidious than anything in the play—a righteousness without rational foundation, indefensible and therefore mute—made a gaudy whore of her. What had she done? Where had she gone wrong? In marrying him in the first place, a fool might say. How simple! One escaped from one jail to another and then to another and another until one escaped to the tightwalled grave. Oh, she might have done better—might have married a man who would not have padlocked her legs together, or anyway tried to, but there was no real escape, not for a woman. And therefore no escape from the guilt of destruction that had nothing to do with the man destroyed—an act of nature, the teeming universe, things and their motions. There was only progression, the old orchard giving way to the new. And was it sane to call the new orchard a betrayal of the old? Yet how well she understood their feeling! It grieved her that the old orchard was old. But she would not be deluded. Her father stood in the church doorway, smiling and holding out his arms to her. "Poor baby," he said, "my poor, pretty little girl." Oh, how she had loved him! But she'd grown older, through no fault of her own, a victim of time, like any tree, and he too had grown older, and the vital spirit in him had shrunk, and little by little he had died and had been replaced. And so it had been with Will, too; for whatever they might think, those casual observers so ready to judge, she had loved him with all her heart for a little while, after that night in the orchard. She had schemed to get him, and not for himself but for his name. Nevertheless—and not ironically but inevitably, she understood now—she had fallen in love with him. For all her tears, only partly feigned, she had laughed at him that night, and had been pleased with him and with herself. And later—after they were married, in fact—there had come that same vaulting joy she had felt with Ben—the same yet altogether different. She was lying in bed watching his reflection in the mirror as he undressed, and all at once she had found him, framed by the mirror, to be beautiful. It was a discovery more than physical: an entirely new way of seeing the world, as if, for the first time in her life, she was seeing with her own eyes, not the eyes of other people. Ben was bronzed from his forehead to the line of his belt and from the hem of his shorts to the soles of his feet—bronzed like a figure on a poster. But Will was tanned—or reddened, really: as red as new brick—only where his workshirt, overalls, and boots didn't cover him: red of face and neck, but below the red V at his collar, white as grade-school paste: and yet not sickly—not at all!—because the muscles of his shoulders and arms were square and awesome, and below his wide chest his waist was (in those days) small, and below his bellybutton the parallel muscles of his abdomen were firm as a boxer's, and each of his thighs was as thick with muscle as the waist of a young girl. His body hair was black as crows' wings and curly and thick, and the hair on his head was brownish, bleached by the sun. It struck her with terrific force that his head did not go with his body—seemed more socialized, tamed, more "advanced," less her secret property, exactly as his thought belonged to her less than his feelings did, or anyway his feelings as her new, loving husband. What he felt on other matters was in those days of no importance. He snapped out the light and came to bed naked, as he always did in those days, and she, naked too, put her arms around him and pressed herself to him and said, "Will, I can't believe my luck, getting you for my husband. When I think how close I came—" She let it trail off. He lay still, thinking—wondering, she knew, if he could believe her. "I love you very much," he said formally. She laughed and kissed him, delighted that even with his muscular body tight against hers he could be formal. After a long time he said, "Millie, did you ever . . . with anyone besides . . ." Her heart beat lightly and quickly, partly from fright, and she moved her hands gently over his body. At last she said, "Will, will you hate me if I tell you something?" He waited, and she said, "I was lying to you—about Ben. It was you I wanted. Right from the beginning." And after another moment. "It's the truth, Will. Can you forgive me?" For all she knew, perhaps it really was the truth. He said nothing for so long she began to be frightened. "Will?" she whispered. Then, as if a dam had broken, a great sob came from him. "All along!" he bawled. "Oh, Millie! Millie!" They had both loved each other from the first. They clung to each other like children and wept and rutted half the night and swore they would always be faithful, and at last they slept. But days passed; seasons; and as Luke, not yet born, would one day howl above the hellfire jangle of his banjo, love grows colder.

In her abstracted state she hardly noticed, at first, the bearded man walking up the driveway out of the shadow of the trees into the sunlight of the yard. When she awakened to his approach she was struck by something familiar in his walk—strikingly familiar—but when she tried to place it her mind seemed to shy from what she knew and she could not explain to herself the sense of sudden discovery. He came to the door and let himself in. When he saw her he paused, flustered, but at last nodded to her, the stocking still drawn down over his face, and then, without a glance at the inert Luke, he went on upstairs.

## 2

He paced. She heard him going back and forth over her head and she remembered dreams of someone walking on her grave. Luke was awake now, sitting with his head in his hands, his face white, saying nothing. Nick sat on the couch, the gun in his lap, cleaning his fingernails with the greatest possible concentration. She too sat silent and almost motionless, waiting. The footsteps overhead went slowly back and forth, from one end of the house to the other, loud on the hardwood of the hallway over the kitchen, softer when he came to the wide old boards of the bedroom floors or the Runians' throw-rugs. She lit a cigarette, and Nick looked at her. The Sunlight Man had told her not to smoke. She sat with the cigarette hanging between her fingers, waiting for Nick to decide, and finally he looked down. "You want one?" she said. He glanced up, then away again. When he'd thought about it a minute he nodded and she reached one toward him, then lit her own and threw him the matches. Then silence again. Two o'clock. She closed her eyes, thinking nothing in particular, wondering if Luke would be better off if he ate something, and when she opened them again—after nearly an hour, she would have sworn—only twelve minutes had passed. She sighed and closed her eyes again. Seven minutes later, Luke said, "I'm going out."

"You can't," Nick said. "That's what you think," Luke said. But when he moved toward the door Nick leaned forward, half-standing, aiming the pistol directly at him, and Luke was afraid. As for Millie, she was terrified; it was as if all her insides had turned to loose pudding. "For the love of God, stop it, Luke," she said. "Nick, put that damned gun down." They obeyed, both of them, instantly, grateful to escape the test. She wiped sweat from the bridge of her nose, and again for a long time they all sat silent.

The police arrived at four. As the black and white car turned in at the driveway the bearded man came down the stairs lightly, the stocking still over his face, his hands in the pockets of his suitcoat, and nodded to Nick. "Come with me," he said. And then, to Millie, "Don't say a word. Be sensible. Show them whatever they ask to see, and remember—" He curled his fingers at her, like claws, as though it were all some joke. "—I'll be right here beside you, invisible." The police car had gone around to the back now. The Sunlight Man made a quick inspection of the kitchen, then went down the cellar steps, pushing Nick in front of him. The knock came, and she breathed deep, trying to think. She heard the cellar door opening again and knew he was somewhere behind her.

"Afternoon, Mrs. Hodge," the policeman said. He slid his hat off. It was the one called Miller.

"Afternoon," she said. Her voice was very faint, and she was sure she had given it all away. She couldn't tell whether she was glad of it or not.

"Everything all right here?" he asked. He was looking at her closely, and she realized she must be pale.

She wet her lips. "Oh yes, fine," she said. Then, hastily, "Luke's been ill. My son. He has—these headaches."

The policeman glanced at Luke, and the shorter policeman with him nodded, sympathetic. "It's a hell of a thing all right," the short one said. "My first wife had headaches. Migraine."

"These are histamine," Luke said stupidly.

Miller said, "Mrs. Hodge, you seen anybody around here? I guess you know—" He let it trail off, and she nodded.

"I heard. It was terrible."

"We thought he might head for here."

"That's what we thought too," she said. "I could hardly sleep last night. And that storm, on top of it." Her shudder was real enough.

He slid his lower lip over his upper and looked at his boots.

"Would you like to come in, officers?" she said. She tried to think of some way of signalling to them.

"Yes, thank you."

Luke sat down in the chair by the fireplace and covered his face with his hands.

"You're sure everything's all right?" Miller said.

She nodded, faint with indecision.

"You don't mind if we look around?"

"No, of course not. We'd be grateful."

He was moving toward the kitchen, his eyebrows lowered and she had a feeling he was straining his ears, listening. Suppose they found him on their own and she had nothing to do with it. Would the Sunlight Man blame her, in that case? If say, he escaped them—shot his way out of it, as they said on TV—would he turn on her then, if she'd done nothing? *Dear God, please let them find him*, she thought. The second policeman had gone to the diningroom and stood now at the window looking out.

"We've been so frightened," she said.

He studied her, smiling with only his mouth. "You look guilty as hell. Been up to something?"

She knew her alarm showed. *A wink would tell him*, she thought, but she did nothing.

Still he was looking at her, but with another part of his mind he was listening to something far away. Could he hear them, down in the cellar? He said, "What is it? Come out with it."

"Really," she said. She gave a little laugh. "I can't imagine . . ."

The other policeman had gone into the downstairs bathroom to look there. He came out holding a bottle. "Look at this," he said.

Miller unscrewed the cap and smelled the pills, then broke a little piece off between his fingernails, watching her as he did it. He ground the powder between his thumb and first finger and tasted a little.

"What you think?" the other policeman said.

Miller screwed the cap back on and shrugged. "I think the druggist's label came off," he said. "Get back to work. Don't get side-tracked." The other man went back through the livingroom toward the stairs, and Miller leaned toward her.

"Look, we got bigger fish than that to fry, right now, so you're in luck. But throw it away or something. Understand?"

She managed a sickly smile.

Miller studied her.

"What's in here?" he said.

"That's the door to the cellar."

He opened it and looked down. "There a lightswitch?"

"It's here." She reached in past him and turned the stairway light on. The stairway was crooked and worn and had no railing. She could see the dim, cobwebbed stone of the wall, and on the floor two inches of water from seepage and last night's rain.

"Stinks," he said.

She nodded.

"These old cellars always stink," he said thoughtfully, looking at her. "You should smell mine. Rats?"

"Hundreds of them," she said. "Sometimes at night you can hear them swimming around."

Miller made a face. He went halfway down the stairs and leaned over to look around. There would be nothing to see, she was sure. The shelves of ancient mason jars full of long-ago rotted tomatoes and peaches and pears, all black now; the old wood furnace with its side caved in; the cobwebbed pipes leading out from the furnace; the chutes for wood, the doors to the apple bins, empty for years. He came back up the stairs and called to the other one. They both went down. They were there for a long time, but they found nothing. They found nothing upstairs either. Was it possible that he really had become invisible? The shorter one went out to look in the barn. Again, nothing.

"You haven't seen or heard anything?" he asked when they were getting ready to leave.

"Nothing," she said feebly.

Luke was rubbing his eyes with both hands, and she could feel his frustration and anger like a shock running through her. She refused to be thrown off. *I exist, no one else. . . .*

"Ok," Miller said. "Sorry to take your time." He said something more, and she watched his mouth move, trying to concentrate on the words, but her mind seemed to have snapped off, she could not make herself listen to anything but the silence of the flooded cellar.

Then they were gone, and she and Luke were alone again,

staring at each other with the old dull hostility, weary to the heart.

"Well, what more could I do?" she said.

"You could have winked," he snapped. "You could have slipped him a note."

"And you *couldn't?*" she said.

Luke said nothing.

They heard something moving through the water in the cellar, then coming up the stairs.

## 3

He returned from the cellar a changed man—exuberant, expansive, tyrannical. He stalked back and forth through the kitchen in his bare feet, his wet shoes and stockings on the oven door beside Nick's, and he bounced up and down as he walked, making a kind of dance of it, his huge rear end protruding and his beard jutting forward. "We were superb," he said, "we were brilliant! Millie, I underestimated you!" But he would not let her have a cigarette or a drink. "Cigarette smoking may be hazardous to your health," he said. "Get your mind off it. Sing after me." He threw out his arms and sang, still in the false, high squeaky voice:

*"Mae swn yn Mhortinllaen, swn hwylie'n codi,*
*Blocie i gyd yn gwichian, Dafydd Jones yn gweiddi;*
*Ni fedra'i aros gartre yn fy myw;*
*Rhaid i mi fynd yn llongwr iawn ar Fflat Huw Puw!"*

He said: "That's Welsh. Magnificent language. Magnificent song, too, as you can hear. All about Huw Puw's boat. Let's do it again now. First phrase. All together! *Mae swn yn Mhortinllaen . . .*" He drew himself up and glared at them. "I'll say it just one more time." The pistol appeared in his hand, and he aimed it at Millie. "*Mae, swn, yn, Mhortinllaen . . .*" She tried, feebly, to sing with him. He shook his fist. "What's the matter with you people? You sing along with Mitch. I hear you. You sing along with Lawrence Welk. But I ask you to sing a simple little boatsong, the most ridiculous, simplest little song in the world, and you act like you've gotten a sliver through your tongue." Abruptly he stomped away, curling his toes as he raised his feet. "Forget it," he said. He whirled and pointed his finger at her, the gun in the other hand aimed at the ceiling like a starter's pistol. "The trouble with you is, you're rotten," he said. "I see those magazines you read. 'Horoscope for Weight-Watchers.' 'Barbara Walters Visits Princess Grace of Monaco.' 'FDR's Secret Affair.' 'How James Bond Destroyed My Husband, by Mrs. Ian Fleming.' 'Foods Everyone Loves.' 'The Truth about the Best Seller List.' 'Why Teen-Agers Rebel.' *Gyuck!* How can you improve your mind, reading tripe like that? Heads stuffed with cotton candy!" He bounded closer, like a fencer, and shook his finger under her nose. "Everyone should learn at least one Welsh song, if only for the double *l*'s. The guttural noises clean out the throat and help to prevent brainless cooing. Now. One more time. He moved the revolver slowly toward her forehead until the metal pressed against her skin. Her heart pounded violently. "Repeat after me," he said. *Mae swn yn Mhortinllaen, swn hwylie'n codi."*

She repeated it.

He smiled. "Good. Excellent! We may have discovered an important new educational method!" He swung away. "As I've said, my object is to make you a saint. I do what good I can as I pass, you know. After we've learned 'Fflat Huw Puw' we'll learn 'The Dream of the Rood' in Old English." He looked at his hand as if surprised. The gun was gone. He shrugged. "I understand how you feel," he said. "But we mustn't waste valuable time, simply because we're imprisoned here. Keep the mind alert, I always say. Try to learn something new and significant every day." He tipped his head, crafty. "What do you know about manure?" he said.

She waited and became aware that she was wringing her hands.

"A well-kept manure heap may be safely taken as one of the surest indications of thrift and success in farming," he said in the voice of a lecturer. He leaned toward her. "Neglect of this resource causes losses which, though little appreciated, are vast in extent. According to recent statistics—or anyway recent in 1906—there are in the United States, in round numbers, 19,500,000 horses, mules, and burros, 61,000,000 cattle, 47,000,000 hogs, and 51,600,000 sheep. Think of it! If all these animals were kept in stalls or pens throughout the year and the manure carefully saved, the approximate value of the fertilizing constituents of the manure produced by each horse or mule annually would be $27, by each head of cattle $20, by each hog $8, and by each sheep $2. 1906 prices, of course. You didn't know that, did you? You'd be surprised how much I could teach you about economy, the fine art of getting ahead if you ever catch up. Take burdocks—those weeds right out there across the driveway—also known as cockle button, cuckold dock, beggars' buttons, hurr-bur, stick button, hardock, and bardane. Worth money! Around 50,000 pounds of burdock root are imported annually from Belgium, for medical purposes. Or were in 1904. Or take common mustard. The imports into the United States of black and white mustard together during the fiscal year ended June 30, 1903, amounted to 5,302,876 pounds. Three to six cents per pound for the seeds. The Lord be praised!"

"Listen," Luke said.

The Sunlight Man drew himself up. "It is interesting to note that in South Africa pumpkins are often given to horses as green feed."

"I need a drink," Millie said.

"Did Teresa drink? Did St. George drink? I withdraw the question."

He went on and on, and whenever any of them tried to leave the room he stopped them and demanded their attention. Exactly at seven o'clock he bowed from the waist and said, "Students, I bid you good evening. I must go make a phonecall," and without another word he went out. They watched him hurry down the driveway toward the road.

When he returned, half an hour later, he was again completely changed, it seemed to her. He was not wearing the stocking over his face now. He had a wide red hat embroidered in what might once have been white—it had gone through last night's rain, apparently—and dark glasses. His suitcoat was stuffed with plants he'd found along the road. He began making supper.

"Where did you phone from?" Millie said.

"Phonebooth," he said.

The nearest phonebooth was five miles away. "That's impossible," she said.

"Not at all. There's a special kind of slug you use. The phone company spends millions a year on slug detection, but one little slug they just can't beat. Like this." He drew from his pocket a washer approximately the size of a quarter, with a little piece of tape across it. He winked.

"You're a strange man," she said thoughtfully.

"Have to live by my wits," he said. He pointed at his temple. He laughed. "But then, don't we all!"

"Can I help you with something?" she said. He was leaning over the sink now, washing the roots and leaves he'd brought in. But her mind was far away. He powerfully reminded her of something or of someone, or perhaps simply, in a general way, of her childhood.

"Why yes, thank you," he said. "Get the hamburger out of the refrig."

She did so absently, trying to locate the center of her unrest. As she was unwrapping what was left of the hamburger she said aloud without meaning to, "What happened to us, I wonder."

His hands stopped moving for an instant, under the faucet, then moved as before. "You belong on TV," he said. He smiled, bowed, clutched his red hat and tipped it to her.

She watched his antics and said nothing. In the bathroom Luke was filling a glass of water, taking a pill. His headache was back, then. She should have known. Nick Slater lay on the livingroom couch asleep. She watched the stranger mixing the hamburger and the chopped-up plants in a yellow plastic bowl. Out of nowhere it came to her that he was Taggert Hodge. She knew it but didn't believe it. If he'd been burned like that they would have heard, wouldn't they? The false voice, the absurd gestures—were they all meant to fool her? Hardly breathing, she watched now his hands, now his eyes; but she couldn't be certain. It was fifteen years. *Taggert did card tricks,* she remembered. *He was good.* But she thought the next instant, *Not that good.* The Sunlight Man was a pro, as good as anybody, and there was all the difference in the world between a few tricks with cards and the unbelievable things he did—the huge solid gun appearing in his hand from nowhere, certainly not from, say, his sleeve. Her heart began to race before she fully understood what she was about to do. She said, "Poor Tag."

He showed no sign. None. Merely turned his head, saying, "Tag?"

"My brother-in-law," she said. "I was thinking about him." He nodded, uninterested.

She couldn't tell what to believe.

He didn't talk at supper, nor did they. She was still uncertain. Luke ate nothing. Nick got out his cigarettes afterward, and when he lit the match the Sunlight Man started violently. She said nothing, merely filed it to think about later.

Then the Sunlight Man pushed back his chair. "Rise up and follow me," he said. Nick rose slowly. Luke did not stir, merely sat pressing his temples with his fingertips. The Sunlight Man leaned down to him. "Are you deaf?" he hissed. She said, "Stop it. It's his head." But now Luke came awake and looked up at him, squinting. The Sunlight Man said coldly, "Come with me." It couldn't be Tag. He went toward the cellar door. After a moment Millie followed. "Go down," he said. She obeyed, and then Nick and Luke came too. Looped in his left hand, the Sunlight Man had clothesline. "What are you going to do?" she said. He smiled. "You'd never believe it."

Suddenly she knew. Perhaps it was because he forgot to change his voice, or perhaps in her blood, though not in her mind, she had known the truth all along. She went cold all over. "*You!*" she said.

His eyebrows lowered and he met her eyes—or looked through them; she could not tell.

"Don't do this," she whispered. "Luke's *sick.*"

He seemed to reflect. His burnt face showed nothing. Then, eyes vague, he came down the steps toward them. In his right hand he had the gun.

*I exist,* she said in her heart, *and no one else.* She drew back her mind from the pain of the tight bonds on her wrists and ankles and around her waist, from the cold of the water around her feet, and from the gag biting deep into the corners of her mouth. *I understand the reasons for your viciousness, your madness, but they're yours, not mine: I have a life of my own, griefs of my own, and I warn you, I can match all your magic tricks sleight for sleight. I have no time for complications, I've spent too much already. Let all the rabbits in your hat—and all the false boxes, trick handkerchiefs—come out and save you from the things that are coming upon you.* Luke writhed, banging the back of his head on the post he was tied to. She closed her eyes. *What do you want of me? What?*

They had found her brother Gil in a pile of straw in the corner of the barn, and he looked as if he were sleeping like a baby, they said, but he had killed himself. At the funeral she'd kept a face of stone. Hadn't she talked with him, stewed with him, done everything in her power to prevent it? But in the end he had not thanked her for it; he'd grown to hate her. He couldn't get a driver's license because the first time he tried to kill himself, an overdose of sleeping pills, she'd made Will drive him to the hospital, and after that the thing was on his record. But she'd accepted his hatred, had shrugged it off as easily as she shrugged off Luke's hatred, or Will Jr's. Self-preservation. It was all one could find to cling to. It was enough.

She could hear him banging his head against the post, exactly as he'd banged his head against his crib when he was a baby. *Die,* she thought. *Smash out your brains and die.* Then: *No, that's stupid. We'll beat him yet.*

It came to her that she was shaking from head to foot. She was afraid.

She remembered: *The first completely by accident, the lady in the car. Then the next one a little less by accident. Then last night the third one, only just barely by accident.* Gil said: "Each time it comes closer, don't it. Each time I come closer to really meaning it, really wanting to be dead. You can see where it's heading." "Be still," she said. "Gil, baby. Be still." She closed his eyes with her fingertips.

When she'd said, "Luke's sick"—his own nephew—he had looked at her and he'd thought about it, and after a minute he'd drawn the gun. His eyes weren't human.

She understood where it was heading.

# XIII

*Nah ist—*
*und*
*schwer zu fassen*
*der Gott*

---

*I only know things seem and are not good.*
—Thomas Kinsella

## 1

Driving down the road with his jaw slung forward and his
heart full of possibly righteous indignation—for though he did
not ask for justice (no man gets justice, not even a king: the
most powerful tyrant may demand his fair share, but not even
God, the Lord of Hosts, can force those around him to think
of Him as He deserves to be thought of), he *did* ask, at least,
that he not be treated as an absolute fool—Will Hodge Sr
grumbled and ground his teeth and said, "All right!" He had

the accelerator clear to the floor, so that the Plymouth was roaring down the pot-holed macadam, steering wheel shaking like a house in an earthquake, at fifty miles an hour. It would smash the A-frame. Let it! Something in him, long idle, unsure of its use, had snapped into gear. For better or worse, he was a new man. All his life he'd been picking up other people's pieces, accepting responsibilities that he knew very well were not his own—his brothers' debts, his wife's mistakes, his sons' opinions, his own failure to measure up—and always, whatever he did, it was wrong, he was the fool, the clown, the villain: him, not them. "All right," he said. "Be pragmatic." The word had suddenly come to be full of meaning for him. John Kennedy's genius, he'd read somewhere, was that he worked out one problem at a time. Kennedy knew that each solution might raise twenty new problems, the writer said; nevertheless, he sought no grand vision, no return to some state of the nation long gone, impossible to recapture. He dealt, one by one, with the troubles of the sick, the poor, the oppressed, sought not what ought to be but what would do. All right! So Hodge, too, would work. It was a thing his father the Congressman would have understood. He would have laughed at them, patching gray barns which time had stripped of use—the slaughter shed and smokehouse, the cider barn, the elegant three-story chickenhouse, impossible to heat, impossible to clean, too dark even on a sunny day for proper egg production. It was a glory to the eye, that chickenhouse: high, narrow windows with small panes (the glass in those days was more brittle than now, and the labor of building such complex sashes and puttying in all those hundreds of panes did not cost then what it would today); on each floor, square, high-ceilinged rooms on either side of a narrow hallway, doors neatly hinged and better constructed than the doors in a modern subdivision house: a veritable hotel for chickens!—and comfortable, darkly grandiose as a gentlemen's club in the warm, obstructed light of a summer afternoon. But not for its beauty did Will Hodge Sr preserve that chicken house. It was a fine barn, like the others; worth a small fortune, and not just in cash but in family memories as well. A man shouldn't let things go. And so, in short, he had patched the barns and had patched up lives, as well as he could. But in the end his daughter had burned down the chickenhouse, lighting papers in the incinerator when the wind was wrong, and for all his work the secret process of ruin that whispered in every leaf, that gnawed inside walls or boldly howled in the woods at night—the process of death, to name its name—had outraced him. And therefore he would live no more by grand visions he couldn't understand, would no more seek the connections of things or grieve that, ignorant of them, he might be more guilty than he knew. "One mouse at a time, like a cat," said Hodge.

He wasn't over his indignation at Clumly's refusal to admit what had obviously happened last night at his, Will Hodge's, apartment. He should be grateful, no doubt; Clumly's stubborn blindness gave Taggert a break. Will Hodge wanted his brother to escape, of course: what they would do to a man involved in a policeman's murder was terrible to think of. Not that Taggert should get off scot-free forever. Taggert wouldn't want that himself, if his mind were right. But much as he wanted his brother to escape their hasty violence of pistols and rifles, he could not keep his mind on that. Taggert would never have gotten into jail in the first place, likely, if it weren't for his knowledge that in a pinch there was always old Will to haul him out. "They use me," he said aloud. He thought: *with scorn.* With unspeakable scorn Chief Clumly had said, *Hooligans. That's what it'll be!* And Will Hodge, though he knew it was Taggert he was trapping if he forced Fred Clumly to the truth—but knowing too, with the force of dynamite blasting through his veins, the rage of being taken for a fool by a muddled old fool like Clumly, and knowing in his numbed and prickling skin the indifference of Miller and the other policemen to whom he was merely the apartment owner, a clumsy obstruction to be walked around—but, worst of all, the shocking indifference, even scorn, yes, of his own brother, Tag, who had walked out quietly into the night, fallen angel once loved, leaving propped against the wall the horrible corpse of a woman who if she wasn't a friend was anyway someone Will Hodge had known—Will Hodge, burning up like coal, had boomed out: *Hooligans my hat!* Small as two nails were Clumly's eyes. The rain howled down in horror, slammed out of heaven. But what Hodge thought was: Tell a man often enough he's dirt and sooner or later he'll be mud in your eye. He smiled grimly and tightened his two-fisted grip on the steering wheel.

That was not all there was to it. When Will Hodge had awakened at the motel this morning, mind full of fury like hot

red light, he was assaulted not only by the image of Clumly
struggling to cover his stupidity and the old woman's dead ac-
cusing eyes, but also by painful images of other times and
places that were now all one with the hour in the apartment
last night. And one image especially: in the yellow-beige motel
room as sterile and gross as a doctor's office he lived through
again the mockery and wrath of the woman in Clumly's office.
He understood. Who wouldn't be distraught, hearing of the
murder of her son, seeing his shattered face in the morgue? He
forgave her. With anger and forgiveness mingling in him like
two writhing seas he had resolved to go see her and tell her in
no uncertain terms that whatever he could do he would do, to
the limit of his ability and, needless to say, at no cost to herself. He had dressed carefully, had even taken pains to cut the
hairs in his nose ("Obscene," his wife used to say; "not even
pigs have hairs coming out of their noses!")—and had cleaned
his battered, chipped fingernails and polished his crooked
shoes and checked his tie for stains and had gone to the house.

It was dark green. Cardboard in a second-story window.
You expected Negroes in the houses next door, but this street
was still Italian, mostly new Italian though, just off the boat.
He rang the doorbell several times, then realized that perhaps
it didn't work, and so he knocked. Even now no one came. He
glanced at his watch. Seven-thirty. He felt a blush prickling up
through his neck and was tempted to step out of sight before
anyone came. But he stayed. There wasn't a sound from inside
the house, and he went on waiting, gazing down the street toward the corner grocery store. Only seven-thirty. In the same
way, once when he was a child of ten, he had agreed to ride to
school on his wooden-wheeled bicycle with a group of friends
from neighboring farms, and he'd gotten up and gone to their
houses one after another and had waited and waited and finally had left without them, baffled and wounded by their cruel
betrayal; he had found when he got to the school that he was
hours ahead of his time. He held his watch to his ear now and
found that it was running. At last he tiptoed down the porch
steps and out toward the street. He'd have breakfast, though
he wasn't hungry. Then, behind him, he heard the Italian
woman's voice, thick with sleep: "Well?"

"Ah!" he said. He tipped his hat and on second thought removed it and held it over his belly. Then, coming a step toward the porch: "Excuse me. I didn't mean to get you up."

She was wearing man's pajamas with a black plastic rain-coat over them, no doubt the first thing she'd been able to lay her hands on. "What you want?" she said. She was holding the screen door open, and he could see beyond her the yellowed wallpaper of her livingroom, dark in the corners as the skin around old people's eyes. The house behind her was sound asleep, like the neighboring houses. The whole city lay silent. The only sounds were the roar of a bus starting up a quarter-mile away and the twittering of robins.

"I'm sorry to bother you so early in the morning," he said. If he were his brother Ben he might have carried it off by sheer gentleness of heart; if he were his father he would not have made the mistake in the first place. But he was, for better or worse, himself. Without preamble or excuse he said, "I wanted to tell you that whatever you may think of me, I intend to do everything in my power to bring your son's murder-er to justice."

She looked at him for a long time, her mind apparently still cobwebbed with dreams. She closed her eyes. "Jesus."

"Do you mind if I come in?" he said. "I haven't got a war-rant." His laugh was like a bark (A fool to laugh at such a time, he realized.)

She seemed to consider it. Finally she said, "Come on." She rolled her head toward the door. The coarse, curly hair falling over her shoulder was like an Indian woman's.

Hodge took off his hat and followed her through the living-room to the kitchen. There were toys everywhere. It was a large family. In the livingroom there was a little girl's stove, a sink, a long shelf of old but carefully preserved toys—boxes of games, sets of dishes, stuffed animals, matchbox cars on the coffee table. There were old newspapers and magazines: *Mechanix Illustrated, Horoscope*.

When he was seated at the narrow formica table in the kitchen, Hodge said, "I have sons myself, Mrs. Salvador."

"You want coffee?" she said.

"That would be fine." He said: "Mrs. Salvador—"

"All we got is instant," she said.

"That's fine."

Her brown eyes looked past him, unalive. "What you think you can do? He's dead. What do you want?" She put the pot of water on and turned up the gas. Before he could answer, she said, all in a burst, "You came to tell me you didn't mean to help kill him. Is that it? Forget it. I was upset. I'm still upset, yes, but today better. It wasn't your fault. You do your job. Ok. So do I. We all do. You got kids of your own, and if you was me . . . Ok. What difference, to blame or not to blame, when somebody dies? No good to talk about it."

Hodge rubbed his legs and avoided her dead eyes. "I only came to say—"

"Ok." She was far away, not listening.

"Your idea about attorneys—"

"Ok." She had her back to him and stood as still as a woman withdrawing into stone. The plastic raincoat was cheap, slick black. Today he felt, as he had not felt yesterday, that he really was in some unclear way responsible.

"Mrs. Salvador," he said, "if there's anything in this world—"

The change was sudden and terrible. One moment she was like stone or old iron; the next, she had collapsed into grief, becoming a young girl, destroyed and helpless. She stood bent as a hunchback, her hands pressed to her face as if to keep it from shattering as the boy's had done, and her back shook. He thought of leaping up and going to her, enclosing her in his arms; but he was not his brother Ben or his father, he could only sit, sick-hearted and formal as a woodcarving, waiting. He stared at the range, the circle of blue flame under the pot, steady black iron and blue flame against the jerking of her back, and at last he said, "There there, Mrs. Salvador."

"Why?" she whispered. "*Why?*"

How could he answer? He rubbed his legs. "If there's anything in this world—" he said.

She did not hear.

He wanted to say, "My dear, my dear, dear *child*—"

"What do you want from me?" she moaned.

From upstairs someone called, "*Chi è?*"

She said, "*Niente, Mammà. Dormi, dormi.*" She threw him a look of panic. "She takes it hard. She's eighty. An old witch. But how can you say to her, a time like this, Mama, you old witch?"

"Your husband's mother?" Hodge said. He had meant to ask if he could send her some money.

Again, she did not hear him, she said weakly, "You want sugar and cream?"

"Thank you," Hodge said.

"Thank you yes or thank you no?"

"Thank you yes."

She fixed the coffee and handed it to him. Then she fixed one for herself.

"If there's anything at all I can do—" Hodge said.

She sat down across from him.

"I have sons myself," he said.

"That's good," she said. "God protect them. May they all grow up and be President."

After that they sat in silence, drinking their coffee. He looked at her young but wrinkled hand on the table, looked at the gray of her pajamas where the raincoat collar opened to reveal it, looked at the suggestion of hair on her upper lip. His heart went out to her. Then he heard the old woman's slippers on the stair, after a while she appeared in the doorway, gray hair straggling down around her face like bad rain, fat shoulders bent from the miserable weight of a lifetime.

*"Eh," she said. "Il caffè s'è raffreddato; o e troppo freddo o è troppo caldo. Ma a te che t'importa?"*

"Mama, this is Mr. Hodge," the girl said. "The lawyer."

*"Sarà inverno presto,"* the old woman said. *"Di giorno è troppo caldo, e così pare che di notte si sta bene, e a letto si gela."*

"Mama," the girl said, "have some coffee." To Hodge she said, without troubling to look at him, "Mama's deaf as a post. Good thing, for everybody."

"Coffee," the old woman sneered. "Coffee for Mama. *Cara Madre. Diamole caffè e puo darsi che muore, e noi faremo una festa.* Good morning."

"Good morning," Hodge said.

She stood at the stove rubbing her rear end with both hands and scowling bitterly. "Coffee," she said. "God forgive." Then she was silent, looking around her shoulder at him, taking his measure. He realized he had his thumbs hooked inside his suspenders like a banker, and that his glasses were far down his nose. You couldn't blame her if she didn't understand that he came to them as a servant. Nevertheless, she came sideways from the stove toward the table and extended her hand, twisted and veined like old cypress root, to the back of the chair at the end. She had her coffee in the other hand. Slowly, steadying herself on the chair, she came the rest of the way. Over her old yellowish blue nightdress she had a black afghan.

*Sta buona, Mammà,"* the girl said.

The old woman let herself into the chair. She pointed at Hodge. *"Chi è lui?"* she said.

"Mr. Hodge," the girl said. "The lawyer."

She pursed her lips as if to spit. *"Dapertutto,"* she said. *"In tutti gli armadi, in tutte le foglie."* She studied him, and he took off his glasses to polish them on his shirt. The girl, the dead policeman's mother, seemed not to be listening any more. She sat with her hands over her eyes, her back no longer shaking, not a muscle twitching in fact; it was as if she were holding her breath or maybe refusing to draw it in. The old woman stretched out her hands like gray branches, and the gray hair hanging around her head was like oak moss around stone. At the ends of her powerful arms, her hands shook like leaves. "When we came to this country the lawyers is all waiting: 'Mortgage! Mortgage!' 'Mortgage you,' we say. And the police say, 'Can't dump the trash. Ten dollars.' And the priests say, 'Ten dollars for your sins.' 'What sins?' we say, 'what sins we made?' I could tell you. In all the leaves, all the cupboards. We go down and get water, there's a lawyer sitting there waiting in a boat. We get coal by the tracks, it's almost dark, all gray in the sky, nothing moving but the what-you-say . . . pigeons, and there's a freight car with the door open, it's full of police. *Madonna mia!* At night in the house we are looking out the window and there's priests. All over the yard, little priests all bones and black cloth and eyes like fish. I could tell you."

*"Mammà,"* the girl said, *"sta buona."*

"You think crazy old woman? Ignorant old wop?" she leered.

> *"Nel mezzo del cammin di nostra vita*
> *Mi ritrovai per una selva oscura,*
> *Che la diritta via era smarrita.*
>
> *E quanto a dir qual era è cosa dura*
> *Questa selva selvaggia ed aspra e forte . . ."*

"She knows all of it—so she says," the girl said.

Hodge said, "What is it?"

"Who knows?" the girl said wearily. "It's long."

> *"Tanto è amara, che poco è piu morte:*
> *Ma per trattar del ben ch' i' vi trovai,*
> *Dirò dell' altre . . ."*

The old woman had her eyes closed now, hands folded under her chin, head tipped up as though the thing she was saying were a prayer.

"It takes days," the girl said. "She gets started and she won't stop. Her father made her learn it for a punishment. This country, they call her a ignorant old wop."

"I'm sorry," Hodge said.

"Ah," the girl said indifferently. "Nobody's fault."

He looked at the coffee and couldn't drink it. The old woman mumbled on, spitting a little, her eyes clamped shut. He hadn't eaten since yesterday morning, he remembered. Even so, he wanted nothing.

*"Mammà,"* the girl said. It had no effect. Outside the kitchen window the light was yellowing after the early gray. It was going to be hot. The narrow stretch of yard between Salvador's house and the next was unnaturally green after last night's rain. You could feel the sogginess of the earth underneath. Sparrows flew by and vanished beyond the wire clotheslines at the side of the garage.

He said, "Can I give you money?"

The corners of the girl's mouth turned down, and the old woman mumbled more loudly for a moment.

"I feel—responsible," he said. "You were wrong to say it's my fault, maybe, but I feel, just the same—"

The old woman bowed her head, shutting him out.

> *"Allor fu la paura un poco queta*
> *Che nel lago del cor m'era durata*
> *La notte ch' i' passai con tanta pieta."*

"Please go," the girl said. "What can you do? It's all right. Today I am ok." She stood up.

Hodge nodded and, after a moment, obeyed. On the porch —the old woman still muttering behind them—Hodge said, "If there's anything—"

"Nothing," she said. *"E' la vita."* Her eyes were dead. It was as if he had left already.

And so Will Hodge drove angrily now, wounded with helpless wrath and frustration, heading west toward the Indian Reservation.

He hardly noticed at first the figure hurriedly walking beside the road a half-mile ahead of him—looked at the figure, took in all the details, yet hardly noticed it was there. It was a small, more or less unbelievable man in a wide black hat, the kind Amish men wear, and he was hurrying mightily, short legs bobbing, cheerfully stomping through the world, fists swinging harmlessly, big feet toeing out, back bent as though it were imperative that he get there first with the tip of his hat and his (head tipped sideways, like the head of a swimmer) nose. When the Plymouth came in range the young man turned and stuck out his thumb. Will Hodge slowed down, still without thinking. He was hardly more than a boy; in his twenties. He had a beard, wide moustache, some kind of perhaps Indian trinket hanging on his shirt. His face was hidden, because over his eyes he had enormous round sunglasses as black as the Amish hat crammed down on his dangling black hair. Under his left arm he had a black metal box, a suitcase.

"Indian Reservation?" Hodge said.

"Yeah!" the young man said with surprising enthusiasm. "I'd appreciate that!" His head bobbed.

He swung the car door open and jumped in, nodding with pleasure, bowing like a Chinaman, and settled the black box comfortably in his lap. Hodge mused. The young man was not an Indian. He was one of those wild young people they have in big cities. "Is that where you were going?" Hodge said.

"Yeah, great!" the young man said, nodding again and grinning and reaching up with a jerk to tip his hat. "I *would* have been going there if I'd knew."

Hodge frowned and pulled back onto the road. He stole another quick glance at that hat, the glasses, the metal box. At last Hodge said, "Where are you from?"

"New York," the young man said. "And San Francisco. All over the place. Things really happening!"

"Mmm," Hodge said. The boy continued nodding, bobbing his head to some rhythm going on inside it and, after a little while began to whistle. He had a button on his chest beside the trinket. *Fun City Needs the Feenjon,* it said. The boy smiled, delighted, and leaned toward him and put his finger under the button to turn it so Hodge could read it better, and as Hodge read it again, screwing his mouth toward his right cheek, the boy smiled more broadly still. Then he folded his hands and went back to whistling.

Hodge drove on. There was an excitement in his chest. The boy's showing up exactly when and where he had seemed portentous—whether portentous of good or bad he could not say. He said, "Excuse me. What are you? That is, are you Amish?" He knew he was not.

The boy nodded with extreme pleasure. "I'm sorry, excuse me. My name's Freeman." He reached out with another quick jerk to shake Will Hodge's hand.

"Ah!" Hodge said. "Yes. My name's—" For a second he couldn't remember. "Hodge. Will Hodge. I'm an attorney."

"Great!" the boy said. "You live around here? And do your practice?"

"Batavia." He said it with satisfaction, though why he felt so satisfied he could not have explained. The boy's clownish pleasure in things put a spell on him.

"Great little town! I was in jail there," the boy said. His hands leaped out to grip imaginary bars and his face filled with horror and amazement. Then he smiled. He bobbed his head again and now he was singing. "Indian Reservation!" he said abruptly. "Great! A visit? Or is that where you do, uh, your thing?"

"Why," Hodge said, "actually—" It all came flooding back over him, and he felt his jaw go tense. He could feel the young man's strangely friendly scrutiny, and it made him more tense than ever. As if to make things easier, the boy pulled off the huge black glasses, folded them carefully, and opened the box in his lap to put them away. Inside the box there were compartments covered in red velvet, frayed but still noble, and in the compartments there were objects. There was a carefully shined flute, some brightly colored stones in a plastic bag, some rattlelike things, dried lilypods perhaps, a toothbrush, numerous bits of glass, wire, metal, wood, flower seeds, and plastic. Hodge looked hastily back at the road and jerked the steering wheel to avoid the baked-mud shoulder.

"Excuse me for being so personal," Freeman said, "but you're acting—like up-tight. Is that because of me?"

Hodge looked at him in alarm. "No, no," he said. "Not at all." They passed bright yellow fields where a week or two ago there had been wheat, and overhead the sky was amazingly blue. The maple trees between the fields and sky were bright green.

"What country!" the boy said. "Psychedelic!" He waved both hands. "I lived in country like this one time, with a friend of mine that's in Los Angeles now. Kentucky then. But it was different, right"—his hands were describing it. Then, suddenly, he grew still with thought. "Man, you send out bad vibrations. Trouble?"

Hodge felt panicky and angry at the same time. The macadam stretched away ahead of him, straight and blue. It was a startling thing, he was finding out—as Miller and Ed Tank had found out before him—though Hodge didn't know about that yet. The boy's queer directness, openness—rudeness it would be in the world Hodge knew—stood outside all the rules he understood. But long before he understood it, Will Hodge felt, perfectly clearly, what it meant: they had dropped—Freeman's kind—the defenses constructed by centuries of civilization: they did not need them: they had nothing to defend. Only their hats, the clothes on their backs, their toys. Hodge, like any man of sense, might scoff at such notions in the abstract. But there was no resisting that childlike openness except by denying that it was real, and Hodge was not one to deny that the real was real: a cow, a chairleg, the dilated pupil of an eye.

The boy too stared at the road, Hodge knew without looking. "Listening to troubles is one of the special numbers I do," the boy said. "I can also do a thing where I sit like a toad and mind my business." When Hodge glanced at him the boy was watching him out of the corner of his eyes, his innocently grinning head tipped forward, meek. His hands and feet seemed to have grown larger.

"Sometimes talk's no great help," Hodge said sternly. He watched the yellow fields sliding past, a farmer's lane with a wooden bridge, a patch of dark woods smoky with fog like the long thin sigh of a dragon, a black-green pond. *Like a child*, he thought. He'd heard that that was what they were like, though he hadn't believed it. He remembered the word for them: *hippies*. Free lovers, he'd heard; yes, like Millie. Except, the boy was all gentleness, not like her. More like a sacrificial lamb or, say, a loyal dog, except that he would take the beating from anybody, not just a master. Like a child, then, that was it. Moving from place to place to duck the draft, maybe, because he wouldn't kill and wouldn't fight the Government either. He'd heard they did that. (But the yellow and green land sliding by, so beautiful in the hippie's eyes, had gophers and gopher-snakes in it, chickens and foxes, cannibalistic fish in every creek, and in a month the bright green trees would be red with death.)

"You have parents?" Hodge said, squinting.

Freeman nodded and suddenly smiled. "They're beautiful people. Hung up here and there, like anybody, but beautiful." His head began bobbing again, full of joy.

Hodge drove on, thinking now of his own father, how he'd followed his father through fields and woods, carrying the gun or the bait pail, his child-arm aching from the weight of it and his side aching from walking farther and faster than he could. He was afraid to drop behind. There were wild things out in these woods and swamps, and at night the high hills over his shoulder would furtively change their places.

He thought of the Italian woman mumbling her poem. She'd go on like that for days, the girl had said. A shudder passed through him.

"Life's strange," Hodge said grimly.

Freeman agreed. He took off his hat and put it on the box and waited seriously, with his long, violin-shaped nose tilted.

Hodge said, "A woman was murdered in my apartment last night."

"No!"

"Mm," Hodge said. But he frowned. That was not the point. "My father was a Congressman," he said. "That's not directly related—" He frowned again. Freeman nodded encouragingly, not pressing. His wide-open eyes were like a doe's, or like one of the Congressman's German shepherd cowdogs. "Nevertheless," said Hodge, "he was a Congressman; good one. He represented—embodied, in fact—almost everything that was, for his time and place—" He winced. He was making a fool of himself with all this talk, he knew well enough. But he said, "Where was I?"

"He embodied."

Hodge nodded, remembering, and glanced over to see if he was being mocked. "Embodied all that was good. For his time and place. Or at any rate, he had a theory." His stomach made a turn. "That is, it was my father's belief that society is made up of disparate parts, if you know what I mean—elements, different groups, so to speak—and that they did not have any one single end. Each wanted, that is, his own special—" He searched for the word; his heart was beginning to race. He felt foolish, or stuffy; clumsy as a thing of wood.

"Thing," said Freeman.

Hodge nodded, dubious. "For instance," he believed that the Jeffersonian ideal of the politician was unsound." He cleared his throat, formal. "Believed that a man who tried to work out by his own lights what was best for mankind would inevitably come up with what he himself thought best, and that this was against the welfare of the whole. The spirit of Democracy. My father believed in pressures. Checks and balances. Like Spinoza. He would have been annoyed by the modern idea of getting out the vote—having Boy Scout parades and all the rest, to make people who have no real interest in government go to the polls and pull levers. He'd argue that those who have something at stake are the people who ought to vote, so that the Negro would vote when he finds himself—"

"Raped," said Freeman.

"Yes," said Hodge, uncomfortably, "or the farmer would vote when a specific program—you see what I mean."

The young man solemnly nodded.

"I'm boring you," Hodge said. And he knew it was true, or ought to be—Millie, at any rate, would be bored, and rightly, rightly. So would a reader if this were all a novel. He screwed up his face and glanced in the rear-view mirror.

"No," the boy said.

"The theory was . . ." Hodge said. (Incredible talk, Hodge recognized, on a blue country road through yellow fields, beneath a blue, blue sky. Some of the houses were paintless and overgrown. There would be owls in them, and woodchucks under the floor. But there were hollyhocks in the rank yards, and grapevines thick with bitter grapes—mindless, pale survivors.) "The ideal politician, from this point of view, was not a man with some special insight into justice but simply a man talented at sensing, dispassionately, the specific desires of the people around him—experienced enough to guess what people from somewhere else would think about that specific desire, what roadblocks their representatives would throw up—and, finally, most important of all, shrewd enough to guess what would happen to the whole fabric if that desire were . . . met. Met. That was the theory."

"Yeah. Great!" He nodded enthusiastically. But he was pay-ing attention not to the words but to something else. To Hodge, Hodge had a feeling.

"Well, straying from the point. I have a son: he's been ac-tive in all this. That's why it's on my mind. He's an attorney too—like me. I think I said. Point is, my father's theory is not as comforting as it used to be, not that I disavow it. It's not so easy to be sure any more. The whole thing so big and complex . . . I read in the paper about how youth is following a man named Ginsberg. Who is Ginsberg? How is a man to keep up?"

"Ginsberg," said Freeman. He tipped up the hat and scratched in through his hair.

"But that's not it," Hodge said thoughtfully. He saw again the dead woman in his bedroom. "The idea of pressures—or-der establishing itself that way—as if society were a pond in a field, where natural balance comes about by itself—so many tadpoles, so many water bugs, so many thises, so many thats —that is to say . . ." He paused, searching. "Things kill each other," he said at last. "You look at a pond and you think, 'How calm,' but things are eating things all the time. Take my father's family. He was a talented man. Everything he did, he did as if he was born to it. But he had a brother who commit-ted suicide, and another one was ordinary all his life. And as for his sons, well, none of us—" He reflected on Ben's falling barns.

Hodge had missed his turn. He slowed down, scowling, and turned in at the first farm lane, backed out, and started east again, Freeman seemed hardly to notice. "All right," Hodge said. "So you begin to think what's needed is an ordering intel-ligence." He nodded to himself, and the boy riding with him waited, reserving judgment. "You begin to think pressure alone's not enough. What's needed is a king. A benevolent des-pot. And the same in the family—the old idea of the father, the judge and punisher, so on. A wife that keeps her place ex-cept when things get extreme. In my father's family now. There's a story they tell, when he was trying to learn Greek." He told the story. For the first time the story came clear, or anyway clear in a new way. They came in sight of the steeples and chimneys of Batavia, and almost without interrupting himself, Hodge turned around and headed, once more, west, back toward the woods.

"So that's what it is," Hodge said. "All my life I've been patching up, trying to keep machines running that were worn out already. I suppose I should have asserted myself and invented a new machine. But I wasn't an inventor. And yet you have to. There it is." He told the story of Taggert.

Freeman shook his head, drumming his fingers on his hat. "The times are out of joint," he said.

Hodge puckered his lips and brooded on the possibility that it had always been so, since the first age. Since Cain. "You have to do something, whether you're fit for it or not," he said.

"That's it if that's how you feel about it," the boy said.

"Dad burn it!" Hodge said. He shoved on the brake and backed up and made the turn. "Almost missed it again," he said.

"Well shit," Freeman said encouragingly.

The car jounced over ruts and pebbles and clattered over the wood and old iron bridge, but Hodge hardly noticed. "Well all right," he said, collecting his thoughts. "You have to be an ordering intelligence, whether you're fit for it or not, whether or not you can see any kind of order."

"Right," said Freeman, "could be."

"Vietnam, now. People say we shouldn't be there. All over the world there are people that say that. Well maybe we shouldn't, I've heard the arguments. But somebody has to be responsible. And who's more fit for that than the United States?"

Freeman scratched his chin through the beard. "Hmm," he said. He had a guilty look.

"We've exhausted every honorable alternative, isn't that so?"

"Hmm," Freeman said.

They had begun to pass Indian houses now. You could tell by the names on the mailboxes—Steeprock, Blue-eyes, Black It was hilly country, and the houses were like houses anywhere, but odd. Some were far back from the road, indifferent to winter, set on the crowns of hills above driveways that would be impassable after the first of December; some were log cabins with elaborate extensions—new sections of tarpaper or asbestos shingles; one was no bigger than a large doghouse, a scale model of a real house but in fact a toy, like the houses set up on the Blind School lawns at Christmas—but there were people inside and a man sitting on a rocker on the porch, his bent head scraping the porch ceiling as he rocked. Hodge drove on, and when he came out of the woods he was in sight of the Longhouse, where the meetings were, and beyond that stood the U.S. Government Activities Center, just off Indian land, where the troopers could get at it. He pulled up in front of the Activities Center and parked under the willows. He was still talking. There was a man in a felt hat with a hole in it, sitting on the long porch in front. Hodge's rider leaned toward the windshield to look the place over, but he was still listening, nodding from time to time, shaking his head.

"All right," Hodge said. "It's not my fault that it's part of my profession to give the criminal the full benefit of the law. And it's not my fault that the Chief of Police is a half-senile old coot who's got no more business in his job than a scarecrow's got in church. My hands are clean of the whole thing. But it's got to be somebody's fault."

The Indian had put down his comic book and was coming over toward them, shirttail hanging out, long, thin shoes untied. He had a face that looked run over. "Don't think I'm doing all this because I like it," Hodge was saying. "If the police would do their job there's nobody would be happier about it than me. Just the same, it's a fact that the boy's got something to do with me—because of Ben, that is. Ben, my brother, the one on the farm."

Freeman nodded.

"And because of my boy, Luke. They wash their hands of him, the Indian I mean, Nick, and there he is out roaming the countryside with a gun in his possession—what am I supposed to do?"

The Indian tipped back the hat and put his hand on the fender and looked at them. "Hod do," he said.

Freeman tipped the hat and smiled. "Good morning."

"Help you people?" the Indian said. He had a wrinkled cigarette between the first two fingers of the hand he leaned on.

"My son Luke, now," Hodge stared past his fists on the steering wheel. He mused.

The Indian said, "You looking for somebody?" He took a drag on the cigarette. Behind him the sky was sharply blue. One of the willows was dead.

"We want to see somebody?" Freeman said.

Hodge leaned toward the window. "You seen any sign of Nick Slater?" he said.

The Indian showed nothing. "Slater?"

"You know him," Hodge said. "A young fellow, thin." He tried to think how to describe him. But he was thinking of Luke.

The Indian scratched his stomach.

"There'd be a bearded man with him," Hodge said.

The Indian drew his mouth down, then slowly shook his head.

Hodge looked toward the willows. At last he said, "Chief around?"

"Lives in the woods," the Indian said. He frowned. "You mean Nicodemus?"

"Who's Chief?" Hodge said.

"Two chiefs," the Indian said. "Nicodemus is the Chief according to him. According to the old women Sun-on-the-Water's the Chief."

"Well, whichever you think," Hodge said.

Freeman nodded, satisfied.

"Sun-on-the-Water's in the woods," the Indian said.

"Well," Hodge said. He waited.

The Indian thought about it. After a minute he said, "Wait here." He walked slowly back toward the porch. As he opened the screen door he glanced back, sharp-eyed.

Hodge turned off the motor and spoke of his sons. After a long time (not long to Hodge) the screen door of the Activities Center opened and a boy came out—a lanky Indian in jeans and glasses and a red shirt. He came to the car.

"Hi," he said. "Welcome." He bowed.

Hodge nodded.

"This is the Activities Center," the boy said. "We have many exhibits."

Freeman said, "It's nice!"

Again the boy bowed. "You're looking for Nick Slater, I understand. The Chief will be glad to help, I'm sure. So therefore follow me and I'll take you to our leader." A second too late, he grinned.

Freeman laughed. Hodge pretended to smile.

"Concerning Chief Sun-on-the-Water there are many stories," the boy said. "If you prefer, I will tell you some as we walk to where he is."

"Great!" Freeman said.

Hodge felt for the doorhandle and took a deep breath, preparing to get out and walk.

Inside the woods of the Old Part it was dark and still musty from last night's rain. The woods were full of brush, and there were young saplings everywhere, pushing against each other, struggling upward. In the old days, the boy said, the Indians used to burn out the brush and leaves every year, but no one bothered any more. No one lived here now except Sun-on-the-Water and some of the old women. The others lived in the new houses toward the edge of the Reservation, where they could get out to the gypsum mines and the tannery when they wanted to. The children went to school in Akron now, and when they were through a lot of them left the Reservation. The older girls went to colleges, and the older boys got jobs down south toward Olean or moved to Idaho. Nobody spoke the old language any more. Some of them could if they had to, but they never did. The trail was so narrow they had to walk single file, and Hodge was now too far back to hear more than a phrase now and then. It was just as well. The heat of his indignation at Clumly had passed and had left behind it a gloom like the gloom of the woods, a memory of pleasant times so long gone he could no longer believe in them, memories of hopes proved years ago to be ashes in the wind. He saw again in his mind the performance Chief Clumly had put on last night, trying to distract them from the truth. One could see well enough what he was up to. Before you knew it he would be saying there had been no escape at all, maybe even believing it. Yet a good man once. He'd spoken to the Lions Club sometimes, and it was a pleasure to hear him. But now you could never be sure he would even remember to come, and if he came you could not be sure he would have his speech ready or, if the speech was ready, whether the facts would be even approximately right. Hodge felt more and more depressed. Let Miller worry about it, he thought. But Miller had pretended to go along with it, standing there nodding like a puppet, and who could blame him? Ordering intelligence, he thought. One of Will Jr's phrases, something he'd picked up in college. He sighed. His shoes squished in the mud. The sticks across the path seemed to have lain here for years; they were soft as bread. But he could see the greenish light of a clearing ahead of them, and as they came closer he saw what appeared to be a cabin.

The boy was saying, "He never comes out any more. They even have to cart his whiskey in to him. Old woman lives with him, some say it's his sister. They use to cut wood and sell it, but his tractor gave out and besides he got too old to haul it, and also he drank, so therefore he left it go and now the buzz-saw just sits there growing vines and moss and the tractor just sits there behind the house growing vines and moss too, and they don't do anything, as far as I know, just wait for people to come in with the whiskey. Sometimes Mr. Bailey comes in and asks Sun-on-the-Water to have a meeting at the Long-house, but Sun-on-the-Water says no, they don't need no meeting, and they let it go, or else Nicodemus has a meeting. Nico-demus isn't even an Indian, or anyway not a Seneca, that's what my father says. But he runs things, since nobody else will. He sold off half the land to the telephone company for nothing but free telephones for whoever wanted one. A lot of people were mad about it, but nobody used the land anyhow and they let it go. Nicodemus said we should all be proud, and some of the people took his side—I don't exactly understand the whole thing—but anyway, after that Nicodemus said he was the Chief and some of the people said ok. Mr. Bailey said Sun-on-the-Water was Chief, and so did Mrs. Steeprock, but Sun-on-the-Water wouldn't come out of the woods, so there-fore that's how it was."

"Maybe we picked the wrong Chief," Freeman said. He looked back along the trail and scratched his beard, but he was still hurrying, each step a little kick, exactly as he'd been walking when Hodge first saw him.

"That's the place," the Indian boy said. "He's prob'ly asleep."

Hodge nodded.

"The Senecas use to be a independent nation," the boy said. "In the War of 1812 the Seneca army declared against En-gland and they saved the Port of Buffalo, people say. They say the United States Army promised to meet them there and help fight the British, but then the United States Army got thinking and they decided to wait and see how the Indians made out, so they waited and the Indians fought the British theirselves, and after they'd won the victory the Americans came and gave them congratulations."

There was no sign that anyone lived in the cabin. The Indian boy and Freeman stood looking from the rim of trees, and when Hodge came up to them he, too, stopped to look. There was a rain-whitened chair in front of the black opening. On the eaves of the house there were wasps' nests.

"I know Nick and Verne," the boy said. He smiled, eyes glinting. "They're friends of mine."

"Have you seen them?" Hodge said. "I'm not the police, you know."

But the boy was looking at the cabin. "I guess they've left," he said. He took it lightly.

"Aw come on," Freeman said. "The Chief of a noble old tribe wouldn't just up and leave." He started for the cabin. "They'll be inside," he said. The Indian boy smiled.

Hodge followed, slowly and heavily, and the Indian boy walked beside him.

"This your first visit to our people?" the boy said.

Hodge grunted.

"There are many interesting stories about Sun-on-the-Water," the boy said. He squinted, perhaps seeing if Hodge was listening. "I know all the stories, but usually when I tell them there's a small charge."

Hodge nodded.

"The story of Sun-on-the-Water and the bear, for example, is short and amusing, so therefore I only charge a dollar. On the other hand—" They were within ten feet of the open door now. Freeman had stopped, a little ahead of them, and stood looking in with his hands in his pockets and his head tipped, dubious, as if afraid there might be snakes. There was a faint stink, of, perhaps, rotten food.

"Anybody there?" Hodge called.

"I don't *hear* anybody," Freeman said.

Hodge came up even with him. "We may as well go back," he said. "Wild goose chase. If Nick came out to the Reservation, Sun-on-the-Water wouldn't know."

"Sure quiet," the Indian boy said. "Maybe he's in there waiting for us."

"You want to go first?" Freeman said.

"It doesn't matter," Hodge said. "You go ahead, if you want."

The walls of the house were rotted and pieces of light came

in through the roof. He wondered if perhaps there was no such man as Sun-on-the-Water.

Freeman said, "Maybe Jack here should go in first. He brought us."

"I don't care," the boy said.

"Well, somebody better go in first, if we're going."

"It doesn't matter," Hodge said. "You can see there's nobody here."

"Right. We might as well go back," the boy said.

"We can't do that," Freeman said. "Maybe they're sick or something."

"Maybe he's lying in there drunk," the boy said.

Freeman looked at Hodge. In the clearing's yellow light the black hat and glasses made Freeman seem obscurely dangerous now, anyway alien, more in league with the woods—or with Mars, it might be—than with them. He said, "You going in?"

Hodge rubbed his chin.

"Well shit," Freeman said. He splashed his hands out with disgust and jerked forward. Hodge followed.

At first, they couldn't see a thing inside. When their eyes adjusted to the dark they could make out a white-with-age table and chair, a wash basin, a great many empty whiskey bottles. In the corner there was a bed with a mass of rotten covers on it. Freeman moved toward it, the Indian boy a little behind him, then stopped abruptly. Now Hodge too could see it. There was a man on it, and he'd been dead for a long, long time, long enough that he didn't smell. Dogs had gotten to him. There were only bones and some black stuff.

Freeman took off his hat. "Wrong Chief," he said.

The Indian boy was smiling.

"You did this on purpose," Hodge whispered.

"But I didn't charge you," the Indian boy said. His teeth were white and as large as the teeth of a horse.

## 2

"Truth is stranger than fiction," said Freeman. "Nevertheless, this is all pretty God damn strange."

"What?" Hodge said.

He repeated it, but Hodge did not listen the second time either. He drove with his head tipped down, jaw forward, brooding. He, of all people, trapped in an allegory!

"Thing is," Freeman said, "you got all up-tight, you know? They kid around with you, so ok, so that's their thing. Go along with it, that's the way you gotta do. But no, you get all up-tight and you wanna go *bam bam pow! Zuk!*" He made motions like a fighter. "Choo," he said. He shook his head. "I guess that's where it is."

Hodge drove.

"Man I was there, you know what I mean?" Freeman said. "I was this student, see—" He made the motions of a student, reading and writing. "Yes ma'am, no ma'am, ah ha! now I grasp it! Zing. Gonna cut through the waves man, arch the treeompf. Zap. 'Wanted: smart young man.' Ok." His hands were a smart young man cutting through the crowd. "So I worked, see, and when I was finished with the books I was a house-painter and a carpenter and a butcher. And after that I would walk where the rich people's houses were." He showed how it was to be a young man walking, looking with vast admiration at swimming pools and shrubbery and gables. "Hoo!" He shook his head. "But pretty soon fella comes out of the sky and he taps me on the shoulder and says, 'Hey baby, excuse me for being so personal, but that ain't where it's at.'"

"The sky," Hodge said, merely registering it, like a man showing he's listening. He drove.

"Something like that. Top of a building, maybe. You know how it is. So anyway, I put it all away for a while—you know, put it in a neat little pile for later—" (his hands quickly fashioned a neat little pile) "—and put the pile in a box and kissed my mother on the cheek—" (he kissed the fond air) "—and started down the valley of the numerous shadows of death, to speak pentameter. Not up-tight. You know what I mean?"

"Not up-tight," Hodge mused. "In other words, you decided to reject—"

"No no! Not reject! That's the other guy." He pointed behind them, and Hodge looked back, then scowled. "I'm for *all* of it, understand? I kiss the sunset wherever it's pretty, even setting over swimming pools and the topless towers of Indianapolis, *Mmmmooch!* I pat the world. *'Good* dog, *good* cow, *good* bush, *good* trombone. See what I mean? I mean I'm the encourager. Keep the gears oiled, you understand? 'Atta gear! Good baby! Spin, spin, spin.' MMMMMMMM."

"Hmm," said Hodge. "It's all right if you don't have a family."

"Right!" Freeman said. "So I meet the right lady and zoom: Tie—vest—" He showed how it would be when he put them on. "Get out the paintbrush and the butcher-knife and the schoolteacher books and *whee!* down the valley of the shadow of work!" He showed how he would go.

Hodge, after he'd thought about it, sighed.

They'd reached Batavia now. Hodge said suddenly, "I never asked you where you wanted to go. I guess my mind—" He let it trail off. "Do you want to get out somewhere?"

"Me?" Freeman said.

"Well, that is," Hodge said, "If you had any plans—"

"Oh no, I'm not in any hurry. I'll stick around and help you."

"Well, actually," Hodge said.

"Don't think twice." He grandly waved away all petty considerations. "I'll just straighten things out for you, good as I can, and then *psst!* like air from a tire."

"Hah," Hodge said.

Freeman came alert. He hurriedly put on the hat and glasses and bent his nose close to the windshield and sniffed. Then he turned to Hodge and smiled, pointing slyly. Hodge saw it too now, Clumly and another policeman coming out of a store, Clumly writing on a pad, looking grim and as crafty as the devil. "That's him?" Freeman said.

Hodge nodded.

"Hole up," Freeman said, "I'll see what's on."

Hodge had hardly slowed down before Freeman was out, sneaking along the line of parked cars, darting, clownish, from bumper to bumper, impossible not to notice, until he was opposite the store from which Clumly and the other policeman had just emerged. They went into the next store, The Palace of Sweets. Freeman darted in behind them, and a moment later darted out again and came ostentatiously sneaking, smiling joyfully, back to Hodge. "They're investigating," he whispered. (There was no reason he should whisper.)

"What?" Hodge said, It was queerly pleasurable, this stalking, and this lunatic was, for mysterious reasons, good company, at least for the moment.

"Investigating," he said again. "They're showing pictures of the Sunlight Man and asking the storekeepers if they know him."

"Are they?"

He nodded, then seemed unsure, then, decisively, nodded again.

"How the devil you find out?"

Freeman looked sly. "My smiling eyes and ears," he said. He studied Hodge thoughtfully. "Pull your shoulders back," he said. "Pull your stomach in."

"Do what?" Hodge said.

"That's better. Good."

It took Chief Clumly and the other man nearly all morning to go the length of Main Street, showing the picture and asking their questions. Hodge parked and waited while they made each block, then drove on and parked in the next block, if he could find a space, or in the block beyond if he couldn't. From time to time Freeman jumped out and ran to listen to make sure they were doing it the same way, then came back and reported. Otherwise they sat and talked.

Freeman said, "Well yeah, ok. I guess it is a little funny, when you stop to think about it—spying on the cops, things like that. But you know how it is. Lots of things are funny. Like being a dentist. Why would anybody be a dentist?"

"Nevertheless," Hodge said, "dentists are useful. If there were no dentists—"

"Right!" said Freeman. "That makes sense! Right!"

Hodge studied him.

"Also beauticians are useful."

Hodge nodded.

"And morticians. And opticians."

Hodge considered.

"And statisticians. Dieticians. And *pat*ricians."

"*Pat*ricians?" Hodge said.

"You a Communist?"

Hodge was still dubious, however. He glanced at his watch.

"In any case," Freeman said, "not everything is useful. Some things are, admittedly. Such as pigs' snouts and scuttles of coal and scaples and strings and salad forks. And some things are useful for their relaxative value, such as roller-coasters and Rolaids and ribticklers—"

"And target pistols," Hodge said tentatively.

Freeman shook his head. "It has to start with *r,*" he said.
Hodge considered.

Freeman said, "Other things are aesthetically useful, appealing to the beauty-loving faculties of man, such as pictures and
prints and poetry and pot-boilers and policeman-watching and
playing the harmonicum."

"Policeman-watching?"

"The aesthetic response is in large part a response to order as
moral affirmation," Freeman said.

"Hmm," Hodge said. After he'd thought about it he said,
again, "Hmm."

By lunchtime Clumly and the other policeman had made it
to the Miss Batavia Diner, at the east end of town. They went
in to eat, and Freeman slipped in behind them and listened to
their talk. When he came back he said, "That Clumly's insane,
you know that?" Then, after a moment: "Ah well. Why not?
eh?" He smiled.

Clumly went to Clive Paxton's funeral that afternoon. Will
Hodge mingled with the cemetery crowd, talking quietly, extending his sympathies, visiting, while Freeman hid behind a
tree and kept a close watch—from under the wide black brim
of his hat—on Clumly. Ben and Vanessa were there, of
course.

"Will!" Ben said. He put his hand on his arm. "Good to see
you, boy."

Vanessa was weeping. "Beautiful funeral," she said.

Will Hodge, bending forward, hung onto his suspenders and
nodded.

She was holding to her husband's upper arm with both
hands, leaning her heavy face against his elbow. Her eyes widened and she said, "What an awful thing, last night! We've
been trying to get you on the phone all morning, but you
weren't at your office. No surprise! Poor woman! Cold blood!
When I think, we had him right under our roof—"

"Now Vanessa," Ben said.

"Oh I know," she said, "innocent until proven glit—" She
gave a little kick. "Ploop!" she said.

"Sh!" Ben said. The minister was praying. All the rest of the
cemetery was hushed and solemn, the wide-boled trees dignified and calm (but behind one of them Freeman crouched)
and the light came down through the trees in yellow stripes.
The Paxtons were a tableau beside the grave, the old woman

in her wheelchair, the sons calm as trees behind her. Clumly stood a little to their right, holding his handkerchief over his nose, blowing with hardly a sound. The Professor stood to the left of the wheelchair, shrunken head bowed, just perceptibly shaking with palsy. Between his huge white hands he had a leaf he was secretly tearing to tiny shreds.

When the prayer was over the people stirred, and some of them went closer to the grave, so that Will could not see any more.

"It was a terrible thing," Will said. He told them how it had been, suddenly seeing her dead body sitting by the wall. "Then Clumly and his men came," he said and winced. "Clumly insisted it was hooligans. He's out of his mind."

Ben was looking at the limbs of the trees. "Well," he said, "someone tried to set Salways' on fire last night. Clarence Pieman saw them—he was patrolling the alley. They'd put some papers up against the wall and lit them. They got away, because Clarence had to put out the fire, and by the time he'd finished they were gone like last year's weeds. Been a lot of that lately. You never know."

"Well in *this* case you know," Will Hodge said. "They shot her with a gun wrapped up in a blanket—the blanket off my bed. Hooligans don't do it that way, if they shoot at all. This was somebody knew what he was doing."

"Blanket!" Vanessa said. "Not Grandma's quilt!"

"No, another one," he said. "One Millie left."

She put her hand to her heart in relief.

"Strange things happening in the world," Ben said. "That boy on the tower in Texas, shooting people for no rhyme or reason. Fellow that killed those nurses in Chicago. Nazis in Chicago carrying signs against the Negroes. It all—" He mused. "It makes you wonder."

An old woman popped her head out beside him. "The Fifteen Signs," she said.

Ben nodded and touched his hatbrim politely.

"It's going to be an early winter," Vanessa said. She sighed.

"Who was that?" Will said.

"Her?" Ben looked where the old woman had been a moment ago. She'd gone away into the crowd now. He shrugged.

"The Fifteen Signs," Will said. It sounded ominous to him.

"Bill Hyde says there's somebody in Oakfield saw an alligator," Vanessa said.

"Wal now," Ben said kindly, patting her hand, "Bill Hyde says a lot of things."

She closed her eyes. "Poor Mrs. Palazzo," she said.

They nodded. Elizabeth Paxton was coming toward them in her wheelchair, her sons and Professor Combs and Chief Clumly a little behind her. Clumly looked up, alarmed. "Afternoon, Will."

"Hah!" Will said. He reached out to shake Clumly's hand.

Behind Clumly, walking with his eyes rolled up and his hands pressed together like those of one praying, came Freeman. He gave them a solemn wink.

"Who was that?" Vanessa said.

Will Hodge blushed. "Who was who?" he said.

"Friend of the family, likely," Ben said. He studied the ground and mused.

## 3

Will Hodge sat alone in his car, a block from the police station. Freeman had set off for Critic's to get them some supper. They'd be able to drop their vigil soon. The light was still on in Clumly's office, but any time now, unless he had still more lunacy plotted, he'd be going home to bed. If Freeman had his way, they'd have dropped the vigil already. He'd sat staring at the dashboard, shaking his head—refusing to look out at where Clumly crouched in the bushes like a toad, beneath Mayor Mullen's window and he'd said, "I dunno," and scratched his ear. "If *I* was in charge we'd cut out. Man starts falling apart, like, it seems to me you should let him do it in private. You got no pity?" But Hodge had said, "Do what you like," set his jaw. "You're free to go when you choose." Freeman had stayed, shaking his head. Hodge thought: *No pity!* A lifetime of pity was what he'd had, pity like a rope around his neck, and all of them tugging it—Will Jr, Millie, Ben, Luke. . . . *What would you know, a mere child, about pity?* It was dark now. Main Street was stinging with neon. There was a crowd in front of the Dipson Theater, the late show about to start. *The Russians Are Coming!* The traffic light over the middle of the street a little ahead of where Will Hodge was parked went mindlessly from red to green again and again, and in his memory of its changes time became as palpable as the shiny-topped cars passing under it or the dark upper stories of the buildings on each side of the street. On the sidewalk to the right of his parked car people walked past saying words to one another that Hodge couldn't catch. Their heels clicked sharply for a time in the darkness and then grew faint, drawing away toward the cheerfully lighted firehouse with its dark red trucks, where there were firemen sitting on the sidewalk in front, on wooden folding chairs. Chief Uphill was there, standing with his hands folded in back of him, chin thrust forward, gazing toward the police station. Beyond him a tractor-trailer came onto Main Street, off the Walnut Street Bridge, brakes whooshing, motor growling at the stoplight like a tiger. On the door Hodge saw a white word he recognized without being near enough to read it: PAXTON.

No pity. He who had watched their world falling board by board, who had patched toggled wheedled bullied wept in secret, cursed, had paid through the nose and gotten nothing. No pity.

He was a man who had understood too much, if anything, though not in Millie's way or for that matter his father's: not in words not in myths but by common sense and by that eldest-brother love and justice that ran in his veins instead of blood. He deserved nothing as far as he could know, and therefore he could not fight for his rights. They too deserved nothing, as far as he could know, but he loved them and so he must fight for them, raise them up when they fell, eternally forgive. Had gone to Paxton full of wrath knowing Paxton no more in the wrong than Taggert but undaunted by that because Taggert was his brother, and not even Millie's predictable conviction that she'd forced him to go there could keep him from it (she'd be wrong, clear as it might seem to her; her scorn at his failure to go earlier had not driven him to it but had merely made it occur to him for the first time that he could go) and had stood in old Paxton's office like a boulder, jaw slung forward, thumbs in his suspenders. "I'm bringing suit against you, Mr. Paxton," he said. Clive Paxton, seated at his desk, still clean and efficient as an axe at sixty-one, showed only the faintest trace of irritation. The window to his right was bright with the snow's reflection. He did not bother to ask what Hodge was suing him for. "You'll have to talk to my lawyer."

Hodge nodded. "I will. I also plan to ask for an injunction to keep your trucks off State Street Road after five p.m."

Paxton's white eyebrows lowered slightly. "You'll never get it."

Again Hodge nodded. "Maybe, but you'll have to fight. And one thing more. I'm suing your wife for libel, and that one I'll win for sure." Elizabeth Paxton had told a woman named Briggs that all the Hodges were crazy, something congenital, and the Briggs woman had told half the people in the Presbyterian church. "I'll have you tied up in the courts for the rest of your life," Hodge said. He waited.

Paxton leaned back in his chair slowly and turned his head a little to look out the window (a view of big quonset huts, red and white gas pumps, a stack of old tires half-hidden in snow, flatbed trucks, big tractor-trailers, dirty green oil drums with snow mounded on the tops) and even now he showed no anger except that he was pale. It was sign enough. Will Hodge knew where he stood. He grew calm and ready as a switchblade fighter (or so he imagined in his overconfidence). He'd say this for Millie: live with that woman for five, ten years and you could take on God Himself.

But Paxton knew that he was ready (whatever else—private sorrows, weariness, righteous indignation—might be stirring behind that iron mask), and at last he said, "What are you after, Hodge?" "Nothing but justice," he said, and forced a rueful grin. "You trying to make me look like an extortionist?"

"All right all right," he said. And now his anger rang clearly in his voice. He was tighter than new-stretched fence.

"It's no joke," Hodge said. "My complaints are legitimate; they'll stand up in court. You'll see. That's all I came to say." He turned then, abruptly, as if to leave.

Without hurry, Paxton stood up. "But you'll settle out of court." Not a question, a statement. The old man understood the game. He'd played it all his life, both fair and foul. If he was lucky he might get away without paying Will Hodge a red cent—and old Paxton would rather pay blood than money: his mediocre fortune was his love and his chilly god—but win or lose he would pay through the nose for the battle. He could afford it all right—and Hodge could too, as his own lawyer.

Paxton could choose to fight, if he wanted, for righteousness'
sake. But when he'd won he'd have new fights to face, for Law
is never spent, and when a man has decided to tie up your life
in court contention he will kill you in the end, though he may
perhaps kill himself as well. If the man means business,
enough to devote a lifetime to it, you have only three choices:
to settle, to murder, or to commit yourself to a tedious and un-
endable war of attrition. Paxton would not murder, though
possibly he might have once, in the days when he was hiring
scabs or trucking black-market hogs; and despite his anger at
all Hodge's house, he would not commit his old age to futile
war, not even for righteousness' sake. His predictable move
was to try for the least painful settlement he could get.

"Only if the terms are fair," Hodge said.

Paxton bent his head, looking at the desktop, touching it
lightly with the tips of two fingers. Without looking up, still
thinking, he said, "I ought to fight you."

Hodge said nothing. He understood, but he wasn't budging.
If Hodge gave an inch, the old man would no doubt boast of it
later, would believe like Millie that he'd won by craft what
had fallen to him as a gift. Face reddening to flame, Paxton
opened the desk drawer—for an instant Hodge had the ludicrous fear that like one of those villains on television he was
reaching for a gun—and took his checkbook from it. Then he
slid the drawer shut and sat down again. The redness of his
face faded. He looked up. He seemed totally emotionless now.
"How much?"

Hodge bent his head and looked up-from-under at him
through his shaggy eyebrows. He slid his jaw out. "Write it to
Taggert Hodge," he said.

The old man blanched. Hodge had expected something like
that, had more or less expected the jerk of the lips, too, and
the closing of the checkbook. "My lawyer will be in touch
with you," Paxton said.

Hodge nodded. "Fine."

But as once more he turned to leave, the old man said,
"What's your game, Hodge? You knew I wouldn't do that."
Eyes mere slits.

Hodge pursed his lips. At last, slowly, as if thoughtfully,
watching his stubby, cuffed shoes as he moved, he crossed to
Paxton's desk. The old man waited, and though he seemed in
command as usual, Hodge could sense that all his power was

drained from him now, because for once in his life he couldn't tell which battlements to defend. That was what Hodge was counting on, though now he was already suspecting he'd made a mistake. But Paxton's hands were liver-spotted, his mouth pale. Wolf without teeth. It could work, he thought, and doubted it. He put his hands in his suitcoat pockets and balled them to fists. He said, "You control grown sons like babies. They haven't got a dime of their own."

"That's my business," Paxton said, baffled. He wasn't confident of it. You could see the wheels spinning in his head.

Hodge met his red-veined eyes as still as dust and pressed quickly. "Set them up in something. Put them on their feet."

"You know I can't do that. What in hell are you talking about?"

"Why can't you?"

Paxton hung fire. "My sons hired you?"

It was a question he'd forgotten to expect. He said again, "Why can't you?"

After a moment, quietly, the old man said, "Because they're sick, irresponsible, and dumb."

Hodge nodded, panicky. "I'll see you in court." The phrase, totally unplanned, pleased him and gave him a feeling of hope.

But Paxton shook his head. "Wait up." He took a deep breath and then another, the deep breaths of a man very sick himself. "What have they promised you?" he asked.

"Nothing." It was the truth, strictly speaking, but he was on bad ground. The sons had said they couldn't help Taggert with Kathleen's treatment, because the old man held the purse-strings. He'd thought at the time, *They're weaklings. They'd do it if we found the right pressure.*

Still the old eyes searched him, cunning and baffled and something else too; after an instant Hodge caught what it was: wounded.

"Little fools," he said. "Going to you of all people! I never would have believed they had the guts."

"But you'll take the deal," Hodge said. He had lost.

Paxton shook his head, but it didn't mean no; not yet. "They're fools," he said. There was pity in it as well as disgust. Then, icily: "You should have advised your clients they'll be disinherited. You warned them?"

Hodge had gone too far—the old man would talk to his sons and the whole shabby trick would be out. "My clients?"

he said, clumsily. "Your sons are no clients of mine. You jump to conclusions."

Paxton's rage flared up and died away again in an instant. A semi came rumbling past the window, and whatever it was that the old man said to himself Hodge missed. The phone rang on the desk. Paxton ignored it. He closed his eyes for a moment, frowning, and breathed deeply again. "I see," he said at last, and Hodge knew it was true. Assuming all motives in the world were hate and selfishness, Paxton had guessed right again. "You think you can get them to support their sister." He did not bother to look up for confirmation. He was himself again, firm and full of lightning. "You miscalculate. They'll be bankrupt inside six months." He remembered the checkbook. As if in terrible weariness or worse, he opened the desk drawer with his right hand and with his left slid the checkbook over and let it fall in. He got up and went to the window to look without interest at his truckbarns. "You all think I'm wrong," he said. "All of you. Even her." Hodge couldn't tell if he meant Kathleen or his wife.

The old man's office was cold. Hodge lowered his chin to his chest and waited for it to be over.

But then something happened, inside Paxton's mind. Hodge would never know what, though he had his guesses. Without turning from the window, Paxton said, "All right." A silence, and then, after another moment, "You win." He took another deep breath. He would say no more.

Hodge withdrew. He had succeeded, he had not won. But he'd gone there, at least he'd done that.

It was in April, two months later, that Paxton went into the hospital with the first of his heart attacks. Hodge understood.

Now he frowned. Stores were closing, the lights of the city dying out. It came to him that in his moon-gathering—his self-pity, to name its name—he had failed to register the arrival of the square dark red Hudson, shiny as wine, which he recognized instantly, now that he noticed it, as Judge Sam White's old car. It was parked in front of the police station, empty. He'd gone in, then; no doubt to talk to Clumly. It was not usual for the Judge to come out in the world except for brief midday visits to his office. Uphill was gone from in front of the firehouse, and so had most of the men who'd been sitting there. Hodge tipped his head, musing, then opened his door quietly and got out. Hands in pockets, he walked in the direction of the firehouse until he had a clear view of Clumly's office through the window. He couldn't see the Judge, but Clumly was there all right, standing in the middle of the room, nodding to someone and looking at a paper in his hands.

Behind Hodge, someone said, "Funny things going on over there." A high thin country voice.

He turned. It was one of the firemen, a young man with milky white hair and thick glasses. Hodge nodded, trying to make out the fireman's features. He gave the fireman no answer, and the silence grew.

"Winter's coming," the young man said at last. "They'll be hoarfrost soon. You wouldn't believe it, a hot night like this, but it's coming. First hoarfrost. After that—ice."

"It's hot all right," Hodge said. "Not a breath stirring."

Clumly was still there, nodding at the paper in his hands.

"The horses have long coats," the fireman said. "Happened early last year, too. Storms coming, bad ones. We'll be fighting fire and they'll be ice on our boots. I don't like it."

Hodge looked at him. Still he could make out no features, only the whiteness of the young man's face and hair against the darkness of the firehouse wall. The glasses glittered with pinpoints of light. At last Hodge grunted as a sign of agreement and moved away toward his car.

"You believe in omens?" the man called after him.

Hodge sucked his upper lip under his lower and was silent.

Ten minutes later, Hodge seated in his car again, the Judge came out, walking slowly, as if not from age and drunkenness but by laborious choice, and climbed tortuously into his car and ground on the starter, with the key off perhaps, and at last got the motor going. Oil fumes billowed up. The square car started very smoothly and inched down the street, solemn and oblivious, like an old Phaeton carriage from another time and place, unhurried, dire of purpose.

Then Clumly's office light went off, and the same instant—not by coincidence, Hodge had a feeling—the bearded Freeman appeared beside the Plymouth, opening the door.

"You brought food?" Hodge said—though even now, after all this time, he wasn't hungry.

"I forgot," Freeman said lightly and shrugged like a minstrel-show Negro. He was watching the police station.

Clumly came down the steps, glancing left and right. He

came hurrying, bent forward at the waist, but he did not go around the side to the garage but continued walking, out to the Main Street sidewalk and then to the left, toward the center of town. It must be after eleven by now. Hodge watched him hurrying along, bent and suspicious, and not until he was nearly out of sight—beyond the darkened theater marquee, and beyond the blue light that fell across the sidewalk from the clock in Brenner's Jewelry Store window—did Hodge start up his car. He pulled over again and switched off the headlights in front of Fargo's Dairy Bar, dark except for the night-light. Clumly hurried on, his head down, his mind far, far away. Hodge started up the car again, then realized that the old man was turning toward the Presbyterian church. He switched off the ignition.

"We'll walk it from here," he said.

Sadly, Freeman shook his head.

"You can stay, you understand," Hodge said.

"I'll come," the young man said. "Shoot."

They started out. When they reached the corner Clumly was standing on the church steps, smoking his cigar. Hodge stepped back out of sight, drawing Freeman with him. Again, sadly, Freeman shook his head. When Hodge peeked around the corner, Clumly had vanished.

"He went in," Freeman said.

"How you know?"

Freeman shrugged, infinitely sad.

Hodge nodded grimly and murmured, "Let's go."

And so they sat in the muggy darkness, peeking down out of the balcony, squinting unbelieving as spectators at a witches' dance. Will Hodge sucked deep for air, as Paxton had done fifteen years ago and, like Paxton, could not get it. "They're both stark raving mad," he whispered. The boy's face was frozen to a wince. Again Hodge sucked for air, but he was drowning. The church walls rang with Taggert's voice as they would to a tolling of bells. Hodge had been grief-stricken enough at sight of the police photograph, but that had been, all the same, abstract. He had not recalled until this moment, his brother's rich voice ringing sweetly and terribly in the darkness of the church, the unbearable pain of love. So, once, like Paxton, he had sucked for air in his bedroom, in the darkness, looking out on the brightly moonlit lawn where under the walnut trees Millie stood naked and beautiful and the boy he had hired three weeks ago, Raymond, stood six feet away from her, naked, erected, advancing slowly, like a dancer (a boy he too had known from the start to be gentle and wise in a boy's way, graceful, not eager to cause him pain: whom Hodge had for three weeks watched her seducing, gently, gently, or he'd watched the boy seducing her—for who could say where the blame belonged, since each of them was playing the game by rules not clearly understood, playing it toward an outcome neither of them anticipated except in secret, an end they no doubt imagined would never come, not in life, could come only in books: so that only he, Will Hodge, had known the whole deadly process with certainty, by the knotting of his belly, and he'd done nothing, hadn't known what to do—had barked "Millie!" once when she overleaped all the bounds of decorum (but overleaped only in play of course, play)—and had once said, "Millie, stop teasing that boy," but she'd said, "Why not? Good God, I'm old enough to be his mother!" which wasn't true, strictly, and he'd said so and had been made a fool of, as usual, because she was wrong by only—"Bald-headed Jesus!" she said—"three years!"—had had no choice but to do nothing because if he tried the only thing possible, an appeal to tradition, common decency, shame, it would make him appear just the stodgy fool he was: it was only *play*). When Raymond went to the movies after work—set off with some pretty, harmless girl from some neighbor's farm—Millie would say lightly, "Give us a hug good-bye, Ray," and laughing, playing, he would hug her, then he would come over blushing and would soberly, fondly, grip Will Hodge's hand. Hodge stood at the window, his stomach gone lead, his chest so light he felt he was falling endlessly, and he knew himself helpless and moreover guilty and foul. He could shoot them, he thought ruefully, and he would have smiled if it weren't for the pain at his heart. And wondered if there were really men so stupid and vicious as to shoot their unfaithful wives and their wives' lovers. He understood that he hated them both fiercely, and fiercely loved them. He was overcome with sobbing. They clung to each other—Hodge stood watching the blurred white image—and then, gently, gently, went down on the grass.

He said nothing, afterward. She grew more loving and tender than before and he thought that it had been good for her, his own puritanical ideas were wrong and pernicious. Sometimes, after that, she would go walking with Raymond, or would ride into town with Raymond when he went for feed. Hodge walked gingerly, whenever they were gone, and was sick with jealousy and grief, and watched the clock. At supper Millie and Raymond would joke, their quick wits leaping, their eyes bright as stars, and Hodge would feel dizzy with love and joy that would fall away later like a stone down a well when he awakened in the middle of the night and found her gone. When he heard them talking in the kitchen he would creep up on them, heart hammering, convinced that they were doing it again. They never were. When he questioned her, as cautiously as possible, she was evasive, sometimes smiled. He had done nothing, could find no purpose, no justification except his pain, which perhaps was self-pity. He would close his fists on the pillow, full of tears.

Taggert seemed to explode. Something darted backwards. There was red light and smoke and then nothing, only poor old Clumly staggering to his feet and groping forward toward where the flash had been, Freeman leaning, far far forward, trying to make out where Taggert had gone; but he'd vanished. Clumly was at the pulpit now, moaning his outrage.

"Jesus," Freeman said. "What do we do?"

"I don't know," Hodge said. It was not sufficient, he understood. It was what he'd been saying all his life—what he'd said when Taggert was first beginning to dip into the till, what he'd said with Millie, with Luke, with Will Jr, with Ben, with Mary Lou's husband. One had to act, for better or worse, act. But act against whom? A pitiful policeman gone crazy? His own mad brother? "We'll keep watching," he said. Conviction flared up. "We'll follow him." Taggert would leave soon, yes; flee to some retreat. When he was gone, out of danger, they would go to the police, reveal the whole thing, put Clumly away where he belonged and bring Taggert back when the men at the police station were calmer, less likely to shoot and ask questions later.

Like an old Egyptian priest, Clumly came slowly down the aisle toward them, carrying a black box. Hodge ducked down and drew Freeman after him.

"That's it," Hodge said, knowing he was dangerously wrong, as usual, "we'll keep an eye on him." They heard the door open, below, then close. Hodge stood up. Freeman, almost invisible in his black hat and coat, went on sitting. "Are you coming?" Hodge whispered.

After a time Freeman said, "No. I'll stay."

"Why?" Hodge whispered. He realized that they were alone and said it aloud. "Why?"

Above the pulpit hung a cloud of dead gray smoke. The pale light of streetlamps shining through the stained-glass windows along the side wall threw shadows over the room. Nothing stirred. It was as if time had ended, and the world were not motion after all but an engine broken down.

"Don't you believe in omens?" Freeman said.

"You were listening," Hodge said. "You were watching when I talked to that fireman."

"Yeah," the boy whispered. "And I *do* believe in omens."

Will Hodge inhaled. The night was hot. *The sky god was misanthropic,* his brother had said, *and the underworld god was totally indifferent to man.*

He saw their two white bodies in the moonlight, slowly dancing, reaching toward each other as if in sorrow. "Omens," he said. His voice broke. Suddenly, boldly, seizing the word with all his force, he said: "Bosh!"

Then, trembling, Hodge left the church.

# XIV

## The Wilderness

*And Misery's increase
Is Mercy, Pity, Peace.*
—William Blake

### 1

3 p.m. Louise Hodge stands at the window in her husband's study, once the sunporch, looking out, unseeing, at the street. Danny is asleep upstairs. Madeline still at school. Louise holds the Pride in one hand, the dust-paper in the other. It is useless to try to clean up in here—folders, files, manilla envelopes everywhere, even the papers on the floor sacrosanct, the wastebaskets not to be dumped except by Will himself. Yet she comes, from time to time, full of high resolve, partly because standing here in Will's cluttered study (the old pipes he has not smoked in years clumsily lined up in the crudely homemade piperack which stands on the windowsill, pipe-cleaners sticking out from the pipestems) she can sometimes feel her life is not, after all, completely senseless.

He'll drive himself crazy, she thinks. He works night and

day and hates it, or anyway no longer has any faith that the work he does makes sense, yet likes nothing else either—except singing in the choir, which he no longer has time for, or playing the cello, except that the longer he goes without playing the more frustrated he is when he gets to it again. Once we used to go to movies; not now.

She shares his indifference. Every time they go there's some tiresome picture about sex—the hilarious adventures (as the posters say) of some girl who bats her eyelashes or some would-be gallant who cannot erect, or some fool who has too many fiancées (each and all indescribably dull)—or they go to some art film, some profound and daring psychological analysis (the posters claim) of a nymphomaniac or frigid woman or a rapist or molester of children. Is there nothing else left to talk about? What is worse, one cannot even admit to one's boredom. The parties—the few they go to—are worse than the movies.

"What's the matter with them all?" Louise Hodge asks the street. Their party friends, she means. It was better at home, in her childhood, when all people talked about was neighbors or accidents or the shortest route to Cincinnati, or they quoted long conversations that had no point, or told of their kidney stones.

But she knows well enough what the trouble is. They don't know the same people, living, as they do, in twenty different suburbs—all identical but having nothing in common, nothing human anyway: not Mrs. Wartz, ninety-two, who just fell down the cellar stairs, or Charley Parish who married that girl from Rome, Italy, and her not half-grown. They could talk, if they talked of such things at all, only in wearisome abstractions, not of neighbors but of what neighbors in general are like—the coffee klatches, the crabgrass business, the children in the yard. Not of particular places but of the abstract idea of a shopping center, and then sometimes a spurt of excitement when you mention some huge, dull store where everybody's been. And to complicate matters, one is—their circle is—polite. Too much comparison of neighbors or shopping centers can turn into rivalry. Undemocratic. What the women want to talk about the men find disgusting; what the men would say bores the women to tears; and for the men to leave the women would be unchivalrous. Or worse, would reveal that what all conversation turns on, sex, is fit only for the dark.

We were going to visit India, she thinks. Why India she has no idea. Neither does Will, probably. But for some reason they talked about it, and she can recall the excitement it stirred in them once—how long ago now?—eight years?

She thinks: What *would* the men talk about, if they talked? But she knows. Law.

Nevertheless, he devotes himself to it as though it were much the most interesting thing in the world. He scoffs at it at the dinner table, talks pipe-dreams of going into teaching, dropping the rat-race, yet after dessert goes into his study (on the days he comes home for supper) and opens fat books and fills one long yellow tablet after another, and won't go to bed. We two have no more to talk about than the people at our parties, she thinks.

Abruptly, with a stubborn, determined look, she crosses to his desk and picks up the sheaf of papers on top of the pile, in the middle of the mess. She reads. After a minute she sits down, alarmed, concentrating.

MEMORANDUM TO TAX DEPARTMENT    Sept. 2, 1966
RE: WILLIAM B. HODGE, JR., IRS Claim for Penalty Tax
   (re. Flemming)
   The following is a summary of my activities with respect to Flemming Construction, Inc. Everything is included which seemed at all relevant to the question of the capacity in which I acted with respect to the company from time to time. In connection with the preparation of this memorandum, I have read all of the files (our closed files 31471 through 31477), the minute book of the corporation and the time slips. References to the particular documents in the files are made as "[1-101]", referring to the closed file involved and the number of the document in the file as set forth on a list I have prepared. References to information in the minute book are indicated as "[MB-date]" and to time slips as "[TS-date]".

For convenience, this memorandum is divided into the following parts:
   I The period expiring 12/31/63
   II The period January 1, 1964 through September 21, 1964
   III September 30, 1964 to date
   IV Summary

*Par.* 1 *Date* 5/2/61 Certificate of Incorporation filed. Standard By-Laws subsequently adopted [MB with Article IV, Section 5, specifying duty of Secretary and Assistant Secretary]:

PART I—The period expiring December 31, 1963

> "The Secretary shall issue notices of all members of stock-
> holders and directors where notices of such meetings are re-
> quired by law or these By-Laws. He shall attend all meetings
> of stock-holders and of the Board of Directors and keep the
> minutes thereof. He shall affix the corporate seal to and sign
> his signature and shall perform such other duties as usually
> pertain to his office or as are properly required of him by the
> board of directors."

*Empty language, insanity,* she thinks, but she reads on. There
are twenty-one pages, typed, single-spaced, and she knows—
though she doesn't know what it's for—he's spent months on
it. He has a keen mind she knows for sure, because sometimes
Will has turned it against her; nevertheless, the idea continues
to molest her thought, destroying her concentration: *It's all
empty, insane.*

> 57 9/30/64 At about 5:00, Finsker asked me to come with
> him so we could talk a moment. We went to Mr. Evans'
> office. Finsker advised me that he did not believe that
> Caulke could carry out the agreement he was making with
> Sand because of the severe financial position of the com-
> pany and advised me then, for the first time, that the com-
> pany had not paid its Federal taxes for a month. He said
> the balance was about $30,000. I advised him, strongly, of
> the consequences of this and asked him to say nothing un-
> til we could talk to Caulke later. We rejoined Caulke as
> the meeting at Porter's office was breaking up and went to
> supper with him at the Hotel Buffalo. I advised them then
> of the situation as I understood it and the possible civil
> and criminal consequences. I said that from this point on,
> no money remaining in the company could be paid for
> any purpose other than taxes and that they would have
> to issue a check for the balance available payable to
> IRS. . . .

After this, pages of unpaid bills, increasingly desperate at-
tempts to keep Flemming Construction afloat, then this:
"Flemming,"

> In correspondence, I did not always carefully speak in the
> third person (referring to "our client", etc.), but sometimes
> merely used the collective "we"—with respect to Flemming.
> See, e.g., letter to Milfort 5/17/65, p. 3. Worse yet is an oc-

casional use of the first person singular in such a way as to suggest that I might have control. E.g., ltr to Milfort, 12/17/64. Fact is, however, that FCI had already decided to sign anything Louie wanted it to, so that when I said I would see that everything was done just so, I was trying to prod Louie merely to say what he wanted. I doubt that the pronouns should create any substantial problem.

Like the cluttered room, the immense mass of facts—"items" —in Will's attempt to defend himself (that much she understands clearly) drains her of strength.

Underneath the sheaf of papers, a letter.

> Dear Mr. Hart:
>
> My client informs me that your check #651 dated September 1, 1966 in the amount of $151.13 has again been returned by your bank because of insufficient funds.
>
> Frankly, Mr. Hart, my client is getting rather fed-up in the way you are handling your account.
>
> I therefore notify you in my client's behalf that he demands the balance of $1526.42 by return mail in the enclosed envelope.
>
> M&T does not wish to carry your account any farther, nor have any further business dealings with you.
>
> Sincerely yours,
>
> [signed]: W. Hodge
> Attorney-at-Law

Carefully, she replaces the papers, then rests her forehead on her fists. She feels momentarily nauseous, involved in what she has called the insanity of it all, and terrified by pronouns. Outside the study window, she knows without looking, the afternoon is unnaturally bright, teeming with grass and leaves and the infinite webwork of bark on trees, and the air is full of noise: children, an air-hammer six blocks away, the whisper of creatures in motion, destroying and building, crawling through the grass.

## 2

Will Hodge Jr's trip to Chicago was a total waste: Kleppmann's man was just ahead of him, as usual, and had liquidated his stocks that very morning. It gave Will the feeling (standing at the file in the oppressive Chicago First National office, reviewing the figures a fourth time, as though repetition might change the result) that everyone around him was in on the deal. They looked as if they might be. The man called Fleet, with the reddish-purple face and eyes starting out of his head like eyes on a drowned man, or one with bubonic plague, his collar too tight but elegant, silk, his tie silk too, on his fat red fingers an enormous set of rings (And what kind of wife do *you* go home to, Fleet?), fat legs filling the ridiculous pin-stripe funeral-parlor trousers; the other called Ottla, Attila to Will, huge, solemn man with a red moustache, slightly luminous, like a child's hair on a summer day, his spectacles low and loose on his nose, and behind them, glazed gray eyes like a lunatic's. "No luck?" he asked softly. He could bellow like a bull if he wanted to, but he spoke as though the deep-blue carpeted room were the public library. Will shook his head. "Ah," said Attila, "those people!" He bent forward slightly, ominous. Turned away.

He could get a plane out at ten-forty, be back in Buffalo a little after midnight, or he could wait for the one at seven or so in the morning. He lowered his eyebrows and swung his jaw out, trying to decide, still gazing at the figures as if expecting from them some sign. His return was urgent: he must reach some decision. If they knew who their so-called Sunlight Man was, their attitude might be substantially changed. That was possible. Moreover, as long as he kept what he knew to himself, there was the danger of his father's getting foolishly involved. Not a practical man, he was easily confused or put off by his bungling feelings. But one could phone them, of course. Why not? Not Clumly, no. But one might get hold of the other one, Officer Miller.

Will scowled. It made sense, yet something he could not put his finger on made him resist.

Buz Marchant was here in Chicago, old Wooster friend. It was a long time since Will had seen him, and for certain reasons . . . This wasn't the first time he'd thought of Buz. All day the idea of calling him when he reached Chicago had been nagging at the back of his mind. What harm? But he knew what harm and toyed with it in the back of his mind and hung now undecided, closing the folder deliberately, as if with satisfaction. "I wonder," he said, "do you mind if I use your phone?"

He could not make up his mind to phone Batavia. He would think about it. He phoned his friend Buz.

In the taxi, afterward, he sat with his fingers interlocked, dark suitcoat open, sucking at the pipe he'd for some reason bought at the airport this morning (it was bitter as alum: he'd never yet had a pipe that wasn't, and the taste made his stomach knot tighter than usual—when he'd searched his pockets, a minute ago, he'd found he had only a half-roll of Tums remaining: have to stop at a drugstore, he'd thought, but despite the rage of his stomach he'd forgotten it already), a BBB, one of the best pipes made in England, according to the man at the counter, the band sterling silver, a steal—pure highway robbery—at fourteen dollars. Nevertheless, he felt like an attorney, sitting with that pipe in his mouth. So, long ago, thus subtly disguised, he had felt like an attorney. It came to him that his Uncle Tag had had a pipe. It was never out of his mouth. An oral fixation, possibly? Was that the secret? Deprived too early of sweet mother-love, snatched too quickly from her soft breast (it was hard to imagine: she was old when Will knew her) and hurled into the old man's grand, unalive, uncommunicating study? But that was not his uncle's life, he knew, it was his own, and the breast, though he couldn't remember it, was probably not soft. Nor was anything ever snatched rudely from that tit. For her sake, too, it came to him, he must get his call through to Miller. God knew what his mother might get in her head when she learned it was dear old Tag. For a moment he closed his eyes.

He seemed to think nothing whatever now, looking out the window, experiencing an indifferent, vaguely disturbing wash of half-ideas and sensations. He could not shake his feeling that the cab was being followed. They were driving under the elevated railroad, a long tunnel of darkness with startling daylight on either side, clear as welding light by contrast, as if it were no mere Chicago day but a day in San Diego or Hawaii. Every second or so they sped through slits of light from above. A train went over, shaking the earth, pushing its roar of sound along ahead of it, machine-gunning storefronts to the right with its hurrying shadow. Through gaps in the wall of buildings he saw tall buildings beyond, gray, brown, red, black; majestic. That was where he'd live, if he had his way: the heart of the honeycomb. His windows would look out on windowed towers, and the sunlight would not touch him except at

noon. He would never hear his neighbors' names, would have
friends as secret and private as himself, would have nothing to
say to the garbage man but " 'Morning." *That* was safety. As
hidden and free as a pigeon on a crowded roof, a bee in a
hive, a stinger in a sea of watchful stingers.

*Baldwin,* he read. He'd been meaning for years to get a new
piano for Louise. He had a fond image of her sitting stoop-
shouldered at the new piano, leaning forward to read the music and stretching her hands for the hymn-tune chords, the
only piano music she knew how to play. Now they were passing steak houses, and now, swinging out from the shadow of
the el, scruffier stores—a pet shop where moulting parrots
stood waiting for old-woman love above their dung, and squirrel monkeys, cowered, eating their fingers in the shadows. On
the sidewalk, a thickset Polish girl with heavy ankles and a
wide, square ass. He reached up to touch his pipe and pursed
his lips and thought, philosophically, of her crotch. At the
corner an old man in a faded plaid shirt stood leaning on his
newsstand, waiting. Beside him on the rack, bold headlines:
MOTHER BUTCHERS FIVE. He thought of speaking to the driver.
The hair on the back of the man's head was filthy and untrimmed, hanging almost to his collar as if to cover the white
scar shooting from his neck down his back. It flickered
through his mind that the driver was an impostor, a murderer.
He wiped sweat from his lip and studied the driver's picture. *It
was not the same man.*

He calmed himself.

It *was* the same man.

Yes.

"I was sorry to hear about the divorce," Will had said on
the phone.

Buz Marchant had laughed. "Life begins at alimony."

"Ha." It was a thing he'd forgotten, that eternal labor at joke-
making. People laughed for him, though, because the voice
was right, the cock of the eye; who cared if the joke was stupid? "I take it your heart's not broken," Will said.

"I'll tell you all about it. 'Mon out."

They were leaving the business district now. He held the
cold pipe in his hand and closed his eyes again, thinking how
good a martini would taste. He thought of Louise, who disap-
proved of martinis, and whose anger and distress when he
drank filled him with fright like the fright he'd felt when he'd

done wrong in his childhood. When he opened his eyes, much later, the taxi was gliding up a winding street with trees on each side. The houses were low and expensive and had diamond-shaped windowpanes. The driver slowed down, looking up at street numbers, then slowed more and pulled over. "That's it," he said. He nodded up at it. It was big, modern, and even from outside it had the look of an overpriced doctor's waiting room. Will got out, paid the man, and—hitching up his trousers, straightening his coat—started up the flagstone steps. Before he reached the first step of the porch itself, the porch light went on. A moment later, when he reached for the doorbell, the button lit up before he touched it, and he heard the bell ring inside. Then Buz was there, beaming. "Dr. Harold Marchant at your service," he said, and that too, his position in life, delighted Dr. Marchant. He'd gotten fatter since Will had seen him last, had grown a moustache, and had balded slightly. But he still seemed boyish—unnaturally so, now that he was in his thirties—short, pushy, a kind of bounce or dance in his step. He had a red and black paisley vest.

Will grinned, troubled, thinking of Louise.

There was folk music hooting from the stereo in the living-room. It was ungodly—such was Will Jr's opinion—a rattle of banjos and iron guitars and what might as well have been hammers banging oil drums. The singers sounded like owls. He thought of Luke.

"So come in," Buz said. "Maid!" he howled above the music, "bring our guest a—a what?"

"A martini." Blood prickled in his neck.

"A martini." He caught Will's hand and pulled him joyfully through the door. "Take the load off," he said. "Look around. Make yourself 't home." He snapped his fingers and a light went on in the corner over the red leather chair. Buz beamed again.

"Pretty clever," Will said. He should ask to use the phone.

Then the girl was there—the maid, as Buz called her—a short, dark-haired girl with a squeezed-shut face, huge bosoms, an excellent butt. She had a silky shirt, red as the furniture, and a black skirt with a slit.

"This is Caroline," Buz said. "Caroline, my old friend Will Hodge. From college."

Will nodded, taking the martini (clear and frosty-beautiful

as a glass rose), and Caroline smiled. She had a second martini for Buz and one for herself.

"Caroline works at the hospital," Buz said.

"I see."

"She helps out. Straightens up and things, now that I batch
it. All the girls have been great, just great." He beamed and
the girl smiled prettily again and, through her deep tan,
blushed. "Have an M&M?"

The bowl had passed Will before he registered. The girl
took a handful, her eyes bright, and shyly kissed the air.

"Well, well, well," Will said heartily, terrified. His blood
more than his brain remembered: So his mother had kissed
the air in the direction of her lover once, old friend of the
family, and his father had stared like a donkey at the floor. As
soon as the memory came it shot away again, like a light
glimpsed through the window of a hurtling train.

He forced a sardonic grin. If Mama Louise could only see
him now!

"Hey!" Buz said. "You got to see the bedroom!"

The girl blushed and smiled again and then, as if because
she too could find nothing to say, gave Will a wink. They were
on their way there, by this time, Buz hustling Will by the arm,
the girl following a step behind. "Let there be lights!" Buz said
grandly, and the hall light went on by itself. He threw open
the door at the end and said, "Now!" Slowly, a reddish light
came on in the bedroom. Will glanced uneasily at the girl. She
smiled, and her lashes dropped slightly on her brown, shining
eyes. The bedroom walls were of red flocked wallpaper, and
the bedspread was red and black. The bed was enormous, with
a carved head and foot, and on the ceiling there were mirrors,
round ones in the corners, full-length mirrors hung sideways
along the sides of the ceiling. Over the head of the bed hung
an obscene variation on the Buddha.

"Hmm," Will said. "Well, well."

"Like wow, eh?" He poked Will's belly with his elbow.

Will laughed, experimental. "It's got to be a joke."

"No joke," Buz said. He put his arm around Will and ush-
ered him out again, and the girl stepped back smiling, sipping
her martini, as they passed.

"Well, well, well," Will said. He was filled with a strange
annoyance, as though he had been—or someone close to him
had been—insulted. But Buz was all kindness, unmistakably

glad to see him. They came back in range of the music. "I'd say you two have quite a little pleasure palace here." He closed his hand around the pipe in his suitcoat pocket and reflected on whether or not to get it out. He thought of his uncle and was momentarily racked by guilt.

"All the girls have been great." He cocked his head, smiling, moustached like a cat, cat's eyes humorously watching Will, and, nervously, Will smiled back.

At last Will said, "They . . . know about each other?"

Buz laughed, reaching around Will's heavy shoulder to pat his back. "Know *about* each other? Sometimes we do it six in a bed—I bet you can't believe that!"

Will cleared his throat, and still Buz was smiling.

"The sheer logistics of such an undertaking—" Will began.

"Come let us fix you another martini, and I'll tell you the whole secret."

"Do," Will said. It came to him that his fingertips were numb already. He had a sudden, fierce hunger to tell him about Kleppmann and the tragic madness of his Uncle Tag. "Yes," he said, "do. By all means! Yes!"

## 3

At the corner of the house, standing in the twilight shadow of hundred-year-old oaks and eight-year-old maples, in the cool perfection of pointlessly curving stone walls and wide slate shingles, the Senator paused and pointed across the broad, flawlessly mown and deeply shaded lawn toward a long stone building as handsomely gabled and ornately dressed as the house itself. "Old mews," he said. "Left empty for years, but my son-in-law's been fixing it up. He's the City Manager in Ferguson. Great future ahead of him. Well, he's got horses in it now. Thurbreds from Texas. Beautiful animals, horses!"

R. V. Kleppmann looked at the mews, and his expression of mournful patience and scorn did not change. "I was bitten by a horse once in Europe," he said as if innocently.

"They're known for that," the Senator said. He grinned. "But I like an animal with spirit."

Kleppmann went on staring, standing with his hands in the pockets of his cheap gray coat.

"My father kept Tennessee Walkers," the Senator said. He had his hand on Kleppmann's elbow again and was guiding him toward the long, wide, gracefully curving driveway where Kleppmann's Ford was parked. "Beautiful animals. Beautiful. But every man to his taste, I say. *De gustibus*." He laughed, orbicular by study. "Now this birdbath here," he said abruptly, stopping and extending his arm toward it, "came over here from England over seventy years ago. Came from a church. Just the base is old, originally part of a cross or something. Chiseled out by hand, as you can see. Now that's something! Notice the interlace. Proves its antiquity. Anglian, I think they said. You can tell it's hand-carved because these squares here are all different sizes. They *look* pretty much the same, you see, but if you look there closer you can see there's no two of 'em alike. Like snowflakes."

Kleppmann bent down, grieved and indifferent, to look.

"Well, everybody likes something different," the Senator said. "One man's meat is another man's poison."

Kleppmann straightened up and turned to look at the Senator mildly but critically. "I never noticed that," he said. "Seems to me everybody wants the same thing. Curved driveways whether or not there's anything to curve around. Wife that looks half-starved to death. Dogs, cats, horses."

"Come now, Mr. Kleppmann," the Senator said, "you like expensive things yourself."

Kleppmann shrugged as if meekly, like a Jewish tailor. He patted the Senator's arm in a way he knew the man would find offensive, and said, "I suppose I do. I suppose we're all made of the same stuff under the skin."

He ate his dinner—a cold hot beef sandwich and a glass of milk—in a small, filthy hash-house in south St. Louis. The potatoes were lumpy, the beef underthin and overcooked, the gravy watery; but Kleppmann did not notice. He was not simply indifferent to food, he was fanatically indifferent. He knew good food from bad, expensive from cheap, and he could use his knowledge to impress his business associates, as he called them, when necessary; but he had no respect for what is known as fine food—meats cooked with wines and spices brought in flaming, as though they would look and taste of decay in their natural state; vegetables chopped or diced or shredded in the decadent French manner, as if for the toothless gums of superannuated uncles and aunts of the royal house. It was not the food itself that disgusted him: it was edible enough, though not appealing. What turned his stomach—and turned his stomach violently—was the people who admired such food: piglike people (whether they were fat or thin, he saw that pig's-eye glint in their piggish little eyes) who prided themselves (as even pigs do not) on knowing which marination was considered superior by persons of superior discernment. What turned his stomach was people who took one sip of wine and glanced expertly at the corner of the room and passed judgment with the greatest solemnity, as if the head of the winemaker hung on their sentence—"nutty," or "tart," or "bland," or "smooth," or some other perfectly obvious designation of a perfectly obvious, wholly unimportant sensation. As for those who could say, and with a fair measure of accuracy, "1963," or even "1937"—a thing he certainly could not do himself—he felt a kind of moral outrage he could barely hide from even the most obtuse observer. It was not simply the connoisseur, the snob, that Kleppmann detested. He was equally revolted by people who took smacking delight in fried chicken or porkchops or Christmas ham, or by people in the suburbs who ate rare barbecued steak and could not help wincing when asked by a guest for a piece "well done." (Kleppmann unfailingly asked for his steak well done, in the hope of offending.) He was no more pleased by the "simple Negro" with his affected and self-conscious taste for chicken necks and gibbets (or giblets or whatever they were called); and he hated with equal intensity the Occidental who learned to eat with chopsticks and the Oriental who ate "naturally," that is, with his mouth at the level of his plate and his sticks slightly higher than his head. For these reasons and others, Kleppmann ate alone whenever possible, just as he went to the bathroom alone, and paid no more than he had to for the privilege.

His wife was of a different inclination, of course, not only with respect to eating but with respect to almost everything in life. She liked big houses, beautiful views, and parties where dinner was served by candlelight. Kleppmann suffered her as he suffered the rest of mankind. She was of use. Nevertheless, when there were no guests and therefore no reason to bend to the ridiculous and annoying fashion of eating by light one could not see by, Kleppmann took dinner in his room, as he called it (his wife called it his study), in solitude. He made no pretense of loving her and never went to bed with her. It was a business arrangement, by no means mutually satisfactory or for that matter more than tolerable on either side. She loved luxury and had so little taste that he could pawn off on her the most disgusting baubles. As for Kleppmann, he liked making fools of people (though he did not like that or anything else in this world very much), and his wife not only provided a willing subject, as quick to sit up and beg as any fawning, stinking lap dog, but also helped him to make fools of other people.

The diner was alone when he entered it—he might not have entered it otherwise—but when he was halfway through his clammy hot beef sandwich two teen-age girls came in. One had blue pock-marks; the other was tanned and pretty except for a suspicious, slow-witted, cowlike look, a slightly affected pout, and large, square ankles. Kleppmann wiped his mouth on the paper napkin and pushed his plate away. Leaving no tip —he never left tips except to impress—he carried his restaurant check to the ornate, ostentatiously large black cash-register, long obsolete but still very grand, counted out the exact change, and went out to the street without a word. He walked to his car, unlocked it, and got in. A freight train stood on the siding across the street, and Kleppmann shuddered, went pale, averted his eyes.

At home, among other messages awaiting him, he found this:

*W.B.H. has a tax claim against him, in amount of $40,000. Own firm has advised him to buy them off, case too chancy.*

Kleppmann nodded. He crossed to the window, picked up his *Barron's Weekly*, and sat down on the stiff, plain wooden chair he always used for serious reading—a chair fit for a monk.

4

What happened was obscure to Will, afterward. He had, strange to say, no particular regrets: it was all hardly more real than a dream, and though he would never have imagined that he would feel that way, he found that it scarcely occurred to him to feel guilty. It was if, taking a wrong turn of no particular consequence, he had found himself in a sweet shop where the air was heavy with the scene of candies, and display cases were piled high with pink and yellow and white things and chocolate things and things in fancy wrappings. They stood in the kitchen, he remembered, the music howling in at them from the livingroom, the girl perhaps in bed somewhere —he'd lost track of her—and Buz was saying, holding up the martini pitcher to watch the level, pouring in gin, "Say what you like, there's nothing in this world more fantastically beautiful than each of your hands on a different girl's breasts and your legs wrapped around two more sets of breasts, and one of them sucking and another one giving you a kiss with a taste of gin." He cackled with pleasure.

Will watched the martini turning round and round in the pitcher.

"Right," Buz said, nodding as if Will had spoken.

Will's head was not as clear as he would have liked. He felt stimulated by it all, and the sexual stimulation was the least of it. He felt new worlds were opening up before him, and what he wanted at the moment was not to explore them, plunge into the raw adventure of it, but think out, boldly, without shrinking, the implications. Buz handed him his martini, surely knowing he was already drunk as a skunk. "May be too wet," he said, "try it." He beamed. Will sipped and nodded—at that moment he might as quickly have approved plain kerosene. He lifted the glass toward the ceiling and said, "The world is round!" "Round!" Buz echoed. They drank to rotundity.

He remembered saying later, slowly and carefully—several drinks later it must have been—"It's immoral, that's my obshection to it."

"That's right," Buz said. "Immoral."

However, there was another side to it, no question about it, and they spoke of it in lofty phrases. An aesthetic side. (They were sitting out on the lawn now. He couldn't remember coming out, but he was here: Buz in the aluminum lawn chair across from him, growing more quiet, more dignified moment by moment, and mentioning often how much he valued this rare opportunity for conversation.) "There is an aesthetic side to the question," Will said. He solemnly belched. "Note the frequency of extraliteral relationships—" Extraliteral? he thought. He decided to brave it out. "Of extraliteral relation-

ships among painters and poets and the like. It's *very
interesting.*"

"Right, I'm glad you mentioned it," Buz said.

"Now painters and musicians, we may safely presume—"
He slung out his jaw and frowned, judicial. "Painters and musicians have a marked aesthetic proclivity."

"Exactly! Exactly *right!*" He banged his fist on his knee.

"Good. *Bien. Bongiorno.*" He giggled. "So far so good."

"Right."

"If the Universe is apprehended *aesthetically,* which is to
say in terms of sensation—"

"Exactly! Sen*sa*tional!"

"—then any cur*tailing*—"

"Exactly!"

"—of the aesthetic proclivity is, in one word, immm-oral!"
The idea filled him with righteous rage.

"Whooey!" said Buz. He agreed. Then, realizing Will had
finished, he looked slightly puzzled.

Will leaned toward him and spoke more confidentially. "We
must live life fully."

Buz nodded, musing.

"We must understan' that there are situations which entail
commitment, and there are situations in which no commitment
is implicated."

"None."

"Nothing different from eating with a person, or playing a
game of golf with him, or, as the case may be, her."

"Not a parcital." He laughed, then looked sinister. "Or a
tracklium."

Will laughed too. "Rise *above* ourselves."

"Excelsior!"

"Shaving cream!"

"What?"

"Nothing." Will pursed his lips but the belch came anyway.
"I better go bed," he observed.

"Excellent," Buz said. "You want company?"

Will frowned, dizzily waiting.

Buz said, leaning forward and touching his knee, "It would
give me great pleasure—" The word came out badly and he
formed it again. "*Pleasure* to unzip your pants." He smiled
like a dog, his face very blurry, like a white flower under water.

"What?" Will said. He tried to stand up.

"You said yourself—"

"You monster!" Will said, deeply shocked.

Buz shrugged, slowly and loosely. "Well."

"I'm as*ton*izzhed!" Will said. "Astonished." That's better.

Buz brought out, just intelligibly, "You weren't astonizzhed when I told you about burying a girl in feathers, or pouring syrup over them—"

"Stop!" He had made it to his feet now. "This is horrible," he said. "What's the matter with you people?" With what he knew himself was ludicrous premeditation, he raised his martini and dashed it, glass and all, to the sidewalk. The noise rang through the night more loudly than he'd expected. Buz laughed sadly, and after a moment Will laughed too.

"Help me up, old college frien'," he said.

Will went over to him carefully, and carefully bent to help him up out of the chair. Then, very slowly, reeling with every tilt and lurch of the wobbly planet in its fall through the void, they worked their way to the porch steps. On hands and knees they made it up to the porch, and the light went on. "Just joking, Will old friend," he said. They laughed and scratched at the door.

"I understand," Will said. "A cunning joke. I must try, tomorrow—" He'd lost the thread.

Hours later, as it seemed to him, a girl in a yellow bathrobe opened the door for them. They laughed and patted each other's backs and rolled in. (It came to him that his suitcoat was gone.) The door closed behind them, and the girl disappeared. He had an impression—but he couldn't be sure—that the girl was not the same one. Then he must have passed out. It must have been sometime after that that he awakened to the half-dream half-reality of lying naked in a dark room, with a naked woman pressing her bush to his face, thighs clamped to his head, pushing at him, her smooth back arched and one hand closed around his penis. He never saw her face and afterward he sometimes was not quite sure that she was real. It was all, well, very strange.

And sitting in his office in Buffalo, giving in once more to bemused staring, eyes passing over his closely reasoned, now meaningless page, he knew what it was about it that was weird. He could see nothing either wrong in it or especially right. He'd betrayed people before, from time to time, in trivi-

al ways, like any man—though he'd never betrayed Louise before, not sexually—and he would have said he knew very well what betrayal was, by his chest. But if so, this was no betrayal. He felt nothing, not even disgust. If she learned about it, which she wouldn't, he knew, he would be sorry about it, but not unduly. If she took it for more than it was, then that was her problem. It was all exactly as people claimed—a trifle, a thing one could easily get used to, not at all the shocking and terrible sort of experience he had imagined. It would be different, perhaps, if the girl were someone he believed he loved. But sex, pure sex—"like food," Buz had said, or a game of golf—it was merely a pleasure, meaningless and harmless. Or was it he himself who'd said it? The fact that all his life he'd guessed wrong about how it would feel, was a shock to him. And more shocking yet was the fact that it seemed, afterward, only a dream. He understood clearly, all at once, that if he did it a hundred times, a thousand, it would still be mere dream, as vague in his mind as his morning recollections of love-making with Louise. That was the reason for the ropes, it struck him, and the six-in-a-bed, and the rest. The pleasure was unspeakable, but only for a moment, like the unspeakable pleasure of dinners forgotten long ago.

He was arrested by a memory, sharp as a vision, of Danny talking with the Indian boy at Uncle Ben's farm. They were in the chickenhouse, and the Indian was hunkering in front of Danny, teaching him to whittle. The word was musical on the Indian boy's tongue, and Will had remembered—as if all the time between had vanished in smoke—how the word had sounded when he himself was a child and someone—Uncle Ben, or maybe his grandfather, or some hired man at Stony Hill, he couldn't remember any more—had bent down to show him how. Danny took the knife in one hand, carefully, the stick in the other, and Will kept in his uneasiness about a four-year-old's handling a jackknife. He watched the small face, haloed in light from the chickenhouse window, furrowed with concentration, tongue between teeth. The knifeblade cut in and moved slowly, jerkily, down the point of the whittling stick. *I was whittling willow,* he remembered with a start. *I was going to make a whistle. It was Uncle Ben. He kept his hand on my arm, and not to steady me, but because he wanted to.*

And now, fists clenched, remembering the pistol in his briefcase, Will thought: *What makes it die? Wordsworth. Trailing glory. And when it's dead—mere duty, is that it? To what?*

He found the new package of Tums and opened it and ate one. Still staring at the papers on his desk, he hardly noticed June, his secretary, when she came in with the collection forms for him to sign. He was aware that all lines were sharper than usual this afternoon, that his eyes were curiously sensitive to trifling detail—dust specks in the air, the pages of the book on the desk beside the papers—and he was sensitive to smells as well. It was her scent that made him glance up at her, raising his eyes only to the level of her waist, where the hip-flesh jutted out. He looked up at her face. She was looking a little past him, lifelessly pretty. It had begun to come to his attention, recently, that every women in the world was sexually attractive.

"My, you're all dolled up," he said. She was not. Her eyes snapped into focus on his face and she looked alarmed and pleased. Will Jr looked down, flushing. *She would do it,* he thought. His chest filled with a pleasurable panic. *Horrible,* he thought. But he couldn't think of why.

It was just as he was leaving, a little after seven, that Mrs. Kleppmann called. He was alone in the office and answered it himself.

"Mr. Hodge, please," she said.

"Who is this?" he asked, though the voice was unmistakable.

"Oh, Mr. Hodge," she said, "it's you."

"Who is this?" he asked again.

"I need to see you," she said. "About my husband. It's urgent. Is it possible?"

"Where are you?" he said.

"Just listen. I can't talk long. Have you a pencil?"

He stared a moment longer, mind a blank, then took out his ball-point pen and clicked the head into position. "Ok," he said, "shoot." He chewed his lower lip and wrote it down. Afterward, the memory of her walk came over him, and he had a sensation like fear and like joy, a shortness of breath. He reached in his pocket automatically, with his left hand, for the Tums.

Will had something on his mind, she saw at once. At first
she thought it was the meeting tonight, one of those Civil
Rights shows he was always getting himself involved in, but
when she mentioned it at the supper table she discovered he'd
forgotten that.

"Aren't you going, then, Willie?" she said. "You don't *have*
to," she said. "Plenty of people don't, you know. If you don't
see any sense in it—"

"Not the point," he said. A piece of spaghetti dropped from
his lip and he tried to catch it with his fork, missed it, and
spattered his tie a little. "Damn," he said.

"Christ's sakes," Danny said, smiling.

Will glanced at him, then down again at his plate.

"You're really in a mood," Louise said. "You're really fun.
A million laughs."

"Oh lay off, will you?" He chewed harder, angry and guilty,
and she knew she could drop it but decided the hell with it.
She was tired. Danny had been rotten all day, and Madeline,
ever since she got home from school, had been making hay on
it, playing the goody-goody. There had been times Louise had
wanted to throw a pot at them both, or drown them in a tub
of boiling oil or something. She had held herself in, saying
only—in a voice like jagged iron—*"Can't* you watch car*toons*
or something?" Maddie would vanish for a while after that,
but then there she would be again, hovering beside her when
she worked at the sink, or flitting around at her heels like a
shadow just thick enough to trip you, consoling her for her
sad, sad life in a tone that weighed on Louise like chains, half
honest sympathy no doubt, yes, but also half pleasure in showing herself sympathetic. "If you really want to help, wash the
lettuce," she snapped. And then, close to tears, wanted to
laugh. It was like throwing good plates at a ghost. For fifteen
minutes, there stood Maddie, ineffectually washing the lettuce,
then the carrots and radishes, prattling until Louise felt ready
to explode, and tying up the sink, and trying so hard to be
good, Louise felt, that it wasn't fair to be anything but kind.
She'd taken an aspirin and a glass of water and had relaxed
for a minute in the livingroom, exactly as the TV commercials
advised, but that too was a joke. Her minute of rest, supposed-
ly refreshing, was shattered three times by cries from Danny

—he'd gotten his finger closed in a drawer he knew he was not supposed to be in, and then he'd spilled milk, trying to pour it without taking it out of the refrigerator, and then—what?— yes, had gotten slapped by Maddie, allegedly for trying to bite her. To which Will, coming home, had contributed only his abstracted look, his deafness, and the stink—after all these years—of a Goddamn stupid pipe. "What in hell are you smoking?" she'd said.

"I take it it doesn't quite sweep you off your feet," he said. He didn't bother looking up from the *Evening News*.

"It makes me want to kill and things like that. Is that good enough?"

"Look, Mommy Louise, I'm tired," he said. It was supposed to console her, that "Mommy Louise." It was what he'd said long ago in college, the first time she gave him a tit. Well it didn't console her. It was *sick*.

" 'Mommy Louise, I'm tired,' " she mimicked. "Nobody else can be tired, of course." Then to Danny, coming in on the tri- cycle she'd told Will he shouldn't let him ride in the house, "Danny, you get that damn thing out of here, Daddy's tired."

Danny looked up at her, then at Will.

"Will, *you* tell him, once."

"You heard Mommy, Danny. Do what Mommy says."

" 'Mommy,' " she mimicked. She wanted to spit.

"Well Jesus," he said, jerking the paper away from his eyes to stare at her, "You're in a mood all right! What's *your* ex- cuse?" In a minute she'd be crying.

She had taken a deep breath, sucking down rage, then had turned and gone back to the kitchen. A minute later she could hear him talking with Madeline. She was giving him her goody- goody stuff, and he was gulping it down like dog-sick. "You bastard," she thought. "You *bastard*." But she had controlled herself then, had calmed down and had come out of the kitch- en smiling, or more or less smiling, talking lightly of the an- tiquing kit that had come this morning from Sears. She was meaning to fix the chest of drawers and the dresser in the mas- ter bedroom. And even when he'd ignored all she said, she'd managed to keep her spirits up, though God knew what the point was. Now, suddenly, with his growl wrecking dinner, turning the food sour in her stomach, she felt herself letting go, relaxing into rage.

" 'Lay off,' he says. Why should I? So I can leave you alone

to never look at your family or play with them or tell them a
story or so much as give them a spanking? So you can stay out
every night till God knows when with June or Lagoon or
whatever her name is and never come to bed with me—as if I
was a leper or some fat old whore that the muscle's all gone
out of—"

"For Christ's sake, Louise, the children!"

"What children? *What* children?" *Now tears, you fucking
bitch,* she thought. But she was crying just the same.

*Poor babies,* she thought, sobbing into her hands, *that bastard not stirring.* They sat white-faced and far away as they always did when explosions came, and she wept, terribly, stupidly, with a feeling like mountains giving way. Danny began
sobbing too.

"Sh," Will said, white, his fingers trembling so the fork
shook. "Now stop blubbering, Danny, and eat your nice potatoes."

The room went blindingly white and she leaped from her
chair with a whoop and ran to the livingroom to hurl herself
like a cannonball at the couch. She lay clutching her mouth,
gasping, and suddenly was rigid, as if something had locked in
her mind and everything had stopped. When she could think
again he was sitting beside her, rubbing her back, and his eyes
were remote, objective. She'd slept a long time, perhaps. She
was calmer.

"I love you," he said with the kindness of a priest.

" 'Love,' " she said. But she caught his hand and said, "I'm
sorry."

"It's all right," he said. "I'm sorry too." Objective, cold as
shit.

*Where are you, Will?* she thought. *Come back.* "I don't
know what happened," she said, and for an instant knew she
would sob again, but hung on. "I'm sorry."

"It's all right," he said again. He put his arms around her.
Cold.

The lights were off in the diningroom. He'd sent the children upstairs.

"Can I get you something, Mommy?"

She shook her head.

"Maybe sleep would help."

She felt a flicker of anger, a last weak flitting of lightning
after the storm is over, then felt it die into indifference. If he

wanted to get rid of her, put her in bed as though she were merely a cross, unreasonable child, it was fair. She was. And tired, so tired she wasn't sure she could lift her own hand. She let him help her to lie down again, her head on the cool pillow. She lay still, with her eyes closed, for a long time, and she could feel his hand resting gently on her back. And then another flicker came, not anger this time but something almost remembered. She concentrated, tensing the muscles of her eyelids.

"Will?"

He grunted, patting her.

"What's that paper, about taxes?"

He patted her again, exactly as before, but she had the impression, too distinct to be wrong, that he'd suddenly moved back from her, physically even, though he hadn't moved a muscle.

"It's nothing," he said. "Don't give it a thought."

"Are you sure, Willie?"

"Would I lie to you?"

She thought about it. What an odd thing for him to ask. Of course he would. She let herself go calm. Comfortably, barely moving her lips now, she said, "You ought to call your mother, Will. We haven't written in months."

"You call her," he said. "She likes you more than me."

"I tried." She collected herself. "She was out all day. Yesterday too, and last night. I tried when you were gone, just to talk to somebody, even her."

"With Luke?"

She shrugged, just the flick of a muscle or two. She was going to say *I tried that, too,* but it didn't seem worth the effort. It was unbelievable how limp and relaxed she felt. *We must try and have more scenes,* she thought, and laughed mournfully inside her mind. Will was stroking the fleshy insides of her legs, pulling her feet apart a little.

When she awakened next, the whole downstairs was dark as a coal bin, and she was chilly. The record was still turning on the record player and in the sleeping house the whisper of the needle in its barren track was frightening—*kh-sst, kh-sst, kh-sst* . . . Then she remembered where he was. He'd gone to his Civil Rights thing. *Us, Will?* she thought without hope. *Could you march for us?*

# XV

## The Dialogue
## of
## the Dead

*Vite, évelle-toi! Dis, l'âme est immortelle?*
—Paul Verlaine

### 1

"Ben," Vanessa Hodge said when he came in for supper, "you've got to do something. I still can't get hold of Millie. No one's seen her. And I can't get Will either, he hasn't been in to the office since Sunday. I can't even get hold of Luke. Something must've happened."

One look at her face and he knew what it was she thought had happened. Her skin was sweat-streaked and puffy and, around the eyes, dark. He hadn't seen her look so bad since the boy was killed in the war. A wave of sorrow swept over him. "Now, now," he said gently. He went to her, put his big arms around her, and, laying his crusted, sunburnt hand around the back of her head, pressed the side of her face lightly to his chest. "I'll go look 'em up right after chores, Vanessa." He looked past her, out the kitchen window. It was six o'clock, but you'd have thought it was midafternoon. He could be finished with his chores by eight, if he hurried supper. (There was a smell of boiled potatoes and applesauce and meatloaf, probably the last of old Ellabelle, slaughtered a year ago November. She'd kicked him.) It would be darkening by eight and beginning to cool, a beautiful time for riding the motorcycle. "Maybe I'll go on the bike," he said.

"And leave me here?" She drew back her head.

"Now Vanessa," he said.

"Sometimes I think you're just not in this world at all," she said. "I'd be petrified, here all alone."

"Why, Vanessa, I've been plowing till way after midnight the whole time this thing's been going on. You never said a thing about *that*."

"Well that's different," she said. She drew away from him, feeling she had something urgent to do, and turned to the sink and put her fist to her chin, trying to think what she was after. The applesauce was there, cooling on the drainboard, and she ran her finger around the edge absent-mindedly, having a taste. "I'm not the only one," she said, "don't think I am." She took another taste. "There isn't a person for miles around that would go to bed with his doors unlocked these days. They even leave their lights on. He was seen clear over in Perry. Did you know that?" She glanced at him. She'd frightened herself. "He was seen on the same afternoon in Bergen and Brockport. I heard it on TV."

Hodge carried the pan of potatoes to the sink and drained them, his eyes vague, then dumped them into a green plastic bowl. He set it on a clear space on the table and turned back for dishes and, with a big, lead-colored spoon, dished up the meatloaf. He stepped into the bathroom then and pushed his sleeves up and filled the sink with cold water (there was no hot), washed, still staring at nothing, rinsed his face, and dried himself hard with the grayblue, scratchy towel. All the while, Vanessa went on talking, frightening herself with rumors. What would she say, he wondered, if he were to tell her it was Tag?

"Is David eating with us?" she said, pausing.

"He'll be in. Putting the milking-machines together and getting out silage."

She stood with the refrigerator door open, trying to remember that what she needed now was milk, then at last did remember and brought it over to the table in its long green pan. It needed skimming. "Skim the milk," she said, to fix it in her mind. She went for a spoon and cream cup and tried to think what she'd come to the silverware drawer for. "Skim the milk," she kept saying to herself, over and over, but she couldn't think what she was after.

"You have to keep ahold of your mind at a time like this," Ben said. His sermon voice; nevertheless, it was musical and quieting. "It's like the bobcat scares. Somebody sees one, or thinks he sees one, and pretty soon everybody's seeing them. There may be something to it, at the bottom; but you can count on it, it's nine-tenths imagination. Everything is."

It made her feel calmer. His solidity alone, the way he would stand, childlike, with his arms crossed and his head tipped on his brick-red bull neck, had a way of making her calmer. He was looking out the window now, wondering what was keeping David, or looking beyond the milkhouse and barn toward the valley and the woods, golden green in the afternoon slant of the sun. She found she was holding an egg in her hand. "Pididdle," she said, disgusted with herself, and opened the refrig door to put the egg back. She wasn't usually as bad as this! When the back door opened she jumped; but it was David.

"All ready to tear?" Ben said.

The boy smiled past her, towering above her, his teeth as pure white as his heart. The smell of sweat and silage coming off him choked the room. "Pooh!" Vanessa said, batting the smell away. He slipped past her toward the bathroom, smiling.

When they were seated, Ben said, "Fatherwethanktheevorthisvood,blesstoouruseandustothyserviceandmmndammndawaythouthaviscoAmen. We forgot the butter." Vanessa got up. Ben said, going back to what he'd been saying before, "For nothing's either good or bad but thinking makes it so."

She came back with the butter and sat down again, and they ate. Absent-mindedly, Ben glanced around for the newspaper and found it, after a moment, peeking out from under the throwaways and the torn-open letters from Vanessa's friends.

He drew it toward him, shaking off the other things. "What's this?" he said.

Fred Clumly scowled out at him from page one, his white, wolfish face a mass of wrinkles, a long black smudge on his cheek. POLICE CHIEF CORNERS MADMAN. "Good Lord, they got him!" Ben Hodge said. But the first line of the article told him he was wrong. It said, "The escaped prisoner known to police only as 'the Sunlight Man' narrowly escaped capture this afternoon. In a daring, single-handed maneuver, Batavia Chief of Police Fred Clumly tracked the escaped man, officially described as armed and dangerous, to a tent-like structure suspended from a railroad underpass near here. . . ." He went back to the beginning and read the whole thing aloud to Vanessa and the boy. On page 9A there were more pictures. The stopped train, tent dangling just in front of it; trainworkers holding up the tent for the cameraman, showing the symbols on it; Fred Clumly peering over his shoulder as though he were the one who was crazy. Clumly himself had, he told reporters, "no comment at this time."

"Armed and dangerous," Vanessa said. "Gyuck!"

"Oh, anyone that's got a gun is called armed and dangerous, honey. It's just to be on the safe side."

"After all those murders?" she said. She decided to try Millie again, but he said:

"Let it go, Vanessa. You're stewing, working yourself up. Just let it go, and I'll drive on over later. I'll leave David here with you." She did not insist on going. He was in luck.

The motorcycle hummed under him and roared when he accelerated and popped and crackled when he cut back the spark for a sharp curve or the crest of a hill. The swath of the headlight flew ahead of him, sharp against trees or the white, three-cornered posts on turns, and the motor's echoes rang to either side of him, closing in suddenly when he passed a car or crossed a bridge with steel walls, falling away toward silence when the road pierced open countryside where the only trees were far away and the houses too were far away and the creek lay glassy and pale beneath the stars. He would rather ride than almost anything he knew. Wind in the sleeves of his old sheepskin coat, beating at his helmet, whipping away his voice if he happened to sing, which tonight he did not. He was alone on the road, he might have been the last man left in the world, and he was so much at peace with the dark hills, the trees, the lighted farmhouses, cowbarns gray in the hazy glow of their security lamps, that he could almost imagine he *was* the world, the scenery around him a projection of his mind. He came in view of the prison's glow and a little later the prison itself, opening out below him as he rounded a turn overlooking the entire valley. He increased his speed and then, half a mile short of Luke's place, switched off the motor and headlight, coasting in as far as he could get. The sudden hush was awesome, and his speed up the pale road seemed to leap so that, familiar as the illusion was, his heart ticked lightly for an instant. He began to lose speed. The steering grew clumsy, and it was an effort to keep the wheels on hard dirt between the small, loose stones that might throw him. At last, rods from Luke's driveway, he eased the brake on, came almost to a stop, and swung off to walk the machine into the hedgerow coming at an angle to meet the road. He walked the rest of the way, hardly making a sound.

They were there, he saw when he reached the driveway mouth. He stood half-hidden behind a tamarack. The lights on the lower floor were on, and he could see people moving around. No one seemed to be watching for intruders. But he was afraid. He'd been afraid all along, but now he couldn't keep his mind off it. Neither of them, he was fairly sure, would shoot him if they realized who he was. But everything depended on his seeing them first and making himself known. If one of them was watching from the woods to the right of Luke's house (huge boles and branches, high brush in under the eaves, a flicker of lightning bugs within—the kind of woods he'd have run from in terror, in his childhood, and maybe could yet), then he was done for. He had no definite plan for what he would do when he got to the house, if he did. Something would come to him. *No use just standing here,* he thought. But he stayed. Chickens sat in the branches of the trees near the house.

He stood in the darkness at the mouth of the driveway for a long time, watching. If there was someone in the woods keeping lookout, sooner or later the one there would reveal himself; that was partly why he stayed where he was, Ben told himself. But there were other reasons too, and he began to face them. Who was in there, after all? Luke, Millie, the Indian, Tag, possibly Will. They were his flesh and blood, all but

Nick, and it was true, he wouldn't want harm to come to them. But surely neither Nick nor Tag would harm Luke: he'd be sick from the stress of all this, sure as day, and they wouldn't hurt a boy half out of his mind with pain. And it was unthinkable that Tag would let any harm come to the brother who'd been his favorite. So that it was for Millie that Ben Hodge must go up to them, if he went. He merely stared at the recognition for a moment, then got down on one knee, squinting.

Maybe it had seemed to him that he loved her—once. It was so long ago now, and he'd been so young then, that he couldn't tell for sure. He remembered standing in the horse-barn, combing his father's old sorrel mare, his riding horse. One moment he was working alone (the light soft on the mare's shiny coat, her smell and the smell of hay and molasses rich in his nostrils), and the next he had a feeling he was not. By the stirring of his blood he knew it was Millie, but he didn't turn. He heard her come nearer. Her hands came onto his shoulders and he grew still, not moving the comb, in fact not breathing. After a long time she kissed him, light as a feather, on the back of his neck. Then he turned. "Don't, Millie."

Her eyes shone, and because she was beautiful, or because of his shame at what he'd almost done to her in the quarry that night, his heart raced. She smiled and flashed the dimple. "Why so petulant, lover?"

"I'm not your lover, Mil," he said too softly, blushing.

"But petulant you are," she said. "Well, cheer up. I bring good news."

"What?" he said.

She turned away, coy, and walked around the back of the mare, running her hand lightly over its rump.

"You'll get your ass kicked," he said.

"Ooh! Shame on you!" she said. "And to a *lady*."

Ben said nothing. As always, his mind turned in on him and filled him with bitter remorse. It was not her fault that he'd tried to seduce her or even that he might have succeeded, and not her fault that he was ashamed of himself—whether because he'd gone that far or because he hadn't gone all the way, he couldn't tell—and not her fault that he was wounded now by the sight of her. It was perhaps true that she loved him; he believed it. It might even be that she was the one he would love, finally, if he could get his feelings straightened out. But it was happening too fast, and he had meant it to be clean and beautiful, not like this. Yet her mockery showed pain. She teased him exactly the way Ruth would do when her feelings were hurt and she was damned if she would show it.

He said, "I'm sorry, Millie."

She waved it off lightly. "Ah well, these things—" She was still moving her hands on the horse's rump, smiling, brandishing the dimple. "Do horses feel sexy when you touch their you-know-whats?"

"For Christ's sake, Millie."

She laughed and went around to the other side like a dancer, then ducked down, putting her hands on her knees, to look under the horse's legs at him. "Guess what," she said.

"What?" Her collar hung open and he could see the hollow sweeping down from her throat, the smooth white rise on each side. He did not look away.

"Sweetie-pie, that ain't no guess."

"I give," he said.

"That'll be the day!" she said, and then "Ooh! The ole rake blushes."

*"Millie,"* he said.

She put her hand to her collar and he blushed more deeply, knowing she knew he'd been looking down inside, and suspecting, in the same instant, that that was why she'd gone around and bent over to look up through the horses legs in the first place. She'd been planning it for days. She was a whore, a bitch; God only knew what diseases he might have gotten! But he knew he was lying. It was his own fault, all of it. The next instant she was coming under the horse to him, knowing very well that the sorrel was skittish (if lifted a hoof, hesitated, tentatively set it down) and she smiled at him, standing between him and the horse, and touched his arm with the fingertips of one hand. He touched her waist with his left hand, holding the stupid curry comb in the other, and after a long time their mouths came together and a shock of her sweetness went through him. He let the comb drop and clung to her, kissing her hard, pressing his body against her, sick with hope and shame. Millie pulled back and sucked her lips in between her teeth as if they'd gone numb. She shook her head slowly, lips parted. "Have you guessed?" she whispered.

"No." He searched her eyes.

She said, "I'm getting married to your brother Will."

His stomach jerked as if she'd jabbed it. "Don't, Millie," he said, "that's not funny."

But she drew her head back, still holding him. "It's the truth, Ben."

"It's not. It's dumb."

And now she was not smiling. "It's the truth." And he realized that it was. She waited. She was not soft and coy now but awesome to him, outwardly the same but in her mind dark, ancient, and terrible as a stone tower under stars of ice; and if there was something she wanted him to say, there was not enough of him left to say it. Even the punishments his father dealt out did not leave his heart so shaky. The mare breathed deep and sighed, letting her back sag, infinitely weary of all man's paltry machinations, and Ben Hodge, servant of sunlit visions, whose heart was set on holiness—like the girl in the story his father told, who threw roses in the air—was silent. She looked down, smiling again, though her eyes had gone wrong, then turned, went back slowly through the tack room, as she'd come, lightly trailing her fingertips over the leather of the saddles on the row of wooden frames.

At the other end of the barn, at the foot of the stairs leading up to the haymow, Art Jr stood in the shadows watching with his arms folded. He came out now—Ben had no idea how long he'd been there—and stood by the old sorrel's head. Art Jr was constructed all of squares—square face, square chest, square fists, square feet—and his mind was a diagram. He said, "She wanted you to fight for her." Ben shook his head, baffled by the linear simplicity of his younger brother's world. It was true, no doubt. About the relations between *A* and *B* he was never wrong. Ben said, "How *could* I?" and Art Jr said, "I wouldn't know," as if that was that.

And so Will and Millie had gotten married, and Ben had held out, had matched, later, with an otherworldly gentleness and eyes-turned-inward passivity like his own, pale light unto pale light. They had lived in peace, a haven for Will's sharp scapegoat pain, looking on from a distance at Millie's resounding destructions. And he had thought sometimes that they were there, Will and Millie, as a foil to his life, a shadow that made him clear. There was no need, no use for such rage and pain as they suffered except that it made his serenity distinct. (But Vanessa said once, for she was just and merciful, though sometimes jealous, "She might have been different with you, though, Ben. That's possible." To which he'd replied, "I'd as soon have married my dad!" He was not sure how much Vanessa knew.) In any case, whether or not he had ever felt real love for Millie, he would not have his life any way but as it was. It was to Ben and Vanessa that their children came—Will Jr, Luke, Mary Lou—for a chance to grow up whole, or nearly whole. To Ben, not to the eldest of the sons, that their mother had come in her last months, to die. Vanessa would read to her hour after hour, the same passages over and over, for her intelligence was gone, or Ben would sit up with her, hearing her ramble through past and present, now that all times had collapsed to one. Once, sitting in the dark beside her bed, at peace with himself, just as she was once again at peace, the green nightlight close to the floor throwing her terrible features on the wall, he had remembered vividly that when she was young she was beautiful. She had red-auburn hair that she wore piled high on her head, and her flesh was white and soft. (He'd lain in bed, pretending to be asleep, watching. They were going out, and so he'd cried, and though his father roared, she'd brought him here to her room where she could be with him a little longer.) She had on only her undergarments, as she called them; and now his father stood beside her, fully dressed, elegant, huge and dangerous and beautiful (to Ben's child-eyes) and fearsome beside that gentleness and softness; but he stretched out his hand toward her as if timidly and touched her shoulder, looking over her head into the mirror at her, and after an instant she turned her head, gracefully, bending forward slightly, the way a blooded mare would turn its head to a groomsman's touch, relinquishing nothing, though submissive, and she brushed his hand with the side of her face. "I think I'll move Ben to his own room," his father said. She smiled. "Do," she said. Her permission and command. *That's what it all means,* he'd thought that night long afterward, remembering and now understanding as he gazed at the terrible shadow of her profile—a silhouette of barren mountains, a bombed city. In peace like that in her own house once, she had died. There was no other life he'd have chosen in preference. If he'd loved Millie once, the part of him that had inclined, overmatched, toward darkness and war was long dead and buried, and he was grateful. He could pity her, forever torturing herself and Will and the children, but he need not

approve her, need not return her good for the evil she'd done
him and all his family. She had not earned from him any right
to protection. For that matter, she probably needed none. No
doubt she could manage Taggert as easily as any other man.
No doubt she had tied his balls in knots already.

The woods were unmoving and hushed. There was no sound
anywhere but Taggert's far-away voice inside the house, a
stream of words—you might have thought he was auctioning
something—a monologue never broken by a sound from the
others. There were no lights on in the upper-story windows.
The gables of the house stood out against the sky, darker,
more solid than the trees surrounding, but not more motionless. The air was pleasantly cool. He remembered sleeping out
on the lawn with his brothers, in his childhood, and sitting up
in the middle of the night to look toward the house like a
watcher from a distant planet, hearing his father's voice in the
study arguing with a guest. And he felt again the feeling that
had come to him then, that all was well, though he himself
was not part of it; the feeling a man might have if he could
come back from the grave and find life not changed by his absence. Then the voice in the house stopped. The trees waited.
The dark gables appeared to take on weight, grow older.
Kneeling with his forearm resting on his leg, his head bent, listening with every nerve, Ben Hodge breathed more lightly and
shallowly, and then did not breathe at all.

Then he heard the shot and thought *Millie!* and in the same
instant was running up the driveway, farm shoes thudding and
crunching on the stones that lay spattered on the driveway like
mountain scree. He was gulping as if he'd been running for
hours (trees still motionless, house unmoved, as if only Ben
Hodge, no one else, were alive). With his eyes on the door he
was aware of the motionless limbs yawing over, above his
head, black against starlight, and when he came to the door it
fell open an instant before he touched it, and he saw the gun,
then felt it in his belly and knew, calm and cold, that he was
finished. He met the bearded man's eyes and, though they
were murderous, knew them, and at the same time, without
looking away, he saw Luke and Nick and Millie on the couch,
white but safe, and a gaudy magician's table, goldfish bowl,
something hanging from the far wall, and he understood that
the shot was part of a magic trick, though now that understanding did not matter. He waited for the shot that would kill

him and in parting grief saw Millie's change: the gray that
mocked the dye in her hair, on her puffy face black bruises.
Bags under her eyes, chapped lips, no lipstick. But Nick and
Luke looked worse. They were broken, like old men; Millie,
just battered. She'd never be broken, chances were; would
merely vanish one of these days, or her wrecked body would
be found sitting upright and severe, abandoned like a house.
Now again he was meeting his brother's eyes, the face he had
known now sunken to hair and scar, and no longer was he
sure that the eyes had murder in them. Still Taggert said nothing, and the gun poking into Ben Hodge's belly was firm. Millie said—a whisper—"Who is it?" Ben glanced at her, then
once again met his brother's eyes, and he understood, perhaps
at the same time Taggert did, that he was standing in darkness; they could not see him from inside the room. The pressure of the gun lessened.

At last Taggert said, directly to Ben, as if speaking to him,
not the others, "There's nobody here. Not a sign." And then,
slowly, as planets pass, he turned away from Ben and closed
the door.

"I heard running," Nick said, low.

Then Tag's voice. "It must have been a deer, or a cow, maybe. There's nothing there."

Ben stood in the darkness rubbing his arms.

## 2

One of the prisoners was singing, in the cells in back. Figlow leaned on his elbows, dark eyebrows low with wrath. Tom
Sangirgonio sat on the railing beside Figlow's desk, relaxed,
long-boned, his small round head tilted to listen.

"Shit," Figlow said, tightening his fists, and the boy glanced
at him, smiling.

"You need a vacation," the boy said.

A few words came through. *Ah got mah mah jawwng wuk-
kin . . .*

"Vacation hell. It's worse at home," Figlow said. "My kid in
school with you?"

"I know her," Tommy said, and smiled again. His smile was

like his father's, warm and at the same time ironic. His eyes,
like his father's, were sharp and black as an Indian's.

"Little bitch is somethin else," Figlow said. It was a joke,
but his mouth jerked over to the right, and the boy knew he
meant it.

He shrugged. "She seems ok though. I don't know."

"At you all the time," Figlow said. "I mean it."

"Yeah, well. You know. Girls."

*"Madonna mia!"*

The singing stopped for a moment, and they waited. It started again.

"Shit," Figlow said. "People are somethin else. You see that
wreck this mornin? Them showdogs? Shit. Dead dogs all over
the fuckin street, or draggin theirselves around with broken
legs and heads tore open. I went past it. I wasn't on duty yet. I
seen the truck-driver, talkin with Pieman and Lewis—they
were the first ones there. He didn't look happy, I can tell you.
Expensive dogs." He jerked his lip as if with scorn. "You
could tell. Other guy got killed. Some guy from Pennsylvania.
Man, he hit that thing like a bat out of hell, I mean he was
driving at a high rate of speed. Shit."

"I didn't see it," Tommy said.

Figlow shook his head, wincing, maybe seeing dead showdogs in his mind. After a minute he said, "What they say
about her, kid?" He winked

Tommy smiled again. "Whom?"

"Come on, whom-shmoom, my kid, that's whom. She pretty cute, eh?" He winked and moved his shoulder a little.

Tommy pursed his lips, thought of teasing, and then
changed his mind. "They say she's a really nice girl."

*"Shhhhtt!"* Figlow said, pleased, suspicious. He tipped his
head, raised two fingers to motion Tommy nearer, but Tommy
merely smiled. Figlow winked again. "In the showerroom, boy,
with their hard-ons in their hands."

He blushed, smiled, shrugged. A chill went through him.

" 'She's a really nice girl,' that's what they say. *Eh?"*

Panicky, he smiled on and nodded.

Figlow rolled his eyes up. "This generation!"

And when his father was there, coming out of Clumly's office with papers in his hand. "Hey, Figlow, how you like to go
kill a few those bastards back there, hey?"

Figlow lit up with mock pleasure, grabbing for his gun.

Miller said, "He'd do it, yeah?"

Tom grinned.

Figlow got up from his desk and went back to the cellblock. When he was out of sight, they laughed.

"You need help, Dad?" Tommy said.

"Not now. I'll be with you in a minute, providing nobody runs over anybody the next ten minutes, or shoots up a movie house." He let his eyes rest a moment on Tom, then grinned and turned away. "Hold the fort," he said. Then, looking out the front door, he went still all over, and instinctively Tommy moved closer.

A heavy Negro woman with gray hair was coming up the walk, alone, moving slowly, like a burned-out star. She stared straight ahead of her but did not seem to see them. When she came into the light thrown from the office they saw blood on her arms and all over the front of her dress. Miller went down to her and took her elbow without a word, and helped her up the steps. She came through the door, and Tommy turned his face away. Her forehead was torn open.

She took a deep breath. "I killed a gentleman," she said.

### 3

The Sunlight Man sat rubbing his palms on his shirt. Luke lay on the couch in the livingroom, unconscious. He'd been out when he'd gone down to untie him. The Sunlight Man had stood racking his brains, leering obscenely for Millie's benefit and Nick's, but he'd thought: *Enough. No more. It has to stop.* He'd said, "Ah! Out like a light! That simplifies matters. Carry him up, boy. I'll bring Granny Goodwitch." And gave a laugh. But her eyes showed nothing, no anger, no hope, and he' had to look away, thinking: *Even you, Millie? Then everything in the world can be broken, can't it.* As he untied her he' let his hands rest a moment cupped around her breasts and he'd pressed his face close, smiling at her, showing his teeth; but her eyes showed nothing, she stared straight ahead. *Like one of those damned Jews,* he'd thought. And then: *Cheer up, they build weapons later, and use the blitz against the Arabs.* He said solemnly, "He he ho ha, Millie. How sad you look! We must try and remember to get you a comb, the kind they use for horses' tails. And some paint, by all means! What color lips would you like, old sweetie? Black, maybe? Bright black to match your heart?" When he pushed his face forward to kiss her she half-turned her head and the eyes turned with it. For an instant he believed she'd gone mad. But he calmed himself. She was all right.

She would still say nothing, sitting at the table, head bowed, eating the hamburger he'd fixed her. Even when he poured himself bourbon she merely looked at it, then down, and kept her silence. "You're a crafty old bitch, Millie," he said. "You watch and wait, like a Christian." She showed no sign that she heard. Nick ate with his head close to the plate, fork upside down, scraping it in, and never looked up at them. "And our brother the murderer, he too watches and waits. Astute! He studies his teacher's every move"—he took a bite, then continued with his mouth full—"except that his manners are bad, of course. That's unfortunate. Draws attention." He leaned toward Nick, pointing with his fork. "The first rule is, be inconspicuous. Like me!" Nick glanced at him, full of hate, then down.

But the fact remained, she was a sight. It might be she was past repair already. "My dear Millie, we must try to get more sleep," he said. "When we sleep, our metabolism helps us to get rid of waste products in the skin and restores essential ingredients—minerals, vitamins, hormones. Yes indeedie! Cut down on sleep and you impair circulation and contract the capillaries, which causes hydration and sagging. The skin is robbed of saline solutions, the tissues sink, and the collagen becomes alas! increasingly visible. In other words, dark circles. Do think about it."

She said nothing but moved her eyes to his face and gave a trace of a smile. It was he who looked down, this time. He said, "Still a spark of life, eh?"

Nick said, "We got to leave."

"When it's right," he said.

"Tonight. No shit."

"Go when you like," he said. "You're free. Millie, *you* know about these things. Explain to the young man about freedom."

She said nothing. She put her fork down and dropped her hand into her lap. His heart sped up.

"Tell him about the gratuitous act, Millie," he said. He bent toward her, fierce. "Tell him."

Her voice was thick from disuse. "There's no such thing."

"Ah!" He turned to Nick. "Listen well, boy! There's no such thing!" He turned back to her, eyebrows lifted, eagerly waiting.

"There's no freedom," she said. She met his eyes. "There's only commitment and confusion."

"A philosopher! A lady philosopher!" he cried with glee. But he said no more. His voice was not in control.

She shifted suddenly to French, her eyes ice cold, and he understood that she did it to give him pain. They'd talked French together long ago at Stony Hill, when he was just learning it. She was still better at it then he was. *From whoring around in Paris*, he thought. But that was wrong, he knew; her French was bookish, and what gave him pain was not the memory of Stony Hill but the revelation of her alter-soul's entombment: She came alive, speaking French; all her humor, irony and wrath came suddenly together like fire and powder, and the Millie who'd survived went dark and fell away, and the woman she'd once meant to be rose out of the grave of abandoned hopes, came striding forth, as confident as a smiling ghost at dusk. He tried to think how to stop her, but nothing would come.

"*Tu es un meilleur professeur que tu le saches*," she said, soft and fast. "*Si quelqu'un peut se vanter de la franchise, de l'acte gratuit, c'est moi. Mais le cerveau est toujours croche à l'animal, petit frère; on dit au cerveau, 'Ne le haïs, cerveau!'* —Comme on dit sur la croix, 'Pardonnez la merde, il ne sait pas ce qu'il fait!'*—mais le corps est en feu, et le coeur pompe, 'Haïssez! Haïssez!' Et même si tu libères l'âme, aliènes en esprit et voyages des lieues et des siècles, chéri, le corps que tu as laissé dans son lit se levera quand il aura faim; il mangera ou fera la cour ou tuera quelqu'un par plaisanterie.*"

"Is that why we do it, Millie?" he said, heart thudding.

"*Tu dis.*"

Nick said fiercely, "They're coming. You know it, and you just sit here and listen to jabbering."

"Shut up," he said. "Not tonight."

"*Il en a tué trois*," she said. "*Combien tu en as tué?*"

He sucked in breath. "Stop it. That's enough."

*"Ou est-ce que tu simplement fais le fou? Pourquoi?"*

"That's enough, I said." He caught hold of the table and meant to heave it toward her, knock her to the floor; but he stopped himself. "Keep that up and I'll tie you in the cellar."

She said no more, but her mouth—not her eyes—smiled.

After a long time he said, almost a whisper, "There are no laws, my boy." He did not look at her. "Only the laws of man, which are easily beaten, and the laws you make up for yourself, which may be obeyed, once they're made up, but only then. That is my lesson for this evening."

*"Une leçon sotte,"* she said under her breath, but he heard it; no doubt he was meant to.

"Not really," he said. "One ought to be *engagé*, I admit it. But the state is not always attainable—like the state of grace. In Rome do as the Romans do, yes. But if you live in the garbage dump, my dear—" He let it trail off, looking again at Nick. "The next man you kill, it's on purpose," he said. "But also, the next man you *don't* kill *that* will be on purpose, too."

*"Pas vrai,"* she said.

He looked at Nick. "Maybe not," he said at last. He stood up. "I have work to do. You'll keep an eye out?"

Nick nodded and glanced up. "Leave the gun," he said.

The Sunlight Man shook his head. "Not this time." He went to the garage and began his preparations. An hour later, running behind time and beginning to feel panicky ("Like any common laborer!" he thought), he went in and, evading the question of what to do with Millie, demanded Nick's labor. "No," Nick said. The Sunlight Man was forced to draw the gun and strike him on the cheek. Afterward, breathing hard, he said, "I'm sorry. You'll see it's for the best. Now get on out there." "No," Nick said. He raised the gun again; the boy changed his mind. Time, the Sunlight Man realized, was running out on him fast.

"Millie, you should be on my side," he whispered, "not theirs."

"You have no side," she said.

"Not so, sister. My actions misrepresent me. The pressure of events. It's happened to me before, if I tell you the truth."

"To all of us," she said.

He had, suddenly, a terrible urge to embrace her and sob, ask for help, but he said, "I have terrible urges to embrace someone, cry out for help." He laughed, "My whole nature howls 'Stop! Why can't we start over, fresh?' In the graveyard, for instance, when I knew for sure . . . almost for sure . . . that my sons were dead. 'This can't go on!' I said. 'We're human beings, a common cause! We ought to present a united front against the wolves and the trolls and the Worldsnake.' Yes! I resolved to confess my terrible guilt to Mr. Paxton. However—"

She closed her eyes.

"—I thought better of it. I decided to turn instead to a life of art.

> *Millie Hodge in whites and pinks,*
> *Reads hard books and thinks and thinks,*
> *Lives life fully, learns it stinks,*
> *Longs for long lost stoves and sinks!*

You approve my decision, of course?"

"No comment," she said. Lights swept over the wall. He paid no attention, then suddenly snapped awake. Millie, too, came suddenly alert. He glanced at the clock on the mantel. *No time for this*, he thought. *No time to spare for trouble*. Nick waited like a cat.

### 4

She hardly noticed the lights passing over the wall behind his head, thrown there by headlights coming up the driveway; hardly noticed even the grinding motor of Hardesty's panel truck. He too, the Sunlight Man, had been off his guard for once. His hands stopped moving and his eyebrows lowered. Though he seemed on the surface, even now, indifferent, infinitely calm, she could feel his concentration in the chill of her blood. There was hardly a chance that Hardesty had not seen him. When the knock came at the back door, the Sunlight Man said, "Let him in."

What happened was very clear to her afterward, but why it happened was not clear. She would never know why he'd said simply, "Let him in," had not even bothered to move out of sight but had waited, holding the pistol in his left hand, standing with his back to the woodshed door but his head partly turned so that he could watch when Hardesty came. Hardesty opened the door a foot and stuck his head in, beaming, neighborly, fat cheeks shiny as varnish under his squint, and he said "Hoddy," his limp hat hanging from his hand. Then he saw the Sunlight Man and they stared at each other, and Nick Slater stood with his hands held away from him as though they were wet. Suddenly, with a jerk of effort that made his face look wild, Hardesty pulled his head back and pulled the door shut behind him and ran out.

"K'out the way!" the Sunlight Man said, coming at her, and he had the gun in his right hand now. She flattened against the refrigerator and he went past her and jerked at the door, and then Nick Slater was beside him, going out after him too. "You wait here," Taggert said.

"No," Nick said.

"Don't!" she yelled, "Please!"—but she wasn't sure afterward whether she'd yelled it aloud or only in her mind.

Luke came staggering to the kitchen and over to the window, eyes screwed up tight, and he looked out into the darkness with his hands at each side of his head like blinders to cut out the windowpane reflections.

"They're going to kill him!" she said.

It came to her that his footsteps had gone toward the chickenhouse, to the south of the garage, but the Sunlight Man had gone north, toward the barn. She could hear them out there shouting, Nick and he, circling through the burdocks so that if he was in the barn he wouldn't get away. It wasn't more than forty feet to the chickenhouse from the garage back door, and it was dark there. Beyond the chickenhouse, the grove began; from there you could make it to the road without being seen. Before she knew she would do it, she kicked off her shoes, slipped out into the garage and through the back door, and began to run. The grass was wet and deep and her feet weren't making a sound. When she got to the high weeds along the side wall she dropped to her knees and pressed into the wall's darkness. She could still hear them, calling to each other. She inched around to the rear wall and whispered through the cracks, "Mr. Hardesty." He'd be gone already, she realized then. There was nothing to stop him from running on through the woods and out to the road. But she whispered again, "Mr. Hardesty, it's me. Millie."

His answer came from so close it made her jump. "In here."

She could peek through the chicken-run door, but she couldn't get in. It was dark as a pit inside. Then her eyes began to adjust. He had his head bent down on the other side of the wall to look out. Beyond him she could see straw and cobwebs and part of a cornplanter someone had stored here, and on the wall a darker place that she knew must be nestboxes.

"You should have run for the grove," she said. "Come around."

"There's no back door," he whispered.

"You have to come out the front, the way you got in, and come around."

"They'll see me sure."

"No they won't. They're by the barn. But hurry."

But they weren't by the barn. She heard Luke's car starting up. They had figured it out and were heading toward the road to cut him off.

"They're leaving," she whispered. "You can cut through the back lot."

But that was wrong too. Only one of them had left: the back door of the garage opened, and through the cracks in the chickenhouse wall opposite her she could see light. After a moment she could feel him coming toward them.

"He's coming," Hardesty said.

"Sh!"

She lay still, feeling the cold softness of the dirt. She dug her hands into it, and it felt good. The lines of light coming through the barn wall looked soft and alive, and where the light touched old straw and dust it made everything sharp and distinct. He took forever to cross the grass place—taking a step, listening a minute, taking another step, it must be. She remembered sleeping in the mow at her grandfather's when she was a child. There were mice and rats there. There would be mice and rats here too, probably. She would sleep in the softness of earth and dew-wet grass and not notice them.

The hinges of the chickenhouse door creaked and Nick said quietly, "Mr. Hardesty?"

It seemed to her that she could hear Hardesty's breathing on the other side of the wall. She tried to breathe without a sound. Then his feet and something he was holding, a pipe maybe, came into view, inside the chickenhouse, and it came to her with a jolt that he would see her. She didn't move. Right now, she knew, he was seeing Hardesty.

Hardesty said softly, "Don't. Please."

She heard him move a little, only his arms perhaps. Nick stood still, directly facing him.

"Please," Hardesty said again.

He won't do it, she thought. There's no reason for him to. Beside Nick's foot there was a pail and a mess of something, old burlap. Light from one of the wall cracks made two little glows on the rim of the pail, like a pair of sights. Her neck ached from holding her head rigid in the same position and she wanted to lean on her arm but she stayed as she was. He'll tell him to get up and come with him, and it will be over, she thought. He'll take him back to the house with him and that will be all.

Hardesty said, "I was startled, that's all. It was crazy to run away like that." He tried to laugh.

He said nothing, and again she could feel him thinking, and then she heard a crack, like the sound a bat makes. Hardesty was screaming, and then she heard the crack again, and she remembered her name was Millie Jewel and Gil was in the barn with his hands tied to the wagon wheel and her grandfather puffing her name Millie Jewel and Gil was in the barn with his hands tied to the wagon wheel and her grandfather puffing her name was Millie Jewel and his hands were tied to the wagon wheel; her grandfather puffing. Gil was her brother. His hands were tied to the wheel spinning in the dark were tied to the wheel her grandfather puffing

The Sunlight Man said, "Come back in the house, Millie." His feet were far apart, and his trousers were wet.

## 5

"Ahem," said Clumly.

Esther was working on the dress she'd been working on for years, sewing and unsewing and sewing.

"I have to go out tonight," he said.

Her lips stopped moving and she turned her face toward him. She sighed. "Will you be late?"

"I don't know." He sucked at the cigar—it had gone out again—then removed it from his lips and glared at it, focusing on it the whole force of his anger. "I imagine I won't be too long. There's no telling, I guess."

She nodded and said nothing. He was grateful for that. The case was making him an old man, cutting the wrinkles of his jowl deeper, darkening the bags under his eyes, wasting his flesh away. She couldn't help but see it, and no doubt it seemed to her her business to worry about it. He'd lost nine pounds in the past two weeks. And it wasn't just the stewing or the physical exhaustion. There was something wrong with him. He ate like a hog, had the trots all the time, and he went on losing weight. Ate from sickness, not love of food. The very smell of food was revolting to him. He felt as if he had lead in his stomach, and when that confounded speech for the Dairyman's League came into his mind, or the thought of Miller standing in a doorway watching him, or the memory of the papers piling up on his desk, or Will Hodge Sr forever turning up in unexpected places, staring at him, Clumly's whole chest filled up, or so he imagined, with greenish gas.

Esther said, as if to herself, "When will it be over?"

"Not long now," Clumly said heartily, and added, "one way or another." And then, because that sounded ominous: "We pretty well got it wound up, Kozlowski and me." The thought of Kozlowski, like everything else, stirred the green gas feeling in his chest. He'd felt free at first, a kind of joyful release, letting Kozlowski in on it. Kozlowski was a man who stood back from things, looked them over, so to speak, and came up with his own private judgments. That was exactly what Clumly had thought he needed. It wasn't even that he wanted Kozlowski to corroborate his own suspicions. The man's presence was enough, gave Clumly something to hang on to, as you might say. And best of all, Kozlowski was no talker. Whatever his private opinions might be about Clumly's manhunt, he would say nothing to the others. He was safe as a bank. Or so it had all seemed then, when Clumly had made his decision to let him in. Not now. Because this afternoon when Clumly had come out of his office to go home, Kozlowski and Miller were talking by the desk, and at sight of him they stopped talking. Kozlowski had nodded his greeting to Clumly, and Miller had called with exaggerated cheerfulness, "Cutting out, Boss?" "Going home, yes," Clumly had said. "Say hello to the wife,"

Miller said, and showed his grin. Clumly had nodded. They'd watched him out the door. At his car, Clumly had stood fiddling with his keys, heart racing in his chest, a belch forming, inexorable, and he'd wanted desperately to sneak back and spy and find out what they were saying. Crazily, he'd looked along the ledge below the window. He could climb up the corner of the building, where the crossed corner blocks formed a kind of natural ladder, and he could get up on the ledge and inch across. . . . He'd be out in plain sight, where anybody driving up Main Street couldn't help but see him, and the next day, who knew? he might open the paper and see a picture of himself crawling on the jailhouse ledge, and some lunatic caption: CHIEF TRIES TO BREAK INTO JAIL. CLAIMS HE LOST HIS KEYS. And so he'd climbed into his car, nerves twitching, and had driven slowly home. Trust *nobody*, he thought. But the thought brought a ghastly smile. He was beyond that now, had no choice but to trust Kozlowski. He'd told him to come pick him up here at nine, to go with him to his appointment with the Sunlight Man. It was now five minutes to.

He got up out of his armchair wearily, hesitated a moment, from habit, to let the hint of dizziness that always came when he got to his feet pass through him and subside. Then he went to the clothespress for his coat and hat and revolver. When he opened the door a shock of alarm ran up his arms and legs. He thought there was a man there, waiting among the coats. A mistake, of course. He rubbed his mouth with his right hand, giving his heartbeat time to slow down, then put the gunbelt on, the hat, the coat. He thought, *Suppose I were to leave before Kozlowski shows up, like the pig in the story.* Kozlowski didn't know where the appointment was.

"Someone's here," his wife called from the livingroom. "A car just drove up."

"Mmm," Clumly said. "One of my men. I'll be right there." He turned his head to glance craftily at the kitchen door, behind him, and then he glanced over at the diningroom window. He too could hear the car motor. *Still time*, he thought. *A man could be over to that window and out* . . . But she would hear him—what's-her-name, his wife. Who would understand? In the morning the Mayor would be waiting for him, and the men in white coats would be with him, maybe. No. Now there came a knock at the door. He heard her crossing to it, drawing the door open. "Hello," she said. "Fred says he'll be right out." He took a deep breath. *Take a Deep Breath,* he thought. Title for a speech.

"Lot of people might get the wrong idea about this, Kozlowski," Clumly said. He sat with his elbow out the window, head thrown back, cold cigar in his right fist. "There's different ways you go about investigating. You follow me? It all depends on the situation. Sometimes you go after a criminal right away, sometimes you give him rope and let him hang himself. It's like a farmer." He squinted at the branches above the street, lighted up by the streetlamps and the prowlcar's headlights, and he pursed his lips. He shot a glance at Kozlowski, then squinted upward again. "It's like a farmer," he said again. He'd started it with confidence, but now, in panic, he realized he could think of no example. "A cow starts crowding you when you're milking her, moving over on you, you know what I mean. Well sometimes you give her a knee in the belly, and sometimes . . ." No, that was wrong. You had no alternatives, in that case. "Or like a dog that chases cars," he said, "or a horse that nibbles the stall." He nodded, thoughtful. The hell with it. Let Kozlowski figure it out if he was so smart.

"Pull in here," he said.

Kozlowski looked surprised, but he slowed and turned left and came to a stop at the cemetery gates.

"Hell of a place for a meeting, eh, Kozlowski?" He chuckled.

Kozlowski turned his black-socketed eyes toward him.

They sat with the headlights shining in, throwing bars across the grass and the nearest tombstones and the trunks of trees. He tried to think how much he should say of what Kozlowski might expect of the cracked magician. He framed the beginnings of sentences in his head, but he couldn't decide to let them out. "Gate's probably open," he said. "That would be like him. I'll see." He opened the car door and got out and went around to the front and pushed at the gate. He'd guessed right. It opened away from him, creaking. "Might's well drive in," he said. He forced a smile. He stepped back to the right, and Kozlowski drove up even with him and let him back in.

"Want the gate left open?" Kozlowski said.

"Might's well," he said, studiously off-hand. They'd park the car in plain sight. Yes. It looked crazy coming to the meeting at all; at least they didn't have to look like they were sneaking. "Park here," he said. "Kill the motor."

Kozlowski switched off the key and turned the lights out. "Ok," Clumly said. He clapped his hands softly. He made no move to get out. He felt short-winded. For a minute or more they sat in the cemetery's hush, behind them the long curve of the cemetery drive, the wrought-iron fence, the blank, abandoned blackness of the old Massey-Harris plant and, above it, the yellow-red glow of the city. Nothing stirred anywhere. Clumly sighed. "Ok," he said again. "Here's how it is. I'll go over where he's waiting—that little crypt over there, with the fence around it."

Kozlowski nodded.

"Give me two, three minutes, then you follow and wait by the door. I'll get him talking, let him babble about anything he wants. If we're lucky he'll let something slip, something that tells us who he is, where he's worked before, what he's up to —that kind of thing. You just stand there and listen, don't make a move unless I yell. If my guess is right he'll pull one of those disappearing acts, sooner or later. You keep your eyes and ears peeled, don't miss a thing, and *zap!* we've got him. And keep out of sight. If anybody shows up to help him, see who it is, find out where they go. You got it?"

Kozlowski nodded.

"And don't touch the radio." He took the flashlight from the glove compartment. "Anybody calls, don't answer it—unless they ask for me. Then it's ok."

"Yessir."

He pressed the flashlight button, testing it. It worked. He put the flashlight inside his shirt with the tape recorder. Then he lit the cigar. "Ok." He saluted. Unnaturally official. It was as if, he thought, he were trying to pretend to himself that the whole thing was regular. He opened the car door, got out, and closed it quietly.

"See you," Kozlowski said.

He felt moved by it. Touched. He nodded solemnly and started across the dew-wet cemetery grass toward the crypt.

Both the wrought-iron gate and the studded iron door to the crypt itself stood open. Clumly bent forward, his hand on the side of the door, and peered in. He could see nothing. It was cold here at the doorway to the crypt. A shiver passed over him, and he could not tell whether it was the chill in the air or childish fear or outrage. *Damned clown,* he thought. That was what made the whole thing so infuriating. Not the fact that he'd chosen a cemetery crypt, a gloomy night, but the fact that the Sunlight Man loved clowning, took monstrous delight in playing with a human being as though he were a toy. It was the incredible ego of the man that made you sweat. Who could say when he would stop being amused and end the game? But that was nonsense, of course. He could admit to himself that it was nonsense, but he wasn't yet admitting why he'd come. "When all's known," he thought, seeing if it sounded at all convincing, "it may prove that every word that man said about the Negro boy and the store full of salesmen is true. Who can say? I may be matching wits with a Master of Crime." He glanced over his shoulder, sheepish. He felt for the handle of his pistol. Still there. But he didn't really expect he'd be allowed to keep it. His enemy was everywhere at once. A thousand tricks, But a man had no choice. No choice. It was a comfort.

His eyes had somewhat adjusted to the darkness now. He could make out, just barely, the slabs of the crypt floor, the iron exfoliation on the arched window of the crypt's back wall, the shelves of concrete, two on each side, and the four enormous wooden caskets, gray with age. He calmed himself. "Are you here?" Clumly said. The thick concrete walls gave a boom to his voice, and again he felt a shiver of mingled terror and indignation. "Piece of foolishness," he thought. "Damned nonsense."

And then—ridiculous! height of indignity!—something whirred past his shoulder and struck the far wall and stuck fast. He whirled, drawing his pistol, but there was no one. From the crypt to the cemetery fence nothing stirred. To his right the police car sat waiting in the darkness, Kozlowski sitting in the driver's seat as though nothing had happened. Cautiously, pistol still drawn, Clumly entered the crypt and moved toward the far wall, pulling out the flashlight and snapping it on as he went. Low on the concrete wall he found an arrow, a child's arrow with a suction-cup tip, and attached to the arrow, a note. It was written in pencil, in childish block letters: WELCOME. As he frowned and read, the paper shaking under his flashlight, the crypt door behind him swung shut, slowly—but he could not move quickly enough to prevent its closing—and the lock clicked. Clumly leaned on the chilly wall, shaking, believing he would faint. He stood leaning for what seemed five minutes, and ice-cold sweat ran down his face and neck.

Thank God for the flashlight. At length, without a sound, the lid of the coffin on the upper shelf to his left lifted three inches and a white-gloved hand, limp as the glove of a vaudeville clown, groped along the edge. Clumly was beyond horror now. He felt only the profound, hopeless disgust of a man repeatedly victimized by moronic jokes, with no sign of hope on the horizon.

"Don't shoot," a timid voice said. It came from all around him.

Clumly smiled like a dead man, still training the flashlight beam on the limp white glove. He was morally certain that if he fired he would find there were no bullets in his gun. He was tempted, almost overpoweringly, to try it. Slowly, the coffin lid opened the rest of the way, and the Sunlight Man sat up. He was dressed as before, in the same moth-eaten black suit, but he had on a ludicrous derby now, and his face (horrible!) was painted white.

When he was upright, the Sunlight Man said, not moving his lips, as far as Clumly could see—perhaps because of the thick white paint on his skin—*"Now* you can shoot."

"Don't be ridiculous," Clumly snarled. He lowered the gun and moved closer.

"No, do. I beg you."

Before he'd quite thought about it—the prickle of heat running down his arms took the place of thought—Clumly obeyed. In the small, sealed room, the pistol was no louder than a capgun, or so Clumly imagined. The Sunlight Man took on a look of dead surprise, then slumped over the side of the casket and hung there, one arm dangling. Horrified, Clumly slipped the gun to its holster, leaped to the man, and caught at the white glove. It came off in his hand, dry cloth. The arm was straw. Clumly clutched his head between his hands and bent his knees, grinding his teeth. And now, behind him, the Sunlight Man said happily, "That was good, right? You were mystified. Admit it!" Clumly went rigid. At last he turned his head slowly and looked up between his fingers. The Sunlight Man sat upright in the coffin across the room from the first, dressed in the same black suit, the same derby, his face the same white mask. In his hand he had Clumly's pistol. He blew across the mouth of the barrel. "Now," he said. Then, after a moment: "You're all right?"

Clumly dragged deeply for air. "Get on with it," he whispered. "For God's sake get on with it!"

The Sunlight Man heaved a sigh. "Ah well," he said. He looked away and, after a moment, smiled. "You brought the tape recorder?"

Dutifully, Clumly drew it from his shirt.

SUNLIGHT: To begin with, don't worry about the door. When the time comes, it will be opened, you will be delivered. Have faith. As for the fellow outside, he has orders to wait. And now to business. Let me get comfortable, though. There. What were we speaking of last time? You remember? You've studied the tape, I imagine?

CLUMLY: I've listened to it.

SUNLIGHT: I think we were speaking of the astrological houses.

CLUMLY: Mmm.

SUNLIGHT: And of freedom, a man's responsibility to maintain his freedom at any cost. You've thought about all this?

CLUMLY *(after a pause)*: Some.

SUNLIGHT: Ah! And you've reached some conclusion?

CLUMLY: I think it's nonsense.

SUNLIGHT: Ah ha! Expand!

CLUMLY: I'd rather not. I'd rather hear it to the end. That is, I'm interested to hear what you think you'll . . . *get* out of this.

SUNLIGHT: Very good! Fine! In other words, to what extent is the action itself individual—a personal as well as a universal expression.

CLUMLY *(without conviction)*: That's it.

SUNLIGHT: So we come to the subject of the Mesopotamian dead.

CLUMLY: Hah.

SUNLIGHT: Are you familiar with the epic of Gilgamesh? A splendid epic, but very obscure, difficult for people like us— undramatic, one thinks at first glance. A technique made up of careful segmentation, with elaborate echoing, repeating and counterpointing, with texture enriched still more by rare and artificial words. You understand me, I take it? A kind of poetry naturally suited to elaborate description and oration and hymnic address, symbolic dreams, and armings. Needless to say, its poetry not suited to dramatic actions which move the story forward. Lifeless, people call it. And they observe with sorrow that in Akkadian historical writing—prose—the battle of Sennacherib, for instance—there's splendid *brío*, a clear delight in the joy and furor of fighting. "Make 'em laugh, make 'em cry, make 'em wait" was the rule for historians. But for poets hobbling on the clumsy crutches of their intricate technique, the rule was, "Make 'em snore." Ah, pity! one might say, if one were sentimentally inclined. But the Akkadian artists are dead, praise God, and no grand vile hicks can poke their bellies with the pointed stick of brainless criticism! What was I saying?

CLUMLY: Actually—

SUNLIGHT: Yes of course! The Akkadian technique. They were concerned with larger elements of form. They played scene against scene, speech against speech. Lovely! It makes you want to march! This interests you?

CLUMLY: Not really.

SUNLIGHT: Very well, then. To the point.

Eleven of the twelve tablets tell of Gilgamesh's life and adventures during his unsuccessful quest for immortality.

CLUMLY: Mmm.

SUNLIGHT: The poet sets up two parallel scenes—one at the beginning of the first tablet, the other at the end of the eleventh tablet—as a frame which symbolically establishes the futility of the quest. He focuses on an image of walls—the walls of the city Gilgamesh has built, Uruk. There are parallel lines, at the beginning and end—the poet's description and comment in the introit that the walls will be the hero's only immortality (but his name will cease to be connected with them)—and Gilgamesh's own description, an echo. The poet goes farther. The same walls that are the hero's only glory seal his doom. To get the walls built, Gilgamesh is forced to make all the inhabitants of his city work for him like slaves. The people cry out to the gods, the gods are enraged and resolve to destroy him. There you have the paradox. The rest of the epic elaborates it, describing the kinds of immortality Gilgamesh tries for and misses—eternal youth, lasting fame, and so on. The twelfth book tells of Gilgamesh pointlessly ruling the pointless dead. It's introduced—not by accident—by the tale of the universal Flood, the final destruction from which no one escapes except temporarily. Enough. One can't say everything.

In Babylon—I leap to essentials—personal immortality is a mad goal. Death is a reality. Any struggle whatever for per-

sonal fulfillment is wrong-headed. Mankind is walled in from
the outset: the very walls man builds around his city to lock
out his enemies are the walls around his tomb. The pursuit of
Youth is ridiculous, the Babylonian says. Compare America:
"Come alive! You're in the Pepsi generation!" Doll-faced fifty-
year-old boys and girls on bicycles-built-for-two smoking Sal-
ems (sign of Spring), heavy-headed with cosmetics, weak-wit-
ted from dieting. I speak of things general. Youth be damned!
We die of it! The pursuit of fame, equally mad. Compare
America. Every girl in gradeschool wants to be a movie star, a
famous doctor, the inventor of radium, the lady riding the fat
white horse in the Shriners' Circus—and when she's old, ah
woe! a misery of failed ambitions: cooking dinner in her curl-
ers for her 2.4 children and the sullen grouch in the crewcut
watching "Ripcord." Or if you're good you can be John Kennedy, and Mexicans will buy your head in handsomely gilded
plastic in the shops of Tijuana. Fame! The same for the pursuit of lineage—Gilgamesh died without issue, being a city
man. And the same for the building of great palaces, or the
writing of symphonies, the amassing of wealth. As for the pursuit of Heaven, the answer in the Gilgamesh is that if there's
an afterlife it's sealed up, brothers, walled in, sisters, like life.
And so, in answer to your question, one acts to maintain the
freedom to act, but the ultimate act, the act which comes
when the gods command it, is utterly impersonal, a movement
of the universe, a stroke by, for, and of sole interest to—the
gods.

Why act at all then? you may ask. Very good! Because action is life. That's the importance of the twelfth tablet; the "actions" of the dead king among the dead. The question is not
shall I act or not act, but how shall I act? Even indecision is
an act, after all: a choice not to act in either of two alternative
directions. Is all this clear?

CLUMLY: Clear enough.

SUNLIGHT: Good. Good! Then we come to the crux.

Once one's said it, that one must act, one must ask oneself,
shall I act within the cultural order I do not believe in but with
which I am engaged by ties of love or anyway ties of fellow-
feeling, or shall I act within the cosmic order I *do* believe in,
at least in principle, an order indifferent to man? And then
again, shall I act by standing indecisive between the two orders
—not striking out for the cosmic order because of my human

commitment, not striking out for the cultural order because of my divine commitment? Which shall I renounce, my body—of which ethical intellect is a function—or my soul?

CLUMLY: This is all very long-winded, you know. And confusing.

SUNLIGHT: Pure chaos.

CLUMLY: Hard to follow, I mean.

SUNLIGHT: A veritable labyrinth!

*(Pause.)*

Listen.

I was once a famous French-horn player.

CLUMLY: That's ridiculous!

SUNLIGHT: My word of honor! Have I ever lied to you? I graduated from the Eastman School of Music, studied with Arkady Yegudkin, first horn in the orchestra of Czar Nicholas. Fled Russia in 1918, on a railroad flatcar, with his wife. Played all over Europe. Famous for what's known as the "smiling embouchure." Affectionately called "the General" by his students. You can check. I'll give you even more detail— I'm not unaware that my time is running out. I played first horn for seven years with the Dallas Symphony. It was there, by the way, that I first began to dabble in magic. Learned from the famous Thurston. You've heard of him?

CLUMLY: Never.

SUNLIGHT: You're difficult to reason with, you know that?

CLUMLY: I'm sorry.

SUNLIGHT: Well, to make a long story short, I fell in love. A dancing girl in her thirties . . . No, I remember now . . . An operatic singer.

CLUMLY: Good God.

SUNLIGHT: You're distracting me.

CLUMLY: I'm sorry.

SUNLIGHT: No, I'll tell you the truth. She was a striptease dancer. I saw her first in an obscene movie, one of those things in obscenacolor. She was beautiful, truly breathtaking. Naked, of course. They had a Kodiak bear strapped to a table, muzzled . . .

CLUMLY *(violently):* That's enough! I'm an old man. I'm tired. Open the door. Do you hear me? *Kozlowski!*

SUNLIGHT: Shut up. Sit down.

CLUMLY: I'm telling you—

SUNLIGHT: But that's absurd. I've got the gun!

CLUMLY: Then shoot. *(Shouting:) Kozlowski!!*

SUNLIGHT *(wearily):* All right. Take it easy. I was lying. There was no bear.

CLUMLY: You make me sick.

SUNLIGHT: It's because I'm a criminal.

*(Silence.)*

That stops you, doesn't it.

*(Silence.)*

You think, "The *waste* of it!" *(Pause.)* But *is* it waste? Shall we be honest, Clumly? I'll tell you a story that's absolutely true. You'll know it at once, no need whatever to check it. I was once a policeman. -

CLUMLY: Stop it!

SUNLIGHT *(patiently):* I was once a policeman. I got old, out of touch. The plain truth—I knew it as well as I knew my own name—was that I was about to be fired, there was absolutely no hope. And then one day I arrested a kind of nut, a man with a beard. A sort of crazy idea came into my head. I could *use* him. I had a feeling in my bones that the man was destructive, somehow fundamentally evil—you know what I mean? No one believed me, but I knew. The man was dangerous—whether because of something he'd done already or because of something he was capable of doing, I couldn't say. Nevertheless, I was never more sure of anything in my life. Besides, he was my only chance.

CLUMLY: You're wrong!

SUNLIGHT: Not quite. I began to hound him, think of nothing but getting him and thus vindicating myself, clear myself with the Mayor—who was a fool anyway—and, more important, clear myself with my men. They were like sons to me. The thought that they might have to pityingly let me go was more than I could bear. I was proud, in short. *Hubris* of the specially deadly, Christian kind. And yet on the other hand, I was right: the man *was* evil. He hounded me as cruelly as I hounded him. It was his pride, it came to me. His incredible ego. A twisted kind of ego that wasted itself on idiotic, spectacular tricks. I pretended to myself that he was what they would call in those old-fashioned thrillers "a Fiend," but I knew the truth all along. He was merely a queer duck, a crackpot philosopher who'd slipped out of the society he lived in and detested it for surviving without him, yet he couldn't really act, blow it up, destroy it; too feeble. He made me his sounding board, tried to use me, as I used him, to save himself. I thought: "Nobody can save himself. Salvation has always come from outside—from prophets, from wives, from children." And then I thought: "But *he* doesn't know it." And then I knew I had him. He could outsmart me, trick me, mock me until he was blue in the face. Finally he was the mouse, and I was the tiger. And then one night—we were talking about towers—he stupidly gave me the gun. I knew who he was, by that time, and I knew that, as far as the law was concerned, he was a thief, public enemy, accessory to a killer. I could be vindicated. What do you suppose I did?

*(Silence.)*

I said, what do you suppose I did?

*(Long pause.)*

CLUMLY: Tell me what to do.

SUNLIGHT: How can I? We're friends. I've told you that all along. But the fact remains, you are a policeman. You have a wife to think of—and more. Your feeling for your men. And for yourself. I'm an accessory to three murders. Not to mention other crimes of a lesser nature. Plenty. If you act on the side of the universe—if you follow my half-wit metaphor—you'll blink, turn your face away. If you act for humanity . . .

CLUMLY: I don't understand.

SUNLIGHT: You're supposed to ask, at this point, what *I* do if I act on the side of the universe, and what I do if I act for humanity.

CLUMLY: Go on.

SUNLIGHT: If I act for the universe, I may kill you. If I act for humanity, I kill you and then myself.

*(Silence.)*

CLUMLY: There must be a choice. There's *always* a choice!

SUNLIGHT: If only we weren't so stubborn.

CLUMLY: I'm willing to listen.

SUNLIGHT: But *I* am stubborn. *(Pause.)* It's time for my trick.

CLUMLY: Wait!

SUNLIGHT: Consider! I lie down in my casket. I close the lid.

CLUMLY: Wait! One more minute!

SUNLIGHT *(muffled—inside the casket)*: Hark! A trumpet! *(Sound of a trumpet, muffled. An instant later, sound of an explosion.)*

CLUMLY: Wait!

While the smoke still billowed from under the coffin lid, he leaped toward the casket and opened it. Inside he found nothing but his revolver. To his left, the door of the crypt swung open.

"You ok, Chief?" Kozlowski said.

Clumly turned slowly, squinting. He closed the casket lid and dropped the pistol in its holster. "God knows," he said. "You saw him?"

Kozlowski shook his head.

Clumly put his hand to his nose and pursed his lips. *Three murders* the man had said. He couldn't be counting the woman killed by the car wreck. Someone else must have been killed, then. *My fault,* he thought. *That's it. Enough!* His knees went weak. After a moment Clumly said, "Let's head for home, Kozlowski."

They started out. The crypt door closed, again by itself, behind them.

# XVI

## Love and Duty

### *1*

*who would gladly have spared him all this if I could (God knows, no lie) and was innocent once, full of mystery, magic, made cherryboughs bend (so it seemed to me once) in my father's orchard when I stood squinting up with my milky-white eyes at where light bent the branches down lacy, sweet-smelling, and cherries fell ripe to my outstretched hand; yes, not a dream I think, perfectly real; and my father and mother stood back from me, watching and I think were smiling, too far in the wash of bright green for*

No, a dream.

What right have I to set myself up as his keeper?

But he had no right.

She wipes away blindwoman tears, puts her sewing away in the woven basket, the ancient ruse of her long wait, house empty, barren of children lovers tradesmen friends, her husband still gone, vanished from the world like a sailor, no one knows where. She turns her virginal back to the room, gropes

593

for the doorknob, opens the door, steps out. She walks quickly, fingers trembling, knowing she is perhaps wrong, turning on him, a false wife, but can no longer chance doing nothing, she may even now be too late. She moves down LaCrosse, head stiffly erect, drawn back a little, sharp elbows out like drawn-in wings. She comes to Lyon Street, turns hesitantly left. Miss Buckland calls for her cat. Birds warbling.

A momentous decision, she understands, though she does not know what hangs on it, has no way of guessing that time has stopped, hangs ready to reverse as old Hubble's bubble prepares to collapse, a new stroke of the giant heart; or at any rate that human hearts, caught and locked in their wide thrombosis, hardening, dark with indecision, will tremble to the prick of her wellmeant revolt and life will move again, rush down its channels, roaring.

At the police station she asks to speak to Miller.

2

She found him, at last, in her husband's office. "Hello," she said. She stood listening, heart beating fiercely. It was already growing hot. The fan was on, but the air did not stir. As far as she could tell he was the only one there.

"Mrs. Clumly," he said guiltily, as though she'd caught him at something.

She stood irresolute, mind racing. *If it were merely that, another woman . . .* At last she said, "Could I speak with you a moment—alone?" She waited.

"Why sure," he said then, heartily. "Figlow, you'll excuse us?"

It made her jump a foot. She was slipping. The man who'd been standing as quiet as a statue now crossed without a word and went past her. He smelled of stale cigarettes and sweat. The footsteps stopped a little behind her and she heard the door close. Then he went on. She heard the other door closing now. Then Miller said, "What can I do for you, Esther?" It was all starting out wrong somehow. For the hundredth time she was unsure of herself, afraid her butting in would only mean embarrassment and trouble. She took a deep breath and

closed her hand more tightly on the handles of the sewing bag.
"Sit down, Mrs. Clumly," Miller said, growing formal. He
touched her arm—she had not realized he was standing so
close—and guided her toward the chair.

"Thank you."

They waited.

Miller said, "Long time no see, Mrs. Clumly."

She laughed nervously. "That's what you said the other
night."

He too laughed. "So I did."

They waited again and eventually both spoke at the same
time, apologized, waited. Esther balled up her hanky between
her two hands to dry the perspiration. "Mr. Miller—that is,
Officer—I had a visitor early this morning."

"I see," Miller said.

"Perhaps I should explain." She paused, thinking where to
begin. "Fred and I have been husband and wife," she began
carefully, "for a long time."

"Yes."

"We—understand each other, about many things." She corrected the impression quickly. "We understand each other, but
of course my husband doesn't always tell me everything, naturally, being in the line of work he happens to be in. He doesn't
like to worry me needlessly, you know."

"No, naturally."

"I'm sure it's the same with you."

"Of course."

She rolled the hanky more rapidly between her palms. "I
have always been very grateful to Fred . . . to my husband.
Because of course it's difficult, you know . . . with my handicap. That is—"

"Yes of course," he said. "Either way, that is, handicapped
or not, as you say, a husband that's a cop can be a problem."
He laughed.

"Yes." She thought about it. "That's true. But I meant, really, it's not easy for him either, you know. He's always been
very patient and he never criticizes. I almost—forget myself."
She let the words hang in the air a moment, reverberating oddly in the room; then: "I've felt I could never deserve, that is,
repay . . . I think you see what I mean."

"Come now," he said, "that's a heck of a thing!"

"Yes. Well, in any case, I *hear* certain things—that is, cer-

tain *rumors* have come to my attention—and this morning a
visitor . . ." She bit her lips and leaned forward. "Officer, I
have reason to believe there is a plot against my husband. I'm
going against his wishes in telling you, no doubt. But I must
think of myself, too, mustn't I? Don't I have a right?"

She waited. Miller said nothing.

"I trust my husband implicitly, Officer Miller," she said softly. "But I'm not sure he's always as cautious as he might be.
I'm not sure he's aware of—the dangers. And at times I've felt
he has a tendency to, well, go off on his own, as you might say
—to do things without telling other people, so that if something were to happen, if he were to be, say—" She hesitated
only for an instant, then plunged. "If he were to be shot in an
alley, no one would know he was missing. That's why I've
come."

"Now now now," Miller said. "That's ridiculous, Mrs.
Clumly."

"He's been gone since last night," she said in a rush. "When
I called here this morning, no one had seen him. I realize he's
not away with some woman, of course." She hurried on. "But
that means . . ."

He laughed lightly and yet kindly, the way men are forever
laughing at the fears of women. "He's with Kozlowski," he
said. "He was just on the radio." She felt a violent sense of relief, then uncertainty. Miller did not seem to her as confident
as he wished her to believe he was, and she knew, suddenly,
that she'd done the right thing in coming.

"Officer Miller," she said, "doesn't it strike you as *odd* that
a maniac such as this Sunlight Man should be able to elude
you all for so long, and stores be robbed and people murdered
and none of you able to stop it—*you*, I mean, people of proven
ability? Doesn't it seem that there might be more than meets
the eye? Officer Miller, suppose there *were* a plot—suppose
people of influence were involved in these . . ."

She waited, hanging in space, but he only cleared his throat.
He too was worried, she saw. She closed the hanky in her right
hand and came out with it. "Officer—Officer Miller—I believe
the Mayor knows something about all this." Tears came, and
she struggled against them. "I believe he's *behind* it," she said
fiercely. "I have reason to think so. Anyway, I have reason to
think my husband has been secretly investigating some mysterious goings-on at the Mayor's house, some kind of political I-

don't-know-what, not Communists, perhaps, but something. And Will Hodge is in on it. That's who came to visit, and he asked a lot of questions that sounded very suspicious, it seemed to me—he came when Fred was away, you know, and he *knew* Fred was away, and in fact it wasn't the first time, either, because when he drove away afterward I realized I'd heard that car before, prowling around, sometimes in the middle of the night, you know. What kind of people prowl around in the middle of the night, I ask you?"

"You're excited, Mrs. Clumly," Miller said. "Take it easy, now. Stay loose." He touched her hand, and again she was startled to find he was so close.

"I have reason to—" She stopped and swallowed and did not continue until she was sure she could control her voice. "I think I have reason to be excited," she said. "I haven't told you the worst. He wasn't alone."

"Who?" Miller said.

"Mr. Hodge, the lawyer. He came and asked these questions, and he pretended he was all by himself, but right outside the door, right on the porch, or beside the porch, I'm not sure, there was someone listening—taking it all down, I think."

"Taking it down? How could you tell?"

"Well, I'm not sure," she said. "But I had the distinct impression. Sometimes people in my situation—" Again her voice failed her and she waited, swallowing. He patted her hand. "And there have been other things," she said. "Someone came from the Federal Government, late at night. Or anyway they said that's what they were, if I remember. He sounded Russian, a little. He left a message, a strange one. I hardly dare—"

"Strange?" he said.

"Well, it was written on a paper airplane." She waited for Miller to laugh, but he was silent. It frightened her.

At last he said, "I'll look into all this, Mrs. Clumly. I give you my word. I've been so blasted busy . . . Meanwhile, don't fret. All right? Go home and take a hot bath—or buy yourself a hat—take your mind off all this. It's nothing, I know that already, but I'll check. Ok?"

"I'm not finished," she said.

After a while he said, "All right, go on."

She drew the tapes from the sewing bag. "I found these. They're his. I think they're the evidence. I don't know. I thought since he trusts you—since you've always been a very loyal, well—I thought you should know they exist."

Again the frightening silence. At last he sighed. "Mrs. Clumly, if the Chief wanted me to hear these things he'd bring them to me."

"Yes I know. But as I said—"

Miller shifted in his chair. "I can't take them. I'm sorry. I understand how you feel, but it's impossible. Really."

"Then listen to them at least," she whispered. "Please, Mr. Miller. Then if anything happens—if the people behind all this do something awful to him—at least there will be someone who knows. I beg you."

"I can't. That's final. As a policeman—"

"As a friend! That's all I ask. Just listen."

"Look," he said. He thought a moment. "If I believed in this plot, as you put it, then all right, that would be something else. But I don't. You see? You found them hidden in the house, right? He didn't want you to see them, or me, or the Mayor, or Jesus, or anybody. Right? How can I just plug in the machine and—"

"Please," she said.

She heard him getting up, moving away from her. After that, silence. He was staring at her, or staring out the window, or standing with his eyes shut, she couldn't tell. At last, quietly, but like an explosion, he said, "All right." She listened to him moving toward her, and without a word she held up the tapes to him. He took them, and after a moment she heard him putting the first of them in the tape recorder on the desk. She heard the button jump in, and then whirring, a sort of groaning noise, several sharp thumps. Now the tape ran quietly, and there were voices, far away and muffled. Miller made them louder.

Then, very clearly, they heard the words: *What are you fiddling with, there inside your shirt?*

"Jesus," Miller whispered.

"What?" she said.

*I might have known. Very well, just as you please.* Then a laugh.

Miller switched off the tape.

"What is it?" she said.

"Nothing," he said. She could hear him unwinding the tape, taking it off.

"What is it?" she asked again, sharply this time.

When he spoke his voice was too even, and she knew that, whatever it was she'd done, she had ruined her husband and had made it impossible for even Miller to help him now. "It's the Sunlight Man, Esther," Miller said. "The man we're after."

"Then Fred's found him," she said desperately. "He's *talked* to him."

"That's right," Miller said. "But he hasn't talked to us." He put the spool of tape very gently in her hand. "Here," he said. "Put it where you found it. Or burn it. Do what you want with it. I don't want to know it exists."

"Is it so bad?" she said, knowing.

"I'll drive you home," he said.

She stood up, listening with the back of her mind to the crackling of the radio in the other room. "I'd rather walk," she said. "Thank you."

"Whatever you like." He put his hand on her arm, thinking of saying more perhaps, but nothing more came. The hand went away, and a moment later she heard the door come open behind her.

"I'm sorry," she said. She pressed the hanky to her mouth.

Miller was silent.

Mr. Uphill, the Fire Chief, said, "What *is* all this?"

Esther jumped.

"Nothing," Miller said.

"Nothing my hat!" Uphill said.

She backed away, her hand over the tapes in her sewing bag.

"Now hold on, Miller," Uphill said. "You listen here."

Miller touched her arm. "It's all right," he said.

And so, at midnight, after walking the city streets restlessly the whole day, she stood alone in the bare third-floor room of the empty house, not crying now, only her chest crying, one hand lightly resting on the side of the window that stood open before her, tall blind eye looking at the darkness of the city (she could hear traffic, far away, an occasional whisper from the leaves of the trees around the house), her lips moving, not making a sound, not even making any sense any more, a movement independent of what thoughts passed through her head, it seemed; and she remembered years from some other life, far away and trivial and sweet as a fairytale, a young girl's sorrows over trifling things, a mother's sweet and touching madness, a sailorboy walking through a wood with her, holding her hand with a sweet and ridiculous tenderness, and they made pictures with stones and he talked of the weather and she said with, oh, infinite righteousness, that she did not believe in indiscriminate kissing (but she was going to have an operation, and afterward, who knew? perhaps she would see as well as anyone, and then it would be she who talked of the weather—ah, how eagerly! how little he saw, really saw!—and, tenderly pressing her mouth to his, she would teach him that all his life he had been blind); but it had failed. "Sorry," she whispered. The dark street heard her—or so it seemed to her momentary fancy—and the earth, cooling from the heat of the day—and a wind came, warm and comforting, and some neighbor coughed, struggling futilely to clear the grit and sludge of his long day of smoking, and she thought of Clumly coming home from his concubine, finding her there on the lawn—or dangling, it might be, from the roof of the porch—and, in short, for better or worse, she could not act. She had meant to be his comfort, his intercessor, but she had destroyed him. She bowed her head. "Sorry," she whispered again, unable to weep. "I too have a life, don't I?"

Then Esther Clumly went down to her bed and lay there, with all her clothes on, even her shoes, nose pointing at the ceiling, arms at her sides, inert and absurd as . . . She furrowed her forehead, trying to think what it was that she looked like, lying there, and suddenly she knew, and the insight was almost pleasing because it was so right. "Like a chicken," she said, and sobbed. "In this house of tragedy, lying here like a horrible, stiff chicken."

# XVII

Benson *versus*
Boyle

> *Yet thanks I must you con,*
> *That you are thieves profess'd; that you work not*
> *In holier shapes: for there is boundless theft*
> *In limited professions. Rascal thieves,*
> *Here's gold.*

—Timon of Athens

## 1

Walter Benson had a bad cold. His nose dripped and his chest ached and his eyes ran so badly he could hardly see. It made him cynical and cross, and in a hundred ways it interfered with the resolve he'd made the night before last, the night of the thunderstorm. He'd thought then, oh yes, of throwing all caution to the winds: he would call the Batavia police and tell them all he knew, and if by involving himself he ended up exposing himself, then so be it. The Lord is Just! It had been an exhilarating idea, at the time. But when one thought about it, really thought about it, it was nonsense. And another thing which contributed to his change—or rather, relapse—of heart was this: whenever he had a cold his wife Marguerite was always unusually kind and solicitous, forever bringing him sweets, offering him orange or grapefruit juice, plying him with candied pills and sugary syrups freighted with aspirin and codeine and milk of magnesia and heaven knew what; or she would read to him out of the *Saturday Evening Post* or *Field and Stream* (which he did not like but which it flattered him to have people think he would be the type to like); and she would ask him if he wanted the Venetian blinds adjusted or if he needed the hotpad turned up or wanted more Vicks on his chest. He liked all this, especially now, when he knew it was pure hypocrisy, and the more he growled and fretted and whined, the harder she struggled to please him. He revelled in his illness and his jealousy both, and pretended to himself that both were considerably worse than they were, and he said to himself, with a testy curl of the lip, that he would think about "that other" sometime when he was better, his heart not breaking in two, as it was just now, and his nose not plugged.

Also, his wet trudge home had abruptly brought the house back to normal. Marguerite and Ollie Nuper were behaving as if nothing had happened between them, and actually, of course, when you really thought about it (he began to confess to himself, little by little), nothing had. It had been, of course, a blow to Walter Benson's self-esteem. Of course. And a terrible shock, terrible! But that was the world, you know, you read about such things every day; they were all, after all, adults. The thought made him weep and blow his nose.

And so he padded around the house in his slippers and robe, with a turkish towel wrapped around his neck and Vicks on his chest and pushed up into his nostrils, or he sat with the electric blanket around him, in front of the television, or lay in bed with the hotpad under his hump and read the paper.

Today Ollie Nuper was all polite respect and thoughtfulness. He came into the livingroom with a bundle of dowel pins under his arms (he used them for signs) and he paused, seeing Walter Benson sitting unshaven and red-eyed and crochety in front of the television, and he leaned the bundle on one hip, tipped his head-like-a-sheep's and put on his sad look. He said, "Feeling better this morning, sir?"

"Doh," Walter Benson said and fiercely rubbed his nose. His eyes filled with tears again.

"I'm sorry to hear that," Nuper said with great sincerity. "Well though, time heals all."

Just then Marguerite came in from the kitchen with a plate of crackers and some Limburger cheese. She set them on the wide, flat arm of his chair and then, seeing his expression, tried to help him by changing the television channel, but it did no good. The only half-interesting program all morning was "Captain Kangaroo." What she got this time, to Walter Benson's horror, was the news. They were showing, again, the picture of the Sunlight Man.

"Still loose," Marguerite said, alarmed. "It's terrible!"

Nuper scratched his chin.

"Do we *have* do watch the dnews?" Benson said, angrily starting to get up.

She meekly changed the channel, giving him a smile. It was a quiz program. He settled in his chair again grumpily and blew his nose. After a moment he glanced over his shoulder at Nuper, and Nuper gave a little jerk, glanced at his dowel pins, remembering himself, and slouched, studiously indifferent, to his room. Benson concentrated on watching the program, thinking nothing whatever, but it was difficult. *East Bethany,* he thought, suddenly panicky for no reason. *Attica. Alexander. Leroy. Medina.*

Just after lunch something very unsettling happened. The new mailman came to the door, and when Benson answered, the mailman asked him who he was. For a moment—it was this that was so upsetting—Walter Benson (or Boyle) could not remember. As sometimes happens in such cases, the whole thing got out of all proportion, and he stood hemming and hawing, evading the question, for a full minute. He clutched the collar of his bathrobe in his two fists and shook it up and down and said, "Why, why, I *dlive* here! Can'd you see dthat?"

"Ah," said the mailman, all apologies.

But Benson, crazily, was still trying to remember which was his thief-name, which his other one. He spluttered, "Do I look like some kide of a prowler, standding here id my bathrobe?

Hah?" He leaned closer, winking obscenely. "Do I look lige the milgman or subthing?"

"I'm sorry," the mailman said. "I beg your pardon."

It was astounding! The name absolutely *refused* to come clear in his mind! He rolled his eyes up for divine assistance, and that made him remember the night of the thunderstorm, his hour of conversion, and he tried to think which of them the conversion had come to, as though only one of them, the citizen, presumably, could have undergone a conversion. But it was no use.

The mailman said, "I have this letter that needs postage, is all. And if your name happens to be Walter Benson——"

Benson's eyes lit up and he pounced with joy. "Well what *else* would id be?" He folded his arms, triumphant.

It cost him five cents.

After the mailman delivered the letter up to him and went away somewhat nervously down the street (frowning and pursing his lips and pushing his cart with exaggerated care, as though he thought the packages all had bombs in them and he mustn't hit a gopher hole or a stick or a bump in the sidewalk), Benson went back into the livingroom and tore open the letter, pacing back and forth in front of the television (hundreds of cowboys were shooting at each other from behind huge rocks), and tried to blow his nose and read the letter at the same time. His eyes ran, and even what he could make out of the scrawled words on the page made no sense to him, that is to say, though he stated the words to himself one by one, they fell into no meaningful order, for he was thinking of other things. He thrust the letter in front of Marguerite, who was sitting with a root beer in front of the television watching meekly (aware of his violent pacing behind her and aware, no doubt, of her sin), and he said, "Whad's this say? My confoudded eyes . . ." She took it from him, lowered her glasses on her nose a little (he looked at the great bulge of lily-white fat on the back of her neck) and read it aloud, but even now he caught none of it—a word or two: "as a priest," "would be so pleased," "among us all," "heaven's love"—and when she finished he blew his nose violently and nodded and said "I zee" and went up to his room.

It was, in plain truth, a dangerous situation. Walter Benson —or rather—that is—Walter Boyle?—was no psychologist, but he knew there was something wrong with him. The violent ups and downs alone were an indication. It was Marguerite's fault, no question about it, and Nuper's, and the Sunlight Man's (in some obscure way), but the problem was not so much whose fault it was as what he was going to do about it.

He was trying to pace back and forth in the bedroom now, and it was difficult. The room was small, the double bed enormous. On one side the bed pressed up against the wall, on the other it stood only a foot and a half from the dresser. At the foot of the bed the highboy began, and it went halfway across the foot, then gave way to a four-by-six empty space, or a space that would have been empty except for the chair and the sewing machine. If he were more conscious of his surroundings just now, Benson would have moved something. But he was lost in anguished thought, so he merely squeezed between the dresser and the bed, went as far as the window, turned around and squeezed back toward the sewing machine, squeezed around behind it to the closet door, then turned back toward the sewing machine, the dresser and bed, the window.

He remembered very clearly the sense of wholeness and purity he had felt the night of the thunderstorm, sitting in the abandoned house and swearing he would change his life, but he also saw now, as he had not seen then, the other side of the nickel, so to speak. Shame, the loss of his worldly possessions, perhaps even prison. He shuddered.

He sat down on the bed abruptly and hunted through his bathrobe pockets for a Kleenex. He could find only one which had to be carefully unfolded and hadn't a dry place anywhere. He blew his nose. He saw the corner of a *Parade Magazine* peeking out from under the bed and he reached for it and opened it up and sat perfectly motionless, as though he were back in jail, pretending to read it. Now his mind was a blank. He couldn't read a word, but the pinked edge of the paper, the blurry, luminously red black print, the colored pictures steadied him. And then, for no reason, he was seeing once again the Indian boy and the Batavia Chief of Police, the pistol going *crack!* against the boy's fat brown jaw. Benson's hands shook. He remembered the guard with his head blown half off, slumping to the floor and reaching out slowly, out of all control, with the involuntary-looking movement of a penis or a snake. The opposition came suddenly clear to him—the violent, lawless bearded man, the violent policeman. It was, he saw with unspeakable clarity, a picture of his life. He, in the shape of Walter Benson, had been about to murder in cold blood the young man who had been toying with his wife's affections!

He leaped to his feet and began to pace again, rubbing his nose painfully and gnashing his teeth and gesturing with his left hand. A man could not be both Benson and Boyle. It was more than confusing, it was immoral! He stopped in his tracks, struck by a thought even more telling. What had he ever gotten out of life anyhow, as Boyle? The men who cleaned the sewers got more money than Boyle, and got retirement pay when they were old. Even the Chief of Police would get retirement pay! His knees were suddenly weak and he had to sit down.

That moment Marguerite peeked in and said timidly, "Would you care for some tea, Walter?"

Instantly, his face squeezed shut and tears ran down his cheeks and he held out his arms to her. "Marguereed!" He wailed.

Her eyes grew round and she came in hurriedly with the tray. "My poor baby!" she exclaimed.

But he could not tell her what was troubling him. He hardly knew himself. Old age. Poverty. His terrible jealousy and something more than that, too, his awful sense of something wasted—a misspent youth, a betrayal of ideals. Waste.

"I don'd wan' any tea," he said. His mouth and eyes turned down and he sobbed and sobbed and clung to her hand. Afterward, he slept and she slipped downstairs to clean up a little bit.

When he awakened at suppertime he felt no better. He got out of bed, however, and put on his checkered light blue suit. He had a vague intention of drowning his miseries at a movie or walking in the park or looking through the bars of the locked-up Buffalo Zoo. Marguerite said nothing when he came out all shaved and dressed up. It was as if she'd expected it, more or less, and he tried to think if there was somewhere they usually went on whatever night this was (Wednesday? Friday?). But that was nonsense. Where did they ever go, he and Marguerite?

He stood in the kitchen with his head tipped back almost to his hump, taking nosedrops while Marguerite finished the cooking, then followed her in to the dining room while she set the table and laid out the napkins, looking up at him and smiling meekly from time to time. He carried in the food. When everything was ready she went to the foot of the stairs and called, "Oh Mr. Nuper! Dinner is served."

There was some bumping and scuffling, and then he came pounding down the stairs, agile as a tiger, his curly long hair flopping around his ears, a cigarette in his mouth. He had an armload of signs with him, and the one on top said BLACK POWER. Benson frowned.

"You're going out tonight, Mr. Nuper?" Marguerite said.

He nodded, almost bowed. "A meeting, yes." He rubbed his hands. "Scalped potatoes!" he said.

"And Spam," Benson said.

Marguerite looked at him, wounded. Just the same, it was Spam. Truth is truth.

## 2

Dinner was eventful.

Marguerite said, "What kind of meeting is it you're going to, Mr. Nuper?"

"A demonstration, sort of," Mr. Nuper said. He was leaning down way over his plate, sliding the scalloped potatoes in with his fork.

Benson pursed his lips and looked at him, and the paperback book that had been on the table came back into his mind. "Against what?" he said.

Something in his tone gave him away, so that Nuper said only, in a clipped sort of way, "*For,* not against."

Benson squinted and wrinkled his nose. "For overthrowing the Goverdment, maybe? Throwing bombs into rich people's houses?"

"Not a bad idea," Nuper said, grinning an instant, then scooping in potatoes and staring straight ahead of him at the wall between Walter and Marguerite.

Marguerite said, "Boys."

"I dode believe in demonstrations, myself," Benson said. He meant to leave it at that. He could feel the blood rising in his neck. He cut himself a small bite of Spam.

"I thought not," Nuper said.

Benson flushed. "Because I'be rich? Because I'be got a little money in the bank?" It occurred to him that that was not exactly true.

Nuper glanced at him—just a flick of the eyes—then away. "Oh come on," he said. "Let's forget it." It was a gesture of charity, Benson would know later. Nuper was a pro at this kind of thing, Benson merely a passionate ignoramus.

"Young people," Benson sneered. He hunched his shoulders and cut his Spam into tiny pieces as if it were Nuper's heart. "They think they ode the world. They think the whole world odes them a living. Eat, dring, add be merry, that's all they do. Run aroudd half-naked and dance rock-n-roll and complain about the Goverdment and take drugs and have riots and whine about the Atom Bobb and play guitars—"

"Walter!" Marguerite said.

He chewed angrily.

There was a silence, and then both Nuper and Walter Benson spoke at once.

$$\left\{ \begin{array}{l} \text{"If that's how you feel—"} \\ \text{" 'Black Bower' he says!"} \end{array} \right.$$

They both broke off, and each of them waited for the other one to speak first. They were both still staring straight ahead in white-hot fury, chewing, forking in the food.

"Would someone please pass the rolls?" Marguerite said.

They both reached. Nuper deferred.

Nuper said in a conciliating tone, "Actually, if one looks closely at the school districts in Buffalo—if one examines the character of each school—one makes the discovery that the schools are monolithic. That is to say, segregated. As the Supreme Court has stated in no uncertain terms, separate but equal is a logical contradiction. Do you believe a Negro child has a right to an education?"

Benson sulked.

"Well he's not getting one in Buffalo, I'll tell you that."

"You'll get hib killed, that's what you'll do with all your signs," Benson said.

"Really," Marguerite said. "Why can't we eat supper in peace?" She was close to tears.

"The city's been warned," Nuper said. His eyes got a curious glint. It made you think of a man watching a building burning down.

"I dode know about all that. Pass the potatoes."

"But it doesn't keep you from talking." Nuper smiled.

"I'be a peaceful man, and I live in a peaceful city. Add I'll tell you something."

"Sure, by keeping the nigger in his place."

"I'm not against niggers—"

"Then how come you call them that?"

"*You* called them—"

"Boys, boys, boys!" Her face was all pulled out of shape with grief and fright.

"I was imitating *you*."

"I haddn't said it yed!"

"Well, you would have."

Benson slammed the table with his fist. "There are ways add ways of doing these things. And the way you people dake, starting riots and getting wibben add children killed—"

"And men." Again he sounded conciliatory, and it threw Benson off.

Benson said, "I'm for peace. I believe when a city has a probleb—"

"It should face it." Nuper smiled and chewed.

"No."

"It should *not* face it." He leaned back and winked at Marguerite, and it was that, that horrible, sneaky, filthy—(words failed him)—*wink* that drove Benson wild. He leaped to his feet and slammed the table so hard his milk tipped over.

"You dode *care*, do you! You just dode *care*. It dode matter to you who's ride or wrong, you just win whatever way you can. You're like all of them. Irresponsible! What have *you* god to lose? *You* dode have to live here. You just cub in and stir up trouble and have your fun and then you're gone, and we're the ones do the cleaning up. Citizens like me. You cub in here —" He spluttered, red-faced, eyes bulging. "You cub in—a city like Buffalo—you rile up—you, you rile up the niggers, the Negroes—you throw bobbs around and start frights in the street." He stopped himself. He was shaking all over, and Nuper was sitting cool as a cucumber, eating his lettuce with sugar on it, and Marguerite was pushing back her chair with a look of witless grief and rage, leaving for the kitchen. Benson tried to make himself calm and, bristling, watched Marguerite leave.

Benson said, voice steely, "I dode like the way you argue."

Again, Nuper smiled. His upper lip went out of sight and his teeth showed, teeth like some kind of an animal's, tiny and yellow. After a moment he said. "I'm sorry I made you angry, Mr. Benson. And I'm sorry your wife—"

"Dode you talk to me about my wife," Benson said. He spit the words out so fast, with such rage, that Nuper looked at him and went white for a moment.

"If I've offended—" he said.

Benson sat down and put his hands in his lap to hide the shaking. He was frightened. It wasn't like him to speak out like that, lash out as if tomorrow would never come. He could give himself a heart attack that way, or get the neighbors down on him, and they might call the police, and the police might have a picture, or there might be some cop from out of town. . . . He sat with his shoulders tightly hunched, his hands pressed together tight between his knees.

After a long time Nuper said, "Mr. Benson, you have the wrong idea about me. Seriously." He spoke gently, all apology. "I realize you don't approve of my activities, any more than I approve of yours . . ."

Benson looked at him, alarmed.

"But I think you should judge me without prejudice. We must all follow the dictates of our conscience, don't you agree?"

The names of towns came into Benson's head. He tried to listen, in spite of them, to Nuper's talk. He found himself concentrating on the way Nuper's chin ran into his throat, the way his ears peeked through his thin, rumpled hair, the way his upper gums showed when he talked. His nose was really amazingly like a sheep's.

"Mr. Benson, how do *you* explain the poverty of the Negro?"

Benson's lips twitched inward but he said nothing.

"Be frank. Do you think it's because they're lazy, or stupid, or—as you say—irresponsible?" He held up his long yellow hand. "It's all right, you don't need to answer. Let me tell you something that may surprise you. I *agree* with you. You expect me to ask, 'But what *made* them lazy and stupid and irresponsible?' and you expect me to answer, 'The system! Environment! And so on.' " Nuper leaned forward, smiling, showing his tiny teeth, his eyelids halfway lowered. "Well I say nothing of the kind. I say what every white man knows in his heart: it's because *they're closer to the ape!*" He sat back, triumphant, smiling broadly, with his lips pressed together.

Walter Benson stared, slightly confused.

When he was satisfied that he'd made his effect, Nuper raised his eyebrows into a long inverted V and opened his hands, the heels pointing inward. He looked, for an instant, like Jesus at the Last Supper. "I don't like them, you see. I don't like them at all. But I like them better than *civilized* people, if you understand my meaning."

Marguerite stood in the kitchen doorway, wringing her fingers and sniffling. *"Please,* Walter," she said. "Why can't we watch TV or something? Why do we have to argue."

He ignored her and stared intently at Nuper, waiting for what he was saying to come clear. He wanted with all his heart and soul to answer him. The hunger to shout him down, make a fool of him, even physically tear him limb from limb made all Benson's muscles tense, but he could not make out yet what Nuper was saying. *Olean,* he thought involuntarily. *Endicott.* It was as if Boyle were taking his body and brain away from him, creeping up insidiously inside.

"What is civilization?" Nuper asked softly, rhetorically. "Civilization, honestly defined, is the enslavement of the many by the few. Put it this way. What do we think of when we think of a civilized man? A man who understands paintings and music and litiracha—a man who plays chess or polo or what-have-you. *A man who does no work.* Now, how does such a man come into existence?" He waited. "You know as well as I do, Mr. Benson. He corners some market. Usually he corners land. Russia under the Czar. South America. Even the United States—though here it's tricky. Here everybody had land at first, but little by little Bell Telephone and Heath Candybar and the rest are taking over. With the Government's help, of course—tax cuts and so on. All right then. There's your civilized man, your man of endless leisure. In the old days it used to be that every minute he spent in his hammock or his kidney-shaped swimming pool was a minute he stole from you or me. Not now. Now he has machines, he can make his mint without even giving you the satisfaction of earning your broth and bread. He can *kill* you, Mr. Benson. But he doesn't. *That's* what's terrible. He throws you sops. Poverty programs. Handouts. Social security. He can keep you just well enough fed that you rest contented in your shanty. And *there*, my capitalist friend, is where the Blacks come in."

Benson has listened closely, waiting to pounce. His muscles felt so tight he had a feeling he couldn't untie himself if he tried. He felt monstrously cheated. It was a mistake to listen to people like Nuper, he'd always known that. He knew what Nuper was, all right. He knew that, for all his fine arguments, the man was a lying, cheating, slimy . . . Again he could find no words. Suddenly and loudly, as if inspired, Benson said, "*I* dode feel that the house I live in is a shanty."

"Ah!" Nuper said. "And yet it is, isn't it. A shanty compared to what the Kennedys live in. A shanty compared to—"

Marguerite said, offended, "The Kennedys have all those children."

Nuper exploded into laughter.

"Stop that!" Benson roared. The sudden exertion loosened the stuff in his nose and he hastily covered his lip with one hand and fished for the handkerchief with the other. He blew his nose.

"I'm sorry," Nuper said. "I apologize. But really, for heaven's sakes—" He laughed again. "Forgive me, Mrs. Benson."

She pursed her lips, deeply hurt, and her chin was as big as Nuper's whole head.

"We better get these dishes washed," Benson said petulantly. He got up, blew his nose again, and picked up his plate and silverware to take them to the kitchen.

Nuper said, "I really didn't mean to get into all this. I really am sorry." Again, infuriatingly, he was laughing. "—all those children," he said. He laughed again.

Marguerite said tearfully, "If you feel this house is a shanty, you ought to leave."

"Dear God, Mrs. Benson!" Nuper said. He shook with laughter.

"Get out of here," Benson said. "I suggest you go to your riot."

Nuper laughed and laughed and laughed.

*I'll kill him,* Benson thought, raising his eyebrows, startled. *This is my house.*

When he came back from the kitchen for more dishes, Ollie Nuper was standing up, shaking and snorting.

"Get out of here," Benson hissed. He took a step nearer. "Get out of my house."

He was standing at the sink washing dishes in his suitpants and white shirt when Ollie Nuper went out to his car with the signs. Benson scowled into the soapsuds, not thinking, his mind a perfect blank. Like a man in a trance, he wiped his hands on the dish-towel and went into the dining room for his suitcoat.

"Where are you going, Walter?" Marguerite said.

"Business," he said.

He heard Ollie Nuper's car start up.

Marguerite's lips were trembling. He ignored it and hurried to his car.

## 3

On one side stood an old, dirty church of reddish stone, with an enormous stained-glass window, lighted, some of the pieces of glass broken out long ago and replaced with something that did not let the light through; on the other side, a brick school that had an abandoned look, a playground surrounded by cyclone fence with barbed wire at the top. The park between was small, crowded with people. Some of the trees were dead and the swings had no seats in them. He had never seen so many Negroes gathered together in one place. Some of them looked poor—old men whose trousers hung low at the crotch and whose shoes were lumpy; old, fat women wearing two or three sweaters and kerchiefs over their heads; boys in T-shirts that were badly stretched out of shape at the neck and trousers with flies that no longer buttoned; young women with enormous rear ends and cheap, shiny shoes that let most of their feet show through—but most of them didn't look poor, in fact they looked rich, to Benson, rich and directly dangerous: a man just ahead of him with a goat's beard and the curved dark glasses murderers wear on television; a group of fat young Negroes a little to the right of him, black as coal in their white shirts and thin little ties; a huge black man in a striped winter suit who kept wiping his forehead and neck with a great white handkerchief. The old people were mostly to the back of the crowd, around Benson—he was not in the crowd at all, in fact, but on the street, well out of range of most of them—and the younger boys, too, kept to the back. They seemed hardly interested, darting in and out among the old people, calling to each other, sometimes cuffing each other in a way that might or might not be playful, Benson couldn't tell. The people at the heart of the crowd were college age or a little older, and more of them than he would have expected were women, loud, belligerent girls of a kind he had never known existed: they had the pretty faces of the girls who waited on him in restaurants or sat reading quietly on buses, and they had the sweet voices of the girls he heard singing on the television with Mitch Miller and the rest, but tonight their pretty faces were full of authority and dire intent, and the sweetness of their voices was irrelevant to their calls and shouts. The young women were the ones, or so it seemed to Benson, who ruled the crowd. It was one of them, a tall, flat-chested girl with large and radiant teeth, who first got up on the speaker's platform. She held up her hands and after a long time the crowd became silent. She raised the microphone, then lowered it a little. Someone on the ground in front of the platform tried to help.

"Can you hear me?" she said.

The crowd murmured, and the loudspeaker made a high, droning noise, then quieted again.

She began to speak, but at the same moment a high voice right at Benson's elbow asked, "You got a light, boss?"

Benson jumped, then hunted through his pockets nervously. The man was short, and his face was like a blackened skull. He had a red straw hat with a wide white band, far back on his head. He held a cigarette between two long purple fingers.

"Ah," Benson said.

The man took them without touching Benson's fingers. "Whoo," he said.

Benson said, as nervous as ever, "What's all this about?"

The man shook his head, held the lighted match to his cigarette, and blew upward. "I 'on't know, man. Shit, man, Ine jis' passin' thoo." He grinned.

Benson took the matches back, put them in his pocket, and

folded his hands to listen. He could feel the black man looking at his ear.

The girl was saying: "—much to be grateful for. In Chicago they throw rocks at us, in Mississippi they throw bombs in our churches and shoot at us from passing cars, but not here, not in Buffalo, New York."

The crowd murmured. Someone yelled, "Tell 'em!"

"In Alabama they have to use the State Police to see that black children can walk to school without being shot at, and in Wisconsin they have to use tear gas to keep the blacks and the whites from murdering each other—but not here. And you want to know why?" She leaned close to the microphone and spoke softly. "Because we're not moving yet, in Buffalo, New York. We're still darkies, here. We stay in our place, like lizards under the porch, and we stand in line when they tell us to stand in line, and if they happen to step on our toes, we apologize."

The crowd cheered, except for the people in back. The old people merely stood there.

"That CORE, man," the Negro at Benson's elbow said, "they muthuhfuckuhs every one of 'em, and the same thing for SNCC. Shoo." His breath smelled of whiskey. He tipped up his head and blew smoke.

Benson said, "What are they meeting about? Are they going to demonstrate?"

The man smiled with ominous teeth and rolled his eyes. "Man, Ine jist passin' thoo."

He tried to see Nuper, but he was nowhere in sight. He was somewhere up near the speakers' platform—at least that was where Benson had lost sight of him.

The girl was saying, "—but they don't want your child to matriculate with their children up here in Buffalo either, make no mistake about it! And they don't want your face in their neighborhood! They want your money and your sweat and your blood in Vietnam, and after that—*they—want—you—dead.*"

The crowd roared.

There was a police car coming around the corner, cruising slowly, seemingly indifferent to the crowd. The policemen were Negroes. When they came up to Benson and the man at his elbow, one of the policemen said, "Don't stand in the street, buddy."

"Sorry," Benson said.

The Negro in the red straw hat looked at them with his head tipped back and one leg thrown forward. The cigarette between his fingers was burned down to the last half-inch. The car moved away. Another great roar came from the crowd.

"We'd better move back," Benson said.

The Negro shrugged. He dropped the cigarette and stamped on it, making a little dance of it, then touched his red straw hat cocking it forward, and started across the street toward the side away from the crowd. Benson pursed his lips, then followed. When he came to the sidewalk he took a place a few feet away from the Negro. There were people standing here watching, leaning up against the sooty, scarred buildings and observing the meeting as casually as they'd have observed a crew of construction men at work. The crowd in the park began singing. Someone on the platform had a banjo. Now Ollie Nuper was on the platform too, clapping his hands and nodding up and down. And now the Negro with the red straw hat was at Benson's elbow again, standing on tiptoe, saying, "You thirsdy, brother?" Benson turned, and the man pointed with his thumb at the green padded leather door directly behind them.

"I don't drink," Benson said.

"Me neither," the Negro said. "But sometime I do take a Coke and a liddle bitta rum." He smiled.

Benson pinched his nostrils together, then on second thought got out his handkerchief and blew his nose. At last, suddenly realizing what the Negro wanted, he got out a fifty-cent piece and gave it to him. Again their fingers did not touch.

"God bless you!" the Negro said. "I accept your bribe." He smiled again and turned toward the door.

Nuper's speech went on for what seemed hours. From what he said one would not have guessed that he thought them apes. His talking was full of facts and figures, yet so simply put, any child could have understood it. It was so convincing, at least to Walter Benson, that he began to believe all Nuper's talk at the supper table had been a grim joke at Benson's expense. Benson stood leaning forward, straining to catch every word. His concentration was so intense that he did not notice the penguinlike man until he spoke.

"Brilliant, isn't he," the man said.

Benson collected his wits.

It was the nose, mainly, that made the man penguinlike. As for his eyes, they were wide and blue as a baby's, and he had eyebrows permanently lifted as if to say affectedly, "How charming!" He looked twenty at first glance; but he was probably past thirty-five. He had a large jewel of some sort on his ring finger, and, as if to advertise it, he fluttered his hands almost perpetually and when he rested them, did so with the fingertips pressed together so that the ring was clearly displayed. It struck one immediately that there was something odd about him, some definite quirk that set him apart from ordinary humanity—some elusive quality or singular madness which, once found out, would make everything about him clear. One knew what it was the moment he said it. He was a Quaker.

He stood with his back arched, his weight on one leg, his left hand pressed to his waist, bent at the wrist. "Brilliant," he said again. Don't you think so?"

Benson said noncommittally, "He's something."

"Nuper's his name, you know. Oliver Nuper. One of the professionals." He spoke rapidly, with excessively precise pronunciation. "It's pure hogwash of course, every word he says, but he does it superbly, in my opinion. I've seen them all. It's a kind of hobby of mine—a bachelor, you know, sick and tired of the movies and those eternal cocktail parties and the rest. And of course I have students mixed up in all this. It's inevitable, you know. Youth. Enthusiasm." He showered down laughter.

"Ah," Benson said.

"Excuse me, I ought to have introduced myself. My name's Veil, as in *Vile*." He made a face. "Ridiculous, I know, but that's my name. Professor John Veil, Department of English, University of Buffalo. And you are—" He waited, head cocked, smiling with lifted eyebrows.

"I am . . ." In horror he realized that again he couldn't think of his name. "I am," he said, blushing, "very interested in these demudstrations."

Professor Veil threw up his hands. "Then you've come to the right place. I know all about them!"

"Ah," Benson said.

"That fellow over there, the one with the guitar and the beard and the thick, thick glasses—you see him? That's 'Baron

Von Badger'—so he calls himself. Actually his name's John Jones or something. Comes from way out West someplace. Crazy as a loon, I assure you. I've had him in class, as a matter of fact. He sits in the front row and looks at me through binoculars turned backwards. That's mad, don't you think?"

Benson considered it.

"His father's rich as Midas, so they say. One of those rice kings or something. He doesn't sing, the Baron, that is. He uses the guitar as a kind of drone for his lunatic chants." The Professor suddenly stooped over like an ape, head thrown far forward, arms surrounding an imaginary guitar.

> *I been on this road a long time,*
> *and the road's been on me, O Lord, Lord,*
> *and I don' know who's walking this road and O*
> *it is a road Lord,*
> *is it me, Lord,*
> *is it a long time Lord or is it*
> *Lord are you there*
> ARE YOU THERE LORD, LORD, I
> *been on this*
> *road's been on*
> *Mankine have mercy on my soooo-oo-OOL!!!*

The Professor straightened up, eyebrows lifted, smiling. "Mad, you see."

Solemnly, Benson nodded.

The crowd was clapping. Nuper shouted, "People tell me the Muslims are gonna wipe us out, us *lib*-erals, the white men that are marching on the side of justice for the blacks. What do I say? I say *then let them do it!* In every war mankind has ever fought, there have been mistakes. Korea! We lost whole battalions from our own air support—and I'm not counting the black battalions that were shot by white infantry from behind. No sir! There are always mistakes! Napoleon made them! Caesar made them! For all we know, maybe *Moses* made them! It don' matter! When a war gets started you've got to fight it out and don' look back. And the white man's driven the black to war, and that's the truth! And if you don't believe it's war I tell you you're yellow-bellied! Yeah! And if you don't like my standing here saying it to you, don't you look at me, brothers, you just look at the white men that think it and never say a word to you, No! they just sit there and smile and smi-ile!" The crowd roared.

The Professor said, "That man could make a fortune selling used cars."

"He's the devil," Benson said.

The Professor smiled. "Well, yes, so he is, of course. But aren't we all?" Still smiling, but only with his lips, he scrutinized Benson's face. At last he said, "See here, you know something? You have the look, right now, of a murderer!" He laughed. "I'm quite serious! Something about—" He fluttered his fingers around Benson's nose. "Your eyes, I think. Heavens. Listen! You must be calm, contain yourself. Look at me!" He held out his hands, smiling, supremely calm.

Benson said grimly, "I know that man—Nuper."

The Professor pursed his lips, and after a moment his fingers fluttered up to them. "I was afraid you did," he said. "I'm a member of the Society of Friends, myself. I abhor violence, and I denounce people who advocate it. But I wouldn't dream —" Again he was scrutinizing Benson's face. He tapped his upper lip lightly, thoughtfully, with the knuckle of his index finger. "You're an interesting type," he said. "You had me completely fooled, at first. Completely. I'm interested to meet you. It's very curious, really." He looked away and stood like a man analyzing the quality of a pain in his abdomen. Whatever the question was that he was asking himself, he apparently found the answer. He smiled more brilliantly than ever. "It takes all kinds, doesn't it," he said. "Good day." Quickly, without another word, he stepped off down the sidewalk.

## 4

The meeting dragged on. Walter Benson's feet ached from standing up, and he'd shifted so often from one leg to the other that he had no way left to rest himself unless, like some of the people around him, he should choose to sit on the fender of someone's parked car. One of the white men standing with a beer bottle said to the man beside him, "They gonna march or something? They just going to talk all night?" The other man said, "Don't you worry. Those people that organize these things, they know what they're doin'." What *are* they doin', Harrison?" another man said. The second man nodded and winked and merely repeated, "They know what they're doin', don't worry." But people were beginning to leave, the old people first, and then some of the fat men in fancy clothes. For all the shouting, it was going to come to nothing. The police continued to drive slowly and without interest around the park. "Just letting off steam," a man to Benson's left said. He kept tapping the brick wall with his ring, like an impatient man waiting for someone. "It's like one of those summer band concerts, only louder. Makes them feel good, talking about how much they hate the son-of-a-bitching whites." He spoke as if to himself, but when he saw Walter Benson looking at him he jerked his chin up, a kind of tic, "Takes the place of church, a lot of 'em. They've seen through all that stuff, a lot of 'em, and now there they are, all dressed up and no place to go." He jerked his chin again and tapped rapidly, in the rhythm of some almost recognizable song. He said, "Don't look at *me*, buddy. *I* didn't take away their religion."

The leaders seemed to realize that the meeting was coming to nothing. Or maybe, as one of the observers in front of the tavern thought, the leaders hadn't meant it to come to anything in the first place, it was a simple show of numbers. In any case, they were winding it up. Then there was a brief period of confusion. A big-shouldered white man with sideburns was on the platform, shouting into the microphone, "Is this a public park or isn't it?" Several people close to the platform answered him at once, but their voices didn't come over the loudspeaker. The man with sideburns said, "I just want to talk for one minute. Let me have—" The rest of his sentence didn't come through. People were pulling the microphone away. Someone else's voice said into the mike, "It's a rented speaker system. You want to have a rally, go rent yourself a speaker. This one—" More lost. The man with sideburns: "—pay you, then." There were bumping noises through the loudspeaker as they tussled over the microphone. The man with sideburns started hitting with his fists. "Heil Hitler!" he yelled, not through the mike. And then through the mike someone yelled, "*Nah Hitler uns!*" People down by the platform were yelling. The police car rolled indifferently by between Benson and what was left of the crowd. In a minute or two it was over. People began singing again, and now everyone was leaving.

Benson walked back to his car to watch for Nuper to come

to his. According to the clock on the dashboard, it was five-to-two in the morning.

"Why are you doing this?" he asked himself.

But he knew the answer, or knew, anyway, that there *was* an answer, but one too complicated to unravel. Again and again he had wanted to say to the guard in the jail, "Be careful. Don't be so trusting. They're after you." But he had said nothing. He had wanted to say, "They're going to break out. I can feel it coming." But he'd said nothing. And they had said, "What did you see?" and he had said—had almost believed—"I was asleep."

All that had nothing to do with Ollie Nuper, though. And it had nothing to do with his straining, tonight, to hear what the speakers were saying, or with the feeling of elation that had come to him during the thunderstorm. It was simply that he was restless, full of a tortured sense of something waking up inside him, whether good or evil he could not make out. He coughed, then coughed again. The tickle in his throat was still there.

He suddenly remembered the old woman, the poetess, whom the Batavia Chief of Police had taken him to see. She looked a thousand years old, and peering in her eyes he had seen to his horror that there was nothing, no one in there: an empty husk. It made him remember a time, more than forty years ago now, when he'd gotten himself locked up in the Buffalo bolt factory at closing time. He couldn't get out, and as darkness came on he'd wandered back and forth through the vast silent rooms where all day long there was a roar of big machinery and a bustle of men, and the belts were all turning and there was a constant gurgle of oil pouring over hot steel. Now nothing stirred, the big machines were still, and he felt like the last survivor on a dead planet. And suddenly—not because of shadows or imagined creatures in the dark, not because he was alone and only a boy—he was afraid.

The Negroes were still leaving, but there were only a few of them left now. They too made him think of the abandoned factory he had thought he'd forgotten, though he couldn't say what the connection between the factory and the Negroes was. Their walk was slow and deliberate, and you could not tell, to look at them, that they had somewhere definite to go.

He caught sight, at last, of Ollie Nuper. He was coming this way, carrying a box and an armload of his signs, walking with a giant, well-dressed white man, some kind of politician, it looked like. When they got to the sidewalk they paused, about to walk in different directions, and they talked rapidly, trying to finish their argument. The big man had his back to Benson. He seemed extremely angry. Something about him was familiar—it seemed to Benson that any moment the recognition was going to burst into his mind—but try as he might, he couldn't make out where he'd seen the man before or who it was he looked like. Finally the big man turned and came striding toward Benson, and for an instant Benson knew him: it was the Sunlight Man. But it was a mistake. It was some stranger. He was clean-shaven and so angry his temples looked swollen. Benson followed him with his eyes as far as the corner, then lost him to the shadows.

The light went on in Nuper's car and Nuper got in and closed the door; the light went off again. Benson switched on his ignition. The car parked directly behind him started up at almost the same moment. The overhead light went on as the driver reached across to open the door for a friend, and the friend got in. They had black bands around their arms. The light went off. Now Nuper was pulling out of his parking place. When Benson pulled out the car behind him followed. The headlights weren't on. "What is this?" Benson whispered. "Good Lord, what's happening?"

# XVIII

## The Dragon's
## Dwelling-Place
## and the
## Court for Owls

*But Yudhisthira was resolute and
would not enter heaven without his dog.*
                              —The Maha-Bharata

## 1

*Regardez.*
*Nous considérons aujourd'hui un homme perdu.*
*C'est triste. Misérable.*
*Condition de vie.*
*Mais oui, et c'est misérable.*

Outside, fog. Drone of the engines, aisle lights very dim,
stewardess asleep no doubt, or smoking a cigarette in her tight

barren cloister musing on a dress she has half-finished, folded
up in her closet to await her return, hidden carefully, sullenly,
like all other signs of her existence, because her roommate has
gentleman friends when she is gone, a working agreement:
when she returns, exit roommate, and when she leaves again
she vanishes utterly, like smoke. Or no. *Avec sa mère. Va de
temps à temps aux maisons des amis. Ta ta, Mama. Je retour-
nerai. Et la mère? Est-ce qu'elle aussi a les amis?* "Good evening Mr. Hodge." Jumped half out of his skin. And did the
regulation kind eyes see, the regulation soft lips draw down,
momentarily distressed by an intuition of damnation? Ha!
*Nous considérons ce soir un homme perdu.*

Mr. Kleppmann, I will be open with you. You enrage me.
No longer a question of just doing my work. Been beyond that
for months. I no longer remember what line I'm in, professionally speaking, at least with the part of my mind I hunt
with—the other mind will click on again when I've caught
you, no doubt, will feed in words like cartridges, official, metal
against metal, clean. Ping. Whooey! I no longer remember
even why you enrage me, or why I'm afraid of you—why I
start violently when I'm sitting on the can and a stranger's legs
appear below the door and the stranger tries the handle. Fantastic way to die. Be found sitting upright, leaning back on the
wall, head tipped, pants at the ankles, and on the nether beard,
the limp prick, martyr's blood. In every airport, railway platform, crowded room, even in the sanctuary of the church in
Albany, or in the flower shop in Syracuse, or on the street—always, on any street, in the gray lath morning or the cheerily
lighted graveyard dark two hours after sunset—the blood says
*Ici! Il est ici!* Some hunter. Scared as hell. Turning suddenly,
seeing that face—wide, white, benign, expressionless as a planet depopulated by fire and flood and war and plague—eyes
like a bubonic rat's, the hat high, high on the forehead yet perfectly level, like a child's fedora placed, *très amusant*, on the
head of a fat, new corpse. Crowd closes. The face is gone. I
run toward where I think it was. (*Votre pardon, madame.
Pardon moi, monsieur.* Sonny.) But there's no one, of course.
An apparition, terror projected to a point, *Très bien.* But I
continue. Yes. Surely you are impressed by that, Kleppmann.
Brother. Perhaps you can say a simple word, be rid of me—
but maybe not, too, eh? Perhaps your man will miss the first
time, and if he misses once I'll have the pistol out, aiming it at

him with my two hands wobbling, or perhaps even aiming as though I knew what I was doing, the second piece of the brain clicking in, an old memory of military training, *whooeee*, Pvt Hodge!—and the room will explode a second time with the noise of a pistol, and he will fall, could be. And then you, Mr. Kleppmann, in time. Surely you must be impressed, Mr. Kleppmann. As shitless scared as I am.

Louise said, "You're never home nights any more."

"Half-crazy with work," I said. "Have you any idea?"

"You'll be crazy all the way. You don't play with the kids. You have nightmares night after night after night. Sometimes I'm afraid of you."

"It will be over. Take it easy. Be patient. *C'est la vie.*"

"And your French is horrible," she said.

Hawes said, "Take an extra day, Will. Listen. Let me lend you my bunny key." Bent closer. "Fantastic place, that club in Chicago. Girl named Molly. Watch for her. Tell her Clarence sent you."

"Ha ha ha."

"I mean it, ole pal."

"No thanks. Got things on my mind. I recommend the same. Get your mind back on mergers. What were this last year's total assets for the Dansville First National? What's the population complex? New industry coming? Farm loans secure? Got to have it by heart Hawes. Got to make the Feds say 'hmm!' Got to wake 'em up with the tragedy of it all. Monumental injustice. They get bored, that's the secret. You'd be bored too, sitting there reading a thousand pages of crap that's no interest to anybody. So they come to the hearing and they're half-asleep. Try cartoons in the margins. Dirty pictures maybe. Wake 'em up."

"Take the bunny key."

"No. Got things on my mind."

Perdu.

Voices:

*Circuit court, Division Nine, now in session. Honorable Christ the Lord, Judge.*

*Good morning, gentlemen. Young fellow, call the docket..*

*Heaven and Earth versus William Hodge.*

*Would you care to make an opening statement?*

*We would, your Honor.*

*Proceed.*

Room very large, excessively bright despite the layers of blue-green smoke, mercurious, stiffening to mare's tales before the tiered dais. *The Judge is bored. Beware of a bored Judge, Counsellor. A bad beginning. This bodes ill, oh ill! for William Hodge, acting in his own defense. A fool. Colossal idiot. It is impossible to act in one's own defense. Miserable. Well,* C'est la mort.

— I will not be judged by Him.

— Kleppmann is my judge. O lead us not into Milwaukee, deliver us from Pittsburgh.

Sholly hoolibash! Niscera willy-bill bingle-um gimpf!

Don't mock, me, Kleppmann. We're past that, you and I. Another martini?

Don't mind if I do. You're paying, of course?

Naturally. Or my firm is. Naturally.

Smile.

You had me running for a while there Kleppmann, I'll give it to you. Well, that's over.

The pistol in his hand (so he imagines) is utterly still and comfortably warm.

A woman with a sweet voice mumbled something, and he smiled, and she mumbled it again. He opened his eyes.

"Fasten your seat-belt, please, Mr. Hodge. We're landing."

"Is something wrong?"

She smiled and tipped her head. She had not heard him. *'Les amis' my foot. Secretly married, quintuplets in the stroller, at home with her husband who was born in Ely, Iowa. At heart a pig grower; by trade, a bicycle mechanic.*

He could see the lights of St. Louis shooting out behind the wing like sparks, stretching out forever, beautiful. And then the plane was diving, as it seemed to him—now leveling again. Before his stomach was ready for it, the landing-gear bumped on the runway.

He caught the train south (with an hour to spare) and sat reading of earthquakes and the walls of Jericho. It made him remember, more vividly than he would have thought possible, his cousin Ben Jr, head tipped nearly to his shoulder, grinning, arguing about whether God, like Merlin, was so powerful he could make a cage so strong He couldn't get out of it Himself. Or was the Merlin story another of Ben Jr's lies? And then he was remembering a song Ben would sing—irrelevant, surely.

*King David was my dancing man,*
*And a juggler too as well;*
*The way he thrown his balls around*
*I'll dance with him in hell!*

2

In fact, he had no idea what it was he expected. It was as if
he had thrown away his compass, in the classical way, and had
ventured into the thickness of the woods prepared for whatever he was destined to meet (Phaiakians?), including the man
with the gun in the public lavatory. She had said she wanted to
talk to him, and it was pleasant to think it was really that—
pleasant not so much in any sexual way as metaphysically, if
that was not too big a word for it: pleasant to think she might
innocently tell him the truth. But he didn't expect it.

He was pleasantly numb from the martinis on the train, but
not so drunk he was entirely indifferent to matters of, as the
expression goes, life and death. The pistol was not in his briefcase but in his pocket.

He was almost alone on the concrete platform. A few students had gotten off—it was a college town—and there was a
man with a sunken, Southern mouth, an engineer's cap, a
frock, and pantlegs limply cylindrical, walking along beside
the train looking under it, as if watching for a rabbit for his
hounds. It was a small town, and, after the hurtle of motion
he'd endured this past hour, he had a sharp sense of its spatial
isolation—the expanse of bare farmland on every side, the
profound darkness outside the pale rim of dead white light
from the depot lamps. Against the wall there were taxi drivers,
but they did not call out to him or even, as far as he could tell,
notice his presence on the platform. He put the pipe in his
mouth, self-consciously solemn, and walked toward the wait-
ing-room doors.

"Thank heavens," Mrs. Kleppmann said from the shadow of
the pillar where she waited, "you've come!"

It rang false—but everything was ringing false. He nodded,
smiling politely, and moved toward her. She took his hand.

"Thank you," she said. Perhaps she meant it. He felt queerly indifferent.

"It's nothing," he said.

"This way." She drew him toward her and down the wide-boarded hall.

They came out on a parking lot lit in gray-white, like the platform on the other side of the depot, and she led him to a long blue station wagon that he might have known at once belonged to Mrs. Kleppmann. It had no chrome, no decorations, no radio, even, and he could not tell what kind it was but knew it was expensive.

"Nice car," he said.

"Thank you."

"What's up, Mrs. Kleppmann?"

"Later," she said. She nodded toward the man in the driver's seat, waiting for them. He had his hat off because of the heat.

They got in then and arranged what little he had in the way of gear—not much: his briefcase, the hat he for some reason felt he should carry, not wear, the raincoat Louise had insisted on his bringing. The driver switched on the motor, quiet as a vacuum cleaner, and the car slid back out of its parking slot and as if without change of direction, smooth as a barque turned in the wind; started forward. Soon the pale light of the town sank behind them and they were moving through a darkness deeper than any he had seen since earliest childhood.

"You're a long way from civilization," he said.

She reached over, matronly, and patted his hand. "Farther than you think," she said. Not sly. She meant him to understand it.

"I'm sorry," he said.

She laughed.

They flowed into what might have been the limits of the world, the depths of the Midwest, oakwoods and farmland where St. Louis was a dream and Chicago an old wives' fable, Cimmerian country. There was no sign of the moon, only mist and cloud, and it was hard to believe that in the morning there would be sunlight.

"You sounded worried," he said. She had, in fact, but he understood the game.

"I am."

In the darkness, Will smiled.

At last there was a yellow glow in the mist—the sharp yellow of mosquito bulbs—and there were pillars and lighted windows.

"That your house?" he said.

He felt, rather than saw, her nod in the darkness. She closed her hand on his more tightly, and he understood that for her it partly wasn't a game. More the pity for her then. His armpits itched, and he thought, *I'm afraid.* And yet he was not. It was as if he had nothing more to do with the fears of his common mortality.

She withdrew her hand.

"You had nothing to say to me?" he said. "—For the record."

After a moment: "Nothing."

Will sighed and slipped his hand into his pocket where the gun was. And now, suddenly, he saw how absurd it was: the gun was no protection, a weighty inconvenience. "I'm a fool," he thought.

"Do you think so?"

He had not meant to speak out loud.

They were up in the driveway turn-around now, and the car had stopped. Time, too, seemed to have stopped. He saw Kleppmann's huge barn, clean-lined against the mist, windows lighted as on a Christmas card, and Kleppmann's long chickenhouse of cinder-block, and to the east, the ornate, absurd old house, sheltered by maples. The grass was white from the mist; the light coming out through the windows was orange. With the motor off, the world was as quiet as the North Pole. Kleppmann bowed, opening the door. "Ah yes," he said. "You've come."

Will bowed back, abstracted and polite. "Certainly." His stomach closed as if what he confronted were not a man but an upright crocodile.

Strange meeting. One saw too much television, no doubt. In any case, it took him a long time to get used to it. He had come half-prepared to kill or be killed, but Kleppmann was having a party. The guests moved all through the house, talking, their voices blending to a roar as indefinite as the overhanging mist, and Kleppmann the Terrible stood on the front lawn like an elderly serpent looking after his barbecue. Like a middle-class merchant. He was cooking not on a barbecue grill of the usual sort but on a long, wide trench with cinderblocks around the edge and, across the middle, steel rods and chickenwire. He stood in his white apron, pouring wine on the meat like a drink-offering to the newly dead—or, to be precise, pouring beer first, and afterward wine, and after that, when the fat began burning, water. Finally he sprinkled flour on the meat, his fluttering fingers incongruous against his somber death's-head face. Grimly, as though any humorous gesture were the farthest thing from his mind, he intoned: "Amen." Tentatively, watching his eyes, Will smiled.

"We usually have nothing but steak," Kleppmann said. "Young heifer. But these people—echh! My wife's friends, as you've guessed. However, for you a coal black ram without a spot." He pointed with his fork.

"I wouldn't have known the difference, you know," Will said, and smiled again.

"You are a wise man," Kleppmann said.

"Not really." He shrank back then, an instant late. The old man was angry, overflowing with hate, or anyway seething, waiting; and Will had been a fool to expect it to be different. He studied the face gray-orange and still as lead cooling in a smelter's mold, Kleppmann bending toward the fire, looking in, and decided abruptly that he, too, could wait.

"Join the party if you like," Kleppmann said. "Don't let me keep you."

"I may do that," he said, but remained. He became conscious of the rumble of a train now, somewhere in the distance. No light from it reached him.

Kleppmann was making no further pretense of talking. Will took a Tums and moved away a little to stand looking out into darkness. Casually, he asked, "What have you got on me, Kleppmann, that makes you so brave?"

Kleppmann gave no sign. "Brave?" he echoed politely.

"This property's yours all right," Will said, looking up into the trees. The branches and the leaves were sickly yellow from the mosquito bulbs on the porch. "The car's yours too, and the horses or chickens or whatever's out there in the barn."

"I never mean to take advantage," Kleppmann said. It seemed to Will—but it was hard to be sure—that the directness made Kleppmann uneasy.

"It can't be merely the long hours I put in," Will continued as if Kleppmann hadn't spoken. "You're a foxy old man, so I imagine you see through the long hours. They're not struggle for survival, not a pain in the neck that would make me vulnerable to, say, some gratuity from you. They're for pleasure."

"It's a good thing when a man likes his work," Kleppmann said. He was a dead man, all mechanical good manners, or the Wizard of Oz, his mind far away, behind some curtain pushing buttons and watching with tiny, sharp eyes. He needed jarring.

"I know now! The business in Chicago."

Kleppmann glanced at him, then away.

Will's voice was not booming with confidence now, or so it seemed from inside, but it made no difference. He wasn't bluffing. His hatred swelled his chest; not anger but the feeling one has toward things with cold blood. "The drinking, the orgy. I suppose you know about all that. Well, I'd be sorry to have it come out, that's true. For the children's sakes, and Louise's." He frowned, checking his emotions to see if it was true—if anything at all in his attic of old opinions, as Uncle Tag used to say, was true to his feelings. But the question was hard, and he put it off. "Not for my own sake though, not for myself. That is, I wouldn't drop pursuit of you merely to keep that quiet. It doesn't strike me as sufficiently evil, though I suppose I know how other people might feel—so I wouldn't pay. Also—" He folded his hands around the glass he was carefully not drinking from and sucked at his teeth, collecting his thoughts. "Also, fact is, I believe my wife would feel the same, ultimately. We're not desperate, like some, for complete approval from everybody on the block." ("Love," she'd scornfully echoed, he remembered, meaning "What is love?" It was a question people were always asking nowadays, scornfully—at the cafeteria where he ate with Sol and Hawes and the others, in the tiresome art films, at parties. It infuriated him that he couldn't snap out the answer at them. It seemed to him he had it on the tip of his tongue. Just the same, he thought, I love her, as well as I can. Such things exist.) Then, less than certain that the troublesome shade was at rest for good, he returned his attention to Kleppmann and the fire. "In short," Will said, "if it was in your mind that you might blackmail me off your ass, so to speak, with the Chicago business, forget it."

Kleppmann smiled, still hiding behind his curtain pushing buttons. "These are shameless times," he said.

"Maybe. Yes, certainly, I suppose. But you get me wrong, I think. I'm no scoffer, proud of having risen out of my middle-class morality. I have no pentecostal urge to declare the new dawn of fornication—no such thing! I have merely lost my feeling for what I have believed." He pursed his lips, struggling to be precise. "It happens to many people, I suspect. I have known some." He nodded. "And it seems to me it could be dangerous to pretend, when the feeling dies, that it's there. There was a woman in our family—generations back, this was —who had a child that wandered off and was never seen again. She kept his room for him, dusted it and kept things tidy for years, and one day she began to see him when he wasn't there, so they locked her up. That's how it would be." His expression went stern as it came to him that he'd run on more than the conversation required. But when he looked at Kleppmann it seemed to him that the old man understood that Will Hodge was not talking to him now, Kleppmann, but to himself. And strangely enough, Kleppmann had taken on a human look, though his eyes were not friendly. He was listening.

"Shameless, no," Will said, "I'm not that. Taking my middle-class values from me is like pulling teeth, and when the value's gone, how dizzying and jagged the abyss revealed to the tongue! But holes must not be denied."

Kleppmann nodded, smiling again, a nervous flicker. "Up-mobility, it's called."

Will scowled. "It's what?" Then: "Nonsense. Are you *purposely* misunderstanding?" Absurdly, he was furious. "I tell you the truth, Mr. Kleppmann, as a believer in Law. Law in the old sense, Justinian. I have never for one minute, so far as I know—" He was shaking his finger, and noticing the ridiculous gesture he lost track of what he was saying. Kleppmann was piling the meat onto trays. It was black. Will remembered again, abruptly. "I'm not social-climbing. Another thing entirely. I am stubbornly trying to understand, in my own rational middle-class terms, why it is that I no longer feel what I believe."

Three men with white faces stood watching like birds at the rim of the fire's influence.

"You say it again and again, though, don't you. 'Middle-class,' 'middle-class,' " Kleppmann said.

"That's pride, Mr. Kleppmann. My family's been middle-class for centuries. Doctors, lawyers, ministers, farmers, a Congressman once. We're all very proud of that."

For the first time all night, Kleppmann looked at him level-ly, not merely snatching an impression to manipulate with from behind his curtain, but scrutinizing his face. "We're somewhat alike, you and I," he said. He bent down for the meat.

It was not until hours later that they talked again. Klepp-mann, at his wife's suggestion, was showing Will to his room. Will still had the pistol, a great bulge in his suitcoat pocket which Kleppmann could not possibly have failed to notice. It seemed now more ludicrous than ever, as Will sat on the side of the bed in the large, farmhouse room, and Kleppmann stood remote but curious at the door.

Will said, "It's come to me, I think. It's the money. The tax business. They'll beat me, you figure—because though God knows justice is on my side, I was never a 'responsible officer,' merely a legal consultant, whatever the fancy title they gave it, it's not so clear that Federal law is neatly squared with jus-tice."

Kleppmann bowed as if to acknowledge that it might indeed be something along that line.

"You forget what ego-gratification I get out of honesty," Will said.

Again Kleppmann bowed, admitting it might be so.

Will stood up and went to the window to look out. He felt cramped, here inside the house. But the fog was thicker now. He could barely see to the pillars of the high portico.

"Ego-gratification," Will said with disgust. "I sound like the rest of them."

"Ah well, one may as well be honest," Kleppmann said. It sounded as though he were mimicking someone, and at first Will couldn't think who. He remembered then. He could feel his neck swelling.

"Scoff if you like," he said. "But consider this. You can't get me through the tax business either. It's true, they may beat me, and it's true that I haven't got even the cash to buy them off. Nevertheless, and you can call it what you like—ego-grati-fication, whatever—I'm as indifferent to jail as to scandal." It sounded grandiose, and he tried to think of a better way to say it. He looked at his hands, white and soft as a woman's. "I have this image of virtue. Idea of nobility. Something."

Kleppmann nodded. "And you actually feel it," he said.

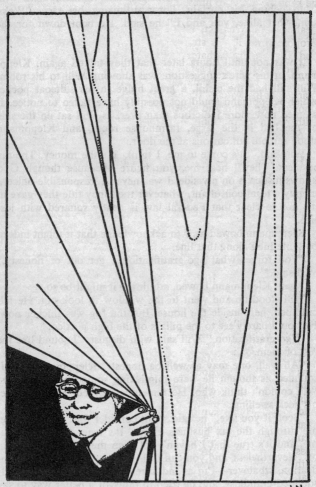

J.N.

"Sometimes." He was not sure that even that was true, but he kept the doubt to himself.

"I understand, of course. Yes. If you were caught in shady dealings—not, in fact, that I have anything of that kind to propose, for all this strange talk of yours—it would be the end. Disbarred, or whatever the phrase is."

"Good night," Will said.

"You're right." He tipped his head, slow and poised, and glanced at his watch. "It's after two. Forgive me." He drew the door partway shut and added, "I look forward to talking more with you in the morning."

And so, at last, he was alone.

He lay in the dark, drifting gently between daydream and nightmare.

One final question, Mr. Hodge.

There are no final questions.

One. I grant, and without reservation, that you are invulnerable. Yes. I can offer no reason under the sun why you should capitulate to my insidious suggestion. But let me ask, indifferently, for mere logic's sake, is there any reason on earth why you should not?

"I know what I feel," he whispered. In the deathly still farmhouse, the sound was like fire in straw.

And what do you feel for sure? the echoes asked.

There was an answer to that. He could not quite put his hand on it, but it was there, he would have it in a moment. He must wait.

The girl at Buz Marchant's had a squeezed-shut face. She was a good girl, no doubt. Pretty, kind in the usual ways. Not intelligent, no, but not all saints were intelligent either. The thing was—he struggled to get hold of it, nail it down once and for all—but again it came merely to this: she had a face that marked her, singled her out not as the bearer of any particular virtue or defect but as, simply, the bearer of her singleness. In adolescent dreams one coupled with radiant beauties with indefinite and lovely faces, but then one day it all turned real, no longer airy wet-dream vision—a girl one knew, with a name, brittle hair, a chin just a little too deeply cleft. That was love, if it was anything. Not the other. Not the sunlight but the sunlight entrapped in the cloud.

"Bullshit," he whispered.

636 The Sunlight Dialogues

Nevertheless, what was true of the girl was true of Mrs. Kleppmann too, and of Kleppmann. An objectness neither significant nor beautiful but there, singular; and they spoke words to him neither significant nor beautiful either; and by agreement, he understood them.

He understood, suddenly, what had gone wrong between him and Louise, and between him and his children, between his own mother and father, between, even, the Congressman and his sons. A kind of power failure, a sickly decline into vision. As simple as that. The discovery ran through his body like a shock and made his skin tingle, the way music did sometimes, or a brilliant point perfectly timed in a piece of litigation. All rhythm, he thought in wild excitement, pure matter in its rhythm. His head filled with an image of atoms going off, on, off, on, spinning—or planets, maybe, there was no telling now. He felt himself swinging in a wide arc around—someone. The face was obscure, a threatening shadow.

In the morning, what he remembered of all this seemed the usual dim-wittedness of dream, when the circuits are weak. Kleppmann spoke casually of horrors in Germany and scoffed at trials of war criminals as self-congratulation. They could not agree. Will Jr boarded the train for St. Louis at noon, integrity intact (conventions intact), though he had not had time, as yet, to work out his reasons. He would think it out on the train and plane, he told himself. But he didn't. The truth was, there was no need. Kleppmann had chosen—for whatever reason, evil or good, despite his habit in such cases, and despite the hatred that flickered inside him like summer lightning, a hatred of life itself, perhaps (but tradition be damned) —to send him home alive.

# XIX

## Workmen in
a Quarry

*The Caverns of the Grave I've seen,*
*And these I show'd to England's Queen,*
*But now the Caves of Hell I view,*
*Who shall I dare to show them to?*

—William Blake

### 1

Miller said, "They want you over at the Mayor's at ten o'clock."

Clumly nodded and moved on toward his office.

"I got some stuff for you," Miller said.

"Bring it in." He opened the door, took his hat off, and went to his desk. Miller came with his clipboard and two or three folders in the crook of his arm. Chief Clumly sat wait-

637

ing, his elbows firmly planted. The two small eyes at the peak of his white, mole's nose were as red as a wolf's. It was nine a.m. One hour yet before Mayor Mullen's "investigation."

Miller said, "Lot of activity last night. Some kids beat up a couple in a parked car, behind the racetrack." He handed the reports to Clumly. "And somebody got into Salway's Hardware last night. Took some money and some papers out of the safe and also—" he held the sheet to Clumly "—twenty-six guns, seventeen of them rifles. Got in the same way as at Francis and Mead. Could be the same outfit. Professional work."

"You know when it happened?"

"Not for sure. Ed Tank was on prowl. He discovered it at eleven-thirty. There's more."

"Go ahead."

"Early this morning, around five-twenty-five, a guy went into Greco's Garage in Darien, took a whole lot of car parts. He must've hauled 'em off in a truck. The State Police—"

"How you know the time?"

"Trooper called in at five-twenty-five, said he was at Greco's, going in to investigate. Then nothing. They found his car there burnt to a cinder."

"Find the trooper?"

"Not a trace."

Clumly half-closed his eyes, and they looked more than ever like a wolf's. "Dead, you think?"

"I don't know."

Clumly said, "Sounds like vigilantes. You think so? Guns. Parts for bombs."

Miller nodded. "That's what it sounds like. The State Police have already got hold of the Federal."

"Ok, that's all?"

"Not quite," Miller said. "You wanted a description of the man who registered in Paxton's name at that ranch in Colorado. We got it. Man with a scarred face, yellow hair, and a yellow beard."

"The Sunlight Man."

He nodded. "As for the stone—the little white stone you gave me—it's out of a deer. Very rare, they say. Forms inside the deer's stomach, one deer in a thousand."

"Anything else?"

"That's all so far on the stone. But this: your hunch was right about Kathleen Paxton. She was transferred from the place in Palo Alto on August sixteenth. Shipped to Rochester. Papers signed by her brother."

"You've got the address?"

Miller nodded and handed him the paper from his clipboard.

"Good work. First-rate. That's all for now. Have Kozlowski wait for me. There's just about time for—" He paused, thought better of it. "That's all," he said with finality. "Have Kozlowski wait."

Miller brooded a moment, then nodded. He said, "Your wife was in." After a moment: "She had some tapes she wanted me to hear."

"You heard 'em?" He kept himself calm.

Miller nodded. "So did Uphill. He was right outside the door."

Clumly tipped the desk with one finger. "All right," he said. A whisper.

Miller nodded again, then saluted and went out.

Now that he was alone, Clumly jumped up and paced and made no attempt to contain his anger. The Sunlight Man had been laughing at him all the time. Taggert Hodge! No doubt had the whole damn family working for him. Keeping him up all day and night, wrecking his health, ruining his brains, robbing him of his job, robbing him even of the dignity a Chief of Police ought to have when he retired. No doubt out there someplace watching him right now. Disguised as a fireman maybe. How else would Uphill have known?

Clumly paused at the window and scowled, then abruptly went to the door and called Figlow. "I want that firehouse raided," he said.

"What?" Figlow said.

"You heard me. Raid the firehouse. The Sunlight Man's there, in disguise."

Figlow put his fist on his mouth, eyebrows lowered. "Yessir," he said.

Clumly stormed back to his desk. The paper the Judge had brought for him to read still lay there. He looked away from it guiltily. "Ok, my magical friend," he said aloud, "you were right. Your time's running out," He looked at his watch. 9:30.

Appointment with the Mayor at ten. Uphill would be there.
Fred Clumly's time, too, was running out.

"Kozlowski," Clumly said, "we're in an age of technology.
A great time to be alive, but also a dangerous one."

Kozlowski kept his eyes on the traffic.

"A time of great prosperity. Enormous buildings, enormous
businesses, factories, institutions of learning! And what's in the
shadow of those glorious buildings? Hovels, Kozlowski. Misery
and crime and despair. More violence than ever before in history. More sorrow and hopelessness and rage. America leads
the world in it. The Russians are hurrying to catch up, of
course—they'll be mass-producing cars by next year, I read,
and also refrigerators and I forget what-all else: turning out a
glorious civilization by technology, push-button factories
where no humans need apply. Ha. It's something to think
about. Khrushchev tried to boost the economy, but he was
cowardly, come right down to it. There's why Koseygen or
whatever-his-name-is took over. Gross national profit has
jumped this year, matched by gross national violence. Fact.
They're catching up with us!" Clumly rubbed his hands. "You
ever stop to think just exactly what happens in slums, Kozlowski? They start out a little pocket of Negroes, say, who are
living there while they look for a job that will move them out.
No jobs. In 1900, fifty-six per cent of the total employed population was engaged in farming and fisheries and forestry.
Now that's down to I think it was seven per cent. Mechaniza-
tion, Kozlowski. Technology. No matter what price supports
you put in, no matter what kind of advertising you put on the
doors of your pick-up truck—like DRINK MORE MILK—it's
over. Finished. Going to be six, seven companies doing all the
farming in the whole damn country. As for industry, used to
be in 1900 almost half the population was engaged in that, but
it's slipping by leaps and bounds. Industries bigger than ever,
but now they're mechanized. Telecontrol in the shop—you
know what that is, Kozlowski? One machine, a man sitting in
an office running all the whole damn plant, with maybe six,
eight men with brooms and college educations keeping an eye
on things in case anything happens to go wrong. And as for
the office, who needs secretaries? They got computers can
make out the check for the man at the telecontrol! What's to
happen to all that labor that's no longer needed? Government,

you say. But just think about it. 1900 there was sixteen per cent of the people in State and Federal government jobs. Now it's forty per cent and rising. Doing what? Maybe sixteen different agencies all doing the same damn job, checking up on each other—providing they happen to know about each other's existence. That's insanity, boy. When a whole country's got nothing to do but watch somebody, well sir, that's insanity. Big brother, they say. Shoot! Watch the *little* brother! *That's the* dangerous one! Keep on putting labor in the only place left for it to go and in another ten years there'll be eighty per cent of the U.S. population in Government jobs, paying theirselves with their own taxes. That's called incest, Kozlowski. You know what results when brothers and sisters reproduce?"

Kozlowski spit out the window. "You're really feeling chipper this morning," he said.

"I feel horrible," Clumly roared—and well he might! However, he felt very good, there was no denying it. "Look there," he said.

On both sides of the road the fields were piled high with wrecked cars; rusty, murdered-looking in the staring sunlight.

"That's violence, Kozlowski," Clumly said. "Say an average of one dead man to a car, or one dead woman or child, whatever you please. There's a couple thousand dead men in there. Could be us, you know that? Man could come wheeling around the curve up ahead—"

The blood drained out of his face. As if he'd caused it to happen, a cattle truck careened around the corner and shot past them. For a time after that, neither of them spoke.

"All right," Clumly said. "That's violence. It's everywhere you look, from kids in school to the President of the United States sending thousands of men to go die in Vietnam when it isn't even a war. Never been declared. You cognizant of that, Kozlowski? And more dying that you never even hear about. Manchuria. That's how we clean the slums. Turn left up there." He pointed.

Kozlowski turned.

Clumly said, "They come off their run-down tenant farms that the Government's taking over for a park or a Job Corps center or some industry is taking over to run big scale, they come North from their shanties where they grew up with nine, ten brothers and sisters and, not a job in sight, they look for work. No work. They're black, for one thing, and not the right age, for another, and for another thing they're full of impatience, so's if they get a job they have a fight right away, or they come to work drunk, and they lose it. So then somebody like you or me goes in and arrests some kid for climbing a transom and they start shooting guns at us, and a crowd builds up, and then pretty soon the looting and burning starts. All the two-bit grocers and pawnbrokers and bartenders lose their places and collect their insurance and scram to someplace safe, and then the insurance companies say 'That's enough of that!' and they quit insuring in places where there might just conceivably be trouble. Think of it, Kozlowski. Ghetto skins along by pawning and whining to the grocer to keep the kids alive, buying groceries on credit—no serious business anywhere in sight except for the houses of ill repute and the junky line—can't even slip over to the posh sections for the stealing business, no cars to get there—and the place getting thicker and thicker with people, all boiling like white-hot lead, half of them ready to kill you on sight from pure jealousy and imaginary or real persecution—and now the insurance people pull out, pawnshops, and grocers and taverns shut down, no more hope for them, nothing in sight but violence. They come crawling out into the city like rabid dogs, spilling over their limits, mugging people on daylight streets, killing people for sport, and raping women. We take shots at 'em. What do they expect? We catch 'em drunk and we throw the book at 'em. Why not? Violence on violence! But not here, you say. Thank God, not in Batavia." He sucked in and out on the cigar, getting it going again. Kozlowski was scrooched down behind the wheel looking up at where the road wound into the trees at the top of the hill.

"Paxton place is up where the pine trees are," Clumly said. He let out smoke with the words. He said hurriedly, "But noplace is exempt. Batavia may not be Rochester or Buffalo, no riots here, Negroes still finding jobs, one kind another. Grocery stores, cleaning out garages, mowing lawns, picking at the dump. But they know people in Buffalo and Rochester, they got friends there. Heat up one piece of a minority group and you heat up all of it, like a frying pan. And meantime you've got the country kids whose families have moved into town, had to sell off the farm. And then you've got the sons of the doctors and lawyers and preachers, with all the money they want and nothing to believe in. Drunk-driving the big cars their daddies bought 'em, no ideas in their heads but that they're better than somebody else—tougher, smarter, more sex power. We had a case last year would've made your hair stand up. Couple kids pulled in at the Checkerboard Drive-In on West Main, had a girl in a blanket in the back seat. Good families, all three of 'em. Parked right next to one of our men—to mock him, must be. Cop got suspicious, reached in and pulled the blanket down. Naked she was. Turned out they were having a contest, they'd screwed that girl twenty-three times between them since noon. How 'bout that, Kozlowski?"

"My goodness," Kozlowski said dully. He'd come to the driveway now. He turned in and drove up to the porch, switched off the motor.

"It's a hell of a world, Kozlowski," Clumly said. He squinted at him, trying to see what he was thinking, but Kozlowski showed nothing. He merely nodded. Clumly looked up at the house, heart ticking painfully, and opened his car door. "Les go," he said. "It's almost ten. We better hurry this."

Professor Combs met them. He was wearing the faded red bathrobe Paxton had had on when he died, or such was Clumly's guess. He showed no embarrassment or alarm. He was old, and though he dyed his hair, he'd been through too much in his time to be bothered by the more trivial details of life and death.

"We've been expecting you," he said. He had a wide, white nose, powdered-looking, perhaps just with age, and there were liver-spots on his temples. His cheeks were unnaturally red, maybe rouged. White hair grew out of his ears. He said, "I'll take you to Elizabeth."

"I hope we're not getting you up," Clumly said.

The Professor did not answer. He probably didn't hear it. They stepped down from the entryway to the large white livingroom where apparently no one had spent more than half an hour in twenty years. The furniture hadn't been dusted in months. The fireplace was empty except for a few scraps of paper that had been there so long they looked as if they'd been rained on.

"This way," the Professor said.

They found Elizabeth Paxton on what had once been the

first-floor sunporch, now a makeshift bedroom for the summer. The Professor's clothes were there, hanging in the back of a peeling kitchen chair. The old woman's own clothes lay in a heap beside the bed. She lay with the covers pulled over her, shoulders bare, bruised. But what was more shocking than all the rest, to Clumly, was the woman's face. She made no effort this morning to hide the birthmark. She seemed to flaunt it. It was purple, brownish around the edges, and it stretched from the corner of her left eye across her wrinkled cheek to the right side of her chin.

"Good morning," she said. She did not bother to smile and she showed no embarrassment.

Clumly nodded.

"Professor Combs told me to expect you," she said. "Because of all your questions at the cemetery." If she was annoyed or disgusted, she did not show that either. The professor sat down on the edge of the bed and she reached out to cover his hand. His colored face was like a doll's.

"You've been ill?" Clumly said.

"Not at all," she said. "What makes you think so?"

He thought about it. It was as if whatever feeble life still remained in the big old house had slid toward this room, the two old people sharing one bed like corpses pushed in a ditch. He wiped his forehead with his sleeve and squinted.

"You came . . . for the funeral?" Clumly said.

The Professor didn't hear it. He turned to Mrs. Paxton.

"For the funeral, yes," she said.

"And he moved in, then?"

She had no intention of explaining. "Moved in, yes."

"Mmm," Clumly said. He glanced at Kozlowski. He was standing with his back to them, looking out at the lawn, where three sparrows were standing on the rim of the birdbath, drinking.

Nervously, Clumly said, "I wonder, if it wouldn't be too much trouble—" He cleared his throat. "Could you show me the study, where he died?"

"You need both of us?" she said.

He bit his lips. A stupid question, and she knew it.

She got the Professor to understand that she needed the wheelchair. He brought it over from the corner where it sat waiting, glossy in the sun, and before Clumly knew it would happen she pushed away the covers, shockingly indifferent to Clumly's eyes on her sagging, bruised skin. He caught only a glimpse before the Professor bent over her to lift her, as if tenderly, into the chair. When he had her in place he covered her again and moved slowly around to the back. "This way," he said. They moved toward the study.

Clumly said, squinting, covering his chin with his hand, "All those bruises . . . excuse me . . . what the devil—?"

She turned her head, but not far enough to see him. "Love," she said. Her laugh made his back run with chills, and the same instant he saw, vividly, that same word painted across Oak Street, official and absurd.

"Shocking," he whispered.

"Yes." A hiss.

The Professor said nothing; perhaps he had not heard.

Clive Paxton's study told Clumly nothing he had not known already—or at any rate, nothing important. He too saw in the full morning sunlight the deadness of the place, the grim actuality of every line and tone, the effect she'd mentioned at the cemetery. A vision of death, she'd said. The room did not need his corpse to make it that; the living dead would do—the Professor, the widow, Fred Clumly himself, for that matter, ten minutes late for an investigation of his incompetence! He could have laughed. He said, "He was sitting over there?"

She nodded.

But he did not look at the chair. He tried the lock on the rolltop desk, then the lock on the bookcase. "These were locked when you came in?"

"The bookcase, not the desk. I locked that later. He always liked everything locked. He was bitter, afraid of everything. Well he might be."

Clumly nodded, cutting her off. "But the window was open."

"No. That was locked too, I think."

"You said it was open."

"When?"

"At the cemetery. You told me you thought you would faint, that morning, but the breeze coming in from the window revived you. You said that. You said you were kneeling by the window."

She thought about it. "That's true. How clever you are!"

"Then you went over and closed his eyes."

She nodded.

"Then what?"

"I made a telephone call." She hesitated. "Is this important?"

He nodded.

"I'm tired," she said. "I'm a sick old woman."

The Professor put his hand on her shoulder.

Clumly turned his back, angry for no reason. "You called your daughter, is that right? But she wasn't there. So then you made more calls, right? To Phoenix, for instance—to your former son-in-law? But he was gone too."

She said nothing for a long time. At last: "I won't tell you a thing. You don't know what you're doing. There's no reason!" It was a whisper.

He turned back to her, all his muscles limp. Slowly, he drew two of the little white stones from his pocket. "What are these? You seen them before?"

"Never," she whispered. But her eyes remained fixed on them, and her chest heaved. Her hands closed like claws on the arms of the wheelchair, and the Professor, startled, bent down closer to her. It took Clumly longer than it should have to see what was happening. Kozlowski was in front of him all at once, lifting her feet up and shouting something—far away it sounded, a voice in a dream—"Call the hospital! Jesus! Help me get her to the car!"

But the next instant she was breathing again. She opened then closed her eyes.

"You'd better go," the Professor said softly.

Clumly frowned, absent-minded.

"Let's go," Kozlowski said. He took Clumly's arm.

Halfway back to town, Kozlowski said, "You damn near killed her."

Clumly nodded.

"I guess you figure it was murder. That it? The old man, I mean. Paxton."

He nodded again.

"Who?"

"I don't know," he said. But he knew.

"The old woman and the Professor?"

"Could be that."

"But you don't think so."

Clumly said, "How much did you hear last night?—that talk we had in the cemetery, me and the Sunlight Man."

"None of it. Just a rumble, sort of, through the wall."

"You be interested to hear?"

Kozlowski glanced at him.

"I have a tape-recording," Clumly said. He thought about it. "After you get off this afternoon, come by my house. I'd like you to hear it. Tell me what you think."

Kozlowski watched the road and said nothing. For two minutes neither of them spoke.

Then Kozlowski looked at him, frowning. "You notice something?"

It came to Clumly now. The radio was dead. He picked up the microphone and flicked the switch off and on. There was nothing. Kozlowski took it from him, and still there was nothing.

"I'll be damned," Kozlowski said. He hung the mike on its hook.

"It gives you the sweats, don't it," Clumly said.

Kozlowski said nothing.

They went over the Oak Street bridge and turned left onto Main. At the firehouse, the raid was on. He could see them lined up, hands against the wall, policemen frisking them. Clumly smiled. "Drop me off at City Hall," he said.

Kozlowski nodded.

Clumly adjusted his cap, looking hard at the lifeless mike. "Stay in the car," he said. He sighed. "Keep an eye out."

Kozlowski pulled up to the curb and Chief Clumly got out. They saluted, careful now of forms.

*2*

"Sorry to be late," Clumly said. He took his cap off and held it over his belly.

The Mayor scowled. "Well, not serious," he said. But it was

serious. "Mr. Uphill just got here himself." He backed out of the way, giving Clumly a view of the three men, the photographs on the far wall, the dead flowers in the window, the scummy Silex. "Come on in," he said. "You gentlemen have met, I take it?"

They all nodded. Uphill's face was dark red.

They sat waiting, solemn as cobras at a funeral. Two were members of the City Council. Mr. Peeper was bald and heavy, a pharmacist. Known for endless talk, an uneasy smile. Hater of unpleasantness; but he would be the one who wrote up the formal charges, when it came to that, and the dismissal. The second one was Mr. Moss, lean, unhealthy brown; he had a bad liver. He saw very little good in the world but rarely said so, merely asked questions, turned over stones and observed, unsurprised, the grubs. As for Uphill, he had a red face, silver hair. A dedicated man, an idealist. He'd been an Army Major once.

"Good," Mayor Mullen said. "Fine and dandy. Well, since it's late we might's well get right down to business." He went around behind his desk. "Sit down, gentlemen."

Only Clumly was standing. "Wittaker, bring the Chief of Police a chair." He looked sternly out the window while he waited. Wittaker came in with a chair, and Clumly sat down between Peeper and Uphill in the semicircle around Mayor Mullen's desk. Moss was to Clumly's far right. "Excuse me," Clumly said. The three men nodded in unison, formally, again like cobras, as Clumly saw it. The Mayor dusted his hands. "That's better," he said. He opened the manilla folder on his desk.

"As you know, gentlemen," he said, "this is not a formal hearing, it's just an investigation."

They nodded, slow and formal. Clumly got out a cigar. Their heads turned and they looked at him and he quickly changed his mind.

The Mayor pursed his lips and moved around the side of the desk and behind them, so that they had to—turning slowly —crane their necks. "Now one problem," he said, "has been partly taken care of, and that is the problem of communications. As I explained to you gentlemen before the Chief arrived, for a while there the Chief wasn't speaking to me. But I got three letters from him this very morning, delivered in person by one of his own men to avoid any needless further delay, and I'm grateful for that."

Clumly kept his face blank, but he knew he had not signed the letters.

"That's good," Peeper said. The uneasy smile.

"But we don't know the improvement's permanent, do we," Moss said. He shrugged, and his mouth hung down at the corners, trying to smile, sorrowfully failing. "I'm just asking," he said.

"That's a point," Mullen said. "And also, of course, exactly why he chose to write those letters right *now*, with the whole town in an uproar from all these robberies and murders and I don't know what—is a mystery, frankly. But no doubt there's some explanation."

"Surely," Peeper said.

Moss said, neither kind nor unkind, "There's never a right time, is there. Wait for the right time and you could be dead before it came, right? I only speak from my own limited experience." The tragic smile. "It's like the lady who kept hoping to be raped, right?" He dismissed the untold joke with a mournful wave.

They all laughed; all but Uphill and Clumly. It was as if the whole fool room were laughing—the dead flowers, the chairs, the desk, the Silex on the hotplate. Peeper, to Clumly's left, said grimly, "Nyeh heh heh heh!" Mullen said, "He he he he!" Clumly scowled.

"Well all right," the Mayor said. "No harm in a little joke, ha ha."

"Nyeh heh heh."

"He he he."

Uphill glared.

"Well all right," the Mayor said. His face grew sober. "Hurry on, then. We got to hurry along with this. Ah! Coffee's ready." He poured five cups, still talking. "So as to the first complaint, we can more or less forget it, it's all in the family, so to speak, and the Chief's shown he's willing to do better, or so it appears.

"The second complaint—I'm saying all this very frankly, so we can get someplace, not just set here jawing around, if you see what I mean—the second complaint is that the police department has not been fully cooperating with our other facilities, such as the fire department, for example. Not yet Fred. You can answer the complaints in a minute. Cream and sugar? Ah." He passed them around.

"Look here," Uphill said.

"The third complaint is, the Chief's not always where he's supposed to be, and where is he? He's out checking up on his men or—" He paused significantly. The cobras hung poised, on target. "Or worse," Mullen said. "Let's let that one ride for a minute. Can't delegate authority, then. So his men say. Whole lot of unrest and bad morale, if we want to face facts.

"Which brings me to the next problem. The crimes just isn't getting solved. I have a chart on my desk. . . ." He drew it toward him. "Now. What was I saying? Ah! I have a chart. Crime's up thirteen per cent over last year, here in Batavia. It makes you stop and wonder, don't it. And it's getting to have a professional look—you agree with that, Fred? Francis and Mead's Jewelry Store, for instance? Or that Boyle fellow you let go from jail, few days ago. You figure those are signs of professionals coming in?"

"You asking my opinion?" Clumly said.

"Not yet. I'll give you time to say your piece."

"We've got all day, right?" Moss said despairingly. He sucked in his cheeks and looked down at his sharp, crossed knees.

Clumly nodded. He sipped the coffee, not really intending to drink it. He got out his cigar again and, this time, lit it. Moss, two seats over, on his right, turned his head slowly, looking, then lit a cigarette.

"Just one more remark," Mayor Mullen said. "We talked with your subordinate, Sangirgonio. We asked him some straight-from-the-shoulder questions. I'll tell you frankly what it comes to. He doesn't trust you. There it is."

Clumly squinted.

"I'd just as soon not release the details on that, right at this time," the Mayor said.

"No need," Moss said. "Mere instances." Lip slightly curled, sad, he looked at each of them for confirmation. "Distrust is universal, right?"

The Mayor looked down at his cup. "Well all right," he said, "let's hear your side of it, Fred. What about all that mail, the speeches you forget to go to? What about the questions people ask you and you don't even hear them, or that crazy little escapade out by the railroad trestle—pictures in the paper and everything, no rhyme or reason, made the whole dang town a laughingstock. What about those *tapes?* And what about what's going on at the firehouse right now, those men standing in their *underwear*, I heard, being searched like thieves? What about it?"

The red of Uphill's face darkened.

"You're changing the charges," Clumly said. His hands shook.

"Don't you go logic-chopping with me, Clumly. I'm asking you to explain to us why we should let you go on with this confounded circus, not ask for your resignation."

"Times are changing," Clumly said. He said nothing more.

They sat leaning forward, necks craned, motionless, watching him with beady, dusty eyes.

At last the Mayor said, "Is that all you got to say?"

Clumly thought about it. "Times are changing," he said.

The Mayor and the three men waited, unimpressed.

"That may seem like nothing to you," Clumly whispered. "I'm not surprised. You're well-off, no real dealings with troubled people—poor people, people with bad tempers, people sick to death of their life." He thought of Elizabeth Paxton and the Professor. "You're responsible for it, if you want the truth: it's because of your kind I have to deal with the other kind, but you don't know it, you don't know they exist. That's your advantage. You're responsible, but you're not *responsible*. It's your laws they hang by, and if one of you slips over from your side to their side, it's your laws *he* hangs by. You, for instance. Peeper. Say you suffer reverses. Your wife commits suicide, sick to death of your stink of fat. You find out she's been playing the ponies for fifteen years. Hundred thousand dollars in debt. Your money. You say you won't pay it. 'Hell no,' you say, 'I'll take it to court!'"

"I certainly would," he said. His mouth seemed to move much too slowly for the words that shot out.

"Correct. Your house burns down mysteriously. And your son gets kicked out of college, they say he's a fairy, been sleeping with his teachers." (It could happen.) "All right, you slip over to *their* side. These gentlemen here will be sorry, correct? But sooner or later they'll send me after you. The responsible one. And I don't have to think about it any more than they do. No sir! I enforce the law—whichever of their laws you broke —I pull you in, I leave it to the court. And *they* don't have to think about it either, right? The lawyers can look up their precedents, they can hang you because they hung some poor devil in 1866. And after I've turned you over to the courts I can go on making speeches about law and order, and after they've hung you, there in court, they can go home and work on speeches about law and order, and nobody has to think. Nobody! That's democracy, you follow me? Like a huge aluminum dome made out of a million beams, and not a single beam is responsible, everything hanging on something else. And if an earthquake comes, or a tidal wave, or a good fat tornado, what's it to beam number nine-hundred-seventy-two? Ha!" The room was bright, their figures dark, like a negative.

Mullen leaned forward slowly. "What are you talking about?"

"Mouse turds," Clumly hissed. "Horse manure."

"You're like a madman."

Clumly nodded. "It's the Times." At last he fell silent.

Moss said, "What he's saying makes sense." His eyes fixed on Mullen.

"But is he competent?" Mullen said. "I'm talking very frankly, you understand. This is just an informal chat."

Moss drew back, then turned his head to look once more at Clumly.

Uphill said, "I'll lose men because of this morning. And don't fool yourself. That's the reason he done it."

"I've got work to do," Clumly said. "If you're through with all this—"

Mullen's head turned. "All right, Fred. You may go. You can wait in the hall."

Clumly stood up.

"I'm sorry about this," Mayor Mullen said. His head was thrust forward and tipped.

"I can see that. Let me know what you decide."

The Mayor looked at him. "I'm truly sorry."

"You sound like you've decided already."

Nobody spoke. Clumly turned to the door.

It was Moss who brought the news. He stood with his head tipped, weight despairingly on one leg. He smiled, gently cyni-

cal, cigarette poised in his lean hand, between his thumb and
four fingers. "It was a foregone conclusion, right?" he said. He
looked past Clumly's shoulder. "Who can escape if he's investigated? *I* couldn't. Nobody could, right? Our best judgment is
that you should step down. We realize it may be a mistake. We
all make mistakes."

Clumly nodded, his right hand clutching his left.

"Finish out the day," he said. He looked off into space, and
it was as if he was thinking what he would do in Clumly's
place. He would finish out the day. He did not seem to guess
that his heart would be broken.

*An informal investigation*, the Mayor had said. Clumly
wept. "He lied to me," he said. "The Mayor told me"—he
sobbed—"told me a lie."

Clumly cried for a long time. Mr. Moss brought him coffee,
and Mr. Peeper went out and got him two donuts and would
not hear of letting Clumly pay for them. "It's just one of those
unfortunate occurrences," he said miserably. "This whole business is a *mess*," he said. At last Clumly went to the room
which said GENTLEMEN and washed his face.

Kozlowski said, "You got a message. On the radio. I wrote
it down." He held out a slip of paper.

"Good morning Chief Clumly," the message said. "I invite
you to one last conference. Here are my instructions . . ."

Clumly read no further. Mouth open, heart drained, he
looked at Kozlowski.

"You going, Chief?"

Clumly could not think. He said, a kind of whimper, "Quit
fooling with me, Kozlowski."

Kozlowski pursed his lips, at last realizing what had happened. "Sorry," he said, then: "They found the trooper."

Clumly scarcely heard it. "When you listen to the tapes . . ."

"The Sunlight Man?" He looked incredulous. "He'll kill
you. It's a fact."

"I don't know. Sometimes I think—"

"He'll kill you."

"It doesn't matter." He would have wept, if he weren't wept
out. He said abruptly, "Come with me. Watch."

"Not on your life. Not alone." He switched on the motor,

shifted, pulled out onto the street. "What are you after? Tell the truth."

For a long time Clumly said nothing. At last he sniffed. "You make a man think, Kozlowski."

Kozlowski cracked the door, like a farmer, and spit. At last he said, "It's a funny feeling, riding around with a dead man."

### 3

He went on as before, but he looked preoccupied. That afternoon they visited Kathleen Paxton. The sign on the iron gates said *Pleasant Hills*. The gates stood open. Kozlowski drove in. Once out of the trees, the driveway dipped sharply and they could see the broad, mercurial Genesee River, and, right up against the river, on the nearer bank, the high, many-gabled house. "Used to be the Bell place," Clumly said. "Canal money. I don't know how long it's been a hospital. Ten, fifteen years."

A furtive old man stood in the turn-around with a watering can. As they drove up, he ran away.

"Like a prison," Kozlowski said.

Clumly said vaguely, "People say it's a snakepit. I wouldn't know. Lot of shock treatments here. Lot of people say they're a medieval torture. They work the same way as a blow on the head with a hammer. Some psychiatrist says. Read it in the *Reader's Digest*. Then there's other people say a shock treatment does some good, reorganizes the brain patterns, something. It makes you wonder. You know that in any profession there's bound to be some incompetents, dishonest people, people full of malice—schoolteachers, doctors, lawyers, dentists. So you know it's possible these shock treatments really are a kind of crime against the public. But then again, you know there's always the radicals, too—teachers that don't think there should be grades, the ministers who say you should quit paying taxes if the money's going for war. Hard to tell which is which if you're not some kind of a specialist. It's like high-speed dentist's drills." He sighed. "Some dentists'll tell you a high-speed drill is the only thing to have, and then others'll say it breaks down the structure of the tooth. What's a man to do?

Things work 'emselves out, eventually—the right side ends up winning, I s'pose—but that's no help if you're sitting in a dentist's chair before it's been decided." Again, a sigh. "It used to be you could tell when a man was wrong just by the way he went at it: you could tell those American Nazis were wrong by how red their faces got. Same with the Communists. But this House Un-American Activities Committee, for instance— what's a man to do when on one side there's all those kids with beards and on the other side that man from I think it's Texas? I saw on TV where one of those rioters from Berkeley stood up in front of the camera and told how her parents were hypocrites and liars and how she was better, shacking up with some long-haired dope addick or whatever, and I thought, Now there's a lunatic if I ever see one, but then I read about how all these professors are right there behind her, saying all how a university is the experiment grounds for the future and how it's not enough to theorize about how society ought to be fixed, you have to act, even if some of the actions don't turn out. It's hard to know where you stand any more. The same thing with shock, if you know what I mean. You feel like you ought to be doing something, come out, one side or the other. But who's to say? I went in the drugstore, couple days ago, I ordered a ham on rye. Came out all fat, not enough meat for a horsefly, and a piece of lettuce looked like maybe they found it on the floor behind the stove. I says, "Wait a minute now, this ham on rye's not fit for a person to eat." Waitress says, "Don't look at me, sir. I just work here." *Everybody* just works here. If the sandwiches are gonna be fit to eat, somebody's got to behave as if he owned the place. Suppose it was your kid they were gonna give shock treatments to. You willing to leave it to the specialists? But what's a man to do! What's this world coming to, Kozlowski?"

"Should we go in?" Kozlowski said.

"Mmm," Clumly said, startled. He opened his door. He got out and waited while Kozlowski came around and stood beside him. Clumly hooked his thumbs inside his belt and squinted at the porch. He couldn't see too good. He sighed.

Slowly, as though they were personally to blame for the misery and pain inside, they went up the steps, rang at the locked door, and stood with their heads bowed, waiting.

"Lot of the people they keep here are drunks," Clumly said.

"Mostly women. But a few true crazy people, too. I remember they had a woman here kept biting people. I never met her myself, but someone was telling me—I forget now who. She'd be talking along just as sensible as you please and then all at once she'd stop and look up and *snap!* Her teeth in you. So her husband committed her. It was just the eternal annoyance, you know. She didn't bite really deep. And then there's a young boy they tell of, all he would eat was hay. What you think does that to people?"

He shook his head.

The door opened inward, and a square, muscular head, vaguely female, poked out to look at them. After a moment the door opened wider and they could see the woman's striped uniform, powerful legs, lumpy black shoes. The key to the door hung from a chain around her waist.

"Come in," she said. "We've been expecting you."

The ceilings were high, traversed by ten-by-ten oak beams. It had all been elegant long ago. The entryroom had almost no furniture in it, though it was large—a parlor—two cheap wooden chairs, an overstuffed chair of ancient mohair, on the far wall a desk with nothing on it but a green blotter and a fluorescent lamp. The stairway curving around to the left had no runner on it, only rubber treads torn at the corners and re-nailed. The mannish nurse guided them past the foot of the stairs to the double-width doorway underneath the stairs, opening onto a sunlit livingroom as plain as the entryroom, though not as sparse. Threadbare rug of the sort found in Methodist Sunday school rooms. Two couches, standing metal ashtrays, a cheap blond coffeetable, small plastic radio (white), old magazines. *The Zodiac.*

"Wait here," she said. "The doctor will see you in a moment."

Clumly sat down and opened a three-month-old copy of *Time.* Kozlowski went to the window and stood looking out. Pictures of dead soldiers, the headless body of a child. He turned the page.

"I guess you know the story of Taggert Hodge," he said. Kozlowski gave no sign.

"About forty now," Clumly said. "Left Batavia sixteen years ago—1950. He was a lawyer, got disbarred. I don't know what all was involved in it. He was the youngest of the Congressman's sons. He was a hero in the Army. Minor sort of hero, but he got a medal, I remember. Well anyway, it was during his time in the Army he married Kathleen Paxton. Prettiest thing you ever saw. Old man was rich of course. Clive Paxton. One they just buried. She was a schoolteacher. (I'm talking about Kathleen, now.) But that faraway look in her eyes was because she was more'n half-crazy, just plain not in the world about half the time. I could tell you something about that, too. That girl's parents never laid a hand on her, her whole life. They never even yelled. She had a room you'd put a princess in—all pillows and white and gold paint and stuffed animals and dolls. . . . Why that place would've turned a Marine into a helpless little flower, or else some kind of wild animal running through the world ram-pant, or maybe both. Anyway, what happened to Kathleen was this: she got to be the softest sweetest gentlest thing on earth except she had a temper that would stand up your hair, same as her dad, and one thing more: she got full of suspicions. When the whole thing blew up, sixteen years ago, she wrote letters to the paper that the Communists had her husband locked up in a cellar, whole town full of secret agents, according to Kathleen. It was sad."

Kozlowski still showed no sign that he was listening. He stood motionless, hands on his hips, staring down toward the river.

Clumly cleared his throat and collected his memories. "Well, Taggert Hodge married her, and they went away on a trip together, over to Europe and I guess Japan and India and all over, I don't recall. He found out how it was with her, all right. They say young Tag went to Clive Paxton about it, he wanted to send her to an analyst, more money than the Hodges have had for a goodly number of years. Old Man wouldn't hear of it. Had his crazy streak himself, you know. Stubborn as the side of a mountain and cold as a iceberg. They say he thought if Kathleen was part crazy it was nobody's fault but Taggert's. Tried to get the marriage annulled, even made some inquiries about getting Taggert locked up in a hospital himself. You can guess the rest. Taggert Hodge was too smart for his own good, and all his life he'd been too lucky. He thought he could get away with some number juggling. I don't blame him, mind you. I'd've done the same thing myself, if I thought it would work. And he didn't just think it would, he knew it. Only it didn't, on account of Kathleen. She was already seeing the analyst, by that time, but it wasn't working fast enough, and one night in the middle of winter, about eleven o'clock, she went into that office of Tag's, where he was working late the way he always did—that boy worked seventeen, eighteen hours a day, and that's the truth—you see it wasn't just juggling numbers that he was up to: he was making money however he could, and that included working himself half to death. Well then, all right. She tried to set his office on fire—covered the floor with gasoline—she had her two children right there with her. But somebody stopped her. Well, life's full of ironies. She wrecked the rug or something, and Will Hodge, he was in the office too, he tried to collect insurance. There's some think he knew all the time. For some reason that meant they had to go through the records, get everything straightened out, and the number juggling showed up. What could Tag Hodge do? He lit out, left the wreck to his brother—they were partners, Tag and Will Sr—because it was either that or jail, and the poor devil still had hope he could save that poor crazy girl. Well he couldn't. Clive Paxton did get the thing annulled then—I don't know what grounds—and so he won, if you call it that. They had her locked up. But Tag Hodge kept in touch, or so the rumor goes. Oldest brother was pretty much on Taggert's side as to how it should be done, and someway they got her away from the Old Man. They been moving her around for a number of years, we found out this morning. My guess is that's Tag Hodge's work, or the brother's, or all the brothers and Taggert too. Old lady didn't know it, I know that much, and I doubt that Clive Paxton knew it either until just lately, though that's just guesswork. He was a coward, some ways. He loved her all right, I grant you that, but I don't think he could look at her after she got the way she was."

"How was she?" Kozlowski asked, distant.

"You'll see," he said. "So where was I? Ah. They moved her around, keeping her out of the Old Man's reach, and they tried to get her treated, but none of 'em had money. The Paxton boys weren't businessmen. We found that out too. And Taggert neither. You know what he's been doing since he left here that night—as good a lawyer as Batavia ever had? He's been working used-car lots, Kozlowski. Sweeping up at some

church. Peddling. Fixing televisions. He was even school janitor awhile. And worked at his magic, of course. He couldn't
stand that humiliation, naturally. Hurt his pride—and who'd
blame him? Truth is, *you'd* feel robbed in a situation like that.
It wasn't for something he'd done for himself. He did it out of
love for her—or maybe worse yet, did it after her craziness
had made loving her impossible, which means he did it out of
duty, something like. Smashed because he wanted to be noble.
Like his father, Old Nobility himself."

Clumly leaned forward, pointing. He was talking to himself
now, thinking out loud. "Listen! You'd think back, a time like
that. You'd commence reconsidering all the fine phrases, the
high-minded speeches about duty and unselfishness and the
rest. Maybe you'd say, 'Ah, ah! I stepped outside the law,
there's the heart of it! Oh Dad, Dad, you were right all along!'
Maybe you'd say that, but then too maybe not. Listen. If I'm
standing waiting for a red light to change and some kid walks
out in the middle of the street, some toddler, say, you think I
go on waiting for the light to change before I run out and drag
him away from where it's dangerous? Listen. Some ordinary
citizen, say—not a cop, mind you, some barber, for instance
—some ordinary citizen picks up a man with a broken skull
and drives him in to the hospital. If the man drives sixty miles
an hour, through red lights and all, with his hand on the horn,
why there's not a judge in the country would say he did
wrong. Law and Order is important, no question about it, but
it exists for a reason—protection of life and property—and
when the law runs counter to the *reason* for law, why it's no
longer law at all. Correct? Maybe it seemed to him a case
where he had to settle an either-or: property—other people's
property—versus life—the life of the girl. So he made the
choice, maybe made it knowing the odds that he wouldn't get
away with it, and what happens? The law comes down on both
their heads, his head the same as hers. He's outcast, in a way,
you might say; killed. In the conflict of property and life,
property's won. How would you feel about that, Kozlowski?
What would you make of you?"

Kozlowski mused.

"Bitter!" Clumly said. "Except that that would depend on
how much pride you had, wouldn't it? And how much temper?"

Kozlowski said, "You think he was right?"

Clumly rubbed his chin, forehead wrinkled as a bulldog's. "I don't know. There's something wrong with it, but damned if I can catch it."

"It's unchristian," Kozlowski said, possibly joking. Clumly couldn't tell.

Three minutes later the doctor came in.

"I'm Dr. Burns," he said. He was small, excessively cheerful, very young. He wore a beard and plastic glasses with one side wired up. "You must be Police Chief Clumly."

Clumly nodded. "This is Officer Kozlowski."

They shook hands. The doctor spoke as if with pleasure of the run-down condition of the hospital, the limited staff, the barbarism of his colleagues. Clumly shook his head politely, not listening. Abruptly and irrelevantly Clumly said, "You don't approve of shock treatments, then?" The doctor looked startled. "Everything's relative," he said. He smiled. There was an awkward pause. Then: "We go this way."

He led them back to the entryroom and toward the stairs. As they went up, the doctor taking two steps at a time and sorting his keys, Clumly said, "How is she, doctor? What is your—" He hunted for the word.

"Prognosis," the doctor said brightly. "Well, you'll see. Not good, I'd say. As you may or may not be able to observe at a glance—it all depends—she hears voices. Projections, you know." There was no one in the hallway that opened out at the head of the stairs. The doors to the left and right of the hallway were closed, perhaps locked. Not a sound came from any of them. "Her conscious mind is seriously crippled, possibly destroyed. The projections—the voices—are of course the unconscious mind at work, stirring up memories of old sensations—as for present sensation, she's cut off from it entirely, you see. She, uh—" He selected a key and fitted it into the lock on the last of the high, peeling doors. He turned the key and opened the door an inch but paused, looking down the hallway, and went on with what he was saying. "She has emotions, sensations, and intuitions, but in all cases old ones, nightmarish memories, so to speak. As for intellect, it's reduced to ashes. Ashes. The voices that mumble are, as you might say, dreamlike representations of the old emotions and so on. I'm telling you this to prepare you."

Clumly nodded.

"Each case is different, interesting in its own unique way. The ordinary layman would be amazed at the infinite variety of psychotic avenues—no two exactly alike. Like snowflakes, you know, or crystals. Because of course no two people are alike, not even identical twins. Put it this way. We receive sensations—you do, I do, Officer Kozlaski here does. You feel the rain falling, you see green leaves, you hear a frying pan fall off the sink. Well now some people have a more acute sense of feeling than other people have. Some people *hear* more acutely, others *see* more acutely, and so on. All this can be measured, at least relatively: a cathode in the brain can register the degree of psychoelectric charge an individual gets from any given sensation—A440 extended to thirty seconds, for example. But sensation is the ground of our experience, not so? First we sense things: a bull in a field, say. Then we ratiocinate. After that—or before that (there are several theories)— we emote. Finally we intuit. To be healthy, normal people—if we may use the expression—we need a balance of sensation, ratiocination, and the rest. Or if not a balance, then an adequate compensation. A fascinating business, let me tell you. The Germans—"

"Excuse me," Clumly said. He pointed tentatively toward the doorknob with one curved finger.

"Yes of course," the doctor said. He opened the door.

"The Germans are far ahead of us in this. They did some really magnificent experiments during the War—induced neuroses, then altered the sensation-field, by blinding the subject, for instance, or terminating his hearing, et cetera. It's incredible, the ways in which neurotics compensate. And if that's true of a neurotic, you see, we can hazard that it's equally true of the so-called normal psyche.—Oh, don't worry, she can't hear a thing. At least not from the outside.—Kathleen?" He clapped his hands.

She sat perfectly still, hands lightly folded in her lap, her back against the wall. Her eyes were open and contained no life. She was so much like a corpse, in fact, that Clumly caught his breath. There was nothing whatever in the room, only the bare floor, the bare, chipped walls, the naked window.

She smelled of urine. Her hair was gray, cut short just at the middle of her ears. Some of it had fallen out, over her temples. The face was old.

"She never move at all?" Clumly said.

"Almost never. The layman might think her an absolute vegetable, but actually that would be an oversimplification. She may possibly have a fine intelligence in there, fast asleep. If there were time enough, it might be possible to rouse it. But there isn't of course. With five years of concentration on no patient but her, using violent pleasure and violent pain, I might be able to get her to smile when I enter the room. Five more and I might be able to get her to play with blocks, say, or rock a doll. Five more—well, you see how it is."

Clumly put his hands on his knees and bent down closer, squinting into the eyes, looking for some spark. There was nothing. "How do you know she hears voices?"

"Ah!" the doctor said. "An excellent question.—Shall we go down now?"

They followed him to the door. He held it for them, then closed it and locked it.

Clumly said, looking at the doorknob, "Why do you lock the door?"

The doctor wrinkled his nose with disgust. "Rule," he said. "An idiotic rule." He dropped the keyring in his pocket, and they started down the hall. "So," he said, "the voices. We don't know what she actually hears, of course, we are entirely in the area of theory. We know she *used* to hear voices, and we assume—it's all very complicated really, but one can express it simply without altogether distorting the matter—we assume she has relinquished her hold on external reality out of preference for the actuality of her voices, if you see the distinction." He pinched his own cheek—an odd sort of gesture, it seemed to Clumly—then went on with great interest in his subject. "At certain periods outer reality does seem to reach her: the nurses find her sitting in the middle of the room, for example. A clear indication that she is aware of the walls—and resents them, needless to say. Feels bombarded by them. That's the effect of reality on us all, you know. A constant blitz." They were going down the stairs now, Kozlowski in front, then Clumly, the doctor behind. "And we all have our periods of withdrawal, of course. At a time of sorrow, for example. When a loved one has died the whole world seems full and terrible, you know what I mean? The trees are suddenly more *oppressive,* intolerably so. A car horn has a nightmarish kind of effrontery, or a birdsong. Not the tripe of poets, I don't mean anything like that. No no! Sorrow, which is to say violated memory, a crack in the armor of our individuality, takes precedence for us. Thus in the moment of the catastrophe sights and sounds are unusually clear, unusually violent and distinct, an imposition. But after the first shock we withdraw to the point where sights are barely seen, sounds barely heard. Interesting?"

Clumly nodded. He thought a moment, then nodded again.

"This way," Dr. Burns said. "I'd like you to meet my son." He led them down a hallway opening to the right off the entryroom, a series of doors exactly like the doors upstairs, but here the doors had metal signs, some of them the names of doctors. "Kathleen's a fascinating case," he said. "I wish I could give it the time it deserves. I have some theories, actually. But this is no place for trying out one's theories. We barely get the taxes paid." He came to a door with the name *Orr* on the plate, and got out his keys. "This is my office," he said. "The nameplates are old. It's been years since there was a Dr. Orr in this place." He laughed, then shrugged a little fiercely, and unlocked the door. "Are you familiar with the Jungian theory of the stages of life?"

"I don't believe so," Clumly said.

The door swung open. The office was very small, comfortable. On the wall there was a picture of a Coast Guard ship, with the number W738.

"You were in the Coast Guard?" Clumly said.

"P.H.S.," he said. "Public Health Service." He glanced at the picture. "Spent six weeks on her. Beautiful."

Clumly nodded.

"Adam?" the doctor called. There was obviously no one in the room. The window was open. The doctor went over to it and looked out. He frowned, then thought better of it and smiled. "Climbed out the window," he said. "He's a devil, that's the truth. Sharp as a tack though. His mother is also a psychiatrist. Gets it on both sides, poor little fellow. We'll go this way." He led them back into the hall and toward the glass doors at the end. With his hand on the doorknob he paused, reached up rather suddenly and once again pinched his cheek. "The stages of life," he said. "Yes. Right. According to Jung life is like the daily course of the sun. He says—" The doctor closed his eyes a moment, thinking, then quoted carefully, shaking his finger as if at an imaginary class, " 'In the morning it arises from the sea . . .' no, 'the nocturnal sea of unconsciousness and looks upon the wide, bright world . . .' something, something '. . . expanse that steadily widens the higher it climbs in the firmament.' Ah, I forget the exact words. Anyway, point is, sun rises in the morning, the world expands before it, and it's in the expanding world that the sun discovers its own significance. It imagines that reaching the greatest possible height, where it can disseminate its blessings most fully, is its life goal. But at noon the descent begins, and the descent means the reversal of all the ideals and values that were cherished in the morning. The sun falls into contradiction with itself. It's as if it should draw *in* its rays, instead of emitting them. Now, it's the same with life, Jung says. You rise out of the unconsciousness of babyhood—he'd go farther back than that, in fact—and you learn who and what you are in youth, reacting with the world, and you build more and more consciousness, you think you can judge everything, meet all demands. But at a certain point you learn that the more you learn the more you'll never know! You begin to shrink back from thought—life has bombed you, and you flee forward to the unconsciousness of senility. You understand all this?"

Clumly tipped his head, lips pursed, hand on his chin. Kozlowski stood looking through the glass.

"Well now this is my belief," the doctor said—excitedly. "I believe one does not *regress* in neurosis. I believe one progresses too rapidly through life. Bombed by experience, one hurtles through life—*snap!*" He snapped his fingers as he said it. "What is the doctor's job, then? *Not* to move him back to childhood, make him live through his traumas over again, this time with understanding. The doctor's job is to rejuvenate! Turn back the years!" He was leaning far forward now, snapping his fingers again and again, eyes narrowed to slits.

"But how?" Clumly said.

The doctor straightened up, became absolutely calm. Then he smiled. "Hypnosis," he said. He beamed. Then: "Come meet my son." He threw open the door. Chief Clumly scratched his head.

It was a small, enclosed yard with a dark-leafed mapletree in the center, around it long soft grass. The boy sat in a swing, looking sadly at his knees. He had long, dark hair, pale skin, blue eyes as colorless as glass. "Adam," the doctor said. The boy turned his head just a little. "Child," the doctor said. He stood with his fingertips together, his head thrown forward, on the peaked face a look of anguish. "Come and meet our guests," he said.

The boy did not stir.

"What am I to do?" the doctor whispered. "Do you think I don't know what damage I can do him by punishing him? Do you think I don't know what damage I can do by *not* punishing him? His mother, now. We are separated. We cannot live together—a grotesque mismatch of slightly paranoid personalities. So we should stick together for the sake of the child, and our arguments eating him alive? We should break up, then, and deprive him of love?" He stretched out his hands to Clumly. "Advise me! What should I do?"

Clumly studied the doctor in alarm.

"Adam!" the doctor called suddenly. "I said to get over here!" His fists closed.

"We have to go," Clumly said timidly. "We really can't—"

"Is that your solution? To go!" He stopped himself. "Yes of course. Fair is fair. I'm sorry. I'm sorry I've been no help. As for the boy—it's not as bad as it seems, not at all. He loves me as much as he hates me, and he's young, flexible. As for his mother—" He stopped abruptly and mopped his forehead. Then, like a child, he smiled. "You must think we're all mad here. And me the maddest of all. My dear sir, life—" He shook his head. For no apparent reason, the boy dropped from the swing and came over to take the man's hand. "Full of surprises, isn't it," said the doctor. "That, if I may say so, is my professional opinion." He patted the boy's head.

"Good luck," Clumly said humbly. They turned back toward the door.

"You haven't asked about the husband."

Clumly waited.

"He came by, once, you know. A strange-looking man—I think mad, in fact, or very close to it. You know him?"

Clumly stole a glance at Kozlowski. He had not exactly wanted it to come out in Kozlowski's presence, for reasons of his own.

"Taggert Hodge. A kind of magician—very good. Very. I suspect if the truth were known he might be directly responsible for . . . the patient's condition."

"He comes here?" Clumly faltered.

"He's been here twice. You want my diagnosis?"

"We thought he was still in Phoenix," Clumly said. Kozlowski did not seem fooled by it. Clumly wiped the sweat from the back of his neck.

"He's here all right. My opinion is, he's right on the edge of violence. Whether it will be directed outward or inward . . . But this is just guesswork. I have only watched him. To tell the truth, I believed he was going to kill me. We've hardly spoken."

"Thank you," Clumly said. He turned away.

For a moment the doctor said nothing. Then: "Good luck. As you say. To all of us. God give the world good luck."

Abruptly, the boy jerked away from him and returned to his swing. They went back inside, leaving the doctor to brood on his difficulties, and walked hurriedly down the long hallway to the entryroom and front door. It was locked. They rang for the nurse, not meeting each other's eyes.

At last, in the car, Kozlowski said, "How come you keep pretending, Chief? You knew who this Sunlight Man was from the beginning."

"Not from the beginning," Clumly said.

"The others?"

"The other whats?"

"The rest of the Hodges know?"

"I don't know. Be strange if they didn't."

They were approaching the iron gates now.

"You think Will Hodge knew, that night he found the corpse in his apartment?"

"People are strange, Kozlowski. Full of surprises." He turned in the seat to look back, and Kozlowski, at the same moment, glanced into the rear-view mirror. Will Hodge Sr's car pulled onto the road.

"Still with us," Kozlowski said. It was the first either of them had said about it. "What's he after, you think?"

Clumly lit a cigar and scrooched down in the seat to media-tate. At last he said, "It comes to this. If he knows, he's following us to watch after his brother. And if he doesn't know —" He let it finish itself, but Kozlowski looked at him, waiting. "All right, Kozlowski," Clumly said, "say you're in the woods and you see somebody tracking something. What's he up to?"

"I guess he's hunting," Kozlowski said.

Clumly blew out smoke. "You guess he's hunting."

It did not matter, now that Clumly had seen her. He was ashamed of having hoped for a parade.

## 4

Clumly was in plain clothes. A blue serge suit. Trousers with enormous pleats in them, a double-breasted coat, dark brown shirt, wide tie, black hat on his head. On the wire hanger in the closet of the otherwise empty room he had his black winter coat. He stood by the window, leaning on his knees, in the third-floor room where he went to listen to the tapes, and to look at him you would have thought he had taken on still more weight, the past few hours: he might have weighed tons and tons, like one of the damned. When Kozlowski had let him off this afternoon, Esther was out. Clumly had come up at once to where he had hidden the tapes, and he'd found that the tapes were gone.

"Impossible!" Clumly had said. "My own wife!" He'd run down to the bedroom (still wearing his uniform) and hunted there—through his shirt drawer, his underwear drawer, the drawer in the highboy where he kept his father's old shaving equipment. He looked in the closet, in the box he kept under the bed, in the medicine chest in the bathroom. He stood patting his cheeks, trying to remember. He looked downstairs. Useless. Life is full of deadly ironies.

He went back up to the bedroom and closed the door behind him and leaned on it, thinking. Well, he'd known, hadn't he, that his time had run out? There would be criminal charges no doubt. Correct. (It flitted through his mind that the Sunlight Man was a natural for "The Most Unforgettable

Character I've Met." He shook his head crossly to get rid of the thought. *Getting old,* he thought. Even his mind would allow him no dignity.)

*Where was I? Yes. They've got hold of the tapes, so they know.* "This is irregular, Clumly." "I'm aware of that. Yes." "Highly irregular. Negligent." "Yes, yes, yes."

Someone had died, he remembered again, through his incompetence.

He thought of the stages of life the psychiatrist had mentioned. Strange to say, he had heard it all without listening. Clumly was in the twilight stage. Not that sixty-four was old, exactly. He still had his teeth. He'd be going strong at ninety. Good stock, as Miss Woodworth would say. But twilight, nevertheless. No longer fit for the world. One further injustice. Was a man no more than a monkey? Young monkeys played games, learning the tricks that would keep them alive when playtime was over. They reached maturity and they reproduced, and they used what skills they had to protect the young. Then the old monkey died. Not so with man. At the Tonawanda Reservation—and it was the same everywhere with Indians, or with those African savages you read about—the old people were the keepers of the law, the guardians of the mysteries: it was not a case of mere sinking into the unconsciousness of childhood, it was a further progress, a final stage in the sun's long ride into darkness, and in that final stage the sun carried all it had known before, all its intellect and activity, but now surpassed mere intellect and activity, surpassed mere propagation, mere earning, mere things of nature, and rose to the things of culture, to civilization! Not so with us. "What is the wisdom of the American old man?" asked Clumly of the room. He contends with the young. For all his pot belly and his ashen skin, he throws on his bikini and parades himself at the edge of the pool. He colors his hair, reads dirty books, perhaps; drinks beer. A sobering thought. He went over to the bed to sit down on it, and when he looked up he saw himself in the mirror, a shrunken old cop with handsome teeth, still wearing his uniform. Thoughtfully, he unknotted the tie and unbuckled the collar. Then, though he never wore ordinary clothes except every second Saturday, when he had his day off, and Sundays of course, he changed into street clothes. He had stepped down, as Moss would express it. He would meet the

Sunlight Man, tonight, as Fred Clumly, Citizen. Or less. As Fred Clumly, merely mortal, nothing more than—without any grandiose overtones—a man. Then, carrying his coat on his arm, not because he would need a coat but because it was a business which demanded the greatest formality, and, lacking his uniform, he could not endure it without, at least, the black coat handed down to him by his father, he went up to the third-floor room to watch and wait.

He stood by the window, leaning on his knees, and you would have thought he weighed tons, like the devil himself. Here, above where the trees intercepted the sunlight, there were certainties, including certainties of doubt. He doubted that he had been a good husband, for all his devotion to duty and justice with respect to his wife. He doubted that he had been honest with himself or honest with his wife either. There was a good deal he could have done and should have done. He should have sailed around the world, should have bought himself a boat on Lake Ontario. The unrealized life lurched and groped inside him like some primeval creature in an ancient jungle, and its presence inside him mocked and poisoned the life he had lived. "Nobody's life is perfect," he said. But there were reasons for that. Any life a man chooses, Clumly mused, betrays the life he failed to choose. And now it was no longer important, it was enough to know that it was so. "Good luck," he said aloud, seeing again in his mind's eye the physician who could not choose which harm to inflict on his son. "And good luck to Kozlowski," he thought. Because Kozlowski would come for him, would imagine it was his solemn duty to escort the old man to this last conversation with the Sunlight Man— with Taggert Hodge, condemned. But Clumly would not be there when Kozlowski came. He would be gone, dressed as an ordinary man, and whatever he learned or failed to learn would have nothing to do with law and order in the common sense. He had promoted himself. He was now Chief Investigator of the Dead.

*Ladies and gentlemen, I would like to speak to you tonight on Law and Order. No subject could be more familiar, and more strange. What do we mean by Law and Order? Think back to the time when you and I, not human yet, bumped our blind way through this world as fish. . . .*

Looking almost straight down, just over the gable of the

porch roof below him, he could see, between the branches of
the nearest tree, a small patch of grass and sidewalk. Four
boys ran into the area framed by roof and leaves, one of them
wearing a bright yellow jacket, and then the next instant they
were out of it again, bounding up onto his porch and along it
to Clumly's right and then away, out through the garden.
"Stop!" he thought. But though his policeman's instinct was
strong, he did not stir a muscle. A moment later a man with a
stick came into the small space Clumly could see and paused
there, looking left and right. Clumly thought of raising the
sash and calling down to him, but still he did not act. The man
went off to the right, still looking around. There were voices
now, two adults, the words distinct. Clumly felt queerly removed from it all, emotionally as aloof from the world where
hooligans ran through people's yards as he was physically
aloof from the street.

It was half an hour later that Esther came home. He
watched her come slowly up the walk, her white cane in one
hand and, in the other, her sewing basket. She too, you would
have said, had taken on weight. Esther had taken the tapes.
Her reason was unimportant. When he heard her coming up
the stairs toward the second floor he tip-toed out of the third-
floor room where he'd been waiting and went up the splintery
attic stairs to wait while she replaced the tapes, if she'd
brought them back, or changed her clothes, if that was her intent. Nothing especially mattered but that she not see him just
now, not trouble him with a confession of error, or with malice, or with freighted silence, or with anything ordinarily human. He heard her coming on toward the third floor now.
Around him, rafters with cobwebs, boxes, trunks, the furniture
from Aunt Mae's sunporch—it had been here for years and
years—lamps, mason jars, rope, his father's violin. He'd forgotten about that, the violin. He'd sit in the kitchen in the gray
shingled house they'd lived in then, on the Lewiston Road,
and, bow lightly hanging from his plumber's fist, he would
play for hours and hours. He played well. Fred Clumly's
mother would sit under the clock darning, nodding her head.
It was dark outside, and inside there was only the comforting
yellow of the oil lamp's light above his mother's elbow. When
she nodded her shadow would extend itself on the wall, then
quickly retract. "Good luck," he whispered to the dead.

When he was safely outside, with the tape recorder tucked inside his shirt, he hurried through the garden and around in back of his neighbors' houses and came out on Oak Street, a hundred yards from where the Sunlight Man had weeks ago painted the word *love* across two lanes. Then, jaw set, he set off on foot toward Main and, eventually, the police station garage. He could not risk taking his own car from his own garage; Esther would wonder why he hadn't spoken to her. Let her think he'd worked late, or let her think—because he'd left his uniform and gun—let her think whatever she thought. There would, perhaps, be time for reparations. It did not matter.

The walk took him half an hour. He listened outside the garage door. They were not talking about him. He went in.

He drove slowly through town in the gathering dusk, and when he saw the funeral—*Mrs. Palazzo,* he thought—he did not pull in. The crowd was small. She had not had many friends. Her eyes were those of a cruel, self-pitying old witch, and the heavy wrinkles going down from her nose were black. Her hair was black, though she was old, and she had traces of beard and moustache. Manlike, she was. Like the nurse at the mental hospital, or like Salvador's mother. Mrs. Palazzo was so ugly, in fact, that she made a man stop and think. She grew more manlike every year, just as he, Fred Clumly, grew more womanish. Her thought hardened like barnacles around her few selfish ideas as Clumly's mind softened, expanded, grew lax. Was that the usual case with old women and men? A part of the general order? It was not the case with Esther. As she lost one by one all the outer signs of her womanhood she gained—if it could be called a gain—an increasing femininity of mind. *Like the sea,* he thought. He hadn't the faintest idea what he meant by it. He had an image of a calm and placid sea where nothing stirred, where the water was clear and pointlessly beautiful, but always darker than a man imagined, and down inside its darkness things were stirring, omens and portents. To tell the truth, he did not know her. Never had. Clumly tipped down his black hat more and squinted. "Strange thoughts," he said.

## 5

JUDGE: Clumly! Sir! You look like hell!

CLUMLY: That may be.

JUDGE: Well come in. Good Lord! Have a chair. Let me give you a whiskey.

CLUMLY: No need. I'm not a drinking man.

JUDGE: No of course. Sorry. What the devil's happened?

CLUMLY: You heard about the informal investigation.

JUDGE: Why, no.

CLUMLY: I think you may have.

JUDGE: I give you my solemn word I had nothing to do—

CLUMLY: No matter. What's done is done.

JUDGE: It's not about that, then? I'll tell you the truth, Fred—

CLUMLY: Never mind.

JUDGE: As you please.

*(Silence.)*

JUDGE: You looked over the article on Houdini? The one I brought by?

CLUMLY: No.

JUDGE: No?

CLUMLY: I was not very interested.

JUDGE: Ah! But I thought, since you're dealing with this mad magician—

CLUMLY: And since he was the writer of the article . . .

JUDGE: You've found out, then.

CLUMLY: No thanks to you.

JUDGE: Don't be harsh, now. I've been close to the family for years. As long as there was a chance the boy would do the sensible thing, disappear, you know—

CLUMLY: Naturally.

JUDGE: It's been hell on you, I can see. But it's a funny thing. It's done you good. No doubt that seems unfeeling, but it's a fact. It's changed you. Made you, I don't know—

CLUMLY: Ferocious.

JUDGE: Yes. *(Thoughtfully.)* Yes. It's ironic. Just when it's time to step down, you become—

CLUMLY: "Step down." Yes.

JUDGE: Pardon?

CLUMLY: A funny world.

*(Silence.)*

JUDGE: It's made a better man of you. I wasn't sure of myself, at the beginning of all this. But I must admit, it's turned out, some ways. Though it's terrible, of course.

CLUMLY: So you always say. Your schemes have always turned out, since the beginning. However terrible.

JUDGE: You're angry. That will pass.

CLUMLY: Yes, I'll forget.

JUDGE: We all forget.

CLUMLY: That's Nature. It's no respecter of persons.

JUDGE: Ha ha. *(Silence.)* Well, you've brought that worse news I predicted. You recall?

CLUMLY: I recall. It was a guess.

JUDGE: A judgment of character, more like.

CLUMLY: A guess about character, maybe. Not a judgment. From an old drunk?

*(Silence.)*

JUDGE: It's made you bitter.

CLUMLY: Tired.

*(Silence.)*

JUDGE: You're wrong, Fred, those suspicions. I defended you. I refused to act. They wanted me to, all right. They couldn't move me.

CLUMLY: More's the pity.

# XX

## Winged Figure
## Carrying
## Sacrificial
## Animal

*After these first warnings, signs of death will
quickly multiply, until, in obedience to
immutable laws, stark winter with its ice
is here.*

—The I Ching

She had underestimated hate.

For three days, off and on, he'd kept them in the wet and
dark of the cellar, in dark water where rats swam, bound
tightly hand foot and waist. An act of madness, partly—of
monstrous sadism. But when she said to him, "Why are you
doing this?" he said, "Because I'm busy. Otherwise engaged.

675

Do you imagine I have nothing else in all the universe to take care of except you?" True and irrelevant, though he believed it. It was his only possible alternative to killing them, yes, assuming the course he'd embarked on. When he was out doing whatever it was he was doing—something increasingly urgent and increasingly unbalanced, she knew by his eyes—he could not be troubled with worries over what they were up to at the house. And it was not any longer strange to her that even Nick should be tied in the cellar. Voluntarily, for reasons no longer mysterious to Millie, the Sunlight Man had taken up Nick's cause; voluntarily he had brought him out of jail to his present freedom; but he never made Nick his equal, and never would: their minds were worlds apart, as differently built as the minds of an elephant and a horse. And so they were here, half-starved, in pain, frightened, heads drooping, miserably bound to their three splintery cellar posts. She believed she caught, sometimes, the Runian sisters' voices, ghostly echoes from an earlier violent time.

Sometimes Luke would twist his head over his shoulder and roll his eyes at her. "So explain why he simply buried Hardesty without a word," his furious eyes said.

"Because," she said in her mind. She heard chickens outside. She was surprised that Luke still had any. They ran in the yard, she remembered. He never fed them.

The Sunlight Man never slept, and his eyes were as baggy as an ape's; yet what it was he was busy at, no one knew. All day long they could hear him sawing and hammering up in the garage. And at night after he'd brought them their supper he would dress up as if to give a concert or attend a formal ball. Sometimes he would come down the cellar steps and bend over, near the foot of the stairs, hands on his knees, to look at them as though they were animals he was tending. (The Runian sisters watched timidly from the shadows.) Then again, sometimes he would take off his socks and shoes and wade toward them, holding up his pantlegs, his bearded and long-haired head thrown forward, eyes squinting like an inventor's, and would scrutinize their faces, one after another. Once, twice, he had taken them all upstairs for an hour and a half, to give them a rest, he said. When Luke and she were seated on the couch, numb and weak, he'd sent Nick upstairs with a snap of his fingers (and Nick had gone, dutifully, too weak to chance fighting), and when Nick came back he was wearing a gold vest and gold slippers and a turban. They were made of what looked like the cloth from an ironing board. The Sunlight Man clapped with a grotesque parody of delight, twirled away from them and out to the kitchen, then emerged not more than a second later, as it seemed to her, in a black and red cape, with a high silk hat balanced on his ratiocination-colored hair. "You're hungry?" he asked with an obscene leer. "Eggs, Nicodemus!" Nick bowed from the waist as if to leave, then straightened again, and when he extended his hands to the Sunlight Man he had four eggs between his long fingers. "Hah!" the Sunlight Man said. He took the eggs quickly and nimbly but not nimbly enough: one fell to the rug and broke. He shrugged and looked sheepish. Then he snatched off his hat and held it up like a bowl and with one hand cracked and dumped the remaining eggs down inside it, and tossed the shells to Nick. He snatched a plain lightbulb from his suitcoat pocket—he was babbling all the time—"Observe! Watch closely! We proceed to step C of our experiment!"—held the lightbulb under the hat, where it went on, as if from electricity inside his hand, then triumphantly held out the hat to them. Down inside there was an omelette. "Take, eat!" he said. "Et cetera." There were hairs in the omelette, but Luke seemed not to notice them. As for herself, she was so sick with hunger she could barely get the stuff down.

When they'd taken a bite or two he said, "Pick a card, any card! Superb! Beautiful! The seven of farts! Tear a corner off! Marvellous! You'll recognize the card? You'll know, when I've put it through fire and water, that the corner you hold in your hand fits the mutilated card?" He snatched it from her, matched the two pieces, thrust the card back. "Beautiful!" He spun away, cape whirling out, and when he turned back to them he was holding the gun. "Now!" he said. "Allah, the incinerator!" Dully, full of hate, Nick handed him a small stone dish, and the Sunlight Man tore the card to bits, dropped the pieces in, sprinkled something like lighter fluid on them, and lit them. They burned to ashes. (Luke went on eating the omelette, stubbornly not watching. He breathed in awful gasps. The Sunlight Man glared.) "Very good," he said. "Would you kindly hold the pistol, madam? Upright. That's it. We'll pour the ashes down the barrel, you see. Hah!" He conjured a funnel and poured in the ashes. "Nicodemus," he said, "you may dispose of the incinerator now." He went away to the kitchen,

with it, then on out into the woodshed. "Now behold," said the
Sunlight Man. She heard him moan. "You see before you a
common nail, except of course that it's solid gold, or a reasonable facsimile. (For all is illusion, ladies and gentlemen. Nothing is as it seems. All tricks out of hell!) Will you mark it,
kind sir. With a cross, if you don't mind. A powerful symbol,
and we need, in this dark pass, the most powerful of symbols!
Excellent! Sublime! You are an artist, young man! A very
Giotto of crosses! I kneel to you! Good. Now madam, your
kind cooperation. Would you drop the nail in the pistol?
Fine!" Then turning, aiming the pistol at the wall: "Nicodemus, you fool, the fishbowl!" He came with it, drew the coffee
table over by the wall, set the fishbowl on the coffee table a
foot from the edge of the drape, then stood back and bowed.
The water in the bowl moved from side to side, and the Sunlight Man waited for it to settle, not saying a word now, dangerously silent, aiming straight at the bowl. Then, deafeningly,
the gun went off. The same torn card was nailed through the
drape to the wall. "Bring it here," the Sunlight Man said, and
Nick brought it. The two pieces matched. Outside, there was a
sound of running. The Sunlight Man smiled, bending toward
her, and his dark ringed eyes showed mysterious satisfaction.
"Praise the Lord of hosts," he said, but he was listening, "in
whose name these miracles are performed. And applause for
Nicodemus, who is His prophet." He turned suddenly to the
door, holding the gun, and snatched it open. There was no one
there, or so he said. She could no longer trust her wits.

After that he did tricks with handkerchiefs, tricks with
rings, more tricks with cards—"Take a card, any card!" He
dealt her a living mouse. He worked more swiftly, as if in
frenzy. He made a chair stand unsupported in empty air, put a
spell on a rooster so that even the blowing of a trumpet would
not awaken it though with a snap of his fingers he could bring
it back. And then when her mind was swimming he said, "For
my next trick, I will do the resurrection. Dear lady, let me borrow your bird."

"My bird?" she said.

He took from just inside her collar, as it seemed to her, a
living bird, a sparrow. "You have heard it said that not a sparrow shall fall?" he said. "Behold!" He put the sparrow on the
coffee table, produced the pistol and, with the barrel not a foot
away from the bird's breast, shot it dead. "A trick, you think?"

he said with a wild look. "Touch it, dear lady! Do not pick it up with your coarse earthly hands, but touch it. Your finger-tips know the feel of death. Touch!" She obeyed. The bird was unquestionably dead. He went nowhere near it. "Bird," he whispered. "My beloved, my leman, O symbol of the soul's eternity, rise! *Rise!*" After a long moment, the bird seemed to move. There was blood on the coffee table. "Stop it," she whis-pered. Nick was bending close, wringing his hands, but he too went nowhere near it. "Rise!" the Sunlight Man whispered, and now there was violence in his eyes, all the violence of thunder and rage. There was no mistake. The bird was coming to life. "Stop!" she said. A shout, this time. The bird twitched violently and struggled to stand up and at last succeeded. It stood trembling, bleeding and twitching and completely alive. The Sunlight Man bowed his head. "Resurrexit," he said.[1]

Sometimes it was in the middle of the afternoon that he would leave. Once, perhaps twice, he took Nick with him. "Where do you go?" she said. "About my father's business," he said. "My *real* father." He winked.

Down in the darkness of the cellar, where there was never a sound except the occasional stirring of a rat, an almost un-heard plosh as one of them slipped from the edge of some moldy shelf into the black, still water, she sometimes believed she was losing her mind, that that was in fact his purpose. For she did not believe, as Luke did, that he had no purpose. She stood hour after hour, or hung limp from the binding ropes she could no longer feel, trying to think, remembering trifles of no sense or significance. She remembered Will's snoring,

[1] Because this illusion may seem improbable, the editors have thought fit to append this explanation of how it is managed:

#### TO SHOOT A SMALL BIRD AND BRING IT TO LIFE AGAIN

In this experiment take an ordinary fowling-piece, and put the usual charge of powder into it; but instead of the common charge of shot, introduce a half-charge of quicksilver. When a small bird ap-proaches, fire. Although it is not necessary to hit the bird—if the bird is struck by the minimal charge, blood will be produced—it will be found so stunned and stifled as to fall upon the ground in a state of suspended animation. As its consciousness will return at the expiration of a few minutes, avail yourself of the interval in declaring your intention of bringing it to life again, and your declaration will come true.

Will Jr's preaching to the others in the orchard—poor, pitiful
Will Jr!—remembered darning socks for her mother, children's socks so worn there was hardly a place sturdy enough
to hold the thread. (She remembered the smooth, heavy darning ball, lovely to the touch.)

Sometimes, with their eyes, she and Luke fought, or so she
imagined.

Luke's eyes said, "So make love to him. That's the trick.
Love conquers all, *et cetera, et cetera*. All *you* want, anyway."

"Stop it," she hissed in her mind.

He stood relaxed against the post, no longer resisting the
ropes that bound his hands and feet and chest, the gag biting
into his cheeks. Nick Slater stood tied to the post beyond, with
his back to them. To look at them he had to twist his head
over his shoulder, and that was too hard. He simply stood
hour after hour with his head dropping, still and silent as the
moldy stone wall. For Nick it had not been so long as for
them, because sometimes when he came back the Sunlight
Man would untie him and take him upstairs with him, whisper
and laugh and teach him tricks, sometimes striking him when
he turned sullen. At times the Sunlight Man would talk to him
as though nothing had happened.

"Me," Luke's eyes said, "I like it as much here as anyplace
—though I wouldn't mind getting some dinner now and then."
They couldn't tell how long it had been since they'd eaten.
Maybe as much as a day. The casement windows were so dirty
you couldn't tell morning from afternoon. "That's the advantage of being a poor crippled bastard, you know." He laughed
shrilly with his eyes. "You learn to ask for nothing. No delusion. You, now. You've had the illusion of being free as a bird;
but me, I'm used to where I am—I almost like it."

"You whine too much," she said. She'd have struck him if
she could.

"Yes, yes! say it cheerfully then. What does she want?
*Power* she wants. Vroom vroom! Be her own boss! She goes to
college and gets her a paper. Self-supporting now. Vroom! She
wants ice-cream, she goes out and buys herself ice-cream. She
wants sex, she goes out and buys herself—"

"Luke!"

"Yes, yes! Quite right. Talking that way to his own shitass
mother! But that's the price, you know. Price of liberty! You

collects the merchandise, you gotta pay the fee. I was quiet a long, long time, after all. But the lesson finally got through to me. Yes. Think of Number One. From you I learned it. Now I think of Number One, which from my point of view is me, and I guess Number Two will just have to smart a little. Which is you. C'est la vie."

"That's stupid," she said. Pious little idiot! Did he really imagine he'd made the discovery all by himself, that it hadn't been one of the grand old clichés for a thousand thousand years?

"Maybe. So then enlighten me, Mama. How come you can walk on whoever you want to, and me, I'm supposed to live by the Guilty Rule?"

"I don't want to talk about it."

*Shame on him! Shame!* The ghosts said.

But she could have told him, if there were so much as a prayer that he would listen. It was not her fault that Luke was the victim of a dream, a romantic image of a world that never was. It was not she who'd given him the image.

*It was the same with us,* the Runian sisters whispered. They referred to their murdering nephew. She smiled. It gave her comfort, this fantasy (for she knew it was that) in which she and the dead sisters were in league against him.

The sentimentality of youth, she thought. And more than sentimentality: overweening pride. Born to save the world ruined by their parents, they prated. Where did it come from —that tiresome idea? That was what the Sunlight Man had said yesterday morning, in effect—or the morning before—except that he'd said more than that, too. Standing up to his ankles in the water, pantlegs rolled up, his hands in the pockets of his suitcoat, studying them as though they were mannequins in a store window. "There's only rule or anarchy," he said. "Talk about anything between as 'freedom' and you engage in insignificant speech. There's much to be said for anarchy, to tell the truth. Consider, please. For the child's safety he learns to stay out of the road. A rule. And for his health he learns to eat both foods he does and doesn't like. A rule. Nevertheless, grown men can walk in the street if they please, and they can go without food for days if they have their reasons. Sooner or later even the rules which keep a man alive—keep his kind alive—come up for nearer inspection, so to speak, and every generation—and every man of it—is alone. Abandoned to life. The wiser a man grows, the fewer his iron bonds. So it seems." He mused, looking first at her, then at Luke. "It's strange, isn't it, the curious counter-movement. How we long to get home again. When I was a child—" He closed his eyes and, after a moment, nodded, deciding on a different tack. "Punctilious old men think back to the easy freedom of their childhood. And long-toothed beatniks in their cups hone for the rituals of right and wrong their bourgeois fathers taught. I was once told that the antidote to the escape through marijuana is brown sugar; another person told me peanut butter. I don't know which is true, if either. But though very little is more pleasurable than a marijuana buzz, it is a curious fact of experience that the higher one goes, the more ardently one longs for brown sugar or, alternatively, peanut butter."

A rat swam toward him. He watched it come, its small legs churning with all their might, stirring the heavy black water, and when it came within six inches he lifted one bare foot and shooed it. The rat turned and continued on its way. He too continued. "With respect to life, I can say this: The greater the freedom I personally achieve—the greater the distance I put between myself and the common run of mankind—bus-drivers, judges, policemen, men of science, and the like—the more I find myself admiring them. I could listen all day to the sober good sense of an upholder of the law. I take my hat off to them, I go down on my knees to them and ask their benediction. Like wicked Jacob in Esau's hair. All are sinners."

She said nothing. It was impossible to know whether he was reasoning or raving, seriously questioning her or mocking her.

He waded over to Luke and bent his face forward till his nose was two inches from Luke's forehead. "And which way will you go, my child?" he whispered. No answer came. The Sunlight Man nodded. "Either way, you have my blessing." He made a cross in the air, then sadly shook his head. "So much revolution in you," he said, "so much hatred for order, so much hatred for anarchy—and so much love. How terrible! Where can you run to? I tremble for your soul." Then, slowly, solemnly, he went down on his knees in the water at Luke's feet and, after long meditation, kissed Luke's shoes. After that he sighed, like a man who has finished an unpleasant task, and straightened up and tightened the cords around Luke's wrists.

He gave them all a little wave. "Think positive," he said. He slapped Luke's cheek to see if he was conscious. His trousers were soaked to the crotch. He turned back to the stairs, whistling under his breath, and went up and turned the light off.

He brought them no breakfast the following morning, and they believed he had abandoned them for good. They could hear no sound of hammering and sawing in the garage, no sound of pacing. "Maybe they caught him," Nick's eyes said. Luke snarled inside his gag like a dog, then cried for a long time. She listened to it and hated him. She'd had nightmares last night. The Sunlight Man did not appear with lunch for them. She looked up at the flooring and began angrily to talk to it—or, really, to talk to the demonic spirit which might or might not be beyond the flooring, resting, or possibly hanging dead (she had half-convinced herself by now that he would kill himself), and at last, experimentally at first, she began to shout inside the gag. Hardly a sound. Luke too shouted, but only with his eyes, sometimes at the Sunlight Man, sometimes at her, sometimes at Nick. At last they were all shouting, their eyes resonant in the wet, stone-walled room. They stopped. Millie wept as Luke had. "At a time like this, you learn what the really important things are," she said in her mind. "That's stupid," she said, enraged.

And then at last, just as the light was going out of the casement windows, they began to hear noises upstairs: pacing, the sound of doors and cupboards opening, sounds of cooking. She tried shouting again, but the man would not be hurried. She fell silent again and stood now, head straining forward, eyes rolling upward, listening intently for any sound of hope. At last it came. The cellar door creaked open and light shot down the stairs and then the cellar light clicked on and his feet came in sight. When they could see all of him they saw that he was dressed in a blue suit of terrible dignity, wearing horn-rimmed glasses that made him look like a college professor, and smoking an elegant pipe. He dusted off one of the cellar steps, then sat down on it, took off his shoes, rolled up his pant-legs. Then he came and, without a word, untied them and half-carried, half-led them from their posts back to the steps. Upstairs he wiped his feet and lower legs on a kitchen towel, rolled down his pantlegs, and put his socks and shoes back on, then showed them to the dining room. The table was beautifully set, as if for a party: linen tablecloth, china, crystal (where he'd gotten it heaven knew), long slim candles.

"Would you care to freshen up?" the Sunlight Man said. He bowed toward the bathroom. "Meanwhile, I'll fix us a drink," he said. "Sainthood cannot be taken on all at once." He laughed, and the laugh startled her. It was Taggert! Then she remembered that she'd realized that before. And again she could hardly believe it, and, full of alarm, held back from seizing the discovery, waiting to be sure. She glanced at Luke, trying to see if he knew, but his eyes were vague as a madman's; he was a thousand miles away. She looked then at the Sunlight Man, and she was dead certain. Yet nothing about him, not even the way he stood, was right for the man she knew he was; and even now her mind would not close on it. "Thank you," she said suddenly, and she went into the bathroom and closed the door, and in the mirror she saw her face. She wept. Monster, she thought, over and over, and she did not know who she meant, the man or herself. She could hear someone moving in the upstairs bathroom, directly over her head. The next thing she knew, she had fallen asleep and someone was knocking on the bathroom door, calling to her.

She felt herself growing stronger. "A minute," she whispered. She gazed into the mirror and could not tell what she felt. She washed her face. No feeling in the skin. She'd been mistaken. She'd imagined that he had partly grown used to going around like some ugly, drunken tramp, shirttails hanging out, beard a rat's nest, shoes worn over till the sides supported more than the soles; because when he wanted he could make himself kempt, almost respectable except for the ruined face. But now, remembering the way he'd covered that face with his arm, she understood his hatred. She remembered the safety razor in the medicine cabinet and squinted, imagining herself slipping the blade into his throat. She opened the cabinet. (Behind her father's house, when she was a child, there had been a woods where there were the remains of a road not used in years—an alley through the trees, merely—and alongside that road that was no longer a road, there were the ruins of a house where a couple named Springer had lived, long ago; a young man and his bride. She had killed him with a razor, because she loved someone else and never intended to marry him, but was forced. Once Millie had been out in the garage playing—she must have been twelve or thirteen at the time—and had all at once been overcome by a profound, completely inexplicable grief, thinking of the Springer girl. She could see the girl very clearly in her mind now, just as she had then—a tall blonde, with hollow eyes and high cheekbones, wearing a cotton print dress faded almost to white from many many washings. But the Springer girl had in fact been plump, Millie had heard later. She had thick lips and dimples, and she used to swim naked with boys.)

The soft knock came again, and Millie started. In the mirror she caught herself gaping like a witch (a second Millie observing the first), saying, "Yes." She thought with sudden violence, surprising to her, *I too would have swum naked with boys.* She'd come too late to her sorceries. After the first green dawn. "Yes," she thought soberly, and opened the bathroom door.

Luke and Nick, too, had washed and had not combed their hair. Luke stood at the piano looking at the keys, holding a martini in his shaky left hand, his mind miles away, or gone entirely. Nick sat on the couch, suitcoat open, with bourbon in front of him and on the ashtray a cigarette he did not seem to have lit himself. The Sunlight Man—no, Taggert Hodge (but that too was wrong: he was no longer Taggert) held out a glass to her, a martini like Luke's, with a small piece of lemon peel in it. She ignored it. He put it in her hand and closed the fingers.

"Ravishing," he said.

She was stone. She could look out and see the glow of Attica Prison in the sky. *All those policemen down there,* she thought, *and he's here, comfortable, prepared to go on for weeks.*

"A beautiful night," he said.

She turned to look at him again for a moment, then shook her head, numb. She remembered him suddenly as he'd been behind the chickenhouse, standing over her after Nick killed Mr. Hardesty, and her back tingled. It passed.

"Yes," he said. "It puzzles me too. But no doubt there's some perfectly reasonable explanation."

"What are you talking about?" she said.

He raised one finger to his lips. "What does it mean, if anything, to say that we're cruel beasts?" he said. He leaned closer and whispered, "It's shocking. The fantastic insignificance of it all."

"All?" she said.

He winked. "As for my own investigations, I'm inclining more and more to the persuasion that the center of it all is Time." Cliché from one of those modern novels. She realized, briefly, that she was merely a character in an endless, meaningless novel, then forgot.

She nodded again. "Time."

"Precisely. It makes us suspend our disbelief. We live by instants, that's human nature; and if we judge, we judge on the basis of the past. But tentatively, because there's always the future, p. 622. Are you actually trying to understand all this rubbish?"

"Trying—?"

"By instants. Exactly! What we are, instant by instant, is a part of a system of relationships. As in classical ballet. I stand in such and such a relationship to you: that is my meaning, my significance. If I go over there and stand by your son, my significance must change. I kiss him. I slap him. Insofar as there are common elements in all these situations, there is continuity, which is to say, I begin to embody values. And insofar as both of you, or both kiss and slap, also embody these same values, we three have reason to suppose these values are a part of the common core."

She said nothing.

"It's very moving, in a way, to be part of the common core. That's what religion is. The Ten Commandments, that sort of thing."

She pretended not to hear.

"But only tentatively moving, because of the Future. Everything may change. We expect it won't, but it may. I've known myself characters whose lives seemed absolutely stable, and whose values therefore seemed absolutely clear. But then, unexpectedly, everything changed. You follow me, don't you? This is a difficult line of reasoning." He hurried on: "So, probability failed them. They became questioners, testers, gadflies to divinity. They discovered that life was—" He leaned close to whisper: "—vastly insignificant." He smiled. "They therefore *imposed* meaning on life: they became, in other words, as rigid as possible, so that in all particular instances they were as much like themselves in other instances as they could manage to be. For example, in all situations (I speak of *one* example now), one of these people made a practice of turning the conversation to politics, on which he could say exactly what he had said before, with the same expression. This was very comforting to him, as you can imagine. He became skillful at interpreting each new political situation exactly as he had interpreted all past political situations. Eventually, and of course predictably, he took the extreme position, that is, he died. Another such maniac—"

"Wait a minute," she said.

"I'm a palmist, too," he said. "Were you aware of that? Give me your hand. Very good, wonderful. Fingers lightly curled. Good. Are you ready?" He closed his eyes and began to move his fingers over the palm of her hand slowly, like a man feeling out a page of braille. "Pointed and Sensible Suggestions to Guest and Hostess," he read. "Avoid controversy and argument. Do not monopolize any good thing. Do not overdo the matter of entertainment. Do not make a hobby of personal infirmities. Go directly when the call or the visit is ended. Do not forget bathing facilities for the traveller. Make yourself at home, but not much so. In ministering to the guest do not neglect the family. Conform to the customs of the house, especially as to meals. Let no member of the family intrude in the guest chamber. Do not make unnecessary work for others, even servants. Be courteous, but not to the extent of surrendering principles. Do not gossip; there are better things to talk about. When several guests are present, give a share of attention to all. Introduce games and diversions, but only such as will be agreeable. Better simple food with pleasure than luxuries with annoyance and worry." He opened his eyes. "Shocking," he said. He looked alarmed and let the hand fall. "Nevertheless, you and I are not so dissimilar as I had imagined, my dear. Shall I refresh your glass?" She had not drunk from it. "I too have a great respect for facts. For instance, it is of no little importance to me that a closed room is bad for sleeping in because air once breathed parts with a sixth of its oxygen and contains an equivalent amount of carbonic acid gas. Air breathed six times will not support life. And I care very much that red hair is of that color because it has a larger proportion of sulphur than black hair. If a fishbone gets stuck in your throat you can get it down by swallow-

ing a raw egg. A red-hot iron passed over old putty will soften
it so that it can easily be removed. A teaspoonful of Borax
added to cold starch will make clothes stiffer than anything
else I have ever tried, and it adds no polish. Let me refresh
your glass."

He poured. It ran down over the sides.

"And so, dear Millie, it comes to this. I've pursued the
whole question as far as I care to, and I'm ready to leave. I
pray you may come to understand yourself and may continue
joyfully on the road I have started you up—or down, depend-
ing on your point of view. Just one thing more. Your son must
drive us, preferably in the tractor-trailer. That might require
your maternal influence. Convince him, dissuade him from
jokes and tricks, and we'll call the whole thing even."

"Even?" She turned away.

Luke had turned partway toward them. He was listening,
pretending not to.

"Nothing personal," the Sunlight Man said. "You won't believe that. Most people wouldn't. Nevertheless, I have watched
objectively, partly because of the accident of my having been
cut off from intervening, and partly, I suppose, because of my
nature. I've observed every move of your chess game with the
Old Man, and maybe I've sympathized with both sides, at
times. In any case, he was right, as you see, and you were
wrong. You brought down his house, made fools of his sons,
and even grandsons, your own sons. But law was on his side."

"What are you talking about?"

"Religion."

She searched his eyes. He really did seem to imagine he was
talking sense, and she wanted to grasp it. But it was useless.
She watched the moving lips, the undeniably insane smile. She
remembered the razorblade tucked inside her bra.

"All the walls mankind makes can be broken down," he
said, "but after the last wall there's still one more wall, the
final secret, Time. You can't get out of it. The man in the back
room, as who's-it says—sitting with head bent, silent, waiting,
listening to the commotion in the streets: the Keeper of the
Kinds. You and I, Millie, we were going to run naked in our
separate woods and play guitars and prove miraculous. But
outside our running the bluish galaxies are preparing to collapse, and inside our running is the space between the pieces
of our atoms. And so I won't kill you for your destructions, or

kill the police for theirs. We'll have dinner, like civilized people, and then your son will drive us away to where we can hide for eternity, like Cain."

She looked at Luke. Before she knew she would say it, she asked, "Luke, can you?"

"Did I ever have a choice?" he said.

She tried to think. "Do you know who this is?"

After a long moment, Luke nodded. She believed him.

"Then you understand?"

He smiled ironically. "At least as well as you do."

The Sunlight Man was smiling too.

"What do you mean?" she said. "Both of you. Luke, what are you talking about?"

"Dinner's ready," the Sunlight Man said. "Will you join us, beloved sister?"

"It's terrible," she said softly. "What your loving people has done to you, I mean. That's it, isn't it."

He laughed. "Ridiculous!" Luke, too, suddenly and horribly, laughed.

But Millie was above error. She was ugly as a witch, and could not be beautiful again. She was ugly, and the father-in-law she had too much admired was dead, his house in ruins. The war was over.

She had underestimated love.

# XXI

The Dialogue
of
Towers

---

## 1

Even now that he had fled them, Luke's scornful laughter rang in his ears. Luke's was the worst crime: youth, innocence. But demented as he knew he was, or anyway twisted out of the sane but not to the comfort of the not-sane, he knew the crime was not merely Luke's but one they must all live down. "It's terrible, what loving people has done to you," she'd said; and so at last they were face to face. He'd made her a foul old witch for her crimes, and now he was chief victim of her witchcraft. Or she'd been a witch before and he had exorcised her demon, had brought her gaze down from grand visions of sex and subtle wit to the bare earth where he stood. Either way, she had seen him clear, "as if scales had fallen from her eyes"—the brittle scales of her theory on how to *"be"*—and

691

she knew him, and knew herself, so that he too suddenly knew. He'd backed away in terror. "Ridiculous." And laughed, faking scorn. She understood. But Luke's scorn was real, and hurt her, and the callouses he'd carefully grown to wall off his nerves from other people's pain were torn away to the roots by her words; the image he thought he had sealed off—an image now familiar and tiresome, infuriating as a tubercular's cough, yet no less dreadful for his having endured it a thousand times, awake and asleep—the image of fire, leapt up again in his mind or, as it seemed, in the corners of the room: turning quickly, with a sudden bow to prove to himself as much as to them that he was still in command, he had fled.

He stood in the old woods beside the house, leaning on a tree trunk, hands over his eyes. When he let himself look again, there were no more flames. The woods, like the house behind him, were unnaturally quiet, and the late slant of the sun made the colors mellow. *Jadis,* he remembered, *si je me souviens bien . . .* They had read it together, he and Kathleen. Was it still there, buried in that brain closed up in stone? A brilliant girl once. Quick-witted as Millie but delicate, as light as the incense-filled garden old Rimbaud lost, like Luke, like Millie: garden of unreality.

The doctor had told him of Nazi experiments, had prattled stupidities while Kathleen sat dying little by little, and Taggert had thought *I could kill him; no one would know, no one would miss him* but had listened on, or pretended to, constructing difficulties: the doctor's detachment was a professional necessity; he might otherwise go mad himself; and how was one to strangle professional necessity? Nevertheless, it was he who had pumped the shocks through her skull, he who had made her this. But then again it was Paxton who had hired and paid him, against Taggert's plea. Then he had seen the two graves, and had seen the gentle, forgiving Ben, though they did not speak; and in his sorrow Taggert had fallen out of wrath. He had resolved to visit her father. He would say, he remembered thinking, "Mr. Paxton, I come to make peace between us. God forgive me for all I've done to you and you to me. We loved her, both of us, and whatever terrible things we did—" There his memory broke down. He was planning it, walking down Oak Street, tears brimming, heart hammering, and then, paintbrush in hand . . .

There was an old man sitting on a stump not fifty feet from

him, reading a book. He was well dressed, incongruous here in the woods, but Taggert could not stop just now for puzzlement. Something had happened, he was realizing for the first time, his mind finally ready or almost ready to face it. He'd been walking down Oak. It was late afternoon. The next moment he was painting a word on the street, and it was morning. One whole night had dropped out of his mind. He wiped away sweat and went through it more carefully. "It's coming back," he whispered. He screwed his eyes up tight. "I reached his house, yes. But I walked by, didn't have the nerve. I stopped." There was a tricycle in the yard, he remembered. He'd stood looking at it.

The man in the clearing went on reading. There was another man now, approximately the same age but heavier, enormous in fact, with shocks of white hair streaming out around his ears. *It's my father,* he thought. *He's not dead.* But the next instant he knew he was wrong, his father was dead. For the man on the stump was Clive Paxton. He was looking up, greeting the ghost of Taggert's father. They began to talk, warmly, like old friends. (He could hear their voices.) *It's not real,* he thought. *I saw my father buried.*

Then, at last, he remembered putting his hands around Clive Paxton's throat. It was all he could remember, but he knew it was not an illusion.

Now the clearing was empty. The ghosts had disappeared.

## 2

Stony Hill. Late afternoon.

A square wooden silo of a sort once common in Western New York. A gabled roof where gray pigeons nest. Fred Clumly parked under the walnut trees on what had once been the Congressman's lawn—now a place of high weeds, the September air full of insects—and walked toward the silo, ignoring the lighted house to his right, the Negro faces at the windows. The silo was dark, its silhouette distinct and imposing against the luminous gray of twilight. The air smelled of apples, and the smell brought to Clumly's chest a keen sense of memories just beyond the reach of his conscious mind, a sense of time lost. With his hands in the pockets of the enormous black coat—the skirt of the coat six inches above Clumly's shoes—he walked toward the silo. As he approached, a faint light began to glow inside, just visible through the vertical cracks in the silo wall, and the closer he moved, the brighter the light seemed to burn. It was a pleasant trick, and he felt comfortable with it. He was no longer afraid. It was not that he expected no danger now, not that he had come to a firm belief that the Sunlight Man was harmless. He was a madman, close to violence, according to the opinion of the psychiatrist, and Clumly could believe it. The poor man's experiment had failed. But Clumly, in black coat and hat, his hands in his pockets, was no longer afraid. As he stood wondering where the entrance might be, a small door opened directly in front of him, and he found himself looking in at a clean, neatly swept room where an oil lamp burned. He went to the door, hands still in his pockets, stooped a little, and went in. The Sunlight Man stood with his arms folded, waiting. He was wearing the same black suit as before, and in one white-gloved hand he held a cane. "Welcome," he said. Clumly nodded. The lamp was on an old chair in the exact center of the silo floor. The arrangement was too obviously theatrical to be mere chance. "On time as usual," the Sunlight Man said. Again he nodded. "As usual."

Abruptly, the Sunlight Man moved to the chair. "The light's not good, I realize," he said. "I do the best I can, but you see the difficulties." He bent forward slightly, and in the glow of the lamp his eyes were dangerous. "It would be better up higher, you think?"

Clumly smiled, tight-lipped.

The Sunlight Man pointed the cane at the chair and with his left hand motioned it to lift. Nothing happened. "My mind's fatigued," the Sunlight Man said. "I'd be glad if you'd help. Concentrate on making the chair lift. Be sure to keep it level."

"Look, friend," Clumly said. Almost kindly.

"Concentrate!"

Clumly sighed and looked at the chair, pretending to concentrate. The chair began to move. It gave a little jerk, then began, slowly and steadily, to rise. It all seemed to Clumly a foolish waste of mind, these paltry illusions, magic tricks. But he was impressed, in a way. It was handsomely done, although he could see the wires. He could almost have believed that it was the very perfection of the magician's pantomime that made the chair rise.

"That's very good," Clumly said.

"Sh!" When the chair was level with his waist the Sunlight Man stopped the lift and turned as if for applause. He turned back then, quickly, and ran his cane through the seemingly empty air in a crafty circle around the chair. "Would you like to examine it yourself?"

"I trust you," Clumly said.

"That's a little unwise." He smiled. Then: "But we have nothing to sit in!" He crossed quickly to Chief Clumly and removed from his inside suitcoat pocket, as it seemed, a long, bright red cloth. He stepped back with it, shook it violently, then held it open at shoulder height, so that the bottom touched the floor, and he seemed to offer it for Clumly's inspection. Then, like a man unveiling a statue, he whipped the cloth away. Clumly blinked. There, quite impossibly, in the center of the room where a moment ago there had been nothing, stood the Indian boy.

"Bring the chairs, Nick," the Sunlight Man said.

The boy nodded sullenly, walked to the corner of the room, then paused. "They're gone," he said.

The Sunlight Man laughed. "How stupid of me. They're right here under my nose." Though he had not moved, Clumly would have sworn, it was true: they stood one on each side of him, good parlor chairs with blue plush seats. The Sunlight Man smiled with satisfaction, then reached out and took a pipe from the empty air. With another wave of his hand he had matches. "Sit down," he said. Clumly obeyed. He sat with his feet planted firmly, hands still in his pockets. The Sunlight Man seated himself opposite and lit the pipe. When he had it going to his satisfaction he said, "One last illusion, and then to business." He turned to the Indian. "Fold up that cloth for me, would you?"

The boy stooped for the red cloth the Sunlight Man had dropped on the floor and raised it in front of him, holding it by the corners.

"Watch closely," the Sunlight Man said. "As far as I know there are only two other magicians who know how to do this." He paused and looked annoyed. "What's wrong, Nick? Fold it." He went over to help, then paused, a foot away.

The top of the cloth dropped of its own will, as though invisible hands held the cloth by the middle, one hand on each side. The Indian was gone. Clumly bent farther forward, watching as the cloth folded itself upward from the bottom, forming a rectangle, then halved to the left, forming a square. Then it formed a triangle, then another and another. The Sunlight Man stood up, went over to the cloth, ran his cane around it, then took it from the invisible hands and stuffed it in his pocket.

Clumly nodded. *Surely, only in a book . . . ,* he thought.

"Now to business," the Sunlight Man said.

He nodded again.

"You brought the tape recorder?"

He reached inside his coat for the machine, set it on the floor, switched it on.

"Tonight I'll tell you about the towers," the Sunlight Man said.

Chief Clumly slid his right hand back into the pocket of his coat.

## 3

SUNLIGHT: The towers of Babylon! The crowning achievement of ancient civilization!

No, start with this. Imagine a Mesopotamian city. It's on a hill, normally—or on a range of hills—a city not so vast as New York or London or Rome, but you wouldn't know that to look at it: it stretches as far as you can see, hill after hill, or the breadth of a whole valley. It's surrounded by gigantic walls —a hundred feet thick at the base, and on top a road so wide you can drive four chariots down it side by side—and the whole city's white as snow, with magnificent buttresses and arches, and there are buildings six stories high and at every story a hanging garden so that what you see when you first come over the mountains or the endless plain is an incredible explosion of light and color—the white of the walls and houses, the green of the gardens everywhere, the red and yellow and purple and blue of flowers, the blue of the sky. But more magnificent than all the rest together, crowning the city as the city crowns the hill, the towers of the temples.

All the city's made of mud—bricks of mud stamped to astonishing density—coated over with white and colored plaster and decorated with enormous murals or with mosaics. As for the towers, they're strange, multistaged buildings wound around with steep outside stairways, and they rise terrifyingly above the whitewashed temples. At times the sanctuary extended into the core of the tower so that the niche with the image was located within the base of the temple tower.

All right. Enough. You get the picture. What were they for? What did the towers mean? Can you make it out?

CLUMLY: What do *you* think?

SUNLIGHT: I don't know. It's a mystery. To the ancient Jews their height suggested a wish in man to become like to God—Babel, for instance. Mad human pride. But it's not in the top of the tower that the god has his place. It's true, Herodotus tells the story that the priestess of Bel passed a night at the top of the temple tower to wait for the deity to alight—but there's no reference to any such business in the cuneiform texts. Sounds like a tale told by a dragoman. Fact is, the god is in the base, a kind of inner mystery from which the towers ascend. Could it mean this: *(a little wildly)* from man's own inner mystery, the destructive principle in his blood—his knowledge that he's born for death—his achievements ascend—his godly will, his desire to become at one with the universe, total reality, either by merging with it or by controlling it?

CLUMLY *(dubiously)*: Mmm.

SUNLIGHT: It might, yes. A reasonable hypothesis, at least.

CLUMLY: Reasonable.

SUNLIGHT: Very well, then I say this. It's a matter of fact that we can never control the secret powers of the universe or even match their force. Sexually, socially, politically—any way you care to name—our civilization is doomed, in the same way all civilizations have been doomed. And so I cannot join you. It's not that I mind doom, you understand. It's because I have a vision of what would be possible in a better culture—one I do not expect ever to arise in the world. And yet I'm torn, I confess it. How can I openly turn against the culture I was born to? I have ties. And something else. I was right to set him free, hold out new life. But you see what has resulted.

Let me tell you a vision.

The age that is coming will be the last age of man, the destruction of everything. I see coming an age of sexual catas-

trophe—a violent increase of bondage, increased violence and
guilt, increased disgust and ennui. In society, shame and
hatred and boredom. In the political sphere, total chaos. The
capitalistic basis of the great values of Western culture will
preclude solution of the world's problems. Vietnam is the beginning. No matter how long it takes, the end is upon us, not
only in the East but in Africa too, and South America. Civilizations fall because of the errors inherent in them, and our error will kill us.

CLUMLY: But what *is* the error? Excuse me.

SUNLIGHT: It's man, Clumly! Man!

You want to know the future? I'll tell it to you! I see towers
of magnificent beauty and awesome height—towers of white
and gold and blue—towers stretching from hill to hill and valley to valley as far as the eye can see—the towers not of men
but of gods, you would swear: but the sky is dark behind
them, and the earth at their foundations trembles and cracks.
The people of the city are blinded and they speak in a babble
of tongues, and around the towers there are luminous clouds
full of dazzling colors, and the air stinks of brimstone. There
is no Zoar to run to, and if there are five good men living they
have no more chance than a Jew's fat wife. Hell's jaws will
yawn and the cities will sink, and there will not be a trace. I
promise you all this. I give you my word as an official wizard
to the king.

CLUMLY: You can't believe that.

SUNLIGHT: I've seen it.

Abruptly, full of a confused sense of pity and anger, Chief
Clumly stood up. He went to the low door and stood there,
bent down, looking out, his hands in the pockets of his coat.
At last he turned and said, "I saw your wife today."

The Sunlight Man's face showed no sign of changed emotion. "So you know." He laughed, ironic.

Clumly nodded.

"And so tonight you will try to arrest me." Again he
laughed.

Clumly thought about it. "I knew all along that—" He
paused to think again. "I knew from the beginning that you
were . . . an irregular outlaw. I sometimes foolishly imagined . . ."

The Sunlight Man reached out suddenly and took from the

empty air a nickel-plated pistol. He cocked it. "Perhaps I'm more regular than you think."

Clumly cocked his head, squinting. "Perhaps," he said.

"You were stupid to come."

He nodded.

"I of course realized how things stood when I found you'd come unarmed tonight."

"Of course. Unarmed. Yes."

"You're not afraid?"

"No."

"And yet you know I may kill you."

Clumly looked at him.

He saw the mistake at once. "You know I *will* kill you."

But it was too late. Clumly sighed. "I know it's possible. I don't mind. A mood I'm in."

The Sunlight Man's hand shook. "I'd like not to have been forced . . . to make a choice."

"It's up to you."

The Sunlight Man wiped his forehead with the back of his glove. "You're still alive, yes." Then, getting himself in control: "All right, we have to go now."

"We."

"Both of us. No grand disappearance. You force me."

Clumly nodded and turned to step through the door. When he looked back the Sunlight Man was looking at the pistol, scowling. At last he came out and closed the door behind him. The thought of the suspended chair inside, the oil lamp still burning, was vaguely unsettling to Clumly.

"To your car," the Sunlight Man said.

Clumly went to the driver's side and put his hand on the door-handle, then waited. The Sunlight Man said nothing. They both looked back at the silo, and at last the Sunlight Man said, "I could destroy all that with a wave of my hand, you know. As easily as I could destroy you."

"I believe you."

"Perhaps you don't," the Sunlight Man said. He frowned, wrestling with some problem, then abruptly laughed a little wildly. He stopped as suddenly as he's started. "Well, get in."

Clumly opened the door, and the Sunlight Man went around to the far side, aiming the gun at Clumly as he went around the hood. When he'd gotten in, he said, "But I think I'll let you destroy it. Look at the silo again."

"Don't be a fool," Clumly said. And yet—idiotically, he would tell himself later—he looked. The instant his eyes struck the place it seemed to explode into flame. It was as if all the walls had been bathed in gasoline. And yet Clumly had smelled nothing, inside it—or nothing but the Sunlight Man's stench. "There was no need," he said.

The Sunlight Man smiled, looking at the fire, and that instant, responding to an instinct he had forgotten he had, Clumly shot out his hand and closed it on the gun. It came free easily, and though the Sunlight Man started, the wild look that came over his face seemed as much one of pleasure as of alarm. A second later, as if nothing had happened, he was looking again at the fire. Everything in the car or around it was yellow-red, reflecting the glow. "My wife and I climbed that silo once," he said. Then: "My move, isn't it," the Sunlight Man said. "I move the horsebarn next."

This time Clumly did not turn, but he heard the explosion. The glow was more intense now. He said, "Why?"

The Sunlight Man looked at his gloved hands. "A demonstration," he said. "You see, your next move is to let me go. Otherwise, I move the house. And there are people inside."

It wasn't true. They were out on the lawn, standing bunched together in horror, their figures reflecting the churning red light. For some reason the Sunlight Man could not see them. He was seeing nothing whatever. An image in his mind.

"You wouldn't burn the house," Clumly said.

The Sunlight Man laughed.

He glanced at the house, then back at the man. At last he said, "You're free." Then: "I'm outside my jurisdiction in any case."

"Ah, justice!" the Sunlight Man said. "Ah, duty!" Then he grew serious. "An unfair accusation. There are no obligations, I realize that. There are merely unconstrained acts of holy love and hate, that is to say, of life and death, both of which are selfless, and between them . . ." He brooded on it. ". . . gloomy confusion."

"You think too much," Clumly said.

He nodded. "That's my crime."

"You'll be caught."

The Sunlight Man nodded. "You think I'll be arrested by 'higher' authorities?"

Clumly thought. "I *believe* so," he said. He rubbed his jaw.

"Yes. That is what I believe." He listened to the roar of the fire. The siren was howling now in Alexander.

"It's time for you to get out. I'll need the car."

He nodded and felt behind him for the handle, then opened the door. When he was out and the Sunlight Man had slid over to the driver's seat, the Sunlight Man rolled down the window. "You realize you're letting me go. I mean, I wouldn't want a misunderstanding. You're freeing me." He was staring past Clumly at the fire.

Clumly nodded.

"Good. Well, good evening, then. I want you to know, I feel friendly toward you, Fred." Clumsily, he started the car.

Clumly put the pistol in his pocket. The siren was coming closer. He watched the prowlcar cross the overgrown lawn like a drunken animal and pull out on the road. When the taillights were out of sight he started toward the porch. Kozlowski came from the darkness of the trees behind him.

Clumly looked at him. "Why didn't you interfere?"

"I'll drive you back," Kozlowski said. "Car's the other side of the house."

"Why didn't you interfere?" he said again.

Kozlowski put his fists on his hips and looked at the ground. "Interfere with which of you?" he said.

They walked to the car. The house was red. The silo toppled and sparks flew up like receding stars. The barn beside the silo was now on fire too. Flames wheeled upward high into the night. A timber fell, silent in the roar of the fire.

# XXII

## Luke

*Hidden dragon. Do not act.*
—The I Ching

As soon as it was dark Luke Hodge got up from the couch and, without a word to any of them, went out to the woodshed piled high with junk and took his heavy driving shoes down from their nail beside the door. The shoes were squaretoed and soft from many applications of crankcase oil, and the laces were clean new thongs as soft as chamois. He bent down and pulled the shoes on, tugged each of his socks up snug inside, then sat down on the stone step between the woodshed and the kitchen, straightened the tongues of his shoes and, at last, as meticulously as a racing skater preparing for a meet, laced the shoes up tight and knotted them. Next, as deliberately as he'd put on his shoes, he pulled on his light denim jacket, his gloves, his driving cap. When he was finished he went down the steps into the garage, stood there a moment with his hands on his hips, looking around at the clutter of bolts, wrenches, electric wire, old machinery, grease-soiled boxes, tools, rags, bicycle tape, scraps of leather, discarded manuals, weldingrods, bits of crockery, like a man taking his last look at home. He bent down to pick up a screwdriver from the grit and sludge on the garage floor, dropped it on the loaded work-bench, then walked up the hill toward the barn to bring around the truck.

It was cold tonight, and the dark barn had a forlorn look already, as though it had been years ago that he had left. The whippoorwills were calling as usual, down at the corner of the lower pasture, and the chickens were already settled for the night, only the leghorns visible, queer puffs of white in the plumtrees to the right of the driveway. When he looked over his left shoulder he could see the lights of the prison, stretched across the valley like a village. Cars passed now and then on the highway, a mile below him, and somewhere over his head there was a plane; he couldn't see it, but he could hear it. He could see the glow where Stony Hill was burning. He shook his head and looked back at the ground and, after a moment, took a breath and quickened his step.

What was strange was that he had known from the beginning that he would be the one. It figured. He was the one who'd been put in the middle, the one who had no choice but to understand both sides, however he fought; no choice even when he wanted to hate them all but to understand they were not hateable, merely human, short-sighted, limited, tired, stupid. At the cottage on Godfries' Pond one time he'd sat on the little gray rowboat dock with Will Jr and Ben Jr—he remembered it as if it was yesterday: a night like tonight, chilly, a kind of dying of summer, sky full of lifeless, opaque light, a large, vague circle around the moon. The water moved listlessly against the palings and the pebbly shore, and now and then a boat would bump softly against the burlap on the dock or a fish would jump. Behind where the three of them sat there were radios playing softly in the cottages, and people talking, occasionally a laugh. Will and Ben were in their teens then, and he, Luke, was no more than four or five. And yet even then he'd known, without having the words for it, that he hung helpless between them the same as he hung helpless between his father and mother. He could no longer remember what Will and Ben had said or even what it was they were talking about; he could remember only the feeling of being between them, knowing what both of them meant (however wordless his knowledge was, a knowledge of their faces more than a knowledge of their talk), and knowing they were both right but mutually exclusive, as antithetical as the black trees hanging motionless over the motionless water and under the dead, luminescent sky. Will was going to do splendid things—rebuild Stony Hill maybe. It might have been that. He talked about that sometimes. And Ben, Ben was going to do nothing—seize the cachexic day, understand himself, transmogrify into a hayfield standing in the rain. No matter what it was they said. It might have been about girls, or war, or it might have been about their fathers, or beer, or college. No matter. Luke had known, as if the knowledge were implicit in the trees and sky, knowledge beyond mere words or even feelings, that all their high and narrow hopes were doomed: each would glide toward the other one's death as the two sides of the pond glided gently and relentlessly toward the grassy outlet where the streams crossed and fell away to the river. He had said it with bitter irony in the past, but not tonight: *In the beginning was the Word and the Word was with Luke. . . .* From the beginning he had been the one marked—by brute situation as much as by any gift of his—to understand them all; and finally—he could say it now without pretentiousness and without a self-deprecatory curl of the lip, for he knew at last, knew he had never hated any of them, the hatred was mere self-defense, the howling of a child not yet ready to put on his destiny like an old wool coat—finally, he knew, he was the one who'd been marked. His luck.

He slid the barn doors open and climbed up into the cab of the truck and started it. Then he sat, leaning his elbows on the steering wheel, letting the engine warm up. The barn was full of motor echoes, like music. Warm, gassy air came up through the maze of slots on the gearshift beside him, to the right of his hip, and he thought fleetingly of dropping a rag over it, but he decided not to bother, to wait until the air got hot and oppressive. He shoved the clutch in and eased into first. The clumsy old Road Ranger shuddered and after a moment, like a cracking dam, began to move. He flicked on the lights, switches 4 and 7. Holy numbers.

They were waiting for him when he pulled up next to the house. He set the emergency and got out to open the sliding side door in back. As soon as it was open, Nick Slater came out, as quick and silent as a shadow in the woods, darted through the patch of light from the kitchen window, and slid the rifle into the truck, then climbed in after it.

Taggert stayed where he was, leaning against the garage door, looking thoughtfully at the truck. Luke's mother stood on the woodshed steps behind him, ugly as death, her white arms folded.

"You coming?" Luke said.

His uncle looked at him exactly as he'd looked at the truck. He probably couldn't have said himself what prevented his getting in, it seemed to Luke; still, he hesitated. His lower lip was drawn a little, his eyebrows lowered, in the look of a man trying to remember something. Abruptly, as if coming to himself, he nodded. He picked up the suitcases, one in each hand, half-turned his head toward Luke's mother in a kind of nod, then came to the truck door. He set the suitcases down, then lifted the larger one up toward where Nick was reaching for it, trying to hurry him up. Luke helped him with the second one —they were as heavy as bags of concrete—then bent over and interlocked his hands to help his uncle in. His uncle put his hand on Luke's shoulder but again hesitated. When Luke glanced up at his face, the eyes had a glitter in them and the lips were pursed. Luke said, "We better move."

He nodded, and lifted his shoe to Luke's locked hands. The man got in easily, almost without any effort on Luke's part, and Luke reached for the door.

"Leave it open so we can see," his uncle said.

Luke obeyed.

His mother said quietly, behind him, "Be careful."

He nodded, irritated, and walked to the cab. Then, just as he was about to get in, he changed his mind, turned abruptly, and strode back to where his mother stood watching. Before she knew what he was going to do, he kissed her cheek and took one of her hands and pressed it and tried to meet her eyes. He couldn't. He looked at the line where her forehead met her hairline—looked hungrily, the way he'd looked, earlier, at the cluttered garage.

"Are you all right?" she said.

He nodded, a brief jerk back and to one side, then turned and ran back to the truck. He jumped in, eased into first, switched on the headlights, and started up. He drove slowly, getting into no gear higher than sixth, until he reached the highway. This was not the time to be stopped by some trooper. Then, when he'd turned onto 98, he moved up through the gears to twelfth. His chest filled with excitement and fear.

He was curving up into the mountains now, coming sooner than he meant to to the place. He loved the rough old battered road with its sudden curves and jolts and dips, its lazy towns with their yellow lights and enormous, comfortable trees, and between the towns glimpses of moonlit river, black and white cows in the blackness of a field, isolated farmhouse lights, once in a while a gas station with old-fashioned handcrank pumps. He'd driven it often, carrying gypsum, or television parts from Sylvania, or batteries, or cameras from Eastman. In the valleys he came into feathery patches of fog, and he would slow for them, but then as the road rose higher he came to open spaces incredibly wide and beautiful. He saw shooting stars. He could no longer see the glow of Stony Hill.

He was not afraid. He had no regrets. Yet even now he went over and over it, trying to know for sure that he was right.

She'd made his father read books, whatever books were popular with the college professors she slept with that year, and he would read them, impatient and irritable but gutless, and he would find them stupid and would know no words to express his feeling, or none she understood. They were tripe, he said. Just tripe. They had nothing to do with anything. And she would take it for a proof of his stupidity and would not even tell him why she thought—why her college professors thought—they were masterpieces. But sometimes he—Luke— or Will Jr would read them, and they would talk about the books and his father would listen and suddenly break in, trying, as feebly as ever, to say what he meant. They talked about *Pierre*. Will Jr said it was full of pointless froth, mere tiresome palaver, a tiresome rumble of symbolism. She said it was profound, the story of their life. Will Jr said Pierre was Melville and if Melville denied it he was a liar or, more likely, a fool. Suddenly, explosively, his father said, sitting watchful in his corner, "Hah!" which meant he agreed. She said fierce- ly, hardly turning in his direction, "For heaven's sake stick to things you understand!" He was abashed. But Luke had cried out, close to tears, "He's right, anyone can see he's right." And

then Will Jr came into it, defending his father, and she made
quips and smashed every word he said and fought him with all
the viciousness she knew how to muster—she knew plenty—
and all at once Luke, the one perpetually caught in the middle
—was defending her, talking about symbolism. Though he
might have as easily taken Will's side, because he too was
right, they were both right but on terms that could never be
reconciled. It was a stupid novel, it was a brilliant novel. She
always won, and she always had to win again, and she never
could win. And as for his father, he worked and slept and
grew fatter and fatter, let his hair grow out in his nose and
ears, carried a smell like a Polish wedding, could not tell a
painting from a hole in the wall unless it was a painting of
horses or a barn, went to sleep and snored like a bull at the
movies, called the bathroom the restroom, wore armbands and
suspenders and smelled of tobacco, and her objections to all
this were to him not only foolish but dangerously immoral.
Will Jr had not had to judge it: he'd grown up with Uncle
Ben, before they were in a position to bring the family together, so he, Luke, who'd spent only three summers with Uncle
Ben, was the one driven to understand them. He could understand—how could he help it?—why she had to destroy all her
husband's name meant, why she'd gotten Stony Hill and sold it
to the Billingses, why she'd mocked him and tormented him
and tried to stir up enmity between him and his brothers. And
he could understand why his father hated her, believed her insane, even toyed once—but tentatively, clumsily, robbed of all
confidence in himself—with having her arrested. And so all his
life he had alternated between trying to make peace between
them and hating them both, and in the end he had found he
had no choice but to cling to them stupidly, voluntarily allow
himself to be pulled apart, snarling first at one, then at the other, with angry love. He was now repulsive to them both. To
each he seemed the image of the other.

They were wrong. He was himself. Or rather he was the impossible union of both of them, the closing of the circle. More
than that.

What was incredible was that it was he, of all people, who
was going to achieve their crackpot dream. He became more
keenly aware of the wind rushing by, the vastness of space before him and time behind. It was as if the idea came not from
his own mind but from someone seated in the truck beside

him, eagerly dictating thoughts in his ear. *You, Luke, are the
ghost. That's what they've wanted, what all of them struggled
toward and missed and fell away from into disillusionment, or
self-hatred, or compromise. Because of a simple error, the notion that when it came it would be what it was the first time, a
thing of this world.*

He leaned forward over the steering wheel, peering ahead,
searching out the thought. He'd come to another small town
now, a few houses, all with their lights out, a store with only
the neon burning in front, a single traffic light. It turned red as
he watched, a quarter-mile away in front of him, and it
dawned on him, but only dimly, far in the back of his mind,
that he was going more than sixty. He hit the brake and shifted down and got stopped just in time, an instant before it
turned green. He shifted up again, automatically, his mind never leaving its hurtling train of thought, and before he reached
the outer limits of the village he was almost back on sixty. The
whispering dictator hurried on, snatching at straws.

*The Old Man knew the secret, that was all. He knew how to
see into all of them, feel out their hearts inside his own, love
them and hate them and forgive them: he understood that
nothing devoutly believed is mere error, though it may only be
half-truth, and so he could give them what they needed. That
was what it meant, the line his father was always quoting ...*
*"There are always politicians. Good politicians. The people
turn this way and that, unsure what they want, unsure how to
get it, unsure whether it's good for them . . ."* Something like
that. *He got up outside himself to where he could act as
though he himself, his own life, were irrelevant. That's all it's
ever taken.*

He was coming to the place he'd decided on, and was
afraid. He felt as he'd felt a thousand times in his grandfather's barn or his Uncle Ben's, perched on a beam, uncertain
whether or not he had the nerve to leap into the hay ten feet
below—except that it was worse now, an uncertainty so violent his body rose up in revolt. Sweat ran like rain between his
eyebrows and pasted his shirt to his back and trickled down
his belly. He had a headache coming on, rushing over him
faster than a headache had ever done before, sharp points
pressing in through his skull from every side. He had to squint
to tolerate the headlights. But in spite of all that, his mind was
clear, it seemed to him, clearer than it ever had been before,

and he knew he was not wrong, not fooling himself, not crazy. He was no Jesus Christ stretched on a rood for the salvation of mankind, but he understood the joy of that, and the terror and pain. He had no grand cause: a petty joy for a petty creature. Better than Ben Jr, who'd died in a war he didn't like; better than Old Man Hardesty who'd gone down almost without knowing what had hit him.

Now he was there; the long bridge opened out ahead of him, an eighth of a mile away, silver girders reaching out across the silent pitch-dark valley, the black further side of it just beginning to come into view—up over his head, stars, motionless and perfect as the infinite span between the heartbeats of God. He bore down on the accelerator and flexed the fingers soaking wet inside his gloves. The bridge rushed toward him, and he was conscious of the rush and at the same time conscious of the infinite time it took the truck to reach the place, and now suddenly all his pain vanished as if by magic and he was reading the sign twenty feet from the bridge—35 MPH—as though he had all eternity to read it. He heard himself saying aloud—very loud in the hollow darkness of the cab —*I'm sorry*. Then a jolt, a tremendous tearing noise of steel behind him, and he was weightless, falling, hair flying in his eyes, the truck turning over and over like a lop-sided boulder. A shock of violent heat and light went through him and he saw the ground and a tree, and the same instant he was dead.

Nevertheless, the sacrifice was in vain. The Sunlight Man and Nick Slater were not in the truck. They'd jumped out in the last little village, taking the suitcases with them. The Sunlight Man could not have said himself why he did it. A hunch that pulled like a cable. Another piece—he might have said— of luck.

Except that the Sunlight Man wouldn't have made that mistake, even for a moment. His luck had already run out long ago. Though he didn't die in the crash, it was of course Luke's crash that killed him.

# XXIII

## E silentio

### 1

The old man stood on the bridge, big as an elephant, shaking with sobs, staring down with tear-blinded eyes at where the lights were, the air around him still filled like a cup with the smell of the truck's explosion in the bottom of the valley, and on the ground beside him lay the bloodsoaked gloves the police had brought up for identification, and the ridiculous Eagle Scout ring and the shoe and the half-burnt cap. He sobbed in great whoops. He was a huge and erect man, at least as ordinary mortals run, and his voice boomed out all the length of the night to beyond where August stars were falling like scratches. If he was guilty of limitations of foresight, or subtlety, or humor, or taste—if he had been foolish in his time and partly unworthy—his grief was anyhow absolute and most profound and better than justice or mercy or wisdom or any of the other great words of the ancient schools.

He knew all right why his son was dead, and who he had meant to protect and redeem, and why. Hodge waited, bellowing his grief at the night, until they brought him the certain

711

word that there were no other bodies, only Luke. Then, little by little, his sobbing stopped and, empty of heart, indifferent to all but his grief, he was able to think in ways that had been closed to him before. He thought clearly now, with absolute indifference to himself, beyond the pleasure or pain of vengeance, beyond any taint of satisfaction or reward or even common dignity, beyond even shame at his having failed to act directly, impersonally before. His son's sacrifice, however impure it may have been, had purified Will Hodge. He was indifferent to the hunt, indifferent to the crimes already committed or yet to be committed, whether the crimes of cops or of robbers: it was necessary, merely, that order prevail for those who were left, when the deadly process had run itself down; necessary to rebuild.

He said (he could not see the man he talked to, had only the blurry impression of a youngish face, a State Trooper's cap, a cigarette), "He wasn't driving on—business. He was helping your so-called Sunlight Man and the Indian boy escape. If they're not in the wreckage, they're somewhere on the road between here and Attica, or they're riding with some travelling salesmen as hitchhikers. You'll get them. It hasn't been long."

"You're sure of all this?"

Hodge nodded. "Chief Clumly can tell you." After a moment: "He's been meeting with your Sunlight Man. Been having long talks."

"Meeting him and doing nothing? Letting him go?"

Hodge scowled. He said, "No doubt he has his reasons."

The trooper stood in front of him a moment longer, as if thinking about it, then took the cigarette from his mouth and went around the side of the car to his radio. Hodge turned, blinking the tears from his eyes, hands behind his back, and walked away. His mind was full of images.

Luke had been blond when he was a child. Beautiful and odd and unnaturally gentle. You could put him in a room . . .

Once—a matter of days ago, but it felt like centuries—it had seemed to him urgent that he do as he'd done, that he act, finally, take the bull by the horns, not simply gaze timidly from behind his tree as he'd done all those centuries upon centuries before. But now all that seemed trifling, a kind of delusion of grandeur. Not where it was at, Freeman would say.

Because of course he had *not* acted, had merely put himself in position to act, watching them all, out-guessing them, growing fatter and fatter on his sense of power, unmoved by any argument for ending the hunt.

He stood with his hands in his coatpockets, studying emptiness.

To the stars he said, "You wanted to see me on my can, is that it?" It was all right, if that was what it was. What mattered was that it might be that it might not, because it was possible that stars, too, had happened to notice how the world stretched out from a broken bridge—had seen it all in ant's perspective—or that they knew beforehand, without ever having had to see from the bridge where Hodge had stood.

Freeman's voice said, inside his mind, or Ben's, maybe, "You can't just walk out. But then again it's no good to get up too close. You know what I mean."

Hodge scowled, then got in the car. Little by little his system learned to tolerate what he'd seen. He stopped at a gas station and phoned his wife, that is, ex-wife, to tell her what had happened. He would know only long afterward that Tag had repaired the line no more than an hour before. After that, he drove to the police station in Batavia to wait. There he tried to phone Will Jr to tell him, but he was away. Hodge told the policemen, Clarence Pieman and Figlow, the news, wept and told the whole story, with all the details, and told how the troopers were hunting for them now, and wept, and moved beyond his vision of distances. His mind held, not as warring principles but as a solemn resolution, the length and breadth of the valley stretching out as if endlessly from the burning wreck, and the close-knit pattern in the wallpaper of Will Jr's livingroom. Figlow sat at his desk, silent, and the desklight shining on his tipped-down forehead made his eyes seem only shadows. Beyond him, Hodge could make out vaguely in imagination the hairy intellectual face of Freeman, who could walk out and who, also, had no doubt wanted to see Will Hodge, Attorney, on his can. Which was all words.

He looked at the clock over Figlow's desk. He felt weightless. It was as if the earth had dropped from under him or had fallen, dragging him with it, off balance with the sun.

## 2

The phone rang, loud in the emptiness of the house, and Millie Hodge turned to stare at it. She had not known it was fixed. She thought a moment, eyebrows lowered, then raised herself carefully from the couch and crossed, turning the ice around and around inside the glass, to answer it.

The connection was bad, and at first she could not recognize the voice. The small of her back knew before her brain that it was Will. She half-closed her eyes.

"Millie?"

"This is Millie. Is that you, Will?"

"I have bad news," he said.

"Talk louder." She leaned over the phone and pressed her lips closer to it. "I can't hear you," she said. She had a weird sense that the Runian sisters stood listening behind the door.

She heard him clearly now. "Luke's dead, Millie."

She was silent. She heard, or imagined, the dead sisters' sharp intake of breath. *Oh my! No! The poor woman!* The voices were clear and distinct. Was it only the wind?

"Are you there, Millie?"

"I'm here," she said.

"Luke's dead. Do you hear me?"

She nodded, silent.

"He ran his truck off a bridge. The others—"

She waited.

"They got out. They must have suspected. There was only one body."

It wasn't possible to cry.

*One body?* the sisters exclaimed. *Only one?* They tipped their heads together like weeds in a wind.

"Will," she said.

"I'm sorry, Millie," he said. That was all. The connection broke. She listened to the wind, and there were no ghosts' voices now. No time for fantasy. The house was empty. She turned mechanically away from the phone. The room was cold, for the hot summer had at last broken, and autumn was descending in a rush, as always in Western New York. She drew the ragged old red and purple afghan from the couch and wrapped it around her shoulders. She stood at the window with her arms crossed over her bosom holding the makeshift robe in place. Stony Hill was burning, a red glow northeast of the prison's flat white light. She stood looking. Her arms were white, her elbows like daggers. Her eyes were like emerald, her lips like amethyst, and in her mourning she was beautiful again; she was calm as stone.

### 3

She sat on the bedside wringing her hands while Clumly dressed. She could have told him, at least, she was thinking in anguish. But she hadn't, and the anguish was pointless, not that that did a thing to make it less: She was not going to tell him even now, and she knew it. You can't ruin a man after all those years of living with him and then tell him, "Oh, say, I ought to tell you something." She had asserted her rights, had surrendered herself to whatever waves must carry them now; she would wait it out, and suffer with him or for him or from him whatever it was she must suffer, whatever was right. *My duty*, she thought. The word darted in and away again and hovered somewhere in the dark of her mind like a mysterious bird that could change its color, and there in the dark, outside her reach, she could feel it changing, teasing her toward a thought. She clenched her fists beside her knees, resolving to wring her hands no more, then instantly forgot. But he saw nothing of it as he dressed, lost in thought.

A meeting, he said. A speech to the Dairyman's League. Was it true? But whether it was true or not no longer mattered. He had a life of his own, it was none of her business. A life to spend or squander as he saw fit, as independent of her as she was of him. That was what she'd learned, a startling and terrible but also exhilarating discovery that brought with it a sudden sense of vaulting joy, of freedom—an escape into wilderness and boundless time: she could kill herself if she pleased, she had realized, standing at the open window dreaming of it; because the pain was hers, not her husband's, whatever pain of his own he might feel. The decision was hers, and if she chose against it for his sake, she did it voluntarily, as his equal. So he too, long ago, might have chosen to stay out of weakness, from dependence on her dependence on him, yes,

but even then, *his* weakness: she was not, after all, his prison.
She felt prepared almost for joy, but first she had tonight and
tomorrow and perhaps next year to stumble through.

He was mumbling something as he dressed, and she closed
off the back of her mind to listen.

"My friends, I'd like you to think back to the story of Cain
and Abel," he was saying. "I know that sounds like a minister
talking, and I know a man's known by the company he keeps
—" Something was wrong with it, he seemed to think, and he
muttered it again, with a slightly different expression. More
heavy-handed, in her personal opinion.

"Should you really say that, Fred?" she said.

"Esther, please," he said.

She sighed.

"—and I know a man's known by the company he keeps,"
he whispered.

*Well anyway, he does have a speech to make. It's not likely
he'd stoop to an outright lie. Something wrong with a marriage
where people can't help but suspect each other.* She thought of
all those years when again and again she'd wondered with an
aching heart if perhaps there was someone else he loved more
than her. The Indian girl with the blue eyes. And others, a girl
he stood talking to once at a School Board meeting. The waste
of it all, she thought dismally.

But that was wrong, of course. There was always some
waste, it was the method of Nature, and besides it was none of
her business. She listened to him swallowing, pulling his tie
snug, and then the almost inaudible yet to her ears distinct
scrape of stiffly starched cloth as he put his cufflinks on. He
went over to the closet in his stocking feet and she heard the
squeak of coat hangers: then he came back, and the suit came
down on the bed beside her and she caught the clean smell.
She heard him straightening the trousers, then putting them
on. He drew in his breath, slipping the belt on, buckling it.
Then he leaned toward her again for the coat. "You look
tired," he said.

Before she could answer, the phone rang. She touched her
forehead with the fingers of her left hand, meaning to get up
for it, but Clumly put his hand on her shoulder gently. "I'll get
it," he said. "Don't trouble."

"It's no trouble, Fred," she said. But she didn't get up.

He carried the phone from the hallway into the bathroom

and closed the door, and when he spoke it was too softly for her to hear. She sighed. Her heart felt drained and withered. But after the first words he no longer kept his voice at a whisper. "Dead?" he said. A moment later: "Go on." He listened again, and then he said, "You've got everything in control then? I'm supposed to give—" Another long pause. "Ok. Check. I'm supposed to give a speech, so if you need me I'll be at the Grange. Right. Ten-four. Right. G'bye."

He hung onto the receiver a moment before he put it in its cradle. Then he came slowly back down the hall, put the phone on its shelf, and came back into the room. "Luke Hodge is dead," he said. "It looks like suicide."

"No," she said. The room was full of distances, sounds farther off than they ought to be, as though it were the room, not the news, that was not to be believed. She could feel Luke's presence distinctly, unquestionably alive; but she knew he was dead.

"He drove his truck off a bridge," Clumly said. "The State Police are there, and Miller's going over. His father's at the scene, too, Figlow says."

"The State Police reported it?"

A silence. At last he said, "Funny you should ask that. No, as a matter of fact. Luke's mother reported it. Got it from his father. The troopers—" He stood thinking, staring into space perhaps.

"What?" she said.

"Nothing. Kept it under their hat, that's all. Not even on the radio. Funny."

She nodded. If there was something wrong, something mysterious going on, she was to blame. Such is the language of the blood.

But Clumly had his shoes on now, and the suitcoat, and he was getting out his good wool coat, though the night was warm.

"Do you really think you should wear that?" she said.

"Now Esther," he said, "you just leave that to me. There are some occasions when a uniform just isn't needed, and tonight is one of 'em."

She was startled. It was not what she'd meant, and his misunderstanding after all these years in the same house, saying the same words at the same time, thinking the same very thoughts, made her suddenly suspect—oh, more than that, *know*—that they'd struck something. *They expect him to come in his uniform,* she thought. *He refuses.* She said, "Dead. I can't believe it!"

A silence.

"It's tragic," Clumly said.

She nodded.

They held their silence like years stretching backward and forward out of sight, like a vast space of quiet ocean at night. He put his hand on her shoulder and, strange to say, with the thought of death enclosing them like the space beyond the farthest stars, like the shell of an empty house, Esther felt safe.

"Be home early," she said.

"I always do the best I can," he said.

"I know that," she said. She patted his hand. She could feel how old it was.

She got up when he started downstairs, and she went down behind him, sliding her hand on the banister smooth as the one at City Hall, and felt comfortable with the closeness of the walls around her and Clumly's presence below her and, in the air, the scent of his passing, a mixture—mysteriously pleasing to her, almost holy, in fact—of cologne and Ivory soap. She saw him to the porch, listened to his footsteps crunching on the gravel, going down the driveway behind the house to where the car was parked. She heard the door, then the motor starting up, and he backed to the street. She closed the door and turned the key in the lock. She switched off the lights.

They used no sirens, but she could feel them coming, moving toward her like subterranean creatures pressing mysteriously upward out of darkness into the cellar and on to the kitchen where she sat, to nibble her bones. She heard their cars purr softly to the curb out in front of the house, heard the doors open, the occasional mutters of the radio—two cars, perhaps, or possibly three, or one. She closed her hand more tightly on the neck of the bottle. *I am not quite as sober as intended,* she thought with dignity, stock still. *This is unusual. I am not, generally speaking . . .* She lost the thread. For a moment she couldn't remember whether she'd turned off the lights. She went through it again in her mind—Clumly's leaving, her quiet listening there on the porch, her return. *I locked the door, switched off . . .* She heard them coming up, their boots loud on the porch steps. Voices. "Nobody home, looks like." "Ring the bell." "I don't know. I mean the house all dark—" "Maybe we should wait till tomorrow? You know what I mean?"

She thought sadly of her life, but the details were a trifle confused. She reached out to touch the pistol, making sure it was there. But she didn't take it in her hand yet, merely waited. They were still talking, on the porch. *Poor Miller,* she thought. She knew pretty well how it must be for him. After all those years, he and Fred there together, "serving together," as Fred would say, as much like husband and wife as like father and son. She was sorry. She nodded in the dark of the kitchen. The doorbell rang. She touched the pistol again and, after a moment's thought, picked it up. It was surprisingly heavy now, as heavy as the cast-iron spider she cooked his eggs in.

Perhaps she was going to die. There was no telling. She knew only that they could not have the tapes. She had no idea whether the tapes would seem worth the trouble to them, but if they were, they would have to shoot her to get them. Her mind was made up. How absurd it seemed now, all those years of self-pity when she'd thought she must even the score with him, pay him back for what had no price on it, no more than her own devotion had a price. The ho-hum evenings, the long triviality of breakfasts and suppers, the conversations without talk. *Nobody's life,* she thought, *is perfect.* Fred's expression. How true! Yes, yes, how true!

Again, the doorbell.

They had loved each other, she thought, frowning. Again the bird in the back of her mind stirred and fluttered. *Duty,* she remembered. But duty was merely turning love into a thought. Without love—if there was no love—then duty

*Meaningless. Evil.*

"Duty is evil," she said aloud. She smiled. *Drunk as a pig. If anyone should see me*

They were pounding now. Banging on the door like the Gestapo or something. It amused her, the thought of poor gentle Miller and wordless Kozlowski and that trembling little tame rabbit John Figlow, or whoever was there, banging the door like the whole German army under orders to kill all Jews.

"Just a moment," she called.

The banging stopped.

She moved toward the dining room, holding the pistol in

one hand, the bottle in the other. *I feel better now, thank you,* she thought. *Quite sober.* Standing in the livingroom she said, "I'm sorry, you can't come in."

"Mrs. Clumly?" someone called. A voice she couldn't place.

"I'm sorry," she said. "It's my duty to keep you out. You don't have a warrant, do you?"

Silence.

Eventually, Officer Tank's voice: "Mrs. Clumly, we need to talk to you."

"I'm sorry," she said.

Another silence. Then, loud as gunshots, a knocking.

"For Christ's sake, Esther, let us in." It was Miller this time. She smiled.

It might have been all civilization, for all she cared, out there banging and asking admission. She said, "What do you want?"

"We want to talk," Miller said.

She waited.

He was quiet for a long time. They were whispering something.

"Mrs. Clumly," Miller said softly, almost too softly to hear. "It's about—what we talked about. You remember?" Another silence. She could hear the house waiting, observing with detachment but a certain remote curiosity. In the cellar, nothing stirred. Then Miller's voice: "Esther, the tapes."

She squeezed. The explosion filled the room and the gun kicked into her stomach so hard all her breath went out, and the world was full of the violent smell of the gunpowder or whatever it was as she fell down gasping and amazed. She heard plaster falling from the ceiling. And then they were howling as if they'd all been shot in the left hind leg, and there were doors opening all up and down the street, and the second explosion was louder than the first and the third explosion still ten times louder, and Ed Tank screamed as if he'd gone stark crazy, "Mrs. Clumly put down that gun before you kill yourself!" They were banging again. She heard the hinges break.

At last, with vast satisfaction, as though huge iron chains had been sawed from her legs and her eyes were opened and her womb filled with life, she fainted. *More brave than was intended,* she said in her mind.

## 4

Arthur Hodge Jr, brother to Will Sr and Ben, sat, all triangles and squares, hooking colored wires together in a pattern so intricate no ordinary man could have read the chart. He was making what he called, by some queer lapse of mind or twist of humor, a Victrola, to anyone else a stereo phonograph. He was a lover of music and did not understand, since he'd forbidden it, that what his seven daughters would play on his machine would be music by, at best, the Jefferson Airplane. The phone rang. His oldest daughter answered. She brought him the news.

"Terrible," Art Jr said. He frowned, reaching a judgment. "It's a mistake."

## 5

Walter Benson, sometimes Boyle, was not sure even now what his opinion was. It was a comfort to have Mr. Nuper dead, and it was surprising to find how little anxiety he felt about ever being caught for his part in it. Nevertheless, even though it was done now, which theoretically ought to have ended it, it was still not exactly settled in Benson's (or Boyle's) mind whether or not he'd done right. It was a foolish question to be worrying about, but he felt cheated. A man deserves to have some feeling about what he has done or hasn't done. As he'd stood that night in the squishy, clayey mud of the creekbed, ruining his good shoes, panting and puffing as he struggled to get the dead-weight, incredibly uncooperative body (in death as in life) down into the mouth of the sluice, he had thought, "What kind of man are you, Benson, or Boyle, to have no feeling at a time like this?" But it was useless, he felt nothing. It was a fact. He felt—(he squinted in the darkness, analyzing)—a certain panic, for though the road was isolated, some lovers might come along, or some fool who'd taken the wrong turn, looking for Niagara Falls. But he did not feel *much* panic, actually. No more, certainly, than he felt when he slipped through the door of what might or might not be an empty house. The main thing he felt was a kind of generalized annoyance—at the squishyness of the mud, which made him fall twice onto one knee, smearing his trousers and the hem of his coat; at the way Marguerite would keep wondering, now, whatever had happened to that nice young man; at the general irresolution of life. He found himself thinking, almost angrily,

> But the gingham dog and the calico cat
> Wallowed this way and tumbled that,
> Employing every tooth and claw
> In the awfullest way you ever saw,
> And, oh! how the gingham and calico flew!

Nevertheless, he finally got the whole body in; the next few rains would dispose of it. He worked his way back up to the road, got into his car and sat there a moment panting, waiting for his emotions to return; but there was nothing, or nothing but the jingle banging in his head.

> And some folks think unto this day
> That burglars stole that pair away!
> But the truth about the cat and pup
> Is this: they ate each other up!
> Now what do you really think of that?

And all the way home the jingle went on jingling, no matter what he tried to think of.

I never got around to that book, he thought now. A book on Cuba that Nuper said it would do him good to read. He, Benson-boyle, had known well enough it would do him no good, but he'd more or less meant to read it just the same, heaven knew why. He'd meant to look over the bills, too. How many days had he been home now? But they could wait, like everything else.

Poor Benson! Or Boyle. He sits humpbacked at his dining-room table, squinting at his newspaper as though he's been sitting here for centuries. He can hear his wife puffing, moving around in the livingroom, straightening up. He doesn't move a muscle. Someone in Texas has been murdering people from a tower, shooting women and children and college professors. In Chicago someone has been killing nurses. There will be more, he thinks. Someone does something like that, and pretty soon all the other lunatics start on it too. Young punks. Crazy people. Sometimes it seems as if everybody in the world has gone insane. It frightens him, to tell the truth. He thinks of the policeman with eyes like two bullets, beating the Indian boy with the butt of a gun, then of the men in the black armbands, protectors of their noble vision, swinging even with Bensonboyle's car on the narrow road, then pulling past Nuper, forcing him to the shoulder.

"Walter?" she says. She pokes her puffy white head through the door.

But he concentrates. There was something important that he meant to do, or meant to decide on. The light coming off the imitation cut-glass salt shaker distracts him a little, and he concentrates harder, until he hardly notices the light. Absurd syllables come into his head:

> *I dimly guess from blessings known*
> *Of greater out of sight,*
> *And, with the chastened Psalmist, own*
> *His judgments too are right.*

It is not what he was groping for, and he thinks, angrily, that he too seems to have gone insane; but he hasn't, of course. He was never more sane in his life, God knows. Nevertheless, there was something he had to get done that he hasn't done.

When she calls again he has a momentary sense of disorientation, cannot think what room he's sitting in, and so understands that he must have dropped off there, for a minute.

"Are you coming to bed?" she asks. And then: "Walter!"

"Ah!" he says, not turning.

It has all come back to him, all at once. He was standing in a place where the sky was dark green—an eclipse, perhaps—and there are black towers, and men moving about, workmen. One touched him on the shoulder—an old, old man with sparse white stubble and tiny, close-set eyes—and called him by his name.

Benson shudders. Whatever the message was, delivered to him in that queer, sudden dream, he has lost it now. No matter.

The doorway behind him is empty now. Marguerite has gone upstairs. He can hear the radio directly over his head.

Sooner or later he must get her out of the house, he knows, and in her absence get rid of Nuper's things (must figure out how to dispose of them too, of course, sooner or later) and then tell her he came back for them. Let it slide and sooner or later she'll begin to worry and call the police. When is it that she goes shopping? he wonders. What day is today?

The trouble is, he feels mysteriously weary all the time now, more tired when he wakes up than when he goes to sleep. Dreams, perhaps. But if he dreams he cannot remember afterward, usually. The truth is, he is half-dreaming even now, sliding off into the sunless, underwalter world where the workmen are moving about, taking down scaffolding of some kind, muttering to themselves, never looking at him. Tomorrow, he thinks suddenly. Tomorrow. He is back in the familiar, gloomy room.

And now Marguerite is calling again. "Walter, come listen to this!"

She has the news on. He hears the rumble of the voice, but not the words.

When she calls again he stirs himself, pushes back the chair and lifts his vast (as it seems to him) weight and makes his way to the stairs.

"It's over," she says when he comes in. "You should've been quicker."

"Over?" he says.

"They caught that Indian boy," she says. "He's back in jail. The one that broke out, you know, down in Batavia. They found him in a barn, down near Warsaw, and he gave himself up. They haven't caught up with the other one yet."

He nodded.

"Five miles from where they found him, there was an accident. A truck driver killed. The police believe there may be some connection."

He nodded, standing carefully balanced, touching the doorframe.

"The truck driver was—something. His guardian or something."

He nodded again, and after a moment it came to him that he'd seen him, he'd come to the jail.

"It's funny," she said, "the way that other one keeps getting away. It's not natural."

He nodded again. "Well, they'll find him," he said. "They'll trace him down . . . They always do." His voice came out weak, and she seemed to notice it.

"They don't even know who he waves," she said.

"They'll find out all right. Someone—" This time the voice was too loud. He shrugged and closed himself up as he would in jail. He looked hard at the radio beside the bed as if to watch the music coming out.

He'd kept driving, of course. The men with black armbands weren't people to get mixed up with. And half a mile farther on he'd pulled into the woods and switched off the motor and lights and had waited. And he heard a car coming and saw that it was Nuper's but had the fleeting impression that Nuper was not driving. Then the other car passed. He'd sat thinking a long time; then, cautiously, he'd gone back to the place. Nuper was sitting on a stump, naked, blind-folded. He'd been shot through the back of the head. A car passed on the road, and he thought *The police!* If anyone had seen him here—had seen Benson, that is, or Boyle—there would be hell to pay. They'd discover the body, put two and two together . . . What could he do? What would any grown man who'd seen a thing or two in this wicked world . . . And it was of course not exactly a murder, all things considered. An execution. He was sweating rivers.

At last she turned her prying eyes away. After a moment she put her puffy hands to the sides of her blurred face and shook her head. "I wonder what ever happened to Mr. Nuper," she said. "Sometimes I think—"

He laughed, startling himself. "He'll turn up. They always do," he said.

Much later, suddenly opening his eyes wide in the darkness, he thinks, "I was one of them, yes. We were digging for something, a deep, deep hole, and it was dark as pitch. And one of the workmen said, 'Here it is! A hand!' We scraped the dirt off the arm and shoulder and then the head, and we looked at the dead face (and yet it was still dark, I think—a strange dream; illogical) and someone said, 'Why it's *him!*' and the others all looked and nodded and shook their heads the way you would at a funeral, but I looked and looked and I couldn't make out who it was. 'Who?' I said. 'I don't recognize him.' And then they were all looking at me in the darkness and—then I woke up. What can it mean?"

Nevertheless, he felt no guilt, as far as he could tell. One can get used to anything, it came to him. In a week, a month, the whole thing would no doubt be almost drowned out of his mind. Such things happen, no doubt. He felt again the momentary sensation of nausea he'd felt that night when he first saw Ollie's body sitting white as a young girl's on the stump. *Fssss,* he thought, and—*horrible!* He closed his eyes and almost instantly he was dreaming again, walking very carefully on the glass roof of a greenhouse. Down below him, in the dim, aqueous light, fronds moved back and forth slowly, like thinking creatures. It was perhaps all just as it should be; he was of two minds. *And there will I keep you forever,* he thought.

> *Forever and a day,*
> *Till the wall shall crumble to ocean,*
> *And moulder in dark away.*

His heart sped up. It was a beautiful poem. Beautiful.

## 6

"It's damned foolishness, that's all," Kozlowski said. "You don't need me there, and this is a hell of a night to tie up a man that might be some use."

"Maybe so," Clumly said. He was in no mood to be giving out explanations, not that he had one. "Turn the radio up." Kozlowski obeyed, but they were saying nothing important now. It was five minutes ago that word had come through that the Indian had given up. They were still out there, beating the bushes for the Sunlight Man, but you could see they were already beginning to get it: he'd given them the slip, as usual. Maybe he was right there with them, helping them hunt. It was a thought. It was the kind of thing he'd think funny. Clumly took the cigar out of his mouth and held it up toward the windshield to look at it. "Maybe he's right there with them," he said, "helping 'em hunt."

Kozlowski thought about it, chin tucked down, mouth wry. At last he said, "Should I call 'em?"

Clumly shook his head. "Let it go. Bad guess." He studied the cigar again.

"It might be worth a try."

But Clumly was sure now. "No, not tonight. If my hunch is right—"

"Well?"

"Nothing." Then: "Get Figlow back."

"Again?"

Clumly nodded, and Kozlowski called in, but there was nothing. They hadn't come in yet with the Indian—had a car on the way—and the place was like a tomb. "Well, keep your cool, Figlow," Kozlowski said, and signed off.

"Cool?" Clumly said.

"Figure of speech," he said. "Spade talk, or something."

"Spade?"

Kozlowski nodded. "Like in poker."

Clumly frowned, full of gloom, but he let it go. The squad car swung into the alley, fenders slipping past the gray-black bricks on either side as smoothly as the walls of a boat in a dark, narrow channel, and after a moment they came out in the dead-white brightness of the parking lot like a stagnant sea. There were a lot of cars, on the far side, and the front door of the Grange, where the Dairyman's League was meeting, stood open. The light in the entryway was yellow, as if it were lit up by candlelight, and you could see the beginning of the stairway. "Park up in front," Clumly said, and Kozlowski slid past the glinting rows of cars and pulled in at the No Parking sign where the sidewalk began. He turned off the motor, the radio still on, crackling, and they sat.

Clumly said, "You ever listen to that Oswald stuff?"

Kozlowski looked bored. "No sir."

"You know what I mean," Clumly said. "What's-his-name Oswald, the one that shot President Kennedy. It's very interesting. You realize all ten of the newspaper reporters or whatever they were that interviewed Ruby—all ten of 'em are dead now? Car accidents, things like that? It's very interesting."

"That part of your speech?" Kozlowski said.

"I was just mentioning it, that's all. Not in the speech. Listen." He leaned forward and partly turned in the seat, to face him better. "What do you make of those three frames of that movie that are in there backwards? Somebody turned 'em around, I mean. J. Edgar Hoover himself says so. They make it look like he was shot from behind, but if you put 'em in frontwards—in the right order, I mean—it appears he was shot from in front."

"What's the difference?"

"Well hell you *know* what's the difference. It means Oswald didn't—"

"No, I know that. I mean what's the difference if Oswald did it or not? I mean, you drag me here to be your bodyguard or something, and the troopers are out hunting for the Sunlight Man, and you sit there and talk about Oswald."

"It's interesting, that's all." He sulked.

"Sure."

"Suppose it *was* a conspiracy," he said. He could see well enough in Kozlowski's face how absurd it was to be sitting here stewing about such a thing tonight. But the urge was on him, and he was not in a mood to shake it off. "Suppose it was," he said again.

"I'm supposing."

"Who would it all be pointing to, in that case? The way it was all done so smooth, I mean. The way not even the F.B.I. can figure it out. And the What's-its-name Commission, the way they just called in certain witnesses and not the others, so people say. That look like the Russians to you? They can't all be Russian spies—the whole U.S. Congress. So who does it point to?"

"You're off your damn rocker." He pushed back in his seat a little, getting out a cigarette.

"Tell me the truth, that's all," Clumly said. Two men and a woman went up the steps and into the hall. Four or five more were standing under the trees around the side, smoking cigarettes. "I just want *truth*. I'm too old for all the rest. *Who?*" Clumly said.

Angrily, Kozlowski said, "You want me to say it was Johnson, right? Ok. It was President Johnson. Ok?"

Clumly sucked at the cigar and brooded. "He's from Texas," he said.

"Jesus," Kozlowski said. He threw his match out the window and spit after it.

"The trouble with you, Kozlowski," he said, "you're afraid to face the possibilities. You believe in flying saucers?"

"Look."

"I read about a town in New Hampshire—"

"You going in? You'll be late."

"I'll just finish this smoke," he said. He sulked. "A man should know the truth."

"That cigar'll take you half an hour if you don't get it lit first."

Clumly laughed, dry as a dog's laugh, and hunted for a match.

At the police station, Figlow sat at his desk going through his reports. The coffee in his blue tin cup was cold, but he went on sipping at it from time to time, to drive down the bite of his cigarettes. The coffee had a skin of silver on it, like oil-slick.

When Ed Tank came in and stood in the doorway with his motorcycle helmet hanging under his arm, Figlow looked up sharply, then nodded and said nothing.

"No more news?" Tank said.

He shook his head.

"Seems like they'd be here with the Indian by now. You think anything could've went wrong?"

"They'll be here." He looked at his watch. "Be half an hour yet anyway, maybe more." It was true, they couldn't possibly make it in less than that, but he too had been wondering where they were.

"Beautiful night," Tank said. He rolled his head a little, pointing over his shoulder.

"Harvest moon," Figlow said, "yeah. Night for were-wolves." He laughed.

Tank came over and pulled himself a cup of coffee and sat down beside Figlow's desk. "That all you heard?" he said at last. "The kid just gave up, that's all?"

He nodded and looked back at the papers. "Somebody saw him go in, I guess. That's what they say. Troopers circled the barn and put the light on him and he came out. All there was to it."

"I'd like to been there."

"Sure."

"Anybody would, I guess." He lowered his square head toward the cup and lifted the cup just off the table and sipped.

Figlow looked back at the papers. "Not me," he said.

"The hell you wouldn't."

"I'm telling you. Suppose he'd come out shooting."

"So?"

"So look." He stared at the bitten-off end of the pencil a moment longer, then laid it down on the paper. Then, frowning, he swivelled his chest and clumsily reached over his lap with his left hand, unsnapped his pistol and drew it out. He held it sideways toward Tank. "Look at the thing," he said. "Look."

"Shoot, man, I seen guns."

"Right. Feel how heavy. No, take it. Feel how heavy the damn thing is."

"I got my own."

"Sure, sure. But feel the damn *weight* of the thing."

Tank studied him, then bent his head toward the coffee again.

"I don't know," Figlow said. He was thinking—not seriously, just playing with the thought—that if he were, say, crazy, he could turn that pistol and before Ed Tank knew what was happening he could blow Tank's head off. He was no more going to do it than fly. The thing was, he *could*. He knew how solid the line was between thinking about it and doing it—as solid as the line between thinking off-hand about suicide and driving off a cliff. Nevertheless, he was thinking about it; wondering. They were bringing back the Indian boy, and who knew? Maybe the Sunlight Man would come and let him out again, or try. And maybe Figlow would be sitting here alone when the Sunlight Man came.

Tank drained the cup, raising his head as he did it, and steam went up past his forearm toward the light. "It's these desk jobs," he said, and wiped his mouth. "Out on a bike, a night like this, you don't get spooked like that." He stood up, grinning.

Figlow grinned back and gave a half-nod. Then he pushed the gun to the front of the desk and picked up the pencil again.

Chief Clumly said, sitting in the car with Kozlowski, "Because I need you here. Is that good enough? If something comes through on this radio while I'm in there making my speech, I want to know about it, that's why. And don't you say, 'Nothing's coming.' I know different."

Kozlowski turned his head, slightly tipped.

"And don't ask me how I know either," Clumly said testily. "Say it's a hunch I've got."

"Is it?"

"I don't know. No. Not a hunch."

"That's what Miller said. Been expecting it all day. Saw three crows over his left shoulder or something." He spit out the window.

They were all inside now, waiting for him, maybe. But Clumly went on stalling, waiting for the news. They'd have a business meeting first, probably. They did that sometimes, and after the business they had the speaker to finish them off. When he leaned toward the windshield and looked up he could see sky above the Grange Hall, wide glodes full of moonlight, and around them, though there was no breeze down here, swiftly moving clouds. Cold weather coming, it might be.

"He's run out of time, see?" Clumly said. Then, thoughtfully: "Both of us have. Anyway, he knows it's over, for now, for here."

"For here?"

"Maybe he'll head out. If he does, that's the last we'll hear of him—till we read about him turning up in Mexico, say, or Peru, maybe, or Australia. And then again maybe he won't."

"And if he stays?"

Clumly shook his head. "Don't know," he said. And yet it seemed to him that he did know, had gotten that close to inside the man's head—or if he didn't know would anyway recognize after he saw it that it was right, exactly as it had to be. He concentrated, trying to see what it was that he knew was going to happen; and though it was ridiculous, like straining to remember the future, it seemed to him he almost had it, but it wouldn't come quite clear. The yellow light inside the Grange looked for an instant like fire.

"You better go in," Kozlowski said. "You got people enough on your back."

"In a minute I will," he said.

Ten seconds later word came that they'd picked up Millie Hodge at her son's place, Luke's, and gotten her story. Two policemen and a couple of neighbors were digging behind the garage for the murdered man's body. Clumly listened in silence. He said at last, "Poor fool."

"He won't get away then?" Kozlowski said.

"Either way," he said, "poor fool just the same." And then,
as though the news from Luke's farm were somehow a conclusion, Clumly tamped out his cigar, sighed like the old man he
was, and opened the car door to get out. He stood a minute
straightening his coat and tugging at his trousers below the
pockets—his underwear had gotten twisted up around him—
all the time staring at the Grange Hall door with a mixture of
dread and determination (because, it came to him, they'd all
be in there, they were always at the Dairyman's League meetings, political reasons likely—the Mayor, maybe the Fire
Chief, somebody from the *Daily News* as well—and one way
or another he must brave it out, act out his last official act as
though nothing were out of the ordinary), then, heaving another sigh, he started up the walk.

To Kozlowski, sitting in the car behind him, his bent-for-
ward walk looked like stealth, and he thought, "Poor old nut."

All Figlow knew was this: he was sitting alone, no longer
pretending to do paperwork, giving all his attention to the infuriatingly slow reports that came by fits and starts from the
snapping, humming radio, and wondering where the devil they
were with that Indian. Twice he went back to the cells, troubled by the silence there, but there was nothing wrong. The
man that had dirty magazines at the G.L.F. feedstore was sitting on his bench, leaning against the back wall, staring, and
the drunk-and-disorderly Pieman had brought in this afternoon was asleep. The next cell was empty—the firebug had
gotten off on bail, in the care of his parents. In the end cell the
younger of the Indians sat reading his one battered comic, as
usual. He looked up when Figlow came in, but only for a minute. The Indian almost never spoke any more. When the Presbyterian minister came to visit him, he'd go right on reading,
and even when May Bunce came, from Probation, he ignored
her.

As he was sitting down at his desk again, Figlow remembered he'd left the gun out and swung his eyes to where he'd
left it. How he hadn't missed it when he got up in the first
place, from the unnatural lightness of his holster, he could
never say, later. Mind on something else, it must be—the stut-
ter of news from the State Police and from Luke's house, or

the business with Ed Tank, the talk that must've made Ed think he was dealing with a madman. Whatever it was, he swung his eyes now to where he'd put down the gun and his heart stopped. He leaned forward slowly, like a man leaning over a cliff a mile high, looking where the gun would have fallen if it was that, and at the same time he saw there was nothing on the floor he became aware of the smell in the room, thick as death. The skin of his face was stinging from the pounding of his blood and he had no strength in his legs, but he managed to sit down. The front drawer was open a little, and though he knew it was not where he'd put the gun— and knew, in fact actually seemed to see through the back of his head, that the Sunlight Man was directly behind him, standing in front of the file cabinets, smiling at him out of a face burnt black as coal—he opened the drawer farther and groped inside it. The gun was there. His fingers closed around it but had no more feeling than pieces of wood, and he thought, It's some crazy joke! If he spun to fire he would be dead before he got the shot off, and if he didn't spin, he would be dead with a hole in his back. He seemed to think all this slowly and deliberately, and to think, at the same time, a thousand things more—about the weakness spreading all through his body, and the line between thinking of killing and killing, and about how he hadn't had his supper and how his daughter had baggy eyes and dust-dry hair, might very well be pregnant —but in reality only a split second elapsed between the moment he closed his fingers on the gun and the moment he turned, caught the stupid, weakling smile, the crossed arms, the body tilted far off balance, as if standing in shoes firmly nailed to the floor. What made the smile terrible was that the eyes were weeping. And it came to Figlow that it *was* a joke. The Sunlight Man had no intention of shooting him. He had come to give up, broken by grief, but in the madness of his trickster vanity or maybe just human vanity he could not resist one final laugh at the childish credulity of man, one last indifferent or partly indifferent sneer, or maybe one final ridiculous pretense that he was still indifferent, still had dignity. By the time the joke came clear, it was too late. Figlow had shot him through the heart.

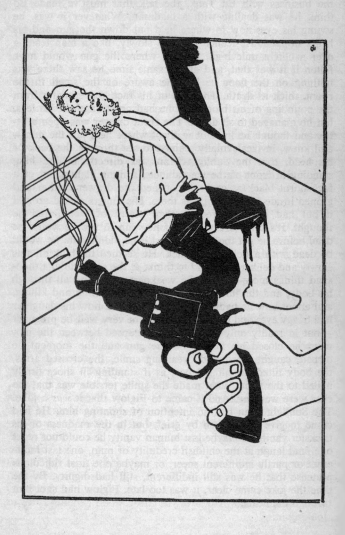

## 7

Ben Hodge sat stunned in the roaring, flickering grist room, sitting on the piled-up bags of oats, hands on the oatbags on either side, legs wide apart and as solid as pillars, chin thrown forward, neither rueful nor belligerent, merely and finally itself. No grain poured down the chute now; the machine ran empty, howling like all the damned at once, and in front of the shed the tractor running the gristmill belt roared angrily, full of empty malevolence. Above the roar, or under it, like a sound of hurrying water under ice, he could hear David beating out rhythms on the pumphouse pipes. Through the open door he could see night sky and Orion like a huge man bending to look in. Ben Hodge's mind was full of memories and pain, not separate instants and not a flow of time either, but all his life without walls or progression, like a small idea of eternity, or like the state sometimes induced in very sick people by powerful sedatives. His brother was dead, and he could make of it neither an abstract truth nor a story; it was itself, an event outside time, complete as an apple. In his blood, not his mind, he heard the drumming rhythm from the pipes, and in them too he could hear no progression: time flowed around them like a river around a stone: each beat stood eternal and inviolate, leading in no direction, implying nothing. *I am,* the drumming said, *and nothing else.* The final truth, he seemed to understand by this queer twist his brain had taken, had nothing to do with human thought or human story; unspeakable. He could look into the gristmill's open side, and he knew the knives were spinning at incredible speed, might snip off his hand if he reached through the hole, and the hand would be as if it had never been; yet the knives were invisible, almost unreal at that speed—not knives, in any case: a dangerous ghost.

He only half-registered the lights flashing across the barn wall opposite the grist room. In the same trance, he understood without knowledge that a car door had slammed and that someone was coming toward him. The dark of the sky went darker and a man as big as Orion stood bending forward looking in.

"Uncle Ben?"

He understood that it was Will Jr who had spoken. He would answer in a moment; for now he said nothing.

The shape went on standing in the doorway, the eyes no doubt searching through the dim and flickering room that opened out around the underfed lightbulb and perhaps made him out at last. (He could not see Will Jr's eyes.) After another moment the shape withdrew. The roar of the tractor changed, became freer; he'd shoved the clutch in. Then the motor went off. The belt went on turning for a while, strangely quiet. Will Jr came back.

"You heard?" he said.

Hardly aware that he was doing it, Ben nodded.

"What a thing," Will said.

That was right. Thing. He nodded again. Now Will came over to him. He bent down, leaning on his knees.

"You ok, Uncle Ben?"

"I'm all right." His voice was soft, a little creaky, as if from lack of use. Then, slowly, like a man coming to life again, he raised his hands to his face. There was no feeling in his fingers. "How are you?" he said. An absurd, trifling question, he might've thought if he stood outside it; but it was not trifling. It was as large and self-contained as the death, and it was the walls of the room that opened out from their two solid figures, the walls of night that opened out around the barn, that was trifling.

"I'm all right," Will said. "You scared me."

He nodded, then reached up, and Will helped him to his feet. "Your wife?" Ben said. Another tentative step behind the world.

"Just fine." Will Jr frowned for a second, thinking about it, then said with curious finality. "We're all fine, Ben. Fine." He took Ben's arm and they started toward the doorway. Then, standing outside where there was a cool breeze and they could look up at the slanting barn roofs and the tops of the tamaracks and the wide flat roof of the big brick house, Will Jr said, "How the devil did it happen?"

It was a hard question. His mind fumbled with it for a moment, then let it fall away. He listened to the drumming. It had grown linear again, like a horse crossing a field. "It's a long story," he said evasively. They started toward the yellow lighted windows of the house. Everything was blurry, like print one could not break past to the word.

"Are you all right, Will?" he asked. Almost a whisper.

"We're fine," Will said, and Ben understood that it was true.

In the kitchen Vanessa talked and talked, turning the whole thing over and over, trying to make out the sense in it. Ben and Will Jr were as quiet as two old rocks in the Genesee.

# XXIV

---

## Law and Order

---

*Darum, ich bitte euch, wollt nicht in Zorn verfallen*
*Denn alle Kreatur braucht Hilf von allen.*

—Bertold Brecht

"Ladies and gentlemen," Chief of Police Fred Clumly said—
his hand was shaking violently and he knew before it fell that
the note they'd handed him was going to fall, though he could
not feel it as it slipped between his fingers, all his physical sensations squeezed down and focused to a burning white point at
the pit of his throat, could not even know after it had fallen
that it had, not even by the eyes of the people who sat silent,
dutiful, and sleepy, his own eyes swimming (for he was, whatever else, good-hearted)—"ladies and gentlemen," said Clumly, "I have the sorrowful duty to tell you the terrible, tragic
news that one of our number is dead."

Silence stood in the room like a barn owl watching, and then, little by little, the whispers began. He raised both arms. "Please," he said, "please!" And once more it was silent. "Ladies and gentlemen," he said, "tonight, a little more than ten minutes ago, the Sunlight Man that we've all been reading in the papers about—" Again he raised his arms for silence and it came, "—the Sunlight Man was shot tonight, dead." It was as if the silence grew in pitch and power until it roared. In any case, the people were all talking now, and after he'd held up his hands for a full minute, to no avail, he let his hands fall and bowed his head and waited for them to calm down. At last they did.

"I have the notes to a speech here," he said, "which I don't know whether I should give or not." He leaned on the table, looking down at where, somewhere in all that blur, he knew the notes would be lying, and, sad of heart, he waited for a sign. Someone coughed, out in front of him, and he took it for one and said gravely, "If it's all right with you, I'd like to depart from my subject somewhat—" He stopped to think it out. "I'd like to deviate from my subject somewhat in order to communicate with you all here tonight, this crowd of friends and neighbors I've known all my life, good people, all of you, the kind of people that can sympathize with whoever gives them a fair chance, if you follow me, and can give the Devil his due, good *farm* people, the salt of the earth, as the Good Book says—" He frowned and stammered, trying to get the thread again. But he was grieved, he was grieved deeply, crying out in his mind "My God, my God! The injustice of it!" and the word *injustice* (printed like a headline in his mind) had a power over him even greater than the thing itself, as is the way of words, and tears brimmed over and fell on his cheeks and his throat tightened to a whimper. He whispered, "Friends," and waited for control, for the help of the Lord, then said again "Friends, I said I'd talk to you about Law and Order, but that's a hard subject for me right tonight. It's hard." He bent over, put his hands to his wide mole's nose and, unable to stop himself longer, sobbed. Someone put his hand on Clumly's shoulder, he would never learn who. He knew very well how absurd he must look, oh yes, yes, he understood their bafflement—the Chief of Police standing there weeping, crying his heart out, for a man he'd been hunting like a wild animal for days and days and days. Yes. He raised one hand, still standing with his head down. "Sometimes," he said and paused and little by little knew he was in command again, would be able to speak like a responsible being. "Sometimes it seems as if there *is* no justice. A man dies—shot through the heart, the message said—a man dies and you think, *Lord, Lord, where is your justice?* Was that what he was born for? Or any of us was born for—to be mortally shot through the heart and killed? Do you think when he was a little baby they supposed he was going to be shot through the heart like that, mortally, and killed? Do you think when he was a child of say five or six years old he wasn't just as fine looking and lovable as your children or mine, if I had any? Listen: We see people that are lucky and that live their whole lives in the shelter of Law and Order and the whole community looks up to them, and they work like any decent person and they start their family and buy a house pretty soon and they mature and prosper before Man and God, and one of these days they die and we go to their funeral, and we all say, 'Rest in peace, Sam,' or Henry, or whatever the case may be. And we go out there to the cemetery with his last remains and we stand by the grave-side and our hats are off to him, and the minister opens his book and prays for him. You know what it's like, all of you. Our hearts are full of sorrow, a time like that, but there's a calm in it too, you all know that. All the man's family there, standing around the grave, and his grandchildren standing there all dressed up, and his friends standing around crying and wringing their hankies and remembering all he ever said to them or did for them. That's order. That's right to the heart of what Order is. Because all his life he obeyed the law. And now all the people that ever knew him come together and give him the dignity of that last final order. That's what it's all about, you know. Order. Correct. It's a beautiful thing, the or-der in a man's life, and sometimes you wonder if that's not the only time it's visible, after he's dead and it's there beside his grave."

Fred Clumly put his hands on the table and he looked out at them but not at them, over their reasonable, patient heads, as if he were reading it all on the wall, from the angel's hand, cut in the plaster like runes from a stylus. They sat motionless as rocks and stumps, as if they too were aware that the angel was there, or the angel's hand, outrageously condemning them for doing nothing wrong. Clumly drew his breath. "Well this man won't get such a funeral as that, and we all know why. He didn't obey the laws. *Our* laws that we've put on the books for the benefit of all, or anyway the benefit of almost all, all of *us*, anyway. And in all fairness to the people who do obey the laws, or anyway don't get caught disobeying, or got forgiven in time, at least, we can't honor him with the kind of order we give those others. If he had any family (I don't say he did and I don't say he didn't, because what will be will be, and you'll find it in the papers the same as I will), if this Sunlight Man, as he called himself, had a family, they won't lay him away in the earth with ceremony; they'll be too ashamed. But I'll tell you this: they'll be sorry, some of them, or sorry in some ways, some of the time. It might be he was of good stock, as people say. It might be he was from one of the best old families in the country, maybe some family right here in Batavia, who knows? I can say this, anyway. I talked to him, and it was the finest mind I ever talked to, some ways. Sometimes you could hardly understand him when he talked, and sometimes you could understand him just fine and you grieved in your heart to hear the terrible way he was talking, so disrespectful of everything. I've seen that man do magic tricks as good as any magician I ever yet saw on the stage in all my life, and I've seen more than two or three, I can tell you that. And I've heard him quote foreign languages just as if he was born talking 'em, even dead languages that nobody knows how to speak any more or whether he's saying the words correct or not. I don't know if he was saying it right, I'll admit that to you, but I'll say this: if you heard him you'd believe him. That's the kind of authority he spoke with. But now he's dead with a bullet in his heart, mortally killed. Where was justice? you might ask. Well, I can't answer.

"I can say this: I'm proud of my boys that tracked him down, insofar as they did, and I wouldn't have it otherwise. They have a public trust, your police department, and I'm as proud of those boys as I could be of my own sons, if I had any. I know they did the best they could to see true justice triumphed, and justice *did* triumph, and we can be proud that we live in this great free country where that can happen. Yes! But also justice didn't triumph, in a way, of course. I can't explain that if you don't see it in your heart, it's just the way it is, maybe always was and always will be. You have to have laws, the best you can, and this is democracy, as we all know, and we're dedicated to the idea of liberty . . ."

He paused again, muddled for the moment. "The boys in your police department are the Watchdogs of Society," he said.

He paused again.

"Ladies and gentlemen," he said, "we all live in the hope and faith that, although there may still be some faults in our society, and sometimes things aren't all we wish they might be, we're trying to get better, doing our level best in that direction. It's a little like the Einstein universe, as I understand it, which is reaching outwards and outwards at terrific speed, and the danger is—if I've got this right—the danger is, it can get cold. Turn ice. Ladies and gentlemen, we mustn't let that happen, I feel. I feel we must all be vigilant against growing indifferent to people less fortunate . . ."

He bit his lip, pausing a moment, and hungered for a cigar. Would they mind? he wondered. Would they even really notice if he took out a cigar and lit it? When he looked at them this time they seemed to him farther away, as if the whole room were receding—not swiftly, but slowly, definitely, determinedly receding. He got out the cigar and, after a moment, lit it.

"Well things are getting better, some ways, we know. There are supermarkets in India now, or so I read—'super bazaars,' they call them. You can buy such things as pressure cookers, egg slicers, meat grinders, and packaged varieties of food—all made right in India. Everything's got a price tag, which is very important *as nobody knows better than the farmer* (There! he'd got *that* in!), and it's all self-service which, as we all know, is the best way to do it, and the truly American way. But then on the other hand there are signs that things are getting worse. A thousand people a day dying of famine right there in India for instance. Or for instance take the problem of advertising. It's getting so advertising's so plain outright obscene you wonder if it's bad for children's minds, such as, 'Does she or doesn't she?' and 'Had any lately?' and that shaving ad for Noxema where the lady is saying 'Take it off, take it all off.' And there's the problem all over the world of juvenile delinquency, for instance, even in Russia. I forget the statistics on it, but they're something staggering, believe me. And yet it seems like the worse things get the harder it is for us to arrest a criminal. In San Francisco, California, according to what I read, every time they arrest a person they have to hand him a card that tells him what his rights are. If that makes you nervous, well I can't say I'm surprised. It does me too."

He paused again. It was none of it exactly what he'd meant to say. It had nothing to do with his feeling about the man who'd been killed, and nothing to do with his own feelings either, for that matter, his own feelings about being here, talking with friends— He felt his mind fumbling, lost.

"There's been a lot of talk," he said. "About me, about the Mayor, about the people over there in the fire department . . ." He felt himself getting angry, and he wasn't sure why. "We do the best we can. You know that. And I want to say I know *you* do the best you can too, or anyway some of you do, and I have the utmost confidence that the people of Batavia will not go off half-cocked about a lot of false rumors." He wished they would turn the lights up more. He could hardly make out the people at the table beside him. "There may be those—" he said. He squinted. Someone was whispering. "There may be those who condemn what happened tonight with the Sunlight Man. I won't hide it from you. I'll tell you right out. He came barging in there to give himself up and the man at the desk got panicky and shot him, that's all there was to it. A terrible mistake, plain murder, you may say. And it was. But let me tell you this: It ain't easy, sitting in there listening to the radio crackle and knowing there's crimes going on in this city and you can't be everywhere at once. It ain't easy to know they're gunning for you—following you around, dogging your footsteps, ready to topple you the first time you go and put your foot down wrong. Think of it! You're sitting at the desk, nothing happening, mind full of stories of the Sunlight Man—murdering, robbing, scaring people in their beds, so the rumors have it anyhow—and all of a sudden whop!!" —he banged the table—"he's right there in front of you like magic! You *know* what you'd do. Don't you *fool* yourself, mister. It's the same all around us. The Negro problem! Or the China problem! Face the truth! Juvenile delinquents setting fire to your store, or dogs hunting children in the streets of the city, or somebody poisoning your calves with paint, or lightning striking, or the end of the world!" whop!! It filled him with exhilaration and he banged the table again and then again. WHOP!! WHOP!!!

Then he put his hands down, shaking all over, collecting his thoughts.

"We may be wrong about the whole thing," he said. "The whole kaboodle. If we could look at ourselves from the eyes of history—" His voice trembled. He squinted, panicky, momentarily believing they had all disappeared and the hall was empty. But they were there, leaning on their knees, listening, eyes as bright as the eyes of birds of prey, far in the distance. He wiped the sweat from his forehead.

"We may be dead wrong about the whole kaboodle," he said wearily. He thought of the Sunlight Man shot through the heart, how he'd said when the Universe told him to jump he would jump; and now—because Luke was his nephew, it came to him: Luke was his brother's son, and he would be alive today if it weren't for the anarchist Taggert Hodge—now, because Luke was his nephew and had died on account of him —he had jumped. "We may be wrong," he said. "We have to stay awake, as best we can, and be ready to obey the laws as best as we're able to see them. That's it. That's the whole thing." His face strained, struggling to get it all clearer, if only to himself. He thought of Esther. "Now there's a fine model for us all," he said emphatically, pointing at the ceiling. They all looked up, and he was flustered. He should go home. Then they were watching him again, as wide-eyed and still as fish. "Blessed are the meek, by which I mean all of us, including the Sunlight Man," he said. "God be kind to all Good Samaritans and also bad ones. For of such is the Kingdom of Heaven."

Then, abruptly, Clumly sat down and scowled.

No one clapped, at first.

The silence grew and struggled with itself and then, finally, strained into sound, first a spatter and then a great rumbling of the room, and he could feel the floor shivering like the walls of a hive and it seemed as if the place was coming down rattling around his ears but then he knew he was wrong, it was bearing him up like music or like a storm of pigeons, lifting him up like some powerful, terrible wave of sound and things in their motions hurtling him up to where the light was brighter than sun-filled clouds, disanimated and holy. The Mayor was there at his side, surging upward, it seemed to Fred Clumly, and crying happily, "Bravo, Clumly!" and the Fire Chief said happily, "Powerful sermon! God forgive us!" And Clumly, in a last pitch of seasickness, caught him in his arms and said, "Correct!" and then, more wildly, shocked to wisdom, he cried, *"Correct!"*

All this, though some may consider it strange, mere fiction, is the truth.

**CERTIFICATE OF DEATH**
STATE OF CALIFORNIA—DEPARTMENT OF PUBLIC HEALTH

STATE NY
FILE 40766A
NUMBER 100539

LOCAL REGISTRATION
DISTRICT AND
STATE NUMBER

| | | |
|---|---|---|
| **DECEDENT PERSONAL DATA** | 1a. NAME OF DECEASED—FIRST NAME Tagert | 1b. MIDDLE NAME Foxley | 1c. LAST NAME Hodge |

2a. DATE OF DEATH—MONTH, DAY, YEAR 9-13-66
2b. HOUR 10:05 PM

3. SEX M
4. COLOR OR RACE W
5. BIRTHPLACE Batavia, NY
6. DATE OF BIRTH 2-8-26
7. AGE 40 YEARS

8. NAME AND BIRTHPLACE OF FATHER
9. MAIDEN NAME AND BIRTHPLACE OF MOTHER
10. CITIZEN OF WHAT COUNTRY
11. SOCIAL SECURITY NUMBER

12. LAST OCCUPATION Teacher
13. NUMBER OF YEARS 2
14. NAME OF LAST EMPLOYING COMPANY OR FIRM Public Schools, Phoenix, Ariz
15. KIND OF INDUSTRY OR BUSINESS Public School

16. IF DECEASED WAS EVER IN U. S. ARMED FORCES unknown
17. SPECIFY MARRIED, NEVER MARRIED, WIDOWED, DIVORCED M
18a. NAME OF PRESENT SPOUSE Kathleen Paxton
18b. PRESENT OR LAST OCCUPATION OF SPOUSE teacher

**PLACE OF DEATH**
19a. PLACE OF DEATH—NAME OF HOSPITAL Genesee Memorial
19b. CITY OR TOWN Batavia
19c. STREET ADDRESS North St
19d. COUNTY Genesee
20. LENGTH OF STAY IN COUNTY OF DEATH less than 1 YEARS

**LAST USUAL RESIDENCE**
20a. LAST USUAL RESIDENCE—STREET ADDRESS
20b. CITY OR TOWN
20c. COUNTY
20d. STATE
21a. NAME OF INFORMANT W. Hodge, Sr.
21b. ADDRESS OF INFORMANT 42 Summer St. Batavia

**PHYSICIAN'S OR CORONER'S CERTIFICATION**
22a. PHYSICIAN: I HEREBY CERTIFY THAT DEATH OCCURRED AT THE HOUR, DATE AND PLACE STATED ABOVE, FROM THE CAUSES STATED BELOW, AND THAT I LAST SAW THE DECEASED ALIVE ON
22b. CORONER: I HEREBY CERTIFY THAT DEATH OCCURRED AT THE HOUR, DATE AND PLACE STATED ABOVE FROM THE CAUSES STATED BELOW, AND THAT I HAVE HELD... Same
22c. PHYSICIAN OR CORONER—SIGNATURE F.S. Schiffer, MD
22d. ADDRESS West Main & Rd. Batavia
22e. DATE SIGNED 9-23-66

**FUNERAL DIRECTOR AND LOCAL REGISTRAR**
23. SPECIFY BURIAL, ENTOMBMENT OR CREMATION country
24. DATE 9-17-66
25. NAME OF CEMETERY OR CREMATORY country
26. EMBALMER—SIGNATURE W. Turner 4A0522
27. NAME OF FUNERAL DIRECTOR
29. LOCAL REGISTRAR—SIGNATURE Ann Biggs

**MEDICAL AND HEALTH DATA**

**CAUSE OF DEATH**
30. CAUSE OF DEATH
PART I. DEATH WAS CAUSED BY: IMMEDIATE CAUSE (a) 410-416 Rupture of the heart due to trauma
CONDITIONS, IF ANY, WHICH GAVE RISE TO THE ABOVE CAUSE (b) 410-414 Gunshot wound of heart
DUE TO (c)
APPROXIMATE INTERVAL BETWEEN ONSET AND DEATH inst.
PART II. OTHER SIGNIFICANT CONDITIONS CONTRIBUTING TO DEATH BUT NOT RELATED TO THE TERMINAL DISEASE CONDITION GIVEN IN PART I (a)

**OPERATION AND AUTOPSY**
31. OPERATION—CHECK ONE
32. DATE OF OPERATION
33. AUTOPSY—CHECK ONE ✓

**INJURY INFORMATION**
34a. SPECIFY ACCIDENT, SUICIDE OR HOMICIDE
34b. DESCRIBE HOW INJURY OCCURRED police action in pursuit of order
35a. TIME OF INJURY HOUR 10:05 pm MONTH, DAY, YEAR 9-13-66
35b. PLACE OF INJURY Police Dept.
35c. CITY, TOWN OR LOCATION Batavia, N.Y. COUNTY Gen. STATE N.Y.
35d. INJURY OCCURRED WHILE AT WORK / NOT WHILE AT WORK ✓

Rev. 1-1-58 Form VS-11

## About the Author

Born in Batavia, New York, John Gardner attended Alexander Central and Batavia High School. "I grew up on a farm and wrote poems, novels, and plays on the typewriter in my grandmother's law office and under the tractor in the back lot when I was supposed to be plowing.

"Went to DePauw University, where I thought I was a chemist; left after two years and went to Washington University, in St. Louis where I thought I was a great poet and was going to die tragically young. Went to the State University of Iowa where I worked hard and wrote worse than in my childhood. Became, by accident a medievalist," writes Mr. Gardner.

He has taught creative writing and medieval literature at Oberlin College, Chico State College, Chico, California, and at San Francisco State. Since 1964 he has taught Old and Middle English at Southern Illinois University.

Mr. Gardner has written several articles, textbook, and six novels. He lives on a farm with his wife and two children in Illinois.

# The
# Best Modern Fiction
## from
# BALLANTINE